EXTRAORDINARY ACCLAIM FOR GLENN MEADE

THE SANDS OF SAKKARA

"Meade weaves well-developed characters into a complex plot that moves at a brisk pace. His vivid descriptions of the sights and sounds of Egypt made me feel like I was back at Sakkara."

—*San Francisco Examiner*

"Compelling."

—*Raleigh News & Observer*

"Meade captures the flavor of the era, the war and the people."

—*Daily Oklahoman*

"A non-stop World War II thriller that will prove much enjoyment to fans of the sub-genre. The story line uses authentic events, which enhance the speed of the novel . . . Glenn Meade is quickly attaining a reputation for historical thrillers."

—*Midwest Book Review*

"A sizzling read, packed with action, great characters, and adventure writing of the highest caliber."

—*Irish-American News*

"A heart-wrenching tale of friendship, love and treachery set against the exotic and intriguing backdrop of wartime Egypt."

—*Sullivan County Democrat*

more . . .

BRANDENBURG

"Fast, sly, and slick, this thriller delivers the goods—tension, action, plot twists—until the smoke finally clears."

—Booklist

"Chilling . . . Another literate and suspenseful thriller from an estimable storyteller who proves that beginner's luck had nothing to do with his impressive debut."

—Kirkus Reviews

"This is a terrific book. I confidently predict that it will enjoy a triumph and that we will see many more bestsellers from the same pen. Sheer, nail-biting suspense, a tour de force—Hitchcock would have filmed it as it stands, without changing a single detail."

—The Sunday Telegraph

"BRANDENBURG is a skillfully plotted and grippingly exciting thriller. BRANDENBURG is a book that I can confidently foresee in the bestseller lists for months to come."

—The Sunday Press (Ireland)

"BRANDENBURG by Glenn Meade is certainly one of the best thrillers I've read this year. It has all the signs of a bestseller. First-class plot, credible characters and dialogue, and exotic settings—definitely a winner."

—Ted Allbury

ST. MARTIN'S PAPERBACKS TITLES
BY GLENN MEADE

Snow Wolf
Brandenburg
The Sands of Sakkara

THE SANDS OF SAKKARA

GLENN MEADE

St. Martin's Paperbacks

First published in Great Britain by Hodder and Stoughton, a division of Hodder Headline PLC.

THE SANDS OF SAKKARA

Library of Congress Catalog Card Number: 99-12725

ISBN: 0-312-97108-7

Printed in the United States of America

St. Martin's Press hardcover edition / May 1999
St. Martin's Paperbacks edition / June 2000

St. Martin's Paperbacks are published by St. Martin's Press, 175 Fifth Avenue, New York, NY 10010.

10 9 8 7 6 5 4 3 2 1

FOR UNA AND NEAL

We had this incredible plan. It would throw the Allies into complete chaos and ruin their intentions of invading Europe. You can't possibly realise how close Germany came to winning the war.

—WALTER SCHELLENBERG, SS general, in an
interview with his Allied interrogators
at Nuremberg, February 1946

Between friends, there is no need of justice.

—ARISTOTLE

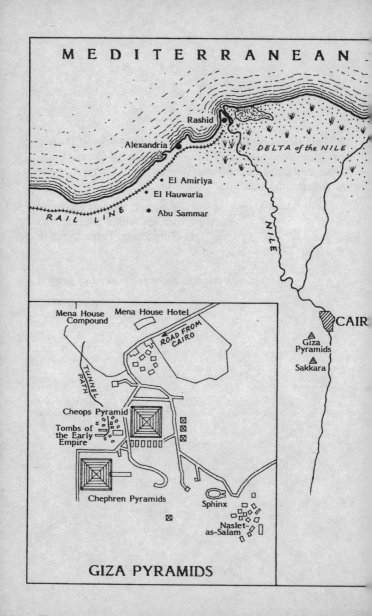

MEDITERRANEAN

Rashid

Alexandria

DELTA of the NILE

• El Amiriya

• El Hauwaria

RAIL LINE

• Abu Sammar

NILE

CAIR

Giza
Pyramids

Sakkara

Mena House
Compound

Mena House Hotel

ROAD FROM
CAIRO

TUNNEL
PATH

Cheops Pyramid

Tombs of
the Early
Empire

Chephren Pyramids

Sphinx

Naslet-
as-Salam

GIZA PYRAMIDS

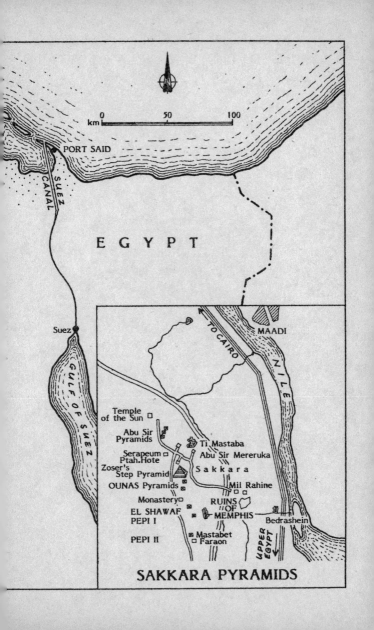

THE PRESENT

ONE

CAIRO

It was April and the *khamsin* was blowing, a howling desert wind that lashed the streets with gusts of blinding sand.

As the taxi pulled up outside the morgue and I stepped out, I wondered again what had possessed me to come here on such a wicked night, and with no more evidence to go on than the corpse of an old man washed up on the banks of the Nile.

"Do you want me to wait, sir?" The taxi driver was a young man with a beard and a mouthful of bad teeth.

"Why not?" It definitely wasn't the kind of night to go looking for another cab.

The morgue was one of those grand, solid old stone buildings you often see in Egypt, a relic of its colonial past, but now it looked quite gloomy and the worse for wear, the granite blackened by years of pollution and neglect. I saw a filthy alleyway at the side, litter swirling in the driving wind. A porch light blazed above a blue-painted door, a metal grille set in the middle. I went down the alleyway and rang the bell. I heard it buzz somewhere inside the building and after a few moments the grille opened and a man's unshaven face appeared.

"Ismail?"

The man nodded.

"I've come to see the old man's body," I said in Arabic. "The one they fished out of the Nile. Captain Halim of the Cairo police told me to ask for you."

He seemed surprised that I spoke his language, but then he opened the door with a rattle of bolts and moved aside to let me enter. I stepped in out of the bitter wind, shook sand from my coat, and went into the hallway. I felt a strange excitement fluttering in my chest. Here I was, a man in my middle fifties, feeling like an excited schoolkid, hoping that at last I might find answers to a bizarre mystery that had haunted me for so many years.

It was surprisingly cool inside, and an almost overpowering smell greeted me. A mixture of fragrant scent and decaying flesh. I could see a wooden archway that led into the morgue itself, the area beyond poorly lit by a dim bulb and a couple of guttering, aromatic candles. Several metal tables were set around the room, grubby white sheets draped over the corpses that lay underneath, and built into the morgue's granite walls were at least a dozen stainless steel vaults, their scratched surfaces pitted with dents.

Ismail stared up at me, a well-practised look of grief on his face. He was small and overweight and wore a faded cotton djellaba. "Are you a relative of the dead one?"

"I'm a journalist."

The expression of grief faded instantly. "I don't understand." He frowned. "What do you want here?"

I took out my wallet, generously peeled off several notes and handed them across. "For your trouble."

"Pardon?"

"Your time. And I won't take up much of it. I'd just like to see the old man's body. Would that be possible? There may be a story in it for me, you understand?"

Ismail obviously did. The money banished any argument, and he smiled as he stuffed the notes into his pocket. "Of course, as you wish. I'm always happy to oblige the gentlemen of the press. You're an American?"

"That's right."

"I thought so. Come this way."

He led me into the morgue. It was very cool inside, the flaking walls painted duck-egg blue and the delicate Arab filigree woodwork on the arches and doors an art in itself, but the place looked shabby and in need of renovation.

Ismail gestured to what looked like a small work area, enclosed by a heavy beaded curtain. "The body is over here. I was just working on it when you rang. Not a very pleasant experience when a corpse has been in water for several days. You still wish to see it?"

"That's why I'm here."

I followed him over and he drew back the curtain. A couple of flickering scented candles were set beside a marble slab, a naked male corpse on top, and next to it was a small metal table with some of the simple tools of the mortician laid out. Waxed cord, cotton wool, some bowls of water. The paraphernalia of death didn't really change much no matter where you were, Cairo or Kansas. There were some clean clothes folded neatly beside the table, an old linen suit and a shirt and tie, socks and shoes, as if they were meant for laying out the corpse.

The old man on the slab must have been well into his seventies and quite tall, at least six foot. His eyes were glassy and open in death, his thinned grey hair sleeked back off his forehead. The skin was white and shrivelled from being in the water, his features tight and horribly contorted. But there was no sign of a long scar in the middle of his chest, evidence that he had been sewn up after an autopsy. In Moslem countries, they bury their dead quickly, usually before sunset if death occurs in the morning, otherwise the following day, and the dead are considered sacred and barely touched. Even murder victims are usually only treated to a necropsy: an external visual inspection of the remains to help determine the cause of death, which is educated guesswork at best.

I felt a shiver go through me, for the scent of the candles didn't hide the stench of decomposition, and nodded at the corpse. "What can you tell me about him?"

The mortician shrugged, as if one more death in a chaotic city of fifteen million souls hardly mattered. "He was brought here yesterday. The police found him in the water near the Nile railway bridge. The identification in his wallet said his name was Johann Halder, a German, and he had an address at a flat in the Imbaba district."

That much I already knew. "Did anyone claim the body?"

"Not yet. The corpse will be kept for a time while relatives are sought. But so far none have been found. It seems he lived alone."

"I take it he's not of the Moslem faith?"

"A Christian, the police think."

"Did he drown?"

Ismail nodded. "The pathologist believes so. As you can see, there are no wounds on the body. He thinks maybe the old man fell into the river by accident, as happens sometimes. Or perhaps he's a suicide from one of the bridges."

He rubbed his stubble. "But it's impossible to know for certain."

"Anything else you can tell me?"

"I'm afraid not. You'll have to ask the police."

"From what I hear, they discovered our dead friend had a second set of identity papers hidden at his flat. They were pretty old, and in the name of Hans Meyer."

Ismail shrugged. "I'm just a simple mortician. I heard nothing about such matters. But I know we have many foreigners living in Cairo, including Germans. You're from an American newspaper?"

"I'm their Middle East correspondent."

"Interesting."

"But not half as interesting as the old man could be."

"You knew him?" Ismail said, surprised.

"Let's just say if he's who I think he is, you could be looking at the earthly remains of a truly incredible man, considering he's supposed to have been dead for over fifty years."

"Pardon?"

"A long story. But if it is him, then you've got a very remarkable corpse keeping you company tonight."

Ismail whistled. "Then no wonder the other gentleman was so interested."

"Other gentleman?"

"He was here not half an hour ago. He came to inspect the body. An elderly American. Used to getting his way, like most Americans. He barged in here and demanded to see the remains." Ismail grinned and tapped the pocket of his djellaba. "Alas, he wasn't as generous as some of his countrymen. When I asked him for a little baksheesh he threatened to cut off my hand."

"Who was he?"

Ismail scratched his head. "Harry Weaver, I think he said."

I was intrigued, felt a strange tingling down my spine. "Harry Weaver? You're *sure* of the name?"

"I believe so."

"Describe him to me."

"Quite tall. In his late seventies, maybe even older, but he seemed to have kept himself in excellent condition. A very capable-looking fellow." Ismail looked surprised when he saw my startled reaction. "You know this Mr. Weaver?"

"Not personally, but I've heard of him."

"He seemed like an important man. Used to giving orders. A military type."

"He was certainly that," I offered. "And you can thank Allah you didn't lose your life, never mind your hand. Harry Weaver is definitely *not* the kind of man to solicit for bribes. He's a model of authority. For almost forty years he was an adviser on American presidential security."

Ismail spread his hands in a helpless gesture. "But baksheesh is the way of our world."

"Don't I know it." I pulled up the collar of my coat and made to go.

Ismail said, "Do you think the body belongs to the German you spoke of?"

I looked down at the corpse. "God only knows. The poor soul's in such a state it's hard to tell which end of him is up. Do you know where Mr. Weaver went?"

"To the house where the German lived. I heard him talk to the taxi driver who waited for him outside."

"This gets more interesting by the minute. Do you know the address?"

"Of course. I went there yesterday to fetch some clothes for the burial, on the instructions of the police." Ismail wrote the address on a slip of paper I handed him.

"The rooms are on the top floor."

"Have the police sealed up the flat?"

"No. It was hardly necessary, the old man hadn't got many belongings worth talking about. But if they bothered to lock his rooms, the landlord has the keys."

As I tucked the paper into my pocket, Ismail said, "Will there be anything else?"

I took one last look at the old man's corpse before I turned to leave. "No, thanks, you've been more than helpful."

Imbaba is a working-class district, parts of it a crumbling shantytown of wooden and concrete dwelling houses near the banks of the Nile. The streets are puddled with open sewers, and the homes are huddled closely together as if to protect themselves from the poverty and squalor all around. The taxi driver found the address without any problem.

The house was built in the Arab style, a big old dwelling, all ancient brown wood and very run-down, the windows covered in shabby, faded net curtains, and there was a rotting, carved wooden balcony jutting out from the first floor. There wasn't another taxi outside but the front door was open, banging in the wind, a dark hallway beyond.

"Wait here," I told the driver, and stepped out of the cab.

The hallway stank of urine and stale food. As I went up the stairs, the wood creaked. I could hear a child crying and a couple arguing somewhere below in the darkness of the house. When I got to the landing I saw that one of the doors leading off was open and I stepped inside.

The room I found myself in was typically Egyptian, but it was shabby and in complete disarray. Drawers were open and their contents spilled out, as if someone had searched the place. Old papers and correspondence, clothes and personal belongings, and a pair of shattered spectacles lay crushed on the floor. A couple of doors led to other rooms, and there was a window that looked out on to the Nile, covered in darkness. I looked through the correspondence and papers, but there was really nothing of interest. As I closed one of the drawers, I knocked over a table lamp. It fell to the floor with a clatter, and then suddenly one of the other doors opened.

When I turned I saw a tall, elderly man come into the room. The bedroom he'd stepped out of was in disarray behind him, papers scattered everywhere, and he held a pair of reading glasses in his hand. He wore a pale trench coat, his silver hair was flecked with sand, and he had a slightly haunted look on his tanned face. I knew he was at least in his early eighties, but he was remarkably well preserved, had a freshness about him that made him appear ten years younger. And he still looked every inch the military type—over six feet, his features finely chiselled, though his shoulders were slightly stooped and his piercing grey eyes looked watery with age.

They narrowed as he took me in. "Who the hell are

you?" he demanded, his accent unmistakably American.

"I could ask you the same question, if I didn't already know the answer, Colonel Weaver."

He seemed taken aback. "You know me?"

"Not personally, but what American hasn't heard of Harry Weaver? A legend in his own lifetime. Security adviser to American presidents for almost forty years."

"And who are you?" Weaver snorted.

"The name's Frank Carney."

He seemed unimpressed, but then something flickered in his eyes and he frowned. "Not Carney the *New York Times* reporter?"

"I'm afraid so."

Weaver relaxed for a moment. "I used to read your columns. Not that I agreed with everything you wrote, mind."

"You must have agreed with some of it, though," I offered. "I was a cub reporter covering Dallas as a stand-in when Kennedy was killed. You were one of his security advisers. You told him not to go, remember?"

"Too many weak spots. Damned holes everywhere in the local security. And he was a sitting duck in that open-top car, despite the assurances of the Secret Service that they could protect him."

"Had Jack Kennedy listened to you, he might still be alive today. I said as much when I wrote about it afterwards."

Weaver shook his head wistfully. "Too late now. But come to think of it, I seem to remember your article. It was a fair and honest assessment of the facts."

"That's because I did my homework. I read what I could about your background at the time. Trust no one and doubt every fact was your personal motto. With a career as long as yours, you seemed like a man worth taking advice from."

"Put it down to experience. The years harden you." Weaver looked across at me, suddenly suspicious again. "None of which explains what the hell you're doing here. This is private property."

"Again, I could ask you the same. Did the landlord let you in?"

"What the hell is it to you if he did? Just answer the goddamned question."

"Oh, I think you can guess why. We were both at the morgue for the same reason. Johann Halder. Arguably one of the greatest enigmas of the Second World War."

Weaver stiffened. "You were at the morgue?"

"Apparently I just missed you. And by the way, the attendant wasn't very pleased you didn't leave a tip."

Weaver's eyes narrowed cautiously. "How do you know about Johann Halder?"

"Egyptology happens to be an abiding interest of mine, which is why I've spent the last five years in Cairo as a correspondent. Quite a few years back I was researching an article on one Franz Halder, a wealthy German collector of Egyptian artefacts. I had it in mind to write a book about some of the priceless Egyptian treasures that went missing from private collections and museums all over Europe during the last war, many of which have still never been found."

Weaver registered interest. "So?"

"Before the war, Halder owned one of the finest private collections in Germany, most of it irreplaceable, and he was a benefactor of the Egyptian Museum. He died when the Allies destroyed Hamburg during a massive fire-bombing raid in 1943. Some time after that, his entire collection went missing. I tried to dig a little deeper, to find out if he had any living relatives, anyone who might have known what became of the collection. So I had a journalist friend in Berlin do some checking for me. There were no relatives still alive, at least none that could tell me anything worthwhile, but it turned out Halder had a son, Johann, who served during the war. The German military records stated that he died in action in 1943, on some kind of mission, but made no mention of how or where. Though my friend did discover that Halder had been recruited by the Abwehr in 1940. That's the wartime German intelligence agency to you and me."

"I know what the Abwehr was, Carney. But go on."

"As a boy, Johann Halder was educated in America, until his mother died tragically giving birth to her second child. After that, his father brought him back to Berlin, though apparently for many years they returned to the States each summer. His mother's family once had a large estate in upstate New York. I visited there some years back, but the place had changed hands many years ago, the house had been demolished, and no one in the area remembered the Halders."

"I'm hardly surprised. You're talking about a long time ago."

"Johann Halder also spoke several languages fluently, including Arabic, and attained the rank of major during the war, though he never joined the Nazi Party. The rest of his military background is pretty much a mystery, apart from a stint spent in North Africa, and there were no details of the mission he's supposed to have died on."

"And what else did you learn?" Weaver said quietly.

"This is where it starts to get really interesting. I thought no more about it until recently, when I interviewed one of the former heads of the Egyptian Museum, Kemal Assan, shortly before he died. I mentioned Franz Halder in passing and Assan said he met his son, Johann, in 1939, when he took part in an archaeological dig at Sakkara. In fact, he said he'd also seen him in Cairo *after* the war. Considering Halder was supposed to be dead, that fact seemed pretty incredible."

Weaver was suddenly very interested. "And what exactly did this Assan tell you?"

"Ten years ago, he was sitting in a Cairo coffee house minding his own business, when he noticed a man seated at the next table. Assan thought his face seemed oddly familiar. When he asked if he knew him, the man simply smiled and said in German, 'We met long ago in another life.' Then he got up and left. Assan spoke some German, and he was adamant the man was Johann Halder."

Weaver's eyes sparked. "Didn't he try to follow him?"

"He tried to, but he lost him in the bazaar."

Weaver looked deflated. "I see. So you believed Halder might be still alive?"

"It's a mystery that's bothered me ever since. I really didn't know what to think—the whole thing was such a puzzle. But certainly I thought there might have been a story in it. If Halder was still alive, there was a chance he might know what had become of his father's collection. Then I came across a mention in yesterday's *Egyptian Ga-*

zette, about the body of an elderly German recovered from the Nile. Apparently, his identity papers named him as Johann Halder, and the police were asking for anyone with information to come forward. When I heard the name I put two and two together, and hoped it might make four."

I looked across at Weaver, who stood there, taking it all in, but he didn't say another word.

"The question is, what are *you* doing here, Colonel? The last I heard you were living in Washington. But come to think of it, if I remember correctly, you've had a lifelong interest in Egypt. You have several archaeological digs to your credit, and served here with military intelligence during the war. But I can only presume the real reason you're here is because you obviously knew about Halder."

Weaver seemed suddenly at a loss for words, caught in a trap of his own making. He sighed, flopped into one of the chairs, but didn't utter a word.

"Was it Johann Halder back there in the morgue?"

Weaver didn't reply.

"Then at least tell me why you're here. And how you knew Halder. After all, it's not every day I come across a story about a man who's been reported dead, and yet might still be alive over fifty years later."

Still Weaver didn't answer.

I stared at him. "I get the feeling I'm talking to a brick wall, Colonel."

He remained sitting there, motionless.

"At least tell me *why* you're here. One simple question. Is that too much to ask?"

Weaver seemed to lose his patience. "*God*, Carney, you're like a dog after a bone. I've had enough of your goddamned questions." He stood up, as if to leave, and said firmly, "You're a stranger to me. And I don't discuss my personal business with strangers."

"OK, Colonel, if that's what you wish. But I'd like to tell you something. Maybe come at this from another angle."

Weaver looked exasperated. "Shut it, Carney. I'm not in the mood."

"I think maybe you'll want to hear what I have to say."

"I doubt it."

"Just hear me out for one minute. The moment I heard your name back in the morgue, I felt a shiver down my spine. I kind of like to think it might be kismet playing its part—fate to you and me, the kind of thing the Egyptians are so fond of believing in."

Weaver's eyes narrowed. "What the hell are you talking about?"

"The article I wrote about you after Dallas. You never asked how come I knew so much about your personal background, when there really wasn't that much information on public record."

Weaver frowned, nodded. "I seem to vaguely recall all the facts were there, all right. But what of it?"

"Does the name Tom Carney mean anything to you?"

Weaver looked totally astonished, as if I'd dealt him a blow. "*Captain* Tom Carney?"

"The same. He was my old man. You served in military intelligence together, and landed in North Africa during Operation Torch, 1943. You were wounded by shrapnel after a mortar hit your reconnaissance unit outside Algiers. He carried you back to American lines, under heavy enemy fire. He got a medal for that one, on your recommendation. He was also wounded twice for his trouble, and got shipped home."

The hardness peeled from Weaver's face, all his aggression gone, and he studied me intently. "Well, I'll be damned. So you're Tom Carney's son."

"My old man talked a lot about you over the years. The feeling I got, you were once good buddies."

Weaver nodded, and his eyes watered, as if he were remembering. "He was a good man. Courageous. Honest. One of the best I served with. I was only sorry we didn't keep in touch. Though I heard he died, what, maybe ten years back?"

"Twelve. And still not a day goes by when I don't miss him." I looked at Weaver steadily. "I like to believe that sometimes lives intersect, even briefly, for all sorts of reasons we mortals can't even begin to comprehend. Maybe it's written in our stars. Like you and my old man. You know, it's odd, but my father used to talk a lot about destiny. And maybe if he hadn't been with you the time you were wounded, things might have turned out very differently, for both of you. Fate's a funny thing, Colonel. And when I heard your name mentioned back at the morgue, I figured it might have been fate lending me a hand. Kismet helping us meet for a reason. This Halder business has been rattling around in my head for quite a few years, an enigma that won't go away, and I'd like to get to the bottom of it. So if there's any way you can help, I'd be grateful. I'm not trying to call in any family favours, Colonel, believe me. But I reckon my father was a man you could trust. I'm simply asking you to trust me."

Weaver was silent.

"Maybe you think I'm asking too much? Two simple questions. Why you're here, and how you knew Halder."

Weaver sighed, a long, hard sigh that sounded like he was trying to expel some kind of pain from deep inside him. "Yes, I knew Johann Halder," he admitted finally. "A very long time ago."

"Now you do surprise me. I know why *I'm* here. But what about you? What's your reason?"

Weaver sat forward in the chair, his hunched frame suddenly making him appear very old, as if my persistence had finally worn him down, and there was a tired, sad look on his face. "Oh, there are lots of reasons, Carney. Lots of them, I assure you." He was about to say something else just then, but appeared to change his mind. "So, you thought there might be a story in all this?"

"I was kind of hoping there might be. And even if not, I might at least be able to put my curiosity to rest."

Weaver hesitated, as if trying to decide something, then he seemed to make up his mind. "I think you could certainly say there's a story, but I doubt it would help you discover what happened to Franz Halder's collection. There's a good chance it probably ended up in Russian hands after Berlin was stormed. Almost everything of value did."

"I figured that was a distinct possibility. But what about Johann Halder? It seems to me he's the only link left in all of this mystery. What can you tell me about him?"

Weaver was uncomfortable, as if the pain he'd tried to

expel had returned. He looked around the room. "Is there a drink in this place?"

"I guess not."

"*Damn.*" Weaver stood and moved to the window. The wind was lashing the tall palm trees along the Nile. He didn't look back as he spoke, almost absent-mindedly. "Cairo used to be quite a place during the war, did you know that? You could even say the fate of the entire world was decided here."

"Really? Care to tell me about it?"

He didn't answer for a moment, lost in thought as he looked out through the window. "I could give you a story, Carney. Maybe the strangest you've ever heard. The real question is, would you believe it?"

"Try me."

He turned back, and his face was deathly serious. "On one condition. You don't publish anything I tell you until after I die."

I was surprised. "You look like a man in remarkably good health, Colonel. That could be a long wait."

"Maybe not so long. I'm an old man, Carney, I can't have much time left. And I kind of guess at that stage the truth of it wouldn't hurt anyone, not with so many years passed. But you know the oddest thing? I've never told my story to a soul. I could have done, wanted to, many times, because it haunted me, but I kept it to myself for over fifty years. And maybe the time's come to unburden it to someone, before it's too damned late." He stared at me. "You could be right about fate, Carney. Destiny playing its part. Besides, having read your work, and if you're anything like your father, I believe you might be an honest man, one who'll abide by my wishes."

I met his stare, nodded. "You have my word."

Weaver glanced around the filthy room, as if suddenly uneasy in his surroundings.

"You mind if we get out of here?"

"I've a taxi waiting outside. I can give you a lift."

"On an evening like this, I won't say no. By the way, I'm staying at the new Shepheard's. It's nothing quite like the old hotel it replaced, but at least it serves pretty decent American Scotch."

"Now you're talking."

Weaver pulled up the collar of his trench coat, stepped out on to the landing, and went quickly down the stairs. I took one last look around the shabby flat, closed the door, and followed him.

The drive to Shepheard's was something of a trial. For some reason, Weaver hardly spoke, just stared out of the cab window, lost in a world of his own. I had a terrible feeling he might have been reconsidering his offer to tell me his story, but when we reached the hotel, he shook sand from his trench coat and said as we entered the lobby, "I'll meet you in the bar in ten minutes. Mine's a very large Dewars. Straight."

He stepped into the elevator and I went into the restaurant bar. The old Shepheard's Hotel had what the guidebooks like to call atmosphere. It had a certain faded glory that suggested *belle époque*, all dark wood and soaring marble columns, rich carpets and antique furniture. It used to be one of the old grand hotels, built to accommodate wealthy Europeans. The modern Shepheard's is a pale imitation by comparison, though it still attracts the tourists. But there were none in the bar that night, just a couple of foreign businessmen chatting over drinks. I took a seat near a window and ordered two large Dewars, then changed my mind and told the waiter to bring the bottle.

Weaver came down ten minutes later. He had changed into a sweater and cotton pants and he seemed more at ease as he looked around the bar. "Damn it, but this looks nothing like the old place."

"Does Shepheard's bring back memories, Colonel?"

"Far too many, I'm afraid," Weaver replied almost wistfully. "And enough of this Colonel business. I've been retired for over twenty years." He studied the room. "Did you know that Greta Garbo used to stay at the original hotel? Not to mention Lawrence of Arabia, Winston Churchill, and half the Gestapo spies in wartime Cairo."

I refilled our glasses and set the bottle between us. "I read somewhere once that Rommel telephoned the front desk to make a reservation after the fall of Tobruk, believing he'd be in Cairo within a week. If memory serves me, the old Shepheard's was burned down during the riots for independence in '52. Apparently, most Egyptians saw it as an irritating symbol of British imperialism."

"It seems you know your history, Carney."

"Which is why something bothers me. If everything I've learned about Johann Halder is true, and if he was still alive after all that time, why would he choose to disappear into hiding and remain such a mystery?"

"I believe there could have been several reasons. One of them being the fact that the United States had good enough evidence to condemn him as a traitor. Probably could even have hanged him."

I frowned. "Whatever for? Halder was a German citizen, surely. How could he have been a traitor?"

"He was certainly a German citizen, but he was American-born. His real name was Johann, though he was better known as Jack. And his disappearance had to do with the mission you spoke about, the one he was supposed to have died on. Probably the most daring the Nazis ever came up with. And it happened right here in Egypt."

"I don't understand."

"Halder led a covert team to assassinate President Roosevelt and Prime Minister Winston Churchill in Cairo, on Adolf Hitler's direct orders."

I was stunned. "Now you really do surprise me. An American-born assassin sent by Hitler to kill the US President? It beggars belief."

Weaver put down his Scotch. "And probably the best American President that ever lived, come to that. Halder's mission was meant to change the tide of the war for the Nazis. And there was much more at stake than when Kennedy was targeted in Dallas. The future of the entire free world, no less. And it happened while Roosevelt and Churchill were attending the Cairo Conference in November 1943, one of the most vital Allied conferences of the war.

"Among other things, the President and Prime Minister were in Cairo to agree on top-secret plans for Operation Overlord, the invasion of Europe. Had Hitler got his way, and had them assassinated, the Allies would have been thrown into chaos, the invasion would never have gone ahead, and Germany would have won the war." Weaver put up his thumb and forefinger, held them the barest fraction apart. "Believe me, Carney, it came *this* close to succeeding. It still frightens me to think about it."

I was overwhelmed. "You're serious, aren't you? It really happened."

Weaver said firmly, "Oh, it happened all right, don't you doubt it. And it was my job to stop Halder and kill him. But it wasn't something that ever got a mention in the history books, it was far too sensitive a matter for that."

I looked at him eagerly. "But I don't understand. Even assuming Halder survived, why would you still want to find him after all these years? So he could be branded a traitor? It's pretty late for that, surely?"

There was a rather sad look in his eyes. He glanced out towards the Nile, before looking back. "No, the reasons are far more private," he said quietly.

And then I was aware of a sudden powerful emotion in his voice. "But make no mistake about one thing, Carney. Halder really did help to change the course of world history."

"You mind telling me how?"

Weaver must have noticed the confusion on my face, but he didn't reply. Instead, he looked out beyond the window and his eyes glazed over, as if he were trying to see into the past. The howling sandstorm had almost died away, lifting the veil off the ancient city, and suddenly you could see the majestic Nile, the houseboats out on the river, the pungent dark alleyways and soaring minarets, the ghostly outline of the Giza pyramids in the far distance. I could easily imagine how it must have been over fifty years ago, a city full of mystery and intrigue.

When Weaver turned back there was a look on his face that was hard to fathom. Grief perhaps, or pain—I couldn't tell which.

"Maybe I had better start at the beginning. You see, I knew Jack Halder long before the war. We were childhood friends. You might even say we were like brothers."

THE
PAST

PART ONE

SEPTEMBER 1939

TWO

CAIRO

Once, they had all been together.

They were young and the place was called Sakkara. An archaeological team had discovered the entrance to a secret funeral chamber close to the Step pyramid of Pharaoh Zoser, near the site of the ancient city of Memphis, almost thirty kilometres south of Cairo. The international group that arrived in early spring to help with the dig was comprised mostly of young people in their twenties, from France, Germany, Britain and America. There were almost a hundred. Some were archaeologists and Egyptologists, others were engineers or eager adventurers, and they all worked hard together under a boiling desert sun, intent and happy in their work and determined to enjoy themselves, despite the gathering winds of war.

For two of the young men, Harry Weaver and Jack Halder, the Sakkara dig was an arranged reunion. The son of a beautiful New York socialite mother and a wealthy Prussian father with a renowned passion for ancient Egypt, Jack Halder was an adventurer by nature.

At twenty-four, he was a year older than Weaver, who had jumped at his first opportunity to travel abroad. His father had worked as a caretaker on the estate owned by the family of Jack Halder's mother, and despite their different social backgrounds, the two boys had formed an immediate friendship that had begun in early childhood and lasted ever since. Even after Halder's mother had died, they had spent their summers together, when Franz Halder came to stay in New York each year. But at Sakkara, there was a problem. Both of them had fallen in love with the same woman.

Rachel Stern was a young archaeologist of twenty-three, just out of university, the daughter of a German-Catholic father and a Jewish mother. Blond-haired and blue-eyed, she seemed to have inherited her parents' intelligence and good looks. They were both noted archaeologists, and her father, a professor, was director of the dig. Rachel Stern liked both young men very much, but she couldn't seem to decide which she loved, so she was content for the three of them to keep company together.

That summer they organised trips to Cairo and Luxor, exploring the bazaars and markets, the Valleys of the Kings and Queens and the ruined Temple of Karnak. They made a habit at weekends of dancing at Shepheard's, or attending parties at the Mena House Hotel, built in the shadows of the Giza pyramids, and dining in the small, intimate restaurants and the houseboat nightclubs that flourished along the Nile.

Once, Harry Weaver had a photograph taken of the three of them together, standing among the tombs in the scorching desert at Sakkara, the Step pyramid as a backdrop, all of them tanned and smiling for the camera, Rachel between the men, her arms around their waists. And though no one ever said it, they each knew it was a happy time, perhaps the happiest in their young lives.

But summer had to end. None of them could ever remember the exact date they had first met, but they would each remember exactly when the shadow was thrown across their path: September 1939. It was the month war had been declared in Europe, Hitler had invaded Poland, and their lives, like so many others, were about to be changed for ever.

Heat shimmered across the vastness of open desert beyond the pyramids that afternoon as the covered Jeep came to a halt and Harry Weaver climbed out. He wiped his brow with the back of his hand, then lifted a battered leather satchel from the back seat, before making his way to the collection of large canvas tents that had been erected around the Sakkara site. Dozens of team members were busy clearing away equipment after the excavation, and were loading it on to a couple of Bedford trucks, and as Weaver strolled towards the activity a grey-haired, distinguished man wearing a bush hat and sweat-stained khaki tropical shirt stepped out of one of the tents.

Professor David Stern had a studious face, but it wasn't without humour, and when he saw Weaver he removed his glasses, wiped them vigorously with a handkerchief, and smiled. "Harry, you're back. And about time. I was beginning to think we'd have to send out a search party."

"Sorry, Professor. I stopped off at Shepheard's on the way to see if there was any news."

"And what's the word from Cairo's principal watering hole?"

"Warsaw's still in flames. German Stuka bombers are razing it to the ground. No one expects the Poles to hold out much longer."

"That fool Hitler," Stern said through clenched teeth. "Before you know it he'll have Europe in ruins. But what can you expect from such a dangerous madman?" He quickly changed the subject as if the present topic were too upsetting, and looked a short distance away, to where a diesel generator was humming away in the searing heat. Electric cables snaked into a large hole that had been opened up in the earth's face with a sturdy wooden safety frame constructed around it, a ladder leading down into the shaft. "We're well on our way. Just the last of the tunnel equipment to be brought up and then we'll concentrate on tidying up the site face. You picked up the post?"

Weaver lifted the satchel. "It's all here, the last mail run. And I made sure the Ministry of Antiquities had the list of forwarding addresses you gave me for the crew, just in case any more mail turns up for us after we've gone."

"Excellent." Stern put his hands on his hips, squinted in the strong sunlight as he gazed around the site. "So, our time at Sakkara is coming to an end. How do you feel about that, Harry?"

Weaver looked sad. "To tell you the truth, I haven't been looking forward to it. It's not often a guy like me gets the opportunity to visit Egypt and take in something like this. I've a feeling this adventure could be the highlight of my life."

Stern smiled, slapped a hand on Weaver's shoulder. "Nonsense. You're a young man. What age are you, Harry? The same as most of the rest of the crew—twenty-three, twenty-four?"

"Twenty-three, sir."

"Then it's all ahead of you. And there are a lot more

interesting adventures to come, I'm certain of it."

"What about you, Professor? You're still leaving for Istanbul?"

Stern nodded. "In four days' time. The temporary lecturing position I've decided to accept came out of the blue, but Istanbul's a wonderful city, so I'm sure my wife and Rachel will find it interesting. All in all, it should keep me busy for a while." He dabbed sweat from his forehead, then held out his hand for the mail satchel, and nodded towards the shaft. "Rachel and Jack, plus a few of the others, are still below. This heat is unbearable, so why don't you go down and help them tidy up and I'll hand out the letters to the crew."

Weaver descended the ladder into the shaft. It was solid rock in parts, a drop of almost fifty feet, and when he came to the bottom several narrow passageways led off in different directions.

The yellow clay walls and ceilings were lined with timber supports, and lit by strings of bulbs, fed from the electric generator up above. The passageways led to the three individual tombs that had been discovered, the ceilings so low in places that a man had to hunch his shoulders as he walked. Compared to the sizzling temperature above ground, the tunnel air was pleasantly cool, chilly almost, and there was a slightly eerie atmosphere, but Weaver had become used to that, and he cheerfully made his way along one of the passageways until he came to the end and heard voices.

A large sarcophagus, once the tomb of a relatively unknown princess from Zoser's dynasty, was set into a recess in the far wall. The mummified remains had been removed after their discovery. The stone coffin lid lay propped against the wall, its surface beautifully carved with hieroglyphics, and several of the crew were in the process of removing digging equipment and electric cables from the immediate area. Weaver saw Jack Halder and Rachel Stern busily working away, their clothes covered in fine dust, and then Rachel turned and saw him.

Her blond hair was tied back, accentuating her high cheekbones, and there were tiny beads of perspiration on her tanned face and neck. Even though she wore a loose khaki shirt and pants, her figure was evident, and she looked startlingly pretty, as always. She offered Weaver a perfect smile, one that affected him instantly. "Harry. We were just talking about you."

"Nothing bad, I hope."

"Of course not. We were simply wondering what had kept you so long." She moved to kiss him on the cheek, smudging his face with dust. "Now look what I've done."

She wiped the dust away, laughing, and at the touch of her hand Weaver felt electricity course through him. Every time he looked at Rachel Stern or felt her touch he was aware of an intense feeling of attraction, and he fought hard to control it. "I called into Shepheard's. The news isn't good. Warsaw's still burning. The word is Poland will be forced to surrender very soon."

"It's all so truly dreadful," Rachel said, genuinely concerned. "Isn't it, Jack?"

Jack Halder had a restless, handsome face, with pale blue eyes and a slight smile fixed permanently in place, one that suggested he found life infinitely more interesting than he had hoped. But the smile was gone now as he shook his head. "It's terrible. At this moment, I almost feel ashamed to be German."

Weaver put a hand on his friend's shoulder. "I think we all feel bad about events, Jack. But neither you nor any of the other Germans on the dig started the conflict. Hitler did."

"I suppose you're right." Halder gazed in awe at the open sarcophagus for a moment, then ran a hand over the lid's smooth surface. "I'll be sorry to say goodbye to the last resting place of our princess. Isn't it incredible when you think about it?"

"What is?"

"For thousands of years she lay here alone, until we found her. Once, she was probably the object of men's desire. And now she's mummified remains, lying in the vaults of the Egyptian Museum, waiting to be dissected and studied, like the others we discovered. And all the important questions you want to ask, for which you'll probably never find answers. What did she look like? What kind of life did she have? Whom did she love? I doubt anyone will ask those questions of us someday. At least she's achieved a kind of immortality."

Rachel smiled. "Jack, you're such a romantic dreamer."

Weaver said with wry humour, "Let's just hope there isn't a curse attached to our princess, or we're all in trouble."

"You don't believe in curses, do you, Harry?" Rachel asked, incredulous.

"Ask me that question a couple of years from now, when we're all covered in massive red spots and dying from some unknown, incurable disease."

They laughed, and there was a sound from somewhere behind them, footsteps on the creaking wooden ladder, and Professor Stern appeared from the passageway. "It sounds like you're all enjoying yourselves, and I hate to upset the mood, but I've distributed the post Harry picked up from Cairo. Most of it's bad news, from what I can gather. At least a dozen of the crew have been conscripted and the general consensus is that they're not too happy about it."

"Harry told us about Warsaw," Halder offered.

"I don't even want to think about it," Professor Stern said, dejected. "It has me depressed enough already." He scrutinised the area. "You've been busy, Rachel, I see. You too, Jack."

"All in a day's work, Professor," Halder answered. "With Harry lending a hand, another couple of hours should see it through."

"Before I forget, Jack, there was a letter for you among the mail." The professor handed an envelope across. "From Germany, I believe."

Halder moved beside one of the light bulbs, tore open the letter, and read the contents. His face darkened perceptibly, so then he slowly folded the pages and stuffed them in his breast pocket.

"What's wrong? Is it bad news?" Rachel asked.

Halder forced a smile. "Of a sort. It's from my father."

He said no more, as if the subject were private. Stern was suddenly brisk again as he slapped a hand on Weaver's shoulder. "Right, we'd better get back to work. I want to have everything finished before dark so that we can enjoy the big party tomorrow night."

"What big party?" Weaver asked, and they all looked at the professor.

Stern smiled. "A secret I've kept to myself, but now it's time you all knew. Remember I told you last week I'd stretched our budget to pay for cheap hotel rooms in Cairo and a meal for all the crew after we'd finished our work here? Well, it's going to be rather better than that. What work remains to be done at Sakkara will be completed by the Ministry of Antiquities, of course, but they've judged our dig to be a complete success, and a party's been organised at the residence of the American ambassador. It's well known he has a keen interest in archaeology, and he's insisted on hosting a gala evening in our honour. There's to be a splendid buffet meal, quite a few distinguished people have been invited, and from what I hear, the ambassador's even arranged a dance band. All very kind of him, I thought."

"Well, good for us," Halder said, more cheerfully.

"That's wonderful news, Papa," Rachel said. "Isn't it, Harry?"

"The best I've heard in a long time."

"I thought it might cheer you up." The professor rolled up his sleeves. "Now, let's get the equipment up the shaft and packed away, and then we can all relax."

The sun was going down, casting a tangerine light over the desert. Dinner had been served by the Bedouin cooks— kofta, saffron rice, and fresh bread—and because it was their last night under canvas, Professor Stern had provided a large quantity of Egyptian beer and wine at his own expense.

They sat around the campfire, but there was little talk of the war, because nobody in the team wanted politics to intrude. One of the Frenchmen played his accordion, accompanied by two young Englishmen with guitars, everyone joining in with the kind of gusto only young people could muster, and by the time the talking and singing was done it was almost midnight, the embers were dying, and people started drifting back to their tents.

Halder was a little drunk as he produced three more bottles of beer, and with a grin handed one each to Rachel and Weaver. "I thought I'd keep us a nightcap. How about we say our last goodnight to Zoser?"

"Why not," Rachel agreed, and the three of them strolled over to Zoser's Step pyramid, in high spirits after the alcohol they'd consumed, Weaver carrying a kerosene lamp to light the way. They sat on the stone blocks at the base, as they'd done almost every night the entire summer, still awed by the beauty and vastness of the five-thousand-year-old tomb. "So this is it," said Halder with genuine sadness. "Our last night at Sakkara."

Rachel was down-hearted. "I hate the thought of leaving. It's been such a wonderful time here, and great fun." She looked at them both. "And it's all been because of you, Jack, and you, Harry. You've helped make it the most memorable time of my life. I want to thank you for that."

Halder said suddenly, "Remember that photograph Harry had taken? The one of the three of us together?"

"Of course. Why?"

Halder took a swig from his bottle and gave a mischievous grin. "You know, I've been thinking. We need more than a photograph to commemorate our summer together. Something that will last for centuries."

"What exactly do you mean, Jack?" Weaver asked.

Halder stood, unsteady on his feet. "Wait here."

He took the kerosene lamp, ambled over to one of the tents occupied by the Egyptian workmen, and came back after a while carrying a tattered canvas bag.

Weaver said, "What the devil are you up to, Jack?"

"Have patience. No speaking, please. Not a word, or you'll distract me. And no looking until I tell you."

He moved a distance away, further along the stone base, put down the lamp, and produced a hammer and chisel from the bag. He sat there working away intently in the lamplight, hammering at one of the slabs of rock, and when he was finally done, he wiped sweat from his face and smiled. "OK. You can see now."

He held up the lamp and they joined him.

All along the base of Zoser's pyramid there were inscriptions in the layers of stepped rock, and on their first day at Sakkara they had marvelled at them; hundreds and hundreds of names and initials carved over the centuries by countless visitors. Even though illegal, it was a custom that no authority had been able to prevent. Some of the inscriptions even dated as far back as Roman times.

And among them, Jack Halder had chiselled: *RS, HW, JH. 1939.*

"Jack," Rachel laughed. "You're not only drunk, you're *crazy*. Papa will be horrified if he finds out you've defaced a treasured monument."

"Maybe, but now we're immortal." Jack smiled. "Just like our princess. Years from now, people will come here and perhaps, just perhaps, they'll wonder who we were. We're part of the mystery of the pyramids."

Rachel touched his arm fondly. "You know something? I'm glad you chiselled our initials. We've had such a special time here, it somehow seems appropriate. Don't you think so, Harry?"

"At least there'll be something to remember us by, long after we're dead." Weaver raised his beer. "I'd like to propose a toast. To us. And to Sakkara."

"To us. And to Sakkara."

They chorused the toast and laughed, then talked for a while, as they watched the lights burning all over Cairo in the dark distance, until finally Rachel stood and dusted down her trousers. "And now, I'd really better get to bed. I'm so looking forward to the party tomorrow night. You'd better both promise me a dance." She kissed them each on the cheek, with genuine tenderness. "Goodnight, Jack. Goodnight, Harry. Sleep well, my loves."

"Don't you want us to guide you back with the lamp?"

"No, stay and finish your beer. I'll be fine in the moonlight." She walked towards the tents, and for a long time Weaver watched her go in the dim silver light as she faded like a ghost, until he looked across and saw that Halder was watching her too, almost in a trance.

"Are you thinking what I'm thinking?"

"I don't know, Jack. Tell me."

"That she's the prettiest, most wonderful woman either of us has ever met."

"You've read my mind, as always."

"Let's be honest here, Harry. The truth of it is, we're both infatuated with Rachel. So why don't we cut out all that manly garbage of not showing our feelings and both say how we feel? It's something we've avoided talking about."

"You want me to be truthful about how I feel?"

"Very. Cards on the table. Promise I'll do the same."

Weaver looked away, towards darkened Cairo. "I couldn't sleep last night thinking about her, especially knowing that these were the last days I'd spend in her company. And not a day's gone by since I've met her that I haven't thought about her, wanted to be with her. Even just to see her face. To hear her voice. She's the first real woman I've ever fallen in love with."

Halder was solemn. "That bad, eh?"

"I guess so. And it won't seem to go away."

"But you never told her even vaguely how you felt, did you?"

"You know I didn't. And that's the crazy thing about it. Something's always held me back. Fear of being rejected, maybe, or of losing her friendship if she didn't feel the same way and my admission complicated things." Weaver shrugged. "Or maybe it was something else. I'm not really sure. So, what about you?"

For a moment, Halder looked suddenly very young, like a little boy, uncomfortable confessing a secret, but then the moment passed. "I'd like to tell you something first. Something I haven't ever told anyone. When my mother was finally dying, she didn't allow my father to see her, to say his last goodbye. Not because she didn't love him, but for the very opposite reason. She loved him so much. Saying goodbye would have been too painful, too final for them both, and she knew that." He turned to Weaver. "Theirs was a great love, Harry. And in a way I've always wanted the same kind of thing. Truly deep, full of honest passion."

"And how do you feel about Rachel? Be honest."

"Sometimes—often—I'd lie awake, restless, imagining all the things I'd like to happen between her and me. I'd picture us together. I'd picture her pregnant with my child, and happy that she was my wife. I'd picture making love to her—not just sex, but real, honest-to-God love. The kind of tenderness a man should feel for a woman he truly loves. And so many times I really wanted to tell her." Halder looked at his friend. "You know how foolhardy and impetuous I usually am, and I can't say I wasn't tempted to tell her such things. But like you, I just couldn't."

"Why not?"

"Probably for the same reason as you. I really didn't want to upset the apple cart."

"What do you mean?"

Halder placed a hand fondly on Weaver's shoulder. "There's another kind of love—not physical, but brotherly, or deep friendship, call it what you will, and it's just as important. You always were the best friend I've ever had. Maybe if one of us had made a pass, it would have ruined everything. I don't just mean between us, because I honestly think our camaraderie is stronger than that, but I mean the friendship we've all had this summer. And I didn't want that to happen."

"I guess I know what you mean. Besides, when you add it up, the three of us had a great time. And maybe that's what's really important."

"Still, Harry, we've both got it bad. And there has to be a practical solution." Halder's drunkenness was suddenly gone and he allowed himself a playful smile. "Friendship aside, what if there's the remotest chance that *Rachel* might be in love with one of us?"

"What do you mean?"

"If it were so, wouldn't it be a shame that we didn't let nature take its course? Otherwise, we could *both* spend the rest of our lives regretting that we didn't tell her how we felt before she leaves. At least one of us could be happy. And Rachel too. It would be fair all round. How do you feel about that?"

"You really think she might be in love with one of us?"

Halder smiled again. "Either way, tomorrow's our last chance to find out."

THREE

The American ambassador's residence was packed with international dignitaries, the cream of Egyptian and European expatriate society, everyone from movie stars to diplomats, senior military officers to academics. The party was in full swing, everyone in good spirits, and as Weaver made his way through the dance-floor crowds, he acknowledged the handshakes from the other members of the team saying their goodbyes. The press had been invited, and a trestle table had been erected in the foyer, two Egyptian policemen standing guard over some of the valuables the dig had uncovered: gem necklaces, scarabs, gold amulets and stone cartouches. As Weaver thanked his well-wishers politely, others pressed in on him, and suddenly he had a desperate urge to be alone. "Would you excuse me, please? I need some fresh air."

He made his way through the throng, crossed to a French window and stepped out on to a balcony. It was cool outside, lotus and bougainvillaea scenting the night air, the window boxes full of flowers. The residency gardens were magnificent, a wooden pavilion in the grounds was lit up with coloured lights, and the majestic Nile lay beyond the walls. But that night there seemed an incredible stillness about the city, the usual traffic noise the merest whisper.

As he stood there, enjoying the solitude and the perfumed air, the door opened and Rachel appeared, wearing a simple black dress that hugged her figure, Jack Halder behind her. He wore a linen suit and held a bottle of ice-cold champagne and three glasses. As he handed a glass across, he smiled. "Quite a party, isn't it? But you look like you've had enough dancing for one evening, Harry. We thought we might find you somewhere quiet. Have another drink."

"Why not." Weaver took the champagne, and when Rachel was handed hers she placed it on the balcony, untouched, a sudden exhaustion showing in her face.

"Tired?" Weaver asked.

She smiled. "I'm afraid you and Jack have worn me off my feet."

Halder said, "By the way, before I forget, there's a few important people who'd like to meet you, Rachel."

"Who?"

"The ambassador wants to pay his respects, and a fellow named Kemal Assan. He's the son of an Egyptian dignitary who's an acquaintance of my father's. There's also a visiting professor from the British Museum who's had far too much to drink and speaks like this—" Halder pinched his nose in a mock gesture, and imitated a perfect upper-class English accent. "They're a boring lot, my dear, so I told the ruddy chaps you're tired and they can't keep you long. Shall I fetch them in?"

Rachel giggled. "Thanks, Jack."

He went out and Rachel said, "So, this is our last evening together, Harry. I'll miss you."

"You mean that?"

"Of course." She looked into his face, and said suddenly, "You know what's strange? I know so little of your background. Jack's is an open book. An American mother and a wealthy Prussian father who's a well-known collector of Egyptian artefacts. Languages and the classics at Heidelberg, and a year at Oxford in between." She laughed. "You can tell—he does that funny, upper-class English accent so well. But you've never spoken much about your past, except for the few things you've told me about. You graduated in engineering in New York, and you and Jack have been friends since childhood." She smiled. "There has to be much more, unless you're keeping secrets. Tell me how you both met. I'd love to know."

Weaver sipped his champagne, looked out over the balcony. "There isn't much to tell. When I was five, my father became the caretaker on the estate belonging to the family of Jack's mother. It's a big, rambling old place in upstate New York. We were the only two children, both only sons, and I guess it was natural we'd either become rivals or friends. But we became friends, right from the very start. Whenever we were together, we'd spend our time getting up to mischief on the estate. The Troublesome Two, his father called us. Sure, his family were wealthy, and mine were just ordinary folks, but Franz Halder always treated us with respect, no matter that we came from different sides of the tracks. He was never a snob and he made sure his son wasn't one, either. Even as a small boy, Jack was always good fun to be with, and a great companion. There isn't a pretentious bone in his body."

"What drew you to Egypt?"

"After I graduated last year, I went to work for a civil engineering firm in New York. But to tell the truth, after a couple of months I was beginning to find it boring. Jack's father liked to keep some of his collection at the estate. As children we'd see the kind of exotic things you'd come across only in books or museums—scarabs, ancient jewellery—and it was all so wondrous we'd spend hours looking at them. When Jack wrote and told me he was coming to Egypt to help with the dig, he asked if I'd like to come along. We'd hardly seen each other in almost six months, he'd been so busy helping his father with family business interests in Germany, and besides, I was ready to jump at the chance to get away from a stuffy Manhattan office. It seemed like a once-in-a-lifetime opportunity. So I decided to scrape together what few dollars I'd saved, quit my job, and take up the offer."

"No girlfriends left behind?"

"No one worth talking about."

"And no regrets about what you've done?"

"Not one. The only trouble is, it's kind of spoiled me. I don't think I can go back to the kind of career I had before. At least not until my money runs out. It's been more fun putting my engineering skills to work on a dig like this, instead of building roads in New York."

"You know what surprises me? That Jack never became an archaeologist."

"I think he's too restless to commit himself to any one thing. He says himself he'll always be just a fanatical amateur, like his father. He brought him here on visits as a child, but I guess you know that. And for as long as I've known him he's been in love with this country, fascinated by it, and not only its history, but everything about it—its culture, its people. I guess the fascination's sort of rubbed off on me."

"You like Jack very much, don't you?"

"He's always been my best friend," Weaver answered honestly. "He's like the brother I never had. And I'm grateful for his friendship. Besides, if it wasn't for his father, I probably never would have gone to college."

"What do you mean?"

"Franz Halder paid for my education. My own father could never have afforded it, though all he had to do in return was to make sure he kept the estate gardens filled with white lilies, the kind Jack's late mother loved so much."

Rachel hesitated. "Is that why you didn't talk about your past? Did you feel beholden to Jack and his family?"

"Not a bit," Weaver said with conviction. "They were simply good people who wanted to help me get a proper education. And I'll always be grateful. But Jack's father isn't the kind to make you feel under an obligation. And nothing like that would spoil the friendship between Jack and me, I'm sure of it. In fact, nothing at all ever has. We've always got on like a house on fire."

"You've never fallen out?"

"Not ever. I guess that's kind of remarkable. Sure, we've had our minor differences, but nothing we couldn't agree to disagree about."

Rachel looked at him, and said honestly, "You know something? I think you're both lucky. To have met each other. To have become such good friends. I thought that from the very start, when I first met you both. It's such a rare thing. Something to be cherished. And I hope nothing ever comes between you." She smiled then, looked into his eyes, but with an inexplicable sadness in her own, and on impulse took a flower from one of the window boxes and placed it in his buttonhole, before leaning over and kissing him gently on the lips. "A small gift from me. Something far less than a college education, but meant sincerely. I'm just so happy you came to help on the dig, Harry. I can't imagine what it would have been like without you and Jack."

Weaver looked back at her, at the striking blue eyes and pretty face. "I'll miss you too, Rachel."

"Will you, honestly?"

"More than I can tell. But I'm worried."

"About what?"

"We hear all this talk about what's happening to the Jews in Germany. If you ever go back—"

He let the sentence hang, and Rachel said quietly, "There's no chance of my parents or me returning to Germany. Not until this war has blown over and the Nazis are no longer in power. For now, Istanbul will be our home, and it'll be safe. My father has a lot of contacts there and he's sure he can get a more permanent lecturing post. But to be honest, it's Jack I'm more concerned about."

"What do you mean?"

"He's bound to go back to Germany, so it's likely he'll be conscripted. But he's being the optimist about how long the war might last. He seems to think the whole thing will have blown over by Christmas, once Hitler has his way and annexes Poland."

"He said that?"

"I heard him mention it tonight. And I suppose it's what a lot of people are saying. The optimists, mainly. But me, I'm not so sure. I think if it carries on, it could be truly awful." She changed the subject, as if to lighten the mood. "Still, at least we all had this time together. It's something I'll treasure and remember. Always."

Their eyes met, and something passed between them, Weaver was certain of it, and he looked at her a long time before he made to speak, wanting to tell her how he truly felt, but then he saw her glance away, towards the party, and suddenly she seemed ill at ease.

"What's the matter?"

"Noth—nothing."

Weaver looked back, through the open veranda door, and noticed a thin-faced Egyptian with a hook nose, wearing a pale linen suit, smoking a cigarette and leaning against a marble column. His skin was pockmarked. He looked faintly sinister, and he directed a darting glance towards them, but when he noticed Weaver staring, he disappeared into the crowd. Weaver looked back at Rachel. "That man—was he bothering you?"

She shivered. "It seems like he's been watching me all evening."

"Maybe I should find out who he is."

She put a hand on his arm. "No, don't bother, he's probably harmless. He just made me feel a little uncomfortable, that's all. But he's gone now."

Just then two men stepped through the open door, led by Halder, one of them the American ambassador, tall and distinguished-looking, the other a formal-looking young Egyptian in his early twenties, wearing the traditional Arab robe, the djellaba, with gold and silver thread.

Halder came forward with a smile. "I'm afraid they're trying to sober up the visiting British professor, he's completely plastered. But allow me to introduce the ambassador, and Kemal Assan."

The ambassador shook Rachel's hand warmly. "Miss Stern, it's a pleasure. I'm a great admirer of your father's work. And Kemal has been looking forward to meeting you all night. He has a keen interest in your excavations, hardly surprising when you consider that his father is one of the most senior officials with the Ministry of Antiquities, not to mention a close personal friend of King Farouk."

Kemal Assan gave the Arab greeting, touching his hand to his heart, then his head. "A tremendous pleasure to make your acquaintance, Miss Stern. My country owes you and your father's team a great debt. You've done wonderful work. I'm certain King Farouk and the government will want to thank you and your family for your efforts and that you will always be honoured guests in Egypt."

"You're very kind, Kemal." Rachel looked out at the lights and the city, aware of the powerful stillness. "I've never known Cairo to be so quiet. It's as if a storm's about to break."

"There's a bad atmosphere in the air, I'm afraid." Assan shrugged. "It almost seems as if the entire city is waiting to hear what more unpleasant news the war will bring."

Jack Halder glanced at his watch and said diplomatically, "And now, gentlemen, I'm afraid I must drag you away. Rachel's got a train to catch to Port Said early tomorrow, and she needs her beauty sleep."

"I hope we see you in Egypt again very soon, Miss Stern," Kemal Assan said.

The ambassador shook all their hands. "Until next time.

And thanks. You young people have sure done a terrific job."

The ambassador and Assan left. Jack Halder sipped his champagne, put down his glass and looked out at Cairo. "You're right, it's as quiet as the grave down there."

Rachel was tired, and glanced at her watch. "I hate to spoil the party, but I'm ready to collapse. And my parents are about to leave. They're both exhausted. It's always the same after a dig, especially in this climate. I think they put their heart and soul into it and they've worn themselves out."

"I'm hardly surprised. They've both been working round the clock." Halder smiled teasingly. "Even while the rest of us were asleep. Only the other morning I saw them crawling back into their tent, looking like they had been up digging half the night. What's the professor up to, Rachel? Has he discovered something he wants to keep secret from the rest of us?"

Rachel smiled back. "Hardly. But you know my father thinks he can never do enough. The work here means everything to him."

Halder winked at Weaver conspiratorially. "Well, Harry, did you ask?"

Weaver shook his head, faintly uncomfortable, and Halder said, "Neither did I."

"What are you both talking about?" Rachel enquired. "Ask what?"

Halder swallowed a mouthful of champagne, as if to steel his nerves, and took a deep breath. "This may be embarrassing. But to hell with it, the moment has come. There's something Harry and I have been mulling over, and we didn't have the nerve to ask. But seeing as you're leaving for Port Said tomorrow, and Istanbul beckons, we thought we might as well be brazen and pose the question."

"What question?"

"Is there even the slightest chance you might be in love with either one of us?"

Rachel flushed. She bit her lip, and for a moment she seemed unsettled. "Why—why don't I make a promise. I'll write to you both and you write back. It would give us all time to get to know each other better. Then we'll take it from there."

Halder looked deflated. "I think you're being very diplomatic."

"No, Jack, just honest. There's so much happening in my life right now. Leaving Egypt, the move to Istanbul—"

"Have we put you on the spot?" Weaver asked.

"No, Harry."

Halder said, "Then why do I feel embarrassed?"

"There's no need. No need for either of you to be. You know I care so much for you both."

"Only care?"

"Please, Jack. This is not the time."

"I'm sorry we brought up the subject, Rachel," Weaver said, and went to take her arm. "I can see that you're tired. I'll go see if one of the embassy cars can take you to your hotel and we'll escort you down."

"No, I hate partings. You both stay and enjoy yourselves, you've more than deserved it." She hesitated, her lips trembling with emotion as she looked at them. "Can I tell you something? It's been the best time of my life. I really mean that. Until we meet again, goodbye." It was very sudden, and there were tears in her eyes as she kissed and hugged them both, and then she was gone.

The band was playing a waltz. Halder picked up his champagne glass. "She seemed pretty upset. But she didn't really answer the question, did she? Me, I feel a little disappointed."

Weaver considered for a moment. "I could be wrong, but it seems to me the offer to write could only mean one of three things."

"What?"

"One, she doesn't want to get involved with either of us, and it's the easy way out. Two, she likes one of us, but we put her in an awkward situation by both being present, in which case she couldn't say outright, for fear of disappointing the other."

"And three?"

"She likes both of us equally, can't make up her mind, and needs some breathing space to decide."

"You think it's that?"

Weaver shrugged. "It's just a feeling I get. Maybe we

should just take Rachel at her word. Besides, she's right. There's a lot happening in her life. Her family can't return to Germany, and Istanbul's a whole new world to come to terms with. And she was exhausted tonight. I think all the hard work she's been putting in has finally caught up with her."

"You seem very blasé all of a sudden."

"I like to think she was being genuine, Jack. She's not the kind of woman to just jump into a relationship. She needs time. So why don't we drop it for now."

"But you're disappointed she didn't give us a straight answer. I can tell."

"Sure I am. It prolongs the torture. But why don't we wait and see what happens, and try not to dwell on it."

Halder forced a smile. "That's the engineer in you speaking. Even when you're upset in love, the practical side takes over. And maybe you're right. I wish I could be like that, but God, I'll miss her. It was such a terrific time, and it's a pity it all has to come to an end. I've had the best time of my life in her company."

Weaver picked up the champagne bottle, refilled their glasses. "Change the subject. When are you leaving Cairo?"

"Tuesday. I'm flying home. I haven't much choice— I've been conscripted."

Weaver was dumbstruck. "So *that's* what your letter was about?"

"I'm afraid so." Halder shrugged. "You know my father's family come from a long line of Prussian officers, some of them founders of the military academy. They'd turn in their graves if I ignored the call."

Weaver put a hand on Halder's shoulder. "You should have told me, Jack. It just all seems so sudden. I'll be worried about you."

"To be honest, I didn't want to spoil the last couple of days by mentioning it. And I've been trying my best to put it at the back of my mind. But don't worry about me. With my background, I'll probably land a boring desk job."

"Do you really believe it'll be over by Christmas, Jack? Rachel said you thought so."

Halder nodded firmly. "I think it will. Ordinary Germans don't want another war. Too many of them remember how

bad the last one was. I'm pretty sure common sense will pre-
vail in the end. And what about you? What will you do?"

"Right now, I feel kind of footloose. Professor Stern
suggested there's still a little clearing up to be done at Sakkara before the site's handed over to the Egyptians, so I
volunteered to help, along with a couple of the others. I've
also had an offer tonight to join a desert expedition, so
maybe I'll stay on for a while, and even try to learn more
of the language. Besides, America declared its neutrality.
We've no part in this war."

"Good for you. Let's just hope it all settles down soon.
But the thing about it is, the whole world's gone crazy."

"What do you mean?"

"The war's already sort of started to intrude. The rumour's been going around that the British dug up a German
radio transmitter hidden in a field along the Pyramids Road.
It seems there are spies already at work in Cairo."

Weaver nodded. "I know about the rumour. But what's
that got to do with anything?"

"After we heard the declaration of war on the radio over
a week ago, I actually overheard one of the British in our
group claim that Rachel and I, and all the other Germans
on the dig, were really enemy agents and up to no good.
Did you ever hear such garbage? I mean, her mother's Jewish for a start. And Professor Stern loathes the Nazis."

"And what do you think of the Nazis, Jack?"

It was the first time they had ever discussed politics, and
Halder was mildly surprised. "Me? I love my country, but
I think you'll have guessed by now I haven't got much
time for Hitler."

"You mean because of Poland? Or because of what he's
doing to the Jews? All these race laws and prison camps
and deportations we've been hearing about."

"Both. And I've no time for that sort of cruel behaviour,
and nor do so many decent-minded Germans. And we've
been friends long enough for you to know I wouldn't con-
done the kind of laws the Nazis have enacted against the
Jews, or the way Hitler has banished so many of them from
Germany. But it's not only that. Hitler talks too loudly and
hasn't a single ounce of humour. Always a bad combination, especially in an Austrian." Halder smiled faintly. "I'm

afraid he's also an arrogant bore. And most important of all, he has the makings of a tyrant. And all tyrants are cowards in the end. Which is why I think he'll back down before it really does go too far."

"I just hope you're right. But do you really have to go back home?"

"There's a German word. *Pflicht*. You may have heard my father use it. It means duty, and more besides. And it's a word often used in the Halder vocabulary. In fact, it's in the family motto. So in a way, I feel I'm honour-bound not to let down the family name. No matter what my father might think of Hitler, I really don't believe he could live with the fact of having a son who turned out to be the first conscientious objector in the clan."

"In that case, I wouldn't worry about what the British say about you being a spy. I hear some of the Germans pointed the same accusations at the French and the British members of the crew." Weaver smiled. "So far, I think I'm the only one who hasn't had a bad word said about him. It has me worried."

Halder laughed, and Weaver scanned the crowds and said more seriously, "There was a man watching Rachel this evening. Egyptian. Thin, about forty, a bit sinister-looking, wearing a linen suit. Did you notice him?"

"No. Why?"

Weaver shrugged. "It's probably nothing. Perhaps she has a secret admirer." He hesitated. "You know what just occurred to me? What if America entered the war, and we were on opposing sides? How would that make you feel?"

"Terrible." Halder shook his head firmly. "But we could never be enemies, Jack. Not ever. At least not personally, whatever differences our two countries might have."

"I guess not." Weaver put down his glass and smiled. "But do you think we'd still be buddies if there's even a slim chance Rachel might choose one of us?"

"Always. No matter what the future brings." Halder's eyes twinkled. "But I have to admit, she's such a desirable woman I'd be almost tempted to fight you for her if ever it came down to it." He smiled good-humouredly, raised his glass. "A final toast, then. To friendship and a wonderful summer."

Weaver lifted his glass. "To friendship. And I'll miss your company, Jack. I really will. So try and look after yourself. I just hope this damned war doesn't drag on too long."

Halder winked. "Me too. But if there really is a chance for one of us, may the best letter-writer win the fair lady's hand."

Jack Halder returned home to Germany via Rome on a scheduled Italian passenger flight out of Cairo. Within a week he had been conscripted into the Wehrmacht and posted to Berlin for officer training. Although no admirer of the Nazis, he was to prove a dashing, adventurous officer, and his sharp intellect and knowledge of languages soon came to the attention of the Abwehr, Germany's military intelligence.

He was personally recruited by Admiral Wilhelm Canaris, posted to the special operations section which dealt with the Balkans and the Mediterranean, and when the war in North Africa began in earnest, was eventually seconded to the Middle Eastern Division, working with Rommel's Africa Corps.

When he didn't hear from Rachel Stern within six months of returning home, he met and fell in love with Helga Ritter, the daughter of a Hamburg doctor. It was something he had never expected or anticipated, because part of him still loved Rachel, and there were many times when he thought of her. But his new wife was to prove as interesting a young woman, vivacious and loving. Within ten months of marriage she gave birth to a son, Pauli.

Rachel Stern never wrote to either young man. Three days after the ambassador's party, she and her parents sailed from Port Said on the *Izmir*, the only paying passengers on board the ancient Turkish-owned cargo ship bound for Istanbul. On the second night out of port she was standing at the starboard rail, still thinking about the momentous summer, when the engine room erupted in fire. The explosion that sank the *Izmir* killed fourteen people. Her mother was one of them.

The surviving crew members had abandoned ship while flames raged on deck. Rachel and her father managed to scramble aboard one of the lifeboats with two badly

wounded Turkish sailors, her father still clutching his briefcase containing his precious maps and notes from the Sakkara dig. They drifted away from the other lifeboats in the
darkness, and a little before midnight a storm blew up.
Their tiny vessel was pounded by ten-foot waves and lashed
by savage winds. The weather improved by dawn, but by
noon the sailors were dead and she and her father were
exhausted, dehydrated, and burnt by a scorching Mediterranean sun.

Late in the afternoon, a grey shape loomed on the horizon and cruised towards them. At first, Rachel thought it
was a British naval boat searching for survivors, but when
it came closer she saw the red-and-black swastika of the
German Kriegsmarine. She and her father were detained on
board the naval vessel after it docked in Naples for refuelling, and two weeks later they arrived in Hamburg, where
they were promptly met by the Gestapo.

Harry Weaver stayed on in Egypt, and for much longer
than he thought, working with an American desert exploration group searching for archaeological ruins, until six
months before Rommel landed in Tripoli in February 1941.
Then he flew to Lisbon and on to London, returning to the
United States via Southampton. He volunteered the day after the Japanese attacked Pearl Harbor.

He had heard about the sinking of the *Izmir* while still
at Sakkara. It was a little after midnight, and someone came
to his tent with a newspaper and showed him the report,
which claimed that the only survivors were four Turkish
crewmen whose lifeboat had been picked up by a Maltese
fishing trawler.

When he read the news in the lamplight, he cried. He
had loved Rachel deeply, and that night on the ambassador's veranda he had so much wanted to tell her, but had
never really got the chance, or had the courage. Then he
did what any grief-stricken young man would have done in
such circumstances. He put aside the newspaper, took a
bottle of whisky from his bag, and got drunk.

But the very last thing he did before he finally fell asleep
was to look at the photograph he treasured, of the three of
them together. Rachel, Jack and himself. Three young,
smiling people, their arms around one another, standing in
the desert sands at Sakkara. It was a happy time.

NOVEMBER 1943

FOUR

It was the hottest summer in thirty-six years. The ancient city built in the shadow of the Giza pyramids had always stunk, but now it smelled like a fetid sewer. All over North Africa and Europe, clear skies and an oppressive heat wave had added an unpleasant discomfort to the rigours of war. And yet, despite the climate, it had been a momentous year for the Allies. The once mighty Rommel had been defeated, the German 5th Army of Field Marshal von Paulus had surrendered at Stalingrad, General Patton's troops had landed in Sicily, and the Reich's second city, the sprawling port of Hamburg, had been reduced to smouldering rubble.

And then came autumn. The weather cooled, the Germans started to regroup, and the war suddenly stagnated. In the cauldron that was Cairo, such news mattered far less than the chilling winds and the welcome rainclouds that finally blew in from the Mediterranean in early November.

To Mustapha Evir, crouching in the shadows of the pine trees, it seemed that the oppressive heat of summer had never gone away. It was a mild night, yet sweat ran down his shirt and back, trickled down his face and chin, and his body felt on fire. It was fear, of course. To try to lessen his anxiety, he toyed with a cheap set of Arab worry beads in his right hand. Considering the danger of what he was about to do, Evir knew that one slip could cost him his life.

He was a small man, lean and thin, and wore a shabby black suit, tatty leather sandals, and a grimy, collarless shirt. His unshaven face had the tired look of a weary old fox constantly beset by hounds. He was in the grounds of a walled villa in the wealthy district of Garden City, an area that quartered some of the grand city homes of foreign ambassadors and their families. He had waited with the patience of a hunter for over an hour, and now it was almost time to move. Sixty paces across the lawns stood the handsome villa that housed the American ambassador. Two armed sentries paced outside the double oak doors, and there were another two at the entrance by the gate lodge.

Evir glanced behind him, down the sloping gardens, past the ornate pavilion and the sentries at the lodge, checking that the guards were still there. Beyond the wrought-iron gates, in the far darkness, he could make out the Kasr-el-Nil bridge and the broad majestic Nile, the ghostly white sails of feluccas gliding over the shimmering, moonlit water. He noticed the tall minaret of a mosque on the far side of the river and said a silent prayer—not that prayer had ever changed anything in his miserable life, but right now he needed to calm himself. The last thing he wanted was to go back to the stinking, crowded cell he had shared with twelve other prisoners, and he begged Allah to protect him.

As he turned back, a chandelier suddenly blazed into life in the villa's hallway, and Evir tensed. Moments later he heard a car's engine start up, then an imposing black Ford appeared from behind the servants' quarters and drew up in front of the entrance. The sentries snapped to attention as the oak doors opened and a man dressed in evening wear came out and stepped into the chauffeured car.

The American ambassador had a well-fed look, and Evir spat in the darkness and despised him. What did he know of having seven hungry mouths to feed? Of living in a stinking hovel? Of how a man had to break his back every day to earn a crust in a harsh city like Cairo?

Evir saw the Ford drive away, and seconds later the chandelier lights went off. As soon as the car moved out through the main gates, the sentries seemed to relax, and the two outside the villa entrance sat on the granite steps and lit cigarettes. Evir crouched in the shadows of the trees for five more minutes, then wiped the sweat from his face, slipped the set of worry beads into his pocket and stood, massaging his aching knees. It was time to go to work.

The American ambassador's residence had a reputation for tight security, but Mustapha Evir also had a reputation. To those who availed themselves of his services he was known as The Fox. There wasn't a house built that he couldn't break into, or a safe made that he couldn't crack. But three stiff sentences in the hell of Cairo's Torah prison, in over thirty years of crime, had cooled his love of the work. After his release three months previously he had formed the intention of leading an honest life, but the only work he could find was back-breaking drudgery, carrying bales of cotton through the steep, cobbled market streets, for a fat cloth merchant who treated him like a dog and paid him barely enough to feed his family. But tonight, this one job could earn him a fortune.

Evir was unimpressed by the security and the sentries. He had watched the villa for over a week, observing the guards, sketching the layout of the grounds, trying to judge distances and anticipate obstacles. So much was at risk, and he couldn't afford mistakes. But it had been simple enough to climb over the residence wall, and the sentries didn't appear to notice as he crawled on his belly across the lawn towards the patio on the far side of the building. He guessed that now the Germans had been defeated in North Africa, the guards were more at ease. He reached the French windows and stood, perspiration dripping from his face. He took a long, slim knife from under his coat, slipped the blade between the window frames, sprung the catch effortlessly, and stepped between some curtains into a darkened, oak-panelled study.

The Khan-el-Khalili bazaar was crowded as usual that evening, the noise and the smell of spices and sweaty bodies overpowering, but as Evir made his way through the throng two hours later, he felt happy with himself. He had done a good night's work. The narrow maze of alleys rang with the cries of street vendors, and cripples begging for alms. Evir kept his hands on the valuable object in his pocket. Even a criminal wasn't safe in the bazaar. There were thieves here who'd steal the coins from a blind man's bowl.

A couple of scruffy beggar children came up to him. "Baksheesh?"

"Away with you, sons of whores."

The boys spat at him, laughed and ran away. Evir didn't even bother to run after them and clip their ears. He had more important things on his mind. Halfway through the bazaar he came to a busy crossroads, with bustling shops and restaurants. The streets and pavements were alive, cafés and shops blaring music, people crowding the trams and buses, passengers clinging dangerously to the rails and running boards.

Despite the war, the blackout restrictions were half-hearted in Cairo; some car headlamps and streetlights were dimmed with a thin coat of regulation blue paint, others not at all. Ancient, dented taxis trundled past. A shortage of parts meant that most of them drove with broken headlamps, damaged fenders and cracked windscreens. The motorised traffic was chaotic, and drivers had to compete with horse-drawn carts and livestock being herded through the streets: goats, sheep, cattle and camels.

To make matters worse, drunken off-duty troops filled the pavements: British, American, Australian, piling in and out of bars and restaurants with names like Home Sweet Home and Café-Bar Old England.

Remembering his instructions, Evir waited at the cross-roads. Clusters of jabbering Arab men sat outside tea rooms, puffing on hookah pipes and playing backgammon as they sipped from glasses. Traffic roared past in all directions. Five minutes later Evir saw a muddied green BSA motorcycle come down the street on his left and slow to a halt.

An Arab sat on the machine. He wore a djellaba, and had a beard. The man gestured for him to join him. Evir climbed on board the pillion seat, and the BSA roared away from the kerb.

The man kept glancing over his shoulder while he drove, as if to be certain they hadn't been followed. He headed towards the El Hakim mosque, weaving through the tight back streets, until ten minutes later they came out on to a cobbled square, ringed with tall brick-and-wood tenement houses. They climbed off the BSA. The man locked it with a padlock and chain, and beckoned for Evir to follow. He stepped into the open hallway of one of the houses and climbed a flight of bare wooden stairs to the first floor. There was a door with three heavy locks, and the man unlocked them in turn with a bunch of keys, led Evir inside and closed the door.

"Well?" the bearded man asked.

"I did as you asked."

The man looked pleased. "You're certain no one saw you at the residency?"

Evir laughed. "If they did, do you think I'd be here?"

He had been in the flat twice before, when the man needed to show him how to use the equipment. It was neat but functional, with a coffee table and some cushions scattered on the floor, a metal stove by the wall, but it smelled musty, and Evir had the feeling the place wasn't often lived in. The man held out his hand. "Give me the camera."

"My money first," Evir demanded.

"You'll get your money afterwards."

Evir shook his head. "I want it now."

"Later," the man answered firmly. "When I'm finished examining your work. If the photographs don't turn out, I want you to go back again."

"Again?"

"Again. Now, give me the camera."

Evir heard the hard edge in the man's voice, saw the threatening look on his face. There was a dangerous air about him that made Evir feel uncomfortable. He took the tiny Leica camera from his pocket and handed it over.

"Wait here."

The man stepped into the bedroom and closed the door. The stand-up closet he used as a darkroom was off to the right, a faint, pungent smell of chemicals wafting out. He went in and pulled the sliding door after him, tugged a string hanging from the ceiling. A red light came on, revealing a shelf containing glass jars of developer and fixer. There was also a stopwatch, a couple of metal soaking basins, an electric fan, and a thin wooden box, topped with opaque glass and underlit with a couple of bulbs. He filled one of the basins with developer, removed the roll of film from the tiny Leica, placed it in the liquid, pressed the stopwatch and waited for three minutes.

Finally he turned on the fan, plucked the roll of film from the tray, and held the exposed negative over the stream of air until it was dry. He flicked on the underlit glass and laid the strip on top. Carefully, he examined the exposures with a magnifying glass. As he studied one of the negatives of the pages marked "Top Secret," he suddenly quivered with shock.

It took him several moments to compose himself, then he picked up a cotton towel and wiped his hands. He must still have looked shocked when he stepped back into the room, because Evir said, "What's the matter? Is something wrong?"

The man shook his head. "Nothing. You've done excellent work." He tossed away the towel. "Now, let's get out of here."

"Where are we going?"

"You want your money, don't you?"

Twenty minutes later they arrived outside a dilapidated warehouse on the old Nile docks. The place was deserted, the wire-metal gates unlocked, and the man turned the BSA into a darkened cobbled yard in front.

Evir felt a pang of fear. "Why have we come here?"

The man switched off the engine. "Come, you'll get your money."

He got off the motorcycle, leaned it against a wall and strode inside the warehouse. Evir reluctantly went after him. The building was a ramshackle, cavernous place littered with bits of rusting scrap metal, the concrete floors covered with puddles of watery oil. There was a dented oil drum in a corner, a storm lamp on top. The man lit the wick and tossed away the match.

The warehouse was flooded with soft yellow light. The man took a thick envelope from his pocket, waved it in his hand. "Before I pay you, I need to ask you some questions. Did you take anything else from the safe?"

Evir saw the man study him intently. His eyes seemed to burn into his face. "On the lives of my children, I did only as you told me."

The man continued to stare. "You're quite sure you're telling me the truth?"

Evir felt uncomfortable, a ripple of fear down his spine. "You said to photograph every document I found in the safe. I did just as you asked. And now I want my money."

"Have patience. And you're certain you told no one about our arrangement?"

"Not a soul. May Allah cut out my tongue if I lie." Evir told the truth. Besides, he had been warned of the consequences.

The man nodded, satisfied, and smiled. "Good. There's just one more thing."

Evir frowned. "What?"

The man put down the envelope and reached into his pocket. When his hand came out the smile was gone, and Evir saw a curved Arab blade with a white ivory handle, a savage-looking thing like a metal claw.

"I can't let you leave. You know too much and you've seen my face."

FIVE

CHESAPEAKE BAY, VIRGINIA
12 NOVEMBER/8:50 A.M.

The sun was hidden behind dark rain-clouds that morning as the vast grey bulk of the battleship USS *Iowa*, all fifty-eight thousand tons of her, the pride of the US fleet, dropped anchor five miles off the Virginian coast.

Captain Joe McCrea watched from the bridge as the tug came heading his way from the shore, bobbing through the gentle swell, escorted by half a dozen naval vessels prowling around it like protective mother hens. McCrea had received the signal twenty minutes ago, telling him the VIP passengers were ready to join his ship. One among them was certainly the most important he had ever carried on board a vessel under his command, in over twenty years' distinguished naval service, and McCrea knew he was about to undertake the most challenging mission of his life.

He turned to the young lieutenant at his side. "Make ready to bring the passengers aboard."

"Yes, Captain."

McCrea put down his binoculars as the lieutenant went down to the main deck. The *Iowa* was like a miniature town in itself, with a crew of two and a half thousand men. It bristled with an impressive array of heavy guns and anti-aircraft weapons, its decks and platforms covered an area of over nine acres, and despite its vast size it could travel at a speed of thirty-three knots, the fastest vessel in its class. Out in the Norfolk Sound, scattered on the gentle grey waves, was her escort, six more vessels with a deadly array of firepower, and their sight was a reassuring one to McCrea that morning. This mightn't be the biggest armada in history, but it was definitely one of the most vital, and secret. He checked his uniform, then made his way to the lower deck to greet his passengers.

When the tug finally pulled alongside, McCrea saw at least a dozen people cramped in the stern, civilians and naval personnel. There was a flurry of activity as sailors on the landing boom grabbed lines and made ready. Because of the height of the *Iowa*, there was a sheer drop of almost thirty feet from the lower main deck to the sea. A small boom extended down towards the waves to enable boarding, but that was where it got difficult. It wasn't every day you got to bring the President of the United States aboard. Franklin Delano Roosevelt was a cripple, wheelchair-bound most of his life, so it posed a particular problem. He couldn't step on to the boom, so a harness had been arranged to winch him on to the *Iowa*.

McCrea looked down into the gentle swell as a succession of Secret Service agents and aides jumped from the tug on to the boom, and then it was the President's turn. He saw the familiar sight of Roosevelt appear, the big, kindly face and the ready smile, as he was helped from his wheelchair. His lower legs were encased in metal braces, the spindly limbs as thin as a young boy's, a legacy of childhood polio which left him in frequent agony. It took two Secret Service agents to carry him to the harness and secure him, and then it was winched up.

It some ways it was a pitiful sight, and one McCrea was dreading. The President of the most powerful country on earth, the man on whom the world depended to win the war, being hoisted aboard the *Iowa* on a harness made of wood and rope davits. But there was no sign of fear or self-pity on the man's face, just solemn determination. McCrea waited patiently, his heart in his mouth, hoping to God there wasn't an accident, that the ropes didn't break and the President of America slip from the harness and drown.

Finally, Roosevelt was helped aboard, and McCrea breathed a sigh of relief. A flurry of Secret Service agents went to his assistance, the wheelchair appeared on deck, and Roosevelt was helped out of the harness and into the chair. One of the agents placed the familiar heavy naval cloak around the President's shoulders. McCrea had noticed the admiration on the faces of his crew as they watched the whole process, young and not-so-young American seamen who had crowded on deck to catch a glimpse of their famous passenger. They looked on in awe and surprise, wanting to applaud, but the order had gone out that no honours were to be rendered when their passengers boarded. This was a top-secret mission, and the *Iowa*'s crew complied to a man. McCrea saluted. "Welcome on board, Mr. President, sir."

Roosevelt smiled warmly, offered his hand. "Captain McCrea. So you're the poor fellow who's got the dubious pleasure of getting me safely to my destination?"

"I am indeed, sir. We've got your quarters all set up. If you'll kindly walk this way and—" McCrea left the words unfinished, suddenly remembering the President's infirmity as he looked at him in the wheelchair. It was a dumb mistake and he blushed a deep crimson. He had been Roosevelt's naval aide for two years, and yet the man's steely determination constantly made you forget that not only was he a cripple, but he also suffered gravely from heart disease.

Roosevelt brushed aside the blunder, warmly took hold of McCrea's arm and laughed. "Don't you worry, Captain. I get around pretty well in this darned contraption, so you just lead the way."

When they entered Roosevelt's cabin on the upper deck, McCrea said, "I took the liberty of bringing along some route maps, to show you how we'll proceed, Mr. President."

The President fitted a Lucky Strike into a Bakelite cigarette holder. "That's most kind of you, Captain."

A Secret Service agent offered a light, before he pushed the wheelchair over to the table. Another agent stood close at hand, carrying a black doctor's bag of emergency medicines; the President's heart pills, his rubbing mixtures for when he became soaked in sweat, which he often did from overexertion, bottles of various painkillers, and—as always—a small bottle of whisky.

McCrea waited until Roosevelt had slipped on his glasses, then pointed to the map. "We've plotted a course south past the Azores, then north-east to the Gibraltar straits, and on to Oran. Our ETA is nine days from now— the twentieth—Mr. President, sir. Then you'll be on your way to Cairo by plane, barring problems."

Roosevelt smiled gently, the cigarette holder clenched between his teeth. "I'll assume you're well equipped for those?"

"We've got speed, and a destroyer escort. Both should prove too much for any German subs. But then you never can tell. It's a risk we take, sir."

Roosevelt shrugged. "The price of war, Captain."

"We'll have our aircraft scouting for submarine activity, and the destroyers will be using their sonar equipment for the same purpose. It's the German U-boats that pose the biggest threat. They're pretty deadly."

Roosevelt removed the holder from his mouth and looked up, his face more serious. "This is an important trip, Captain. You might even say that hundreds or thousands of lives—not to mention the outcome of the war and the future of our nation—depend upon my arrival. You think we'll make it?"

McCrea considered before replying. "It's never easy to predict, Mr. President, with so much enemy activity in the Atlantic. But then again, the Germans don't know our plans and we'll be moving fast, so I'm pretty confident we can get you safely to your destination."

Roosevelt removed his glasses and gave one of his famous lopsided smiles. "Captain, it seems for now my fate is in your hands."

The man wore a pair of dark navy oilskins, the standard issue of the US Coast Guard. He had waited for almost three hours, lying in the sodden grass on the Norfolk headland as the rain pelted down, the powerful marine binoculars resting on his arm. By the time he saw the tugboat roll through the waves and come alongside the *Iowa*, the rain had stopped and the visibility had greatly improved. He lay there, observing the vessels as best he could from such a distance. Five minutes later he tucked the binoculars under his oilskins and quickly made his way back down the headland path. He recovered the bicycle hidden in the long grass, swung his leg over the crossbar, and rode away.

SIX

BERLIN
14 NOVEMBER/8:30 A.M.
Admiral Wilhelm Canaris was an odd man.

He shuffled around wearing carpet slippers, and his office was always in disarray. The obligatory wall portrait of Adolf Hitler was nowhere to be seen, for Canaris—or the "Little Admiral," as the former U-boat commander was affectionately known to his old shipmates—had nothing but contempt for the vulgar and pompous Nazi leadership. It was a contempt he shrewdly kept to himself, for Canaris was also head of the Abwehr, Germany's wartime military intelligence, with responsibility for overseeing almost twenty thousand personnel and agents in thirty countries around the world.

It was almost noon when the young Prussian adjutant knocked on the office door in the Abwehr's headquarters at 74–76 Tirpitz Ufer in Berlin, overlooking the Landwehr canal, and, receiving no reply, entered. The adjutant was a new man, barely a week in his post, but he was already acquainted with the admiral's eccentricity. He saw a small man in his middle fifties with bushy grey eyebrows and a stooped back, who looked like a provincial schoolmaster, wearing frayed slippers and a crumpled naval uniform, kneeling on the floor and feeding a bowl of scraps to two nervous-looking pet dachshunds.

The adjutant coughed. "Herr Admiral."

Canaris looked up, distracted. "What is it, Bauer?"

"A call from SS headquarters, from General Schellenberg."

"And what does Walter want this time?"

"The general requests an urgent meeting at nine hundred hours."

"For what purpose?"

"He didn't say, Herr Admiral. Only that it's urgent."

Suddenly there was the distant wail of an air raid siren. Canaris sighed, patted the dogs to calm them, got to his feet and dusted his knees. US Air Force B-17s had been raiding Berlin during daylight all the previous week, with deadly effect, and by the sound of it they were about to start again. "Very well. I suppose you had better organise the car. And make it quick, before the Americans go to work."

"*Zu Befehl*, Herr Admiral." Bauer shouted the reply, snapped to attention, and smartly clicked his heels, causing both animals to whimper. Canaris frowned with displeasure.

"Do me a favour, Bauer. This heel-clicking and shouting business, it's all very well on the parade ground, but please refrain from doing it in the office. It rather frightens the dogs."

Bauer flushed. "As the Herr Admiral wishes."

When the adjutant left, Canaris looked down at his beloved dachshunds, their snouts stuck in the bowl, and sighed wearily. "No rest for the wicked, my children. I have a feeling young Walter may be up to his tricks again."

Walter Schellenberg was one of the most unorthodox SS intelligence officers Canaris had ever met, and perhaps also the most likable. A young man of thirty-two, and a lawyer by profession, he was dashing and handsome, with a taste for the finer things in life. A graduate of the University of Bonn, he had shrewdly joined the SS after Hitler came to power in 1933, and managed to obtain a post in the SD, the SS intelligence department, where his sharp aptitude and businesslike mentality soon attracted Himmler. Schellenberg quickly rose to become a member of Himmler's personal staff, and was eventually appointed Head of SD Ausland, the foreign intelligence branch, for like his boss he revelled in plots, subterfuges and secrecy, as if they were his very life-blood.

A chain-smoker, he had an easy manner, and he was in a good mood when Canaris entered his office on the third floor, despite the fact that the bombardment was going on outside, wisps of smoke and dust drifting up from the wall ventilator.

"Sit down, Wilhelm." Schellenberg smiled. "As usual you look like you have the weight of the world on your shoulders."

Schellenberg wore his black SS uniform, the cuff-titles bearing the legend RFSS in silver thread. *Reichsführer der* SS. Himmler's personal staff. The sight of the cuff-title made Canaris shiver inwardly. He always detested having to visit the Reich Main Security Office on Prinz-Albrecht-Strasse, the headquarters of the SS and the Gestapo, from which Heinrich Himmler and his deputies presided over their empire of evil. The black uniforms and grim surroundings never failed to send a chill down his spine.

"Sometimes it certainly feels that way," he replied. "So, what is it this time, Walter?"

There was a lull in the bombing and Canaris heard a screech of tyres outside in the inner courtyard as a truck and a Mercedes pulled up in quick succession. Leather-coated Gestapo men climbed out in a hurry and began unloading their human cargo, bound for the torture cellars. Several senior Wehrmacht officers were among the prisoners, elderly men mostly, one or two of whom Canaris faintly recognised. Some were with their bewildered wives and families. The Gestapo savagely kicked and beat them with pistol butts as they were herded towards the basement entrance.

"What the devil's going on?" Canaris asked in alarm.

"A messy business." Schellenberg observed the scene outside. "Suspected subversives, all of them. Himmler has reason to believe there's a group of traitorous plotters working against the Führer. Recent evidence from our interrogations points to an attempt by high-ranking officers to bomb his plane in March of this year. Only by the grace of God did it fail to go off."

"Good Lord." Canaris paled. "You can't be serious."

"Very, I'm sad to say. Who could believe that anyone who has taken an oath of loyalty to the Führer would wish him dead? But we'll root them out, don't you worry. Every last one of them, even if we have to interrogate the entire army, navy and air force."

Schellenberg turned from the window, popped a cigarette in his mouth, lit it, and blew smoke up to the ceiling. "But back to business. The latest ciphers from my SD agents in Persia and the Middle East agents make for rather interesting reading. It appears all the signs are that the Cairo and Teheran meetings of the Allied leaders are definitely on, just as we suspected. And as you well know, Roosevelt has yet to decide on how the imminent invasion of Europe will proceed."

Canaris forced himself to look away from the disturbing scene outside, felt a chill go through him, and sighed heavily, as if he knew what was coming. "Why do I get the feeling you have another of your exotic plans in mind?"

Schellenberg grinned. "My dear Wilhelm, such is the sole reason for my existence. What would life be without a little subterfuge to make it interesting?"

"I suppose you had better tell me."

"First, tell me your opinion of President Roosevelt."

Canaris raised an eyebrow. "What is this? Some sort of trick question to hang me with?"

An uneasy alliance existed between Germany's two intelligence agencies, and Canaris had the unpleasant suspicion he was about to be duped into some sort of trap.

"On the contrary. A simple question for which I'd appreciate an honest answer."

Canaris shrugged. "I have to admit a certain grudging respect for the man, even if he is the enemy. A cripple who's spent most of his life in constant pain and in a wheelchair, but nevertheless still manages to win the presidency for three terms, commands a certain admiration in itself. As far as American public opinion goes, he's probably the most revered President since Lincoln. He took their economy out of the worst depression in history almost single-handedly, and they respect him for that, even though we Germans despise him for bringing America into the war and bombing our cities to ruins."

"An honest assessment." Schellenberg stood, came

round his desk and sat on the edge. "What do you know about my top agent in Cairo?"

"I presume you mean Nightingale? Only that I've heard he's the best you ever had."

Schellenberg laughed and shook his head. "Forget Nightingale, that's far in the past. I'm talking about the present."

"Absolutely nothing. You know damned well you keep that information to yourself."

Schellenberg smiled. "But times change, and now it's time to co-operate. The war is hardly going in our favour right now. Indeed, there are some who say we're on the losing side."

Canaris raised his eyebrows and said mildly, "I really wouldn't express that view too loudly, Walter. Unless you want to whistle goodbye to your career and have your testicles reshaped in the cellars."

Schellenberg threw his head back and laughed. "That's what I like about you, Wilhelm, you always have my interests at heart. But back to matters in hand. Actually, we have two principal agents still active in Cairo. The most important is a man named Harvey Deacon, code name Besheeba. Born in Hamburg, forty-eight years of age."

"He's a German citizen?"

"British, actually. Rather ironical, that, considering he hates the Allies with a vengeance."

"May I ask why?"

"The British were responsible for killing his father."

"Which makes for rather a neat motive."

"Exactly. He's a nightclub owner and businessman. I can also tell you that he's ruthless and immensely capable. He's done rather well for us in the past, extremely well in fact."

"And the other?"

"An Arab named Hassan Sabry. Code name Phoenix. We had him working for Rommel's people, until we moved him to Cairo. Though his real interest is banishing the British from Egypt. However, while both men have the cunning of sewer rats, they're rather limited when it comes to the bigger picture."

"Why are you telling me all this?"

Schellenberg stubbed out his cigarette, quickly lit another. "I need your help. I have a job in mind that requires the assistance of a couple of your people, to work alongside Deacon and Sabry."

"Whatever for?"

Schellenberg looked deathly serious. "Because, my dear Wilhelm, together we're going to kill President Roosevelt."

The room was so quiet that Canaris could hear the clock ticking. He was caught off guard, and when he had recovered said, "Have you lost your mind? What you're suggesting is preposterous."

"*Daring* was the word I would have used. And you forget, only six weeks ago Colonel Otto Skorzeny's SS paratroops rescued Mussolini from a heavily fortified garrison. Before we undertook that mission all the indications pointed to failure—we assessed only a ten per cent chance of success—yet we pulled it off brilliantly. From touchdown to rescue took precisely four minutes, and with not one of our men lost in the action."

The bold liberation of Il Duce from imprisonment at the Hotel Campo Imperatore in Abruzzi in central Italy on 12 September was still being proudly sung about in the corridors of SD headquarters. It was certainly a dazzling triumph, but Canaris shook his head. "What you're proposing is something else entirely. We both know that Roosevelt, like Churchill, has a steel wall of security around him day and night. Such a thing would be impossible."

"Nothing is impossible, Wilhelm. And desperate times call for desperate measures. Besides, it all depends on the planning."

Canaris said wearily, "And how exactly do you propose to assassinate the President of the United States?"

"First, let me show you something." Schellenberg handed across a slip of paper from the file on his desk. As Canaris started to read, he said, "It's a rather important message from Deacon. I think you'll agree he's unearthed an interesting nugget."

Canaris continued to read the decoded signal and looked up, pale-faced. "Is this true?"

Schellenberg smiled. "I thought you might be surprised. As you can see, it virtually confirms Roosevelt will be arriving in Cairo on the twenty-second of this month, eight days from now, before he proceeds to Teheran. There's to be a private conference with Churchill and a senior Chinese delegation seeking more Allied support for the war in the Far East. But Himmler is convinced the real purpose of Roosevelt's visit is to agree the timing of the invasion of Europe with Churchill. If the invasion goes ahead, it doesn't bear thinking about—we'd be fighting on all fronts."

Canaris read the signal again, then held it up. "Can you be absolutely certain of this information?"

"All SD agents abroad were ordered to use whatever means necessary to gather intelligence about the Teheran and Cairo meetings, just as your own people were. One of our American agents spotted the battleship *Iowa* departing Chesapeake Bay two days ago, after taking on a cargo of civilian passengers. Nothing remarkable about that, you might say, but we suspected a ship of the *Iowa*'s class might be used to transport Roosevelt to North Africa. It was only a suspicion, of course, and we needed more information. Fortunately for us, Deacon came up trumps. He managed to get photographs of a top-secret memo which was kept in the American ambassador's private safe at his Cairo residence, confirming the dates of the conference. The microfilm arrived last night via a Spanish diplomatic courier."

"How in God's name did this fellow Deacon manage to photograph the memo?"

Schellenberg grinned. "Some weeks ago he signalled us with details of a special compound being built at the site of the famous Mena House hotel, near the Giza pyramids, and strong rumours he'd gathered that some sort of important meeting was soon to take place. Naturally, he was urgently instructed to collect more information, but all he turned up was confirmation that large numbers of troops and army engineers had been drafted into the hotel area, which was sealed off by the military. It suggested to me it might be the location of the proposed conference. In desperation, I personally ordered Deacon to try to breach security at either the British residency or the American embassy: they were the most likely places information would be kept. It was a tall order, brazen and dangerous in the extreme, but after surveillance he estimated that both locations were too tightly guarded."

"And impossible to break into, I would have thought."

"Which was why Deacon turned his attention to the American residency. The ambassador's home was less closely guarded. He learned from a Spanish diplomat that the ambassador would attend a gala dinner at the Turkish embassy a week later, and so the die was cast. He employed a burglar, one of the best in Cairo, to do the necessary." Schellenberg smiled. "But the kernel of the matter is the American President definitely intends visiting Cairo, and we know the approximate dates. A rather heaven-sent opportunity not to be missed, don't you think?"

"What if the information is meant to mislead us?"

"Come now, do you really think it would be kept in a heavily guarded safe if the Allies actually wanted us to find it? And Deacon is certain no one can possibly suspect that he had the residency burgled and the memo photographed. Which means we have the element of surprise."

Canaris put the signal down, disbelief on his face. "You're serious, aren't you? You're really planning to go ahead with this."

Schellenberg nodded. "I considered an attempt in Teheran during the conference there, but Persia is too hostile a territory. With so many Allied troops about, and Stalin's paranoia, such a mission would be fraught with difficulties. However, Egypt is quite a different matter. Security is more relaxed now that Rommel is no longer a threat. And it's way behind the front lines, so the Allies would never expect us to strike. But naturally, it isn't our only iron. We'll have the Luftwaffe and our U-boat wolf packs in the Atlantic on the alert, in the hope they can locate Roosevelt's convoy and destroy it. But I wouldn't hold my breath, which is why we shall proceed with the plan as if our very lives depended on it."

"And what *exactly* do you intend?"

"Unfortunately, the memo didn't disclose where Roosevelt will be quartered, or his security arrangements, which poses us a problem, but not an insurmountable one. As for the mission, it will break down into two parts, much the same plan we used to get Mussolini. First, we'll send in a small, select team to pinpoint exactly where the President and Prime Minister will be staying and the strength of their protection. Once they've done that, they'll try to find a way in—there are always weak links in any security, as you well know.

"When they've achieved that objective, they radio us. Then begins the second and final phase of the operation. I'll have a couple of plane-loads of Skorzeny's crack SS paratroops ready and waiting at an Italian airbase. A hundred of his very finest specialist troops—the toughest, hardest, most highly trained the SS can provide—and we both know our SS paratroops are the absolute best in the world. The kind of men who are willing to lay down their lives for the Führer without a moment's hesitation. Once we get the signal, they'll be flown to Cairo and land at an airfield near the city, which our team on the ground will have secured beforehand, along with any equipment—trucks, vehicles, and so on—necessary to help Skorzeny's men make their way to the target. If the intention is to quarter Roosevelt at the Mena House, which I strongly suspect, so much the better, and a good omen for us. Skorzeny's SS have already shown they can penetrate such a heavily fortified hotel, as they did in Abruzzi. They'll be in and out so fast, the Allies won't know what's hit them."

"Why not kill Churchill as well while you're at it?" Canaris said, shrugging off-handedly.

"One target is always easier to hit than two. To kill Churchill as well would be a wonderful bonus, and if the opportunity presents itself, I assure you it will be taken. But Roosevelt is top of our list."

Canaris sighed. "I still think it's folly. The Allies' security will be as tight as a bank vault. On the ground and in the air."

Schellenberg smiled. "As we've seen with Mussolini, there are always ways to crack open a vault, my friend. And you fail to appreciate the rewards if we succeed. The death of either leader would be a godsend, but Roosevelt especially. He's the linchpin that holds the Allies together, and their quartermaster when it comes to supplies. With him out of the way, the Allies would be thrown into disarray. And with their President dead, I doubt the Americans would have the stomach for an invasion next summer, as the British and Russians are demanding. It would probably split the Allied powers apart, which would suit us nicely and give us enough time to regain the upper hand. And think of the propaganda value—it would be an incredible boost to our troops' morale. Besides, a lesson is needed here, I think. The Americans will have to learn they can't bomb German cites with impunity, and interfere in a war that's really none of their business. It's about time they had their faces slapped."

"Are you saying the mission is definitely going ahead?"

"Unless our U-boats or the Luftwaffe somehow miraculously succeed in destroying the *Iowa*, you can be certain of it. We already have a name—Operation Sphinx."

"Then you're way ahead of me. Who gave the order?"

"Himmler."

Canaris shook his head in dismay. "Don't tell me the Führer approves of this madness?"

"He's already given the mission top priority. See for yourself." Schellenberg handed across a signed letter from the file, and Canaris saw the signature of Adolf Hitler underneath.

He read the letter and looked up. "A joint operation between the Abwehr and SD is most unusual."

"I agree. But the Führer's still upset about that last fiasco of yours in Cairo—he can't quite decide if it was disloyalty or incompetence—which is why he wants me to take the lead on this one, but with your help. So I'm certain he'd be rather annoyed if you didn't put in your oar and give any assistance necessary." Schellenberg grinned slyly. "Worse still, God forbid that he might be tempted to put you in the same class as those who plot against him."

The Abwehr, while able to think up the most grandiose schemes, was sometimes woefully inept in carrying them out. Their top spy in Egypt, John Eppler, had been apprehended the previous year, caught by the British when the sterling bank notes he was supplied with for his mission turned out to be excellent but flawed forgeries, which ultimately led to his arrest. But there was an even graver mistake Canaris had wisely kept to himself.

The previous year, one of his agents in Spain had got a tip-off that Roosevelt and Churchill were meeting in Casablanca. He radioed the date, time and place to Berlin. But because the agent was a Spaniard, some idiot in the Abwehr translated Casablanca literally, and reported to his superiors that the Allied leaders were planning a meeting, not in North Africa, but in the White House in Washington.

Canaris blushed at the threat as he put down the letter. "It seems I have little choice. Which of my people had you got in mind?"

"First, I'll have need of one of your Egyptian agents. Preferably someone living in a remote desert location, not more than a couple of days' travel from Cairo. Someone entirely trustworthy."

Canaris shrugged. "I can think of one or two who might be suitable. But go on."

"Second, I thought Jack Halder would be perfect to lead the initial team we send in to set everything up. He's one of your best men, knows his way around Cairo, speaks Arabic, and is capable enough to see the whole thing through. He's also American by birth and can speak English with a flawless American or British accent, thanks to his time at Oxford. All of which may be useful when it comes time to get access to Roosevelt's quarters."

Canaris's face darkened. "So that's why his file was requested yesterday by the Reichsführer's office? I thought it had to do with that business in Sicily, months back."

Schellenberg smiled. "You must admit Halder has an impressive reputation. It's almost part of military legend how he managed to infiltrate Allied lines while serving in North Africa. A month in Cairo and Alexandria, in the guise of a British officer, gathering intelligence under the very noses of the enemy? Quite a remarkable feat, I would have thought."

"He's certainly one of my best, but you're wasting your time." Canaris shook his head. "If you've read his file you'll know he's lost his edge after all that unpleasant business with his father and son. He doesn't seem to have the interest any more, and spends most of his time out at a summer cottage his father owned, overlooking the lakeshore at Wannsee. I visited him there last month and he looked unhappy as hell."

Schellenberg said grimly, "Yes, all rather tragic, what happened. But what if I could convince him otherwise?"

"It's still a suicide trap, Walter. You'd be sending him to certain death."

"I assure you the plan can succeed," Schellenberg said firmly. "And those who survive the operation will return safely. Furthermore, I think you'll agree when you're briefed on the details in full."

Canaris knew there was little point in arguing. He shrugged wearily in defeat. "Knowing Halder, I suppose there's a slim chance it could work."

Schellenberg gave a wintry smile. "It's got to. Otherwise Himmler assures me the Führer will have our heads."

"But a week is no time at all to set up a mission like this."

"Which is why things will have to proceed at a very rapid pace from here on. There's absolutely no time to lose."

SEVEN

BERLIN
It was just after eleven that same morning when Schellenberg's Mercedes pulled up outside the secluded lakeshore cottage at Wannsee, ten kilometres west of Berlin. The sleepy village on the edge of the Grunewald was a favourite among senior German military officers, many of whom kept magnificent summer homes there. The rain-clouds had gone and it was glorious for November, with clear skies and bright autumn sunshine.

The single-storey, white-painted wooden cottage looked out on to a perfect view of the lake. It had a picket fence and a small veranda, and Schellenberg smiled when he noticed a woman's bicycle propped against the fence. He went up the steps, carrying a leather briefcase and his officer's silver-topped riding crop.

The front door was unlocked and he stepped into a tiny

living room. The place was no more than a couple of rooms, with a sofa on each side of a stone fireplace, a table and chairs, a tiny kitchen and a single bedroom leading off. There were some books on the shelves, a brass bust of King Tut, and two silver-framed photographs of a rather striking blond-haired woman and a young boy, but the room was in some disarray. He noticed an unfinished bottle of champagne and two glasses on the coffee table, a pair of women's shoes and a grey uniform skirt lying discarded on the floor. There were some fresh cotton towels on the back of a chair.

"Halder? Are you there?"

A moment later the bedroom door opened and a pretty female corporal came out. She wore only the top part of her uniform, her bare legs and underwear showing, a look of surprise on her face as she grabbed one of the towels and covered herself.

"Who in God's name are you?"

Schellenberg smiled. "I might ask the same question, fraulein. General Walter Schellenberg. And you?"

She looked young and ravishing, her hair tousled, as if she had just climbed out of bed, but when she took in the black SS uniform and heard the name, her expression changed and she flushed with embarrassment.

"Hei—Heidi Schmidt, Wehrmacht Nursing Corps."

"Charmed, I'm sure. Relax, Heidi, you're not on parade. Perhaps you can tell me where Halder is."

"He—he said he was going for a run and a swim."

"Is he a friend of yours?"

"We—we met the other night in a bar in Wannsee," the girl stammered. "He seemed quite down, so I—I cycled over here after my duty to see if he was all right."

Schellenberg grinned. "Brought out the maternal instinct in you, did he? Still, I'm glad to see someone's keeping him company. God knows he needs it right now. Is that your bicycle I saw outside?"

"Yes, sir."

Schellenberg bent to pick up the discarded skirt with the tip of his riding crop, and held it out to the girl. "Well now, Heidi. I think it might be wise if you got dressed and ran along. Halder and I have some business to attend to and I really don't want us to be disturbed."

Jack Halder sweated as he ran along the lakeshore. His shirt was off, his tanned bare chest covered in small scars, and he wore plimsolls and a pair of loose cotton training pants. There were touches of premature grey in his hair and the beginnings of wrinkles around his eyes, but the same wry smile was fixed permanently in place, though it looked a little solemn that morning. He clutched a stop-watch in his hand, and when he reached some rocks at the edge of the shore he halted, clicked the stopwatch and looked at the result with dismay.

"Damn it, you can do better than that, Halder."

He started to run again, gave a burst of power, the sweat pumping now after a brisk five-kilometre run. As he rounded the cove and reached the rocks he saw the black-uniformed officer sitting in the sand, a grin on his face, a cigarette in his hand.

Halder came to a halt, took several deep breaths and stared over at Schellenberg, who simply smiled. "Well, Jack, trying to get into shape again, I see. Always a good sign. I had thought of joining you for a swim, but I think I'll give it a miss. Here, you need this more than me."

Schellenberg had a towel in his hand and he tossed it to Halder, who caught it and wiped the perspiration from his face. "You bastard, what the hell do you want?"

"That's no way to greet an old comrade." Schellenberg glanced at Halder's scarred chest. "You seem to have healed quite nicely. And by the way, I rather liked the young lady who's been giving you comfort." Then he said, more seriously, "Did she help ease the pain any, my friend?"

"That's none of your damned business."

"You're quite right." Schellenberg stood, wiped sand from his uniform and picked up his briefcase. "Now, how about we go up to the cottage? There's something I'd like to discuss."

Schellenberg poured the last of the champagne into two flute glasses and handed one to Halder, who shook his head.

"Not for me. What do you want?" He had showered and

changed into a shirt and slacks, and sat on the sofa.

"Just a little chat between friends," Schellenberg answered. "Military business, I'm afraid."

"The last time I heard those lines was over four months ago. You had Canaris have me pose as an American intelligence officer to help rescue one of your SS generals from an interrogation post behind enemy lines in Sicily. I ended up with a bullet in my leg and grenade shrapnel in my chest."

Schellenberg sipped from his glass. "Unfortunate that, but no one could have played the role as believably as you, which was why we needed you in the first place. And you lived up to my expectations and succeeded admirably. You're certain you won't have some champagne, Jack? It's really delicious."

"Go to hell."

Schellenberg shrugged and glanced at the bottle. "An excellent Dom Perignon, '36. You're looking after yourself, I see."

"For your information, the champagne was a gift from a friend."

"No need to explain." Schellenberg plucked a book from one of the shelves. "The *Collected Works* of Carl Jung. Rather depressing reading, his philosophy, I would have thought. Old Carl isn't exactly one for a joke and a laugh."

"It goes with the mood I'm in right now."

"What *are* we going to do with you, my friend?" Schellenberg replaced the book on the shelf and looked at the silver-framed photograph of the woman. He turned back. "You loved her very much, didn't you, Jack?"

Schellenberg saw a terrible grief flood Halder's face, a fathomless sadness in his eyes. He stood and said awkwardly, "The Wehrmacht girl you met, she's just a nice kid. Someone I got drunk with and poured out my soul to. Maybe I finally needed to talk to someone. And if you really want to know, she didn't help ease the pain."

"It hasn't been easy for you these last few years, has it? Losing a young wife, and then what happened in Hamburg. I was truly sorry to hear about your father," Schellenberg said quietly. "I mean that. I hope you'll accept my condolences. I hear the boy's still recovering?"

"And will be for a long time. All water under the bridge now. Let's leave it be."

Schellenberg put down his glass and became more businesslike. "But you're still angry, and quite rightly so. And it's an anger I can put to good use." He undid the straps on his briefcase, plucked out a file and laid it on the table.

"What's that?"

"It concerns what happened to your father and son. Our latest intelligence reports on the Allied fire-bombing raids on Hamburg."

"What about it?"

"It seems the raids had the highest approval of the British and American governments. Both agreed they wanted absolute and total destruction, to teach Germany a savage lesson. It turned out to be the worst single act of devastation in world history. Do you know the full extent of the damage?"

Halder said angrily, "Look, Schellenberg, all I know is I lost my father, and my son's burned so badly he'll be lucky if he ever walks again."

"Your father certainly chose the wrong time to visit relatives in Hamburg with the boy."

Halder was bitter. "I was on my back in hospital, recovering after that little escapade you arranged in Sicily, remember? Pauli was being looked after by his grandfather."

"Not for a moment can you blame me for what happened, Jack. The Allies committed an utterly insane act. Ten square kilometres of Germany's second city wiped out, over sixty thousand dead, mostly civilians, and a hundred thousand injured. The use of incendiary fire-bombs was deliberate, to cause maximum civilian casualties. I hear the city was like a scene from hell—people burning like torches, the heat so intense the flaming asphalt made the streets look like rivers of fire. And the feeling is the Allies may intend the same for Berlin, sooner rather than later. Goebbels has already ordered the evacuation of a million citizens."

Halder ignored the file, a harsh look on his face. "Get to the point."

"There's a matter I wish to discuss. Something rather daring and dangerous that perhaps may put a little life back

into that tortured soul of yours. Canaris has offered to loan
you to me, if you agree."

"I don't work for the SD. And the answer's no, whatever
it is. I'm not interested. Me, I'm content to sit out the rest
of the war in Berlin."

"And then what? Wait for the Allies to hang you as a
traitor? You may be a German citizen, but you're
American-born, and with your war record it's quite a likely
scenario. Where would your son be then? He needs you,
Jack. Even more so now. And do you really think Canaris
could allow you to relax in Berlin? Now that your wounds
are healed, he'd use you every chance he got, especially
with the war going the way it is. Which rather diminishes
your chances of remaining alive. On the other hand, if you
help me with this mission, we'll wipe the slate clean and
you're free to go."

"You mean leave the Abwehr?"

"I mean leave Germany. Get away from the war, if that's
what you wish." Schellenberg saw the surprise on Halder's
face. "You have my word on it, Jack. And Himmler's and
the Führer's. You and your son can start a new life together,
somewhere safe and far from here."

Halder frowned. "And what's the price I've got to pay?"

Schellenberg smiled. "You're ahead of the posse, as they
say."

"So tell me."

And Schellenberg told him.

Halder looked bewildered for several moments, then he
laughed. "Walter, you're definitely going crazy in your old
age."

"I assure you, the plan's feasible. And you know me, I
always do my homework thoroughly."

"The admiral knows about this?"

"It's to be a joint operation. Unusual, I know, but necessary under the circumstances. I shall take personal command of the planning and briefing."

Halder crossed to the window, ran a hand through his
hair, and looked back. "Kill Roosevelt? I know you think
I'm an adventurer, but believe me, that doesn't include a
vocation for suicide. Whoever accepted the mission would

have about as much chance of surviving as a one-legged man of escaping a forest fire."

Schellenberg laughed. "An interesting comparison, but hardly valid. The plan is quite simple, really. Once you and the team reach Cairo, you'd be established in a safe house. Any equipment you might need to move around the city with relative freedom—Allied uniforms and vehicles—should already have been secured for you by my agents, and they'll provide any further help you might need. All you have to do is affirm *exactly* where Roosevelt will be quartered—most likely at the Mena House—and find a weakness in their security that can be breached. You'll also need to secure a small airfield, about ten kilometres south of the Giza pyramids, that's largely unprotected. Once your objectives have been achieved, you radio us. When our SS paratroops land you lead them to the target and leave the rest to them. After that, we get you out."

"How?"

"The same way Skorzeny's men will get out—by air."

"You mean if anyone's lucky enough to survive. And why the hell do you need me?"

"I told you, my agents in Cairo may be cunning fellows, but they would be incapable of handling such a mission all by themselves. You, on the other hand, are a perfect candidate. You've already worked deep behind enemy lines in Egypt, speak fluent Arabic, and you're familiar with Cairo."

"There have to be better reasons than that. You're bound to have agents who speak Arabic and know the city better than me."

Schellenberg shook his head. "Not many, actually, and certainly not of your calibre with a proven track record. You've impersonated American and British officers to perfection many times, so a repeat performance shouldn't be beyond your abilities." He opened his briefcase and unfolded a map on the table. "I've brought along a map to help you refamiliarise yourself with Cairo."

"You're getting ahead of yourself. I haven't decided on anything yet. And you've told me nothing about the rest of the team."

"I anticipate three others—two SS men and a woman."

"Tell me about them."

"The two SS are Major Dieter Kleist and Feldwebel Hans Doring. Both serving with Otto Skorzeny's Commando group."

"Dieter Kleist?" Halder looked across with contempt. "He's a ruthless animal, the worst kind of brute in uniform. I came across his work in the Balkans. He had the nasty habit of shooting suspected partisans out of hand, and raping his female prisoners before he put them out of their misery."

"Perhaps, but even a brute has his uses. He's a very efficient and deadly weapon, our Kleist, recently transferred to Skorzeny's command, and an excellent man in the field. He also speaks reasonable English and Arabic, and he's acquainted with Egypt. He once worked for a German company, surveying for oilfields."

"What about Doring's background?"

"He spent some time in the Middle East before the war, as a driver-mechanic for a German archaeological crew. Now he's a specialist in covert operations behind enemy lines, and comes highly recommended."

"By whom?"

"Skorzeny himself. Himmler insists on having Skorzeny's SS as part of the first team. I'm sure that between the lot of you, you should be able to do the necessary business."

Halder shook his head. "So far, I still don't like it very much. What about the woman?"

"Her name's Rachel Stern."

Halder was thunderstruck. After a long silence Schellenberg lit a cigarette. "Understandably, you're shocked. I believe you once knew her."

Halder was still white-faced and didn't reply. Schellenberg said, "What's the matter?"

"It's been a long time since I heard that name."

Schellenberg smiled. "I've been looking through your file again, with Canaris's permission, of course. Among the archaeological team you joined in '39 were several Germans working for the SD. One of them was code-named Nightingale, the very best agent we had. I checked back through Nightingale's reports out of curiosity. Your name

and the girl's were mentioned. It appears you were quite
fond of her. It was rather daring of you, Jack, considering
the girl's half Jewish. Does my information surprise you?"

"Nothing surprises me any more. Where has she been
all this time? What's happened to her and her family?"

"An interesting man, the professor. A renowned archaeologist with several significant finds to his credit. However,
he was also virulently anti-Nazi. Despite the fact that he
spent much of his time abroad, the Gestapo were anxious
to get their hands on him. They eventually succeeded with
a stroke of luck."

"What do you mean?"

"Four years ago the girl and her father were rescued in
the Mediterranean by the Kriegsmarine. They were passengers on a Turkish vessel bound for Istanbul. It was sunk
by an engineroom explosion, and the professor's wife perished. Since then, the girl's been in Ravensbruck women's
camp, detained at the Führer's pleasure, and her father's
serving thirty years in Dachau."

Halder flushed with rage. "You suddenly remind me
why I started to dislike Hitler."

"Come now, Jack. Not my doing. If the truth be known,
I find this whole anti-Jewish thing quite repulsive. And I'll
forget what you just said—it really doesn't do to broadcast
such remarks."

"What I don't understand is what part Rachel plays in
your little scheme. Why do you need her?"

"She'll be your insurance—think of her as a temporary,
but very necessary, policy."

"What do you mean?"

"Like you, she speaks fluent English and Arabic, and
knows her way around Egypt. But best of all, she's an
expert archaeologist, like her father. No disrespect, but you
on the other hand have never been more than a keen amateur in such matters."

"Why's her profession so important?"

"Simple, really. For the sake of appearances, as part of
the mission, I intend your cover to be that of an international archaeological team, stranded in the Middle East because of the war. My intelligence sources tell me there are
several such groups still languishing in the area because of

the hostilities. Needless to say, I can't go over the exact details of the entire plan until I know you're committed, but you can take it you'd have the usual faultless forged papers and documents that'll pass the stiffest test. Not that you'll need to use your cover story for very long. You shouldn't have to spend more than two or three days in Cairo at the most."

"There are other cover stories you could have come up with. You're sure you're not just using her as another pawn to get me to go along with this?"

Schellenberg grinned. "Perceptive of you, Jack, and valid enough, but actually there is another reason why we need her. And perhaps a very important one, though it'll have to keep for now. You'll be told in good time, if you agree to come on board."

"You're forgetting one important fact. What makes you so sure she'll co-operate?"

Schellenberg smiled knowingly. "There are always ways to entice. Besides, she'll know nothing about our true intentions. As far as she's concerned, it'll be just a little intelligence-gathering operation in Cairo."

Halder shook his head. "I don't like the idea of using her. If she's been in a prison camp, she'll have been through enough as it is."

"I'm afraid there's no one else quite suitable. Himmler's already read her file and thinks she's an ideal choice. And I must say, I agree."

There was a sudden, pleading look in Halder's voice. "Not her, Walter. I'm asking this as a favour."

"I'm sorry, but it's out of my hands." Schellenberg paused, deliberately. "I'm sure the girl would be safer if you went along. Especially if she had to endure Kleist. I'd rather fear for her safety once she'd outlived her usefulness."

Anger erupted on Halder's face. "You're a bastard, Walter."

"And I have a war to win. Sentiment can play no part in it."

"You can't honestly believe this crazy business stands a chance?"

"Quite the contrary. I'm convinced it does. What Skorzeny accomplished in Italy can be repeated in Egypt, and with deadlier consequences. It'll be a hit-and-run operation—our men will be in and out so fast the Allies won't know what's going on until it's too late." He paused. "As regards your team, I'm told Cairo's quite cosmopolitan right now. Crammed with displaced Europeans and lots of Americans, not to mention troops from every nationality. In a big, sprawling city with a population of over two million, a few more faces won't look amiss. You should be able to move around with impunity. And by the way, Himmler's even promised you the Knight's Cross if you accept."

"You can keep the damned medal."

Schellenberg laughed. "I thought you might say that. More importantly, he's agreed to offer you safe passage to Sweden, for you and your son. And onward to wherever you want to go."

"I don't know. It all sounds too risky to me."

"Trust me, it can work. And think about it. A German-American, sent to help kill Roosevelt? Surely it's almost a kind of poetic justice. You know what could happen if the Allies win and you're caught by the Amis." Schellenberg used the contemptuous German word for Americans. "It's either a long prison sentence or a long rope. This way, you have a chance. One last mission and that's it. And there's a bonus."

"What?"

Schellenberg nodded at the file on the desk. "The report on the Hamburg bombings—you ought to read it. Roosevelt gave his complete approval for the raids—in fact, he publicly urged the bombing crews to be merciless. Now Germany has a score to settle and you have the chance to repay what happened to your father and son. Personal, of course, but I always think the personal helps in such matters."

"Who says I want revenge?"

"I can see it in your eyes, Jack. It's written on your face. Your mother's country killed your father and maimed your child. This offers you a chance for retribution."

"And if I don't accept?"

Schellenberg shrugged. "A wise hound will always run

with the pack. But if you refuse, I can assure you Himmler's displeasure will be unforgiving. Think about the girl, too. She'd be safer in your hands, rather than Kleist's."

"Who'd be in charge?"

"The first phase of the operation would be entirely under your command. Kleist and you are the same rank, obviously, but I'll see to it that he's answerable to you, and obeys your direct orders. Until our paratroops land in Cairo, that is. Once that happens, Skorzeny takes complete charge."

"The Allies control the skies over the southern Mediterranean. You'd need either a very brave pilot or a very reckless one to attempt the crossing to Egypt in an unarmed plane, without a Luftwaffe escort. I presume that's how you intend doing it?"

Schellenberg nodded. "I'm sure you're familiar with some of our best fliers, those who've worked on Abwehr missions. So if it's any consolation, I'll let you pick your own." He paused, gave it one final smile. "Well, are you in? This one last thing and then you're free."

EIGHT

CAIRO
15 NOVEMBER/8:30 A.M.
Harry Weaver woke with a blinding pain between his eyes. The window in his bedroom was open, sunlight pouring in, and through the curtains came the din of voices and the hooting horns of morning traffic. He raised himself from the bed and swore.

His body was full of small pains and his head throbbed. He climbed out of bed, ran the shower, and looked at himself in the mirror. His eyes were hooded with pain, swollen and bloodshot, and the flesh on his face looked like folds of rubber. And then he remembered why. He'd been to a farewell party at Shepheard's Hotel, given by a couple of British officers from GHQ who were being transferred home, and the celebration had lasted until three a.m.

He shaved, then stepped under the steaming-hot water

which brought him back to life, before he towelled himself dry and got dressed. He wore the uniform of a US Army lieutenant-colonel. When he went downstairs Ali was in the kitchen making scrambled eggs, bacon and coffee over a wood stove. The house servant was an elderly, grey-haired Nubian.

"Good morning, Ali. Have the others left?"

"They've all gone, sir. You're the last for breakfast. The effendi doesn't look well this morning."

"The gin they serve in Shepheard's, do you think it's real? Someone told me last night that the taxi drivers use it in their cabs instead of gas."

Ali smiled. "Who's to say? But you might be right."

Weaver laughed and went out to the patio. The table had been set, and he picked the shaded end, out of the warm sunlight. There was fresh bread and iced mango juice, and he poured a glass, drank it down quickly, then buttered some bread. He shared the big old villa in Zamalek with two other American officers, a signals lieutenant and a translator at the American embassy. Zamalek was one of the better districts in Cairo, situated on a large island in the middle of the Nile, and the villa had once been the home of a wealthy Italian merchant. It had its own private gardens, well stocked with lemon and orange trees, and a large, stone-flagged patio at the rear with cool palms and a bubbling stone fountain.

There was a newspaper on the table, the *Egyptian Gazette*. When Ali had served him, Weaver glanced through the pages. Several reports caught his interest. The Red Army had crossed the River Dnieper and broken through the German defences; the invasion of Italy had pushed towards the south of Rome, and it was rumoured that the Germans soon planned to loot and evacuate the city. Churchill had claimed that sixty U-boats had been destroyed in the last three months, and President Roosevelt had promised Congress that the US Air Force would continue to step up its bombing of German cities, until Hitler had been crushed or accepted defeat. All good news, though somehow Weaver didn't think any of it was going to make the Germans surrender. But it sure had them on the run.

He put aside the paper, glanced at his watch, and quickly

finished his breakfast. It was way past nine and he was late for work.

"Good news, effendi?"

Weaver drained his coffee, pulled on his jacket, and smiled at Ali. "It looks like we're really winning the war."

Weaver's office was a short walk away at British GHQ, Middle East, on Tolombat Street in Garden City. Known as Grey Pillars, it was a large four-storey building surrounded by barbed-wire fencing, and had once belonged to an Italian insurance company. As a US Army intelligence officer with the attaché's office, Weaver was responsible for liaising with the British command, and he reported directly to the American military attaché, General George Clayton, at the American embassy.

He had been transferred to intelligence a month after completing his officer training, where his specialist background and knowledge of Arabic was soon put to good use, first with the US Army's invasion of North Africa, Operation Torch, and later when he was seconded to the Cairo embassy, with the brevet rank of lieutenant-colonel. He was glad to be back in Egypt, but found intelligence work in Cairo pretty boring. Far from the battlefield, intelligence officers spent their time shuffling papers and engaging in endless bureaucratic skirmishes, a practice Weaver had little time for. There was a hectic social life, of course. Drinks at Shepheard's bar and the Gezira Club, where there was a constant round of socialising, golf and tennis, polo matches, sailing and dinner parties, not to mention beautiful women. Cairo was in full bloom now that Rommel's threat had been lifted.

Weaver took the lift to his office on the second floor and took off his jacket. There was a silver-framed photograph on his desk, the one taken at Sakkara, of himself, Rachel and Jack Halder. After he had learned of Rachel's death he had had a copy framed, and sometimes he liked to look at the snapshot and recall with fondness the best summer of his life. There was also a pile of paperwork on the desk, reports to be filed and written, and he had just started making headway when there was a knock on his door.

"Come in."

A woman lieutenant entered. Helen Kane had been Weaver's aide for the last six months. Despite her name, she was half English, half Egyptian, dusky and faintly exotic, with expressive brown eyes, her dark hair trimmed into a pageboy bob, its ends curling inward, as regulation demanded, just over the collar of her uniform jacket, the green flash of the Intelligence Corps on her sleeve. She had been at the party at Shepheard's and he'd danced with her for most of the night, the first time since working together that they'd had any social contact. He still remembered the pleasant feel of her body against his, the faint scent of her perfume, but he'd been a little drunk and he felt slightly embarrassed.

"Good morning, sir. If you don't mind me saying so, you look a little under the weather."

"It shows?"

"I'm afraid so."

"I hope I didn't make a fool of myself last night, Helen." She smiled back, playfully. "No more than most."

"Is there anything happening I should know about?"

"Lieutenant-Colonel Sanson asks if he can see you in his office."

British military intelligence had two chief sections: the DDMI (O)—for Operational—and DDMI (I)—for Intelligence. Alfred Sanson came under the latter, and was responsible for security leaks. Weaver and he were not exactly friends, but he knew that Sanson had formerly served as a police inspector with the British-controlled Cairo constabulary before the war, having risen up through the ranks. He had a reputation as a tough, meticulous officer, a loner wedded to his job. At Shepheard's the previous night, Weaver had noticed him sitting alone at one of the tables, a drink in front of him, watching Helen and him with more than a passing interest.

"Did he say what it was about?"

"No, sir."

Weaver stood, pulled on his uniform jacket. It was difficult to accept her still calling him sir, after they had danced so intimately the night before. "Then I guess I'd better see what he wants."

Sanson's office was across the hall, a cramped room with peeling walls, a rusting filing cabinet, a scratched wooden desk and a couple of chairs. It was also scrupulously neat, everything in its place. There was a tray of tea and some cups ready on the desk that morning, as Weaver was led in by a corporal.

Sanson stood, but didn't offer his hand. "Lieutenant-Colonel Weaver. Please, sit down. Some tea?"

The Englishman was tall, well built, with a prize fighter's physique and a disfigured face. A black leather patch covered his left eye and there was a thick mass of pink scar tissue on his left jaw. The facial injury had been badly sewn by the surgeon, and gave the impression of a tortured smile. The effect was unsettling. Weaver took a seat.

"Thanks."

Sanson poured a cup and pushed it across the desk. "I take it you're enjoying your posting in Cairo?"

"Sure." Weaver ignored the tea, knowing Sanson wasn't the type to waste time on social chit-chat. "What did you want to see me about?"

Sanson lit a cigarette, opened his desk drawer, and pulled out a file. "Last night the Cairo police recovered the corpse of a man from the Nile, near the old docks. Just the upper torso, to be precise. It was spotted by the crew member on one of the local ferry boats. The remains had been in the water for several days."

Weaver knew it wasn't uncommon for bodies to be washed up on the Nile's banks. The river was noted for suicides and murder victims. "So?"

"Despite the fact that the corpse was badly mutilated, the police managed to identify the man. He was a criminal well known to them, and me personally. His name was Mustapha Evir."

"What's this got to do with me?"

"Evir was murdered. His throat had been cut. When his house was searched, one of the policemen found this hidden among his belongings."

Sanson removed a crumpled-looking piece of paper from the file, smoothed it out, and handed it over. Weaver saw that it was a rough sketch in heavy pencil, a series of boxes and shapes, like something a child might have drawn. It appeared to be of a large house and gardens, marked off inside a rectangular shape. What looked like some clumps of trees were pencilled inside the square, and an odd image, like a small cupola-topped pavilion. There were also two other box shapes that Weaver couldn't figure out. He studied the sketch, then looked at Sanson and shrugged. "I still don't see your point."

"The man in charge of the murder investigation is Captain Arkhan, an old colleague of mine. For a time he was in command of the police guard at the American ambassador's villa. He believes that what you're looking at is a sketch of the same residence. The grounds have a similar distinct shape, and there's a pavilion in the gardens. I also seem to remember there are two sentry huts on the property, which correspond to the two boxes in the drawing. Arkhan wanted you to have a look at it and give your opinion."

Weaver looked at the sketch again. He recalled the layout, the pavilion and the sentry huts. "You could be right. But I still don't see what it has to do with me."

"Mustapha Evir had a reputation as an excellent safe-breaker and burglar. Among the criminal fraternity, he was known as The Fox. But a while back he got caught and served eighteen months in prison. He was released three months ago. He tried to lead an honest life after his release, but he found only badly paid work." Sanson paused. "Captain Arkhan believes Evir intended to return to his old career. That perhaps he meant to break into the ambassador's residence, and that's why he had the drawing. He also had a reputation for planning his burglaries meticulously, though to break into the well-guarded home of a foreign ambassador wouldn't have been typical of him. But because he was murdered, it crossed Arkhan's mind from the information he's gathered that Evir might already have carried out his work, and that it perhaps had something to do with his death."

Weaver frowned. "What information?"

"The police questioned his wife. Evir had little money and his wife was complaining. She said her husband told her he had important business to attend to on the evening he was killed, and boasted that he'd have a lot of money for her that night. But he never came home."

"You're suggesting he broke into the ambassador's home and stole from the safe?"

Sanson pursed his lips, made a steeple of his fingers, and nodded. "Perhaps something valuable. Something worth killing him for. A couple of things you should know. Evir worked to order. Because of his talents, he was usually hired by other criminals, with a particular theft in mind. We also suspected he might have been behind the theft of confidential papers from the briefcase of one of our officers a couple of years ago—carried out at the behest of a German agent or sympathiser, no doubt. But the theft wasn't noticed for twenty-four hours and by then it was too late. Evir never admitted to the crime when we took him in for questioning, and seeing as we had no hard evidence, we had to let him go."

"I haven't heard of any theft from the ambassador's home."

"There's always the chance it went unnoticed."

"I doubt it. The residency is tightly guarded."

Sanson gave a razor smile, as if amused by Weaver's naïveté. "If I've learned one thing as a policeman, Weaver, it's that no security is watertight in Cairo. I've known burglars who could rob a place blind and nobody would see or hear a thing. Besides, Evir wasn't called The Fox for nothing. Most of his burglaries went undetected, until he was long gone."

"Have the police any suspects for the murder?"

Sanson shook his head. "Not so far. Arkhan questioned most of Evir's criminal acquaintances, and he's reasonably certain none of them had anything to do with his death."

"How was he mutilated?"

"His legs and buttocks had been severed by a ship's propeller." Sanson crushed out his cigarette. "His widow claims she doesn't know why her husband was murdered, or who might have killed him. And she says she knew nothing about the sketch. But she belongs to a family of thieves and liars, and you couldn't believe any of them.

However, we might be able to help Arkhan's investigation."

"How?"

"Like most Egyptian peasants, Evir's wife has a grudging fear of authority. Arkhan thinks that the sight of a couple of military officer uniforms might help loosen her tongue."

"You really think that would help?"

Sanson shrugged. "Right now, the case has Arkhan baffled, and he'd appreciate any assistance. Besides, if Evir's wife knows more about this matter than she's telling, or there's been a breach of security, it may concern us."

Weaver raised his shoulders. "I guess it could do no harm."

Sanson reached for his cap. "We can take my car."

It was hot in the olive-green Humber, and Weaver rolled down the window. He held on to the door for safety as Sanson turned the staff car into a cobbled street and swerved past a cart drawn by a camel and loaded down with watermelons. His patched eye seemed to make judging corners fraught with danger.

Since returning to Egypt, Weaver had been surprised by how international Cairo had become. The tight streets were crowded with shoppers and soldiers, the crush of bodies and smells almost overwhelming. Aside from half a million Allied troops of every nationality, there were White Russians, French, German Jews, British, and Greeks. Over a hundred thousand foreign refugees had crowded into the city since the war began, and the streets were a babble of strange dialects. The Egyptians didn't seem to mind; the restaurants, brothels, lodging houses and bazaars were all doing brisk business.

Apart from the uniforms, the war might not be happening at all as far as Cairo was concerned, for there seemed to be no shortage of anything. From tiny cramped shops, competing vendors sold charcoal-cooked kebabs, or juicy kofta from huge bubbling, blackened vats of oil. Merchants beckoned from the doorways of cupboard-sized shops, inviting passers-by for a glass of mint tea or Turkish coffee, ready to haggle over the price of anything from a needle to a camel saddle. Stalls were weighed down with food and spices, cheap jewellery and trinkets, cotton and papyrus, carpets and bales of wool cloth, and an endless variety of brass and copperware. And everywhere, as always, there was the pungent, herbal smell of hashish in the air.

Sanson turned down a littered street with an open sewer and pulled up outside what could hardly be described as a house. It was no more than a ramshackle ruin, in the middle of a row of shanty dwellings. All the windows were broken and had been replaced with tattered cloth and bits of wood. A couple of scrawny-looking children played with make-shift toys in the dusty street, skinny-ribbed, half-wild dogs barking and yelping at their heels.

Sanson led the way to the entrance, which hadn't even a door, just a beaded curtain. "This way."

He pushed through the beads and Weaver followed. The first thing that struck him was the overpowering stench. A mixture of stale sweat and rancid food, and that particularly unpleasant, rotting smell you got in the more destitute quarters of Cairo. The place was a pitiful hovel. There was a tiny fireplace, no more than a hole in the grimy white-washed wall, a rickety wooden table but no chairs, and the floors were bare, filthy concrete.

In one corner sat a wailing, black-robed woman, clutching an infant in her arms. She was surrounded by three grieving females, all dressed in black, despite the terrible heat. Weaver guessed they were relatives or neighbours. Half a dozen noisy, barefoot children were crowded into the room. They seemed unaffected by a death in the house, giggling and smiling playfully at their visitors. Sanson scattered them with a wave of his hand. "*Barra! Barra!* Outside! Outside!"

When the children had scurried out, Sanson had words with the women mourners, and they shuffled out of the room, leaving them alone with the woman and her child. "This is Evir's widow. She speaks no English, naturally. And you may find it difficult to understand her dialect, so I'd better translate."

The woman looked well over forty, her skin lined with wrinkles, but Weaver guessed she was probably ten years younger, six births and a miserable life adding a decade to her face. There was a room leading off that served as the sleeping area, but no beds, just a couple of worn rugs scattered on the floor. Weaver felt something tug at his jacket and looked down. A small boy no more than ten, with big eyes and a cheeky, dirty brown face, smiled up at him. Weaver patted his head and saw to his horror that the child's hair was infested with lice.

Sanson said to the child, *"Barra!"*

The boy clung to Weaver, and Sanson made to pull him away. "No, leave him, he's OK."

"A word of advice from a former policeman, Weaver. The boy here could probably have your wallet before you know it. His type are born with a hand in the midwife's purse."

The child seemed harmless, but Weaver guessed that Sanson was probably right. "I guess you'd better explain why we're here." He nodded at the woman. "You want to ask her if she knows why her husband had the sketch?"

Sanson spoke to the woman as she continued to wail. After a few moments, she babbled something tearfully. It was a tenement dialect, spoken rapidly, and Weaver found it almost impossible to grasp a word.

Sanson looked frustrated. "She says she doesn't know why he'd have such a thing. She says she's puzzled. Not only about the drawing, but why such an important effendi should call at her home."

"Tell her the information could be important. And any help she can give will be rewarded."

While Sanson translated, the boy tugged at Weaver's jacket. He reached into his pocket and handed the child a stick of gum. The boy smiled with delight, peeled off the silver wrapper, and slipped the gum into his mouth.

When the woman replied, Sanson said, "She says her husband never spoke about his private business. And she doesn't know where he might have gone the night he was killed. But the night before his death he told her he was going to meet someone. He left the house about nine and came back before midnight. She wants to know if this helps."

"Who did he meet?"

"She claims she doesn't know. Her husband never told her where he went, or who he met."

"She's sure?"

Sanson nodded. "I'm reasonably certain she's telling us the truth, Weaver."

The woman jabbered something else, and Sanson answered in Arabic, "Be quiet."

"What did she say?" asked Weaver.

"She wanted me to tell you she has a bare cupboard and six mouths to feed, and for any help the effendi could give a widow, Allah will smile on you. But pay no attention to her."

Weaver looked at the baby in the woman's arms, at the pitiful squalor around them, and took out his wallet. The experiences of war had hardened his heart to pretty much everything, had toughened him in so many ways, but he couldn't endure the thought of the woman and her small children going hungry. Sanson said, "You don't have to, Weaver. These people always survive. Besides, she told us nothing really useful."

"No, I'd like to." Weaver generously peeled off several large notes and left them on the table. The woman clutched her child to her breast and rocked back and forth, sobbing her thanks. As he put away his wallet, Weaver felt the boy tug at his coat again.

"Take it easy, son."

The boy babbled something. Weaver looked at Sanson. "What the hell did he say?"

"He thinks he knows where his father went."

NINE

Weaver looked beyond the windscreen as Sanson's staff Humber trundled into the Khan-el-Khalili bazaar. The streets were bedlam, lined either side with cavernous huckster shops, heavily laden stalls, and food vendors.

Harassed-looking waiters ran in every direction, carrying silver trays of tea or coffee balanced above their heads. Children carrying huge bales of cotton scurried past, their

backs bent double like those of old men. The pedestrian
and donkey-and-cart traffic was chaotic. A legless beggar,
wearing cut-up parts of a car tyre strapped to his stumps,
propelled himself past them with frightening strength. Sanson blasted his horn as he inched the car through the throng.

"He says that since his father came out of prison, he
wanted to get to know him again, but he hardly bothered
to even speak with him. So he followed him on several
occasions. Twice he went to a house in Gamaliya, not far
from the El Hakim mosque."

The boy's name was Jamal and he had wanted to ride
up front in the car. He sat between them, and Sanson had
questioned him relentlessly since they had left the house.
Weaver knew the El Gamaliya district. Its narrow streets
contained the Khan-el-Khalili, the area peppered with ten-
ements, cheap lodging houses and belly-dance halls that
doubled as brothels.

"On one occasion," Sanson continued, "he waited until
his father had gone inside the house, then he followed him.
He saw him go up a flight of stairs, and knock on a door
on the first floor. A man came out into the corridor, and
then they both went inside."

"How does he know his father went there the night before he was killed?"

"He doesn't. But he followed him towards the El Hakim
mosque that evening. His father saw him and told him to
go home. The boy thinks that maybe he went to the same
place."

"Did he see what the man looked like?"

"Tall, and he had a beard."

Weaver handed the youngster another stick of gum. The
boy nodded his thanks and slipped it into his pocket. Finally, Sanson turned down a narrow cobbled street that
came out into a small dusty square, ringed with dismal-
looking four-storey tenement houses and crumbling pavements. The area looked totally forbidding to a foreigner.
Most of the buildings were badly neglected, tattered washing hung from balcony windows, and a few shifty-looking
men lazed in doorways and on street corners. When they
saw the staff car slow down, the effect was immediate.
They disappeared.

The boy pointed to a house across the square, its door open and leading into shadowed darkness. "That's the place," said Sanson.

He pulled in and jerked on the handbrake. Weaver told the boy to wait in the car.

"OK, let's take a look."

As they walked across the square, it suddenly occurred to Weaver that he had no gun in case there was trouble. He rarely carried his Colt service automatic, but Sanson had a revolver, a standard-issue Smith & Wesson .38, and as they approached the house, Weaver noticed him release the holster flap.

"Shouldn't we have called your friend Arkhan?"

"Time for that later. We have a few questions ourselves that need answering."

The front door of the tenement was open and they stepped into a cool, dark hallway. The bare floorboards were filthy, and there was a smell of rotting wood. Several doors led off, to individual flats Weaver guessed, and there was a stairway leading up.

"Wait here a moment."

Sanson went down the hallway and knocked softly on the first door. An elderly woman came out, dressed in black. When she saw Sanson's uniform, she seemed alarmed. Weaver couldn't hear the whispered conversation between them, before the woman went back inside, the door closed and a bolt rattled.

Sanson came back. "There's an Arab man living alone on the first floor, matching the description the boy gave. The woman doesn't know him except by sight, and she doesn't know his name. He's been renting the flat for about nine months and comes and goes at all hours. He keeps to himself and she hasn't the foggiest what he does for a living."

"Anything else?"

"She hasn't seen much of him for the last few days." Sanson looked up towards the landing. "Let's see if he's in."

Weaver followed him up the creaking stairs. When they

reached the first landing, they saw a solid door with three sturdy locks.

"He's careful, I'll give him that." Sanson knocked. There was no reply. He banged very hard on the door. When still no one answered, he tried once more. Finally, he said frustratedly to Weaver, "Wait here."

"Where are you going?"

Sanson said simply, "I won't be long."

He went down the stairs, and when he came back minutes later he had a steel wheel brace from the car. In Cairo, a military uniform often carried enough authority for the wearer to do what he wanted, but Weaver was alarmed. "You're going to break in without a warrant?"

"The man may be a suspect in a murder and he could already have fled. The woman said she hasn't seen him in days. Besides, I checked the rear of the building. There's no way to reach the windows without a ladder, and in this neighbourhood you can be sure they're well locked. Believe me, Weaver, this way is quicker."

"But he might be entirely innocent."

"He might also be guilty, and trying to hide. But if he's innocent, I'll apologise and have the locks repaired." Without another word, Sanson wedged the brace between the door and the jamb. He jerked the brace hard, and the wood splintered. Then he pulled out his pistol, kicked in the door, and they moved into the flat.

The place was untidy. It was also empty. Sunlight poured into the room through filthy gauze curtains. There was an old ottoman couch by the window, covered in red velvet, a low coffee table, some cushions strewn around the bare floor, and a metal stove against one wall. Three doors led off, one of them open to reveal a tiny kitchen. Weaver saw a gas stove, a sink, and some cupboards.

The room was pretty bare, and while Sanson went off to check the other rooms, Weaver stepped into the kitchen. There was some tinned food on the shelves, jars of sugar, coffee and a few spices, but the cupboards themselves were empty. He noticed a dark brown-black stain on the sink. He licked his finger, dabbed it on the stain, and brushed it against his tongue.

Coffee.

Sanson called out, "In here."

Weaver stepped into a bedroom. Like the other room, it was pretty bare and functional. There was a mattress on the floor, covered with dirty grey blankets. No pictures on the walls, or personal belongings, except some empty wooden boxes on the floor, and a tattered cardboard suitcase lying under the bed, containing a couple of djellabas.

"Weaver?"

For a moment, Weaver couldn't see the Englishman, but then he noticed a walk-in closet off to the right, a single red light bulb on overhead, Sanson standing inside. He joined him in the cramped room. "What have we got here?"

There was a miniature camera lying on a wooden ledge, some jars of chemicals, and several rolls of film. A stretch of twine ran from wall to wall, with some clothes pegs attached for hanging negatives out to dry.

Sanson said, "It seems our friend has a keen interest in photography." He took down the camera and examined it. "A German Leica. Did you find anything in the other room?"

"Nothing."

"I'll have the flat searched thoroughly, and I'll need a man on duty at the door until I can get it repaired and sealed up. After that, we'll put a watch on the place and see if anyone turns up. There's a phone at the railway station. Could I ask you to wait here while I call headquarters?"

"What happens if the Arab shows up in the meantime?"

Sanson removed his revolver and offered it to Weaver. "You'd better take this as a precaution. I'll be as quick as I can. Ten minutes, perhaps less."

Weaver opened the window. There was hardly a breeze. He looked down into the back alleyway below. A tiny bricked-off courtyard lay behind the tenement house, filthy with stinking garbage. The door leading in was rotted off its hinges. He went to sit on the ottoman, laid the revolver on the coffee table, and looked around the room. The place was functional, nothing more. There were no photographs, no personal belongings, no knick-knacks that showed the kind of man they were dealing with. But even bare functional rooms with a mattress, some clothes and three locks on the front door told them something. The man was secretive, cautious, had simple needs, and lived alone.

The man was also a spy, of that he had no doubt. And ruthless, assuming he had killed Evir. Weaver was intrigued. Why had Evir been murdered? And what was the Arab up to in Cairo? The Germans had recruited agents and sympathisers in the city's clubs, bars and brothels, but since Rommel had been defeated they were pretty much redundant.

Something else struck him. If the man was a spy, he probably had a radio. He knew he should leave the proper searching to Sanson and his men, but his curiosity got the better of him. He stood and went into the kitchen. He rapped his knuckles on the insides of the cupboards, checked the floors and walls, but there were no false panels. He did the same in the bedroom and in the darkroom.

Nothing.

He went back into the front room, tried the same, with no luck. The stove was all that was left. It was unlit, the metal cold. He knelt and pulled at the bricks at the base. One of them came loose, then another. Four bricks later, a recess was revealed. He put his hand inside, felt something and hefted it out on to the floor. It was a small leather suitcase with a sturdy handle and a couple of straps. He undid the straps. Inside was a German shortwave radio set, a pair of earphones, and a Morse code key. He guessed the battery was still in the recess or hidden somewhere else.

Weaver smiled and whistled. "You know something, Harry, I think you're in luck."

Suddenly he heard a faint creak behind him and turned. A tall, bearded Arab stood in the doorway, a Walther pistol in his hand. He wore a djellaba and a livid expression on his face which suggested he was furious that his territory had been violated.

Weaver stood. "Who in the hell—?"

"Move away from the radio," the Arab ordered in English. "Do it very slowly."

Weaver stepped back. Sanson's revolver was still on the coffee table. The Arab saw Weaver's eyes flick to it.

"Don't, unless you want a bullet. Empty your pockets on the table."

Weaver did as he was told. The Arab picked up Weaver's identity card and examined it without expression. "An American. What are you doing here?"

"I came looking for a friend and saw the door open."

"Don't lie to me, or you'll lose your life. Answer the question—what are you doing here?"

Weaver glanced at the radio. "I think that's obvious."

"Hand the radio here."

Weaver closed the suitcase and moved to hand it over. At that moment, there was a clatter of feet below on the stairs. The Arab looked behind, startled. Weaver saw his chance and made a move. Just as the man looked back, he managed to grab the Walther's muzzle, and punched him hard in the face, with a sound like bone cracking. The gun went off, the slug drilled the wall, and the man reeled back. As Weaver struggled for the weapon, the man's free hand came up. There was a flash of a blade and Weaver felt a searing pain in his throat. He cried out and let go of the Walther. The Arab kicked his feet from under him and he fell to the floor.

There were shouts outside the doorway, and moments later two of Sanson's men appeared, their guns drawn as they moved gingerly into the flat, Sanson unarmed behind them. The Arab grabbed the radio and moved towards the window, then turned and fired twice as he clambered out. One of the men was hit in the chest and slammed back against the wall, as Sanson and the second man frantically sought cover.

"Stay down, Weaver!" Sanson roared.

Weaver was bleeding heavily from a gash in his neck, but he got to his feet, grabbed the revolver from the table and staggered to the window. Down in the alleyway he saw the Arab climb on to a motorcycle and kick it to life. He tried to aim with his left hand, but the Arab's weapon came up smartly and spat twice, the shots whistling past Weaver's head as he ducked back inside.

He heard the motorcycle roar away, and when he looked out again the man was already halfway down the alley. Weaver tried to steady his hand against the window frame, but he felt terribly weak. He noticed blood washing down his chest, turning his tunic bright crimson. Sanson was beside him in an instant, prising the gun from his fingers.

"Give me that!"

Sanson aimed out of the window and emptied the revolver in a rapid volley of shots.

The last thing Weaver saw was the Arab's djellaba blowing wildly in the wind as the motorcycle skidded, rounded a corner, and sped away. Then his vision started to go, he felt himself falling, and everything turned black.

TEN

BERLIN
15 NOVEMBER
The hospital in the suburbs of Charlottenburg was a solid-looking redbrick building, built at the turn of the century and set behind high walls. It was just after eleven in the morning when Halder arrived. Several convoys of ambulances and army trucks were pulling up in the gravel driveway, soldiers and medics helping to carry in dozens of injured civilians on stretchers. A staff nurse he recognised came down the steps, all business, and Halder said, "More problems, I see."

"It's those damned British and American bombers," she answered scornfully. "Have they no shame? Most of the dead and wounded are women and children."

A medic went past with a badly bleeding teenage girl, and the nurse left to help. Halder moved up the steps into the entrance hallway. It was in chaos, ringing with the cries of the injured and the shouts of medical staff, orderlies running in all directions. He saw the office down the hall, knocked on the door, and an impatient voice said, "Come in."

A white-coated elderly doctor, well past retirement age and looking under strain, was sifting through some files as he sat behind a desk. "Yes, what is it?"

"I'm here to see about my son, Pauli Halder. He's a patient in the burns ward."

"You'll have to come back. I've got fifty new casualties on my hands, enough beds for only half, and God knows where I'm going to put the rest."

"My apologies, but I thought Dr. Weiss was on duty."

"Weiss and his family were killed yesterday evening in the air raids. His home took a direct hit."

"I'm very sorry to hear that. He was a good man."

"Even doctors aren't immune from bombs, I'm afraid. Halder, did you say? What exactly do you want?"

"The matron mentioned yesterday that Dr. Weiss had wanted to see me. But he wasn't on duty and I got no reply from his home number, so I thought I'd call by in case it might be something important about my son."

The doctor sighed, went to a filing cabinet, and searched until he found the medical report he was looking for. "Pauli Halder, almost three years old, transferred from Hamburg?"

"That's him."

The doctor read the report and shook his head. "Not too good, is he? He's healing, of course, after the skin grafts, but most of his body was covered in third-degree burns from the phosphor bombs, and he's still in pretty bad shape. Injuries like his can take a long time to heal. And he really needs to get out of this environment. The Allies have been bombing close to the hospital recently, and the pounding seems to upset him. Not surprising really, after his ordeal in Hamburg." The doctor sighed again. "There's a note here about the morphine for his pain relief. I imagine that's what Dr. Weiss wanted to see you about."

"What do you mean?"

"We barely have enough drugs for emergency cases right now. We'll have to cut back on his dosage."

"I've been here every day since my son was admitted," Halder said angrily. "I've seen the kind of agony he's in. If you do that he's going to suffer even more!"

"A lot of injured civilians are suffering, Halder, not to mention our troops. Our factories are being destroyed by the bombing—drugs and medical supplies are posing a problem right now. The troops get priority for what's available and our allocation has been reduced. And with these latest raids, we're stretched to the limit. There's nothing I can do, I'm afraid."

The phone rang and the doctor picked it up. "Yes, damn it! I'm on my way." He slammed down the phone. "Look, I'm sorry, I'm needed in surgery."

Halder stormed out of the office and went up to the second-floor ward. It was crowded with new patients. He found the curtained-off bed in a corner. A harassed-looking nurse stepped out, carrying a tray of balm and used dressings. "Oh, it's you again, Herr Halder. I've just been dressing Pauli's wounds. He's resting now, but you can go in."

Halder moved behind the curtain. The little boy was covered from head to toe in bandages, his skin burned so deeply in places that numerous skin grafts had been needed, especially on his legs, which had been horrifically charred. Only his face was visible, some of the tissue bloated and pink and scarred, his eyes closed, the eyelashes seared away. There were beads of perspiration on his forehead, and even in sleep his expression was pained.

"Pauli, can you hear me?"

The boy gurgled something, but was too drugged to make any sense. There was a single chair, and a bowl of water and a cloth on the locker beside the bed. For a long time Halder sat there, gently swabbing his son's forehead with the damp cloth, staring at his tortured face. When he reached out to touch his bandaged hands, the boy moaned in his sleep. There was something deeply disturbing about having to witness a child in such horrible pain, and not being able to do anything about it. Halder felt a wave of anguish sweep over him, and he was close to tears.

A young nurse put her head round the curtain. "Are you Major Halder?"

He wiped his eyes. "Yes."

"There's a gentleman to see you, sir. He's waiting downstairs in the visitor's room."

When he went down, Wilhelm Canaris was sitting on one of the benches. He wore civilian clothes, a shabby dark suit, overcoat and hat. He stood and offered his hand.

"Jack, it's good to see you."

Halder didn't offer to shake his hand, and Canaris said,

"I can imagine you're hardly pleased to see me. I believe you met with Schellenberg?"

"What about it?"

Canaris nodded towards the hospital grounds. "Would you mind if we walked outside? We need to talk in private."

The admiral led the way, down a pathway between some trees, and when they had gone several paces he said, "How's your son?"

"What the hell is it to you?"

"My enquiry is genuine, Jack. Don't take offence."

"He's not too good."

"The poor boy. I'm terribly sorry to hear that."

"What do you want to see me about?"

Canaris let out a breath. "I'd just like you to know that Schellenberg's plan is entirely his own little scheme. I spoke with Himmler last night and tried to convince him to reconsider using you, but it was a waste of time. He's investing a lot in the mission succeeding. Seems to think it has a good chance of working and you're perfect for the job."

"And what do you think?"

Canaris shrugged. "Does it matter? It's just another lunatic SD plot. And like you, I've no choice but to go along. But Himmler's adamant he won't accept failure on this one. The way he sees it, everything is at stake, and by that he means total victory or defeat. If the mission succeeds, he'll keep to his word. He'll give you everything he's promised, and more." Canaris hesitated. "But if you fail—"

"Spit it out, Willy."

Canaris looked at him. "I suppose because of the fact you're American-born, Himmler's a little doubtful about your absolute allegiance to the Fatherland. That's partly why Kleist and Doring will be along—to make sure the job is done. If you fail, or don't put everything into the mission for whatever reason, Himmler assures me you'll never see your son again. There's also the risk that Kleist or his comrade will put a bullet in you if you try to shirk your duty."

A look of anger flashed on Halder's face. "The lowdown, evil bastard."

"It's been said before, and worse, but to no avail.

There's something else. Schellenberg wants you to be the one to speak with Rachel Stern."

"Why the hell should it be me?"

"That black uniform of Walter's tends to put the shivers up most people. Besides that, he seems to think she may be more receptive if she knows you're involved." Canaris handed across a large envelope. "All her details are in there, including Schellenberg's proposal, which may help her decide. You're expected at Ravensbruck this evening, as a guest of the Reichführer's office. I'll have one of my drivers pick you up at seven."

"Do you know how she's been?"

Canaris saw the concern in Halder's face. "These places are never pleasant, but Ravensbruck is not the worst. And for the last few days Schellenberg has made sure she's been well looked after, given extra rations, medical attention, and so on. He also tells me she hasn't been badly treated despite her imprisonment. It seems one of the senior camp officers was a former pupil of her father's. Fortunately, he made sure she was spared the worst and given light duties." Canaris stopped walking and looked at the other man. "Did you love her, Jack?"

Halder glanced away, towards the hospital grounds. "God knows. All that seems a long time ago and another life."

"If it's any consolation, I've told Schellenberg I want to be kept fully abreast of developments—after all, you're one of my best men, and I feel a certain responsibility." Canaris hesitated, his face troubled. "One other thing. Walter may be a reasonably likable rogue compared to some of his SD comrades, but I still wouldn't trust the little shit an inch."

"What do you mean?"

Canaris shrugged. "Call it intuition, if you like, but no doubt it's years of experience in this unpleasant business that's sending off warning bells inside my head—I've got a distinct feeling he may not be telling us the entire story, and that he's up to something behind our backs. You know how much he delights in his cunning little plots. It's like an elaborate game with him."

"Up to what?"

"I'm afraid I haven't the faintest idea. But you've been warned, so tread carefully."

Halder slipped the envelope inside his jacket. "I'll try to. Do me a favour, Willy."

"Anything."

"Take care of Pauli for me while I'm away. And make sure he's looked after if I don't make it back. Promise me that?"

"Of course." Canaris put a hand on his shoulder. "Good luck, Jack. That's really all I can say. And try and come out of this alive and in one piece."

ELEVEN

BERLIN

Ravensbruck concentration camp had been built in 1935 on Heinrich Himmler's orders, one of the first camps exclusively for female prisoners. Constructed on a reclaimed marsh, it housed a variety of political offenders, gypsies and Jews, prostitutes, female prisoners-of-war, captured Allied agents and *résistants*.

It was dark and raining that evening as the Mercedes turned off the Potsdam autobahn and headed north. Sitting in the back seat, Halder wore a black leather trench coat and a slouch hat. The dark evening clouds were lit up by flashes of anti-aircraft fire, and parts of Berlin's northern suburbs were peppered with flames.

"A filthy night," he said to the driver.

The sergeant glanced round. His passenger had the look of Gestapo about him in the hat and leather coat. "And going to get worse before it gets better, by the looks of it. The Allies have been bombing us the last three nights. Dangerous times we're living in."

Halder rolled down the window as the Mercedes turned off the main road. A sign said Ravensbruck, and there was another underneath. *Entritt Verboten.* Entrance forbidden.

At the end of the road was a set of heavy wooden gates, high barbed-wire runs either side, a sentry command post beyond. Halder felt a chill go through him. For some inexplicable reason his heart was pounding in his chest. A couple of SS guards wearing rain capes came out, one of them with a leashed Alsatian. When the Mercedes halted, the sergeant showed their papers and they were allowed through.

A room had been set aside in a draughty wooden hut with a table and a couple of chairs. Halder was alone, and the wait seemed endless as he anxiously tapped his fingers on the table. He had an odd feeling in the pit of his stomach, fear and a strange kind of excitement. The door finally opened and two female SS guards came in, Rachel between them. She looked pale, and wore a drab, striped camp uniform, her blond hair cut short, but not completely cropped.

"Hello, Rachel."

For a moment or two she couldn't seem to take in his presence. "Jack—?"

Despite her pallid appearance, she was still striking— the high cheekbones, the wide, blue eyes, the generous mouth—and Halder was aware of a sudden unbearable tightness in his chest. He dismissed the guards. "Leave us."

When the door banged shut, Rachel stood facing him, silent, and then he slowly crossed the room, put a hand gently on her cheek. "My poor Rachel, what have they done to you?"

"I—I can hardly believe it's you. I'm so glad to see you. So glad."

It all seemed too much for her. He saw tears at the edges of her eyes, and in a moment she was in his arms. He was suddenly conscious of the warmth of her body through the thin material of the camp uniform, and for several moments they remained like that, holding on to each other as if for comfort. "It's all right. It's all right. Please, sit down."

He led her to the table and they sat. "It's been a long time. How are you?"

She wiped her eyes. "Alive. I suppose that must count for something."

"Forgive me, but I only just heard what happened to you and your parents. If I'd known sooner—"

His voice trailed off and Rachel said, "Is that why you came to see me?"

"No, that's not the reason. But I'd like to talk. Do you feel up to it?"

"Talk about what?"

He placed the file on the table in front of him, opened it, and looked up. "You've had a hard time of it, by all accounts. A prisoner here for four years, and your father in Dachau. I'm sure it's been far from pleasant."

For a moment she didn't reply, and then there was an unexpected flash of defiance in her eyes. "Who are you working for, Jack? The Gestapo?"

"Hardly."

She looked at him, noticing the slouch hat and leather coat. "The way you're dressed might suggest otherwise."

He shook his head. "A bad choice, then, I'm afraid. I'm a major in the Abwehr. Military intelligence. I have a proposition for you, Rachel. Or rather my superiors have a proposition they'd like me to put to you. How would you like to go back to Egypt with me?"

He saw the puzzled reaction on her face. "Bear with me while I explain. Do you want to see your father again, and for you both to go free?"

She looked completely taken aback. "Of—of course."

"Then I can promise that he'll be released from Dachau, quartered in an excellent private hospital, and receive the services of a top physician to help regain his health. But best of all, I can promise that you'll both be freed and allowed to leave Germany. In return, you'll agree to be part of a mission. It's a rather straightforward operation—to gather some important intelligence information in Cairo. No doubt you're unaware, but the city is in Allied hands."

"I don't understand. What kind of information?"

Halder shook his head. "That's a security matter, and doesn't concern you. All you'd have to do is be part of an undercover team, on the pretext of being a group of archaeological experts stranded in North Africa because of the war. It's as simple as that. A few days' work at most, and then you and your father are released."

"On whose word?"

"On the word of Heinrich Himmler, Reichsführer of the SS, and Admiral Wilhelm Canaris, the head of the Abwehr."

She stared at him as if he were mad, then suddenly laughed. Halder said, "What's so funny?"

"I'd sooner trust Satan himself. You want *me* to help the Nazis? How can I trust them after what they've done to my father and me?"

"The answer is you can't. But let's just say I'm stuck in the same boat. Caught between the Devil and the deep blue sea."

"How?"

"A long story that doesn't really concern you. For now, all you have to do is decide."

"And what would happen if I agreed?"

"You'd be released and transferred to a barracks in Berlin, where you'd meet the rest of the group and be briefed on exactly what's expected of you. Soon after that, we'd be flown to Egypt. I'd be lying if I said there wasn't an element of danger. If you were caught on Allied territory, you'd run the risk of being shot as an enemy spy. But if everything goes according to plan, the risks should be minimal. When our mission is complete we'll be flown back to Germany. After that, you and your father would be set free and put on a ship for Sweden within twenty-four hours."

"And if I don't agree?"

Halder stood very slowly, crossed to the window. The rain was coming down in sheets. He hesitated before looking back. "If you don't, I'm informed you'll both be shot by morning."

She stared back at him with no expression, like a woman who had long used up all her emotional reserves. He shook his head, his own distaste obvious. "I'm sorry, Rachel, this is none of my doing. I'm simply a messenger, and an unwilling one at that. But if you ask me, a few days in Egypt and a chance of freedom sounds a lot better than a firing squad. I know you're wondering if you can believe the promises you've been given. But you'll have to trust me when I tell you that I have to believe them too."

"You're really serious about all this, aren't you?"

"Very. No doubt you wondered why they gave you extra rations, and the camp doctor seemed suddenly interested in your health. Now you know. But as I told you, I'm just a messenger. The fate of you and your father is beyond my control. Nothing I could say or do would change matters."

He came back to the table and sat down. He felt a catch in his throat. "But there is something I have wanted to tell you for a long time, if it's any consolation. And whatever you choose, I'd like you to know."

"What?"

"Something I never told you because I knew Harry felt the same way. And because we were always such close friends, I didn't want to ruin that friendship. But the first time I saw you at Sakkara, I fell instantly in love. *Coup de foudre*, the French call it. The thunderclap. The most potent kind of love of all."

She didn't reply. There was a strained silence between them. Halder stood, suddenly uncomfortable, and pushed back his chair. He was conscious of a powerful emotion welling up inside him as he looked down at her face.

"I'm going to leave you for a while, and let you think about the offer."

It was after midnight when the driver dropped Halder back at the Wannsee cottage. The rain was still coming down in sheets as he went up the veranda. There was a black Opel sedan parked on the gravel in front of the house, two leather-coated Gestapo men sitting inside. Schellenberg's Mercedes was parked next to it, and he was already waiting in the front room, smoking a cigarette and relaxing on the sofa, the fire lit and blazing, a glass of champagne in his hand. "A filthy night, so I thought I'd make myself at home and help myself to some refreshment. I hope you don't mind?" He grinned. "Well, how did it go?"

Halder shook rain from his coat and said angrily, "She agreed. Though it hardly surprises me, the offer you put to her."

"The way of the world, Jack." Schellenberg seemed excited and got to his feet. He drained the champagne and put down the glass. "It really looks like we're on our way. Excellent."

"I just hope she's up to it."

"Nonsense. She's in reasonably good health. And it's too late to find someone else, even if we could. You'll just have to keep an eye on her, and make sure she does what's expected. Naturally, I'll give her an account of the war situation—having been in Ravensbruck, she won't know the present state of play." Schellenberg smiled. "It'll be a selective account, of course. Just as much as she needs to know."

"I want you to do something for me."

"What?"

"My son needs morphine. The hospital says its supplies have been cut. I don't want Pauli to be in any more pain than he is already. And I'd like him transferred to a hospital outside Berlin, somewhere where there's less bombing."

Schellenberg nodded. "Very well. I'll see what I can do."

Halder flared. "Don't *see*, just do it."

"Temper, Jack," Schellenberg snapped back. "I promised he'd be looked after and I intend keeping my pledge. What's got into you?"

"Let's just say I'm not overly fond of your tactics. And you know something? I've got a bad feeling about this. A very bad feeling indeed."

"Nonsense. It'll work—it has to."

"Another thing. If Rachel Stern gets out of this alive, you'd better keep to your promise. Otherwise, I'll come gunning for you, Walter. On my life, I will. Even if it means a firing squad."

"Harsh words indeed, and I'm not sure I like your tone," Schellenberg answered firmly. "But the promise will be kept, you can be sure of that."

Halder tossed his wet coat on a chair. "What happens now?"

"You get to meet your fellow travellers tomorrow morning. Seven a.m. at Lichterfeld SS barracks. The girl will be transferred there tonight. I'll send a driver to pick you up at six-thirty."

"Then what?"

"Time is against us, so we need to move fast. There'll be a rigorous briefing, starting early tomorrow, for yourself, Kleist and Doring, to explain the plan in detail and go over your cover story—that should take no more than three days—then you'll have the following day to all get ac-

quainted. After that—assuming our U-boats or the
Luftwaffe haven't miraculously succeeded in doing the
dirty deed for us, and with Himmler's final approval—
you'll be flown to Rome and from there on to Egypt, probably on the same night. A detailed message will be on its
way to our principal agent in Cairo, informing him of our
intentions, and with instructions to obtain what equipment
you'll need, and to prepare for your arrival."

"It all sounds too rushed to me."

"Apart from the obvious time constraints, the long-range
weather reports for the Mediterranean regions are pretty
grim. So I want you well under way in case we can't make
the drop later. We simply can't take the risk of having to
delay or cancel."

"Then I'll need to see my son one last time before I go."

Schellenberg shook his head. "Not possible, I'm afraid,
for obvious security reasons. From this moment on, you're
all committed to the mission and under my protection. By
right, you should be sleeping in Lichterfeld barracks tonight."

Halder made to protest, but Schellenberg said, "Forget
it, Jack, you're wasting your time. It's Himmler's personal
instruction, and the two Gestapo men outside have orders
to ensure you don't go anywhere without my permission."
He stood. "And now you'd better get some sleep. You've
a busy day tomorrow." He crossed to the door, opened it,
looked out at the pouring rain. "Thank God the weather's
stopped the bombers." He shivered, pulled up his collar and
looked back, a curious expression on his face. "Do you still
have feelings for the girl, Jack?"

"What's it to you?"

Schellenberg shrugged. "I'm simply curious."

"You can go to hell."

"I take it Canaris told you about Himmler's threat?"

"He told me."

"Old Heinrich means what he says. Unpleasant, I know,
but there you have it. So I wouldn't even think about fail-
ing, Jack, or putting anything less than a hundred per cent
into this. Life wouldn't be worth living, as they say, for
either you or your son." Schellenberg gave a wicked grin
as he turned back towards the door. "But rest assured, the
boy will be well looked after until your safe return."

TWELVE

CAIRO

Weaver tilted his head and tried to sit still as the female doctor stitched his neck. He was in a cubicle in the Anglo-American hospital. A nurse had given him a shot of morphine, and all he felt was a warm feeling of elation. The pain would come later, when the drug wore off.

The doctor finished another stitch, smiled and said, "A wonderful thing, morphine. Makes you forget all your troubles. That's a pretty nasty gash. You're lucky you're still alive." She was British, very attractive, and had sensitive blue eyes. "So, tell me, what happened?"

"Someone cut me with a knife."

"That much is obvious."

The incident was an intelligence matter and not something Weaver wanted to discuss, no matter how attractive the doctor. "Are we almost done?"

"One more to go." She pierced the flesh again, finishing the last suture. She tied the stitch, cut the thread with scissors, then the nurse put a protective dressing on Weaver's neck and wrapped a bandage around it.

"Will I be OK?"

"You'll be fine, apart from a nasty scar when the wound heals. But you're a bit shaken and you'll have to rest up for a week or two. Stick to liquids for a few days, soup and some glucose mixed with water, otherwise swallowing's going to hurt. I'll give you some morphine pills to help keep the pain at bay. In the meantime, try not to move your neck too much, otherwise the stitches might be disturbed."

"Do I really have to rest up?"

"Lieutenant-Colonel Weaver, you've lost quite a bit of blood and the cut's deep. A quarter-inch deeper and you'd probably be in the morgue. So it's straight home to bed."

The door opened and Helen Kane came in. She looked concerned. "How is he, Doctor?"

"He'll live." She handed Weaver a bottle of pills. "Take

two whenever the pain gets too bad. They'll make you a little slow and light-headed, but that's a small price to pay. Try to be more careful in future."

She smiled playfully and went out with the nurse. Helen Kane said, "How are you feeling, sir?"

"Lousy."

"Well, there's one good thing."

"What?"

"I think the doctor liked you. She made a lot of eye contact."

Weaver was tempted to smile back, but resisted. He touched the bandage around his neck. It felt tight. He could barely move his head and he felt groggy. He hardly remembered being taken to the hospital—everything that had happened after the Arab had slashed him was a blur. He slid off the bed and reached for his jacket. Helen Kane put out a hand to support him. "Don't you think you'd better rest for a while?"

"Time for that later. What's happening about the Arab, Helen?"

"Lieutenant-Colonel Sanson wants to see you. He's waiting down the hall."

Sanson was in one of the waiting rooms when Weaver and Helen Kane entered, the windows open, a ceiling fan whirring away. When he saw Weaver's bandaged neck and the dried blood caked into his shirt and tunic, he looked mildly sympathetic. "That looks pretty bad. Do you feel up to talking?"

"Sure."

Sanson said politely, "If you don't mind waiting out in the car, Helen."

"Yes, sir."

When Helen Kane left, Sanson lit a cigarette and watched her stroll into the gardens outside. "She seems to have a keen interest in your well-being, Weaver. Is there something going on between you two?"

"As one equally ranked officer to another, and if you don't mind me saying so, I really don't think that's any of your business."

Sanson reddened. He seemed to take the rebuff personally, his expression icy as he nodded towards a bench. "Take a seat."

They sat near one of the windows. Out on the sun-washed lawns, nurses strolled with their charges, limbless and seriously wounded men on crutches and in wheelchairs, recovering from the fighting in Italy. Looking at the injured patients, then back at Sanson's scarred face and patched eye, Weaver suddenly felt grateful that he had only suffered a knife laceration. The last time he'd been wounded had been in Algeria, when he'd sustained a shrapnel injury to his thigh from an enemy mortar blast. It had been a close call, because he'd lost a lot of blood and his unit was under heavy machinegun fire at the time. He couldn't move, but one of his fellow officers had heroically risked his life, crawling forward under withering fire and helping to get him back safely behind American lines. Had he not been rescued, Weaver would certainly have died, but after six weeks enduring the boredom of recovery in a hospital bed in Algiers, he had been almost glad to return to active duty.

"You had a lucky escape," Sanson said sharply. "My sergeant wasn't so fortunate. He died ten minutes ago in a ward down the hall."

"I'm really sorry to hear that."

"So was I. He was a bloody good soldier by any standards." Sanson was angry. "And I'll tell you something else, Weaver. Something that *is* my business. Had you kept a vigilant watch with the gun and waited until I returned before poking your nose around the flat, my sergeant might still be alive."

Weaver said grimly, "Maybe you're right. But from the look on the Arab's face, he meant to kill anyone who got in his way. All of us who were in the room if he had to. I meant it when I said I was sorry about the sergeant's death. But it could just as easily have been me."

Sanson took out a notebook, all business, and replied curtly, "Forget it, Weaver. Right now I'm not in the mood for arguing. You'd better tell me exactly what happened after I left the flat."

Weaver told him and Sanson jotted down details. "If our friend is worth his salt, he's probably got another safe house, but we'll have to check the hotels, pensions and lodging houses to see if anything turns up. It's probably pointless keeping a watch on the flat—he'll never go back there again. I've also given details of the incident to every police station in Cairo, and we're questioning the other tenants and trying to get in touch with the landlord, to see if he can tell us anything about the identity of this fellow."

"Did you search the flat?"

"Top to bottom. We found nothing, apart from a radio battery hidden under the stove. But it wouldn't stop him from transmitting. A car battery would probably do just as well. I'll try to find out if there's been any unidentified radio traffic out of Cairo recently, and ask Signals to keep a close monitor on the airwaves from now on. By the way, the camera we found is a type that's ideal for photographing documents, and uses a miniature roll of film. With that and the radio, you can bet the bastard's up to serious business. Have you any experience of enemy spies, Weaver?"

Internal security in Egypt was the responsibility of the British; they had the most experience, and the US took a back seat. "I guess not."

"You might say catching them is a personal crusade of mine." Sanson pointed to his face, the patched eye and scarred jaw, an edge of bitterness in his voice. "No doubt you've wondered about this. It was a gift from a chap named Raoul Hosiny, who worked for the Germans. I tracked him down to a flat in Alexandria eighteen months ago, while he was sending a radio transmission to one of Rommel's bases. He was another good one with a knife, was Raoul. So good, he left me blind in one eye and looking on the bright side, permanently."

"He escaped?"

"Not for long. I tracked him down again and shot the bastard dead." Sanson dropped his cigarette on the floor, ground it out with his boot. "Catching Italian spies was always easy—you located the most beautiful women in town, and looked under their beds. And being sensible fellows, the Italians nearly always gave up without a struggle. But the Germans are something else entirely. They have the most ruthless and professional agents you'll ever meet. Hardly surprising when you consider some of them are trained by the Gestapo and SD."

"And what about the Arab?"

"Oh, he's a spy, no doubt about it. The question is, what's he up to? And what did Evir do for him that he paid for with his life?"

"You really think he might have breached security at the residency?"

Sanson stood, towering above Weaver, his tone still icy. "We'd better check and try and find out, hadn't we? But if you want an honest opinion, I'll give you one. I was a policeman for ten years, and my nose is twitching on this one. We both know your President and our Prime Minister are due to arrive next week for a top-secret conference. Our intelligence reports suggest that the Germans have been trying desperately to get details. Why should be pretty obvious. I'd say that's reason enough for both of us to be concerned, wouldn't you?"

The Gezira Sporting and Racing Club was the most prestigious in Cairo, situated on Gezira Island, a small luxury oasis in the middle of the Nile, set in fourteen acres of magnificent gardens, with tennis courts, three polo pitches, swimming pools, restaurants, and several bars. The membership was mostly diplomats, wealthy Europeans and Allied officers, and there was a waiting list for new members as long as the club's racecourse.

The members' bar was still busy with civilians and off-duty officers when Weaver arrived just after lunch. He ordered a Scotch and soda, took a sip but found it an effort to swallow. He had showered and changed into civilian clothes, a light linen suit and an open-necked shirt. Wearing a uniform shirt and tie was impossible with the bandage, and now that the anaesthetic was beginning to wear off his neck felt painfully sore.

He saw General George Clayton enter the bar, his uniform immaculately pressed as always, the polished brass stars shining on his epaulettes. The US military attaché was a no-nonsense intelligence officer with a tough reputation. "Hello, Harry. You look like you've had one hell of a morning."

"I think you could say that, sir."

Behind Clayton came the American ambassador, wearing sweaty tennis whites and carrying a racket and towel. Alexander Kirk was a tall, very handsome man with a flamboyant manner, his friendly blue eyes hiding a wily streak.

"Mr. Ambassador, sir. Sorry for interrupting your game."

"Lieutenant-Colonel Weaver. Good to see you again."

Weaver shook hands, and Clayton nodded towards the empty tables on the veranda. "Why don't we take a walk, where we can have some privacy."

The ambassador and general strolled outside and sat in the cane chairs at one of the tables, and Weaver joined them. A couple of *ghiassa*—Nile boats with huge sweeping lateen sails—drifted gracefully along the river. Beyond the palm and oleander trees there was an uninterrupted view out to the Giza pyramids, twelve miles away, where Weaver knew the American and British army engineers were putting the finishing touches to the special compound being constructed for the top-level conference.

Clayton lit a cigar and dismissed the waiter who approached the table. "So what's this about some Arab trying to cut your throat?"

Weaver explained, and when he finished there was a long silence, until the ambassador said, "You're telling us Lieutenant-Colonel Sanson thinks this burglar managed to crack my safe *without* my staff's knowledge? That seems pretty incredible."

"He believes it's possible, sir."

"The residency has tight security," Clayton remarked. "You know that, Harry."

"And there's been nothing missing from the safe," the ambassador offered.

"Maybe I'd better tell you what we found, sir."

Clayton stopped chewing on his cigar. "Maybe you'd better."

Weaver looked at the ambassador. "There were some faint scratch marks near the latch on the French windows that lead to your study, which could have been made with a knife. And several indentations in the soil under a clump of trees across the lawn. Lieutenant-Colonel Sanson thinks they could have been footprints. We're still checking for fingerprints, but it's too early to say."

The ambassador stirred uncomfortably in his chair. "And what do *you* think, Lieutenant-Colonel Weaver?"

"The fact is, the burglar was murdered, for whatever reasons. And the Arab had a radio, and was obviously prepared to kill me to retrieve it. Which means the radio's vital—so it's likely he's in contact with the Germans. He also had a camera. Maybe nothing was taken from the safe, but any documents kept there could have been photographed. Can you recall your schedule for last week, sir?"

"Monday, I visited the British embassy for a private meeting and was back around five-thirty. Tuesday, I was at home. Wednesday, I attended a gala function at the Turkish ambassador's residence. I left at eight and returned at midnight. On Thursday, I remained at the residency, working late in my study, catching up on some paperwork. Friday, the same."

"How many guards were on duty Wednesday evening?"

"At least a dozen, as usual. Eight in the residency, two on the gate lodge, and two at the entrance. They patrol the entire residence, inside and out, at regular intervals."

"The officer in charge of security claims there was nothing unusual noted in the shift reports. But with your permission, I'd like to speak to the men on duty that night."

"Of course, but I doubt they'll tell you any more than you already know."

Weaver had been avoiding the question. He said delicately, "Would you care to tell me if there was anything of particular importance kept in your safe at any time during the past week, sir?"

"Top-secret documents are usually kept at the embassy."

"I'm aware of that, sir. But with respect, that wasn't my question."

Kirk didn't respond. Instead he turned slightly red. Clayton said, "I think you'd better tell him, Mr. Ambassador."

Kirk cleared his throat, as if embarrassed. "I believe there was a classified, decoded copy of a signal I sent to Washington, left there by the First Secretary."

Weaver said, "Exactly what kind of signal would that have been, sir?"

"It simply confirmed that our preparations here are almost complete for the conference, a week from now, and that the necessary security measures would be in place well before the arrival of our President and the British Prime Minister." The ambassador flushed, and added quickly, "However, there were absolutely no details of the nature of the meeting, or about security itself, I assure you."

Weaver was silent. The ambassador looked uneasy, as if he'd been compromised.

Clayton said, "For Christ sakes, Harry, do you really think that a single Arab spy could really pose us a threat? There'll be over a thousand men guarding the area, and security's going to be tighter than a crocodile's ass. No one gets next to near the place, not even if they've got a pass signed by God and someone to verify the signature. Besides, the nearest German lines are over a thousand miles away."

"I honestly don't know what to think, sir. But I learned a long time ago to suspect coincidence. Our latest intelligence reports from Lisbon and Istanbul indicate the Germans are aware there's something in the air, and their agents have been trying desperately to get information. I'd like to know what our friend with the radio is up to. And I'd rather not find out about it the hard way."

Clayton shot a meaningful glance at the ambassador. Kirk pursed his lips, his face still troubled, and nodded back with a sigh.

Clayton said to Weaver, "OK, you'd better find this guy. I want it cleared up before the President and Prime Minister arrive. But we don't go sounding any unnecessary alarm bells, not until we're pretty sure we might have trouble on our hands. We keep it under wraps for now."

"What about Lieutenant-Colonel Sanson, sir?"

"I want the two of you to take charge of this personally. I'll square it with his brigadier at GHQ—it's their security concern as much as ours. But you'd better let Sanson take the lead on this one. After all, this is British jurisdiction, and it's his turf we're playing on. From what I know of Sanson, he's had a lot more experience in these matters. And like the Mounties, a certain reputation for always getting his man." Clayton stood, crushed out his cigar. "Don't fail us, Harry. That's an order."

PART TWO

16–20 NOVEMBER 1943

THIRTEEN

The agent known as Harvey Deacon, discussed by Schellenberg and Canaris during their talk at Prinz-Albrecht-Strasse, was a naturalised British citizen who had lived in Egypt for over thirty years. A businessman, he owned a Nile houseboat that he operated as a casino and well-known nightspot called the Sultan Club.

Though hardly the most reputable nightclub in Cairo—the converted river steamer had been decorated inside to look like a smaller, cheaper version of the Folies-Bergère, with dim lighting and gaudy furniture—it was definitely one of the most popular. Not only because of the well-stocked bar and the excellent resident band, but because some of the girls performing the erotic floor show were usually agreeable to a little bedroom activity if the price was right. It was a practice Harvey Deacon encouraged, considering that it helped business no end.

He was in his office on the houseboat that afternoon, attending to some paperwork. An imposing figure, with greying curly hair and an impressive physique, Deacon wore a silk dressing gown with a scarf knotted at his neck. A crooked nose added a certain rugged grandeur. There was a knock on the door and he threw down his pen.

"Come in."

The door opened and his Nubian manservant appeared. "A gentleman to see you, effendi. He didn't give his name."

"Don't worry, I know what it's about. Send him in. Make sure we're not disturbed."

Moments later Hassan entered, wearing a djellaba. Deacon had a look of consternation on his face as he plucked a cigar from a sandalwood humidor on his desk. "Well? I'm waiting."

The Arab flopped into one of the cane chairs opposite. His jaw and lip looked badly bruised and swollen despite the beard, his right eye was blackened, and he'd lost a couple of bottom teeth. He grimaced in pain when he spoke. "The boy was Evir's son. I knew I'd seen him somewhere before. He was hanging around the railway station one night when I met his father. He told the boy to go home, but he must have followed us to the flat."

Deacon erupted, flung down his unlit cigar. "Of all the fucking things to happen. You should have been more careful."

Hassan sat back moodily in his chair, and held Deacon's stare in a kind of challenge. "One street urchin looks like another. And remember, it was you who told me to take Evir to the flat in the first place, to show him how to use the camera. If I hadn't gone back when I did and seen the staff car outside, the military would have been watching the building, waiting for us."

The Arab was right on that count, Deacon knew, and had risked his life retrieving the spare radio, but he was still fuming that the man's cover had been blown and the safe house discovered. "They still got the camera and saw the radio, didn't they? They'll know there's a German agent at work in the city. And you probably killed one of their men. It's a bloody disaster. You'd better lie low for a couple more days. The police and military will be looking for you."

"Let them look," Hassan said defiantly. "They'll never find me. Not in a crowded city like Cairo. All they saw was just another bearded Egyptian wearing a djellaba. And they can't know that Evir broke into the residence. They have no evidence—all he took was photographs."

Deacon reckoned there was probably some truth in what Hassan said, but it didn't alter his mood. "It still smells of trouble and I don't like it. The Allies are not fools—they'll know they're on to something. The officer you cut, you said his name was Weaver?"

Hassan put a hand to his jaw. "An American. And next time I see him, I kill him."

"There'll be no next time, not if you've any ruddy sense. Keep well away from this Weaver and his like, or you're likely to lose more than a couple of teeth. What did you do with the motorcycle?"

"I left it at the villa."

"You'll need somewhere safe to kip down. Not the villa—I don't want to risk you being seen there." Deacon thought for a moment. "The hotel in Ezbekiya, the Imperial, seems the best bet. You should be out of harm's way there. I'll call you when I need you."

"What for?"

"There's a reply due from Berlin tonight. And after the package we sent them, I've a feeling they might be up to something." Deacon opened a desk drawer and tossed a handful of notes across. "Here, make sure you can't be recognised again. Shave off that beard, get a haircut, and buy yourself a suit. And be careful from now on, understand? Stay in the hotel until I call you. Just because you think you're bloody invincible doesn't mean you have to put us both in danger."

Hassan took the money sullenly and left without replying. Deacon crossed to the mirror near the porthole window and sighed in despair. The Arab had worked for the Germans in Tripoli until nine months ago, when Berlin suggested he might find a use for him. With Rommel close to taking Alexandria, Deacon had had a frantic amount of work on his hands, and there was no question he had needed help. Hassan certainly had his uses, but he was far too cocky in his opinion, and the last thing he needed at a time like this was arrogance and carelessness, or they'd both wind up hanging from the end of a rope.

Deacon glanced at himself in the mirror, shaking his head at his reflection before he went to get dressed. "The crap you have to put up with, Harvey. It'll be the ruddy death of you."

Harvey Deacon had been born Harvald Frederick Mandle in December 1894, in Hamburg. His father, Klaus, had emigrated to the Transvaal with his only son, hoping to start a new life in South Africa after his wife had died in the devastating flu epidemic that had raged through Germany the previous year.

But an uneasy truce had long existed between the British and the Boer settlers of Dutch and German stock, and no one was really surprised when the South African war started in earnest in 1899. When the Boer forces were almost decimated by the British infantry at Bloemfontein a year later, they began a bitter guerrilla war, mounting commando raids to harry British bases, a campaign that brought swift and brutal retaliation. Settler families were rounded up, their farms and property burned, and their livestock confiscated. Klaus Mandle and his six-year-old son were sent to a camp where thousands of Boer families had been imprisoned, in what became the first of the concentration camps.

Conditions there were wretched, disease and malnutrition rampant—more to do with bad administration and lack of proper hygiene than any deliberate British ill-intent—but over twenty thousand men, women and children perished as a result. When his father contracted TB and died eight months later, young Harvald Mandle stopped eating his meagre rations and withdrew into himself, until finally the camp doctor intervened and found a childless middle-aged British couple willing to adopt the orphan.

Frank Deacon and his wife had emigrated from Birmingham to Johannesburg, where he managed a clothing factory. Delighted though they were with the opportunity to provide a decent home for the boy, the arrangement soon turned out to be a disaster. Their new son was moody and rebellious in the extreme, prone to aggressive behaviour, and unable to form any real bond with the couple.

That same year Frank Deacon accepted a posting to Cairo to manage one of the company's cotton factories, with a generous salary and an option to purchase a handsome Nile villa for a nominal sum after his first year of contract.

"It'll be good for the lad, Vera," Deacon told his wife, still feeling pity for the boy. "It'll change him, help him get over his trauma."

Within five years he had made a great success of the Cairo factory. He was given a directorship, making him a reasonably wealthy man, but the change of scenery did nothing to alter their adopted son's behaviour. All Harvey Deacon saw in Egypt was the same colonial arrogance he had witnessed in South Africa, and he showed nothing but contempt for his parents' new-found acquaintances and friends, most of whom were British upper-middle-class expatriates, until little by little the Deacons realised that their son had a loathing of everything British which was irreparable, almost beyond reason in its intensity.

When they died tragically in an automobile accident while returning from a New Year's ball at the Mena hotel, Harvey Deacon was twenty-six and didn't shed a tear. Left two thousand pounds in their will, and their Nile villa, the first thing he decided to do with his windfall was to go into business.

The Sultan Club was a shabby Cairo nightspot owned by the son of a wealthy Italian wine importer from Alexandria, who had only invested in the nightclub business as an easy way to meet girls. It was going downhill fast when Deacon bought himself in as an equal partner, but things began to thrive when he hired a dozen French and Italian hostesses and an American jazz band, and soon it had a reputation as one of the liveliest places in town.

Commerce had seemed to come easy to him, and he enjoyed the role of playboy he began to cultivate, indulging himself with a wide variety of women. Any connection to the country of his birth was by now non-existent, but by 1936 the Nazis were in power, and no one was more surprised than Deacon when he got a phone call one afternoon from a woman who called herself Christina Eckart. She claimed to be his cousin, in Egypt with a German trade delegation, and working as a deputy minister's secretary. Could she invite him to dinner?

The last Deacon remembered of Christina Eckart was the image of an unattractive, plump little girl of four, standing on the Hamburg docks with a clutch of relatives, bored while she waved him and his father off as they departed for Cape Town. He decided to meet her out of curiosity.

This time, when he saw Christina Eckart, he was stunned. The years had turned her into a desirable, ravishing woman. Slim and pretty, with bobbed blond hair and long legs, she also turned out to be quick-witted and excellent company. She was also surprisingly unmarried, and after they had chatted and drunk champagne all evening, she suggested they might take a walk in private to get some air.

"So, your Nazi employers seem to be doing something right," Deacon remarked as they strolled along the Nile promenade. "From what I hear things are booming in Germany."

It was merely something to say, for the truth was Christina Eckart was driving him crazy with distraction, and he knew he had fallen in love with her. All night he had sensed a strong sexual chemistry between them, and had she not been his cousin, he would definitely have taken it further.

"And it's only going to get better," Christina said with a smile. "The Führer has tremendous plans."

"Something surprises me. You're an intelligent, seductive woman, but you're not married. Why?"

Christina laughed. "I think I'm what you might call a committed mistress."

"To whom?"

"The Nazi Party."

"That surprises me too. Why would a deputy minister take his female secretary on a trip like this? Unless he's sleeping with her?"

She laughed again. "Hardly. My boss's tendencies lean the other way. But let's just say I'm something more than a secretary."

There was mystery in her reply, and before Deacon could enquire further, Christina looked towards the Kasr-el-Nil army barracks as a squad of grenadiers went marching smartly through the gates. "Look at that, not a step out of line. They're damned good soldiers, the British, I'll give them that."

Deacon shivered, bile in his reply. "They act like they're fucking God's gift to the world."

"You still hate them for what they did to your father?"

"They're arrogant bastards. Always have been, always will be."

Christina stopped walking, put a hand on his arm and said casually, "How would you like to work for your Fatherland, Harvey? There's going to be a war, and this time Germany can't make the mistake of losing. We need to plant the seeds of success, have people in place for when the time comes. Sympathisers in every part of the globe who can help our cause." She looked directly at him. "Britain's going to be our enemy again, and Egypt's her colony, so she's not going to be left out of the conflict."

Deacon felt the touch on his arm, suddenly aware of an intense, pleasant sensation in his groin, and wished the hell they hadn't been related. He laughed back. "So that's it? Berlin wants to recruit me as a bloody spy. And who better to do it than someone I know. But why me, for God's sake? What could I do?"

"You fit the bill perfectly. A British citizen, with no apparent connections to the Fatherland, your past hidden behind the veil of adoption. An outwardly loyal citizen of the Crown. You're an ideal candidate. And I have a distinct feeling you could be very useful. Well, what do you say?"

Deacon looked back at Christina Eckart's face, drank in her womanly, handsome figure, knowing he would have done anything for her, then he shivered, remembering his father's last days alive in the camp, fevered and coughing up blood. "What would you have me do?"

There was mischief in her eyes. "First, I want you to fuck me. Then I want you to come to Berlin."

Three months later, Deacon arranged a ten-week touring holiday in Europe. He was met off the train at Zurich station, given a false passport, driven across the border into Germany, and taken on the overnight sleeper to Berlin.

At SD Ausland headquarters, the SS intelligence arm to which Christina belonged, he was subjected to a series of rigorous interviews over three days. He was recruited as an agent and immediately began an intensive training course that lasted two solid months. He learned how to operate a radio and communicate in code, how to read maps, avoid surveillance, and gather intelligence. Above all, he was trained to observe. Where were the enemy arsenals, tank and airfield facilities? Where were troops deployed? Artillery? What size, how much, where was it positioned? Railways? What lines were active, what was in the yards and sidings? It was hard work, but it proved an exhilarating experience, and back among his father's people Harvey

Deacon felt for the first time in his life that he truly belonged.

He also spent the weekends sleeping with Christina, indulging in a frenzied sexual ecstasy even more pleasurable than that he'd enjoyed in Cairo. It was the first and only time Harvey Deacon had ever felt what passed for passionate love in his life. On their last weekend, as he made love to her, she whispered softly in the darkness, "Do wonderful things for the Führer in Egypt, Harvey. And who knows, maybe some day we can be together?" Deacon went back to Zurich and spent ten days touring Europe to maintain his cover, then returned to Egypt.

On SD instructions, and with a draft sent through a Swiss bank, he purchased the Sultan Club outright, expanding the enterprise with a gaming licence. When the war finally came, his venture proved to be a hotbed of gossip and information, just as his masters predicted. Once British troops started to arrive in their thousands to fight Rommel, the bars, nightclubs and red-light districts were the places to which they headed for recreation. There was nothing like drink and women to impress a man into talking, and Deacon kept his ears and eyes open. Soon he had more intelligence material than he could handle, with contacts and unwitting informers in every stratum of society, from lowly army subalterns up to the royal palace itself. What he didn't transmit by radio, he passed on to a clerk at the Spanish embassy, who used the diplomatic bag to send it via Madrid to Berlin.

It was after eleven that evening when Deacon drove his black Packard towards Giza, but instead of taking the road west out to the pyramids, he turned south, out along the banks of the Nile, and ten minutes later he reached the villa.

Maison Fleuve was large and whitewashed, with shuttered windows, two floors with four bedrooms and a small, overgrown garden surrounded by creeper-clad walls. It stood alone, had its own private river mooring, and was originally built by one of Napoleon's campaign generals to entertain his mistresses. It had been rebuilt several times before it had belonged to Deacon's adoptive parents. He hardly ever used it now, preferring his quarters on the houseboat. Besides, most of the villas in the area were the secluded weekend retreats of the city's wealthy, vacant during the week, and the property hadn't even got a telephone.

He pulled in under the shadows of a cluster of banyan trees in the front garden and stepped out of the car. There was a full moon and he could just make out the dark outline of the great pyramid at Cheops ten miles away, flat fields of sugar cane in between, stretching towards the desert.

He unlocked the door and stepped into the darkened hallway. The villa had no electricity, but a couple of palm-oil lamps stood on the hall table, and he fumbled to light one with a match. He locked the front door behind him, and fitted a solid, heavy metal bar into a couple of slots either side, a precaution he'd installed for added security. No one was going to come through the front entrance easily.

He turned towards another door leading off from the hallway and unlocked it. A flight of stairs led down into darkness. At the bottom of the steps was what had originally been a wine cellar, the ancient racks covered in dust and cobwebs, dozens of wine bottles stored there. But the general had found another use for the *cave*: as a secret escape route. At the end of the cellar was a short tunnel, leading to a metal door, rusting on its hinges.

Deacon unbolted the door, opened it, and a breath of fresh air wafted in. Tall reeds lay beyond, a tiny stone jetty hidden among them, leading out to the river, where there was a small wooden rowing boat complete with an engine, covered with tarpaulin. He stepped back to the bottom of the stairs. There was a single chair and a cupboard. He unlocked the cupboard door and removed the radio transmitter hidden inside, ignoring the loaded Luger nine-millimetre pistol beside it, then ran out the wire to the aerial mounted on the tunnel's exterior wall, connected the battery, switched on, and sat in the chair. The small green light glowed on the console, but he still had another ten minutes to wait before the transmission began.

What had happened at Hassan's flat nagged at his mind. Killing Evir, the burglar, had been a messy business, but the man might have talked and that would have jeopardised everything. Even though he'd managed to survive four years of war without detection, Deacon knew the Allies were not fools. From this point on they'd be looking, and looking hard, reason enough for him to be extra careful.

Especially now that Berlin had its proof that Roosevelt and Churchill would be visiting Cairo. With the war going badly for Germany, he had a feeling the information would almost certainly elicit some sort of response—why else would Berlin have urgently wanted confirmation, unless Schellenberg intended to do something about it?

But from his report last night Berlin was also aware of the problem of the safe house being discovered, and he awaited their reply. When the radio had warmed up, he tuned in. A relay station in Rome passed on his messages to SD headquarters, and once he heard the call sign he readied his notepad. The signal was longer than usual this time, and it was over twenty minutes later when he heard the letters AR, meaning the message had finished, then came *"Good luck"* and *"Please acknowledge,"* and lastly K for over. He replied with a series of Rs, to indicate he had received the transmission, and then he decoded.

When he was done, he stared at the message. The enormity of it all was almost too much for him to take in. His mouth went dry. He felt his bowels turn to water and a cold sweat broke out on the back of his neck. He could hardly believe what he was reading, and he whistled aloud.

"Well, blow me," Deacon said, smiling excitedly to himself, "it looks like we're really in business."

At that same moment, Hassan was in the crowded back streets of Ezbekiya, a chaotic district full of lodging houses and greasy restaurants, teeming with Arabs and European refugees.

The Imperial Hotel looked dilapidated, set in the middle of a row of similar cheap hotels and decaying tenement buildings, with peeling shutters and cracked exterior walls. He had stayed here before, when he first returned to Cairo after crossing the Allied lines. This time, he had carefully waited in an alleyway across the street for almost the entire evening, to make sure the hotel wasn't being watched and it looked safe to enter, before he went up the steps into the threadbare lobby.

A stoutly built man, very overweight, who walked as if his feet were precious, waddled up to the counter, munching fresh dates. He wore a fez and a loose shabby suit flecked with cigarette ash, his legs under strain, his heavy cheeks puffing air. He barely glanced at his customer's face. "We're full."

"Cousin Tarik."

The man paled when he recognised Hassan, quickly gestured for him to join him in his private office. He looked aghast at the swollen face. "What happened to you?"

"The army is looking for me. I need somewhere safe to hide."

"What did you do?"

"I may have killed a British soldier."

Tarik smiled. "I have the room you used before. You'll be safe there."

"You have my gratitude, Tarik."

The man grunted, as if thanks were unnecessary. "We are of the same blood, with the same enemy."

The room was on the second floor, small and bare, with just a single bed, worn sheets, a cracked mirror hanging above a chipped washbasin and jug. It looked like a large, converted storage cupboard. Tarik was out of breath after the climb, and unlocked the door with a special key he kept in his pocket. He pointed to a small, round electric buzzer above the door, barely noticeable because it had long ago been painted over with the same cream colour as the walls, stained yellow by years of tobacco smoke. "You remember the warning signal?"

Hassan nodded. Tarik had told him about the alarm button under his office desk. *Once for caution. Twice to get out*.

"Anything you need, tell me," Tarik wheezed.

"Tomorrow, I will need you to shave me, and cut my hair. I will give you money to buy me a suit of second-hand clothes."

"It is wise to disguise yourself," Tarik answered simply. "Remember, the room is very private. It isn't listed on the register, and the staff have no key. To come and go discreetly, use the fire escape at the end of the hall. No one should see you if you're careful. I bid you goodnight, cousin."

They kissed, Tarik gently grazing the injured jaw, and then Hassan was alone. He undressed, lay in the darkness, cradling his throbbing cheek in his hand, his tongue licking at the two tender hollows in his gums where his teeth had been, his mind boiling with thoughts of revenge.

Of one thing he was certain. No matter what Deacon said, the American intelligence officer would pay dearly.

FOURTEEN

CAIRO

Weaver dropped a thick batch of files on his desk with a solid thump, took off his jacket, rolled up his sleeves, and went to work.

The files dealt with Axis sympathisers, at least the ones GHQ knew about. With the Africa Corps' defeat, all the known German agents in Egypt had been apprehended, but the very fact that any V-men—*Vertrauensmanner*, the German term for agents—had operated in the country was hardly surprising. Egyptians had long been pro-German, and scores of Nazi agents had been in place for as long as five years before the war, furnishing their masters with a steady flow of information, much of it of importance.

Weaver had read the file on the most notorious. In 1942, the Abwehr put a spy ashore from a U-boat off the coast of Libya. His name was John Eppler, born in Alexandria of a German father and Egyptian mother, and with him he brought a radio and a suitcase full of expertly forged sterling five- and one-pound notes. He was guided across the desert, a journey of over 1,700 miles, by a Hungarian-born explorer named Count Almaszy, and eventually made his way to Cairo. In the guise of a wealthy young Arab, Eppler rented a luxurious Nile houseboat, lived a champagne life-style, and used a number of alluring women to try to wheedle top-secret information from unsuspecting Allied officers. With a codebook based on Daphne du Maurier's *Rebecca*, he sent his intelligence messages to one of Rommel's listening posts, until GHQ eventually caught up, after tracing the forged banknotes back to him.

Sympathisers were more common than actual agents. These were people whose pro-German support was strongly suspected. They ranged from waiters, bargirls and hotel doormen, belly dancers and taxi drivers, to minor diplomats, neutral businessmen, Egyptian army officers with pro-fascist leanings, and even senior members of the Egyptian government. Some were nationalists—Moslem Brotherhood extremists or patriots, prepared to help any enemy rid their country of the British—while others simply did it for the excitement or the money. Many more sympathisers were known to exist among the 100,000-strong foreign community residing in Cairo, some of whom were war refugees or displaced persons, either planted by the Nazis or willingly pro-German.

During the "flap" of spring and summer 1942, when the British feared defeat, they had rounded up and interned anyone suspected of working for the Axis. But scores of suspects had escaped the net because of lack of any reasonable evidence, or had simply disappeared before they could be arrested, and it was these files that Weaver went through one by one. It was all very well for General Clayton to tell him he had to track down the Arab spy. But what kind of person was he, how was he masquerading, and what was his *modus operandi*? Still, he was determined to find the man who had tried to kill him. Four hours later he hadn't got through all the files but had picked out a half-dozen suspected Nazi sympathisers—five Egyptians and a Turkish businessman—whose descriptions vaguely resembled the Arab.

There was a knock on the door and Helen Kane came in, carrying an enamel mug of coffee. "I thought you could do with this."

"Thanks. Haven't you finished your duty yet?"

"I was just about to leave. Feeling any better?"

Weaver had ignored the doctor's advice to rest up, and was paying the price; his neck felt as if it were on fire. "Not much."

She hesitated, said tentatively, "If it's any consolation I could cook you dinner tonight after you finish up here."

She smiled. "I forgot, you have to stick to liquids. Still, I'm sure I could rustle up something. Even a drink, if that's allowed?"

"That's very kind of you, Helen. You're sure it's not any trouble?"

"If it was, I wouldn't have asked. I'll give you the address of my flat."

As she finished writing the address and handed it to him, the door opened again and Sanson came in, a folder under his arm. He noticed her hand the slip of paper to Weaver, and reddened slightly. "Not gone yet, Helen?"

"I was just leaving."

When Helen Kane had gone, Sanson said sharply, "Well, have you had any luck, Weaver?"

"Have a look at these."

Sanson took the folder from under his arm, sat in one of the chairs and studied the files Weaver handed him. "At a guess, they're probably harmless enough. Most Arab sympathisers are bloody useless to Berlin at the best of times. All talk and no action. Still, we'd better pull them in and have a look at their faces."

Weaver had already questioned the guards on duty at the residency. Nothing unusual had been logged in the shift reports, but the duty officer admitted that on Wednesday evening, about nine, he thought he had heard a noise like a door banging in one of the ground-floor rooms. He had personally searched the entire building but found nothing amiss. It was something but nothing, Weaver reflected. "What about the hotels and lodging houses?"

"We're still checking, but it's going to take at least another day or two before we get through them all. So far, we've drawn a blank. As for the tenement landlord, according to his wife he's in Alex on business. He's not due back for a couple of days, but we'll try and locate him in the meantime." Sanson picked up the folder he'd brought, and Weaver noticed that the cover was marked in red lettering: *Top Secret*. "However, I'd like you to take a look at something."

"What is it?"

"A record of decrypted and untraced transmissions that Signals have picked up over the last year."

Weaver knew that the British "Y" section at GHQ and the US Army Signal Corps unit based in the former Italian colony of Eritrea scanned the airwaves nightly, when most agent transmissions were made. They recorded everything on punched tape, and signals originating in North Africa that could not be accounted for by any of the military services were assumed to be messages from spies, which were then sent to London and Washington for the boffins to work on.

Sanson opened the folder and showed Weaver a radio intercept about troop reinforcements in Cairo. "It was made about a year ago, from an agent code-named Besheeba our monitoring boys stumbled upon."

"What's so interesting about it?"

"Apart from the fact we haven't caught him yet, you'll see a rather remarkable coincidence in one of the signals. But have a look at these others first." He showed Weaver two other radio messages recorded six months earlier. This time, they gave details of the morale of British and American troops stationed in the city, and the arrival of New Zealand replacements in Maadi, a Cairo suburb.

"Is any of this stuff true?"

"The information's faultless. He's not a low-grade collector of rumour and gossip—he's definitely a highly trained pro. Look at his messages. Terse but detailed. Signals have picked him up a couple of dozen times in the last eighteen months, but he usually keeps it short, which makes it difficult for us to get a fix on his transmitter."

"Do we know anything about him?"

"He provides excellent information, probably lives in Cairo and comes into contact with military personnel, and signs himself Besheeba. But apart from all that, sweet damn all."

"What about this coincidence you mentioned?"

Sanson rubbed his scarred jaw. "Now that's where it definitely becomes interesting." He handed Weaver one more intercept. "It was picked up last Thursday morning, just after midnight."

This time the message was long, and just a series of

unintelligible letters and numbers. Weaver looked at Sanson. "I don't get it. It's still in code."

"Shortly after Eppler was caught, the Germans tightened up their operation and Besheeba's code changed. It seems he probably switched to one-time pads which are impossible to decode. Still, that's not the point. Besheeba doesn't transmit that often, and when he does, the information is usually reasonably important. We reckon Evir was murdered some time last Wednesday evening. Not long after, Y Section picked up this transmission. I'm not for a moment saying we've linked the two events, though it's an interesting coincidence, wouldn't you say?"

"But you think Besheeba transmitted the signal?"

"I'd bet my balls on it."

"Why?"

"Not only did he use one of the same frequencies, but every Morse key operator has what the signals boys call a signature. It's a kind of individual style, if you like—a distinct way in which the Morse key is handled. Heavy or light, fast or slow, there's always a certain tempo and emphasis unique to the person working the key, so much so that trained signals personnel listening in can usually differentiate one sender from another, no problem. And the chap who picked up the signal last Thursday morning is an experienced fellow who had heard Besheeba transmit on many occasions before. He knows his signature style, and swears it was him."

"Do you reckon Besheeba might be our Arab friend?"

"God knows, but I suppose it's a possibility. Like I said, he's a pro, and by my estimation there can't be that many thoroughbred Nazi spies left in Cairo." Sanson looked up. It was past nine o'clock and dark outside. He put the intercepts back in the folder and stood. "OK, we'd better call it a day. Let's meet back here at six a.m. You can carry on with the files."

"What about you?"

"There's a pile of intelligence reports we captured when Jerry evacuated Tunis. They're stored in one of our depositories over in the Ezbekiya district. We haven't sorted through them all yet, mainly because there hasn't been much of an urgent need since Rommel got his comeuppance. My German's reasonable enough, but I've arranged for a couple of translators to help me have a look through them, first thing tomorrow."

"Why?"

"To see if there's any reference to Besheeba."

"You think that's likely?"

Sanson shrugged. "Right now it's all I can think of. It's always possible that Rommel's people knew about him, and were picking up his signals direct. It makes some kind of sense. At that time, the Germans were on a roll, and they needed their intelligence information fast—routing it through Berlin could have cost them valuable time."

"When I get done here tomorrow, and if you don't mind company, I'd like to come along."

Sanson raised his good eye. "Are you looking for a medal, Weaver?"

Weaver reached for his coat. "No, just a dangerous German spy."

Helen Kane's flat was on Ibrahim Pasha Street. Weaver showered and changed back at his villa, his neck still throbbing, but he was trying to avoid taking the morphine pills until the pain became unbearable. He hailed a cab in the street outside and took it as far as the Ezbekiya Gardens, where he decided he needed air and some exercise and would walk the rest of the way.

Taking his time, he strolled past the Birka, the notorious red-light district. It was a busy place, riotous with noise and sound, and patrolled by the military police. The area was bounded by white signs with a black "X," denoting that it was out of bounds to all ranks, but that didn't deter the soldiers. Young girls and middle-aged women leaned over little balconies, cooling themselves with paper fans. Most were Egyptian, some were dark-skinned Nubian and Sudanese, and they smiled and waved as they offered their bodies to the men passing below, while their Arab pimps solicited for business. "Hello, my friend, you like that girl? Very nice, very clean. Special price."

Weaver waved them away. On occasion, he'd come to the Birka for comfort, as did most of the officers and men, single or married, but the experience always left him feeling empty afterwards. The truth was, if he cared to admit it to himself, in over four years he'd never got over Rachel Stern. It had seemed the one moment in his life when he had truly wanted someone, felt deeply in love, and everything afterwards was something infinitely less than that. He put the thought from his mind as he walked, reminded himself he was looking forward to seeing Helen Kane.

As always in the streets, officers and enlisted men had an endless obstacle course to contend with. Apart from pimps, they were pestered by cripples, vendors and pitiful begging women with crying babies, their faces covered with dirt and flies. Urchin shoeshine boys ran alongside anyone who looked remotely foreign, pleading for business. A thought struck him: what chance did they have of finding an enemy agent in such a swarming, disordered city?

Five minutes later he reached Helen Kane's flat. It turned out to be a neat and tidy two-bedroom affair, with a tiny kitchen. There was a drinks trolley with a couple of bottles and some glasses. When she let him in, she was still in uniform.

"Jenny, my flatmate, has gone to Alexandria for a week." She explained that the girl she shared with was a typist at US military headquarters. "She met an RAF captain who swept her off her feet. Help yourself to a drink. I was just going to shower and change."

When she left the room, Weaver poured himself a Scotch. The fire in his neck had become irritating, and he swallowed two morphine pills, washed them down, and looked around the flat. There were lots of books on the shelves, mostly on Egypt, and some novels, and he noticed a photograph of an attractive man in naval uniform. The room was hot, and when Helen Kane came back she opened one of the windows. She wore a dark blue skirt and a white blouse and her hair was down around her shoulders. It was the first time Weaver had seen her out of uniform—even at the party in Shepheard's she had been in khaki—and the change was remarkable.

"What's wrong?" she asked.

"You look different, that's all."

"You mean I don't look like an intelligence officer any more?"

"I meant you look . . . very pretty."

She blushed. "Thank you." She poured herself a drink and came to sit beside him. "Do you think we'll find this Arab spy?"

"We've got to. There's no telling what he might be up to. He has a radio. With a radio he could be in contact with Berlin, or with a listening post that relays his messages."

Weaver put down his glass, looked at the photograph on the shelf, and before he had a chance to ask she said, "Peter was my boyfriend. He was on Crete when the Germans invaded, over two years ago. I've heard nothing about him since."

"I'm sorry."

"I've got over it, but it took me a long time."

"Tell me about yourself."

She half smiled and Weaver said, "What's so funny?"

"You, asking me a personal question like that. It's sort of hard to get used to with all the military formality of the office. But there isn't much to tell. My father worked in Cairo for a British legal firm, and met my mother. We lived here when I was a child and then moved to England."

"Where's your father now?"

"He died when I was twelve."

"And your mother?"

"She lives in Boston. She eventually married again, a nice American lawyer." She smiled faintly, then refilled his glass and handed it to him. "Now it's your turn. How did you end up being posted to Egypt?"

He found himself telling her about his time at Sakkara, about Rachel Stern and Jack Halder. There was also something Weaver couldn't ignore, a sexual chemistry he'd been aware of since the party at Shepheard's. He could see the firm outline of her breasts through the cotton blouse, and the way her bare, lightly tanned legs were crossed excited him. This was wartime, death a real possibility, and people took their comfort where they could, but he knew if he stayed longer he might make a fool of himself.

"What's wrong?" she asked.

"Not a thing," he lied. "I guess I'd better be going. Thanks for the drink." When he stood, he felt dizzy. The mixture of morphine and alcohol had proved a deadly combination and had gone straight to his head. He swayed unsteadily on his feet.

"What's the matter?"

"Just a little muzzy, that's all. I'll find a cab."

"Maybe you should rest a while. You lost a lot of blood. I wouldn't like to think of you collapsing in the back of some cab. Cairene taxi drivers aren't the most trustworthy." She hesitated. "There's always Jenny's bed if you'd like to stay."

He looked at her face. It blurred in front of him. "You're . . . you're sure?"

"Yes, I'm very sure."

She led him into a large bedroom with a narrow bed. The room smelled faintly of perfume and there was an unlit candle by the bedside. She lit it, then helped him take off his jacket. The alcohol and the pills were still having their effect. He leaned over and made to kiss her, was surprised when she opened her mouth eagerly. They kissed for a long time, and then she said, "How do you feel?"

"All of a sudden, a lot better."

She laughed, and something seemed to spark between them, her eyes smiling invitingly. Weaver put a hand to her cheek. "You know what they say about Egyptian women?"

"No. Tell me."

"They talk with their eyes. For centuries, it was the only way a veiled woman could communicate her feelings to a man, and the habit's deeply ingrained."

She smiled. "And what do my eyes say?"

"Lots of things." Weaver blushed. "Some of them unspeakable." He gently stroked her face with his fingertips. "Something else I noticed. At the party in Shepheard's, Sanson couldn't keep from looking at you. He and I haven't exactly hit it off, but I also get the feeling he thinks there's something going on between us. And he doesn't like it."

"And is there something between us?"

"I think that's up to you. Tell me about you and him."

"We had dinner a couple of times. He sent flowers, and seemed a little infatuated. He told me I reminded him of his wife. She died, you know. On one of those convoys taking officers' wives back to Britain during the flap, sunk by a U-boat. They hadn't been married long. I imagine that's why he hates the Germans so much. The devastation he suffered because of her death probably hardened him to lots of things, and maybe it's the reason he puts everything into his work. Sometimes it almost seems as if the war is personal, and he's trying to pay the Germans back for what they did." Her voice softened. "I think it took him a lot of effort to ask me out, and I truly liked him—"

"But?"

She put a finger to his lips. "Not as much as you."

Her eyes held his. He sat down on the bed. Slowly, she unbuttoned her blouse, revealing a pair of rounded, full breasts. She undid her skirt, which slid to the floor, and Weaver took in her pale brown skin, her smooth legs, the curve of her hips. He reached out for her, drew her down to lie beside him, and her arms went around his neck, her mouth fastening on his lips, as his hands moved over her breasts and down between her thighs.

As they lay there, she kissed his chest, sucked his nipples, made small flicking movements with her tongue which worked their way down his belly and between his legs, and then he was in her warm, silky mouth, and she was stroking him gently, his pain forgotten, a warm feeling of ecstasy spreading through his entire body.

She looked up, brushed a strand of her hair from her face. "Well? Do I drive you even a little crazy?"

"More than that."

Her eyes met his again. "Come into me, Harry."

For a moment he hesitated, then he moved on top, looked into her face as he lowered himself into her, and she moaned softly with pleasure.

FIFTEEN

BERLIN
16 NOVEMBER/7 A.M.

It was a frosty morning and still dark when the Mercedes staff car pulled up outside the commandant's office in Lichterfeld SS training barracks. As Halder climbed out, he saw

Schellenberg step out of the lighted doorway, his officer's leather coat draped over his shoulders, a briefcase under his arm.

"Well, you made it, Jack, I see. I hope you slept well?"

"Forget the small talk. I'm not in the mood."

"I take it you're still angry about not being allowed to see your boy?"

"What the hell do you think?"

"I'm sorry, but it can't be helped. Right, let's not waste any more time. I have a briefing room organised. Kleist and Doring are waiting. Colonel Skorzeny himself will be along later to meet you."

"Where's Rachel?"

"Asleep in one of the barrack huts. She's been given medication to help with some extra rest, to build up her stamina. You can see her this evening."

"You still haven't told me the other reason she's so important to the mission."

"You'll be told before the time comes for your departure. Follow me."

Schellenberg led the way to a barbed-wire compound, guarded by a dozen SS troops with machine-pistols and a couple of vicious-looking leashed Alsatian dogs. A sign outside said *Strictly Authorised Personnel*. Schellenberg showed his pass and they were allowed through. Across the compound yard was a long, single-storey redbrick building, a floodlight over the entrance. Two SS guards with Alsatians were posted outside, and the men snapped to attention as Schellenberg came forward to unlock the door.

"Security precautions," he remarked as he led Halder inside, then locked the door behind them. "The mission's completely top secret, so we can't be too careful. Anyone who tries to enter without my personal permission will be shot out of hand, if the dogs don't get them first. Those animals can kill a man in seconds."

The building was large and basic inside, and looked like a classroom, with a wooden desk facing three chairs, a blackboard, and a tiled wood stove in the middle. Two men stood beside it warming their hands, both wearing civilian clothes. One was in his late thirties, and very obviously a military man, broad and bullish, with a ravaged face and a flattened nose. He looked a study in brutality, his dark eyes hinting at a savage nature. The second man was in his middle twenties, coarse-looking, with a sharp face and a thin, cruel mouth.

"You already know Major Kleist. And this young man is SS Feldwebel Doring. Meet Major Halder."

Kleist was the first to thrust out his hand. "Well, Halder, we meet again. The last time was an anti-partisan operation near Sarajevo, as I recall?"

Halder ignored the offered hand. "I remember it very well. And I can't say it's a pleasure seeing you again. Not after witnessing how you dealt with prisoners."

Kleist flushed, offended, and his eyes narrowed dangerously. "Harsh methods are sometimes called for in war, Major. You ought to know that."

"I'm a soldier, not a butcher, Kleist. Or perhaps you can't understand the distinction? And I hardly call raping and torturing women an honourable way of conducting a war. Your behaviour disgraced the German uniform. If I had my way, I'd have had you shot."

Kleist raised his eyes and grinned maliciously. "Strange you should have that opinion, considering I ended up getting a commendation for the operation. But obviously the major doesn't have the stomach for such work."

Halder ignored the provocation. Doring, the Feldwebel, had a sly grin on his face, as if amused by the proceedings, and Halder took an instant dislike to the man.

"A pleasure to meet you, sir," Doring offered.

"Charmed, I'm sure."

Schellenberg sighed and placed his briefcase on the desk. "Right, now that it's quite obvious you'll all get on like a house on fire, take your seats, gentlemen, and we'll proceed."

Schellenberg opened his briefcase, took out a number of maps, and unfolded a detailed one of northern Egypt. "I'll give you the exact particulars in a moment, but simply and shortly put, the structure of your mission is this. You'll be flown to northern Egypt and be met by one of our local agents at a disused desert airfield who'll help you on your way to Cairo, under the guise of an archaeological group.

There, you'll meet with one of our Egyptian agents, who'll
accommodate you in a safe house. From then on, and
quickly, mind—we estimate within no more than three
days—you'll do your utmost to discover *exactly* where
Roosevelt and Churchill are located in the city. We suspect
it'll be the Mena House, but we'll come to that later. Once
you manage to confirm the location, you'll need to come
up with a plan that will help us breach the Allied leaders'
security and get close enough to kill them. That done—
assuming you've achieved all of your objectives—the rest
is straightforward. You'll radio Berlin and we'll send in
Colonel Skorzeny and his paratroops, to rendezvous with
you at a small airfield outside Cairo, which you'll need to
have secured before-hand. Once Skorzeny lands, you'll
brief him in detail and transport him and his men to the
location where you've determined Roosevelt and Churchill
will be, and help them get past their security. After that,
it'll all be up to Skorzeny to finish the thing, and you're
out of it.

"I hardly need to impress on you again the importance
of this mission to Germany's survival. It's absolutely vital
that it succeeds. No matter what obstacles you encounter,
your objectives will remain firm: to reach Cairo and carry
out your tasks. Under no circumstances will you abort, unless personally instructed by me to do so. Is that understood?"

"How will we keep in touch?" Halder asked.

"Besheeba, the agent you'll meet in Cairo, has a radio
transmitter. His signals are relayed to Berlin via a receiver
in Rome. Weather permitting, we can usually communicate
with each other within an hour, two at the most. There's
also an alternative listening post in Athens, in case of problems." Schellenberg jabbed at one of the maps. "So, to details. The Italians have surrendered, of course, but our
troops still occupy the northern half of Italy, Rome included, which is less than three hours' flying time to the
North African coast. In four days' time you'll be flown to
Rome to take up your stand-by position. Assuming we have
confirmation from Egypt that everything is prepared for
your arrival, our intention is to land you at a disused RAF
desert airfield, here, near a village called Abu Sammar,

thirty kilometres south-west of Alexandria, at approximately five hundred hours on the morning of the drop.

"The airfield's no more than a flat strip of sand, really, but ideal for our purposes. Deserted, apart from a couple of Bedouin families camped a few miles away, but they shouldn't give you any trouble. Our agent there has already been given instructions to meet you. He'll signal your aircraft from the ground and once you land he'll drive you to Alexandria. From there, you'll board the first train to Cairo which departs at seven a.m., arriving in Rameses station just over two hours later. If everything works to plan, you'll make contact with Besheeba and be taken to a safe house."

"How do we make contact?" Kleist asked.

"There's a popular café called the Pharaoh's Garden, directly across the street from the Rameses station. You'll proceed there as soon as you get off the train, take a table outside, and each order coffee. One of you will leave your ticket stubs in your hatband as a recognition signal. A man will engage you in conversation—he'll be wearing a Panama hat, have a copy of the *Egyptian Gazette* under his left arm, and a rose in his buttonhole." Schellenberg smiled. "An old routine, but then the old ones are always the best. He'll ask you the shortest way to the Egyptian Museum. You'll tell him you're going there and can show him the way. We'll go over the precise details of everything later, including the warning signals, in case you or your contact feel the meeting is in danger, and an alternative rendezvous is necessary. If for some reason you don't make the first train, your contact will return at the arrival time of each successive train due from Alexandria that day, until the first one the next morning. If you still haven't turned up by then, he'll have to assume the worst."

"And what if no one shows up at the airfield?" Halder asked.

"The man who'll meet you is a reliable fellow. He has my personal instruction to wait until your aircraft makes the rendezvous."

"You still haven't said what happens if he doesn't show up."

Schellenberg offered a thin smile. "Ever the cautious one, Jack. But to put your mind somewhat at rest, and in case of any extreme obstacles—which I don't anticipate—there'll be a motor boat waiting here"—he pointed to the map—"on the Nile delta, just outside the town of Rashid. The river's a straight run to Cairo, about six hours away. Again, details later."

Halder checked the map. "But Rashid's at least twenty miles from Alex."

"You're neglecting the point. If there are difficulties overland, and with desert all around, the river route offers the only likely alternative to get you to Cairo, and Rashid is one of the nearest points where you can access the Nile. Besheeba considers the route a safe bet, should you run into any problems. We've also arranged for him to supply any equipment necessary, from weapons to transport, and anything else you'll require." Schellenberg smiled. "I've already given him a shopping list of things you'll likely need. Three American army trucks, to ferry Skorzeny's men from the airfield outside Cairo. And a Jeep and military police uniforms for yourself, Kleist and Doring, along with any necessary transport papers required, which should help you move around the city with ease while you're setting everything up. I'll go over the list with you this afternoon. But there's another reason for the Jeep and uniforms, which I'll come to presently."

"Permission to speak, Herr General."

"Yes, Kleist."

"You're certain this Besheeba fellow can be trusted?"

"Completely—he's a man who's proved himself very useful, and one of our top agents. He'll have help, of course—an Arab, a former agent of Rommel's."

"I never trusted these Arabs," Kleist remarked sourly. "Shifty, the lot of them."

"He's a reliable fellow, Kleist. So treat him with respect when the time comes, despite the fact that he's a mentally inferior class by SS standards. That's an order. Understand?"

"Yes, Herr General."

"Any more questions? Yes, Doring?"

"What about our air transport, Herr General? We'll be taking a big risk flying over enemy territory in a Luftwaffe aircraft."

Schellenberg smiled broadly. "I shouldn't worry about that, it's all been taken care of. In fact, you have an interesting surprise in store for you when the time comes."

"And our papers?"

"Each of you will have an excellent set of forged documents—everything you'll possibly need will be sorted out before you depart. Jack, you'll be assuming an American identity, naturally. Kleist and Doring, you'll be South African nationals. Fraulein Stern will have papers in the name of a German Jewess. Unlike other Germans in Egypt, German Jews have not been interned—they're free to go where they please. Hopefully you shouldn't be bothered too much by the Egyptian authorities. I understand they're quite lax about such matters as checking papers. But to make sure you're all prepared, I've arranged for three of my best counter-intelligence officers to question each of you thoroughly about your cover stories, and the same with the girl."

Halder interrupted. "Back up a little. It's all very well our agent in Cairo procuring these three American army trucks for us to ferry Skorzeny's men from the airfield after they land and get them close to where Roosevelt and Churchill will be. But we're talking about a hundred German paratroops in battle uniform. If for any reason the trucks are stopped at a checkpoint, we'll be finished."

Schellenberg smiled. "We have a little trick up our sleeves that should resolve the particular problem you speak of, if it comes up. But all in good time, Jack. You'll get to know the full facts before you depart. But be aware that Skorzeny's part of the operation will be done at lightning speed, with no hanging about. After the paratroops land, and you consult with Skorzeny and furnish him with all the relevant details he'll need, you'll be transporting him and his men straight to where the targets are, with no unnecessary detours, I hope."

He put aside the map of Egypt, selected a detailed one of Cairo and its surroundings, and spread it out on the table. "And now to the tricky bit, the Mena House at Giza, where we assume the Allied leaders will be staying. All we know for certain is that the area around it has been heavily fortified and put under strict guard. We have some precise details of the hotel layout, from the usual tourist information published before the war, and we'll study that this afternoon. But I expect Besheeba to have more exact information when you rendezvous in Cairo. Estimated troop numbers, defence details of the compound, and so on. However, I repeat, the main point is, before our attack can commence you'll have to find a way of getting inside the compound grounds and confirming that Roosevelt and Churchill are being quartered there. And if so, where exactly. Getting in—and out again with the information you need—is the difficult job. But you've got to do it somehow, and without being detected."

Schellenberg pointed to the Cairo map. "Assuming you can achieve that, you'll need to secure and hold this airfield, here—about twenty minutes' drive from the hotel—so Skorzeny's men can land safely. We had considered parachuting them in, but it's too risky. Their parachutes could easily be spotted from the air and the alarm raised. The airstrip itself is ten kilometres south of Giza, near a town called Shabramant. It's a training field belonging to the Royal Egyptian Air Force, an insignificant organisation that's largely symbolic, and the airfield's only very occasionally used by the British and Americans. From Besheeba's past intelligence reports, it would seem it's poorly guarded, but considering Cairo's about to host a visit from Roosevelt and Churchill, that might not be the case. Again, a problem you'll have to solve once you get there."

"How in God's name are you going to get a couple of plane-loads of SS paratroops past Allied air defences?"

Schellenberg smiled at Halder. "There are always ways and means. And basically it's the exact same way we're going to get you in. It's rather ingenious, really. But as I said, you'll have to wait with bated breath for that particular surprise, and a few others into the bargain. As for getting you out afterwards, I'll give you precise details long before you depart, but at present the intention is you'll make your way back to Shabramant, where one of our aircraft will be waiting to fly you out. Along with Besheeba, I might add. He'll have outlived his usefulness in Egypt after this. If things go horribly wrong at Shabramant—which they won't—Besheeba will have already arranged an alternative escape route for you. He'll give you details when you arrive."

"Surely our departure by air is going to be risky? The Allies will probably have their air defences well up by then."

Patiently, Schellenberg said, "To cover that eventuality, I've arranged for a couple of air raids on Alexandria and Cairo from our bases in Rhodes and Crete as a diversion, just after Skorzeny's men land, so the Luftwaffe should keep things busy for several hours. Yes, Kleist?"

"When do we get to meet the girl?"

"The day after tomorrow, when we distribute your clothes and personal belongings. As I explained she's not going to know the true purpose of your mission, so none of you will discuss anything of relevance in her company. Be particularly careful about that." There was a knock on the door and Schellenberg said, "Enter."

A huge man strode into the room with an air of total self-confidence, as if he could walk through a brick wall unscathed. He towered well over six feet, with bullish shoulders and a hard face that looked as if it had been hewn from rock. He wore an SS colonel's uniform with paratroop flashes, the Knight's Cross displayed proudly at his throat. He gave the Nazi salute and clicked his heels.

"Herr General."

"Colonel Skorzeny." Schellenberg beamed. "What perfect timing. I was just finishing my preliminary briefing. This is Major Halder."

Skorzeny returned a salute and offered a massive hand, his grip like iron. "Major—a pleasure to meet you."

Halder shrugged. "From what I hear, the pleasure should be all mine. I believe the Reich's newspapers are calling you the most dangerous man in Europe. Rescuing Signore Mussolini was quite a feat."

"And one which I hope to repeat, with even deadlier effect. But you have an enviable record yourself, Halder. I must say, I'm impressed. I could do with an officer like you in one of my paratroop battalions."

"Sadly, Colonel, I prefer to keep my feet firmly on the ground. It's a lot safer."

"A pity." Skorzeny shrugged. "But who knows? After

this little adventure, you might change your mind." He turned to Schellenberg. "But my apologies, Herr General. I'm holding up your briefing."

"Not at all. I was almost finished for now." He turned to the others. "Except for the matter of the Jeep and military police uniforms, which I said I'd return to. As you can imagine, guard duties will have to change at the compound, reliefs will have to be made. Besheeba should have more exact details of the guard duty changes when you arrive, but it seems to me that this might present an opportunity to get into the compound."

"How?" Halder asked.

Schellenberg smiled. "An able fellow like you, and with your talents, I'm sure you'll come up with something, Jack. Have any of you more questions?"

The room fell silent. Schellenberg stood there, hands on his hips. "Good. For the next few days you're going to familiarise yourselves with your cover identities. You'll study the maps thoroughly, until you're acquainted with Alexandria and Cairo—we don't want anyone getting lost. We'll go over our plans and the layout of the Mena House with Colonel Skorzeny, and he'll be joining you at intervals over the coming days to check on your progress and make sure you're totally familiar with any details pertinent to his own drop. And just so you'll know, I'll be with you as far as Rome when the time comes, to send you on your way and wish you good luck."

He looked at Kleist and Doring. "As to any questions you might have about the rudiments of archaeology to enhance your cover stories, I've arranged for Major Halder and a couple of other experts to give you a crash course. In the meantime, get to work, gentlemen."

It was raining hard that evening, a real Berlin downpour hammering from the blackened sky. Halder opened the barrack hut door and stepped in, his hat and coat dripping wet. Rachel was there alone, sitting on a bunk. "Schellenberg told me I'd find you here."

"What do you want?"

He removed his hat, shook water from it, and smiled uncertainly. "Hardly the warm welcome I'd expect on a miserable evening like this. I thought we might have dinner together in my quarters."

"I'd prefer to be alone."

"Is there really any need for all this, Rachel?"

"All what?"

"The cold-shoulder treatment. Despite the unpleasantness of the situation, I thought we could still be friends."

She made to turn away, but Halder gently gripped her arm. "Do you really despise me that much?"

"Let go of my arm!"

He let go, and suddenly there was a tired, vulnerable look on his face. "No doubt you're thinking I've sold my soul to the Nazis. But you want the honest truth? A simple case of life not turning out the way you planned—you take the wrong road and before you know it you've gone too far to turn back." He hesitated. "I never told you this, but when you didn't write, I met and married someone else. She was a good woman, very much like you in many ways."

Rachel looked at him blankly.

"She died after giving birth to our son. And none of us has escaped this war unhurt, Rachel—we're all victims. Three months ago, there was an Allied air raid on Hamburg. The worst destruction in history. My father perished, my son survived. If you call being a cripple and scarred for life survival."

Her face darkened. "I—I'm sorry to hear that. Truly sorry."

"Water under the bridge."

She started to say something, but seemed to change her mind. Halder turned to go. "Schellenberg will be along tomorrow to go over your cover story. In a few days, you'll meet the others."

"Who are they?"

"No doubt he'll tell you about them. All you need to know for now is that they're both SS. I'm sure they're hardly your idea of perfect travelling companions after four years in a camp. Nor mine either. But nothing can be done about that. In the meantime, try and get as much rest as you can. You're going to need it."

There was a silence between them. Halder tugged on his

wet hat, turned up the collar of his coat, crossed to the door and went out. Rachel moved to the window, tears in her eyes as she watched him cross the barrack courtyard, his head down against the sheeting rain, and then he was gone.

SIXTEEN

CAIRO
17 NOVEMBER

It was Sanson who found the memo, just as they were about to give up.

They had searched until after midnight and by then they were exhausted. They were in the depository building in Ezbekiya, near the Opera House. A large room on the second floor, with shuttered windows, a wooden table and some chairs. The documents and files were stacked in thick piles on the table and floor. Many of them had been scorched by fire and bore the marks of water damage, others were in a complete mess. German intelligence staff had been caught in the act of trying to burn their papers when the Allies had taken Tunis. Weaver had noticed heavy bloodstains on several. Someone had died trying to destroy these papers.

Sanson studied the memo, suddenly coming awake. "I think we've got something here."

He showed Weaver the page, typed in German and dated nine months earlier. It had been partly burned, but the contents were still readable. The name Besheeba leaped out at him and Weaver looked up eagerly. "What does it say?"

"It appears to be an internal memo from an army intelligence officer, Hauptmann Berger, to his commanding officer in Tunis." Sanson handed it to one of the NCO translators, a young sergeant with black-framed glasses. "Give us an accurate translation, sergeant."

"Yes, sir. *'Rommel urgently pressing for more details: troop numbers, armour and artillery movements. Berlin instructs Phoenix to proceed Cairo at once. Besheeba will rendezvous. Hopes combined efforts will produce more re-*

sults.' " The sergeant looked up. "That's about the gist of it, sir."

Sanson said to Weaver, "It seems our friend Besheeba got himself some help."

"Why was that?"

"Easy enough to understand. Nine months ago, Jerry was having a bad time of it from Monty, and needed all the intelligence he could get. Pretty much everything passed through here—signals, reinforcements, equipment." Sanson shrugged. "Not that it matters much at this stage, except that if they're still working together, we could have a double act on our hands." He yawned, rolled down his sleeves, pulled on his jacket, and dismissed the two NCOs.

"What next?" Weaver asked tiredly. He needed to sleep, had stayed up half the previous night making love to Helen Kane, and his body was full of pleasant aches and pains. In the office that day, it had been difficult to keep their relationship strictly formal. Whenever she came near him, she would give him a knowing smile, and he couldn't ignore the heightened sexual electricity between them. If it weren't for the problem of having to find the Arab, he would have liked to have seen her that night. He looked back as Sanson replied, felt sympathy for him now that he knew his personal tragedy.

"We'll carry on searching here after we get some sleep, in case anything else turns up. And I'll check with the prison camps and see if we captured Hauptmann Berger, or his CO, when we took Tunis."

Despite their discovery, Weaver felt oddly deflated. He knew they were still no closer to finding Besheeba. If Signals couldn't locate him, their chances were even slimmer.

"That sounds like a long shot I wouldn't bet on. We still haven't got much hope of catching him, have we?"

Sanson rubbed his good eye. It stared back at Weaver. "In a city of two million? Not much. But we've got to, Weaver. We've got to."

The Sultan Club was packed that Tuesday evening. There was a band playing on the stage, a group of displaced Frenchmen wearing ridiculous fezzes. Harvey Deacon went down the steps just before ten and clicked his fingers at the head waiter. "Find me a table near the back, Sammy. Number seven would be perfect."

"Of course, sir." The waiter scurried off, anxious to please his employer. Deacon watched as he went over to a group of American soldiers sitting in the back shadows. An argument developed as the waiter tried to convince them the table was reserved. The men grumbled, but eventually agreed to move with the promise of a complimentary beer. When the waiter came back, he led Deacon over to the table.

"I'll have a glass of champagne." Deacon looked at his watch moodily. "What the bloody hell's keeping the performance?"

"It begins any moment now, sir."

When the waiter had poured his champagne, Deacon lit a cigar. He was tense, and had hardly slept in the last twenty-four hours. There were dark circles under his eyes and he felt exhausted, but with it came a sense of elation. The signal from Berlin had been clear and the intention unambiguous. Four people arriving to set up the operation, and then the paratroops. It was certainly a daring plan; only time would tell if it was brilliant. One thing he was certain of. *If it worked, the war was as good as won.*

But just as important, he'd have revenge for what had happened to Christina.

He still felt a chill go through his blood when he thought of how she had died. During the first American daylight raid on Berlin six months ago, her apartment had been blown to pieces. They never found her body, and Deacon had been devastated when he heard the news, delivered via his Spanish courier. The thought of killing Roosevelt *and* Churchill sent a surge of vengeful adrenalin through his veins.

But things had to move fast, and Deacon didn't particularly like the sense of urgency. These were deep waters he was getting into, and he had to tread carefully. But there was no doubt the feeling it caused was electric.

As he sat there a spotlight suddenly went on and the red curtains parted. A half-dozen women paraded on to the stage, wearing tiny sequinned tops and harem pants, and accompanied by the sound of an Egyptian drumbeat. Tanya, the star of the show, was in the middle, and her charms were obvious: long dark hair and dark, almond-shaped eyes, complemented by a voluptuous body with splendid curves and incredible breasts. She was half Italian, half Arab—a potent combination.

The band struck up and the girls danced and peeled away their clothes. The musicians tried their best to keep the whole thing in tempo, but the girls were a pretty hopeless bunch of dancers. Not that the audience cared.

A man wove his way through the crowd, carrying a glass of champagne high above his head, his eyes glinting appreciatively as he watched the girls perform. He was tall and dashing, with a devil-may-care look about him, his manicured hands and expensive Western suit hinting at a privileged upbringing. A Royal Egyptian Air Force captain, Omar Rahman was the son of a senior government minister, and an ardent Nazi sympathiser. He couldn't keep his eyes off Tanya as she undressed. "My God, she's some woman. And those breasts could drive a man crazy with desire."

Deacon smiled indulgently. "Time for that later. You have the information I need?"

Omar deftly slipped an envelope from his pocket, handed it under the table. "It's all there, everything you asked for."

Unseen, Deacon tucked the envelope into his pocket. "Well, Omar, can you do it?"

The captain smiled. "You know me, I'm always willing to take a risk."

"But can it be done?"

"Stealing the aircraft isn't a big problem. Until a few months ago, the British controlled the Egyptian Air Force with a tight first—we couldn't take off or land without their permission, and our fuel was rationed. But since Rommel's gone, they've relaxed things a bit. And I'm certain the plan you suggest is workable. So long as you keep to your end of the bargain."

"You can be sure of that." Deacon beamed. "Good, that's settled, then." The girls' performance was coming to an end. A solitary drumbeat struck up. Tanya stepped forward, completely naked except for a couple of sequinned tassels on her breasts and a tiny pair of flimsy pants. She

proceeded to swing the tassels in circles, at the same time
sashaying her hips and giving a ridiculous rendition of "Let
Me Entertain You." Her erotic gyrations whipped the audience into a sexual frenzy, until the drumbeat climaxed
with a bang and she finished performing. There was a moment of silence, and then the men at the tables went wild,
getting to their feet, cheering and clapping. Tanya took a
bow, her lush breasts even more seductive. Deacon saw
Omar lick his lips.

"You'd like a couple of hours in her bed?"

Omar grinned. "My friend, that would be heaven on
earth."

Deacon laughed. "Come, I'll take you to her dressing
room."

Back in his office ten minutes later, Deacon had finished
reading the contents of the envelope when there was a
knock on the door. Hassan came in. Deacon barely recognised him. The beard was gone, and so was the djellaba, a
suit in its place. He looked like a changed man. The Arab
flopped into the chair beside him. The swelling had gone
down on his jaw and lower lip, the flesh dark and yellow
from healing.

"Well, did you see Salter?" Deacon asked.

"He's expecting us at the warehouse in half an hour."

"Excellent." Deacon relaxed a little. Berlin had been
specific about its needs, and he had a feeling Reggie Salter
could help him solve most of them.

"I don't trust Salter, or that conniving Greek partner of
his," Hassan said moodily.

"Short of stealing the vehicles and uniforms ourselves,
which would be impossible and highly dangerous, we
haven't much choice. He might be one of the biggest gang-
sters in Cairo but he can supply everything we need, and
with a guarantee he won't go to the police. Who can ask
for more than that?"

Hassan gingerly massaged his jaw. "But will he do as
you ask?"

Deacon finished his champagne, crushed out his cigar.
"Let's bloody well hope so, or we're finished before we
start."

MALTA

Twelve hundred miles away that same night, Prime Minister Winston Churchill had just finished a simple meal of boiled chicken and fresh vegetables in the small private dining room set aside for him on board the battle cruiser HMS *Renown*, anchored off Valetta, the Maltese capital, for a brief stopover *en route* to Egypt.

Having spent the earlier part of the evening at the governor's residence pinning North Africa ribbons on Generals Eisenhower and Alexander, he had returned to ship to attend to a hefty pile of urgent paperwork, before a late supper. He followed his meal, not with dessert, but with his customary indulgence, a cigar and a large brandy and soda, poured for him by one of the ship's officers.

"Not so much soda, young man. It bloody well kills the taste." Churchill's gaze swung from the officer to General Hastings "Pug" Ismay, his chief of staff, who had shared his table. "Well, Hastings, shall we stroll back to my cabin?"

"Of course, sir."

Churchill thanked the officer who handed him his brandy, and led the way out on deck, clutching his glass. It was a mild night, a gentle Mediterranean breeze blowing, the moonlit waters lapping against the hull. Churchill, out of respect for fire regulations on board, rightly desisted from lighting his cigar until they reached his cabin. It was quite small, spartan almost, just a bedside locker, a couple of chairs and a metal bunk, the simplicity not at all in keeping with the man's perceived larger-than-life personality, but then few among the public realised what a simple warrior their Prime Minister was, cigars and brandy apart.

"Take a seat, Hastings."

As Churchill slumped into a chair and touched a match to his cigar, Ismay saw that the Prime Minister looked pasty-faced and far from well; a severe throat infection and the effect of his typhoid and cholera inoculations for the trip had already kept him in bed for days. To make matters worse, a punishing three-week schedule of top-secret conferences lay ahead: five days in Cairo with Roosevelt to discuss Operation Overlord, the invasion of Europe, and with Chiang Kai-shek, the Chinese leader, to decide tactics in the Far East and Pacific, then on to Teheran with Roosevelt to confer with Stalin on Allied strategy, then back to Cairo again with Roosevelt to attempt to resolve the tactical considerations the conferences had raised. A critical point had now been reached in the war: with the invasion of Sicily and the Italian mainland, the tide was slowly turning in the Allies' favour. The judgments made in the coming weeks, Ismay knew with certainty, would clearly decide their success or failure.

"You're looking forward to the conference, Prime Minister?" Ismay said, pulling up the other chair.

"I'm growing tired of bloody conferences, Hastings, and weary of war. I wish to God this whole wretched business was over. Which is why we've got to tie it all up at Cairo. Every last thread. Our strategy from Europe and the Balkans, to Russia and the Far East. Then take the ball on the hop and run with it as fast as we bloody can." Churchill gave his chief of staff a steely look, which could have been frightening had it not been meant to convey his complete honesty. "If we don't, I fear we could find ourselves losing the entire war."

Ismay sat forward anxiously. "I know security is going to be extraordinarily tight for the conferences, sir, but have you read the recent intelligence reports from London? Apparently, the Germans have a whiff that there's something in the air. Their spies in Lisbon and Istanbul have been doing their utmost to get information about your movements, and those of President Roosevelt."

"So I read."

"Our intelligence chaps are even suggesting Berlin might be tempted to try something desperate, sooner rather than later, now that we're pushing Hitler hard."

"I read that, too. Kill us, you mean."

"It makes sense. The death of any one of you, Roosevelt, Stalin or yourself, would be a godsend for the Nazis— especially yourself or Roosevelt. It would throw everything in a muddle and likely as not put the brakes on the Allied offensive. Who knows which way the tide might turn if a catastrophe like that occurred?"

"Don't I know it." Churchill eased himself from his chair, crossed to the porthole, looked out, and spoke without turning back. "But personally I've never put much faith in the Nazis' ability to carry out an operation like that."

"But they got Mussolini out of Abruzzi. And very daring it was too. I wouldn't put anything past them, sir. They could as easily have assassinated Il Duce as rescued him. And this Skorzeny chap who led the SS paratroops, you have to admit his entire operation was first-class."

"True. Are you trying to frighten me, Hastings?"

"I doubt I could do that, sir. I'm simply pointing out the possibility of danger ahead, if these reports are to be believed. Perhaps it might be wise, if it's found necessary, to reschedule the conferences?"

"Impossible. It's taken too much hard work, planning and compromise to arrange them in the first place. And it's vital they take place at this juncture, with everything so critical. You know that better than anyone. Lives depend on it. The sooner we can win and finish this battle the better, lest there be more death and destruction."

"But if it's deemed necessary."

"Then it will ultimately be my decision." Churchill sipped his drink, continued to gaze out of the porthole. "But I'm sure I'm in much safer hands than Mussolini. And there's one thing Berlin hasn't figured on."

"And what's that, sir?"

"Rather than succumb at the hands of Hitler's assassins, I have every bloody intention of dying in my sleep, at a ripe old age and with my family around me. There's a lot to be said for it, Hastings."

Ismay couldn't help but smile cheekily. "No doubt with a cigar in your mouth and a brandy by your side?"

Churchill turned back, raised his glass. "That's it, exactly."

SEVENTEEN

CAIRO

The big old warehouse in the teeming market area of the Khanel-Khalili looked on the outside like any other in the bazaar, a shambling brick building with soot-blackened walls.

Inside, it was something else entirely.

A treasure-house of supplies that any merchant or NAAFI stores would have been proud of, packed from floor to ceiling with crates of assorted alcohol, medical supplies, boxes of shoes, bedcovers, tinned food and olive oil, reams of cloth, and just about anything that would fetch an inflated price on the black market.

Reggie Salter was sitting at a desk in the first-floor office, counting through several thick wads of dirty Egyptian banknotes, sweat on his face as there always was when he counted money. He was a small man in his early thirties, stockily built, and wearing a sweat-stained linen jacket, a Browning automatic tucked away neatly in a leather shoulder holster underneath. The heat and humidity were unbearable that evening, and every now and then he wiped his face with a handkerchief.

Across the room, a thin, barefoot Egyptian boy, no more than ten, sat on a couple of sacks of flour, turning a set of bicycle pedals as fast as he could with his hands, working a complex mechanical contraption of chains and pulleys that kept a couple of large wooden fan blades spinning in the ceiling overhead, although the air was too oppressive for it to make much difference.

"Can't you turn those bleeding things any faster?" Salter snapped. The child was lathered in sweat, but did his best to obey. There was a knock on the door and Salter scowled, but didn't bother to look up as he carried on counting the notes.

"I'm busy. What the fuck is it?"

The door opened and one of his bodyguards appeared. He looked thoroughly dangerous, well over six feet, broad and muscular, tiny scars crisscrossing his face like a spider's web.

"Baldy Reed is here to see you, Reggie. And Deacon's arrived. He's waiting downstairs."

Salter scooped the money into a drawer and locked it. "Keep Deacon waiting and send Baldy in first. Then find Costas down in the cellars and tell him I need his arse up here, pronto."

"Right you are, boss."

When the door closed, Salter crossed the room and

jerked a thumb at the boy. "Get out, kid. You're bloody useless."

The exhausted child lowered himself from the sacks, but when he didn't move fast enough, Salter lashed out and kicked his backside. "Are you bleeding deaf? I said out. Now!"

The boy scurried out through the door and a little later it opened again and a shifty-looking man in a British army sergeant's uniform appeared. Wally Reed was no more than twenty-five, boyishly thin-faced, but when he removed his forage cap there was barely a wisp of hair on his smooth young head. Salter came round from behind the desk, flashed a smile, all charm now, and shook his hand.

"Good to see you again, Baldy. And what do you have for me this time? Something interesting, I hope?"

"Two forty-gallon drums of petrol, a dozen bottles of the best claret, and four sides of beef."

"And who did you have to murder to get those?"

Reed laughed. "A man's got to live. Are you interested?"

"How much?"

"Forty quid."

"You're a bigger thief than I am. Thirty, and not a penny more." Salter grinned. "But just to show there's no hard feelings, I'll throw in a bottle of Scotch."

"Done. You want me to drop the stuff off at the usual place?"

"I'd appreciate it." Salter slapped a hand on the sergeant's shoulder and led him to the door. "And do it after midnight, as always. Good to do business with you again, Baldy."

The day Reggie Salter deserted from the Eighth Army, his life changed for the better. It had made him a wanted man, but also a wealthy one. When the North African campaign had begun in earnest, thousands of frightened young troops had fled from their units and hid low in the Nile delta and cities, anxious not to invite a German bullet between the eyes. In Salter's case, it wasn't fear that made him steal away from his foxhole in the middle of the night, but simple common sense.

As many as twenty thousand Allied deserters were in Egypt at the height of the war, not a fact the army liked to admit. The more hardened among them, numbering at least a hundred, had set up very lucrative rackets, using organised groups of renegades to rob civilian warehouses and military stores. Salter had become one of them, and probably the most successful, hardly surprising considering he'd already had a career in petty crime in London before being conscripted. Now he led a gang of twenty armed and dangerous deserters, English and American, aided by a handful of Arabs, operating one of the sharpest and most profitable black-market operations in Egypt.

The door opened as Salter sat perched on the edge of his desk, and a swarthy-looking man with a black moustache appeared. Costas Demiris was the son of a Greek merchant, and like Salter, his business partner, a deserter. His dark eyes were constantly on the move, missing nothing. "What's the problem, Reggie?"

Salter lit a cheroot from a pack on his desk. "Deacon's here."

Costas grinned. "So, your chickens have finally come home to roost. Are you going to pay him the two hundred quid you lost on his roulette table? It's been over a month now."

Salter meshed his fingers together and cracked his knuckles, a sudden vicious sneer on his face. "Like hell I am. Those wheels of his are as bent as a dog's hind leg. He fucks with me and I'll have his balls for bookends."

Costas's grin widened in anticipation of trouble, as the bodyguard opened the door and Harvey Deacon stepped in, followed by Hassan. Salter walked calmly across the room and stuck out his hand. "Good to see you again, Harvey. Drink? I've got a ten-year-old Scotch to die for."

Deacon shrugged. "Why not."

"Pour Harvey a drink, Costas."

The Greek took a bottle from one of the desk drawers, wiped a couple of tumblers with his shirt, filled them, and came over with the glasses. Salter clinked Deacon's tumbler. "Well, what can I do for you, Harvey, old son?" He nodded at Hassan. "Your boy here said it was urgent."

"I'm not his boy." Hassan glared back.

"I wasn't talking to you, sunshine. So why don't you shut the fuck up until spoken to?"

Salter skewered the Arab with a dangerous look, then turned back to Deacon. "So, what's the trouble, Harvey?"

"No trouble. Some business, if you're interested."

"I can always do with that. Well, I'm listening. What are you stuck for, a couple of cases of black-market Scotch?"

"Not this time." Deacon went to sit in one of the chairs. He ran a finger round inside the collar of his shirt—the heat in the warehouse office was stifling—then looked with wry amusement at the crates and sacks of black-market goods packed floor to ceiling. "You know, it never ceases to amaze me how you haven't been caught yet by military intelligence. You move about the city with impunity, and with a bounty on your head. You must have balls of brass, Reggie. Or a guardian angel looking over your shoulder."

Salter grinned and raised his glass. "My secret, old son, but the military has bigger fish to catch than Reggie Salter. Uncle Adolf, for instance."

In truth, Salter's warehouse was one of several he had around the city, almost every one of them a warren of tunnels below ground, with lookouts and runners posted up to three streets away, and he rarely slept in the same bed for more than one night. He also had a line of informers that stretched right to the top at the Provost Marshal's office, a costly service he willingly paid for, since it ensured that he managed to avoid capture and a certain firing squad after eighteen months on the run, despite a price on his head.

Deacon said quietly, "That gambling debt you owe me. How would you like to keep it, and make some extra money into the bargain?"

Salter glanced at Costas, and raised his eyes with a faint smile. "I'd like that very much, sweetheart. But what's the catch, as my old granddad used to say?"

"I need a Jeep. American Army type, with military police markings."

Salter was still smiling. "Is that all?"

"I haven't finished. I'll also want an American army captain's uniform, two MP uniforms, sidearms to go with them, along with a couple of M_3 machine guns. And three army trucks, American, in good mechanical condition. Plus all the right paperwork for the vehicles."

Salter looked amused, and laughed out loud. "What are you going to do, Harvey? Start another bleeding war?"

Deacon took a large envelope from his breast pocket and tossed it to Salter. "That's a thousand pounds on account. Sterling. Just so you'll know I'm not wasting your time."

The smile vanished from Salter's face and he nodded to Costas, who picked up the envelope and riffled through the contents. "It looks kosher, Reggie. A grand sterling, like he says."

Salter checked the money, then studied Deacon. "Who's the stuff for? Not yourself, surely? It's a bit late in the day to start playing soldiers."

"Some customers of mine." Deacon smiled. "Who wish to remain nameless."

Salter grinned back. "In for a dealer's fee, are you?"

"You might say that. The question is, can you supply the necessary?"

"You know me, I can provide anything your heart desires. But it'll cost."

"How much?"

Salter's grin widened. "A lot more than a grand. A Jeep, three trucks, uniforms and weapons? That's a lot of hardware. Let's say three thousand, sterling, the lot."

"A considerable amount of money."

"It's the best I can do." Salter shrugged. "My lads could get shot stealing that kind of gear. Widows-and-orphans fund to take care of, and all that. Take it or leave it."

"There's just one problem. I'll need to know you have the Jeep, uniforms and sidearms within forty-eight hours, by Friday night at the latest. The trucks I'll need a day later."

Salter whistled. "That's a rush job, Harvey, my mate."

"But can you do it?"

Salter shrugged, and finally smiled. "I don't see why not."

"I'll want you to garage them for me until I can pick them up."

Salter frowned. "For how long?"

"Probably no more than a day."

Salter nodded. "So long as you pay storage, not a problem. Say a hundred quid a day for the lot."

Deacon stood. "Agreed. We've got a deal." He stuck out his hand and Salter shook it.

"Don't you need to consult with your friends first, about the price?"

"No need. They trust my judgment."

"Fair enough. I'll want another five hundred when the Jeep, uniforms and weapons are ready for inspection, the rest when I have the trucks. You pay the storage when you take delivery. Where do you want to do that?"

"We can decide later."

"No sweat." Salter tucked the envelope of money into his pocket.

Deacon looked him in the face. "I'm depending on you, Reggie. Don't let me down."

Salter slapped him on the back and walked him to the door. "Don't you worry, I'll see to everything. Just make sure you bring the cash on Friday and everything will be hunky-dory, old son."

Reggie Salter splashed Scotch into his glass, then stood watching from the grimy warehouse window as Deacon and the Arab left the building and disappeared into the bazaar.

He rubbed his jaw. "I wonder what old Harvey's up to?"

Costas joined him. "You think he's telling us the truth?"

Salter sipped from his glass, shrugged, and wiped a film of greasy sweat from his brow. "Could be. But as far as I know, he's not the kind to get mixed up in naughty business. Sure, he'll come to us for a couple of crates of stolen booze when he runs short, but that's about his lot."

"MP uniforms, a Jeep, weapons, and three trucks. That's a lot of ordnance, Reggie."

"And three grand is a lot of shekels. There has to be a return for that kind of investment. A bloody big return. So I ask myself, what are these mates of his up to?"

"Any ideas?"

Salter put down his glass. "A payroll heist, stealing valuable artefacts, robbing King Farouk's jewels, who knows? Remember some cheeky sods did the naval paymaster's office in Port Said three months ago and walked away with a cool ten grand? Deserters, dressed in navy uniforms and driving stolen navy trucks, and good luck to them, I say. It smells to me like it could be something along those lines."

Costas frowned, rubbed his moustache. "I could never imagine Deacon getting involved in anything like that."

Salter looked round. "And that's the point. There's got to be much more to all this than meets the eye. Sure, someone could be using Deacon to do their shopping. Only they're not hardened criminals, or they'd deal direct with the likes of me. But whatever's going on it definitely must be something big, especially with all that hardware involved."

There was a sudden noticeable glint in Salter's eyes, and Costas looked at him with a lopsided grin. "I know that look on your face, Reggie. You're up to something."

Salter winked deviously, cracked his knuckles. "Not yet, old son. But I've got a funny feeling we could be on to something interesting here. And it might be worth a lot more than three grand."

EIGHTEEN

CAIRO
17 NOVEMBER/11:45 P.M.
Weaver studied the faces of the two Arab men standing in front of him. They had been picked up that evening by the Egyptian police and delivered to the Provost's office at the Kasr-el-Nil barracks. One of the men was clean-shaven, the other had a ragged beard, and they looked pathetic creatures as they stood there in handcuffs. Finally, Weaver turned to Sanson and shook his head.

"You're sure?"

"Positive."

Sanson nodded to the two sergeants waiting at the door. "Right, you can take them outside for now."

Weaver had known as soon as the suspects were led into the room that neither was the man who had stabbed him. Their faces bore no evidence of bruising, but even so he had carefully studied both men, especially the bearded one, to be absolutely certain. When the sergeants led the men out, Sanson sat down with a sigh, removed his cap, and opened the folder in his hand.

"As regards the other four suspects you picked from the lists of sympathisers, the police say one of them—the Turkish businessman—moved back to Istanbul almost a year ago, another's been serving a sentence in Luxor for theft, and a third had a watertight alibi."

"What kind of alibi?"

"He's dead and buried. Stabbed three months ago in a fight he picked with a British marine."

"What about the last one?"

Sanson referred to the folder before looking up. "Don't hold your breath. The police have been trying to arrest him for at least five months. He's a Moslem Brotherhood extremist, wanted for attempted murder and arson—he took a pot shot at a Guards officer and stabbed another, set fire to a couple of army trucks, and he's made himself scarce ever since. The police have his home under watch and the word's out that we want him, but the feeling is he's hiding out down south, in Assyut or Luxor. They could be wrong, of course, he could still be somewhere in the city."

"Is there a chance he might be our man?"

"Difficult to say. He's definitely a Nazi sympathiser, and he's fond of using a knife. But Cairo Special Branch are really a bit doubtful that he could be a German spy."

Weaver slumped into a chair. "So we're back at square one."

"It looks like it," Sanson said, dispirited, and slapped the file on the table.

Weaver was beginning to despair. Three days had passed without any leads turning up and he was exhausted, his neck still hurting like hell. He tried to ignore the pain, needing to keep his senses focused, but he knew they were fast running into a dead end.

The landlord had been interviewed and told them that the tenant who rented the flat had given his name as Farid Gabar, and had moved in almost nine months ago. He had always paid his rent on time, but the only information he had offered about himself was that he worked for a well-known cotton merchant in the Old Town, and came from

Luxor, but the landlord thought his accent sounded Cairene. When questioned, the merchant and his staff claimed they had never heard of Farid Gabar. A close watch was being kept on the premises just in case he made an appearance, every cotton merchant in the city was being visited by the police, and Gabar's details had been passed on to the authorities in Luxor, in the hope that something might turn up.

"Not that we should hold out much hope," Sanson had admitted. "The name's probably an alias and he's unlikely to have told the truth about coming from Luxor."

They had gone over each of the statements from Gabar's neighbours. The few who admitted they had even met him said he kept to himself, and had never spoken to them. None could recall the licence number of the motorcycle. Nothing else had turned up in the remainder of the captured German papers, but they had made one important connection. The Arab had moved into the flat six days after the date on the memo.

"We can't really assume we're dealing with the same man, this chap Phoenix, but it's a possibility," Sanson commented. "I've put in an urgent request to Y Section to see if they can get a proper fix if our friend transmits again. They're keeping a round-the-clock watch on the frequencies he used in the past."

There was a knock on the door and a lieutenant poked his head round and said to Sanson, "Phone call for you, sir."

Weaver walked over to the window after Sanson left, and stood there for several minutes, watching a platoon marching in through the barrack gates. There was a bustle of activity in the camp. The Kasr-el-Nil barracks and Camp Huckstep, the American base, were bristling with extra troops, drafted in to help with conference security. He knew the only hope they had now was if Besheeba transmitted again and they had enough time to locate the signal. But that depended on him staying on the air long enough, and to judge by his past performance this was unlikely.

He glanced at the wall clock. Midnight.

He rubbed his eyes. He had barely seen Helen in two days, apart from passing her briefly in the office. She had asked him back to her flat that night, and despite the exhaustion creeping in on him, and the pain still flooding his brain, he was looking forward to being with her again. He found the pill bottle, was about to pop one in his mouth when Sanson came back, looking pleased.

"Some good news for once. I think we've found our memo-writer. According to the POW detention lists, a Hauptmann Manfred Berger of German military intelligence was captured six months ago in Tunis."

"Where is he now?"

"At Bitter Lakes. I just telephoned—they've definitely got him, according to the camp commander."

Bitter Lakes was a two-hour drive south-east of Cairo, a collection of salt lakes near Suez that was a cauldron of heat and mosquitoes. Thousands of Axis nationals were interned there, Germans and Italians, along with prisoners of war.

Weaver snapped to full attention, his pain forgotten. "When can we talk to him?"

Sanson picked up his cap. "As soon as we can get there."

Baldy Reed was drunk. Not so drunk that he couldn't walk back to barracks from the brothel he'd just visited, but he didn't notice the olive-green staff car following him until it pulled into the kerb and a burly man in uniform hopped out. "Reggie wants a word."

Reed swallowed, moved into the back shadows of the car. Salter sat there in military disguise, a British major's uniform jacket draped over his shoulders. The car pulled out. "Baldy, old son. Sorry about the dramatics, but something urgent's come up and I need your help."

Reed wiped his sweating face. "For a bleeding minute there I thought I'd been nicked."

Salter laughed. "Not you, old son. You're too careful." He handed over a wad of notes. "That's five hundred on account. Another five hundred for when the job's done."

Reed frowned. "What job?"

When Salter told him what he needed, Reed paled, suddenly sober, and moved to hand back the money. "Jesus, Reggie. Military vehicles, weapons and uniforms? I'd be getting in the deep end on that kind of thing, honest—"

Salter turned on him. "You do as I tell you, mate. And I want the lot within forty-eight hours."

"Reggie, have a heart——"

The car halted, Salter shoved the money into Reed's tunic, patted him on the cheek, and showed him the door. "It's an important deal, old son. So just do as I ask. Otherwise those balls of yours are going to be dangling on the end of some Arab's worry beads."

NINETEEN

BERLIN

Schellenberg came into the barrack hut with Rachel just after seven that Wednesday morning. It was bitterly cold and dark outside; the tiled stove in the corner was going full blast, but it was still freezing in the room.

"Time to meet the last member of your team, gentlemen," he announced, rubbing his hands briskly. "Allow me to introduce Fraulein Stern. From now on you'll know her as Maria Tauber, an expert archaeologist and a displaced German Jew." He turned to her. "Major Halder you already know. But for the purpose of the mission he's Paul Mallory, an American professor of archaeology. The papers he'll carry are genuine, by the way. The real Mallory was captured by our troops in Sicily three months ago—a lecturer with the American University in Cairo, helping the US Army identify important Roman artefacts our troops liberated in North Africa." Schellenberg gestured to Kleist and Doring. "These are the other two gentlemen I told you about. You'll know them as Karl Uder and Peter Farnback, both South Africans."

Kleist inclined his head, clicked his heel, and grinned. "A pleasure, I'm sure, Fraulein."

Rachel pointedly ignored him, and said to Schellenberg, "If Major Halder is supposed to be an American, why isn't he in uniform?"

Schellenberg smiled charmingly. "A good point, and I'm glad to see you're entering into the spirit of things, but this has already been taken care of. A suitable medical condition was recorded in the professor's papers, which meant he was unfit for army service. Now, let's move things along."

There were several Gladstone bags on the table, and he handed one to each of them, then gave a set of identity papers to Rachel. "Your personal belongings, and your necessary documents. I advise you again to thoroughly familiarise yourself with the cover story you've been given. If you're stopped and questioned on Egyptian soil, the slightest slip could cost you your life, and those of the others. Now, everyone had better examine their belongings."

They opened their bags. Inside were clothes and personal items. Civilian desert kits with water canteens, safari suits and broad-rimmed khaki hats, along with more conventional casual attire. All of the clothing looking suitably well worn.

"I think you'll find the tailors have done an excellent job with the alterations. The clothing and personal items were all taken from Allied prisoners and refugees in North Africa, so they won't arouse suspicion if you're searched. Sufficient quantities of currency will be given to you before you depart."

Halder held up a carton of Lucky Strikes he had removed from his Gladstone bag. "It seems you've remembered everything. Thoughtful of you."

Schellenberg smiled. "The German variety would rather give you away—so you'd better get used to them. Egyptian brands are rather hard to come by in Berlin, as you can imagine. But these will do just as well." He helped himself to a pack of the American cigarettes, removed one and lit it, then put his hands on his hips, all business.

"Now, let's go over things one more time. Just the necessary, salient facts that the Fraulein here will need to be aware of. Then I'll leave you alone to go try on your outfits for size, familiarise yourselves with the maps and routes, and let you all get better acquainted."

Halder was studying a map of Cairo, Rachel by his side, when Kleist came up behind them and gestured at the map. "A long time since I've been in that stinking hell-hole of a city. Not that I ever wanted to see it again—it's a filthy mess."

"A pity you only saw it that way," Halder answered dryly. "You obviously missed out on over six thousand years of history. Perhaps you might have learned something from it."

"For what purpose? The real history's happening here, in the Fatherland." Kleist grinned. "The Egyptian women were all right, though, I'll give it that. Some of the best brothels I've had the pleasure to frequent were in Cairo and Alexandria. In my experience, the women you pay for are always the best."

"No doubt you're an expert in such affairs."

Kleist laughed. "I think you could say that." He glanced over at Rachel. "Schellenberg tells me you and the woman already know each other."

"What of it?"

This time Kleist looked blatantly at Rachel, taking in her body, and leered. "I'm looking forward to getting to know the Fraulein better. I'll even admit that for a Jew she looks tempting."

Halder rounded on him with a steely look. "Let's make one thing clear. You misbehave towards her in any way and I'll personally put a bullet in you, understand?"

"Is that a threat, Halder?"

"Think of it as a friendly warning. And I'd heed it if I were you." As Halder moved to lead Rachel away, Kleist suddenly grabbed him by the arm, pulled him round, leaned in close and stared him in the face. "Is that a fact, now?" The big SS man smirked, but his eyes were hard and dangerous. "Are you sure you can back it up?"

In an instant, Halder's knee jerked up, hitting Kleist in the groin. Kleist doubled over in agony, then Halder grabbed one of his arms, twisted it painfully hard, and pushed him against the wall.

"Let go, for Christ's sake! You're breaking my arm!"

"Next time, it'll be your head. We might share the same rank, Kleist, but just remember who's in charge of this part of the operation. So in future you'll accord me suitable respect as a fellow officer and address me as Major. Is that understood?"

Kleist was white-faced with pain. "Yes . . . Yes, Major. As you say, Major."

Halder let go and pushed him away. There was a frightening rage in Kleist's eyes, and Halder said quickly, "I really wouldn't pursue this any further. Not unless you want trouble. Another outburst like that and you'll have Schellenberg's wrath to deal with, as well as mine. Now get back to work."

Kleist bit back his anger, and went to join Doring.

Halder took Rachel's hand and led her to the door. As they walked across the compound, he said, "My apologies. The man's a bully, who doesn't know when to keep his mouth shut. I'll have a word with Schellenberg before the fool gets out of hand. In the meantime, try to be very careful when you're around him. He's a dangerous animal, likely to kill you if you cross him. If I had my way, he'd be thrown off the mission, but unfortunately I don't have any say in the matter."

"You don't have to stand up for me."

There was a hardness in her voice, and Halder stopped, gently took her arm, and turned her round to face him. "The camp's completely changed you, hasn't it?" He raised a hand to her face. "My poor Rachel."

She pulled away. "I told you before—don't touch me. And I don't need your protection. I can look after myself." And with that she turned abruptly and walked away.

Kleist stood at the barrack window, feeling sick as he massaged his groin. He watched Halder and the woman cross the compound. There was murder in his eyes, and at that moment his hatred was total and overwhelming, and went beyond all reasoning.

Doring came up to him, and they saw Rachel Stern walk away, leaving Halder alone, before he eventually moved off. "Cool bastard, isn't he? Still, the woman doesn't seem all that happy about what he did. I would have thought she'd be glad of someone playing the knight in shining armour."

Kleist spat on the floor. "Maybe she's got a lot more sense than you'd think. Halder's typical of all those rich fucking Prussian aristocrats. And arrogant with it."

"That's his background?"

"Wouldn't you know. The same toffee-nosed type who milked this country for fucking centuries, and kept the peasants under their heels. My old man worked his arse ragged for that lot all his life, and for what? A pittance and an early grave. If you ask me, the Führer should have done to them what he's done to the Jews. The likes of Halder make me fucking sick."

Doring grinned. "So that's it? I had the feeling it was something more personal. Still, he's able to look after himself, I'll give him that. That's the first time I've ever seen anyone bruise your balls and walk away alive."

Kleist turned on him. "Wipe that fucking smirk off your face, or I'll wipe it off for you."

Doring obeyed instantly. "Sorry, Herr Major."

"I don't know what you find so fucking funny. The Halders of this world like to think they're above you and me, but they've kept us down for too long. That type have a lesson to learn. I didn't join the SS to have some arrogant Prussian bastard of the same rank treat me like shit."

"Have you got revenge in mind, Major?"

"Don't worry, I'll think of something." A sinister grin spread over Kleist's face. "And you can mark my words, Halder will definitely get his when the time comes."

TWENTY

BITTER LAKES

The desert road was empty in the early hours, the air chilly, and they didn't pass a single vehicle. Weaver drifted in and out of sleep, napping in the passenger seat until just after four a.m., when Sanson turned off the main road and drove for two miles down a desolate track.

"Wake up. We're here."

Weaver rubbed his eyes and saw a signpost in English and Arabic. *"This area strictly off limits, except to author-ised military personnel."*

They were in a shallow valley, the first rays of dawn barely tinting the horizon, and the place had an eerie feel.

He could make out a vast collection of wooden and corrugated-iron huts, surrounded by barbed-wire runs, watchtowers jutting into the darkness.

They drove up to the camp's main entrance barrier and halted. Two armed guards from the sentry hut examined their papers before telephoning the duty officer and allowing them to drive through. They were met outside the main administration building by a tired-looking British major who escorted them into his office. "I believe you're here to interrogate Berger, sir?" he said to Sanson. "An odd hour for that sort of thing, if you don't mind me saying so."

"It's a security matter," Sanson offered simply. "We'd like to have a look at the prisoner's file."

The major didn't press his enquiry further. "As you wish." He left and came back minutes later with a manila folder and handed it over.

"Do you know Berger personally?" Weaver asked.

"I think you could say that, sir."

"What's he like?"

"A very decent sort of German. You might say a model prisoner." The major smiled. "And a highly intelligent chess-player into the bargain. He usually beats me hands down, every time." He shrugged, as if excusing his fraternisation with the enemy, and the fact that the British generally treated their Axis prisoners with decency, which usually amazed most Americans. "Not much else to do around these parts, I'm afraid. A man could shoot himself for the bloody boredom. I'll give you a few minutes to have a look at his file before we wake him, sir. You won't need an interpreter, by the way. Berger speaks excellent English."

The officer escorted them down the hall to a stark room with just a table and some chairs. After he left, Weaver and Sanson read Berger's details. Apart from the usual name, rank and serial number that he had been obliged to provide to his captors, various comments and notes had been added by his camp guardians; British officers and men with whom Berger had obviously become friendly and made casual, personal conversation. Aged twenty-five, and a career intelligence officer, he was married with an infant daughter and had a degree in mathematics from Dresden University.

After serving briefly in Russia, where he was badly wounded and had his left foot amputated, he had been posted to a desk job in North Africa eighteen months earlier.

Weaver said doubtfully, "Even if Berger admits to knowing about Besheeba and Phoenix, it's unlikely he'd be aware of their true identities, or anything about their backgrounds. A junior intelligence officer wouldn't be party to that kind of information, he'd simply be following orders."

"Probably not. But he's got to know more than we do."

A little later two guards led in the prisoner. Berger was tall and pale, boyish-looking, with a pleasant face, gentle mouth and restless, intelligent eyes. He limped noticeably, dragging one of his feet, an obvious false limb, and wore a ragged German uniform a size too large. His hair was tousled and he seemed confused and barely awake.

"Hauptmann Manfred Berger?"

The young German blinked. *"Ja."*

"I'm Lieutenant-Colonel Sanson, military intelligence. And this is Lieutenant-Colonel Weaver. You speak English, I believe?"

"Yes, fluently. May I ask what this is about?"

"Take a seat."

Berger rubbed his eyes and pulled up a chair facing them. Without preamble, Sanson showed him the memo. "Did you write this?"

Berger studied the flimsy, and a faint look of caution showed in his expression as he looked up. "I could have. As war goes, nine months ago is a lifetime."

"Did you write it?" Sanson repeated.

"I'm afraid I really don't recall."

"Your name's right here at the bottom. Hauptmann Manfred Berger."

Berger shrugged. "Yes, I see that. But in the course of my duty I put my name to many papers, and was obliged to help send many of our agents across your lines. I cannot be expected to remember every one."

"This agent in Cairo, code-named Besheeba, and the other one, Phoenix. What can you tell me about them?"

"I know nothing about either of these people."

"The memo suggests otherwise, Berger," Sanson pressed

him. "You obviously knew what you were writing about, so don't bloody lie to me."

The German blushed at the hint of a threat. He studied both his interrogators. "May I be permitted an observation?"

"You're permitted."

"For Germany, the war is over in North Africa. Whatever agents we had here are no longer of any importance." He raised his eyes, curious. "Yet two senior intelligence officers come here at four in the morning to interrogate me. May I ask why?"

Sanson ignored the question. "I'll ask you one more time—"

"And may I please remind you that under the terms of the Geneva Convention I am obliged only to give my name, rank and number. Nothing more. You are both soldiers, you know this."

Sanson slammed his fist on the table. "I don't give two fucks about the Geneva Convention, Berger. Answer the bloody question."

Berger looked mildly shaken by Sanson's hostility, but then he said quietly, "I'm sorry, I really cannot help you. You should know that minor intelligence officers such as myself are not usually privileged to know the true identities of field agents. That kind of information is confined to headquarters in Berlin."

"Usually, but not always, Berger. And there are always barrack-room rumours floating around concerning the agents who work for you. No matter how small or insignificant that information seems, it may help us. And I'm sure you knew *something* about the operation in Cairo. How did Phoenix get across our lines? Was he taken, or did he go alone? Where did he stay in Cairo when he arrived? How did he rendezvous with Besheeba? So give me answers."

Berger didn't reply, and Sanson promptly flicked open the German's folder. "You were arrested in Tunis wearing civilian clothes."

"I was trying to avoid capture, naturally—"

"A soldier disguising himself in civilian clothes on enemy territory—that suggests he's a spy. Spies are shot by firing squad, Berger. That's the law. Even according to the Geneva Convention."

The German paled. "Me, a spy? You're making a joke, of course?"

Sanson held Berger's stare and didn't flinch. "Am I? You're also an intelligence officer, double proof if it were needed."

"I'm not a spy," Berger answered nervously. "And even if I knew anything about this matter, which I don't, I couldn't help you." He looked at Sanson defiantly, a faint hint of pride in his voice. "I'm still an honourable German officer. I would never betray my country's trust in me to the enemy. *Never.*"

Sanson pushed back his chair with a clatter and stood. "I'll give you five minutes alone to review that trust, and your memory. After that, I want answers, not bullshit, or you'll suffer the consequences. And if I were you, I'd give some serious thought to a firing squad."

Sanson paced angrily up and down the hall.

"You think he knows more than he's telling us?"

"I'm bloody sure of it. He wrote the memo." Sanson stopped pacing. "We're not the Gestapo, but in a situation like this, you sometimes have to forget the rules."

"What do you mean?"

Sanson took a leather truncheon from his pocket. "This. And worse, if necessary."

Weaver saw the cold determination in the Englishman's face. "Beating a prisoner is considered torture. It's illegal, Sanson."

"I don't give a ruddy damn about legal niceties right now, Weaver. Or how nice a chap Berger is. This is war, not a bloody cricket match. Our backs are to the wall. If we had time, we could play the usual games and try to coax it out of him. But we haven't got that luxury."

"And what do you suggest?"

"If he still refuses to tell us what he knows, we take him back to Cairo for further interrogation." Sanson slapped the truncheon hard into his palm. "But either way, if Berger knows anything, by Christ I'll make him talk."

When they stepped back into the room, Sanson blatantly placed the truncheon on the table. Berger looked at it anxiously.

"Well, have you reconsidered?"

When the German hesitated, Sanson had the truncheon in his hand in an instant, struck him a quick, stinging blow across the face. The young German cried out, almost fell from his chair, clutched his jaw in shock. "I—I don't know anything about the Cairo operation."

"We've established you wrote the memo. Which suggests you knew something about the people involved. Let me remind you again what it says." Sanson removed the German flimsy from the folder, and read, " *'Rommel urgently pressing for more details: troop numbers, armour and artillery movements. Berlin instructs Phoenix to proceed Cairo at once. Besheeba will rendezvous. Hopes combined efforts will produce more results.'* "

Sanson looked up. "It's that last line that gives it away, Berger. 'Hopes combined efforts will produce more results.' What results did you hope for? You must have known *something* about these two agents. So tell me."

Berger looked frightened. Sanson said, "Well, Berger, I'm waiting."

"My name, rank and serial number are all you're entitled to—"

"It serves no purpose to continue like this," Sanson said in frustration. "You admitted yourself, the war's over for Germany in North Africa. What can you hope to achieve by not answering my questions?"

"I told you already. I know nothing. How many times do I have to repeat that?"

"You can repeat it all you like but I know you're lying. You're also trying my patience. You could be shot as a spy, or can't you grasp that?"

"Ich bin Manfred Berger, Hauptmann, nummer—"

Sanson was off the chair in an instant, the truncheon in his hand. This time, he lashed Berger hard across the face. The German screamed in agony and collapsed on to the floor. Weaver couldn't stomach much more, was beginning to wonder if Berger could really tell them anything useful. He went to help the German up.

Sanson reacted in a flash. "What the bloody hell are you doing, Weaver? Leave him be!"

"To hell with you. He's hurt, for Christ sakes!"

"I said *leave* him."

For a moment, Weaver thought Sanson was going to hit him, but instead the Englishman skewered him with a frightening look. Weaver stepped back. Sanson moved to stand over the German, hands on his hips. "Come on, Berger. The truth. Out with it!"

Berger lay there, whimpering, a lather of sweat on his face, his false limb twisted hideously. "Please—"

"*Think*, Berger. Think hard. You must know something. Is it worth a beating and a bullet when your country's already losing the war? Think of that child of yours. You'd like to see her again, wouldn't you? Or would you rather your wife and daughter got a telegram telling them you're dead?"

Berger reacted, almost at breaking point, his lips trembling, eyes welling with tears. He raised a hand to protect himself as Sanson started to lift the truncheon again.

"No—please! I'll tell you what I know."

BERLIN
19 NOVEMBER/4 P.M.

Heinrich Himmler, head of the SS and the Gestapo, was an unusually austere and distant man, a former Bavarian chicken farmer who sent millions to the death camps without so much as a second's thought, his dour bureaucrat's face devoid of emotion.

As Schellenberg was led into his Prinz-Albrecht-Strasse office that afternoon, rain was gusting against the windows, an icy wind blowing so harshly it could only have come from the Baltic.

Himmler wore his full-dress black Reichsführer's uniform and customary pince-nez glasses. He was seated behind his walnut desk, a stack of paperwork in front of him, a pen poised in his hand. The office was in half-darkness, everything about it spartan and impersonal, the only warmth coming from a sparking log fire blazing in a corner.

Schellenberg gave the Nazi salute. "You sent for me, Reichsführer?"

Himmler laid down his pen, silently indicated a chair, and in very slow, precise movements cleared his paperwork to one side, except for a handful of reports, as if preparing himself for business. He indicated the remaining papers on his desk with some distaste. "The latest ciphers have arrived from our agents in North Africa, and the progress reports from the Luftwaffe and Kriegsmarine. I think you had better read them."

Schellenberg studied the pages, while Himmler stood and came round from behind his desk. He paused at the fire for a time, warming his hands, then touched a jutting log with the toe of his polished boot, making sparks flare, before finally turning back.

"Well?"

Schellenberg put the reports aside. "They're disappointing, Reichsführer."

"Disappointing?" Himmler flared. "They're disastrous. Our Atlantic U-boats have continually failed to engage Roosevelt's convoy. We've sent out our best commanders, and they've all failed. The most recent Luftwaffe report indicates a large fleet of protection vessels surrounding the battleship *Iowa*, which we suspect is carrying the American President. It was sighted from the air, approximately four hundred miles off the Moroccan coast at midday today, and pursuing an erratic route. Goering says it's too far away for us to attempt a bombing run—the spotter plane was engaged by aircraft from enemy destroyers and barely made its escape. As for the Kriegsmarine, they claim it's completely impossible to breach the heavy naval security."

"I would imagine so, Reichsführer."

"If all that weren't bad enough, our agents are having serious difficulty discovering where exactly Roosevelt's convoy might dock in North Africa—so it could be anywhere along a three-thousand-mile coast. Without precise information, we couldn't possibly effect a meaningful air or sea attack. And once Roosevelt comes ashore, we'll have little chance of knowing how he'll proceed until he reaches Cairo." Himmler sighed with frustration, removed his glasses and polished them methodically with a handkerchief. "So, Walter, it seems it may well be all down to you, after all. Tell me your progress."

"I'm glad to report that everything goes according to plan, Reichsführer." Schellenberg smiled brightly.

"You seem confident. Do you feel certain the woman will be capable of doing what is expected of her?"

"With her father's life in the balance, she'll do her utmost, I'm sure of it."

"You had better be right. And Halder?"

"He's coming along nicely." Schellenberg smiled again. "A little conflict between him and Kleist, but we expected that."

Himmler replaced his glasses, adjusted them on the bridge of his nose. "Ah, yes, Kleist. A bit of a brute, but the kind of man you can rely on. Much easier to predict than this fellow Halder. And what about Deacon?"

"Reichsführer?"

"His progress in Cairo?"

"I expect a signal from him within the next twenty-four hours, informing us of his readiness."

"The troubling matter of this safe house being discovered, it hasn't caused him further problems?"

"Not according to his last report. If it had, I'm certain he would have let us know."

"Halder is aware of this?"

"I didn't think it necessary to trouble him with the information, Reichsführer. He has enough to occupy his mind."

Himmler nodded. "Perhaps you're right. But what if Deacon fails to obtain the necessary transport and equipment at such short notice?"

"I'm confident we can still go ahead. It would be left to Halder and the others to sort out the problem once they arrive. But I'm sure they're quite capable of it."

Himmler made no comment, stared at the fire for several moments, lost in thought. "Very well. Considering the pessimism of the reports you just read, you have my authority to proceed with Operation Sphinx, and with the Führer's approval."

Schellenberg stood, delighted. "As you command, Reichsführer."

"You will take Halder and the others to Gatow aerodrome tomorrow, and on to their stand-by position in Rome, to prepare for departure." Himmler came back to his desk, sat, and carefully replaced the barrier of paperwork in front of him, indicating that the meeting was at an end. "And as always, keep me fully informed of any developments."

BITTER LAKES

"It's not much, but it's definitely something." Sanson lit a cigarette as they sat in the interrogation room an hour later, after Berger had been taken away.

Weaver was silent as Sanson read back through his notes. "We now know for certain that Phoenix arrived in Cairo nine months ago to help bolster the Germans' intelligence-gathering. We also know, from Berger's agreement with our description, that it's probably our friend Farid Gabar. And we know that after he got through our lines he probably stayed one night in a safe house in Ezbekiya—a hotel belonging to an Arab sympathiser working for German intelligence—before making contact with Besheeba."

The information Berger had given them had indeed been slender, but was still significant. He had merely transcribed the signal for his commanding officer, but admitted to having twice seen the Arab that Sanson described, during intelligence debriefings at Wehrmacht headquarters in Tunis. As Weaver had suspected, Berger wasn't privy to the true identities or backgrounds of either agent, and he couldn't tell them anything about Besheeba, except to say he'd heard a rumour he was Berlin's top spy in Cairo.

"So we need to find this hotel. Except it was nine months ago that Gabar stayed there."

"It's the start of a trail, Weaver. And right now, it's all we've got. I'll have a word with some of my informers, and we'll go through the lists of sympathisers again. We might turn up a suspect. If not, we'll get the rundown on every hotel owner in the area until we do."

Weaver stood. Sanson said, "Where are you going?"

"To see if Berger's all right. I think you shook him pretty badly."

Sanson said angrily, "Forget about it, Weaver. And there's something I ought to point out while we're on the subject. You should know better than to show disagreement or weakness during interrogation. That was a stupid thing you did, attempting to help him. It undermined my authority."

"It wasn't interrogation, Sanson. It was torture, whatever the results. The kind of thing I'd expect from the damned Gestapo."

Sanson looked fit to explode. He got to his feet and stuffed his notebook in his breast pocket. "I told you, this is war. Or don't you understand that? If you have a complaint to make about my methods, do so. But in a situation like this, results are all that count. Now, let's make tracks back to Cairo. If we're going to find Gabar fast, we've got our work cut out."

TWENTY-ONE

BERLIN

Two thousand miles away that same day, and at just past eight in the evening, Admiral Wilhelm Canaris was still wrestling with his conscience as he entered the basement *bierkeller*.

It was a smoky place, filled with off-duty troops and glum-looking Berliners, the brass band playing on the rostrum all looking like condemned men, which wasn't surprising. Like everyone else, their nerves were shot from the bombing, the arrogant marching songs they played to an indifferent crowd hardly reflecting the despondent mood of the beleaguered city.

Canaris slid into an empty booth and ordered a mug of beer. He glanced at his reflection in a nearby wall mirror. He looked stressed, exhausted, having hardly slept in the last five days since meeting with Schellenberg. *Oh, what a tangled web we weave, when first we practise to deceive.* No wonder he was stressed. He had kept the secret for many years, and a dangerous one at that. He was a traitor to his country, one of the plotters against Hitler, a defiance that would soon cost him his life, hung by piano wire from a meat hook in Flossenburg concentration camp.

But that was a fact he was ignorant of that evening, and a fate that was months away. He wore shabby civilian clothes, an overcoat and hat, and being a spymaster, he had no problem losing the Gestapo tail that had followed him as he left his home for an after-dinner stroll.

He sipped a mouthful of tepid beer from the mug in front of him and glanced at his watch. The young woman who entered the *bierkeller* two minutes later was slim and blonde, her beautifully sculpted face and even more beautiful body expertly masked by far too much make-up and dowdy, ill-fitting clothes that deliberately hid her charms. She saw Canaris. He had left his hat on the edge of the table, the signal that it was safe to meet. She slid into the seat opposite, smiled. "Wilhelm."

"My dearest Silvia," Canaris said fondly. Had he not been faithfully married, he could easily have fallen in love with this divine-looking angel in front of him. Countess Silvia Konigsberg was the wife of a Swedish diplomat, and an old friend. "You had no problem getting here?"

"None." Mischief sparkled in her eyes. "I lost my Gestapo tail in the Underground. The poor man must be having a fit by now."

Canaris ordered a beer for her, and waited until the waitress left. "So, you fly to Stockholm tonight."

"Midnight. The mail run. Was it something terribly important you wanted to see me about?"

Canaris cleared his throat. Anything in writing was out of the question, evidence that could be used against him. Silvia, on the other hand, had diplomatic immunity and powerful friends, extending up to the King of Sweden himself. Brutal interrogation was out of the question if she was caught. But that didn't mean she wasn't risking her life. The Gestapo was skilled in arranging fatal accidents.

"My dear Silvia, I must entrust you with a vital, urgent message. So crucial, it may decide the fate of the war. Are you ready to commit it to memory?"

Silvia didn't flinch. A brave woman, Canaris thought, with that remarkable Nordic ability to appear calm under the worst duress. "Tell me," she said simply.

Canaris hesitated. He knew that by this very act he was dooming Halder and the woman to failure, even death, and it was a heavy load on his conscience which had racked him for the last five days. But the alternative was simply too horrible to contemplate. "Schellenberg and Himmler have devised a plan to kill the American President and British Prime Minister. They know Roosevelt will arrive in Cairo to meet Churchill some time on the twenty-second—three days from now. The intention is to assassinate them both."

His Swedish angel turned pale and her mouth opened to admit a sharp intake of breath. Canaris said, "You *must* pass on the message to your usual contact. If this insane plan were to succeed, we both know the consequences."

"How—how will it happen?"

"A specialist team to set up the operation will be on its way to Egypt by air within the next forty-eight hours. Even sooner, perhaps—"

At that moment they both heard the wail of an air-raid siren. The band stopped, people panicked, chairs overturned, and the bar staff began ushering customers to the basement cellars. "My God, it starts again," Canaris said palely. "The country will be nothing but rubble." He put a hand urgently on Silvia's. "You're certain you'll make the plane tonight?"

She nodded. "My husband has important diplomatic business in Stockholm. And we have an escort across the corridor, as usual."

It was absurd, Canaris knew. In the middle of the worst war in human history, a Baltic air corridor had been tacitly agreed between the Allies and Germany, for the safe passage of aircraft from neutral Sweden. Outside, the pounding started; the ceiling shook, scattering plaster, and the lights dipped.

Silvia stood anxiously. "I really had better go. If I'm stuck here, I may miss the flight."

"God go with you, Silvia," Canaris said urgently. "And for heaven's sake, be careful out there, and please don't let me down."

Another bomb struck, somewhere in the streets outside, and off-duty soldiers and the *bierkeller* staff screamed at people to move quickly to the basement. "There's more our friend in Stockholm should know," Canaris added quickly.

"There isn't time, Wilhelm." Silvia was moving towards the door.

"But I simply *must* give you some details—" As he took Silvia's arm and helped her towards the exit, a burly Feldwebel came over as a powerful blast shook the building, almost knocking him off his feet.

"Are you two deaf? Downstairs, quickly! Before you're blown to fucking pieces."

As the Feldwebel began to push them towards the basement, without a word Silvia Konigsberg darted past him, out through the door, and up the steps. "You stupid bitch. Are you crazy?" the soldier roared, and started after her.

Canaris gripped his arm. "No. Leave her!"

"She can suit herself, pops, but if you want to live to see your fucking pension, you'd better get your arse down those stairs straight away. Move!"

Canaris saw Silvia disappear up the steps as a cloud of dust rolled through the *bierkeller* and the building shook once again. He put his arm over his mouth to stop from choking. *My God.* What if she was killed in the air raid and didn't make it? And he had desperately wanted to give her more details, to make sure that her British Intelligence contact in Stockholm knew that Halder and the woman were innocent pawns in a deadly game, but he was too late. Silvia was gone and the soldier was pushing him down towards the cellars.

Two kilometres across Berlin, at that very same moment, it was a different kind of cellar General Walter Schellenberg was being led towards. A visit to the basement prison at Gestapo headquarters always depressed him. It was a wretched place, reeking of fear, and full of the screams of torture victims, but he was in an excellent mood that late afternoon as the burly SS jailer led him down the steps.

They walked to the end of a chilly, dimly lit corridor, past lines of iron doors on either side. The jailer halted outside one of the last and inserted a key. Schellenberg lit a cigarette.

"How is he?"

"Better than most here, Herr General. Three good meals a day and no more torture or beatings. But I still think he's not right in the head. He barely responds."

"Has he mentioned his daughter?"

"Not that I'm aware of, sir. He just cries a lot. Hardly stops, in fact."

Just then, Schellenberg heard sobbing, and glanced across the corridor to one of the other cells, from where the noise came. "Wait a moment."

He stepped over, flicked on a wall switch, and pulled back the metal viewing shutter set in the iron door. He saw two young boys, one in his late teens, the other no more than fourteen, their faces badly swollen, huddled together in the corner of the cell as if for comfort, the youngest sobbing uncontrollably. Blinking in the harsh light, they looked pathetic, frightened creatures.

"And what about these two?" he said over his shoulder to the jailer.

"Traitorous brothers, plotters against the Führer, aren't they, Herr General. They haven't confessed yet, but you can be assured they will. And they'll get what's coming to them in the end, no doubt."

Schellenberg shuddered with disgust as he heard a woman's scream from somewhere in the depths of the prison. He closed the shutter, turned back to the waiting jailer and gave a nod towards the other cell. "You can open the door now."

The jailer obeyed, flicked on the light from outside. Schellenberg stepped into the foul-smelling room. There was barely space for two people, a metal bunk with filthy grey blankets and a dented slop bucket, a harsh light glaring from the ceiling. A grey-haired, once distinguished-looking man sat curled up in the corner, hands over his head and face, whimpering like a baby, rocking back and forth.

"You're being treated well, I hear?" Schellenberg remarked quietly.

The man didn't reply or attempt to look up, and the guard screamed, "Answer the general when he speaks to you!"

Schellenberg angrily snapped his fingers. "Leave us! Outside!"

The jailer clicked his heels, instantly obeyed. Schellenberg drew on his cigarette, looked back at the prisoner. "I'm afraid you'll have to forgive these people. Some are worse than common beasts. But I have some good news, which should boost your morale. Your daughter agreed to my proposal. If she does what's expected of her, and survives, this unpleasant business should all be over very soon. Well, what have you got to say?"

The man whimpered, nervously took his hands away from his head. His bearded face was severely bruised, purple sores where old wounds had healed. He stared up like a frightened madman, deranged eyes beyond help, then he started to cry, covered his face again, and rocked back and forth.

Schellenberg sighed with despair, tossed his cigarette on the floor and crushed it with his heel. "I have a terrible feeling you're beyond redemption, my friend. The bully boys have scrambled your brains." He stepped outside, said to the jailer, "Have a doctor come by. Not one of the usual cellar quacks. A proper physician. And I want to see his report."

"Yes, Herr General."

The cell door clanged shut and Schellenberg retreated back down the corridor.

CAIRO
18 NOVEMBER

Reggie Salter was in a foul mood that Thursday afternoon, and for a very good reason. One of his warehouses had been raided the previous night, not by the police, but by a well-organised gang of Arab thieves. They had slit the throat of one of his guards, and made off with over five thousand pounds' worth of Salter's cherished goods.

His men had already buried the guard's body out in the desert, and before long some greedy bastards would be digging their own graves to keep him company. Whoever robbed his warehouse was going to pay dearly, but knowing the Arab criminal gangs as Salter did, he was unlikely to see his goods again.

He was still fuming at the thought of losing five grand when Costas came up the stairs from the warehouse below, wiping his hands on an oily rag. "Deacon's just arrived downstairs, Reggie. You want me to send him up?"

"No, I'll go down. What's happening with the fucking Jeep?"

"It's out in the yard. The boys are checking it over."

"Right. Let's see the colour of Deacon's money." Salter went down the steps to the warehouse, Costas behind him, and they saw Deacon and the Arab waiting by some packing crates on the ground floor.

"Harvey, old son. Good to see you again."

"You have the Jeep and the uniforms?"

"All business today, ain't we? I said I wouldn't let you down, and I haven't. I even got them earlier than expected. Follow me."

Salter led the way through the warehouse to a covered yard at the back. Two of his men were working away under the hood of an American Jeep, while another was busy cleaning the dust off the military police decals on the sides.

"Costas tells me the engine's a good one—almost new," Salter explained. "Not half clapped out like most you'd come across, after being run ragged across the fucking desert."

Deacon looked over the vehicle. "Where did you get it?"

Salter tapped his nose with a grin. "The less you know the better."

"But you're sure the papers are legitimate, and the Jeep can't be traced back to here?"

Salter laughed. "Give us a break, Harvey. Of course I bloody am. If I conducted business any other way I'd be nailed in my coffin by now."

Deacon ran a hand over the paintwork, and Salter said, "Feel free to check the merchandise. You're the customer."

Deacon sat in the Jeep and started the ignition. The engine throbbed smoothly. He climbed out and looked under the hood with Hassan's help. "It looks fine," Deacon pronounced, dusting his hands.

"Would I do you a bad deal?" Salter handed him the vehicle's papers. "All in order, I think you'll find."

Deacon examined the papers. "They seem OK, right enough. What about the uniforms?"

Salter clicked his fingers at one of his men. "Get the other stuff from inside, Joey."

The man went into the warehouse and returned carrying a couple of bulging military kit-bags over his shoulders. Salter opened one and emptied some of the contents on the ground. An American captain's uniform, and a military police sergeant's uniform, both with all the trimmings, including a couple of holstered Colt .45 pistols and two American M_3 "grease gun" machine-pistols, with extra ammunition clips for each.

"Everything you ordered. Better check, though, just to be certain."

Deacon examined the contents of each of the kit-bags, and Salter said, "Happy?"

"It all looks good."

"Another five hundred shekels, I think we said."

"The uniforms and weapons I want delivered to the club later tonight. Use the delivery entrance, and for God's sake be discreet."

"It's my middle name."

"You're sure it's not a problem leaving the Jeep for a couple of days, until I need it?"

"Not so long as you pay the agreed storage it's not."

Deacon removed an envelope from his pocket and handed it over. Salter riffled through the notes, then slid the envelope into his pocket. "A pleasure to do business with you, Harvey."

"We haven't finished yet. What about the trucks?"

Salter lit a cheroot and scratched his jaw. "I'm afraid we're having a bit of temporary bother with those, ain't we, Costas?"

The Greek shrugged. "It seems the army's laying its hands on every vehicle it can right now, Harvey. God knows why, but there's a shortage of trucks about. Don't worry, we'll do our best."

"Your best isn't good enough," Deacon said worriedly. "I have to be certain I'll have those trucks within the next two days."

There was a hint of desperation in his voice that Salter didn't fail to notice, and he said reassuringly, "I'll look after it personally, Harvey, no sweat. They'll be here, and on time, even if I have to nick them myself. That's a definite promise."

"Good." Deacon looked relieved, nodded to Hassan and turned to go. "You'll be in touch?"

"As soon as I have word, old son."

Salter watched them leave the yard, and when they had gone called over two of his men. "You know what to do. Everywhere Deacon goes, anyone he sees, I want to know about it. Fuck this up on me and let him spot you, and you'll be crocodile bait, understand?"

"Sure, Reggie."

The men left. Costas sidled over. He grinned crookedly at Salter. "You think it'll work?"

Salter cracked his knuckles. "It had bloody well better, Costas, old son. We lost five grand to those thieving Arab gits last night and I intend to recover our losses. Whatever's going on, we're going to get a piece of it, whether Deacon and his mates like it or not."

TWENTY-TWO

BERLIN
20 NOVEMBER
The Luftwaffe aerodrome at Gatow was busy that afternoon as Schellenberg's Mercedes passed through the barrier, followed by a covered truck carrying Halder and the others. They pulled up beside a locked hangar, and Schellenberg led them in through a side door. An aircraft was parked inside, its fuselage painted in sand-coloured camouflage, no markings or roundels to identify it. A half-dozen mechanics were working away, while two pilots were busy in the cockpit.

"Vito!" Schellenberg called out, and the man in the captain's seat waved through the window, then moments later appeared at the fuselage door and came down the metal steps. "Herr General."

"And how is our transport coming along?"

Vito Falconi was tall for an Italian, very handsome, with dark curly hair and a fine Roman nose, and rather dashing-looking with it. He was also quite old for a combat pilot, in his late thirties. He wore a Luftwaffe leather flying jacket, a white silk scarf knotted at his neck, his eyes full of restless energy.

"*Bene*. I took her up twice this morning, and she handles remarkably well." He turned to Halder and shook his hand warmly. "Jack, you're still alive, I see."

"Hello, Vito. It's been a while."

Falconi smiled. "And I'm not exactly sure it's good to see you again. Not after I heard it was your idea to pick me to fly this mission. Are you trying to get me killed? So, how are you, my friend?"

"Between despair and middling."

Falconi laughed. "Aren't we all. This damned war has everyone on edge. And what are you up to now? Something so top secret the whole future of the war depends on it?"

"You'd better ask the Herr General that."

"All none of your business, Vito, I'm afraid," Schellenberg said lightly, and made the introductions. "Meet Gruppenkommandant Falconi, your pilot. He'll be taking you all the way to Egypt."

Vito took Rachel's hand and kissed it. "A pleasure, *bella signorina*. And may I say you're the best-looking passenger I've had in a long time."

"Pay no attention to Vito," Schellenberg remarked. "He's a first-class charmer."

Kleist interrupted, a sour look on his face. "Herr General, the pilot's Italian. Why not German? The cowardly bastards surrendered to the enemy. All they've ever done is give us trouble. As for their pilots, everyone knows they're useless. You may as well give us our death certificates here and now."

Falconi gave Kleist a frosty look. "In case you hadn't heard, thousands of Italian dead lie as far east as the outskirts of Moscow and the ruins of Stalingrad. I think that counts for something, don't you?"

Schellenberg glared at Kleist. "Quite so. And I wouldn't worry about the Gruppenkommandant's flying abilities. He's been seconded to the Luftwaffe as an instructor since 1940, and is one of the best we have. He's also had a lot of experience flying in Africa. Since before the war, in fact, so you're in safe hands."

"With respect, you must be doing your recruiting in some low places these days," Falconi said to Schellenberg. "Your friend here had really better improve his attitude. Two minutes in his company and already I've had enough."

Schellenberg said pointedly to Kleist, "Curb your tongue, and watch your manners. I also hear from Major Halder you're getting a little out of hand. Just remember he's in total charge of this part of the operation, so show him the proper respect. That's an order."

Kleist grimaced, and drew himself up. "Yes, Herr General."

"And now, Vito, I suppose you'd better explain about our transport."

Falconi led them over to the sand-camouflaged aircraft and Halder said, "What's this, for God's sake?"

"An American C-47 cargo plane, otherwise known as the Dakota, or rather more affectionately as the Gooney Bird. Probably the best transporter the Allies have. This particular beauty ran out of fuel and ditched in a field in northern Italy, fortunately with only minor undercarriage damage. An SS patrol was in the area and managed to get to her before the pilot could blow her up. She was repaired and transported to Luftwaffe special operations."

"So what's the idea?"

"The Dakota's as common as ditch-water in the Allied air forces. So from our point of view, she's ideal."

"You mean to help us sneak past the Allied air defences?"

Falconi grinned. "Exactly."

"It was Vito's idea," Schellenberg explained. "And there are two more aircraft just like them, for our friend the colonel. This way, we have a chance of getting you to your destination without coming under suspicion from enemy coastal patrols."

"And they're pretty tight at the moment, from what I hear," Falconi offered. "Their Spitfires and Tomahawks are out hunting day and night, and they're damned good. Luftwaffe bomber squadrons based in Italy have been trying to hit Sicily and Alex in the last few weeks, but with considerable losses. Most of the poor bastards have been shot down before they even reached their targets."

"All very ominous for us," Halder remarked. "Won't we need Allied aircraft markings? Surely there's a risk we could get blown out of the sky by one of their air patrols?"

"When we land in Rome for refuelling, American markings will be painted on. We'll have a slight advantage using Italy as our departure point, because the Allies tend to focus their attention on the air traffic from German fields in Rhodes and Athens, seeing as they're closer to North Africa. Once we're on our way, to all intents and purposes we'll look like a US Air Force plane going about its lawful business." Falconi smiled. "And just in case you're worried, we'll be cleared with Luftwaffe command as far as southern Italy, so there's no danger of being shot down by our own side before we even get under way."

"And after that?" Halder asked.

"The route we'll take down to North Africa will be mostly over sea. When we reach the desert airfield, I'll land and let you disembark, then take off again immediately. The Dakota's been fitted with an extra tank, so I'll have more than enough fuel to get me back to Rome."

"What happens if the Allied air defences intercept us and call you up on the radio?"

Falconi shrugged bleakly. "That's a possibility, of course. But if it happens, I'm afraid we'll just have to try to muddle our way through. You see, we really wouldn't know if they tried to call us up on the radio."

"Why?"

"For security reasons, they change their communications frequencies daily, sometimes even for each patrol, so we've no way of knowing what the frequency might be."

"But their aircraft would try to make contact somehow if we didn't respond?"

Falconi nodded. "If normal communications didn't do the trick, they'd try to do it visually with a signal code, either with Morse-keyed lights which Allied aircraft have mounted under their fuselage, or with a Very flare gun. Or then again, they might not even bother with a signal code, and just shoot us out of the skies."

"That really inspires me with confidence, Vito. Any other good news?"

Falconi laughed. "We do have the slight advantage of flying one of their aircraft. They'll be less likely to shoot first and ask questions later. Which might give us a chance to bluff our way out if they think our communications or electrics are dead, and we can make a run for it, if necessary."

"That's hardly a likely option if we come up against a night fighter. They'd have us for speed."

Schellenberg interrupted. "Like I said, Jack, there are risks. But you're well aware Vito's done this sort of run over enemy territory before. You're in excellent hands."

"It's the weather I'm really more concerned about," Falconi admitted to Halder. "The Met reports indicate a pretty nasty front moving in rapidly across the Med. It looks like thunderstorms all the way down to Alex for the next twenty-four hours, and sandstorms along the north Egyptian coast."

"Marvellous."

"But the good news is I'm hoping the bad weather will keep any enemy coastal patrols firmly on the ground."

"You really think we'll be safe?" Rachel asked.

Falconi smiled, all charm. "There's a war on, *bella signorina*. And no one is entirely safe, especially in our situation. But even the Devil has his good days, and since I've lived this long, he obviously hasn't let me down so far."

"And just to lay your minds at rest," Schellenberg put in, "I have a team of the Luftwaffe's finest mechanics waiting in Rome to give the aircraft a final inspection. The last thing we want is technical trouble during your flight—it could prove disastrous. Are we almost ready, Vito?"

"My co-pilot, Remer, and I were just finishing our checks."

Schellenberg searched the faces around him. "No further questions? Good. Climb aboard and stow away your things. We'll be getting under way shortly."

It was almost one o'clock when the Dakota finally lifted off the long Gatow runway. Falconi climbed to fourteen thousand feet before letting the young Luftwaffe co-pilot take over the controls, while he consulted the route maps.

In the back of the aircraft, Halder sat on the floor beside Rachel, while Kleist and Doring sat opposite. Schellenberg was up near the front, stretched out on the floor with his arms folded, his briefcase clutched to his chest, his officer's cap tilted over his eyes as he tried to sleep. The C-47 was pretty basic, with no seats and a lattice of canvas cargo webbing hanging along the fuselage walls. Once they had reached their cruise altitude, Halder began to feel the cold, and he noticed that Rachel looked pale and drawn.

"How do you feel?"

"Tired and freezing."

"It's a long flight. I'll see if I can find something to keep out the chill."

He went to get a couple of the blankets from one of the stowage bins, but when he came back Rachel was already fast asleep, curled up like a child, her head to one side.

Halder placed a blanket over her, then for some inexplicable reason he leaned over and gently kissed her on the nape of the neck. Across the aircraft, he noticed Kleist stare at him and say something under his breath to Doring, and the two SS men sniggered. Then Kleist glared at him boldly, eyes filled with something close to hate.

Halder ignored the provocation, covered himself with a blanket and tipped his hat over his eyes. The drone of the Dakota's twin engines quickly lulled him to sleep.

TWENTY-THREE

CAIRO
20 NOVEMBER/1:45 P.M.

"It's called the Imperial," said Reeves. "Twenty rooms in all. Looks like a proper dive inside. I think I'd rather take my chances sleeping in a rat-infested sewer."

Weaver had just climbed into the back of an unmarked staff car next to Sanson, both of them armed and wearing civilian clothes. They had taken a taxi into the hot, crowded back streets of the Ezbekiya to join two of Sanson's men who had been detailed to watch the Imperial. One of them,

Reeves, a young intelligence officer with a thin moustache, sat in the driver's seat, also wearing civilian clothes.

Across the street, the Imperial looked far from what its name suggested: a cheap, run-down hotel with peeling shutters, cracked exterior walls that looked as if they were about to collapse—four derelict floors sandwiched between a long row of similar cheap hotels and decaying tenement buildings. The painted sign above the entrance was badly faded.

"What's the owner's background?" Weaver asked.

Sanson had his notebook open on his lap. "Tarik Nasser's a small-time businessman with no known convictions. The hotel was visited by the local police three days ago as part of our checks, but they claim the register was in order and the clerk told them no one of Farid Gabar's description had looked for a room. The only reason we reckon Tarik Nasser's a likely sympathiser is the word of one of our informers. During the flap he was overheard boasting that he'd be welcoming the Germans with open arms as soon as they reached Cairo. Hardly unusual, you might say, but it turns out he's probably got a good motive—a number of years ago his younger brother was shot dead while pilfering from British Army stores. And as of now, Nasser's the only likely suspect we've come up with."

Three other hotels in the district were under observation, and Sanson seemed impatient to make progress. "Give me the story," he said to Reeves.

"I asked for a room and the clerk told me they're full right now," Reeves replied. "All twenty rooms bursting at the seams, and not a chance of getting one for another two months. It's the same with all the others around here. You can't get a room for love nor money."

Sanson let out a sigh. The intention had been to get one of the men inside the Imperial to see if they could spot anyone among the guests who resembled Gabar. "That messes up our plans. Which means we probably don't have much option except to raid the place and pull in Nasser for questioning. What about the customers?"

"Mostly European refugees, but some Arabs too, so far as I could see."

"Did you get a look at the register?"

"No, sir. That wasn't possible."

"Did you see *anyone* who might resemble Gabar entering or leaving?"

"No, sir."

"What about Nasser?"

"I asked to see the owner after I tried to book a room, just to get a proper look at him. He came out himself. I gave him my spiel about needing accommodation badly and that I'd pay over the odds, but it made no difference—he told me he was full to the gills. He left just over an hour ago and hasn't come back since. Briggs went to follow him, sir." Reeves looked out of the window. "Hang on a minute. Here's Briggs now."

A man came up alongside the car, wearing a civilian suit and hat, and climbed in beside the driver. "Where's Nasser?" Sanson asked.

Briggs nodded out of the window. "That's him, sir. He went for lunch in a Greek restaurant two streets away. Then he bought some groceries in a store around the corner."

Across the road, they saw a barrel-chested man waddle along the pavement. He wore a fez and carried a bag of groceries, his treble chins rippling as he munched an apple. He turned into the hotel and climbed up the short flight of steps with difficulty, his stubby legs under strain, his fat cheeks puffing air.

Sanson opened the car door. "Right, let's nab him while we can. Reeves, you come with us. Briggs, go round the back. Anyone tries to make a run for it, you drop them, but don't kill the bastards. If they run, they've got something to hide, and I want to know what it is."

Hassan lay on the bed, idly cleaning the Walther pistol with an oily rag.

The tiny room was driving him insane and he felt like a caged animal. A pile of Arab newspapers lay on the floor; he'd read each at least a half-dozen times. He was restless, needed to walk. His stomach rumbled. It was still lunchtime, and the Greek restaurant two streets away served excellent food. Wearing the suit, and with his beard gone, he had begun to feel reasonably secure in his disguise.

He put aside the pistol, got up from the bed, took his tie

and suit jacket from the hanger on the back of the door, and started to get dressed.

Weaver went into the lobby with Sanson, Reeves behind them. The place was threadbare, smelled of stale food and cigarette smoke. There was a wooden counter on the left, a young Arab clerk behind it, idly fingering a set of worry beads, and Sanson said, "Tarik Nasser. Where is he?"

The clerk blinked at his visitors. "I—I don't know, sir."

"Don't lie to me. I saw him enter just a moment ago."

The young man gestured nervously towards a door. "Mr. Nasser's office over there. Perhaps you find him inside—"

Sanson smartly crossed to the door with Weaver and Reeves, pushed it open, and they found themselves in a tiny office. Tarik Nasser was seated at a desk, set against the far wall, looking through some correspondence, and he wobbled uncertainly to his feet at the sudden intrusion. "Yes?"

"Tarik Nasser?"

"Yes, I'm Nasser."

"I'm Lieutenant-Colonel Sanson, military intelligence. This is Lieutenant-Colonel Weaver."

Nasser tried not to swallow, felt his legs begin to shake, as if they were about to collapse under his weight. "To what do I owe this pleasure?"

Sanson nodded to Reeves. "Check the registration book. Be quick about it."

"What's going on here?" Nasser protested.

Reeves left and Sanson said, "Sit down, Mr. Nasser."

Nasser sat, felt sweat rise on the back of his neck, and his heart began to palpitate. He thought of reaching for the buzzer under his desk, but reconsidered. "You haven't told me what this is about."

"Then I'll get directly to the point. You're suspected of harbouring German spies, Mr. Nasser. And of being a German agent yourself."

He *was* in trouble. Nasser felt a sudden pain tightening his chest, but he gave a dry, nervous laugh that didn't sound very convincing. "Is—is this some kind of funny business?"

"Cut the innocent act, Nasser. We have the word of a captured German intelligence officer."

Nasser swallowed, reached for a handkerchief on his desk, dabbed his brow. "There—there must be a mistake, certainly? I'm—I'm an honest businessman."

Reeves came back moments later with a thick guest ledger. "There's no one named Gabar registered for any time over the last nine months, sir. Or at present."

As soon as he heard the name, Nasser's chest pain got worse. He felt like throwing up, but he made to reach for the buzzer instead, his hand shaking. He quietly took it away as Sanson looked back at him.

"We're going to search the hotel. Tear it apart if we have to, and check the guests in every room, one by one. Then we're going to take you to GHQ for interrogation. Before we do so, I'm going to give you the opportunity to confess. Well, Nasser?"

Nasser made up his mind. Trembling, the handkerchief still in his hand, he quickly reached under the desk and pressed the button twice. Sanson grabbed his arm in an instant, twisted it behind his back. "What the devil are you playing at—?"

Nasser yelled in pain.

Sanson heaved him out of the way, searched under the desk, spotted the button. "The clever bastard's warned someone." He drew his revolver. "A pound to a penny the Arab's here. Watch him, Reeves, and cover the lobby. Follow me, Weaver, quickly—"

Hassan had finished putting on his suit. He examined himself in the cracked mirror, almost ready to leave, when he heard the buzzer go off, a sharp, brutal noise that sounded like a giant angry mosquito had suddenly invaded the room.

His heart skipped. He looked up sharply at the buzzer, just as it stopped for a second, then sounded again.

Once for caution. Twice to get out.

In one fluid movement he picked up the Walther, scanned the room to make sure he'd left nothing behind, and moved to the door.

Weaver had his Colt automatic out as he went back into the lobby with Sanson.

"We'll take one floor each, one at a time," said Sanson,

the Smith & Wesson in his hand. "I'll take the first, you the second, then move up from there. And for God's sake be careful."

They both went up the staircase, Sanson leading the way, and parted company on the first-floor landing as Weaver raced up to the second. He found himself in a short hallway, a window at the far end, the same smells and shabby red carpet as the lobby, three rooms on either side.

He saw no open doors. He tried the first, on his right. *Locked.* He moved his shoulder hard against it, pushed, and suddenly heard a noise behind the door. It opened and a middle-aged European man made to come out, a shabby briefcase in his hand. He looked alarmed.

"Get your hands above your head." Weaver pointed the gun in his face and pushed him back inside the room.

"I—I have papers," the man stammered, his hands shaking violently. "My—my name is Josef Esher. I am Hungarian refugee—"

The man obviously wasn't Gabar, and Weaver saw there was no one else in the room.

"I'm looking for an Arab." He described Gabar. "Have you seen him?"

The trembling man shook his head. "I—I see no one like that."

"Stay in your room and lock the door," Weaver ordered, then moved back out into the hallway. The door closed after him, and he heard the lock click.

He tried the next room. *Locked.* He moved quickly to the door opposite, tried the handle. It opened. He was in a tiny single room. The bed was ruffled, an indent in the bedclothes where someone had lain. Newspapers lay scattered on the floor. It looked as if someone had left in a hurry. Weaver noticed a key in the inside lock. He went back out into the hallway. The window at the end was half open. He moved towards it quickly and looked out. A rusting fire escape led down to a back alley, but he saw no one outside.

"Damn."

Suddenly, he heard two pistol shots in quick succession from somewhere below in the hotel, then came another two, which seemed to echo out in the alley. He raced back along the hall and down the stairs.

"He's dead, sir. He tried to escape—made a move towards the front door. I fired a couple of warning shots to scare him and he just keeled over, clutching his chest. Looks like the shock must have given him a heart attack. I tried to revive him but it was useless. The clerk's called an ambulance, not that it's going to do much good."

As Reeves spoke, Weaver looked down at Tarik Nasser's overweight body sprawled on the lobby carpet. The blubbery face had turned blue.

Sanson knelt, felt his pulse to be certain. "*Damn it to hell.* We needed to question the bastard. Did you see anything, Weaver?"

"There's a window open on the second floor. I think someone might have got down the fire escape, but there's no sign of anyone." He looked at Reeves. "I heard two more shots. Where's Briggs?"

"He should be still covering the rear, sir."

Sanson paled, got to his feet. "Let's get out the back—"

As they made to move, Briggs rushed in the front door, panting, his revolver still in his hand, and Sanson said urgently, "Did you get the Arab?"

"He got away, sir."

"Damn it to bloody hell."

2:45 P.M.
Deacon reversed the Packard into the deserted alleyway near the Rameses station.

He was fuming. There were important things he had planned to do that afternoon, before he sent his signal to Berlin that night, but this unexpected disaster had ruined his schedule. It could even ruin *everything*.

He halted the car, jerked on the handbrake, rolled down the window. The alleyway was a filthy, stinking place, not a sinner in sight. He lit a cigar to ward off the stench, before he stepped out of the car and said aloud, "You can come out. It's safe."

A second later, Hassan appeared from a recessed doorway, the Walther in his hand. He slipped it into his waistband. "What kept you? I phoned half an hour ago."

"I got here as fast as I could." Deacon looked enraged. "Never mind that. What the fuck happened?"

Hassan told him, his face puzzled. "I don't understand. I was careful entering and leaving the hotel. How did the army know I was there? Tarik told me the police were searching all the hotels in the city. They called on him a few days ago, but he said they didn't seem suspicious. Perhaps they were, but pretended not to be. They could have been watching the hotel all along."

Deacon said sourly, "There's got to be more to it than that, or they would have nabbed you days ago. You're sure Tarik didn't inform on you?"

Hassan looked insulted. "*Never.* He is my cousin. He saved my life."

Right now, Deacon couldn't think clearly enough to reason things out. He knew only that he had a terrible gut feeling there was trouble brewing.

"Did anyone get a good look at you as you left the hotel?"

Hassan shook his head. "I escaped the back way, over the rooftops."

"That doesn't mean they won't get a second-hand description. Some of Tarik's guests are bound to have seen you in the hotel. You said there was shooting?"

"They had a man waiting in the back alley. I think he saw me climb on to the roof and fired two shots. I heard another two shots inside the hotel. And I saw the American officer, Weaver."

"*What?*"

"I saw him look out on to the fire escape as I waited on the roof until it was safe to move." Malice flashed in Hassan's eyes. "If Tarik is harmed, I will kill the American."

Deacon gritted his teeth in exasperation, unlocked the boot. He had neglected to tell Hassan that he'd been delayed because he'd driven past the hotel on his way, and spotted an ambulance outside, two attendants carrying out a body covered with a blanket. He'd tell him later, once he had found out what had happened. "You'll kill no one. Get in the boot. I can't have you travelling up front in the car, it's too risky. Don't worry, you'll be able to breathe."

Hassan reluctantly made to climb into the boot. "Where are you taking me?"

"To the villa. It's about the only place left. You stay there from now on, until I say it's safe to go out on the streets again. Understand? And start praying no one searches the bloody car if I'm stopped at a checkpoint."

TWENTY-FOUR

CAIRO
20 NOVEMBER/4 P.M.
Weaver sat in the Jeep's passenger seat as Helen Kane drove him towards Giza. "Did Sanson say what it was about?"

"Only that he and General Clayton wanted to see you urgently at Mena House."

They had crossed the English Bridge, and the city gave way to mud-brick villages and sugar-cane fields, until they reached the edge of the desert. Soon they were eight miles west of Cairo, the dusty road busy with American and British military traffic, motorcycle despatch riders speeding past in both directions.

Weaver felt bad about hardly having seen her in three days, and had the nagging feeling he'd overstepped the mark by sleeping with her. "Look, I'm sorry about what happened the other night, Helen."

"But I'm not."

"You mean that?"

"Of course. I just wish you didn't look so troubled about it." She glanced at his face. "My poor Harry. Have I disturbed the ordered pattern of your existence?"

"Something like that."

She smiled, playfully. "You ought to know by now that women are the Devil."

"You don't think it might complicate things?"

"Only if you let it. We're human, there's a war on, and it happens all the time, no matter what the military rule books say. I think we can still do our duty and keep a face on things, don't you?"

He leaned over and kissed her cheek. "You're a terrific girl, you know that?"

She smiled back. "Careful. Otherwise I might be tempted to take it further. If you can spare the time, we could always have dinner tonight."

"It's the best offer I've had in days, but we'd better wait and see what General Clayton has in store. After what happened at the Imperial, somehow I don't think he's going to be in the best of moods."

The mud-brick dwellings of the poor gave way to the luxury country villas of wealthy Cairenes, until eventually they came to the untidy little village of Nazlat as-Saman, at the foot of the Sphinx and the three Giza pyramids. Further up the road from the village, at the end of a broad, palm-lined avenue, was a magnificent white-painted building surrounded by individual guest lodges and set in its own private grounds.

Originally an Ottoman hunting lodge in the last century, the Mena House had been bought by an English couple and transformed into a world-famous luxury hotel, a favourite haunt of royalty and the rich, complete with viewing balconies overlooking the pyramids, swimming pools and lush gardens, all done in lavish colonial style.

"What does a girl have to do to earn a weekend here?"

"I'm sure I could think of something."

She laughed. "I'm sure we both could."

"OK, let's see how good the security really is. Better get your special pass ready."

She swung the Jeep towards the hotel. The long avenue leading up to it had two heavily manned security checkpoints at each end of the track, a hundred yards apart. The road itself was blocked off by red-and-white pole barriers, and there were barbed-wire runs and several machinegun emplacements either side of the track. A sign warned OFF LIMITS TO ALL PERSONNEL! STRICTLY NO ENTRY!

At the first checkpoint a burly American army captain stepped forward and told them to switch off the engine. He examined their papers thoroughly, including the special passes for the compound which the general had arranged for them to be issued with at GHQ, then went to use the telephone in the sentry hut, while half a dozen armed soldiers thoroughly checked the Jeep, using a mirror on a long pole to study the underside of the vehicle.

The officer finally came back, handed them their papers and saluted. "Everything's in order, sir. You're expected. I'll have one of my men accompany you to the hotel."

"That won't be necessary, Captain."

The officer smiled knowingly. "Procedure, sir. Without an escort, the men at the next checkpoint are liable to blow your heads off without asking questions."

They drove forward to the second checkpoint, a sergeant with an M_3 machine-pistol riding in the back seat. The same security drill was repeated with the same thoroughness, before they pulled up at the hotel entrance and parked in the special visitors' carpark opposite the main entrance.

A half-dozen Sherman tanks and armoured cars were parked near the front, and sandbagged machinegun emplacements and anti-aircraft batteries had been set up on the roof and around the grounds. The place was a hive of activity, despatch riders coming and going. There was another security checkpoint in operation in the hotel reception area. It bristled with American and British military police, and near the front of the hotel a detail of army engineers and carpenters was busily testing a mobile ramp, a wood-and-metal contraption on wheels which Weaver guessed was to help get Roosevelt's wheelchair speedily up and down the steps.

"All very impressive," he said to the sergeant as he climbed out. "And definitely not the kind of place where you try to sneak past the concierge at four a.m."

"You ain't seen the half of it, sir. We've put a ring of steel around the area. Watertight ain't the word."

A grim-looking General Clayton came briskly down the hotel steps, Sanson behind him, accompanied by a tired-looking British major with a moustache. Weaver saluted.

"You wanted to see me, sir?"

"Get back in the Jeep, Harry. We need to talk," Clayton said gruffly, and climbed into the rear, Sanson and the major crowding in beside him. The general made the introduction. "Meet Major Blake. He's with SIS."

Blake offered Weaver his hand. "Pleasure to meet you, sir."

Sanson said brusquely, "Perhaps it's time you got the guided tour, Weaver. We can talk on the way." He nodded to Helen Kane. "Take her away, Helen. And be careful where you drive. Some of the areas around here are mined."

It took twenty minutes to drive around the security compound. Weaver saw that the entire hotel and almost a quarter-square-mile of the surrounding desert had been ringed with a barbed-wire perimeter fence, dotted with machinegun emplacements, and was patrolled by armed guards. Army engineers were still erecting tents on the Mena House grounds to accommodate the large numbers of troops. Just beyond the protection of the camp, the Sphinx and the pyramids stood as a majestic backdrop.

"We've got in excess of a thousand men guarding the area," Clayton explained. "By the time the President arrives this place is going to be sealed up as tight as Fort Knox. Each of the delegates will have their own private quarters and additional personal security, depending on rank and status. Added to that, the President will have twenty Secret Service men protecting him, working round-the-clock shifts. And nobody, but nobody, gets inside the area without the proper papers. From this morning, there's a ten-square-mile air exclusion zone patrolled by the RAF and our own boys from the US airbase here in Cairo, and enough anti-aircraft batteries to take out half the Luftwaffe. If anyone dares enter the zone they get blasted out of the sky, no questions asked."

"May I ask where the President will be quartered, sir?"

"In one of the hotel suites. If we have to move him for security reasons, it'll be to the ambassador's private villa, a mile from here. Like the compound, it'll be heavily guarded, but by our own boys. As for the hotel, all employees have been replaced temporarily with military personnel, with the exception of the manager. The Arab staff have all been given a paid holiday. We even had to move several local Bedouin families off their land for the duration. Which brings us to our Arab friend."

The general looked stern, his displeasure evident. "What happened was a disaster. You'll have to do a damned sight better, Harry."

They had come full circle, and Helen Kane pulled up back in the hotel carpark. Weaver saw that the army engineers had just finished working on the special wheelchair ramp, and two of them wheeled it off to one side.

Clayton sighed as he climbed out of the Jeep. "There's also been a very worrying development. Major Blake, I guess you'd better explain."

The major addressed Weaver. "Late last night, one of our intelligence people in Stockholm received an important message, passed through a Swedish intermediary from a high-ranking German source. The information said clearly that the Germans intend to kill the US President and British Prime Minister."

Weaver frowned grimly. "How?"

"The details are pretty sparse, but it seems their intelligence knows for certain that both men will arrive in Cairo some time before the twenty-second, and they've devised a plan to kill them. A specialist German team to set up the operation was to be sent to Egypt within forty-eight hours. Our Swedish contact received the information yesterday evening. So that means it could be any time from then until tomorrow tonight." Blake paused. "That's all we know, sir."

Weaver had turned pale. "I see."

"I guess this puts a serious new perspective on things," said Clayton. "It seems your fears about this Arab were correct all along. We've put extra coastal patrols in the air from this morning, as well as the air exclusion zone. There's some pretty lousy weather due to hit the northern Med over the next couple of nights, a deterrent in itself, but we can't be too careful. The Krauts are desperate and ruthless enough to try anything."

"And not to be treated with kid gloves," Sanson remarked. "Or wouldn't you agree, Weaver?"

Weaver didn't reply, and Clayton said, "You look like you've got something on your mind, son. Spit it out."

"There's nothing, sir," Weaver replied.

Clayton said to the others, "Lieutenant, gentlemen, will you excuse us? Let's take a walk, Harry."

He led Weaver a short distance towards the gardens. "I'm not going to pussyfoot around, son. I get the feeling you and Sanson don't see eye to eye."

"Sir?"

"He told me what happened with Berger. Beating a prisoner isn't exactly your kind of ball game, but it's war, Harry, and we're all tired of it. Like I said, Sanson's had a lot more experience in these matters. And he gets results. So from now on, you'll just have to bow to his judgment. He's in the driver's seat. Understand?"

"Yes, sir."

"If the Krauts are going to try anything, bottom dollar it's going to happen real soon. Gabar, or whoever the hell he is, has got to be involved in some way, so I'm putting it up to you and Sanson to stop this thing in its tracks. Whatever resources you need, you've got. If this Kraut team isn't shot out of the skies first, I want this whole sorry business wrapped up, put in a box and buried."

"I understand, sir."

"I damned well hope so, Harry. The President arrives in thirty-six hours. I want to see progress. You find our Arab friend, and find him fast."

TWENTY-FIVE

GIZA
20 NOVEMBER/4 P.M.
The village of Nazlat as-Saman was no more than a collection of mud-brick houses and ramshackle shops along a dusty main street. The pyramids stood several hundred yards away, and the village existed only because of the tiny shops selling trinkets and an assortment of inferior leather goods to visiting tourists.

Harvey Deacon's car was covered in dust, and as soon as he halted, a half-dozen ragged, barefoot village children crowded round the Packard. He beckoned the toughest-looking boy and gave him ten piastres.

"You get another ten when I return. Allow anyone to touch my car and I'll cut your ears off."

Deacon patted the boy's cheek and turned into a flagged courtyard with a couple of fig trees on either side. It brought him to the far end of the village. He walked across the unpaved road towards the pyramids. The ancient site was on a plateau, with a sweeping view of the Nile valley, and he started to walk up the incline, past a scattered herd of goats cropping at the sparse grass near the edge of the desert. He noticed that sandbags were still in place in front of the Sphinx, shielding the human face of the ancient god of death, a blast wall built by the British to protect the monument from German aerial bombing.

The site was busy. Several military staff cars and a dozen or more horse-drawn gharries were parked near by. Groups of American GIs and British squaddies who had travelled out from the city in the hired gharries were having their photographs taken sitting on Bedouin camels, while dozens of officers and civilians wandered among the ancient mastabas—large rectangular stones that marked the tombs of the pharaohs' nobles and royal princesses—pestered endlessly by local villagers trying to sell them trinkets and paper fans, or offering their services as guides. Most of the tombs dated from the fourth and fifth dynasties, in the third millennium BC. Deacon knew that many had already been excavated, but the work was painfully slow and ongoing, and groups of Arab students and archaeologists were still busily digging among the ruins of several.

There were no troops guarding any part of the site; the only military presence was the off-duty soldiers. He walked further up the incline and halted near the top. To the south he could make out the distant outline of the Sakkara pyramids. He shielded his eyes from the strong sun and stood there, pretending to admire the view down to the Nile. When he was sure no one was watching him, he turned casually towards the north.

The Mena House compound lay below, less than half a kilometre away. He stared hard at the view, made a careful mental note of everything he could see—the outline of the perimeter, the machinegun emplacements, and the daunting sight of several tanks and armoured cars parked in front of the hotel entrance. He would add any differences he spotted to the observation notes he had already made over the last few days, and that night he would send off his signal, informing Berlin he was ready.

What happened at the Imperial still bothered him, but he had made up his mind that it wouldn't deflect his work. He still couldn't understand how the army had located Hassan—it had to have been luck, or chance—but he reasoned that they'd have their work cut out from now on trying to find him. There was nothing to link Tarik Nasser back to either of them. And the man was safely out of the way—dead from a heart attack. A phone call to the hotel on the pretence of booking a room, and a few gentle questions posed to the gullible clerk who answered, had told him enough to figure out what had happened. Feeling reasonably pleased with himself, he walked back down to the village.

The boy was still there, scratching himself as he sat in the sun, guarding the Packard. Deacon tossed him another ten piastres, climbed in, started the engine, and headed south for Shabramant airfield.

5 P.M.

When Weaver returned to GHQ, he went to his office and sat at his desk, totally confused. The handful of staff at the Imperial had been thoroughly questioned, and it was obvious they knew nothing about Gabar. The room had been searched and no personal effects had been found. There were no clues, nothing more to go on that might help them. Briggs had barely glimpsed the Arab climbing on to the roof from the fire escape—or at least he *thought* it was him—except to note that the man appeared to be wearing a suit, not a djellaba, and he hadn't got a look at his face before he challenged him and fired two warning shots. None of the guests who had been questioned had admitted seeing anyone resembling Gabar. But Weaver *knew* it had to be him.

The city brothels were being visited by the police, as well as the alms-houses, and the army was mounting mobile checkpoints in every district, but time was running out, fast. He glanced at his desk, at the mound of paperwork he'd been ignoring for the last five days. His eye caught sight of the photograph taken at Sakkara, and for no particular reason he picked it up, looked at the faces of Rachel Stern and Jack Halder. It all seemed such a long time ago, and a happier time.

"Get out of this black mood, Harry," he scolded himself. He replaced the photograph on his desk and pressed the intercom. Helen Kane came in. "What's happening with the checks on the hotels, Helen?"

"They were completed this afternoon."

"And?"

"I'm afraid there's been nothing. They've drawn a blank."

Weaver sighed. He could think of nothing else to do. He was exhausted, had barely slept or eaten since returning from Bitter Lakes. "Where's Lieutenant-Colonel Sanson?"

"He left word to say he's gone to RAF GHQ. It's something to do with the air patrols the general spoke about. He said he shouldn't be long."

Weaver's neck hurt but he didn't want to take any more morphine. It made him drowsy, and it became difficult to think straight. "The files on Arab sympathisers, I want to have a look at them again. I guess we'll have to skip dinner. Unless we try the Kalafa? Then we can come back here and trawl through the files together."

The Kalafa was only a street away. The food wasn't up to much and the cheap restaurant was usually packed with military staff, but Helen Kane smiled at the offer. "I'll leave word with the duty officer where we'll be, in case anything comes in."

4:45 P.M.

Deacon observed the airfield as he drove past the approach road. There was no proper fence, just a barbed-wire perimeter, no more than a metre and a half high, and he could see the dirt runway with a couple of barrack huts and two hangars near by, two old Gloster Gladiators and another biplane of some sort parked on the tarmac.

It was his second journey out to Shabramant in the last three days, and nothing had changed. The two sentry huts at the entrance were still manned by a pair of Royal Egyptian Air Force privates, sitting in the shade out of the blazing sun, swatting away flies with their paper fans. They looked up lazily as Deacon drove by, barely showing interest.

Apart from a couple of mechanics tinkering away at one of the planes, there appeared to be little activity on the airfield. He knew from Captain Rahman that it was used mainly for training flights—there were no navigational aids, and during the day the place was never manned by more than two dozen men. At night even less. By six p.m. and usually earlier, all of the officers had returned to Cairo, while only half a dozen soldiers remained behind on sentry duty. Deacon knew that even then, security was pathetic. According to Rahman, some of the guards had a habit of disappearing into the local town after hours, or cycling home to the city for the night.

The airfield was perfect—a straight run from there to Giza and the Mena House, a distance of no more than five miles. The question was, could it be safely secured and held until the SS paratroops landed, and without alerting trouble?

Deacon drove past the field and on for two miles towards the dusty little town of Shabramant, where he wasted twenty minutes buying fresh vegetables in the local market, then did a U-turn and came back, heading towards Cairo as the sun began to set.

When he was almost past the airfield again, he had to halt for several minutes until a wizened old man herded some goats across his path, ushering them towards the rolling, parched landscape across the road from the camp. As Deacon sat there patiently, he used the time to etch again in his mind everything he could see, to verify the notes and drawings he had already made from memory: the distance from the sentry posts to the barrack huts, the hangar and airfield; the overhead telephone lines that ran up from the village, and the radio aerial on top of one of the buildings.

But what he failed to see was the motorcyclist who had followed him at a good distance from Cairo, and stopped a safe five hundred yards behind, observing the Packard through a pair of powerful British army field glasses.

5:30 P.M.

The Kalafa was busy, but they got a table near the door. The food was lousy—greasy and overcooked—and as they finished their coffee, Weaver said, "I guess we haven't seen much of each other these last few days. I'm sorry, Helen."

"Don't be." She put a hand on his. "When this is over, we'll make up for it."

The restaurant door opened and Sanson strode up to their table. "There you are, Weaver. Could you excuse us for a moment, Helen? I'd like a private word."

She blushed, took her hand away. "Of course. I'd better be getting back anyway." She looked at Weaver, embarrassed. "I'll get those files ready for you, sir."

When she left, Sanson removed his cap, placed it on the table, and took her chair. "All very cosy. I'm surprised you have time for that sort of thing in a crisis like this."

"We came to eat. What's on your mind?"

"I've spoken with RAF command. They'll let us know immediately if anything turns up. One of us had better stay in the office overnight, in case anything comes in. I thought I'd allow you the honour."

"What about Gabar?"

"At this stage, all we can hope for is that the checkpoints and the brothel and alms-house searches turn up something." Sanson looked bothered. "One other thing. I take it you had a chat with the general?"

"That's right."

"Good. Then you'll be absolutely clear about your role from now on. This is a harsh war, Weaver, and whatever tactics I deem necessary are my business. If you don't like it, by all means take it up with your superiors, but you don't *ever* countermand my orders again, especially in front of a prisoner. Is that plain enough?"

"It couldn't be plainer."

Sanson picked up his cap. "I'll be at my flat catching up on some sleep if you need me. Otherwise, you'll see me bright and early." He stared at Weaver. "I really do hope everything's crystal clear. If by any slim chance the Germans manage to get this team of theirs past our air defences, it'll be our job to hunt them down. Kill them if we have to. The last person I need on my side is an officer who's not prepared to follow orders and do his duty."

TWENTY-SIX

ROME

The Dakota came in over the sea and touched down at Practica di Mare military aerodrome on the coast just after seven that evening. It turned off the runway and taxied towards a large hangar. The doors were open and the inside was lit by powerful Klieg lamps, the area around it guarded by half a dozen armoured troop carriers filled with crack SS troops.

Once the plane rolled inside, Falconi cut the engines and the hangar doors were shut. A half-dozen Luftwaffe mechanics immediately made busy, preparing to give the aircraft a final check, while a paint crew set about rigging up metal gantries to paint American markings on the fuselage and wings. Halder noticed that two other identical Dakota aircraft were already parked inside, freshly painted in desert camouflage and bearing US decals.

Schellenberg led his fellow passengers down the metal steps and across the hangar to a private office that served as a rest room. There was a table and some easy chairs, half a dozen crew bunks, and refreshment of sandwiches and real, freshly made coffee. The co-pilot and Falconi followed them in, and the Italian beamed when he smelled the aroma.

"Real coffee. I don't believe it. You've really outdone yourself, Walter. I just hope this isn't some kind of ominous Last Supper?"

"Let's hope not, so enjoy it while you can."

Falconi filled a cup and swallowed a mouthful. "My God, that's good. You can keep that lousy ersatz stuff they serve in Berlin. I suppose there's no chance of a few free hours to visit the Eternal City?"

"Absolutely not. You're confined to base."

Falconi smiled. "A pity. There's a certain young lady I wouldn't mind seeing again." He took a handful of sandwiches and headed towards the door with his co-pilot. "Try and save some more coffee for Remer and me while we go and check the latest weather reports."

When Falconi and Remer had left, an SS adjutant entered and saluted. "Signal for you, Herr General."

Schellenberg stuck his riding crop under his arm, tore open the flimsy, read the contents, then dismissed the adjutant. "You may leave, there's no reply. But you'd better find Colonel Skorzeny and tell him we've arrived."

"I believe the colonel is already on his way, Herr General."

"Excellent." Schellenberg took Halder aside and said to the others, "And now, please enjoy the refreshments while I have a private word with the major."

He led Halder across the hangar floor to a private office at the back which overlooked the darkened sea in the near distance, closed the door and placed his briefcase on the desk.

"What's up?" Halder asked.

"I had thought I might be able to bring you better news, but our U-boats have still failed to intercept Roosevelt's battleship. The latest indications are that it passed through the Gibraltar Straits yesterday evening, but the convoy accompanying it is heavily armed and altered course so frequently it again proved impossible to get anywhere close enough to torpedo the vessel. By my reckoning, the President should reach Cairo within the next forty-eight hours, even allowing for any stop-offs on the way."

"So that's it. We definitely go in."

Schellenberg nodded. "All we need now is a signal confirming we're all clear for the drop, which I'm anticipating shortly." He unlocked his briefcase. "I told you there was another reason Rachel Stern is a vital part of the mission, and now it's time you knew. As you're probably well aware, the ancient Egyptians had a fondness for secret passages. A practice, I'm told, that has continued until modern times. They say all of Cairo is a warren of secret tunnels."

"What about it?"

"While you were in Egypt in '39, there was a rather interesting and important discovery at the site of the Giza pyramids, not far from the Mena House. A secret passageway was uncovered, one that led towards Cheops pyramid. It seems most of the passageway forms part of a natural underground cavern, and the rest of it was burrowed out by grave-robbers in ancient times."

Halder frowned. "I never heard about that."

"For a very good reason, which I'll explain in a moment. You recall your dig at Sakkara?"

"Of course. Why?"

"The passageway I refer to was discovered by Professor Stern. His wife and daughter worked with him on the excavation. But they kept it a family secret."

Halder looked totally surprised. "How do you know all this?"

"I told you, Jack, I always do my homework thoroughly. The professor's notes and maps were found in his possession when the Kriegsmarine picked him up. The truth came out during his interrogation by the Gestapo."

"You're sure Rachel was involved?"

"Positive. The professor intended to return to Egypt after the war and continue the work at Giza. Rather sly of him, don't you think?"

"And how is this passageway going to help us?"

Schellenberg raised his shoulders. "I don't know that it can exactly, not until you see it for yourself and decide, but it certainly suggests an interesting strategy if all else fails. One which just might help Skorzeny's men to mount their attack with a strong element of surprise."

"Skorzeny's been told about the tunnel?"

"Of course. It was necessary for him to know exactly what tactics he might have to work with." Schellenberg took out a tattered map and spread it on the table. It showed the Giza pyramids and the surrounding area. "The map belonged to the professor. The passageway entrance lies somewhere here, about two hundred metres from Cheops pyramid. It ends under the tomb of an unknown noble, but for some reason the professor found the burial place to be undisturbed. He was looking forward to excavating the tomb, and seemed to think it might have led to an important find, but war broke out and he never got the chance to complete his work."

"You still haven't told me where all this is leading."

"According to Professor Stern, the Mena House was originally a royal hunting lodge. Thousands of years before that, it may have been the site of an encampment for the stonemasons and craftsmen who toiled on the pyramids. Stern considered it possible that certain of the workmen somehow discovered the natural cavern, and might have been greedy and daring enough to risk their lives by using it to help them burrow into the pharaoh's tomb and try to steal the immense riches in gold and jewels contained there, or have grave-robbers try and do it for them.

"All entirely irrelevant, of course, except that used in reverse, the passageway may help you gain entrance to the compound area or, with luck, close to the hotel itself. But you can't know for certain unless the tunnel is opened again and explored. Besheeba confirmed in his report last night that there's still some archaeological activity going on at Giza, which means you may be able to use your cover story to examine the site." He looked at Halder. "What's wrong? You look troubled by something."

"Now you mention it, I seem to remember the professor and his wife had a fondness for disappearing at night."

Schellenberg grinned. "There you are, then. You should know by now you can't trust anyone. But you'd better say nothing to Fraulein Stern for now. At least not until you reach Cairo, and the need arises for her help. Well, what do you think?"

Halder shrugged. "It might be of use. But a lot will depend on how heavily guarded the area is, and the condition of the tunnel."

"You'll have to do infinitely better than that, Jack. I told you, this can't fail. We need to know precisely where we stand before Skorzeny's paratroops can go in. Memorise what you can of the map. You can't take it with you for obvious reasons, in case you're stopped and searched, but the Fraulein will have remembered the details, you can be sure of it."

As Halder studied the map, there was a knock on the door. Otto Skorzeny entered. The colonel carried a baton under his arm, his paratrooper's blouse over his SS uniform. He raised his arm in salute. "Herr General. You arrived safely."

"Ah, Otto. This should interest you." He handed him the signal flimsy, which Skorzeny read.

"So, it's all down to us," Skorzeny replied when he looked up, a slight smile on his face which suggested he actually relished the news.

"It appears so. I was just explaining to Halder about the tunnel."

"An interesting possibility." Skorzeny tapped his baton on the professor's map. "Let's hope it can be of some use." He looked at Halder, his bullish stare almost a threat. "See that you don't let me or my troops down. We're going into the lion's den on this one. So much depends on you accomplishing your tasks. You have two of my best men under your command—they'll do their duty, whatever it takes. See you do yours, Halder."

"I have a question, Colonel. No doubt the Allied defences will include an air exclusion zone around Cairo. How will you manage to avoid the risk of being spotted on radar and shot down?"

Skorzeny smiled broadly. "With relative ease. The two other Dakota aircraft you saw on your arrival are our transport. Fortunately for us, the desert terrain on the lead-in to the city is reasonably flat. Once we're fifty kilometres from the airfield we'll descend to no more than two hundred metres above the ground. Radar detection would be impossible at such a low altitude. The equipment would be useless. And even if the enemy makes a visual sighting of our aircraft from then on, they'll see our Allied markings and think we're going about our rightful business."

"I told you, Jack," Schellenberg said with a smirk. "Ways and means."

"There's also the other tricky problem we discussed," Halder went on. "And one that needs answering. The question of getting the colonel's men safely from the airfield to Giza. What if the vehicles are stopped and searched for any reason? Surely the game would be up?"

"Let's give him his answer, Otto," Schellenberg said.

"My pleasure, Herr General." Skorzeny went to the door, opened it, and barked, "Lieutenant Eberhard, your presence is required."

Halder looked on with surprise as a blond-haired,

boyish-faced young man in his early twenties, who had obviously been waiting outside, smartly entered the room. He
wore a US infantry officer's uniform, summer issue, with
a peaked cap, and carried a Colt .45 automatic in a leather
side holster. He snapped off a neat salute and stood to attention.

"Very good, Eberhard," Skorzeny said. "Tell us a little
about your background in America."

"I lived in Philadelphia for twelve years, sir," Eberhard
replied in perfect, American-accented English. "My parents
emigrated with me when I was a child. My pop worked as
a machine-shop foreman, until he and my mom eventually
decided to return to Germany in '34."

"Open your tunic, Eberhard," Skorzeny ordered.

"Yes, sir." Eberhard undid the buttons of his tunic to
reveal an SS officer's shirt, with silver-threaded runes.

"Button up again, Eberhard. You're dismissed."

The lieutenant closed his shirt, and when he had left the
room Skorzeny turned to Halder with a grin. "Eberhard is
a fluent English speaker, as you heard. And with an im-
peccable American accent. An all-round clean-cut American boy, wouldn't you agree, Halder?"

"With respect, Colonel, one man out of a hundred in the
disguise of a marine, no matter how good his accent, is
hardly going to be enough to fool anybody if those trucks
are stopped and searched."

"I don't think you understand, Jack," Schellenberg interrupted. "When the time comes for the colonel to fly to
Cairo, *all* of his men will be wearing US military garb over
the shirts and pants of their German uniforms."

"I see." Halder raised his eyes. "Again, it seems you've
thought of everything."

"Once they enter the hotel they can discard the American
uniforms and slip on their own SS paratroop blouses, which
they'll carry in kit-bags, along with their helmets and weapons. But until then the subterfuge of pretending to be US
troops ought to help them get inside the building. And at
least a dozen of the men speak English with acceptable
American accents." Schellenberg turned to Skorzeny. "Are
your men prepared, Otto?"

"As they'll ever be, Herr General. Like me, they'll be

anxiously awaiting Halder's signal. Perhaps you would do me the honour of inspecting them?"

"Later, of course. It would be my pleasure."

There was another knock on the door and Schellenberg said, "Enter."

The SS adjutant returned. "Urgent message for you, Herr General."

He handed over a sealed envelope. Schellenberg tore it open, removed two signal flimsies, and studied them, before he dismissed the adjutant.

Halder said, "A problem?"

Schellenberg shook his head. "Quite the opposite. Your contact will be ready and waiting at the airfield near Abu Sammar, as expected. And Cairo has everything in hand and is looking forward to your arrival." He smiled triumphantly at Skorzeny, then turned back to Halder. "Well, Jack, it seems we're just about ready for take-off. Let's get your clothes and personal belongings sorted out, and then hopefully you'll all be on your way."

They had already changed into their clothes when Falconi and the co-pilot reappeared. The Italian was dressed in a flying jacket with a sheepskin collar, over the uniform of a captain in the United States Army Air Corps. The co-pilot wore a lieutenant's uniform under his flier's jacket, and both men were armed with holstered Colt automatics.

"It feels like I'm on my way to a fancy dress party," commented Falconi with a smile. Rachel wore a khaki bush suit, like the others, with a white cotton scarf tied at her throat, and Falconi laughed when he saw Halder's battered felt bush hat, khaki pants and shirt, and high-laced desert boots. "You look like an extra from Hollywood central casting, Jack. Don't tell me, you're off in search of King Solomon's mines."

"Don't laugh, Vito. I'm trying to get into the part."

"I'm sure Cecil B. De Mille would be impressed."

Schellenberg made a final check of their clothes and belongings, rummaging through the assortment of Gladstone bags they had been given.

"Everything seems in order," he announced, when he had completed his check. "It's best to be certain none of you has taken along any personal items you shouldn't. That kind of thing has a nasty habit of giving people away. I lost a perfectly good agent once, all because the fool neglected to remove his German wristwatch before his mission. The error cost him his life. What about the weather reports?" he asked Falconi.

"It seems it could be pretty terrible all over North Africa."

"How bad is terrible?"

Falconi smiled. "Storms, lightning, high winds. Probable desert sandstorms on the ground. Not a pleasant combination. But the good thing is it should keep the Allied air patrols to a minimum."

Schellenberg looked worried. "What do you think?"

"I've flown in brutal weather often enough." Falconi shrugged. "It's just the passengers may find it unpleasant being tossed about."

"We still go, of course," Schellenberg said firmly.

"Then I'm ready when you are."

Schellenberg gathered Halder, Kleist and Doring around him. "Well, it seems this is it. Good luck to you all."

He did a final check on their clothes and belongings, shook their hands, then Kleist and Doring went on board. As Falconi and his co-pilot went up the metal steps, Schellenberg said, "Take good care of your passengers, Vito. They're precious cargo and a lot depends on them."

"Of course, Herr General."

Rachel climbed the steps and, as Halder made to follow, Schellenberg grasped his arm, excitement welling in his voice. "So, it begins."

"Let's just hope there's a happy ending."

Schellenberg touched his cap with his riding crop in a final salute. "That all depends on you, Jack. Remember, nothing less than a hundred per cent will do. Need I say it? As of this moment, the survival of the Reich and the outcome of the war are entirely in your hands."

Halder looked back at him grimly, then followed the others up the steps.

PART THREE

21 NOVEMBER 1943

TWENTY-SEVEN

Achmed Farnad came awake with a curse in the darkness.

He reached over and silenced the source of his irritation—an ancient British-made alarm clock—then screwed up his eyes and checked the time.

Three a.m.

He sat up in bed, scratched himself, and looked over at his snoring wife. The lazy bitch would sleep through an earthquake. He forced himself from under the warm blankets and shivered as he stepped out on to the cold floor, feeling the desert chill in the room bite into his bones. He knew his task that morning was extremely dangerous, and he was aware of a nervous cramp in his stomach. At such an early hour, he also knew that the entire population of Abu Sammar—barely two hundred souls—was fast asleep, but when he heard the howl of a solitary dog he crossed anxiously to the window and peered out through the peeling wooden shutters.

The village was in darkness, streaks of black cloud racing across the face of the quarter-moon. The wind moaned, sand flurries tossing rolls of camel thorn through the deserted streets. Not exactly favourable weather for the important work he had to do. The dog stopped howling and the village became silent again, except for the banshee sound of the wind. Achmed dressed quickly and went downstairs, his excitement mounting.

The Seti Hotel was a decaying six-bedroom inn, but it was a palace compared to the rest of the village's mud-brick hovels, once popular with Arab merchants on the trade route from Tunisia to Egypt. Now the only visitor Achmed saw was the occasional businessman passing through on his way to Cairo. But when the Germans were close to taking Alex, it had been a different story.

Then, the hotel had billeted a succession of British officers, and had once even served as a command post. Ach-

med had gone out of his way to please the officers, sucking
up to them like a faithful dog, and the fools had mistaken
his enthusiasm for loyalty. They confided in him, told him
their failures and successes, and Achmed had learned a lot
about their morale and tactics. What the officers didn't
know was that he had a radio and a Luger pistol hidden in
the barn at the back of the hotel.

The Germans had paid him well for his information, but
he would gladly have done the job for nothing. He hated
the British, and the sooner the bastards were kicked out of
Egypt, the better. Passing the shabby reception desk, Achmed paused to grab a sackcloth bag from behind the
counter. "Time to go to work."

The enclosed yard and the rusting corrugated barn at the
back of the hotel served as a general storage area, a covered
pen for Achmed's chickens and goats, and a garage for his
Fiat truck. A grateful British captain had rewarded his hos-
pitality with the captured Italian vehicle, and Achmed had
lovingly kept it in excellent condition ever since.

Before climbing into the cab, he opened his sackcloth
bag. He had everything he needed—torches and spare batteries. He checked the truck's spare wheel, just to be certain,
and made sure he had the jerrycan of extra fuel. Satisfied, he
crossed the yard and unlocked the back gates.

A savage wind raged into the enclosure, disturbing the
chickens and goats in the barn behind him. Was it his imagination, or was the weather getting worse? He had sensed
the previous evening that the weather might turn bad, but
not as bad as this. He sat in the driver's seat, started the
ignition, and the Fiat roared into life. The wind would help
drown the engine noise, but no doubt some of his neighbours would hear. There was nothing Achmed could do
about that, and he nosed the Fiat out into the unpaved street
before climbing out again to close the gates, then turned
the truck on to the main road leading out of the village. It
ran through the desert, north-east towards Alex, over twenty
miles away, but when he had gone five miles he turned
south on to a desolate minor track.

He halted in front of a pair of steel-and-wire swing-
gates, a barbed-wire run stretching to either side. Sand

grains were tossed against the windscreen, but beyond the gates he could make out the landing strip. With the desert war finished, it lay abandoned, the half-dozen huts and two hangars with rusting corrugated roofs standing like forgotten monuments in the stormy darkness. No one came here anymore, except passing Bedouin tribesmen who scavenged among the dented oil drums and discarded military junk. Achmed climbed out of the truck, opened the unlocked gates, drove towards one of the Nissen huts, and pulled up outside.

Covering his face to ward off the blowing sand, he killed the engine, stepped out of the cab again and moved inside. The hut stank of rotting wood and excrement, and the walls had been defaced with chalk. *"Run, Rommel, run!" "Bert was here."*

Achmed heard a bleating sound in the darkness, and called out, "Mafouz? Are you there?"

Out of the shadows, a small boy of twelve appeared, rubbing his eyes from tiredness.

"Yes, Father."

Achmed could make out the blanket in the corner, the small parcel of food he had given his son. Half a dozen of Achmed's goats had bedded down beside the boy, snug out of the wind. They bleated and stirred, but stayed where they were.

"Did anyone come?"

"No, Father. I have seen no one."

"Good work, Mafouz." Achmed beamed and patted his son's head. He had left him at the airfield the previous evening, pretending to tend the goats. He needed to be certain that none of the Bedouin had come wandering by and taken refuge in the huts, which they sometimes did in bad weather, for that could have upset his plans. Mafouz was completely trustworthy and an intelligent boy; reasons enough for Achmed to delegate the task to him.

"Help me with the torches."

He squatted on the filthy concrete floor, opened his bag, and laid out the four electric torches. Mafouz helped him check each of them again; they all worked. Achmed would use one of the torches to signal to the aircraft that the field was clear and it was safe to land. The other three torches he'd place in an L-shape on the runway, mounted on wooden stakes which he'd brought in the back of the truck, to mark out the landing strip's exact width and length.

Once the aircraft returned his signal, he would switch on the other torches so the landing could proceed, and not before. Achmed checked his wristwatch: four a.m. In just over an hour, hopefully, the Germans would arrive. He didn't know why they were coming—that wasn't his business—but he guessed it had to be something important. They wouldn't operate this far behind enemy lines without good reason. He just hoped the wind had died down by then, otherwise it could make things difficult. A gust rattled the corrugated roof, and Mafouz looked up at him, excitement on the child's face.

"Is the aeroplane really going to come, Father?"

"If it is Allah's will, my son."

Achmed felt the excitement too, but with it came a jab of fear. He had once witnessed a Wellington bomber crash during the *khamsin*, on the very same runway. The aircraft was lifted into the air by a severe gust in the last moments before landing, then its wing dipped, and the plane skewed in a half-circle and exploded in a shower of flames, instantly killing the crew. This wasn't the *khamsin*, but from the sound of the wind raging outside, there could be a bad storm brewing.

Achmed heard the wind rattle the roof again, slipped a set of worry beads between his fingers, and considered the plight of the incoming aircraft. "Let's hope, my friends, you have better luck."

4:20 A.M.
It was cold in the Dakota, and Halder woke from a fitful doze. He was surprised to see Rachel fast asleep, so he went up to the darkened cockpit and found Falconi and the co-pilot, Remer, drinking coffee from a Thermos.

"Can't rest?" Falconi asked loudly, over the noise of the engines.

"It seems not. Mission nerves, I reckon."

"It happens to us all. Here, have some coffee."

He accepted the metal cup from Falconi and sat in the empty wireless operator's seat. When he looked out at the night sky, the quarter-moon gave just enough light to see by. Puffs of occasional black cloud raced past and flurries of rain lashed the cockpit windscreen, bright stars winking in the blackness.

"Where are we?"

Remer showed him a route map opened on his knees. "Just over halfway between Sicily and Egypt, off the west coast of Crete. In less than an hour we should be passing Alex on our left. So far it seems pretty quiet—there's no radio activity at all out there."

"Let's hope it stays that way. What about the weather, Vito?"

Falconi pointed to a thick, ominous-looking bank of dark cloud on the distant horizon, and Halder saw frightening streaks of fork lightning flashing deep in its core, illuminating the night sky. "Christ, that looks bad."

"Bad enough. We'll try to steer clear of the worst of it, but we may get thrown around a little. Nothing we can do about that, I'm sorry to say."

Halder offered round cigarettes, and as he lit Falconi's said, "I thought you would have finished with this damned war by now. Don't tell me you've taken a liking to it?"

Falconi smiled. "Hardly. But it's either fly for the Luftwaffe, or wind up in a prison camp bored out of my skull, and that wouldn't do at all. Or worse still, in a penal battalion on the Russian front."

"You could always try landing in Sicily on the return leg and give yourself up."

Falconi laughed. "I won't say I haven't considered it. Except Remer here might complain. And I have a brother imprisoned in a German POW camp in Milan, since Italy surrendered two months ago. I doubt Schellenberg would take kindly to him if I deserted."

"It seems Walter has us all stitched up nicely."

"You too?"

"I'm afraid so."

"The bad bastard." A sympathetic look appeared on Falconi's face. "He told me about your father and child, Jack. A terrible business. I'm truly sorry, my friend."

Halder nodded, his mouth tight, then turned towards the cockpit door. "I'll go see how the others are doing."

"There's some more coffee in the Thermos if your lady friend wants some."

"Thanks." Halder turned back towards the cabin. "Don't forget to keep your eyes peeled for enemy aircraft."

"It's a milk run, Jack." Falconi smiled reassuringly. "The skies are as quiet as the grave in this weather. Anyway, it's conditions on the ground I'm more worried about—let's keep our fingers crossed we can get this crate down safely, and lift off again in one piece."

4:35 A.M.

Flight Lieutenant Chuck Carlton, from Dallas, was singing "The Yellow Rose of Texas" as he sat in the darkness of the Bristol Beaufighter's cockpit, trying to keep himself awake. In the navigator's seat behind him, Flight Sergeant Bert Higgins could bear it no longer. It was the only song Carlton ever sang, and to make matters worse the Texan had a voice like a chainsaw cutting through metal.

"Don't you know any other songs, sir?" he asked over the intercom.

Carlton grinned. "That's the best one there is, boy. Hell, you British don't recognise a good toon when you hear it."

"With respect, sir, I heard it a hundred times already tonight."

Carlton laughed. A veteran pilot with fifteen years' experience, he was a burly man in his early thirties, with restless blue eyes that seemed full of impatience, as if life were too slow for him. At a mere seventeen years old, he had earned his wings working for a private mail service, criss-crossing America in every weather condition Mother Nature could throw at him. Afterwards, there had been two years flying a crop duster out of Atlanta, and a pretty exhilarating year with a flying circus act, none of which explained why he was still alive and flying for RAF 201 Group out of Alex, except that when war broke out, like many of his American countrymen who had volunteered to fight for Britain, pitching in seemed the right thing to do, and Carlton had longed to see some action.

"OK, our time's nearly up." He eased the stick forward and gently pulled back on the throttle to start his descent from fourteen thousand feet. "Give me a bearing and we'll get this baby home and give those ungrateful British ears of yours a rest."

The Beaufighter was flying night coastal patrol, cruising at 150 knots in cloud. Higgins checked his compass and took a bearing on Alex. They were north-west of the Egyptian port, and he estimated they'd be landed and home in another half-hour.

He looked out at the bank of ugly storm cloud off to his left, the lights of Alex just a dim cluster. There was a sandstorm blowing down on the mainland, the orange-brown swirl just about visible, even though they were seventy miles from the coast. The Met Forecasting Unit of Coastal Command had warned them about the imminent bad weather, but Higgins had checked with the Alex tower every half-hour; the sandstorm hadn't hit the city yet and the runway conditions were still within landing limits. As he finished taking the bearing, the Beaufighter broke cloud at twelve thousand feet. He looked down, and was startled when he glimpsed the dark shape of an aircraft about a mile off his starboard wing.

"Target at two o'clock low!"

Carlton tensed and peered down to scan the black sky. The moonlight wasn't terrific, and there was only a faint glow of dawn on the far horizon, but his eyes were accustomed to the dark after almost three hours' night flying and he noticed the aircraft ahead of them, flying at about ten thousand feet.

"Right you are, buddy. OK, let's go down and take a look."

Carlton nudged the stick down and to the right, and at the same time eased the throttles forward, giving him a burst of power. The nose tilted down and he picked up speed. Carlton loved the Beaufighter. A two-seater, it was a real thrill to fly and one of the fastest in its class. And right now he knew he had the advantage; the target was ahead of him and low, and probably wouldn't see him approach. Within two minutes, he was less than a quarter-mile behind it, and he recognised the unmistakable outline of a sand-camouflaged Dakota C-47, the Stars and Stripes on the wing and tail, and the USAAC legend. He relaxed a little.

"It's a Gooney Bird—one of ours," he said on the intercom.

"I see that, sir."

"The question is, what the hell's he doing up here?" Carlton had requested a traffic update from the tower only ten minutes before, and there was no report of aircraft in the vicinity.

"OK, let's give him a call." He flicked the radio switch to transmit. "C-47, this is coastal patrol on your rear, high at five o'clock, identify yourself. Roger and out."

There was no reply. Carlton tried again. "C-47, identify yourself, please. I'm behind you, high, at five o'clock. Roger and out."

When he still got no reply, Carlton did a quick check on the other three communications channels. One was for the tower and base, and the other two were distress frequencies, used solely for emergencies in case an aircraft was in trouble. He scanned each, just in case the C-47 was trying to transmit. All the airwaves were dead.

"Maybe their radio's out," he said to Higgins.

"What do you want to do, sir? Show him the colours of the day?"

Recessed into the Beaufighter's fuselage were three dome-covered lights; red, green and white. They could be flashed on in different combinations to display a coded identity signal, which was changed each day. There was no way an enemy intruder could know either the code or the correct reply, and by such a simple method genuine Allied aircraft could still identify each other, even if their communications channels were unserviceable.

But Carlton was still cautious. The C-47 could have a technical problem, and the last thing he wanted to do was destroy one of his own planes. But the pre-flight briefing had been very specific. An intelligence report suggested the Germans were likely to try to breach Allied air defences along the North African coast, and *any* aircraft encountered on patrol was to be verified. Carlton intended to flash the C-47 with the colours of the day, but first he wanted to be certain there was no stray traffic in the area. "Hold off on the colours of the day for the moment," he said to Higgins over the intercom. "Call up Alex tower quick, and find out if there's a C-47 in the area."

Carlton heard Higgins call up the tower, and got the reply in his earphones moments later. *"Larchtree, this is Alex Tower to Coastal Patrol Beaufighter. No reported Allied C-47 in your area."* There was a pause, and then the voice said, *"You better bring him back."*

Carlton perked up with excitement. For the last three months he'd seen damn all action. What had started out as a dull patrol was turning into a lively one. The C-47 could still be legitimate, but he knew the Germans weren't beyond using captured Allied aircraft. Either way he was going to find out, and quickly. The C-47 was unarmed and slow. The Beaufighter was fast and had four twenty-millimetre Hispano cannon under the fuselage, another four .303 machineguns in the port wing, and two more .303s starboard. Carlton could easily outrun him and blow him out of the sky, if necessary.

He flicked open the red "Fire" cover on the stick that operated the machineguns. "OK, just to be on the safe side, let's flash our friend with the colours. If there's no response, I'll fire a warning burst and we'll take it from there."

The Dakota hit a pocket of turbulence, then settled again. Rachel awoke in the cold, a dim white dome light on overhead. She looked across and noticed that the two SS men were asleep, just as Halder came down the cabin with a Thermos of coffee.

"I thought you could do with some of this. It'll put some heat into you."

She accepted the coffee without comment, and Halder said, "Am I really that repulsive?"

"Maybe it's the uniform you represent. The man I'm not quite sure about yet."

Halder smiled. "That's a slight improvement, at least." He saw her shiver. "Cold?"

"A little."

He knelt and pulled the blanket around her. "Are you afraid, Rachel?"

"I don't know what I feel."

"It does seem odd, the two of us together again under these circumstances. I can still hardly believe it myself."

She said quietly, "Tell me about your wife. Did you love her very much?"

There was an instant look of grief on Halder's face. She touched his arm lightly, brushed it with her fingertips. "I meant it when I said I was sorry, Jack."

Suddenly there was a sound of machinegun fire, a long sustained burst, and the aircraft rolled violently. Halder said, "What in the hell . . . !"

There was another long burst, the Dakota rocked again, and Halder was flung forward, landing on Kleist and Doring, who came awake.

"What the fuck—?" shouted Kleist.

"Stay where you are, all of you," and Halder got to his feet and moved quickly towards the cockpit.

TWENTY-EIGHT

Falconi looked worried when Halder burst into the cockpit. "What's wrong?"

"We've got an RAF Beaufighter on our tail," Falconi cried over the engine noise. "It came out of nowhere and flashed us with a colour code. When I didn't reply, the bastard fired a couple of tracer bursts across our nose and flew round behind us. You should see him on our starboard side, any second now."

Halder looked out and saw a fighter come abreast of them on the right, the pilot and navigator visible in the cockpit glow. The fighter started to waggle its wings, and moments later its undercarriage was lowered.

"What's he doing?" Halder asked.

"Telling us politely he wants us to follow him into Alex and land. If we don't, he'll blow us out of the sky."

"Terrific. Can you do anything about it?"

"The Beaufighter's got us for speed, Jack. There's no way we can outfly him."

"Can't you try and flash a code in reply?"

"It's pointless, Jack. There's absolutely no way we can

know the correct colour sequence. The Beaufighter's skipper might suspect we have a technical problem, but if you ask me, he's already smelled a rat."

"How far are we from the coast?"

"About thirty miles. Less than ten minutes' flight time."

Halder said frantically, "We have to get away from him, Vito. Do whatever you can."

"Easier said than done." Falconi wiped perspiration from his face and tightened his seat harness. "I'll see what I can do. But you'd better warn the others. Tell them to hold on tight and expect trouble. Then come back up here and strap yourself in. Things may get pretty rough from now on."

Carlton watched as the C-47 lowered its landing gear, its nose tilted down gently, and the aircraft started to descend. Its cockpit was in darkness, but he could just make out the shadowy forms of the crew. He said to Higgins, "OK, he's following orders. Keep your eye on the sonofabitch. Don't lose him."

"Got you, sir."

Carlton retracted his landing gear and flaps and applied enough power to gain on the C-47 by half a mile. "Can you still see him?"

In the navigator's seat, Higgins twisted round, looking back through the laminated glass. "Yes, sir."

Carlton scanned his instruments, pushed the stick forward and began to descend. "OK. Let's take this guy into Alex and find out who in the hell he is."

When Halder came back from the cabin and buckled himself into the wireless operator's seat, Falconi was sweating badly. "You warned the others?"

"Just like you told me."

"How are they?"

"Worried as hell. What happens now?"

Falconi pointed towards the coast. "See that?"

In the faint glow of sunrise, Halder noticed the swirling, orange-brown tint of a ferocious sandstorm, dust rising high up into the atmosphere and stretching all along the desert coast.

"We're about ten miles from land," Falconi explained.

"The only slim chance we have of shaking off our friend is to head straight into the storm. If we go in fast and keep low, we just might lose him."

"Isn't that dangerous?"

"Deadly was the word I would have used," Falconi answered soberly. "A storm like that can be fatal for an aircraft. Sand can affect your engines and before you know it you're dropping out of the sky. And that one looks pretty bad to me."

"Any other good news?"

"Visibility can be down to almost zero. And if we try to fly too low, we risk crashing into a sand-dune. But we really have no option, unless you want to follow our friend and face the consequences?"

"No way, Vito. Can our aircraft take the punishment?"

Falconi shrugged. "The Dakota is reliable enough, a bit of a workhorse, really, but I'd guarantee nothing in these conditions."

They were very close to land, and at eight thousand feet the dark Mediterranean below them looked a churning frenzy of white-topped waves. The coastal wind seemed to be whipping up the desert with awesome ferocity, the orange-brown cloud swirling up to a thousand feet. The Beaufighter was still ahead of them by about half a mile, its navigation lights on. Moments later it banked left, parallel to the coast and away from the sandstorm, heading towards Alex.

"OK, he's about starting his approach. He's expecting us to follow him in, but this is where we make a run for it." Falconi gave a wave to the Beaufighter. "*Arrivederci, amico.*" He looked back grimly at Halder. "Hold on to whatever you can. And if we don't make it, it's been nice knowing you, Jack. Gear up," he called out to Remer.

The co-pilot retracted the undercarriage, and at the same time Falconi pushed the throttles full forward, nosed down the Dakota, and they descended with frightening speed towards the sandstorm. Halder saw the Beaufighter still off to the right, continuing to make its approach, but at the last moment the RAF fighter turned in a tight circle and came after them at speed.

"Damn it, he's seen us!" said Falconi. "Now we really are in trouble."

There was a sudden explosion of machineguns from the Beaufighter as it spewed scarlet flame, tracers arcing across the sky off to their left. Falconi dived down to a thousand feet, quickly levelled out, and flew straight over the coast and right into the storm, the Beaufighter diving after them, guns blazing.

It was like flying through grainy, thick yellow smoke. The visibility was down to several hundred metres and sand flurries crackled against the windscreen, the noise like static electricity. The Dakota shuddered violently in the buffeting and Falconi had to concentrate hard to keep the aircraft straight and level.

Halder saw a scarlet blaze of red-hot tracer fire streak past them on the left. "The bastard's still after us."

"With a vengeance, it seems."

There was another burst, and a couple of holes punctured the left wing as a volley of tracers hit them.

Falconi grimaced, his face bathed in perspiration. "Damn! He's not going to let us off easily. Which means we'll have to try something very dangerous. And if this doesn't work, then I'm afraid it's *ciao*."

Chuck Carlton was sweating. The Beaufighter was being buffeted like crazy in the sandstorm and he knew the engines didn't like it. He hadn't expected the target to make a run for the coast, because it didn't stand a chance, and definitely not in weather like this. He was certain now the intruder was an enemy aircraft, and his adrenalin was flowing, anticipating a kill. The C-47 had a slight advantage: its twin Wasp 1200-horsepower radials were probably better able to withstand a sandstorm than the Beau's twin 1500-horsepower Hercules engines, whose carburettors and oil coolers were more likely to clog. But even so, the C-47 pilot was taking a God almighty risk, flying so low in such extreme conditions. Carlton was determined not to let him get away. Besides, he'd flown in America's dust-bowl, in weather almost as bad, and he reckoned he could handle it as long as his aircraft could.

"He's picked the wrong guy to fuck with," he roared to Higgins.

In the back, Higgins was ashen-faced, watching the rush of golden sand on the laminated glass, barely able to make out the tail of the C-47, dead ahead, maybe four hundred metres from their nose. His nerves were on edge. If the C-47 dropped speed, they'd crash right into his tail.

"Maybe—maybe we should get out of this, sir," he called anxiously over the intercom.

"No way," Carlton answered above the snarl of the engine. He had the C-47 directly in his line of fire. "We almost have the sonofabitch, and I'm going to blow his ass to fucking kingdom come." And with that Carlton pressed the fire button again, the six .303 machineguns crackled across the wings, and tracers zipped towards their target like angry red hornets.

A tracer shot into the right side of the cockpit, and punched its way out through the fuselage. It hit Remer in the side, spinning him round in his seat. He screamed as he clapped a hand on his wound, and Halder went to help him, but Falconi roared, "Leave him! Don't distract me!"

Remer was moaning in pain, bright red blood pumping from a gaping hole in his side.

Halder said, "For God's sake, Vito, get us out of this!"

Falconi didn't answer, his eyes fixed dead ahead, as if he were looking for something in the middle of the frightening storm, and then another burst of scarlet tracer tore past their left-hand side. Falconi nosed down to avoid the blazing gunfire until the altimeter read eighty feet. They were barely skimming the ground now, low sandbanks rolling like golden waves directly underneath the aircraft, and then suddenly Halder saw a huge sweep of sand looming straight ahead, rising up several hundred feet.

"Vito! For God's sake!"

But it seemed as if Falconi had been waiting for exactly this moment, almost expecting it. In an instant his hands were working rapidly, pushing forward the throttles, pulling back hard on the stick, lowering the flaps. The nose lifted sharply and the C-47 barely cleared the sandbank. There was a harsh metallic sound as the fuselage scraped the top, but miraculously they continued to climb.

"Christ, Vito, that was close!"

Falconi's white face dripped sweat. "Too close for comfort. Now let's just pray our friend doesn't see it in time."

Carlton was trying to keep his eyes on the C-47, preparing to fire again, when he suddenly saw the target's tail climb sharply.

"Keep level, you sonofabitch. What the hell . . . ?"

A second later Carlton saw a massive sand-dune straight ahead. *"Jesus Christ!"* He pulled back frantically on the stick.

Higgins screamed. It was the last sound Carlton heard in his earphones before the Beau clipped the top of the dune, the aircraft spun out of control, nosed into the sand, and exploded in a ball of searing orange flame.

"I think we got him." Falconi burst out of the thick cloud at a thousand feet, took in the flaps, glanced back and saw a bright mushroom of flame rise up out of the sandstorm. There was no sound of triumph in his voice. "The poor bastards. God have mercy on them." He wiped a lather of sweat from his face and levelled out the Dakota. *"Mamma mia!"*

"What in God's name were you up to back there?"

"A small game we used to play when I flew mail runs down to Addis Ababa. We'd fly low and skip the dunes, anything to relieve the boredom of flying over nothing but desert. Pleasant, enough fun in clear weather, but in a blinding sandstorm, positively dangerous. You'd better see to Remer."

Halder felt the co-pilot's pulse. It was very weak, his breathing shallow, and he was still bleeding heavily. "He's alive—just about."

"Get the first-aid kit from the cabin, see if you can do anything about the bleeding—and check the others. But be quick about it, Jack. Remer seems in a bad way."

Halder went back to the cabin and saw Rachel standing, clutching the cargo webbing, looking frightened and white-faced. Kleist and Doring seemed shaken after the experience, and there were several holes punched clean through the fuselage, but incredibly no one had been hit except Remer.

"Is the worst over with, or about to begin?" Kleist asked bleakly.

"It seems we're out of the woods for now. Find me the first-aid kit. The co-pilot's badly wounded." As Kleist went to look for it, Halder said to Rachel, "Are you OK?"

"I—I don't know. I'm still trying to recover. That was one of the worst experiences of my life."

"We're still alive, which counts for something."

Kleist came back with the kit and handed it to Halder. As he went towards the cockpit, Rachel said, "Do you want me to help?"

"Not for now, but if I need you I'll call."

Suddenly there was a sickening dropping sensation, and the plane started to lose height. They all heard the engines struggle as Falconi applied a surge of power, but the Dakota barely lifted.

"Stay down, all of you!" Halder went back up to the cockpit and saw that Falconi looked deeply worried. "What's wrong now?"

"Engine trouble. More than likely we ingested sand and it did us some damage. And we're losing fuel, fast. The machinegun fire must have ruptured the fuel lines."

Halder put a heavy cotton dressing on Remer's wound. The man was unconscious, but he groaned in pain. "Can we still make it to the landing site?" Halder asked.

"We're close, maybe eight miles away or less, but there's not a chance in hell," Falconi replied grimly. "I'm going to have to try and crash-land."

"After all our trouble that's all we need."

Halder looked out of the cockpit, but could see nothing. They were down to six hundred feet and back into the sandstorm. Falconi applied full power, but the engines barely reacted. "It's no use," he cried. "She won't respond."

At that precise moment the engines died. There was a frightening silence, broken only by the sound of the wind on the wings, and then the Dakota dipped sickeningly.

"Our engines are out!" Falconi shouted. "Strap yourself in, Jack. And be quick about it!"

"What about the others?"

"There's no time. Brace yourself!"

Halder scrambled into the wireless operator's seat and fastened the harness. There was a terrible sinking feeling, and then the sand flurries thinned and he saw the desert rushing up at them fast. He braced himself for the impact.

At the last moment Falconi pulled back hard on the column, the Dakota lifted a little, but then sank again. They hit the ground with a terrible force. There was a grating sensation as they ploughed across the sand, then the left wing seemed to hit something and the aircraft flipped over.

TWENTY-NINE

BERLIN

It was still dark when Canaris arrived at the hospital in Charlottenburg just before eight that morning. When he saw the carnage and destruction he almost wept. Bodies had been laid out in the grounds in a long line, damp white sheets covering them, looking like an array of ghosts in the light drizzle of rain. The Berlin fire brigade was still working furiously and one half of the building was a smouldering ruin, wisps rising from the charred remains, an acrid tang of smoke in the air.

When his Mercedes drew up on the gravel and he stepped out, a doctor wearing a bloodied white coat came up to greet him. "Herr Admiral, I'm Dr. Schumacher."

"Herr Doctor. Not a pleasant sight. How many dead?"

"Fifty-seven patients and four staff."

Canaris's jaw tightened, but he was hardly surprised by the news. Parts of Berlin he had just driven through were a desolate ruin after last night's raid. "My God, it gets worse. And the boy?"

"He's barely alive, in a very bad way. He was bad to start with of course, but now—" The doctor shrugged helplessly. "You instructed me to call you if anything happened concerning the child—"

"Of course." Canaris sighed deeply. "You'd better take me inside."

An emergency ward had been set up in one of the undamaged basement storage rooms, tilly lamps offering the only emergency light, and when Canaris went in the place was bedlam, with orderlies and staff trying to tend the sick and wounded. The doctor led him to a curtained-off cubicle. A nurse and another doctor were with the boy.

"How is he?" Canaris asked.

"Not too good."

Canaris looked down at the child's innocent face and wanted to weep. His eyes were closed and his head and pelvis were wrapped in bloodied gauze, his breath just a faint wheeze. "Pauli, can you hear me?"

The child didn't react, and one of the doctors said, "You're wasting your time. He's in deep shock."

"What happened?"

"A bomb hit—"

"I know all about the bloody bombs," Canaris erupted. "They haven't stopped all week. What exactly happened to *him*?"

"A shell came through the ceiling of a nearby ward. The blast shattered the walls. Falling masonry crushed his pelvis and caused severe head injuries."

Canaris pursed his mouth. "His chances?"

Both doctors exchanged looks, then one of them shook his head. "Can't you do *anything*?" Canaris begged.

"I'm afraid it's quite hopeless. I'm surprised he's even lasted this long."

At that moment the nurse said, "I think he's going, Doctor."

A few minutes later the child moaned and gave a tiny gasp, his chest deflated and his eyelids flickered. The doctors went to work, but it was useless. The child's head slumped to one side, he went still, and the life passed out of him.

"He's gone," the doctor said finally.

Canaris had seen death before, many times, but the passing of someone so young was a heart-wrenching thing to witness. He was deeply upset as he looked down at the innocent dead face.

"The poor child," he said, and there were tears in his eyes.

Canaris was in his office an hour later, writing a report, when the adjutant showed in a tired-looking Schellenberg. The admiral didn't rise but tossed his pen aside and gestured to a chair. "Sit down."

His tone was gruff, but Schellenberg sat and Canaris said, "You got my message?"

Schellenberg managed to look suitably grieved. "Yes. A terrible calamity. But then what do you expect from Roosevelt and Churchill? They send bombers to destroy our cities, to kill and maim our—"

"Shut up, Schellenberg. I'm not in the mood for one of Goebbels' speeches. You promised Halder you'd have his son transferred to a hospital outside Berlin. He was very specific about that, so why didn't you?"

Schellenberg bristled at the accusation in Canaris's voice. "I'm not sure I like your tone."

"Just answer the question, God damn you. Why?"

"I only got back from Rome an hour ago. There wasn't time."

"You had time before you left."

"Not really."

"Damn you again, Schellenberg! If you'd done what you promised, the boy would be alive now."

Schellenberg stood and pushed back his chair angrily. "I don't have to take this from you."

"Sit down. I'm not finished. You also lied to Rachel Stern."

Schellenberg frowned. "About what?"

"Her father. I checked with Dachau. According to their records, Professor Stern was never delivered to the camp after his arrest four years ago. What's going on, Schellenberg? Did your Gestapo friends do their dirty work after he was arrested? No doubt he was shot or beaten to death in those cellars of yours. Or maybe he's still rotting there? You lied to me, didn't you?"

Schellenberg gave an indifferent shrug. "Lying and subterfuge are all part of this game. You know that as well as I do. True, I didn't tell you the full story. But what of it?"

"So, it all comes out now. You fooled the woman, and you failed to keep your promise to Halder—the one thing he asked of you. His only concern was that his son would be looked after. He loved the boy deeply. You're despicable, Schellenberg, you and every one of your bloody-minded Gestapo and SS friends. You've brought this country to the abyss. But you know what really makes me sick? To know that we're all going straight to hell together."

Schellenberg ignored the outburst. "Don't you want to know the mission status?"

"Oddly enough, at this moment I couldn't seem to care less." Which was a lie, of course, but Canaris strove to hide his curiosity. He was still struggling with his conscience for having had to betray Halder and Rachel Stern, no matter how necessary he considered that betrayal to be, and it weighed heavily on him.

"The Dakota has disappeared. It either crashed, was forced to land on enemy soil, or was shot down. That agent of yours at Abu Sammar whom I used sent a radio message an hour ago, relayed from Rome, to say the aircraft never showed up at the rendezvous. And it certainly didn't return to Italy."

This time Canaris turned pale. *Perhaps his message to Sylvia had got through?* The knowledge that he might have contributed to the deaths of Halder and the woman caused him a painful spasm of remorse. Later, he would certainly wallow privately in his grief for the loss of innocent lives. "I see." He looked shocked and saddened. "It's over, then? They're either dead or captured?"

"I'm afraid so."

CAIRO
7 A.M.

Weaver woke to the sound of a muezzin's cry. He had spent half the night sleeping badly on a borrowed cot bed in his office, and when he stood his body was covered with aches and pains. The clapboard windows were closed, and he had a splitting headache from rereading all the files on Arab sympathisers.

He rubbed his face and opened the windows. Dawn rose

over Cairo, silhouetting the rooftops and the ancient citadel built by the Turks. Just after midnight he had come across something that had roused his interest. An Arab about the same age as Gabar who had worked as a houseboy for the German embassy before the war. He was employed in a radio shop in the Old Town, which had certainly made Weaver stop and think, and he wondered how he had missed the man first time round. His address was in the file. He jotted it down in his notebook. He would check him out first thing that morning. A shower and shave would be in order first, but as he went to pick up his cap to leave for his villa, the door opened and Helen Kane came in, carrying a tray of steaming coffee and a plate of fresh bread rolls.

"I thought you might want breakfast."

"You're in early."

"It's dedication," she said with a smile. "Did you sleep OK?"

"Tossed and turned through most of the night, I'm afraid."

"A pity I couldn't have kept you company."

"Lieutenant Kane, don't even tempt me with a thought like that." Weaver smiled back.

When she put the tray down on his desk, he barely sipped the coffee before reaching for his cap. "I can't stay, Helen. When Sanson gets in tell him I should be back in a couple of hours. I'll be out looking for one of our sympathisers. His file's on my desk."

"But there's a report that just came in you ought to know about. I'll get it for you."

"No, tell me, it'll save time."

"There was a curious incident up in Alex. We received details on the teleprinter from RAF Command just a few minutes ago."

Weaver nodded. "What kind of incident?"

"An aircraft on coastal patrol, an RAF Beaufighter with 201 Group, reported an unidentified American Dakota flying northwest of Alex. The pilot went to intercept, but it appears the tower lost contact and the Beaufighter vanished. There was a pretty bad sandstorm blowing at the time and flying conditions were atrocious."

"What about the Dakota?"

Helen Kane shook her head. "They don't seem to know what happened to it either. Alex Coastal Command are suggesting the Dakota could have been an intruder, and they've asked Cairo RAF HQ to put out an alert for either aircraft, or their wreckage, in case they were destroyed or crash-landed because of the storm. They thought we'd like to know about it."

Weaver went to the wall map. He studied it for several moments as he considered the information, then looked back, mildly excited. "Check with RAF HQ and find out if they've come up with anything more on the Dakota."

"And if they haven't?"

"Ask if they know its heading when the Beaufighter first made contact, and if they've any further information they can give us."

"I'll do it straight away."

Weaver tossed his cap aside, his excitement growing. He could check out the Arab suspect later. "Then call Sanson and tell him to get here as fast as he can."

THIRTY

TWENTY-TWO MILES SOUTH-WEST OF ALEXANDRIA
21 NOVEMBER/5:30 A.M.

Halder woke with a terrible headache, a savage breeze blowing sand in his face. The cockpit glass had shattered and he was still strapped into the wireless operator's seat. The aircraft was turned over on its left side, and his head was badly bruised where it had cracked against one of the overhead panels. Remer hung from his seat harness at a grotesque angle, blood trickling from his mouth, his eyes wide open in death, and Falconi was slumped in his seat and groaning in pain.

Halder shielded his face from the gritty wind, and called out, "Are you hurt, Vito?"

"My foot's caught. I can't move."

Halder undid his harness and moved forward. Falconi's right foot was trapped under one of the rudder pedals, which was a tangle of twisted metal, and there was a deep, bleeding gash below his knee. Halder quickly took off his belt and tied it firmly above the cut to try to stop the bleeding, then attempted to work the foot free, but it was no use. "It's too tight. I'll need help."

Falconi stared at his co-pilot's body. "The poor bastard. He was only twenty-two."

"Not your fault in the circumstances. You did well to get us down."

"Even the Devil has his bad days. I think the port wing slewed into a sandbank, just after we hit the deck."

The storm raged outside and Halder turned anxiously towards the cabin door, Rachel's fate the only thing on his mind. "Try not to move. I'll see if the others made it."

He moved back through the cabin fuselage. It was in better shape than the cockpit, crumpled in places but still completely intact. Kleist was helping Doring to his feet and Rachel was nursing a bleeding cut on her head. She looked to be in shock.

"Are you all right?" Halder asked.

"I held on tight as we went in, but it didn't stop me from being thrown about when we crashed. What happened?"

He told her and she frowned. "I don't understand. Why didn't the plane catch fire?"

"The fuel lines were ruptured and the tanks bled empty. At least you can thank the RAF for that. Let me have a look at your head." He examined the wound. "It doesn't look too bad. How do you feel?"

"Like someone's hit me with a hammer."

He loosened the cotton scarf at her neck, placed it on the wound, and put her hand on top. "Hold on to that until the bleeding stops." He helped her up, then said to Kleist and Doring, "Are either of you injured?"

"A few bruises, but we're alive," Kleist said sullenly. "I was right about those Italian pilots. They're fucking useless."

"Things could have been a lot worse, so be grateful. Get up front and give me a hand. The co-pilot's dead and Falconi's trapped."

They went up to the cockpit and with Kleist's help Halder tried to prise Falconi's leg free of the mangled

pedal, but it was awkward in the confined space and both
men could barely move. Falconi's face was a film of sweat
and he looked in terrible pain. "It's no use, Jack. You'll
need a lever of some sort."

"I'll see if I can find something outside in the wreckage."

"We can't stay here all day," Kleist protested. "Once the
storm dies down, there could be a patrol along to investigate."

"We'll worry about that later." Halder turned to Falconi.
"Where the hell are we, Vito?"

"About six miles north of the drop zone."

"We'd never make the rendezvous on time, that's for
sure. Trying to cross the desert in this weather is only asking for trouble."

"There's an Arab village maybe eight miles west of here.
I know the place from before the war. You could try and
make it on foot. After that, God knows. But you'd better
leave me, Jack. I'd only slow you down."

Halder shook his head. "We free you first, then I'll decide." He turned to Kleist. "Wait here. I'm going outside."

Halder went out into the cabin, but Kleist followed him
and grabbed his arm.

"Listen, Halder, the pilot's going to slow us down once
we try to move. His foot's broken by the looks of it, and
he's losing blood."

"And what are you suggesting?"

"We leave him behind. He said so himself. But better if
we kill him. I told you, I don't trust those Italians. He
probably has it in mind to give us away if the Allies find
him, and try to save his own neck." Kleist gestured a knife
across his throat.

"I'll do it myself. Just say the word."

Halder pulled free. "You're a callous bastard, Kleist."

"Our lives are threatened by remaining here," Kleist persisted. "So the sooner we try to move, the better. That
fighter probably reported our incursion before it crashed.
There could be enemy aircraft waiting to search the area
once the weather clears. If they spot the wreckage, there're
going to be patrols swarming all over this place before you
know it. And remember, we're enemy agents. The Allies
shoot the likes of us, or hadn't you heard?"

"You're still under my command," Halder replied curtly. "I'll have no more talk about killing anyone. And no one moves anywhere until I reckon our chances in the storm. Now wait here. That's an order."

Halder went back through the cabin, past Rachel and Doring, forced open the fuselage door, covered his mouth and nose with his arm and jumped down. The weather was ferocious outside, and he found it difficult to move, but at least the wreckage offered some cover. There was a smell of oil and kerosene in the air. The Dakota had tilted over on one side. One half of the left wing had completely sheared off, and what remained of it was twisted metal. He found a piece of torn-off slat, then quickly made his way back into the cabin and shut the door against the wind.

Kleist waited, looking unhappy. "Well, what's the verdict?"

"We wouldn't stand a chance trying to move, not in these conditions. Better to wait until the storm dies down. Now give me a hand and we'll try to free Falconi."

It took them over half an hour, and by then Falconi's foot was badly bruised and swollen. The bleeding hadn't stopped, and when Halder helped him out of the seat, the Italian cried out, agony on his sweat-battered face.

"For God's sake, easy, Jack!"

They carried him out into the cabin and Halder tightened the belt on Falconi's leg and checked the injured bone. "Apart from a deep cut, it seems you've got a fracture or a break, I'm not sure which."

"Whatever it is, *amico*, it feels sore as hell."

The storm appeared to have died down a little. Kleist went to the cabin door, peered out. He said to Halder, "When are we going to move?"

"As soon as we can rig up some kind of stretcher." He pointed to the cargo webbing along the fuselage walls. "See what you can do with that."

"Get sense, Halder, for Christ's sake! I told you, he's going to slow us down."

"He's right, Jack," Falconi agreed. "You'd stand a better chance without having to look after a cripple."

Halder ignored him and said sternly to Kleist, "Obey the

order." He jerked a thumb at Doring. "And you, give him a hand."

Kleist turned away in anger, and he and Doring began to remove some of the webbing, ripping it from the walls. Rachel found a dressing and a wooden splint in the first-aid kit and bandaged Falconi's foot.

"Grazie, signorina."

"Try not to move, otherwise you'll end up making things worse."

"Are you a nurse?"

"I'm afraid not."

"No matter, you're an angel."

"Don't you Italians ever stop being charming?"

"It's in the blood, I'm afraid." Falconi managed a weak smile. "We learn to seduce women from the cradle."

Rachel went over to Halder. "What now?"

"Vito reckons there's a village about eight miles west of here. How long it'll take us to get there carrying him on a stretcher is anybody's guess. It would have made sense to have tried the landing site first, just in case our contact decided to hang around. He might have been able to get us medical help. But for that to work, we'd need transport, so we'll have to give it a miss."

"What if there are troops in the village?"

"A distinct possibility, but we'll just have to take the chance."

"And if we're challenged or questioned?"

"We stick to our cover stories."

"Don't you think you're being over-optimistic? For one, how do we explain crashing in the desert?"

Halder smiled. "A good question, and I'll try and think of something. Meantime, let's get Vito comfortable."

Kleist and Doring came back with a crude webbing stretcher that almost resembled a hammock. "That's the best we can do," Kleist said gruffly.

"We'll take turns carrying him. What's the weather like?"

"Weakening."

Halder said to Doring, "There's a stand-by magnetic compass in the cockpit. It may come in useful if it's still working. See if you can remove it. If not, we'll have to use the sun as a guide."

Doring went into the cockpit, and Halder beckoned Kleist to help him carry Falconi out through the fuselage door. They placed the webbing on the sand and laid Falconi on top. The wind had died down, the sun had risen, and the visibility had greatly improved. Halder moved around the aircraft. Empty desert lay all around, but he thought he saw what looked like a wadi, maybe a mile away, a few date palms silhouetted against the dawn sky.

He went back. Doring appeared carrying a small, bulbous compass. "Well?"

"It looks like it's still working, but it's difficult to be certain."

"We'll have to take our chances." He told the others about the wadi. "If we're in luck, there'll be water and we can fill our canteens, then we head west. Everyone make sure they have their belongings and let's move out."

Halder and Kleist carried the makeshift stretcher between them. It sagged without any wooden supports, and Falconi had to keep his injured foot hanging over the side. It took them almost an hour to reach the wadi. It was no more than a half-dozen date palms, some rough camel thorn bushes and a few clumps of scorched grass, but there was a small freshwater pool that hadn't entirely dried up.

"You'd better fill your canteens and rest for five minutes."

They drank from the pool and filled their canteens. The heat was already starting to increase. Halder wiped his brow and checked his watch: almost 7:30. Falconi started to drift in and out of consciousness. He didn't look too good.

Rachel felt his temperature. "He's cold."

"It's the blood loss. Let's not waste any more time." Halder checked the compass for west, then said to the others, "On your feet."

They'd hardly gone twenty paces when Doring shouted, "We've got company, Major!"

Halder noticed a vehicle in the near-distance, kicking up a dust cloud in its wake, and his heart sank. They laid Falconi down and watched a British Army Jeep race towards them, its pendant flying, a couple of uniformed officers in front. One of them was standing, holding on to the vehicle's windshield, his pistol drawn.

"Fucking brilliant," said Kleist. "Well, what now, Major? Any bright suggestions?"

Halder wiped sweat from his face. "Just keep your heads." He knelt beside Falconi. The Italian was conscious, but only just. He patted his cheek. "Vito, we've got a problem on its way—a couple of British officers in a Jeep. Can you understand me?"

Falconi's eyes flickered, barely focusing. *"Si."*

"Keep your eyes shut, act like you're unconscious. Moan if you have to, but don't say a word."

Falconi was bathed in a cold sweat, his voice weak. "That—that won't be difficult, *amico*."

"The rest of you, leave the talking to me."

THIRTY-ONE

7:35 A.M.
The Jeep came to a halt and the British officer in the passenger side climbed down. His captain's uniform was covered in dust and he held a Smith and Wesson revolver in his hand. Halder went to move forward but the officer said, "Stay right where you are and don't move. Hands in the air, all of you."

When they obeyed, the captain stepped closer and studied them suspiciously. "Who the bloody hell are you lot?" he demanded.

"Thank God you found us," Halder exclaimed. "I'm Professor Paul Mallory, and these are members of my archaeological team. Our aircraft crashed."

The captain was still wary. "Is that a fact?" He flicked a glance back at his comrade. "You'd better search them, Hugo. See if they've got any weapons."

"Now see here," Halder protested. "We've just come through the worst experience of our lives—"

"Just shut up for now, please. For all I know you could be enemy agents. There's still a war on, you know."

The second officer was a fresh-faced lieutenant in his

early twenties. While the captain covered them with his revolver, he got out of the Jeep and searched each of them in turn, including Falconi, disarming him of the Colt automatic and taking all their wallets and riffling through their identity papers. He came to Rachel last, and looked back at the captain uncertainly.

"The lady, too, Hugo. My apologies, madam."

The lieutenant searched through Rachel's clothes and belongings. "They're all unarmed, sir, apart from the pilot. And their papers look in order, except the pilot doesn't seem to have any."

"Show them here."

"Can we at least put our hands down?" Halder asked.

"You may, but stay perfectly still."

The lieutenant handed over the papers and the captain examined them. "So, you're an American, two South Africans, and the lady's a German Jew?"

"That's right," Halder replied.

"Quite a mixed bag." The captain looked over at Falconi, who appeared unconscious, and studied his American uniform. "What about your pilot? He had no papers."

"They must be at the crash site. He's been badly injured. We had a first-aid kit on board and did what we could, but he's lost consciousness." Halder sounded impatient. "Now, if you don't mind, we'd like some help getting him to a doctor."

"Anyone else injured in the wreckage?"

"The co-pilot was killed. If you could just—"

"Hold your horses, Professor, I'm not finished yet." The captain continued to cover them with his revolver. "Where were you flying to?"

"Cairo, and on to Luxor."

"Part of an archaeological team, you say?"

"That's right."

"Doing what?"

"Working on a dig in the Valley of the Kings."

The captain frowned. "And what the hell were you doing in an aircraft south-west of Alex?"

Halder pretended frustration with the man's questioning. "If you must know, returning from Sicily. We hit bad weather and had engine trouble. The pilot crash-landed in the middle of a sandstorm."

"And what exactly were you doing in Sicily?"

"We were asked to examine an archaeological cache found by the American Army. The Germans stole quite a number of artefacts in North Africa, and took some of them with them when they retreated. A very valuable cache it was, too. Roman, second century AD."

The officer considered for a moment, then frowned in indecision. "Well, your papers seem in order. But I'll still have to check your story out with the proper authorities, back at base."

"And where's that?"

"El Amiriya, less than twenty miles away. When did you crash?"

"About an hour ago."

"To tell you the truth, I saw the wreckage in my field glasses, before I noticed your little group. That's when we decided to veer off course a bit and have a look." The captain glanced over at Falconi. "This chap does seem in a bad way. Did he manage to send a distress signal?"

"There wasn't time. I'll need to get in touch with Cairo and tell them what's happened."

"We can do that at Amiriya, and we've got a doctor there who can attend to your pilot." The captain removed his cap and wiped his brow. He put away his revolver, his suspicion obviously allayed, but he didn't return their papers. "I'd better hold on to these until we get things sorted out. You're most probably telling me the truth, but like I said, there's a war on, old boy. I'm sure you understand." He called over the lieutenant. "Let's get these people on board, Hugo."

"Right, sir."

The lieutenant helped Kleist and Doring carry Falconi to the Jeep. He was still out of it, moaning as he was loaded on. Halder had a sudden and terrible fear that he was really unconscious and might utter something in Italian. The captain produced a cigarette case. "Smoke, Professor?"

"Thanks."

"And you, miss?"

Rachel declined, and when the captain lit the cigarettes,

he said to her, "Damned bad luck, crashing like that, and especially about your co-pilot."

"Yes, it was."

"I studied classics at Cambridge, myself. Always had a keen interest in archaeology. What's the dig you're working on in Luxor?"

"A tomb from the New Kingdom period."

"It's been worked on throughout the war?"

"More or less. With a slight lull when Rommel threatened Cairo." Rachel gave a weak smile. "No rest for us archaeologists, I'm afraid."

"It seems not."

"We were lucky you came along when you did," Halder interrupted. "Were you on patrol?"

"Good Lord, no. We were on our way back to base after a poker session with some army friends in Hammam, but got lost when the bloody storm blew up. Had to sit it out in the shelter of some rocks about five miles west of here. But we're all right now, we know our way home. Right, let's mount up and have a quick look at this aircraft of yours."

"Captain, our pilot is badly injured—"

"I'm well aware of that, but while we're here I really had better check out your story—it'll save a lot of time and trouble afterwards. Besides, it's on our way, and we'll be as quick as a breeze. It'll be a tight fit in the Jeep, but we should just about manage to squeeze all of you in."

Before Halder could protest, the captain tossed away his cigarette and strode back to the vehicle. Halder lingered where he was, turned to Rachel, and gave a faint smile. "You did well. A slight nervousness in your voice to start with, but apart from that you were up there with Marlene Dietrich and the best of them."

"What choice did I have?" she whispered back. "What happens now?"

"God knows, but we'll have to think of something. As soon as our two friends see the tracer holes in the Dakota, our cover's blown."

The captain had already climbed into the back of the Jeep, Doring beside him with Falconi, Kleist up front with the driver, and there seemed barely enough room for all of them in the cramped vehicle. "Are you ready, Professor? Miss?" the captain called over.

Halder tossed away his cigarette, took Rachel's arm, walked across and helped her into the back of the over-crowded Jeep. He climbed in beside her, the engine started up, and they drove away.

CAIRO
7:40 A.M.

"You're sure it was a Dakota?"

Weaver nodded to Sanson. "That's what Alex Coastal Command said when I spoke with them on the telephone. The Beaufighter's pilot confirmed the sighting about ten minutes before he disappeared from radio contact—just after four-thirty a.m. He asked the Alex tower to let him know if there was any known traffic in the area, but the reply was negative. They told him to bring the intruder back to the airfield. But neither aircraft showed up and the Beau-fighter's radio was dead when the tower tried to call him up at four-forty. At first the tower wasn't unduly alarmed— the storm had been causing their communications to act up—but after that they got suspicious."

Sanson stared at the wall map. It seemed his mood hadn't improved since their talk in the restaurant, and there was a noticeable coolness in his tone. "Anything else, Wea-ver?"

"There've been no subsequent sightings of either aircraft in our airspace. Air Command pointed out that the Dakota's usually not armed, and the Beaufighter should have been able to take him back, no problem. They say it's possible both of them were forced to land somewhere because of the storm, or collided in midair."

"Are they looking for wreckage?"

"They're sending up a couple of spotter planes to search the coastal area, and the desert south of it. And they're requesting any air traffic due to fly over the sector to keep their eyes open."

Sanson reflected for a moment. "Those sandstorms can get pretty rough. They play bloody havoc with aircraft. There's probably a good chance they both could have got into trouble and crashed."

Weaver joined Sanson at the map. "But it still doesn't tell us what the Dakota was doing where it shouldn't have been at that hour of the morning. I checked with RAF HQ—there's been no notification of any missing aircraft, British or American, in the last eight hours, from either Egypt, Sicily or mainland Italy."

"What about traffic coming east from Tunis or Algeria, or the chance that some unlucky pilot got blown off course?"

Weaver shook his head. "Apart from air patrols, Alex or Cairo hadn't any scheduled traffic for last night or early this morning—American or British—mainly because of the expected bad weather." He pointed to the map, at the desert areas south and west of Alex. "It occurred to me there are lots of remote, abandoned airfields up near the north coast that would probably be ideal for a covert drop. And it seemed kind of suspicious, the Dakota appearing and vanishing like that—I thought we might look into it."

Sanson turned back. "Contact Alex again. Ask them to double-check the traffic reports for last night and this morning, just to be certain none of our aircraft went missing, apart from the Beaufighter. See if they've got any information that we don't already have, and tell them to keep us posted if anything turns up. And if they spot any wreckage, tell them we want to see it. Get to it, Weaver."

THIRTY-TWO

7:50 A.M.
Halder tried to assess the situation as he sat in the back of the Jeep. As soon as the officers saw the tracer-damaged wreckage, the deception would be over. Up ahead, he could see the crash site looming closer. He glanced over at Doring. The SS man made a fleeting gesture across his throat and his eyes flicked towards the captain, suggesting the obvious. Halder didn't have a chance to indicate a reply, because at that moment Falconi moaned, and shuddered in pain.

Halder felt the Italian's brow. It was feverish, and he

knew Falconi wasn't acting. He saw damp patches of blood
on the bandages; the bleeding had started again. "Captain,
we have to get this man to a doctor, urgently. God knows
what internal injuries he might have."

The captain leaned over and lifted one of Falconi's eyelids, then felt his pulse. "His heartbeat does seems a bit
slow. It's probably delayed shock."

"If he dies, I'll see you're held personally responsible."

"Steady on, Professor. I've got a bloody job to do."

"And this man's life is in danger."

The captain chewed his lip in indecision. "There's a village about half an hour from here. It's closer than our base
and I believe there's a local doctor."

"Then I suggest you get us there as quickly as possible."

"Of course. Just as soon as I examine the wreckage."

Halder made to protest again, but the captain put up a
hand to shield his eyes as he peered ahead at the mangled
Dakota. "Christ, it looks like you had a bad time of it. You
were bloody lucky to survive."

The lieutenant pulled up a short distance from the
wreckage, and the captain climbed down. "I won't be a
moment. Keep the engine running, Hugo."

"Yes, sir."

Halder tensed as the captain moved towards the Dakota.
The tracer holes weren't immediately noticeable in the
tangle of metal, but when he had gone only a few steps, he
turned round, ashen-faced. "This plane's been shot at—"

He reached for his sidearm, but in the Jeep Kleist
grabbed the lieutenant's revolver as Halder's arm went
around the young man's neck and Kleist pointed the gun
at his head.

"I really wouldn't, Captain," Halder said. "Now toss that
weapon over here, quick as you can."

9:20 A.M.

The Avro Lancaster was a robust British bomber, one of
the most successful Allied aircraft of the war.

The one that Weaver and Sanson flew in that morning
was a transporter, its mission ferrying an urgent cargo of
artillery munitions to Italy, with a brief stopover in Alex.

The aircraft had definitely seen better days. Part of the cabin skin had been shot through by flak and left unrepaired, the interior was freezing, and the noise from the four Merlin piston engines sounded like a million angry wasps gone mad.

Weaver tried to ignore the noise and discomfort as he and Sanson sat on a couple of munitions boxes up near the cockpit. They were twenty miles south of Alex, and at five thousand feet they could see the white clusters of flat, mud-bricked buildings where the suburbs began. The Lancaster was buffeted violently by a heavy gust of wind, then settled.

"Couldn't you have found us an aircraft with a safer cargo?" Sanson asked.

"It was the only available flight to Alex this morning—we were lucky to get a ride."

"Let's just hope it's worth all the trouble, Weaver."

They had hit the tail-end of the bad weather during their climb out from Cairo, and there was rough turbulence. Sanson just sat there, stone-faced, but Weaver felt as if he wanted to throw up.

Half an hour after he had contacted Alex RAF HQ, they had called him back. A further check had revealed no air traffic missing in the Med or northern Egypt, nor had there been anything scheduled to fly at that hour of the morning, apart from the missing Beaufighter, and three coastal patrol Tomahawks which had returned safely to base. Something else had turned up. A low-flying Lysander *en route* from Mersa Matruh to Alex had reported the wreckage of two aircraft in the desert, approximately twenty miles southwest of the city, one of them still smouldering.

"Ten minutes to landing," the pilot called over his shoulder, and looked back at Weaver, who was still white-faced. "What's the matter, sir? Don't you like flying?"

"I love it," Weaver replied, as the aircraft bucked in another pocket of turbulence. "Especially in a plane that looks like a sieve, and is packed full of explosives. Definitely the only way to travel."

The pilot laughed, and turned back to set up his approach.

7:55 A.M.

Halder waved the revolver and moved the two officers inside the Dakota. "Remove your uniforms, both of you." He turned to Kleist and Doring. "When they're done, tie them securely to the fuselage. Use some of that cargo webbing."

The officers undressed as they were told. The captain looked astounded, and fearful. "You're Germans, aren't you?" he said to Halder. "You mind telling me what's going on?"

"Questions, Captain, will get you nowhere. Be quiet, please."

When Kleist and Doring finished tying up the men, they secured them to the fuselage. "What do you want us to do with the uniforms?" Kleist asked.

Halder looked at them for size. "I'll take the captain's." He tossed the lieutenant's papers and uniforms across to Doring. "Put that on—see if it fits."

Doring tried on the clothes and they fitted reasonably well. The SS man grinned down at the young lieutenant, who was naked except for his underwear, and tapped his ribs with the toe of his boot. "Well, do I pass for an *Englander*?"

The lieutenant's face was strained, and he was rigid with fear. "Leave him," Halder warned Doring.

"It's all right, Hugo. They're not going to harm us." The captain looked up at Halder as if for reassurance. "Under the rules of the Geneva Convention—"

"I'm well aware of the rules, and you both have nothing to fear. Though I'm afraid we'll have to leave you here."

"We could be dead from thirst by the time we're found."

"I'll give you both a fill of water before we go. I'm sorry, there's nothing else we can do. But I've no doubt one of your patrols will find the wreckage."

Halder indicated for Doring and Kleist to join him outside. When they went out, he jerked a thumb at Doring. "See if there's a map in their Jeep. Kleist, give our friends some water, and a couple of our canteens in case they manage to free themselves. Make it quick, then let's get moving."

"Are you insane? You're going to let them live?" Kleist said in amazement.

"And what would you suggest?"

"We shoot them."

"Forget it, Kleist. They're innocent men."

"They're the enemy, and you're making a grave mistake. They can give their comrades our descriptions. Alive, they sign our death warrants. Dead, the enemy knows nothing."

"I'm not going to murder anyone in cold blood. And we're in deep enough trouble as it is. Now do as you're told. Give them the water and get back here, on the double."

Kleist made to protest, his face livid, but then seemed to think better of it. He hurried towards the wreckage, picking up the water canteens as he went, just as Doring came back. "There's no sign of any map, sir."

"Damn." Halder turned to Rachel. "Quite a mess, isn't it? Still, look on the bright side—at least we have transport." He removed his shirt and pants, pulled on the captain's shirt and uniform, buckled on the Sam Browne belt and holstered the revolver, then tried on the boots. "A bit tight, but they'll have to do for now."

"You might bear a passing resemblance to the captain, but if those papers are checked thoroughly, you'd never pass inspection."

"A fact I'm well aware of, but let me worry about that if it happens."

"What now?" Rachel asked worriedly.

Halder pulled on the captain's cap, set it at a jaunty angle, and touched the peak in a mock salute, impersonating a British accent. "God only knows, my dear, but we'll do our jolly best."

"You're crazy. We'll never get out of this alive."

"Oh, I don't know about that. You always have to live in hope."

Suddenly, Falconi gave a low moan, and Doring said, "I think you'd better take a look at him, sir."

Halder knelt over the Italian. Falconi's skin looked sickly grey, and dark patches of blood were seeping through the bandages. He loosened the belt tourniquet again, then tied it more tightly.

"He's in a bad way. The heat's going to be unbearable in another hour, and he'll only get worse. Without proper medical attention, he'll bleed to death. It's probably still worth trying the landing strip, in case our contact hung around. If so, he may know of a trustworthy doctor who can help." He urned to Doring. "Tell Kleist we're moving out."

Suddenly two shots exploded from inside the Dakota. Halder went white and turned towards the wreckage, knowing instinctively what had happened. "Kleist—you bloody animal!"

When he reached the aircraft door, Kleist was stepping out, the revolver in his hand, a faint plume of smoke rising from its barrel. Halder looked in and saw the twisted bodies of the two young officers, each shot through the head. He grabbed Kleist by the lapels, enraged. "You callous bastard—you killed them in cold blood!"

"If you couldn't do it, I could," Kleist said, unrepentant. "This is war, Halder—"

Halder punched him in the face. Kleist was flung back against the wreckage and dropped the revolver in the sand. He staggered to his feet, his nose dripping blood, hate in his eyes. "You're dead, Halder. Fucking dead!"

Kleist came at him fast, his arms open like those of an angry bear, his full weight hitting Halder and toppling him. He lunged on top and punched Halder savagely, fists slamming into his face. Halder fought back and managed to roll away, but when he tried to unholster his gun, Kleist came at him again.

This time he was ready. His foot came up and kicked Kleist below the knee. Kleist roared in pain and staggered back, clutching his leg. Halder got to his feet and his fists went to work, punching Kleist hard and fast. The dazed SS man was spun round, and Halder's arms locked around his throat, but Kleist's hand came up, gripping Halder's hair, almost wrenching the scalp from his skull. Halder tightened his hold. "Enough, Kleist, or I'll break your bloody neck!"

Kleist managed to scream hoarsely, "Doring—the gun!"

Doring hesitated, uncertain for a moment, then ran to recover Kleist's revolver from the sand, but Rachel tripped him, he fell forward, and she reached for the weapon. As Doring got to his feet, she pointed the gun at his face.

"You bitch!" Doring moved towards her.

"Another step and I'll kill you."

Doring halted instantly. The look in her eyes suggested she meant it. Rachel kept the gun trained on him and said to Kleist, "Unless you want your comrade to die, do as Halder says."

Kleist gave a look that suggested he knew when he was beaten, and did as he was told. Halder pushed him away and pulled out his revolver, as Doring said sheepishly, "Major, I—"

"You stupid fool. I could shoot you for insubordination."

"A grave mistake, Major, I—I didn't think—" Doring stammered.

"Shut up and get over beside Kleist."

Doring obeyed, and Halder levelled his gun at them. "I ought to finish the matter right here. And you, Kleist, you're beyond contempt. You deserve a bullet."

The big SS man wiped blood from his nose. "See sense, Halder. We didn't have any choice." He jerked his head towards the Dakota. "If they were found alive, we'd be caught before we knew it. This way, at least we have a chance."

There was a brutal logic to it, Halder knew, but Kleist's ruthless savagery made him loathe the man. "Except now we're responsible for murdering two British officers. A fact I'm sure will make their comrades all the more determined to catch us. You've put us in even worse jeopardy."

Kleist had no answer to that, and he stood there, sullenly.

"You're also forgetting we have a mission to complete," Halder reminded him. "This is still a military operation and I'm still in charge. Until we're either killed or captured. Is that understood?"

"Yes, Major."

"Now both of you get in the Jeep. Up front, where I can keep an eye on you."

The SS men climbed in, and Halder went across to Rachel and took the revolver from her. "From the look on your face you were quite prepared to use this." He raised his eyes. "What a change war brings in people. Do you really think you could have pulled the trigger?"

"I don't know." She smiled, very faintly. "But at least

the threat of it seemed to frighten the hell out of Doring. Are you all right?"

He rubbed his jaw. "I've felt worse. But Kleist certainly hasn't helped our situation." Halder looked towards the wreckage, anger in his voice. "I'm sorry it's come to this. Those men didn't deserve to die." He turned back to Rachel. "You can be sure it won't be long before enemy patrols are out looking for us. With luck, if our compass is working, we could reach the airfield in twenty minutes. We can only pray our contact's still there. But after that, I'm afraid everything's in the lap of the gods."

9:35 A.M.

There was a military police Jeep with a canvas hood waiting on the airfield when they landed, a British lieutenant and a driver seated in front. When Weaver and Sanson climbed out of the Avro Lancaster, the officer came forward.

"Lieutenant-Colonel Sanson? I'm Lieutenant Lucas, sir, Field Security." He saluted them. "I've been ordered to liaise with you by Captain Myers at Alex HQ. He sends his apologies he couldn't meet you personally, but he has a staff meeting to attend."

Sanson returned the salute. "This is Lieutenant-Colonel Weaver, US military intelligence. He'll be joining us."

"A pleasure to meet you, sir." The lieutenant turned back to Sanson. "Captain Myers said you were interested in this missing Dakota, that it might be a German intruder."

"Have you made any progress?"

"We just had word ten minutes ago, sir. One of our spotter planes sighted the wreckage of an American-flagged Dakota in the desert, about twenty-five miles south-west of here. The pilot also thinks he might have found the Beaufighter, about five miles further north."

"Good. Any signs of survivors?"

The lieutenant shook his head. "Not as far as the Beaufighter's concerned. It's a complete mess, ploughed straight into a sand ridge. And one of the wings appears to have sheared off the Dakota. But the spotter says the fuselage still looks intact, so it's possible the passengers made it."

"Have you sent anyone to investigate?" Weaver asked.

The lieutenant indicated a field radio with a whip antenna on the Jeep's back seat. "I have a patrol on its way, as of five minutes ago, and they'll keep in touch. Military personnel are pretty thin on the ground in that particular sector, but I've put a bulletin out, to be on the alert for any survivors."

"How long will it take us to reach the crash sites?"

"If we push it, less than an hour."

THIRTY-THREE

ABU SAMMAR
21 NOVEMBER/8:55 A.M.
Achmed Farnad was in the yard at the back of the hotel, cleaning the windscreen of his Fiat truck with a tattered leather chamois. The glass was covered with dust and insects after his drive to the airfield that morning, and he really didn't know what to make of the whole confusing business. He had waited over two hours, but the Germans hadn't appeared. The sandstorm had been pretty bad, of course, and he guessed they had either been forced to abandon their mission, or else the poor bastards had been shot down *en route*, or maybe even crashed.

If they had, he hoped for his sake there were no survivors. There was always the risk he might somehow be compromised if they were captured and interrogated, and the uncertainty of what had happened made him feel uneasy. He finished cleaning the Fiat's windscreen, rinsed the chamois and tossed out the bucket of dirty water, then crossed to the barn, scattering the chickens in his path.

He stepped into an empty goat pen and kicked away part of the thick layer of cane-leaf fodder covering the floor. Underneath was a wooden trapdoor, and he lifted it to reveal a neat recess.

A piece of filthy sackcloth lay on top, and when he removed the covering, his radio transmitter was concealed below, a Luger pistol next to it. He had made the coded transmission two hours ago, questioning why the aircraft hadn't arrived, and the signal had been acknowledged, but there wasn't any possibility of a reply until eleven that evening, when he kept his frequency open. At least by then he ought to have an explanation, but for now he wanted to make sure the radio battery was fully charged. As he made to lift it out, his wife suddenly came into the barn, ashen-faced, nervously clutching her apron.

"Achmed, there are soldiers outside—they're coming into the hotel. I think they've arrested Mafouz!"

Achmed's jaw dropped with fright. He stashed away the radio, replaced the trapdoor, and scattered the fodder on top with his hands. "Stay here, woman," he told her, worriedly. "Look busy feeding the chickens. And try to remain calm."

Halder waited with Rachel in the area that passed for reception—a wooden desk with a half dozen keys hanging from a rickety board on the wall—while Kleist and Doring sat outside in the Jeep, tending to Falconi. A group of ragged children had gathered around them, following the vehicle into the village the moment they appeared, and both Kleist and Doring looked uncomfortable.

"It's like the circus come to town," Halder said. "The whole damned village knows we're here. Still, it can hardly be helped."

Abu Sammar was no more than a collection of wood and mud-brick buildings in the middle of nowhere, criss-crossed with unpaved roads and narrow alleyways. Scrawny-looking chickens and goats roamed among piles of rotting refuse, and the entire population of men, women and children seemed to be watching them out of curiosity as they pulled up outside the Seti. The hotel wasn't up to much, a three-storey affair with an enclosed yard at the side, the place shabby with oddments of threadbare carpet and flaking whitewashed walls, the only hotel in a village that looked as if it didn't need one.

"Not exactly the Ritz," Halder said to Rachel. An ancient marble staircase with broken metal banisters led upstairs, and the building smelled of must and decay. There was a bell on the desk and Halder smacked it again, much harder this time, the noise ringing around the walls, before looking down at Mafouz. "You're sure your father's here?"

They had found the boy at the airfield, minding some

goats in one of the Nissen huts, and it didn't take long for Halder to discover what had happened.

"I will find him, sir."

"Good lad." Halder patted the child's head, but as he made to go a thin-built man appeared, wearing a fez and a djellaba. His unshaven face looked waxen with fear, and the moment he took in Halder's British uniform his anxiety seemed to deepen.

"Can . . . can I help you, sir?"

"I'm looking for the proprietor, Achmed Farnad," Halder said in fluent Arabic.

"I . . . I am Achmed."

"An acquaintance of ours in Berlin made a reservation on our behalf, but we were unavoidably delayed."

Achmed definitely heard the words, but in his anxiety he didn't comprehend. He glanced out at the Jeep, before turning back. "Pardon?"

Halder said impatiently, "Don't you understand who we are, man? We came across your son at the airfield."

It took another second for the words to register, then Achmed let out a sigh of relief and wiped sweat from his face, all caution gone, not imagining for a moment his visitors were anyone other than they said they were. He had left Mafouz at the airfield, in case by some miracle the Germans showed up. "When . . . when my wife said there were soldiers, I thought you'd come to arrest me."

"I'll explain about the uniforms later. Right now we have urgent need of your help."

A group of children appeared in the doorway. They giggled at Achmed's visitors, and he waved them away. "Be gone!" He turned to Mafouz. "Get some food and refreshment for our guests."

"Forget that," Halder said. "We're in trouble."

"Trouble?" Achmed paled again, and ushered Halder and Rachel towards a room at the back of the hotel. "Come—this way. We can talk in private."

The grimy, blue-painted annexe looked as if it passed itself off as a dining room, with several low tables and scattered cushions. Achmed led them inside and dabbed his forehead with a filthy handkerchief, still trying to compose himself.

"What kind of trouble? I waited for over two hours. What happened?"

"Our aircraft crashed, five miles from here."

The Arab frowned and took in Halder's uniform again, his eyes begging an explanation.

"Where did you get the clothes and the Jeep?"

"Another unfortunate problem we ran into. A couple of British officers came across the wreckage."

"British officers?" Achmed stared back. "Where are they?"

"Dead."

Achmed looked alarmed, put a hand to his face. "It gets worse. This definitely won't help matters."

"Our pilot is badly injured. We had no option but to come here."

"And in broad daylight. Every tongue in the village will wag."

"Unavoidable. Now, if you don't mind, we'll need medical help. Is there a doctor in the village?"

"The nearest is fifteen miles away. And he's not a man I'd trust—he's friendly with the British."

"Then we'll have to do what we can. I'll need some hot water and clean towels."

Achmed nodded. "I'll have my wife fetch them."

"You'd better find us a room. We'll need somewhere private to attend to our comrade. Have you any other guests?"

Achmed shook his head. "Apart from my wife and son, the hotel is empty."

Halder turned to Rachel. "Tell the others to drive the Jeep into the back yard and bring in Vito—as quick as you can."

When Rachel went out, Achmed wrung his hands. "This is a disaster—the army will have patrols out looking. And before you know it they'll be checking the village. You can't stay here for long."

"I'm well aware of that. But for now, just do as I ask."

Achmed reluctantly plucked a key from the wall. "My life will be at risk, and my family . . ."

"*All* our lives are at risk. Now, that room, please, and the hot water and towels, quickly."

THIRTY-FOUR

11 A.M.

Weaver sweated inside the covered Jeep. They were twenty miles from Alex, speeding along a stretch of open road, the brutal heat of the sun beating down. The endless desert on either side was broken by occasional rocky outcrops and the scattered wrecks of burnt-out military vehicles and tanks, the rusting remains of battles and retreats.

The lieutenant had a map open on his knees, a compass in his hand. "Go left," he ordered the driver, and the man swung out on to the open desert. The lieutenant looked back. "According to the pilot's co-ordinates, the Dakota should be about three miles directly south of here."

They had already examined the Beaufighter wreckage. The patrol the lieutenant had dispatched earlier had located the crash site and radioed back. They were still scouring the area when Weaver and Sanson arrived. There wasn't much left of the aircraft. Its nose had smashed into a sand ridge, the fuel tank had obviously exploded on impact, and the plane had almost completely disintegrated, shards of aluminium wreckage and engine parts scattered for several hundred yards, faint wisps of smoke still coming from a few clumps of debris. One of the soldiers found a charred human arm, fifty yards from the point of impact, but that was about all that appeared to remain of the crew.

"Not a pleasant way to go, but at least it must have been quick," Sanson remarked.

They decided to press on, the other patrol Jeep taking up the rear. Twenty minutes later they saw the Dakota in the distance, and Weaver took the binoculars the lieutenant offered. The aircraft seemed pretty much intact apart from a sheared wing, but the starboard propeller had completely peeled back on impact with the ground. He noticed the unmistakable Stars and Stripes on the fuselage and tail.

"Well?" Sanson asked.

Weaver handed him the binoculars. As they drove closer, he could make out a faint set of tyre marks leading up to the wreckage. "Have a look for yourself. It seems quiet, no movement so far as I can tell."

"We'd better not take any chances." Sanson removed his pistol and said to the driver, "Pull up about fifty yards away. We'll go the rest of the way on foot."

9 A.M.

The room on the second floor of the Seti was a dingy affair, stark as a bone. There was an ancient metal bed with filthy sheets, and the peeling whitewashed walls were stained yellow from tobacco smoke. They carried Falconi to the bed and Halder went to work immediately. He cut away the flying suit and removed the blood-soaked bandages. The leg wound was much worse than he had first thought. Bone protruded through the flesh, and Falconi had lost a considerable amount of blood.

Halder felt the Italian's wrist, then lifted the eyelids and examined the pupils. He slapped Falconi's face, but there was no response. He looked over at Rachel, busy cleaning the wound. "It doesn't look good. He's completely out of it and his pulse is weak."

"Isn't there anything we can do?"

Halder beckoned to Achmed, who stood with Kleist and Doring at the foot of the bed.

"Surely there must be someone in the village with medical knowledge?"

Achmed shrugged. "There's an old crone who passes for a midwife and has the cheek to call herself a nurse. But if you ask me she's hopeless. She also has a mouth that works better than my transmitter. Before you know it, the whole village would know your business."

"How long would it take to fetch the doctor?"

"A couple of hours, assuming he hasn't been called away. But even so, you can't bring him here. It would be far too dangerous, and he'd probably want to inform the military authorities."

"He's right," Kleist interrupted. "Our chances are slim enough. Why make it worse?"

"You'd better ask the old woman if she can help," Halder told Achmed. "Tell her we're strangers who came to you for assistance—as far as she's concerned, our friend's had an automobile accident. Does she speak English?"

"No."

"Then introduce me as a British officer and leave it at that."

"I warn you, the old woman's useless," Achmed advised. "I'd sooner put my trust in the local butcher."

"Beggars can't be choosers. Bring her as quickly as you can."

9:15 A.M.

The old woman was completely toothless, in her eighties at least. She was dressed in black from head to toe, and despite being almost bent double and hobbling on a stick, she looked as if she had an inflated air of self-importance. Achmed and his wife helped her up the stairs, and when she came into the room her hooded eyes regarded them warily.

"Her name's Wafa," Achmed said in English. "I told her as you suggested. She says she'll do what she can to help."

The woman carried an ancient doctor's bag. Her heavily wrinkled face, the colour of walnut, peered out from under a black net veil. Halder couldn't help noticing that her fingernails were filthy. She went over to Falconi and arranged the basins of hot water and the clean towels. As she rolled up her sleeves and made to scrub her hands in one of the basins, she called Achmed over and cackled something in a heavy dialect which Halder didn't understand. "What did she say?"

"She can't work with men looking over her shoulder. She only wants the women to help, the rest of us are to leave the room."

"No, I stay," Halder insisted in Arabic.

The midwife prodded a finger towards the door, scolding him, and this time Halder understood. "Men outside! Outside!"

Achmed shrugged and said in English, "She's a bad-tempered old bitch at the best of times. You'd better do as she says."

"You think you could give her a hand?" Halder asked Rachel.

"I'll do what I can."

"Call me if you need help."

Halder gestured to the others and they left. Before he followed, he spoke to the midwife in Arabic. "Do you think you'll be able to save him?"

The old woman drew herself up self-importantly. "Wafa has helped birth many children in the village—she knows as much as any doctor. Now go—your friend is in good hands."

9:30 A.M.

Achmed took Halder and the others down to a filthy kitchen at the back of the hotel. The table was set with a plate of fresh bread and dates, foul-smelling goat's cheese, and a silver pot of Arab coffee. He poured tiny glass cups of the black treacly liquid for each of them. "Help yourselves to some food. All you can do now is wait and pray."

Halder accepted the coffee, ignored the food while the two SS men ate, and said to Achmed, "On account of our trouble, it seems we may have to abandon our original plan, which was for you to drive us into Alex in the guise of archaeologists. So we'll have to come up with another. Have you any maps of the area, as far as Alex?"

Achmed shook his head. "All I've got is an old Baedeker guidebook some tourist left behind. But it's at least twenty years old, and the maps are not very detailed."

"No matter, bring it here."

When Achmed left the room, Kleist swallowed a lump of bread and cheese and wiped his mouth with his hand. "Doring and me have talked things over. We can't stay here for much longer. Before you know it, enemy patrols are going to be swarming all over the place. We'd be better off splitting up into two pairs and trying to reach Cairo separately—at least that way we increase whatever chances we have. Remaining together would be suicidal."

"What would you suggest?"

"You and the girl, Doring and me." Kleist shrugged. "Or whichever way you want."

Halder considered for a moment. "And what about Falconi?"

"I still say taking him with us would be stupid. Leave

him with the hotel-keeper. If the Italian's caught, at least he might get proper medical attention."

Halder thought about it, then shook his head. "Let's see how he fares with the old woman first, then I'll decide. Meanwhile, we'll have a look at the map and consult with Achmed. He'll know the lie of the land better than us."

Achmed came back with a tattered Baedeker guidebook. He opened it on the table and pointed to one of the maps. "We're here. Roughly twenty-five miles from Alex, if you take the inland route. Several minor desert tracks lead to the city, or you can cut towards the coast road and approach it from the sea, but that way's longer. The direct route, using the main road, is the quickest, less than an hour by automobile."

Halder studied the map. "Are there any troops stationed in this immediate area?"

"Not since the fighting stopped. The nearest camp is at Amiriya, about fifteen miles away."

"How many men?"

"Easily several hundred. It's a large enough base."

"Do they ever come by the village?"

Achmed shrugged. "Now and then they drive through. But once they learn what's happened to their comrades, they'll be like angry bloodhounds, looking for a scent."

"Which is why we need to move as quickly as possible. They could be searching for us even as we speak."

Achmed scratched his jaw. "It seems to me you have two options. First, there's an old camel track Arab merchants used to use, about five miles from the village. Using the Jeep it's a bumpy, slow journey over rough desert, and you'd have to be careful not to get stuck in the sand, but there are several wadis on the way in case you run out of water, and you can reach Cairo in about ten hours."

"And the second?"

"The way I intended getting you there in the first place, by the scheduled train service that leaves Alex four times a day. There's also a rail line that runs along the coast, north of here. The nearest station is El Hauriwaya, perhaps a dozen miles away. If you want my advice, it's probably your best way to get to Alex. The main roads are where the army's most likely to set up roadblocks. The trains are frequent enough, and take you directly into the main city station, where you can make the connection for Cairo. But as you say, you don't know if the army is already looking for you. If not, either way shouldn't offer any difficulties. If they are, only Allah knows your chances."

Kleist looked doubtful. "If we split up, the best bet for Doring and me is the desert route. The oil company I worked for operated south of here, so I'm reasonably familiar with the area. True, it's difficult terrain, but with luck and a decent vehicle, we might make it."

Halder shook his head. "The desert's too open. You're liable to be spotted from the air."

"Maybe, but there's something else to consider," Kleist suggested. "Your English is better than ours. You'd stand some chance of bluffing your way past a checkpoint. Mine and Doring's would be considerably less. I'd sooner take my luck out in the desert."

"You're certain you want to take the risk?"

"Be honest. You'd stand a better chance with just the girl. Two's a couple, four's a crowd."

"I suppose you're right. Well, what do you say, Doring? Are you sure about this?"

"Either way, we could run into trouble. But with respect, I'd sooner go with Major Kleist."

"Very well. The Fraulein and I will try to make it to Alex by the coastal train, then on to Cairo." Halder turned to Achmed. "It seems we're going to split into two groups. We'll have need of additional transport."

Achmed despaired at the thought of losing his beloved Fiat, and he sighed. "I suppose you'd better take my truck. If anyone should ask, I can always claim it was stolen."

"It's going to look suspicious if we drive it out of the village," Kleist said. "Better if you take us out to this camel track and show us the way."

"It's five miles away. How am I supposed to get back?"

"Walk," Kleist said bluntly.

Achmed didn't like the suggestion one little bit, but at least after that the Germans would be out of his hair.

"Well?" said Halder.

Achmed nodded reluctantly. "If I must."

Kleist gave Halder the keys to the Jeep. "We're not

much use here, and the longer we delay, the more the cards are stacked against us. I suggest we leave straight away."

Halder jerked a thumb at Doring. "Go with Achmed. Remove your things from our vehicle and get the truck ready—remember to take plenty of water for the journey."

They left, and Halder and Kleist were alone. "If you make it to Cairo, you know how and where to meet our contact. If any of us are apprehended, we say nothing that might jeopardise our mission. You heard what Schellenberg said—everything depends on us. We carry on, until we're dead or captured. And for what it's worth, good luck."

"The same to you. And I never thought I'd hear myself saying that, Halder. But it seems we're all going to need more than luck."

Halder was unmoved. "You're still a callous bastard, Kleist."

Kleist grinned. "The next time we meet could well be in hell. I'll make sure to keep the fires stoked and ready."

Achmed came back. "My son's helping your friend put your things in the truck," he said to Kleist. "If you come with me I'll give you a couple of cans of water and some food."

"Did you radio Berlin when we didn't make the rendezvous?" Halder asked.

Achmed nodded. "When I returned from the airfield. I told them you didn't show up."

"Send off another signal before you leave. Explain what happened, just the barest details, and that we're doing our best to carry on." Halder slipped the guidebook into his pocket. "I'll keep the Baedeker, if you don't mind."

"As you wish."

At that moment the kitchen door was flung open and Rachel stood there, grim-faced. "I think you'd better come upstairs."

THIRTY-FIVE

When he saw the two bodies, Weaver wanted to throw up. Sanson came into the cabin behind him. *"Jesus Christ."*

When Weaver had recovered, he knelt and examined the corpses. "They're both still warm."

The cabin was in disarray, the floor scattered with debris. He moved up to the cockpit with Sanson. The co-pilot was still strapped into his seat, dressed in a jump suit. His face was grotesque in death, and flies buzzed around a gaping wound in his side. Sanson searched through the dead man's clothes and found a set of dog tags around his neck and identity papers in one of his pockets. "According to these, he's an American flight lieutenant."

Weaver examined the papers. They looked legitimate. He noticed that a trail of blood led from the pilot's seat out to the cabin. "It looks like someone was badly injured."

They both stepped out into the sun again. The lieutenant and the driver dismounted and came over. "Is there something wrong, sir?"

Sanson was grave as he jerked a thumb. "Take a look inside."

When they reappeared moments later, the lieutenant said solemnly, "The two men in the cabin look like they might be ours, sir. They're wearing British army underwear."

"I'm well aware of that," Sanson replied bitterly. "Take a walk around outside, see what you can find."

"Yes, sir."

While the lieutenant searched around the wreckage, Sanson lit a cigarette. "They must be cold-blooded bastards, whoever shot those lads." His voice was thick with rage. "There's no question we're dealing with German infiltrators. The co-pilot's papers might look in order, but you can bet they're excellent forgeries. Well, don't just stand there, Weaver. Have a look around. See if you can find anything."

Sanson kicked among the debris, and Weaver went to look at the tracks in the sand he'd noticed earlier. They led towards the aircraft and appeared to have been made by a single vehicle, but the sand was too dry and powdery for any footprints to have been left behind. Sanson came over and Weaver pointed to the tracks.

"I'll take a guess at what happened. The two men inside spotted the wreckage and came to investigate. They were shot for their trouble and their uniforms and vehicle stolen."

Sanson nodded. "Which means we're dealing with at least two men, probably more. And one's wounded—the pilot by the looks of it."

He called the lieutenant over and they consulted the map. "There aren't that many villages within a twenty-mile radius," the lieutenant explained. "Maybe half a dozen at most."

"Have any of them got a doctor or a hospital?"

"The nearest hospital is in Alex. But there's the army base at Amiriya, which has a doctor, I believe. And there's probably another somewhere in the area who looks after the local villages."

"How far's Amiriya?"

"About twenty miles, perhaps less."

"Get them on the radio and explain the situation. Find out if anyone sought medical treatment there in the last few hours, civilian or military. And tell them we need as many men as they have available to check the villages in the area. I want to know if any local doctor or anyone with medical knowledge was asked to treat a wounded patient this morning, especially someone in uniform. Then call up HQ. I want checkpoints on all roads leading into Alex. We're looking for a stolen vehicle, most likely a military staff car or Jeep, with a wounded passenger on board. Number of occupants unknown, but at least two, and they're probably wearing stolen military uniforms. They're suspected enemy infiltrators, armed and highly dangerous."

"Yes, sir."

"And find out if any patrols or military personnel have gone missing in the area."

The lieutenant ran back to the Jeep.

"We'll make a start on the nearest villages ourselves," Sanson told Weaver. "In this kind of terrain, they haven't got many places in which to hide. We should find them quickly enough. Unless they've already made it to Alex, in which case we'll have our work cut out. What was the name of the lieutenant's CO back at Alex HQ?"

"Captain Myers."

"One of us had better go back and oversee the search from that end, in case we've no luck here." He nodded to the wrecked fuselage. "Let's take another look inside, in case we missed anything."

They moved into the cabin again. This time, Weaver noticed that the aircraft's first-aid kit was missing from its recess, there was more blood on the floor in front of the pilot's seat, and one of the rudder pedals was mangled. As he came back into the cabin, he caught sight of a crumpled white scarf discarded on the floor. He picked it up and saw that the cotton was stained dark with patches of blood.

Sanson came over. "Find anything, Weaver?"

He held up the scarf.

9:45 A.M.

When they reached the bedroom, Halder saw that the sheets were drenched crimson and the old woman was standing over Falconi, desperately trying to stem a faucet of blood from his injured leg, but without success. The woman looked totally flustered.

"What the hell's going on?" Halder demanded.

"She doesn't know what she's doing," Rachel said. "She's only made the bleeding worse, and now it won't stop."

"Get away from him," Halder ordered the woman in Arabic.

"It wasn't my fault," she protested, pointing an accusing finger at Rachel. "She didn't do as I told her. *She's* to blame if he dies."

"**Don't say** I didn't warn you," Achmed said. "The old crone's a fool. You can be sure it was her fault." He jerked a thumb at his wife. "Take the stupid bitch downstairs."

Falconi seemed to become conscious just then, his eyes opening wide, sweat glistening on his forehead, and he gave a low moan. Halder saw to his horror that an artery had opened in Falconi's leg and he was rapidly bleeding to death.

"Give me a towel. Quick!"

Rachel handed one over and felt for Falconi's pulse, while Halder applied a tourniquet again, tight above the knee. The bleeding diminished. "You'd better fetch that doctor," he told Achmed. "We'll just have to worry about the consequences later."

"But your friends need me to—"

"Get going, now!"

"Jack—"

Halder turned, saw Rachel let go of Falconi's hand as his head rolled to one side. "I'm afraid it's too late. He's dead."

10:20 A.M.
They were alone downstairs in the kitchen. Halder lit a cigarette, his hands trembling slightly. "He was a good man, Vito. One of the best I knew."

"Are you all right?" Rachel asked.

He nodded, an edge of bitterness in his voice. "It just seems such a bloody waste, this whole damned war. One death after another, and for what?"

"I—I'm sorry. I only did as the old woman told me. She seemed completely lost."

"I'm not blaming you. I'm sure you did your best." He explained their change of plan. "We're going to try to make it to Alex alone, just the two of us. Pray we have enough of a head start and they're not searching for us already."

Achmed came into the room, followed by Kleist and Doring. "The old crone's gone, blaming everyone but herself. And the mood she's in, you can bet she'll blather everything to the village."

"It's probably for the best the Italian's dead," Kleist remarked. "It makes things less complicated."

Halder gave him a bitter look, but ignored the comment and said to Achmed, "Did you send off the signal?"

"Just now. But in daytime, the signal strength is never reliable. Let's hope Berlin gets the message."

"Repeat the transmission after you return, and again tonight, to be absolutely certain. What about my comrade's body?"

"We can bury him in the desert on our way."

Halder said to Kleist, "Make it reasonably decent. Don't leave him for the vultures, you hear me?" He crushed out his cigarette. "We'd better get going."

They went upstairs to remove Falconi's body, wrapping him in a couple of filthy grey blankets, then Achmed led them out to the back yard. When they put the body into the back of the truck, Achmed's son appeared and opened the yard gates, and Halder and Rachel climbed into the Jeep.

Achmed got behind the wheel of the Fiat, beside Kleist and Doring, then leaned out of the driver's window and gave a wave to Halder. "Allah go with you, my friends."

Halder waved back, started the Jeep, and he and Rachel drove out through the gates.

Achmed watched them disappear in a flurry of dust and spat out of the window. *You poor fools*, he thought, *None of you has a hope in hell.*

"Well, what are you waiting for?" Kleist jerked his elbow into the Arab's ribs. "Move!"

Achmed started the Fiat and pulled out into the street.

THIRTY-SIX

**BERCHTESGADEN
21 NOVEMBER/4:30 P.M.**
Two thousand miles away that afternoon, in the forested splendour of the Austrian Alps, a heated meeting was under way in Hitler's mountain retreat, the Eagle's Lair, attended by a half-dozen Wehrmacht field marshals, two Kriegsmarine admirals, and Hermann Goering, the chief of the Luftwaffe. All had arrived specially from Berlin and had the unpleasant task of reporting bad news.

They were in the large, wood-panelled room used for such meetings. The scene out over the Tyrol was beautiful, clear skies and a crisp autumn day, but everyone's mind was on anything but the splendid view. Field Marshal Gerd von Rundstedt, Commander-in-Chief of the German Army in the West, had been the last to speak, and as he summarised the Wehrmacht reports he deliberately avoided looking at Hitler.

"To outline the main points—our armies are fighting a vigorous delaying action on the eastern front, west of the River Dnieper, and also south of Rome." He gestured with a pointer to the maps, laid out on the large baize table. "I can also report that partisan activity in France, Norway, Holland and the Balkans is posing ever-increasing problems." He looked across the table at Hitler, whose face was a mask of displeasure. "We can overcome all these difficulties, of course, *mein Führer*," von Rundstedt added quickly. "But it's really a question of manpower and supplies. The Allies are destroying our supply lines with increasing regularity, by air and sea. Our resources are stretched to the limit."

"You say delaying action when you mean retreat. Our armies are *retreating*."

Von Rundstedt saw Hitler's unforgiving stare and flinched. "Well . . . quite so, *mein Führer*, but—"

Hitler put up a hand to silence him, before glaring over at the Kriegsmarine admirals, accusation in his voice. "Sixty U-boats lost in the last four months. I believe that's a record, is it not?"

"Again, a question of manpower and supplies, *mein Führer*," one of the admirals replied nervously. "We're simply becoming outnumbered since the Americans entered the war. Even our vessels undergoing repairs are being bombed in the dockyards."

Hitler stood there, his arms folded, his face a mask of contempt, as his gaze swivelled to Goering. "And what does the Air Marshal have to say about all this? Where are the daring raids he threatened over Britain? The ring of steel he promised in the skies around Germany? Or does the Luftwaffe even bother to fly these days?"

Goering, his overweight figure looking ridiculous in his white uniform, cleared his throat. "We do our best, *mein Führer*. But the admiral is right. The opposing forces are becoming overwhelming. Our resources are stretched so thinly we cannot hope to command the skies." He tried desperately to strike a note of optimism. "But soon we will have our new

V-1 rockets and our jet fighters—I'm certain they will give us the advantage."

"We are concerned with the *present*, not six months from now," Hitler snorted, brushing aside Goering's reply with a contemptuous wave of his hand. "Excuses. All of you give me excuses. You say you do your best, but your best isn't good enough." His voice rose hysterically as he spat the words with venom. "Fools! With such incompetence, what hope do we have if the Allies launch their invasion in the west? Next time you come here I don't want feeble answers, I want solutions, is that clear? Now go! You're dismissed, all of you!"

When the humiliated senior officers shuffled out of the room, Hitler collapsed moodily into a leather armchair. Moments later his SS aide entered and snapped to attention.

"Reichsführer Himmler and General Schellenberg are here to see you urgently, *mein Führer*."

Hitler's face was ashen with fury. "No doubt with more bad news." He stood, wiped spittle from his lips. "Very well, send them in."

Himmler entered, followed by Schellenberg. Both men gave the Nazi salute, and Hitler waved for them to be seated.

"I see you still can't manage to wipe that grin off your face, Walter," Hitler commented. "I never quite know whether you come bearing good news or bad."

"A terrible affliction, *mein Führer*." Schellenberg's smile widened despite himself. "But the ladies seem to find it attractive."

Hitler didn't look amused, still in a foul mood as he turned his attention to Himmler.

"Well, what is it you wish to discuss?"

"*Mein Führer*, we have news concerning Operation Sphinx."

Hitler brightened a little, the dark clouds temporarily forgotten. "Our one hope in this entire mess. Well, is it good news you bring, or like my generals have you come with bad tidings? I warn you, I'm in no mood for the latter."

Himmler delicately adjusted the pince-nez glasses on the

bridge of his nose. "The aircraft carrying our agents was intercepted and attacked by an Allied fighter, before crashing on Egyptian soil early this morning."

Hitler's face darkened, but Himmler carried on quickly, anxious to dispel the gloom.

"However, as we prepared to depart Berlin to bring you word, we received another signal from our agent in Abu Sammar. It appears that the flight crew were killed. But Halder and the others survived without injury and managed to make contact."

Hitler stood abruptly, paced the room with growing anger. "More disaster! Does it ever end?"

"Perhaps not entirely a disaster, *mein Führer*," Himmler suggested. "It seems Halder is intent on proceeding with the operation."

Hitler turned on him. "And what about the Allies? They're not fools. Once they discover what's happened, no doubt they'll do their utmost to hunt our people down."

"Even so," Himmler offered reassuringly, "that assumes they would be immediately aware of our exact intentions, something which is highly unlikely. We used an American Dakota, which should help confuse matters for a time—it's not unknown for the Allies to shoot down their own aircraft in error, no more than it is for us. And if Halder is intent on carrying on, he's obviously convinced there's still a chance he can reach Cairo."

Hitler sighed, crossed to the panoramic window. "It doesn't augur well and I still don't like it. Have you informed Canaris?"

"He's aware of the loss of the aircraft, but not the latest news. Walther will let him know when we return to Berlin."

Hitler's face twisted in contempt. "I don't trust the man. I'm convinced he's spreading rumours behind my back, that the war is lost and I'm insane. If he is, he'll pay dearly."

He looked over at Schellenberg. "Still, this man Halder of his seems an able fellow."

"One of the Abwehr's best, and an excellent choice for our purposes. If anyone can accomplish what we intend, Halder's the one to do it."

"And what news of the Jew, Roosevelt?"

"It's likely he'll arrive in Cairo within the next twenty-four hours. Our agent in Oran reliably reported that the *Iowa* docked off the Algerian coast just after oh seven hundred hours, yesterday morning."

"And yet our U-boats failed to destroy the vessel *en route*," Hitler said bitterly.

Himmler had already broken the news of that particular failure the previous evening.

"Our wolf packs tried repeatedly to intercept the *Iowa, mein Führer*. But the convoy was so heavily armed and altered course so frequently it proved impossible to get anywhere near the vessel."

Hitler stood at the broad window for several moments, looking out at the mountains, hands clasped behind his back, rocking up and down on the balls of his feet, as if considering the situation. After a while he turned to Himmler. "So, Sphinx, such as it is, remains our last hope."

"At the best of times, a mission like this is bound to be fraught with difficulties. And the problems we've encountered don't help matters. But I'm convinced there's still a reasonable chance Halder can achieve his objective."

Hitler banged a fist into his open palm and his voice rose to a scream. "A reasonable chance isn't good enough. If the Allied invasion is agreed, then the war is lost. Roosevelt's death would give Germany the most precious advantage of all—time. It will give our industry a full year. With that year we can win the war. That is why this mission *can't* fail. I want immediate reports from now on—any information concerning Sphinx's progress, I'm to be informed at once."

"With respect, *mein Führer*," Schellenberg interrupted quietly, "even if Halder disappoints us, we may still have an ace up our sleeve."

Hitler wiped spittle from his lips and looked across knowingly. "And you'd better pray to God this ace of yours works. Dismissed."

EL HAUWARIYA,
TWENTY MILES WEST OF ALEXANDRIA/
11:25 A.M.

Halder halted the Jeep outside the whitewashed railway station. They hadn't encountered any checkpoints during the fifty-minute trip across the desert, and as they drove into El Hauwariya no one seemed to pay them much attention. The landscape around was flat and endless, the desert on three sides, the turquoise Mediterranean in the very far distance. The village was larger and more bustling than Abu Sammar, but just as shabby, with badly paved roads and a couple of small decrepit hotels, and there was a lively camel market in progress in the crowded main square as they drove past. The station looked quiet enough, but as Halder pulled up he noticed a military police Jeep parked further along the kerb. "Not very promising. You'd better wait here while I have a look."

"Can't I go with you?"

"Best not, in case there's trouble. Besides, an army officer on his own shouldn't attract much attention, but with a pretty woman on his arm people are bound to notice." He smiled and stepped out of the driver's seat, then adjusted the belt of his holstered revolver. "Try not to look too worried. And if anyone asks, tell them your boyfriend's gone inside."

The station was busy, dozens of people waiting around on the platform, mostly Arab peasants in worn djellabas, but as Halder started to approach the ticket desk window, he saw two armed British military policemen, with red hat bands and white ankle leggings, standing off to one side. One of them, a corporal, carried a Sten gun. The sergeant with him was scrutinising passengers as they passed through the ticket barrier. Halder pretended to check a timetable pasted on the wall, but before he had a chance to leave, the sergeant came over and saluted. "Morning, sir. May I enquire if you're travelling?"

Halder frowned, returned the salute, and mimicked a perfect upper-class English accent. "Why, Sergeant? Whatever's the matter?"

The man looked him up and down, reluctant to offer an explanation. "Well, Sergeant, I asked you a question."

"There's been an incident not far from here, sir," the sergeant said. "A couple of British soldiers were murdered by enemy agents."

"Good Lord." Halder noticed the second MP glance over

in his direction as he checked the papers of an Arab couple passing through the ticket barrier.

"I'm afraid you still didn't answer my question, sir," the sergeant persisted. "Are you travelling?"

Halder shook his head. "Afraid not. I'm meeting someone. But I think I got the damned times mixed up. It's the next train."

"I'm sorry, sir, but I'll still have to ask to see your papers."

"Of course, I quite understand." Halder fished in his pocket, pretending to look for his ID, but really trying to gauge whether he could manage to shoot both MPs if it came to it. "Do you know the names of the two chaps who were killed? I might have known them."

"I'm afraid not yet, sir. But I'm sure we will, soon enough."

Halder presented his ID, and before the sergeant could get a thorough look at the photograph, he held out his hand for him to give it back. The man made no move to return the document. He looked up, the watchful eyes under the peaked cap staring into Halder's face. "Captain Jameson, is it, sir?"

"Of course."

"There's a problem with this ID."

Halder felt his heart sink. "What sort of problem?"

"It's out of date by a week, sir." The sergeant waited for an explanation.

Halder promptly took back the ID and examined it. "You're absolutely right. You've got me there, I'm afraid. Must have slipped my mind. What can I say?"

"You mind me asking where you're billeted, sir?"

"At Amiriya." Halder sounded irritated. "Look, is all this really necessary? I can understand you've got a job to do, and my ID's a little out of date, but, good Lord, man, it ought to be evident I'm British, not a bloody enemy agent. Give Amiriya a call if you've nothing better to do. Ask to speak with the CO. If the old man's not in too foul a mood, he'll vouch for me. Carry on, Sergeant, I'll wait here with the corporal."

The sergeant hesitated, pursing his lips in indecision, but the blunt offer seemed to satisfy him. "That won't be necessary, sir. But if I were you I'd get the ID sorted out as soon as possible."

"Of course. Damned negligent of me." Halder slipped it back in his pocket. "Bad luck our two chaps being killed. Christ, you'd think we were bloody safe from that sort of thing after we kicked Jerry out, but apparently not. It all sounds pretty serious."

"Not half as serious as it's going to be when we catch them, sir."

"I'm sure you're right." Halder glanced at his watch and sighed. "Well, I suppose I'd better find something to do until the right train arrives. I wish you luck, Sergeant."

"I'm pretty certain we'll find them, sir. We only got the word ten minutes ago as we were passing through town, but I heard that checkpoints are being set up on every road into Alex. They haven't got a ruddy hope in hell of escaping."

Halder left the station feeling utterly depressed and walked back to the Jeep, slipping in beside Rachel. He removed his cap and wiped sweat from his brow. Rachel said, "Is there a problem?"

"I think you could say that. It looks like they're definitely on to us." He explained the situation, then reached across and touched her hand. "The whole thing's a damned mess. Even if I let you take your chances alone, you'd still be in trouble."

"I'm not so naïve as to think I'll get gentle treatment if I'm caught. I'd still rather take my chances with you. You're sure there's no other way we can get to Alex?"

"I don't see how. The checkpoints on the roads are bound to be thorough. We're caught like rats in a trap, whichever way we turn." He gestured northwards, towards the sea.

"We could attempt heading towards the coast and try stealing a boat from somewhere, but I wouldn't rate our chances of getting very far before the theft was reported. And we'd be sitting ducks out on the water, once the army came after us."

"There must be *some* way we can get on board the train. If we wait around here, we're bound to be caught."

"Short of following in the Jeep and trying to jump on, but that would give the game away." Halder shook his head. "I can't think of anything else, unless we can get rid of our two friends watching the ticket counter."

"What did you tell them you were doing at the station?"

Halder explained. Just then they heard the whistle of a steam engine. Further down the track a plume of thick smoke rose into the air. The train was only minutes from arriving. "Any suggestions?"

Rachel looked over at the Military Police Jeep. "Just one. But will it work?"

THIRTY-SEVEN

Rachel saw the two military policemen as soon as she stepped into the station. The sergeant approached her. "Excuse me, miss. Are you travelling?"

"Yes. Why?"

"Where to, miss?"

"Alex."

"May I see some identification, please?"

Rachel pretended to search in her bag. "I'm sorry, I don't seem to have any with me. I came out in such a rush this morning, you see. I must have forgotten my papers."

"Are you British, miss?"

"South African."

The sergeant said politely, "And may I ask what you're doing in town?"

"I came on an earlier train to meet a friend at the station, but he didn't turn up."

"And who might that be?"

Rachel frowned. "Look, do you mind telling me what all this is about?"

"That isn't any of your business, miss."

"It is if I'm being stopped," Rachel said boldly, and glanced at the corporal beside the ticket gate. "You're looking for someone, aren't you?"

The sergeant's eyebrows rose. "Now why would you ask that?"

"My father's a colonel, serving in Cairo. You get to know when something's up with the military—they get in such an obvious tizzy. Who or what are you looking for?"

"That's privileged information, miss. And I'll need some sort of confirmation of your identity. Otherwise I can't let you board."

"Well, I can't help you, unless you phone my father in Alex. Look, I've had a difficult enough morning as it is. I came here to meet my boyfriend, and he stood me up. His name's Captain Jameson and he's stationed at Amiriya. Perhaps if you could radio the camp and find out what's happened to him? If he's there, I'm sure he can vouch for me."

"Jameson, miss?" The sergeant frowned. "He was here only five minutes ago. Thought he'd got the train times mixed up. But he said he'd be back."

"Really?" Rachel pretended relief. "Well, thank God for that—I thought I'd made a wasted trip."

Beyond the ticket barrier, the waiting passengers were dragging their belongings closer to the platform, and there was the faint rattle of metal wheels. Rachel said to the sergeant, "Look, I hope you don't mind me saying this, but you've done me such a good turn. Is that your vehicle outside?"

"Why do you ask?"

"I just saw two men a few minutes ago, acting awfully suspiciously. They drove up to the station in a Jeep, and when they saw yours they seemed to panic. They got out of their Jeep and took a military staff car parked near by, then drove off in a hurry. The whole thing looked terribly suspect."

The sergeant's face clouded. "What did these men look like?"

"It all happened so fast. I didn't get a proper look. But one of them wore an officer's uniform and the other was dressed in a civilian suit. That's all I remember."

The sergeant pulled out his pistol. Behind him, an ancient black train came alongside the platform in a squeal of metal and clouds of steam. "Did you see which way they went?"

"Out of town, heading east. I hope you don't mind me telling you all this."

"Not at all, miss, you've been a great help." The sergeant beckoned the corporal. "Get out to the Jeep, Charlie, quick as you can. I think we're on to something." The corporal raced towards the exit, and the sergeant tipped his cap at Rachel as he followed him out. "Thanks, miss. Thanks a lot."

Moments later, Halder joined her at the ticket barrier. Rachel had bought two tickets and they boarded. The carriages were ancient and filthy, smelling of stale sweat and coal smoke, many of them filled with noisy peasant families, the overhead racks packed with their belongings—sacks and baskets of farm produce bound for the bazaars and markets of Alex. They had to move to the end of the train before they found an empty carriage to themselves, and Halder slumped into the hard wooden seat as the train pulled out.

"That was damned close. I really didn't think we'd make it." He smiled at Rachel without humour. "One hurdle over with. How many more to go? Up to now, the military didn't know what we looked like. But that'll soon change as soon as those MPs can't find who they're looking for and put two and two together."

"How long will it take to reach Alex?"

"Barring no more problems, about half an hour. Let's hope our two friends are kept busy for at least that."

"But what if there are more police checking papers when the train pulls into Ramleh station?"

"It crossed my mind. Which is why we'll get off one stop before Ramleh and take a train or taxi the rest of the way into the city. According to Achmed, there's a train for Cairo at two-fifteen, which should give us plenty of time to scout out the station and see if the police have got it under watch."

"And what if they have?"

"Let's worry about that if and when we get to Alex. In the meantime, I ought to get out of this uniform, and you'd better change your clothes. Did you have to show your papers to the sergeant?"

"No."

"Good. It might make things a little easier. They won't have a name to go on. Have you make-up in that bag of yours?"

"A little."

"Try to alter your appearance as best you can. I'll ditch my suitcase and put some of my things in with yours—we can't go traipsing around looking like bewildered refugees. And well done, by the way. You must have given a convincing performance. Those MPs drove off like they had a rocket attached to their Jeep."

"I still don't know how I mustered the courage," Rachel admitted.

"That's simple," Halder said. "Just think of the alternative."

THIRTY-EIGHT

CAIRO
21 NOVEMBER/1:30 P.M.
Harvey Deacon was in his office when the telephone rang. He picked it up anxiously. "Deacon." He listened, then thanked his caller. "I'm grateful for your help, Omar. I know I can rely on your discretion. If you get any more information, call me at once."

He slammed down the telephone and sat grimly shaking his head, dabbing his brow with a handkerchief before stepping over to one of the cabin portholes. As he lit a cigar to help steady his nerves, he saw that his hands were trembling. His contacts should have landed over eight hours ago, and arrived in Cairo before now.

He'd gone to the Pharaoh's Garden opposite the railway station at nine that morning, wearing his Panama hat and a fresh rose in his buttonhole, to await the first train from Alex. He'd sat outside on the terrace drinking coffee and reading the *Egyptian Gazette*, but they hadn't shown up. He'd gone back to the café three hours later, before the second train arrived, but with the same result. The next wasn't due until after four, and Deacon had decided to return to the club, a terrible feeling of doom in the pit of his stomach.

As he paced the room, his anxiety deepened. Something had gone drastically wrong, and now that he knew what it was, his nerves were even more on edge. In desperation, he had telephoned the Royal Egyptian Air Force Headquarters and asked for Captain Omar Rahman. The captain had contacts in all the right places, police and army, and ten minutes later he returned his call, this time from a public coin box. Another call half an hour later and Deacon had the information he had been dreading. The army and police were looking for a man and a woman, suspected German infiltrators, whose aircraft had crashed in the desert south of Alex. A massive search was about to get under way.

"They're sealing up Alex as tight as a tomb," Omar told him. "That's all I can find out, my friend. But it sounds serious."

Where the other two Germans had vanished to, Deacon hadn't a clue, and he didn't dare enquire, but the information confirmed his worst fears. He'd suspected all along that Berlin had put the operation together too hastily. Now the whole thing was a terrible mess. A man and a woman, Omar had said. There were supposed to be four people; three men and a woman. What had happened to the other two? There had to be *something* he could do to try to rescue the situation. But if the four had split up and gone in different directions, it wouldn't help matters, and time was against him. How could he even hope to find them before the police and army, let alone get them out of Alex? And if they couldn't make it to the boat at Rashid, they'd almost certainly be caught.

For several minutes Deacon stood at the porthole, his brain working feverishly, until he made up his mind what to do, then he crossed to the wall and pulled a tasselled cord.

His manservant appeared. "Effendi?"

Deacon tugged on his Panama hat, picked up the keys to the Packard. "I'll be gone for an hour, perhaps less. Stand by the phone. If anyone calls looking for me, take their message and tell them I'll call them back."

ALEXANDRIA
12:40 P.M.

"It seems they might have been two British officers, missing from the army base at Amiriya. A Captain Jameson and a Lieutenant Grey."

As Captain Myers put down the telephone, Weaver sighed. He was in Myers's office at Alex Military HQ, while Sanson carried on the desert search.

"That was their CO I just spoke with," Myers added. "He reported them missing an hour ago. They didn't show up for duty this morning, and he thought they might have got into trouble during the sandstorm."

"What else did you learn?"

Myers glanced at the information he'd jotted in his notebook. "The lieutenant was twenty-one. He'd only been commissioned and posted to Egypt a month ago. He and the captain went to a card game hosted by some military friends in Hammam yesterday evening." He looked up. "They were probably caught in the storm, all right, but somehow stumbled on the crash site. The poor chaps walked right into trouble." Myers hesitated. "I trust Lieutenant Lucas has been of help? Sorry I couldn't meet you this morning, but I had a staff meeting to attend."

"Sure," Weaver said distractedly. He studied the wall map and found Amiriya. Myers came round from his desk—a small, barrel-chested man, quick on his feet, with a crisp English accent. "You said you'd like to know what routes these intruder chappies might try and use to escape. That's assuming they don't stick around Alex."

"I don't think we can assume anything, except that they're armed and highly dangerous. But if I was them I'd be trying to lose myself in the biggest city I could find, either here or Cairo."

Myers pointed to a map of the city. "We've got the main railway and tram station, right here in the centre of town. It's called the Ramleh. The trains run to Cairo four times a day, morning, afternoon, evening, and the last one at midnight. There's also the main road, which takes about three hours by car or public bus. The buses for Cairo leave four times a day from the railway station. As does public transport for all other major destinations—Port Said, Rashid, and so on."

"Are there any other routes?"

The captain scratched his jaw. "There's always open desert, of course, which avoids the main roads. But trying to cross terrain like that would be suicidal. Far too many minefields still around that haven't been dealt with, and the journey's slow and difficult. You mind me asking what you think these infiltrators are up to, sir? The nearest German lines are in Italy, and the war's been over in this neck of the woods for months. It seems rather odd."

"We don't know," Weaver lied. "But it's imperative we find them."

Myers shrugged. "The problem is we don't have any idea what they look like, and *exactly* how many there are. You say at least two people, possibly more."

Weaver nodded. "Most likely they're German, but don't discount them being Egyptian, or disguised as Arabs."

"It's all very vague, and that's going to make things difficult. But I can have the rail and bus stations watched, and the main roads. I'll ask the local police to help. We'll see what turns up."

"Remember, they're dangerous and on the run. If they see troops and police all over the place, there could be trouble. So I want a plainclothes presence at the stations, not uniforms, and tell the men to be extra careful. I don't want the shoot-out at the OK Corral and bodies piled on the streets. What about the desert route?"

"Sir?"

"How can we cover that way of escape?"

"It's really too vast an area for us to mount effective patrols. But I can try and get a spotter plane up."

"Then do it. How many airfields are there in Alex?"

"Two main ones, and two more minor airfields towards Port Said." Myers shook his head, knowingly. "They're strictly for military use and security's tight. They'd never get past the gates, let alone board an aircraft without the right travel permit and passes."

"Still, you'd better alert them just in case. Are there *any* other ways out of the city?"

Myers pointed to the map again. "From the harbour. But

it's hardly an ideal choice, even if they managed to steal or get on board a boat. The route's too slow, and where can they go? Our naval patrols carry out spot checks on all civilian vessels in this part of the Med."

"Even so, you'd better detail some men to keep watch on the port."

The captain raised his eyes in mild protest. "That's an *awful* lot of manpower, sir. We'd have to stretch things a bit thin to cover everything."

"Just do it, Captain. And I'll want transport and a driver. The main railway station is the most likely way out of town, so I'd like to keep it under close watch. And I want all the hotels and pensions in the city checked for new customers, especially anyone who's arrived within the last three hours."

"*All* of them, sir?"

"Every damned one, Captain. Big and small. Flophouses included."

The captain looked flustered. "But there are *hundreds* in Alex. That could take days."

"You'll have to work faster than that. The longer we delay, the more likely they are to kill again, and the better their chances are of escaping."

The captain sighed. "Yes, sir." As he reached for the telephone, it rang. He picked it up, listened for several moments. "Right, I'm on my way." He put down the phone, looked up. "We're in luck. It seems we may have spotted two of the people you're looking for."

THIRTY-NINE

12:45 P.M.
The Corniche, the famous crescent-shaped road stretching for miles along Alexandria's coast, was peppered with hotels and nightclubs, sidewalk cafés and cheap lodging houses. There was a certain faded glory about the seafront buildings. Some of the smaller hotels were actually brothels that catered to both sexes, handsome young Arab men and

women sitting outside on the stone steps, trying to entice customers.

Halder had changed out of uniform, abandoning his suit-case under one of the carriage seats, and Rachel had donned a different set of clothes and put on make-up. As the train approached the outskirts of Alex, they saw the clusters of white, red-roofed houses perched on the side of the road, the Greek restaurants with their shady verandas, the blue sea close on the other side, palm trees dotting the coastal sands.

When they pulled into the station before Ramleh, they saw no obvious military presence on the platform, so they walked outside and took a cab. Halder told the driver to drop them off along the Corniche, and ten minutes later they stepped out on to the promenade.

"You'd hardly think there was a war on," Halder commented, lighting a cigarette and slipping Rachel's arm into his as they walked. "It's like another world after drab old Berlin."

Couples strolled along the magnificent sunny esplanade, as trams rattled past the Mediterranean, and there were bright-coloured kiosks selling candy and trinkets. The only obvious reminders of the war were the dozens of ships belonging to the Allied fleet anchored further along the quays, and the sailors and off-duty soldiers loitering outside brothels.

"They used to call Alex the Paris of the Middle East. But then it does have a certain reputation, even seedier than Cairo's. They say the brothels cater to every imaginable taste. Even the ancient Romans named it the City of Sinful Delights."

Rachel noticed two heavily bosomed Egyptian prostitutes trying to tempt a couple of young sailors into a run-down hotel. "It seems things haven't changed much since the time of Antony and Cleopatra. But I'm puzzled that you seem to know Alex so well."

"My parents took me on visits as a child, or didn't I ever tell you? My father always had it in his mind that Cleopatra's fabled treasure palace was buried somewhere under the harbour out there. But the last time was a year ago—I spent a month operating behind enemy lines. It wasn't as dangerous as it sounds. And definitely a lot more pleasant than being shelled by the British in Libya."

At that moment two military Jeeps suddenly rounded a corner up ahead, and came to a halt in the middle of the Corniche. Half a dozen military police jumped out and began setting up a roadblock, stopping traffic in both directions and checking drivers' papers.

Halder tossed away his cigarette. "It could be just a routine spot check, but then again they might be looking for us. Let's not tempt fate." He took Rachel's hand. They crossed the seafront road and turned down a narrow back street opposite the promenade. It was thronged with more brothels and off-duty troops, and reeked of unpleasant smells. "I know it's taking a risk, but we'll have to give the main railway station a try. There's always a chance it mightn't be watched just yet. This time we'll use our own papers."

"What happens if someone tries to arrest us?"

"We get out of there fast as we can, guns blazing if we have to." He saw Rachel study him. "What's the matter?"

"I suppose you know you're crazy, Jack Halder? You seem to come alive whenever there's danger in the air. Or didn't anyone ever tell you that?"

He smiled, faintly. "It must be the Prussian in my blood." He stood there, an odd look of excitement on his face. "But you know the strangest thing? I haven't felt this alive in months." He pointed towards another side street. "The station's about a twenty-minute walk. It'll be safer if we stick to the back streets. Right, we'll get going. And let's try not to look like we're a couple of escaped convicts on the run."

1:10 P.M.
"They sent me on a wild-goose chase, sir. Bloody clever pair, I'll give them that."

Weaver looked at the MP standing to attention in Myers's office. "At ease, Sergeant."

The sergeant stood at ease, put his hands behind his back.

Sanson removed his cap, his face and eye patch flecked

with sand dust. He sat on the edge of the desk. "You'd better tell me exactly what happened."

Weaver had had Sanson radioed as soon as he heard Myers's news, and Sanson had sped back to HQ, leaving the patrols to carry on searching the villages. Weaver had filled him in, and told him about the identities of the two dead officers.

The MP appeared uncomfortable in the presence of three officers. "Speak up, Sergeant," Weaver prompted.

"There wasn't a sight of the two men anywhere. I had some of our lads cover the main roads out of town, but they didn't see any staff car. And there was no report of any other civilian or military vehicle stolen. But when we got back to the station, I checked out the abandoned Jeep. Turns out it belonged to the two officers who'd gone missing."

"What did this young woman look like?"

"Very attractive. Late twenties. Blond-haired, blue-eyed. Slim, average height. And a bloody good actress, I'd have to say."

"She claimed she was South African?"

"Yes, sir. Said her father was a colonel, serving in Alex."

"And yet you didn't check her bloody papers?" Sanson said angrily.

The MP blushed. "She told me she'd forgotten them, sir. And then I reckoned there was no need—not when it seemed the officer could vouch for her."

Sanson made an effort to control his anger. "You say he presented himself as Captain Jameson?"

The MP nodded. "That's what's frightening, sir. He played it as cool as you like. Spoke with a perfect upper-class English accent—" He broke off and glanced at Myers. "Begging your pardon, sir, I meant—"

Myers nodded abruptly. "I know what you meant, Sergeant. Go on."

"He was about thirty, I reckon. Give or take a couple of years. Tall, handsome enough, dark hair and eyes. Capable-looking chap, I would have said. Then, when I checked with Amiriya, they told me Captain Jameson and another officer, Lieutenant Grey, had gone missing. And then I heard they'd been—"

"We know what you heard."

"Would you recognise either of them if you saw them again?" Weaver asked.

"Oh yes, sir. Not a shred of doubt about that."

"What about his papers?" Sanson interrupted. "The photographs couldn't have matched."

The sergeant blushed again. "Sometimes it's difficult to tell with photographs, sir, especially if someone's wearing a uniform and there's a passing resemblance. But he was a cool customer—told me to go ahead and check with his CO when I noticed his ID was a week out of date. He seemed so convincing, I took his word for it."

"He's certainly a ruthless, clever sod, whoever he is," Sanson said to Weaver, and walked over to the wall map. "You say they took the local train, heading west towards here?"

"Yes, sir," the MP replied. "I questioned the station-master. He saw the man and woman board together after I'd left. That's when I radioed HQ."

Sanson said to Myers, "Where's the final stop?"

"The Ramleh, the main station. But they'd have reached there long ago—it only takes about half an hour. I'm assuming, of course, that was their destination—there are several other stops along the way."

"Get some men to the outlying stations on the route and question the railway staff. Find out if anyone saw a couple matching the descriptions get off at any of them." Sanson looked over at the sergeant, his anger at the man's incompetence barely controlled. "That'll be all for now. Wait outside."

The man left, and Sanson said, "They've got only two options. Move on, or stay in town."

Myers glanced at his watch. "There's a train leaving for Cairo in just over an hour, sir. The two-fifteen. And there's another for Port Said an hour later. If they decide to keep running while their luck's good, it might do no harm to keep an especially close watch on Ramleh station, as Lieutenant-Colonel Weaver has suggested."

Sanson grimaced. "You can bet your backside we'll be

watching. Plainclothes only. Don't have your men trooping in together—filter them into the station in twos and threes, through the front and back entrances. Tell them to be discreet—one wrong slip and we could ruin any chance we've got of catching these bastards."

"Yes, sir."

"And you'd better find us some civilian clothes. Arrange it with the stationmaster so that all passengers have to pass through only one or two barriers, so we can keep a close watch on things. Have medical assistance standing by too, in case we need it."

"We're cutting it a bit fine for me to organise all that, sir."

"No excuses, Captain. Just see that it's done." Sanson picked up his cap, slapped off the sand dust. "Anything else you can think of, Weaver?"

"I guess you've covered everything." Weaver nodded towards the door. "Except we'd better take the sergeant along. He saw them once. He'll recognise them again."

1:45 P.M.

It took Halder and Rachel almost half an hour to reach the Ramleh station. There was a small café—the Petite Paris—on the corner opposite, and Halder led them to one of the tables and beckoned a waiter.

"What's wrong?" Rachel asked.

"A little reconnaissance might be in order first. Let's have some coffee. I can recommend the Yemeni, it's first class. And we'd better eat something while we can."

They ordered coffee and pastries, and Halder watched the station entrance across the street. There were the usual soldiers in transit, entering and leaving the massive entrance, kit-bags over their shoulders, and a couple of Egyptian traffic policemen stood chatting on the square. They didn't seem to be paying much attention to anyone, and Halder noticed no obvious military presence.

"It seems quiet enough. But then again, they could have men posted undercover. It's a risk we'll just have to take."

He observed the station for ten more minutes, then finished his coffee. "If there's even a whiff of trouble, you stick close to me. Understand?"

Rachel nodded.

He felt for the revolver in his pocket, stood, looked down, and offered her his arm.

"Time to test the water. Ready?"

She stood and took his arm.

FORTY

RAMLEH STATION
21 NOVEMBER/2 P.M.

The Ramleh was chaotic, a massive stone building with high vaulted ceilings. There were several filthy-looking food stalls just inside the entrance, busy with passengers, mostly Arab peasants. They crowded the station, many of them barefoot and wearing djellabas, accompanied by wives and children, carrying boxes tied with string, wooden crates packed with chickens and pigeons.

Weaver stood behind the ticket barrier, wearing a linen suit loaned by one of Myers's staff. The air was clammy with smells and stifling hot. The sergeant was by his side, sporting a blazer and flannels, his skull-cropped haircut covered by a Panama hat. The train for Cairo left in fifteen minutes, the one for Port Said an hour after. There was only one barrier through which all passengers had to pass to gain access to the platforms, and Weaver and the sergeant stood a short distance away from the uniformed Arab ticket inspector, but close enough to see the faces of everyone who passed through.

Weaver glanced at the station clock. The hands struck two p.m.

A long queue had formed and there were murmured protests from some of the European passengers, but the Arabs took the inconvenience in their stride, used to mindless bureaucracy and delays. So far, the sergeant had spotted no one resembling the couple. Another checkpoint had been set up further down the platform, out of view of the passengers, where two plainclothes MPs were double-checking the identity cards of everyone who was allowed through.

Weaver felt confident that if they spotted the couple they couldn't escape.

It had been a manic rush to organise everything. He'd arrived only five minutes ago through the back way, changing into the borrowed clothes in one of the army trucks parked at the rear. Ten armed plainclothes men were posted around the station, six further along the platforms, and another two dozen uniformed troops were holed up in the stationmaster's office, if needed. Sanson had chosen to position himself outside the main entrance with two plainclothes MPs, ready to block any escape, and a couple of motorcycle riders were parked in a nearby side street, alongside a waiting ambulance and two doctors, in case there was shooting.

The station was a chaos of human traffic, which made the job all the more difficult. Weaver saw Myers and another plainclothes officer lounging against a pillar twenty yards away, smoking cigarettes and standing over a couple of battered suitcases, pretending to be waiting passengers. Myers looked over and Weaver shook his head. They had seen no suspects so far.

Suddenly the sergeant touched Weaver's arm. "There's a couple about twenty feet from the barrier, sir—"

"Where?"

"The lady's fair-haired, wearing a blue dress. The man with her's wearing a light-coloured jacket."

Weaver tensed and glanced down the queue, trying not to make it obvious. He saw the couple. They looked like European refugees. The sergeant said, "They're a bit far away to get a proper look, but there's definitely a resemblance."

"You're not certain it's them?"

"Well—no, sir. At this distance I couldn't be sure. And the lady looks like she's wearing a lot of make-up."

Weaver knew that if it was the wrong couple and they approached them, it could jeopardise everything. Other passengers in the queue would see the incident, and if the real suspects were among them, they might smell trouble and slip out of the queue. Myers and his companion were waiting by the pillar in case that happened, but the queue was so congested and the station so busy, Weaver just hoped the strategy worked. He looked back at the couple. They had moved up in the queue, maybe fifteen feet away, and he avoided looking at them directly. "You still think there's a resemblance?"

"Yes, sir," the sergeant answered.

"When they get near enough, move closer and try to get a better look. Be as discreet as you can."

He gave a faint nod to Myers, waiting at the pillar. The captain tossed away his cigarette, said something to his companion, and they both got ready to move. Minutes later, the couple had almost reached the ticket inspector. Weaver saw the man produce a pair of tickets, and gripped the Colt in his pocket.

"Now," he prompted the sergeant.

While the couple were busy with the inspector, the sergeant stepped closer. As he studied their faces, the woman looked up, saw him, and smiled disarmingly. The sergeant turned, came back and shook his head. "Sorry about that, sir. It looked like the two I saw, but it's definitely not them."

"You're *very* sure about that?"

"Certain."

Weaver felt deflated. He looked over at Myers and shook his head, saw the captain relax.

He glanced at the station clock: 2:05.

Dozens more passengers, many of them Europeans, some military but mostly civilian, were still joining the end of the queue in the final rush to board. Weaver felt on edge and wiped his brow. The boiling afternoon heat that penetrated the packed station was overpowering, and the tension of waiting didn't help. He guessed that if the Germans were out there, they'd try and leave it until the last minute, just before the carriages pulled out.

"Keep your eyes open," he told the sergeant. "If they're going to try and board, it'll happen soon."

2 P.M.

Halder stepped into the crowded station with Rachel on his arm. He looked around cautiously. The only soldiers he saw were obviously off duty, drinking beer at the Arab food stalls while they waited for their trains, others heading towards the platforms carrying kit-bags over their shoulders.

"Everything looks normal enough, but you never can tell." He led Rachel towards a timetable on a pillar near the ticket booths. "Achmed was right. Two-fifteen. We've got fifteen minutes before the train leaves. Think you could buy us a couple of tickets?"

"What if the train's full?"

Halder smiled. "I think you'll find a little baksheesh will work wonders." He gave her some money. "Buy returns—they're always less suspicious than singles. And don't worry, I'll be right here, watching."

He waited as Rachel went to join the ticket queue. He noticed a young man in civilian clothes standing off to one side of the row of busy ticketing counters, idly reading a newspaper. Halder saw him glance over at Rachel a moment, before he returned to reading his newspaper. Halder felt uneasy. The man might be military police, or he could simply be waiting for someone. It was hard to tell. He made no attempt to approach Rachel, or anyone else in the ticket line, but his presence made Halder feel distinctly unsettled. The platforms were too far away for him to get a good look and see if there were any military checks in progress, and he didn't want to leave Rachel alone. He looked at the station clock. It read five minutes past two.

Rachel came back with the tickets, and Halder said, "Any problems?"

"No. Two returns, like you asked."

"Right, here goes. Keep your fingers crossed."

He took her arm again and they walked towards the platforms. There was a long queue waiting in line for just one ticket barrier, which immediately aroused Halder's suspicions. When he looked ahead he noticed two men in civilian clothes standing to one side of the barrier, near the uniformed Arab inspector. As one of the men lifted his Panama hat to wipe his brow, Halder froze. It took a second or two, but he recognised the sergeant from the station that morning.

"Damn it to hell."

He was just about to turn away when he noticed the face of the second man standing next to the sergeant. *"My God, I don't believe it."*

"What's wrong?" Rachel asked.

Halder's eyes were wild with disbelief, and he didn't reply. Instead, he took a firm hold of Rachel's arm, slipped out of the queue, and pulled her into the crowd.

FORTY-ONE

Halder fought his way through the crowd towards the station food stalls, busy with a group of boisterous Australian soldiers. He bought two beers and they made their way to one of the upright tables. Rachel said, "What's the matter? You look like you've seen a ghost."

"Don't look now," Halder said hoarsely. "But there are two men in civilian clothes near the barrier. They're plain-clothes military and they're looking for us."

"How do you know?"

"One of them is the sergeant we sent on a wild-goose chase."

Rachel was stricken. Halder said, "You'd better prepare yourself for another shock—the second man is Harry Weaver."

For a moment she looked totally astonished, then she turned round sharply, looking towards the ticket barrier. It was a distance away, and Halder saw her try to focus. "Don't stare. You'll only attract attention," he warned.

But Rachel was hardly listening. She had noticed the sergeant, standing near the ticket inspector, and from the look on her face she had recognised Harry Weaver instantly. He was looking a little older, and wearing a lightweight linen suit. He was too far away to notice them, preoccupied as he watched the passenger queue.

"Rachel—" Halder's voice brought her back. She was completely stunned.

"I—I can't believe it."

Halder swallowed a mouthful of beer. "It's certainly a small world, full of surprises. The kind of destiny the ancient Egyptians liked to believe in—meeting again in another life."

Rachel made to look round again, but Halder caught her

hand. "Don't make it obvious. It's Harry, all right, no question."

"But—what's he doing *here?*"

"A good question. But I suppose it makes some kind of sense. He speaks reasonable Arabic, so it's hardly surprising he's serving in Egypt. At a guess, he's probably military police or army intelligence." He looked at her. Her face was still confused. "Are you all right?"

"It—it seems so unreal. Seeing him again in these circumstances. I don't know what to think."

"That makes two of us. And I'm pretty sure Harry would be surprised if he knew we were here."

Rachel seemed totally bewildered. "You don't think he knows that it's *us* he's looking for?"

"I doubt it. How could he? But as much as I've always loved Harry's company, I don't think we ought to stick around for a chat." He shook his head, added uneasily, "Whoever would have guessed? Harry and us on different sides of the fence at a time like this. It's a frightening thought, and I'm not sure I like it very much. It makes you wonder if there's someone up there pulling strings and laughing at us."

Halder guessed she wanted to look back at Weaver one more time, but he reached across the table and gripped her hand. "We're going to leave now. Better drink up—you're going to need some Dutch courage. Seeing as Harry and the sergeant are in plainclothes, you can bet there are others close by, and they're probably covering the exits, which could make things difficult. I spotted a man at the ticket booths earlier who looked suspicious. He's probably one of Harry's comrades."

Rachel hadn't touched her beer and Halder noticed that her hands were shaking. "Are you sure you'll be OK?"

"I think so."

"If anyone tries to stop us, let me do the talking. But be ready to move if I tell you."

"You don't give up easily, do you, Jack?"

"I never could see the point." He forced a smile, took off his jacket and loosened his tie. Then he slipped the revolver from his pocket and put it under his jacket.

"What happens if Harry and his friend should come after us?"

Halder's face tightened with anxiety. "Save me the thought. It's bad enough I'm up against the closest friend I ever had. The last thing in the world I'd want is for Harry and me to have to face each other in a showdown. So nice and easy does it, and stay close to me."

As they moved back into the crowd, Halder squeezed her hand.

"Once we make it outside, we'll try to head back towards the promenade."

"You mean *if* we make it."

"Remember that old Arab saying? To survive, you have to laugh in the face of despair. If we look desperate, we're dead. So just try to act perfectly calm and normal, even if we're stopped." He shot a quick glance back over his shoulder, but there was no sign of Harry Weaver or the sergeant following them. He steered Rachel towards the station exit, looming ahead through the mob of passengers. "This is it. Here we go."

The walk towards the exit seemed to take an eternity. Bodies milled past them in either direction, and as they pushed their way through, Halder anxiously watched the crowd for any sign of danger, but they reached the exit doors without anyone stopping them. He paused before they stepped out, trying to scan the busy square outside the station. Buses were lined up on the kerb, but he didn't see any parked military vehicles. The pavement was too packed to get a proper look, but he noticed no one who looked as if they might be plainclothes military or police. The two Egyptian traffic cops he'd seen earlier were still there, chatting and smoking, totally uninterested in anything happening around them. Directly across the square was a maze of back alleyways, the entrance to a teeming bazaar.

"That's where we're headed," he told Rachel. "Everything seems normal enough. Are you ready?"

"Yes."

Halder tightened his grip on the revolver under his jacket. "Keep your fingers crossed. And remember, if anyone stops us, let me handle it."

They pushed into the crowds pouring through the station's massive floor-to-ceiling doors, and stepped out on to Ramleh Square. Out of the corner of his eye, Halder suddenly noticed a tall, well-built man in civilian clothes, off to his left, near the station wall. He had a patch over his left eye and a livid scar on his jaw. Halder knew instinctively that the man was watching the crowds entering and leaving the station, and he saw him stare over in their direction. He felt his pulse race; he had no option but to keep moving.

They'd hardly gone a dozen paces when a voice said from behind, "Excuse me, sir, madam."

Halder turned. His heart sank. It was the man with the eye patch.

2:15 P.M.
Weaver was getting frustrated. So far, the sergeant had spotted no one else resembling the man and woman. The train for Cairo was ready to leave the platform, whistles sounding and the flag men moving up and down the carriages, slamming doors. As the ticket inspector hurried the last passenger through, the sergeant said, "We're not having much luck, are we, sir?"

"I guess not." Weaver called Myers over. "The couple still might turn up. You'd better keep the men posted. When does the train for Port Said leave?"

"In an hour, sir. And the next one for Cairo at six."

"Tell your men to take turns having a break, but to keep watching the local arrivals and departures."

"You want me to tell Lieutenant-Colonel Sanson, sir?"

Weaver shook his head and loosened his tie, feeling totally despondent. The station was stifling hot and he needed air, and a break from the milling crowds. "No, I'll tell him myself."

Halder was trying to decide whether to shoot the man with the eye patch when another burly figure in plainclothes joined him. He spotted a third man in civilian clothes positioned near the entrance, watching the proceedings as he had his shoes polished by a shoeshine boy. He guessed the men were military police or intelligence. The bazaar was only fifty metres across the square, but too far to make a run for it without the risk of being shot.

"May I see your papers, sir?" the man with the eye patch said briskly. His comrade stood beside him, a bulge under his open jacket, one hand on his waistband, ready to move.

Halder tried to look affronted as he regarded the two men. "Who the hell are you?"

"Lieutenant-Colonel Sanson, military intelligence." Eye Patch showed his ID.

Halder said calmly, "Well, in that case, sure." He handed over his ID wallet.

Sanson said, "You too, madam, if you don't mind."

Rachel fumbled in her bag and offered her papers. Sanson scrutinised both sets of documents, as carefully as a bank clerk might study bills he believed to be counterfeit, taking his time as he studied the photographs, then rubbing his thumb on the print. Finally, he looked up, and Halder saw the suspicion in his face. "Were you about to board a train, sir?"

"Why do you ask?" Halder sounded irritated.

"I noticed you both enter the station ten minutes ago. Now you've come out again. I wondered if there was any reason you might have changed your mind about travelling."

"Listen, buddy, we got *off* the train from Cairo earlier. My lady friend here realised she mislaid one of her bags. Now it turns out it's been lost, and we'll be lucky to get the damned thing back." Halder tried to sound suitably upset. "But that's the Egyptian rail service for you. Pretty goddamned useless."

Sanson gave a brief, cold smile. "Your papers say you're an American and your name's Paul Mallory."

"What about it?"

Sanson seemed unsure of something as he looked Halder up and down. "You mind me asking why you're not serving in the military, sir?"

"I hardly think that's any of your business."

"I could make it my business."

"If you must know, a medical condition ruled me out. There's a document in my ID wallet to state that fact. Now, how about you telling me what's up here?"

Sanson found the medical document in the wallet, examined it. Then he studied them both again, still suspicious. "May I ask the purpose of your visit to Alex?"

"I'm an archaeologist, lecturing with the American University in Cairo."

"That wasn't what I asked."

"The chief curator of the Alex Museum invited us to examine some artefacts discovered recently near Rashid." Halder smiled. "But I guess it's really an excuse to visit old friends." He could see that Sanson still wasn't convinced. In desperation, he tried his last card. "In fact, we just bumped into one in the station. Harry Weaver. Seeing as you're in the same line of work, I take it you know him?"

Sanson raised his eye. "You're friends of Lieutenant-Colonel Weaver's?"

"Harry and me go way back."

Sanson appeared suddenly to relax. "I see." He looked at Rachel. "You're German-Jewish, Miss Tauber?"

"Yes."

"Might I ask what exactly your relationship is to this gentleman?"

"We're colleagues. I'm an archaeologist also."

Sanson handed back their papers. "I won't detain you any longer. Thank you, madam. And you, sir."

Halder slipped his papers inside his pocket. "You still haven't said what all the fuss is about."

"There's a major security operation in progress," Sanson answered simply. "Or didn't Lieutenant-Colonel Weaver tell you?"

Halder smiled. "Not a word, but then that's Harry for you. Always plays his cards close to his chest." The smile vanished as he looked past Sanson and froze as Harry Weaver came out through the station doors. He looked away sharply.

"Is something the matter?" Sanson asked.

"Nothing." Halder forced a smile. "I think we've delayed enough. Good-day. This way, my dear."

He held tightly on to Rachel's arm, started to cross the square towards the bazaar, but he knew they were already too late. Out of the corner of his eye he saw Harry Weaver stop dead in his tracks as he came towards Sanson. There was a look of incomprehension on his face, as if he had seen the dead get up and walk. He stared at them open-mouthed, his eyes falling on Rachel, and his face went chalk white.

It happened quickly. Sanson registered their reactions, sensing that something was wrong, but in an instant Halder pulled out his revolver.

Sanson stepped back, fumbling for his gun. *"Christ!"*

Halder shot him in the hand and the big Englishman staggered back, clutching his wound. The square erupted with screams as people ran for cover, and the area around them cleared almost instantly. Sanson's comrade already had his gun out, but Halder fired first, hitting him in the shoulder, and the man screamed in pain and went down. As the plainclothes man near the station entrance tried to get off a shot, Halder fired twice again, punching him back against the wall.

Harry barely reacted. He was still in shock, looking from Jack to Rachel in utter disbelief. Halder raised his gun, aimed at him, but still Weaver didn't move, and then Halder broke the spell and grasped Rachel's arm.

"Move!" And they ran across the square towards the bazaar.

FORTY-TWO

They ran through the bazaar's maze of narrow streets, Halder frantically pushing people out of their way, knocking over merchants' stalls.

It was a nightmare.

In the packed market, bodies pressed in on them, and it was bedlam as they tried to keep moving. Ten minutes later they had left the bustling alleyways behind and the human traffic had thinned out. Halder slowed to a brisk walking pace, both of them out of breath. He constantly checked over his shoulder but saw no one pursuing them, although he knew it wouldn't last.

Moments later his dread was justified.

The high-pitched whine of a motorcycle approached. He pulled Rachel into a foul-smelling lane. "Don't move. Stay absolutely still."

An MP motorcycle rider suddenly roared by, quickly followed by another. Halder waited until they had driven past, then peered out into the alleyway. He wiped a mask of sweat from his face. "I think we've given them the slip for now. But we can't stay here. Take my arm, like we're out for a stroll."

They left the lane and eventually found their way once more into busy back streets, heading towards the seafront, and ten minutes later came out on to the Corniche. Halder saw no sign of the checkpoint they'd seen earlier, and he led Rachel to one of the benches on the promenade.

He saw the strain on her face. "We can't stay here for long. And the longer we hang around in broad daylight, the more likely we are to get caught."

"What can we do?"

"You can bet Harry and his friends will seal off every exit road after what's happened, so it's pointless even trying to make it to Rashid. Once it's dark we'll have to try and slip out of the city, across the desert. It's about the only hope we have."

"Why Rashid?"

"I forgot. You didn't know." He explained about the boat. "It was meant to be a bolthole in case we ran into trouble. Except it's not much use to us now."

"But you said trying to cross the desert would be suicidal."

"I'm afraid we don't have much choice." He consulted the map. "If we could steal a suitable vehicle, a truck maybe, and find a gap in the army cordon, we might get lucky. They can hardly surround the entire city. It's too sprawling, and they just wouldn't have the manpower. So there's bound to be a gap or two somewhere. The problem is finding one."

"And what happens in the meantime?"

"We'll need somewhere secure to stay until tonight, while we work things out." Halder stood, looked down at her. Suddenly she looked very vulnerable and childlike.

"I'm sorry, Rachel. Sorry you ever got involved in this mess."

"What—what happened back at the station with Harry. I still can't quite believe it. It's like a nightmare. I'm still shaking inside."

He put a hand gently to her face, with a sober look that suggested he was trying to contain his own emotions. "Me too. But let's not talk about it now. Please."

Across the sunny Corniche an endless line of hotels, lodging houses and brothels stretched down the curve of the seafront. The buildings were very British, late Victorian and with steps leading up, but most were run-down and in need of repair.

Rachel looked over at them. "The army's bound to search the hotels and lodging houses. Nowhere's going to be safe."

Halder forced a valiant smile. "True." The smile vanished and his face became more serious. "But I have an idea. It's a bit drastic, and probably our only hope, but it just might work if we can both endure the embarrassment."

It was hard to believe that Gabrielle Pirou had once been one of the most desired women in Marseilles. Her sixty-year-old face was heavily rouged, her lips were a slash of red lipstick, some of it smeared on her teeth, and she walked with a pronounced limp. The only reminder of her past beauty was her slim figure and her sensuous Mediterranean eyes, but even they had become corrupted with age, witness to every sexual vice imaginable.

The French toy poodle clasped to her ample bosom yapped as Gabrielle clicked her fingers, assembling her girls in front of the group of men who stood around the brothel salon. "Quiet, Donny, *mon chéri*," she admonished the dog. "Can't you see the gentlemen are trying to make up their minds?"

The "gentlemen" in question were four Allied officers who had dropped in after a bout of drinking in a local bar. The "girls" were a mixture of European and Arab, some in harem dress, low-cut sequinned tops and loose, see-through pants, others wearing pencil skirts and revealing blouses. All were very pretty, two were exquisitely beautiful, and every one of them oozed sex. They smiled and giggled at the officers and playfully displayed their bodies, hinting at what could be enjoyed in the bedrooms upstairs.

"Well, gentlemen, aren't you very glad you visited? The ladies are *trés* enchanting, *n'est-ce pas*?" Gabrielle still spoke with a heavy accent, her sentences sprinkled with her native French. She flicked ash from her ivory cigarette holder, some of it landing on her blouse and her poodle.

The British officer standing beside her coughed politely. "Yes—yes they are, rather."

"And all are positively clean, I promise you. The doctor comes once a month." Gabrielle smiled mischievously. "He's a fastidious man, the doctor, absolutely fanatical about hygiene, so I'm certain discerning gentlemen like yourselves can rest assured."

The officers smiled nervously. They were certainly a little drunk, but more than polite. Gabrielle always preferred officers to enlisted men; they usually didn't drink themselves legless, argue the price or abuse the girls, not like some of the enlisted soldiers, who behaved like drunken savages, so she wanted to give her customers the best of attention and ensure their return. A French officer, middle-aged and overweight, cleared his throat and whispered, "Would madam have two ladies available?" Gabrielle smiled charmingly, glad to double her profit. Whatever the customer wanted, she provided. "But of course, whatever monsieur wishes. Madam Pirou caters to every desire."

The officers began to pair off with the girls, moving to sit in the comfortable red velvet chairs scattered around the pleasantly decorated salon. Gabrielle relaxed, her work done.

She had come to Alex twenty years ago to open her own salon, far from her brutish French pimp who'd left her a cripple. Now she was madame of one of the best, a deluxe brothel along the seafront, with a reputation for catering to a discerning clientèle. And it had proved extremely profitable, especially since the war. Battle-weary troops, hot-blooded and missing wives and girlfriends, panted for sex and company. Business was positively booming.

The doorbell rang out in the hallway. Gabrielle clutched her poodle, gave a regal wave to one of the girls, and hobbled out of the room. "I'll attend to the door, Suzette. Pour some refreshments for the gentlemen. Champagne if they wish. See they're treated royally before the ladies take them upstairs."

When she opened the front door, she received a mild surprise. It wasn't often a couple visited her salon, but it was by no means unusual. A man and a woman stood on the steps. They were a handsome pair, and she smiled politely. "*Qui*? Can I help you?" The man looked apprehensive. "A friend suggested we visit your establishment."

Gabrielle thought: *L'amour* is never simple. Occasionally, adventurous Bohemian couples liked to indulge in a threesome with one of her girls. Usually they were either rich, the husband sexually bored, or the wife had lesbian tendencies, and sometimes all three. This couple didn't look rich, just anxious, but so long as they could pay and didn't harm the girls, they could play whatever bedroom games they wished.

"Please, step inside. We're rather busy this afternoon. I'm not sure you can be accommodated right away."

Gabrielle led them into a lounge off the hall, brightly decorated with several vases of flowers and tasteful, erotic Arab wall prints. She looked at the woman. Very pretty, but a little too much make-up. She prided herself on her judgment of human nature, and usually the eyes told her everything she needed to know, but this one she couldn't figure out at all. Her eyes were unfathomable. The man's were easier to read: honest enough, and he had the look of a military man, despite his civilian clothes.

"Don't be afraid to tell Madam Pirou what it is you desire." Gabrielle offered a friendly smile, anxious to make the couple feel at ease. "We cater to all tastes. So long as one can pay."

It was a gentle question, not a statement, and the man nodded. "Of course."

"And how can madam help you?"

The man faltered, still uneasy, but definitely trying to hide it. "We'd like to spend the evening with a discerning lady. A private room, of course."

"Ah, something to add a little spice to your love life?"

Gabrielle raised her eyes. "But that's a rather long time."

"Money isn't a problem."

Gabrielle brightened at the prospect of a handsome profit. "Then I'm certain we can accommodate madame and monsieur. One of my most pleasant young ladies will be available shortly. She is very comfortable in such situations—*trés* sensitive and rather beautiful. Unless, of course, you would prefer to choose a different girl?"

"No. That would be fine."

"The lady will request five Egyptian pounds an hour for her services."

"How long can we stay?"

Gabrielle gave a tittering laugh as she waved her hand. "As long as you wish, *chéri*, providing you pay in advance. Now, if you'd come this way, I shall arrange a private room and a bottle of champagne. On the house, of course. The young lady will join you shortly and you can enjoy your evening undisturbed."

FORTY-THREE

BRITISH MILITARY HQ/ALEXANDRIA
21 NOVEMBER/4 P.M.

Weaver stood alone at the window in Myers's office.

He felt numb, as if he had just recovered from an anaesthetic. His mouth was dry, and there was a gloss of sweat on his forehead. Outside on the barrack square, dozens of armed troops were climbing into covered trucks. He watched as Myers and several other officers directed the men. A massive search was about to begin, covering the entire city.

Weaver came away from the window, sat at the desk, and put his head in his hands, suddenly overcome with anguish and confusion. If he hadn't seen it with his own eyes, he wouldn't have believed it. The couple outside the station were Jack Halder and Rachel Stern. And there wasn't a shred of doubt in his mind: they were the same pair who had fooled the sergeant that morning. None of it made any sense, none at all. The whole thing was totally insane. His body was shaking, and he was still in shock.

The dead didn't get up and walk, and yet he'd seen the dead. *He'd seen Rachel.*

He remembered the look of surprise on her face the instant he saw her. A face he'd recalled in his mind every day for the last four years, a face he'd wept over, remembering. At that moment, he had convinced himself he was dreaming, or that he'd seen her double. But when he saw Jack Halder, standing there in the flesh, saw him shoot Sanson and the two plainclothes MPs, he knew he wasn't hallucinating.

The question raged inside his head: *How was it possible?*

What had happened at the station was a disaster. Sanson and two men wounded, one of them still in the operating theatre at the French Hospital, a bullet lodged in his chest. Halder and Rachel had escaped in the chaos. He had pursued them into the crowded alleyways, searched the area for almost an hour, but they'd vanished like ghosts. Afterwards, he had even doubted his own sanity, but there were witnesses and there were wounded. The incident wasn't a figment of his imagination. He shook his head in utter confusion, a terrible hollow feeling in the pit of his stomach that made him want to throw up. He felt palpitations in his chest.

There was a knock on the door. A corporal came in, saluted. "Phone call for you, sir."

"Put it through. And tell Captain Myers I'd like to see him when he's finished outside." The phone rang moments later. He picked it up. "Lieutenant-Colonel Weaver."

"Hello, Harry. Can you talk?"

He heard Helen Kane's voice. Instead of being glad to hear her, he felt his heart sink.

"Helen," he said hoarsely.

"You sound strange. Is everything all right?"

"Yes. Everything's fine," he lied.

"I just called to say hello. That I miss you. And to ask if you'd made any progress with the Dakota."

Weaver didn't reply, his mind still in turmoil.

"I'm not interrupting anything, am I, Harry?"

"Look, I'm busy, Helen," he said shortly. "Can we talk later?"

There was silence at the other end. He was certain she was hurt by his abruptness, and he felt bad. But Rachel was alive, and at that moment he couldn't think of anything else. "I'm sorry. You've caught me at a bad time."

"Of—of course. I understand. Goodbye, Harry."

The line clicked dead.

He tried to compose himself when Myers came in. "The men are ready, sir, and we're rounding up everyone we can to help with the search. The police are calling on every hotel and lodging house in the city, and they've been warned to be extra careful. The couple can't have gone far. We'll scour Alex until we find them."

The captain sounded confident, but Weaver knew it wasn't going to be easy. Egypt's second city teemed with refugees of all nationalities. As in Cairo, there were hundreds of cheap hotels and lodging houses that didn't even bother to register guests. It would take days to search them all thoroughly. "Any word about Lieutenant-Colonel Sanson?"

"He's still being attended to at the hospital." The captain glanced out at the last of the men climbing into the trucks. "I'd better get under way. Will you be joining us, sir?"

"As soon as I've called at the hospital. If anything turns up, contact me by radio immediately."

The captain saluted, turned to go, and Weaver said, "One more thing."

"Sir?"

"Try and take the couple alive. Pass the word to your men."

The captain looked astonished. "That might not be an option, or even wise, especially after what's happened."

"You heard me. Alive, if at all possible. Give them every chance to surrender. That's an order."

The captain frowned. "May I ask why, sir?"

"I have my reasons," Weaver said simply.

"I'll do what I can," the captain said grimly. "But they've already killed two officers, not to mention wounding three others. If it comes to the worst, I can't put the lives of my men at risk."

The casualty room in the French Hospital was empty except for Sanson, who was being attended to in a cubicle by a doctor and a nurse. Weaver waited until they'd finished and Sanson appeared from behind the curtain. His right hand was heavily bandaged and he looked pale.

"How do you feel?"

Sanson produced a pack of cigarettes, lit one with difficulty. "Like Boris Karloff, playing the Mummy. Still, I've got all my fingers intact, which is something." He studied Weaver. "We need to talk, somewhere private."

He nodded towards a whitewashed veranda with a couple of wooden benches, and led the way outside. They sat. "You're acquainted with the couple at the station, aren't you, Weaver?"

He said palely, "How did you know?"

Sanson pulled on his cigarette. "I saw your faces. The three of you looked like you'd seen Lazarus rise from the dead. Besides, the man said he knew you."

"What do you mean?"

Sanson explained. "I think you'd better tell me what the hell's going on, Weaver."

Weaver told him how he knew Halder and Rachel. It took several minutes to explain everything and Sanson sat there, showing no reaction, until he had finished. Then the Englishman stood and sighed.

"It's quite a coincidence. But Halder's presence is the kind of coincidence I can understand. He speaks fluent Arabic and he's familiar with Egypt. He also speaks English like a native, obviously has no trouble impersonating a British officer, and I can vouch that his American accent was flawless. He's probably Abwehr, or with one of the specialist German commando forces, so it's hardly surprising he's involved. But it's the girl that really baffles me. Considering what you just said, she shouldn't even be alive."

"I don't understand either." Weaver shook his head, totally perplexed. "None of it makes any sense."

"What was the name of the ship that sank?"

"The *Izmir*."

"And you're quite sure it was the same woman?"

"Positive."

"I'll have the *Izmir* story checked out. On the surface, it seems highly unlikely that someone with a Jewish background would be helping the Germans, unless she's been forced to. But there's always another possibility."

"What?"

"She wasn't who she said she was in the first place. The German-Jewish thing was a cover, and she was working for the Nazis all along—probably your friend Halder was too."

Weaver said angrily, "Look, Sanson, I don't know what the hell's going on here, or why they're both involved. But I know one thing for certain. Rachel Stern and her family were totally anti-Nazi. And I've known Halder's family all my life—they were never Nazis."

Sanson tossed his cigarette on to the veranda, crushed it with his shoe. "Let me tell you something, Weaver. Before this war started, military intelligence and the Egyptian police kept watch on anyone suspected of being a foreign spy or agent. The Germans sent quite a number of their intelligence people over here, posing as tourists or international salesmen, or on the pretence of being archaeological experts. They were feeling out fascist sympathies among the Egyptians and making useful contacts for later use. The reasons should be obvious. They knew North Africa would be part of any future conflict—on the route to the Middle East oilfields, it had to be. The Italians played the same intelligence game. There were even a number of Americans operating here undercover, working for your State Department."

Weaver shook his head. "There's no way Jack Halder or Rachel Stern were spies. I'd stake my life on it."

"I really wouldn't if I were you. Not until we find out if the police knew anything about either of them back then. We can all keep our secrets well hidden, if we need to. And your friend Halder seems a very capable man. Handy with a gun, fluent in several languages, and a killer into the bargain. Quite a deadly combination all round. But at least we know what we're dealing with."

"I can't believe Halder murdered those officers in cold blood."

"Somebody did. And I mean to find them. Halder and

the woman might have company, but so far we've no evidence of that. And there's no question they're anything but enemy agents." Sanson stood, added briskly, "What's happening with the search?"

Weaver told him. Sanson considered for a moment. "You'd better have every church, mosque, alms-house and brothel visited as well. I wouldn't dismiss anywhere that's a likely refuge. Even if we have to tear this city apart, we're going to catch them."

Weaver wiped perspiration from his brow. Sanson came over and felt his forehead, looked into his eyes. "Your adrenaline level's as high as a ruddy kite. You'll need a shot of something to calm you down."

"I'll be OK."

"No you won't, Weaver. You're badly stressed." Sanson turned to go. "I'll fetch the doctor."

"What's going to happen when we find them?"

Sanson looked back. "I think you already know the answer to that. They might have been your friends once, but now they're the enemy and they've got blood on their hands. There's a list of charges a mile long. Provocateurs, impersonating a British officer, not to mention murdering two others, wounding three more and resisting arrest. I'm sure there's a lot more a military court could sling at them. And God only knows what they intended before we were on to them." Sanson shook his head. "Let's face it, Weaver. Even assuming we don't kill them first and they're captured alive, it's the hangman's noose for the pair of them. They'll be strung up so high the buzzards won't reach them. That I can promise you."

FORTY-FOUR

ALEXANDRIA
21 NOVEMBER/3 P.M.
The room was on the top floor. There was a double brass bed with clean cotton sheets, and the luxury of fresh towels in the tiny bathroom leading off. Tall shuttered windows overlooked the rear of the building, a private flagged court-

yard below, complete with a couple of fig trees, an outhouse of some sort, and an arched wrought-iron gate that
led out on to a narrow back street, lined with cheap hotels
and more brothels. A small café stood directly opposite,
rickety cane tables and chairs set outside on the pavement,
the Arab customers smoking hookah pipes.

After Madam Pirou had left, Halder locked the door and
opened the shutters. It wasn't yet evening, but already the
streets were busy, troops and civilians wandering through
the red-light district. He could see on to the landings of
several of the buildings opposite, their windows open, and
noticed a couple of tarty-looking girls leading customers
into rooms.

"Do you really think it's safe here?" Rachel asked.

"As safe as can be. Let's just hope Harry and his friends
stay well away."

"I can't stop thinking about what happened, seeing him
again in these circumstances."

"Me, I'm trying hard not to. Frankly, it's a little too
disturbing right now. And we need to keep our spirits up."
He closed the shutters and cracked open the bottle of iced
champagne, a cheap Egyptian brand, and filled two of the
three glasses the madame had left on a tray. He handed one
to Rachel with a grim smile. "Not exactly vintage, but enjoy
it while you can."

Rachel swallowed hers thirstily and flopped back on the
bed, exhausted. "I never thought I'd be so glad of a bed in
a brothel."

"The question is, how do we avoid the inevitable embarrassment when the young lady arrives?"

Rachel managed a tiny smile and Halder said, "What's
the matter?"

"How did you keep a straight face with the madame?
You talk about me, but you definitely missed your vocation—you should have been an actor. No wonder your
friend Schellenberg picked you."

"He's not a friend, and he didn't do me any favours.
But I'm glad you see the funny side."

"You still haven't told me how you knew about this
place."

"After a month here, undercover, I got to hear of certain

salons by reputation, Madam Pirou's included. Now, let's be serious. Any minute now, a girl's going to appear—"

"If it means saving our necks."

Halder was shocked. "You're not serious?"

"I could think of worse things to have to endure, if it keeps us from being caught. But I'm sure you'll think of something." Rachel slid off the bed, ran a hand through her hair, and moved towards the bathroom, past a stunned Halder. "I need a warm bath and a change of clothes. I'd suggest you do the same while we can."

There was a knock on the door and Halder froze. Another knock, and Rachel suddenly became serious. "I think you'd better answer it."

Halder crossed to the door. When he unlocked it, a very delectable, chocolate-skinned Arab woman stood there. The madame was right, she was quite beautiful, with jet-black hair and dark brown eyes. She smiled at Halder, then looked past his shoulder at Rachel. "Monsieur, Madame. My name is Safa."

Halder hesitated, unsure of what to do, but the girl came into the room, all business, and closed the door. She wore harem pants and a low-cut top that showed off her generous cleavage, and it was obvious from the way she made eyes at Rachel exactly where her tendencies lay.

"You're certain we won't be disturbed?" Halder asked.

Safa smiled wolfishly. "Of course. The room is ours for as long as you want." She ran her fingers playfully down his lapels, but her stare moved hungrily on to Rachel. "Madame tells me you have special needs. I am here to please you both."

"That really won't be necessary," Halder answered.

"Pardon?"

"Where's madame?"

"In her office, taking a nap. Why?"

"Is there a back way out of here? In case any of the customers want to slip out unnoticed."

The woman looked puzzled. "Yes. Why do you ask?"

Halder opened his wallet and produced a generous wad of notes. "We agreed five pounds an hour. I'll give you a hundred to vanish until midnight, and say nothing to Madame or the other girls."

This time, Safa looked completely bewildered. Halder said, "Our presence here can be easily explained. We're trying to escape from an American intelligence officer, an angry and determined man, who doesn't like the idea of his wife having an affair. We arrived from Cairo this afternoon but had to flee our hotel with him in pursuit. You can bet he'll be searching every hotel and lodging house in the area, so we needed a refuge for the evening, until it's safe to leave town." Halder smiled charmingly. "There's obviously been a misunderstanding on Madame's part, one which we gladly played along with. When it comes to delicate matters such as this, we thought it wise to say little. I'm sure you understand?"

Whether the woman did or didn't seemed immaterial. Safa plucked the money greedily from Halder's fingers, tucked it between her breasts, and smiled agreement. "Anything you say, monsieur."

CAIRO
5 P.M.

Deacon swallowed his third brandy in ten minutes. He had just returned from the Pharaoh's Garden, and there was no one waiting on the terrace who looked remotely as if they were trying to make contact.

"It's over, then?" Hassan said. "If the city's surrounded, they're finished."

"It's a complete mess," Deacon said bitterly. "After this disaster, it could be the last nail in the coffin." He put down his glass and took a sheet of paper from his desk. He'd driven to the villa and returned to the houseboat with Hassan hidden in the Packard's trunk; luckily he hadn't been stopped by any checkpoints. He needed Hassan for what he had in mind. "But we're not finished yet. There's something we need to do—"

There was a knock on the door and his manservant entered, looking flustered. Deacon exploded. "I thought I told you I wasn't to be disturbed."

"Apologies, effendi. But there's a gentleman named Salter to see you—he came alongside in a boat, with some men."

Deacon peered through the porthole. Darkness had fallen

outside, but he saw that a motorboat had tied up alongside, a couple of Salter's henchmen on board. Hassan came over. "What's he doing here?"

"If the bastard isn't careful, he'll have the law all over us."

At that moment the door burst open and Salter entered, Costas Demiris in tow. "Hello, Harvey." Salter slowly crossed the room and picked up the brandy bottle from the desk, examined the label. "A '36 Hennessy. Living well, I see. Does a man have to die of thirst before he's offered a drink?"

"Leave us," Deacon said abruptly to his servant, and when the man had left he glared at Salter.

"What are you doing here?"

"No need to get shirty. It's about those trucks you ordered. And there are a couple of things we need to discuss."

"I thought we'd done that already."

Salter grinned as he went over to the drinks cabinet, found a glass, then came back and helped himself to a generous splash of brandy. "Not really, but we'll come to that in a minute. I've got three American trucks, like I promised, and with all the right papers." Salter swallowed from his glass and raised an eye. "What's the matter? You don't look too impressed."

"If you could get to the point and be on your way, I'd appreciate it. Playing the roulette table in my private room after dark is one thing, but if anyone saw you come aboard I risk a visit from the military police."

"Relax, you're safe as houses. No one saw me, I made sure of that." Salter refilled his glass, swirled the amber liquid. "The stuff will be at the warehouse tomorrow afternoon, ready for delivery."

"Good," Deacon said flatly.

"You could try and sound a bit more enthusiastic. You're not thinking of backing out on me, are you, Harvey?"

"The deal's done and I'll pay you. Now, what else did you want to talk about?"

Salter nodded to his partner. "Tell him, Costas."

"You've been a busy boy, Mr. Deacon. Trips out to

Giza, and another to that airfield. We wondered what to make of it all."

Deacon was aware of the blood draining from his face, and felt like an idiot. In his haste he'd ignored the most basic of rules: always watch your back. He was barely able to contain his rage as he looked at Salter. "You've been following me."

"Quick off the mark, ain't you, Harvey? Tell him what else we found out, Costas."

"The airfield belongs to the Royal Egyptian Air Force. It's used sometimes when the government Antiquities Department wants to transport valuable artefacts to Cairo, discovered on official digs down south. The last I heard, some stuff came through there a month ago, bound for the Egyptian Museum. Gold and valuables from a tomb they're working on in the Valley of the Kings. Priceless, all of it."

Salter put down his empty glass with a wicked grin. "Interesting, don't you think, Harvey? Treasure like that would fetch a pretty penny from private collectors once the war's over—it could set a man up for life. You wouldn't happen to know anything about another consignment due shortly, would you, old son?" He studied Deacon and shrugged. "It's the American Army trucks I don't understand—I would have thought Egyptian Army or Air Force was more likely the case. That and your little trip to Giza, which I just can't figure out. Some kind of clever plan in mind, have we?"

Deacon swallowed. "I think you're seriously misjudging the situation, Reggie. Honestly, I do."

"I don't think so, mate, not by a long shot. I reckon your friends are up to no good—like nabbing some priceless treasure out at the airfield—or something tasty along those lines. And I'd like to know exactly what they have in mind."

"I couldn't tell you even if I knew."

Salter stepped closer, jabbed a finger threateningly into Deacon's chest. "Don't try it with me, Deacon. It doesn't wash. Whatever you're up to, I reckon it's worth a lot more than three grand. So we've got a new arrangement. I want in for ten per cent. In return, you get your vehicles and uniforms free of charge, and any extra muscle that might come in handy from me and my boys."

"I told you . . ." Deacon made to speak, but Salter slapped him across the face.

"Don't mess me around. I haven't got the patience. I want to know what these buddies of yours are up to."

In an instant, Hassan was up off the chair, his knife out, but Salter was quicker. He had his Browning out of its shoulder holster and pointed at Hassan's face. "Try it, sunshine, and I'll drill a fucking hole in you big enough to drive a camel through. Now drop the blade, or your boss here is going to need a new carpet."

Hassan didn't move. "I'm not going to ask again," Salter warned.

"Drop the knife," Deacon told him.

Hassan obeyed. Salter's fist came up and struck him a blow in the face and Hassan fell back, his nose bloodied. Salter picked up the knife. "You ever threaten me again, you fucking wog, and I'll carve you."

He tossed the blade away, turned back, and touched the Browning to Deacon's nose. "Have a talk with your friends. Explain the situation. Make them see reason. I can lay my hands on anything they need to pull this off—and I mean *anything*—equipment, uniforms, men, you name it. I want to know by tomorrow night where I stand." He smiled as he put down the gun. "Trust me, Harvey, this can be good for us all. A nice tidy profit all round."

Deacon took the handkerchief from his breast pocket and wiped his face. "You're a conniving bastard, Salter."

"You know, that's the nicest thing anyone's said to me all day." Salter replaced the Browning in his shoulder holster, grinned, and patted Deacon's cheek. "No hard feelings, Harv, but this is business. And a good word of advice. Convince your friends to play ball, and I promise, everything can be sweet. But try to keep me out of this caper, and I'll screw the lid down on you. And I don't think your friends would be too happy if the police got a tip-off telling them to watch the airfield. Get my drift? See you around."

When Salter and the Greek had left, Hassan spat on the floor and wiped blood from his nose. He picked up his knife and glared at Deacon. "Next time, I kill him. And the Greek."

Deacon poured himself a large brandy, swallowed it

quickly, then slammed the glass on the desk. "Drop it.
We've got bigger problems right now. And you ought to
be careful about where you point that toothpick. Salter's
the kind of scum who doesn't take a threat lightly." He tore
a slip of paper from the sheet on his desk, and scribbled
down an address. "The way things are, we don't need
Salter's trucks. And he's not going to like that. Even if I
pay the bastard, he's going to think I'm trying to double-
cross him. But that's another day's worry." He threw across
the Packard's keys. "For now, take my car and drive to
Alex, as fast as you can."

Hassan frowned. "You said it's swarming with the army
and police."

"No one's going to be looking for you there. Besides,
no one should recognise you in that disguise, without the
beard, and you said yourself no one got a good look at you
at the hotel."

Deacon handed him the slip of paper. "Go to this address
and ask to speak with Inspector Sadek. And make sure none
of Salter's men are tailing you."

Hassan looked at Deacon as if he were mad. "A policeman?"

"A retired policeman—he's a Nazi sympathiser. We need
to know whether our friends have been caught. I'll have to
inform Berlin when I transmit tonight. Sadek ought to be
able to find out. If everything looks hopeless, drive to Rashid
as quick as you can, and tell that cousin of yours to get rid of
the boat—we don't need him to hang around the river any
longer. I don't want a shred of evidence to lead back to us if
our friends are rounded up and interrogated, and they tell
about their bolthole."

"Can't you phone this inspector?"

"He doesn't have a phone, not since he retired on a
pension. If Sadek's not at home, ask his wife how to contact
him, but either way find him, and tell him I sent you. If
he's reluctant to help, get him to phone me and I'll handle
it from this end."

Hassan frowned. "And what will you be doing?"

"Visiting the café again, just in case by some marvel our
contacts still turn up."

FORTY-FIVE

ALEXANDRIA
21 NOVEMBER/4 P.M.

Gabrielle Pirou heard the knock on her door. She was in the back room on the ground floor which served as her private office, wearing an old cardigan draped over her shoulders, her feet up and stretched out on the couch, as she dipped into a box of chocolates and fed tidbits to her poodle.

"Enter."

Safa came in. "It's well for some." She tossed a wad of notes on the table.

Gabrielle frowned. "What's that?"

Safa plucked one of the chocolates from the box and popped it in her mouth. "Your share. The couple upstairs didn't want to play games. Turns out there's been a mis-understanding. A pity, the woman looked all right." She explained the situation. "The man gave me fifty pounds to get lost until midnight. So I'm giving my back a rest and taking the afternoon off to do some shopping."

Gabrielle sat up. "You think the couple are kosher?"

"Should we care?"

Gabrielle made a face, then shrugged. "It doesn't sound right. Still, it's money, I suppose." She tucked the wad of notes into her cardigan and looked at Safa. The greedy bitch had probably been given more, but she let it pass for now. She would check with the couple before they left. The telephone rang on the desk and she said, "Be a dear and answer it, *chérie*."

Safa picked up the receiver. "Madam Pirou's salon." She listened. "One moment." She covered the mouthpiece. "Someone's looking for one of the officers who came in earlier—Captain Green. Says it's urgent."

"Who is it?"

"His office at army headquarters."

"Tell them you'll fetch the captain," Gabrielle sighed.

Safa spoke into the receiver, then laid it down. "After

that, I'm off." She went out, and Gabrielle sat there, thinking about the couple upstairs. She had a feeling there was something odd about them. A certain nervousness that suggested all was not what it seemed. A few minutes later she heard footsteps outside and there was a knock on the door. A man came in, red-faced, tucking in his shirt.

"Ah, *capitaine*. An urgent phone call for you. Headquarters, I believe."

"How the bally hell did they know I was here?"

Gabrielle smiled. "Like God, the army works in mysterious ways. I'll leave you in private."

She was in the hallway minutes later, rearranging a vase of flowers, when the officer came out of her room, looking irritated.

"Problems, *capitaine*?"

"I'll say. There's a search on, and I'm wanted back at barracks. Seems a couple of enemy infiltrators are on the loose. They wounded three of our men outside the Ramleh station. Would you credit it? Just when a man's enjoying himself. Bloody thoughtless lot, these Germans."

For a second the information didn't register, then Gabrielle frowned. "Did you say Germans?"

"A man and a woman, and a dangerous pair by the sounds of it."

4:15 P.M.

Halder was lying on the bed, smoking a cigarette and studying the Baedeker, when Rachel came out of the bathroom. Her hair was wet and she had a towel wrapped around her middle. "At least the water's hot and there's real soap. Don't you want to bathe?"

Halder took in her figure, her long legs and delicate neck, the gentle rise of her breasts beneath the towel.

"What's the matter?" Rachel asked.

He looked at her face. "Nothing."

He tossed aside the guidebook, got off the bed, crushed his cigarette and went past her into the bathroom. He ran the bath while he shaved, then soaked in the hot tub, and came out ten minutes later wearing a towel. He took another cigarette from the pack, tapped it moodily, and leaned against the bathroom door. Rachel was sitting on the bed, still drying her hair, and she noticed him staring at her. "Why are you looking at me like that?"

He lit his cigarette and inhaled slowly. "There's something different about you. Something I sensed the first time we met after four years. I've been trying to figure out what it is. Now I know."

She stopped towelling her hair, her face taut. "What?"

"There's a hardness about you I don't remember. You're like a different woman."

She turned away, unable to meet his stare, finished drying her hair and put down the wet towel.

Halder said, "But then again, I suppose four years in a camp can either break you or strengthen you—" He let the words trail away. "I saw the look on your face when you saw Harry again. Of the two of us, it was him you really loved, wasn't it?"

This time Rachel stared back. "You saw shock. Nothing more. And how I felt about Harry is immaterial."

Halder sighed, came away from the door and peered through the curtain. All the windows across the street were closed and shuttered, but below in the alleyway the café was still busy. He let the curtain fall. "I suppose in some ways you're right. Human life is the raw material of war. And whether the two of us live or die really doesn't matter. But it does to me."

"Why?"

"Because I'm still in love with you. I always have been."

Rachel didn't answer. She wrapped her arms around herself, as if to ward off a chill, and went to sit on the bed.

Halder looked over. "Can I tell you something? When my wife died, the only thing that kept me alive in this insane world was my son. But there were often times when I thought of you. Wondered what had become of you— were you alive or dead? Maybe the truth of it was I hoped that someday we'd meet again, and I'd have the courage to tell you how I felt." He crushed out his cigarette, suddenly looked grim. "As for my son, I doubt I'll ever see Pauli again. For all I know he might already be dead."

There was grief in his voice, and suddenly all the bravado was gone, and he turned away, looking totally broken. Rachel stood, came over, put a hand on his shoulder. "You can't give up now, Jack. You simply can't."

"You don't understand. There's no way out of this. And there's no sense in pretending otherwise."

"No. Together we'll find a way."

"I wouldn't rate our chances, not after what's happened."

She put both her hands on his shoulders. "Look at me, Jack. We'll make it. You have to believe that."

He took a deep breath and composed himself. "You're right. I'm sorry."

"You still care about Harry, don't you? Despite the fact that you're on opposing sides. When you pointed your gun at him outside the station, did it cross your mind for a moment that you might have to shoot him?"

"Of course. Except I knew I couldn't have done it." Halder shivered. "But it worries me, the thought that it might come to us both having to face each other with fingers on the trigger. Do any of us know how we'll react if the situation's desperate enough? But there's one thing I do know. If it came to having to kill Harry to survive, I'd have to think twice. Killing your best friend, a man who's been like a brother, that's not the kind of thing you want to face, ever."

Rachel hesitated, looked into his face. "What you said, about our first meeting. A thunderclap. Did you really mean it?"

"Every word. But I told you, Harry loved you too. And I cared about him too much to upset our friendship by being the first to make a pass and tell you how I felt. It's why we both spoke to you on the veranda that night, and asked you if you loved either of us. It was almost a matter of us both wanting to be fair to each other, by letting you make the decision. But then you left and it was over. Except nothing's changed for me—I still feel the same. You know what they say. You can smash the vase, but the scent of the flowers never quite goes away." He looked into her eyes. "And what about you? Did you love either of us back then? Tell me the truth."

Rachel hesitated, didn't reply. She was on the verge of tears, her face a mask of confusion, and then she brushed a finger against his lips. "Even just for a little while I want to be happy in a world that's gone crazy. Kiss me, Jack."

He looked at her. A single tear rolled down her cheek. His eyes blazed, full of raw, intense passion, and he kissed her fiercely on the mouth. She responded, and he pulled away the towel, exploring her body, his lips brushing her neck, her earlobes, her shoulders, his hands moving on to her breasts, down over her thighs and between her legs. She cried with the pleasure, caressing him in return, her fingers moving over his flat, muscular belly, gripping and stroking his hardness.

And then he could bear it no longer. He picked her up and carried her over to the bed. They lay there, touched and kissed with a forceful tenderness that was almost over-whelming, until finally, sensing he was ready, Rachel moved, rolling on top of him, spreading her thighs, guiding him into her.

FORTY-SIX

7:15 P.M.

"So far, we've caught a couple of deserters, a wanted Arab criminal, and two Germans."

The main road from Alex to Cairo was a riot of angry drivers, honking their horns. Cars and trucks had backed up in both directions, and Weaver stood watching as the troops halted all traffic. Nothing could be discounted. Even incoming vehicles were being checked, just in case Halder and Rachel had had accomplices who had managed to evade the desert searches and therefore might still be trying to reach Alex.

Weaver had arrived at the old checkpost site five minutes ago. It had been used to control all traffic into the city when the Africa Corps had been on the offensive. Drivers were being told to step out of their vehicles, which were being searched thoroughly and their occupants' papers scrutinised. An arc-light blazed behind the barriers, illuminating the scene. Weaver frowned at Myers, standing beside him.

"What Germans?"

The captain half smiled. "Before the surrender, some of

Rommel's chaps ditched their uniforms and made it through our lines. There are still a few of them around, sir. They either had Arab girlfriends they didn't want to leave behind, or else didn't like the thought of risking their lives by staying in uniform. We're pretty certain there's still a few skulking about whom we haven't rounded up yet."

"Who are the two you caught?"

"One's barely out of his teens. Been hiding out in a Coptic church since he deserted eight months ago. The second chap was an army cook, a Wehrmacht sergeant." Myers gave another smile. "Turns out he was working in an Arab restaurant, a favourite haunt of our senior staff. The bastard could have poisoned the lot of them if he cared to. There'll be murder to pay over that one."

"You're absolutely sure they're deserters, not enemy agents?"

"Certain. I questioned them myself, sir. Their stories checked out."

Weaver looked out at the darkened road. The traffic was backed up for almost a quarter of a mile, headlights on as darkness settled in, horns blaring irritably as the traffic inched forward at a snail's pace towards the barriers. Army motorcycle riders drove up and down the two lanes, making sure no one tried to make a run for it. Ahead, fires flickered in the hillside villages around the city, while behind him the desert road to Cairo grew darker by the minute. More horns blared and angry shouts filled the dusk.

"They're getting bloody impatient," Myers commented.

"Tough." Weaver strode towards the barriers. "Let's see how the men are doing."

7:20 P.M.

The road was in chaos as Hassan sat in the Packard. It had taken him over two hours to reach the outskirts of Alex, driving as fast as he dared. Now the traffic ahead was bumper to bumper, and he'd joined the queue a hundred yards back.

The army was searching every vehicle. He knew it meant they hadn't found the Germans yet, or at least not all of them. The truck ahead of him, laden with a cargo of melons, inched forward. He slipped into gear and moved up in the line. There was an arc-light blazing at the check-point barrier, and suddenly he jolted with shock.

He noticed two officers, one British, one American, striding towards the barrier. The American who led the way was the intelligence officer he had encountered at the flat.

Weaver.

Hassan swore, and slammed his fist on the steering wheel. The American was unlikely to forget the face of someone who had tried to kill him—they had seen each other close up. He rubbed his jaw. The bruising hadn't completely gone away, more proof if Weaver needed it, so there was a chance he might be recognised, despite his disguise. Hassan thought frantically. He knew the risk was too great, and he made the decision instantly. He had to get away. He started to swing the Packard out of the line, ready to turn round and head back towards Cairo. Suddenly an armed military policeman on a motorcycle roared past, and screeched to a halt.

"Oi! You! Where do you think you're going, mate?"

Hassan shrugged. "The road's too slow and I have an important business appointment. I must go another route."

"Not bloody likely. There's a search in progress. You stay in line, understand?"

"Yes, sir. Of course, sir."

The military policeman glared back, then roared off. Hassan sat there, trying not to panic, but his heart was racing. If he tried to flee, he risked being shot before he had moved a hundred yards. He had no option but to stay in the queue. But if Weaver recognised him, he was finished.

He sweated in the clammy heat of the car, and five endless minutes later he was only one vehicle away from the head of the queue. The truck in front moved forward to be searched, then one of the soldiers beckoned Hassan to take its place.

He was next.

He saw Weaver still at the barrier, his hands on his hips as he watched the soldiers swarm over the truck. But just as Hassan was about to move ahead, the American looked up, past the truck, and stared at the Packard.

Hassan shifted back into the shadows and swore to himself, unsure if he had been recognised. There was no way out. He reached into the glove compartment and removed the ivory-handled knife. Tarik was dead and the American had a debt to pay. He felt the anger well inside him. He made up his mind to kill Weaver and take his chances trying to escape, if it came to it. If he could smash through the barrier and flee towards the outskirts of Alex he stood a chance—the Packard was faster and more powerful than any army vehicle that would pursue him.

The soldier beckoned him again. "Come on, mate. Move it, move it!"

Hassan shifted into gear, and inched the car forward.

7:20 P.M.

Weaver was growing tired, and impatient. He watched as a corporal examined the identity papers of an Egyptian truck driver, while one of his men climbed in to inspect the cabin. Another looked under the chassis with an electric torch, and two more climbed on the back to search through the cargo of melons.

Halder and Rachel had to be *somewhere* in the city, but more than likely they were trying to get out. With so many checkpoints and searches, Weaver reasoned, they couldn't have escaped. His gut instinct told him they had to be out there, somewhere in the long queue of traffic, trying to flee, and probably in disguise with false papers, which was why he wanted to be present to identify them.

And then what? Weaver didn't want to think about that.

But at least he might have a chance of convincing Halder to surrender peacefully, before anyone else got hurt. He sighed with frustration and looked back at the traffic waiting to enter the city.

A big, dark American Packard was next in the queue. A private beckoned for the driver to move up in line and take the truck's place, but he hesitated. Weaver strained to see the driver, but he moved back into the shadows.

The private waved again. "Come on, mate. Move it, move it!"

The Packard finally crept forward, the driver's face still hidden.

Weaver approached the car, faintly suspicious.

Suddenly an engine roared.

Weaver spun round and saw a Jeep speeding towards the barrier, from the direction of the city. It drove on the rim of the road, tilted at an angle, the outside wheels running on sand. Someone was trying to make a break for it.

He wrenched out his pistol, was about to aim when he recognised Sanson in the passenger seat. The Jeep screeched to a halt in a cloud of dust.

"Christ! I almost shot you."

"Get in," Sanson said urgently. He called Myers over. "Follow us, and bring a radio operator."

"What's up?" Weaver demanded.

"We've hit pay-dirt, that's what. The police got an anonymous tip-off. There's a suspicious couple in a brothel near the seafront. I've got two squads on their way to surround the place—there's no way they can escape. If we put our skates on, we can be there in ten minutes."

Weaver jumped into the back of the Jeep. It swung round, and roared away.

Hassan let out a sigh of relief as Weaver sped off. He was certain the American had spotted him, but he'd been saved by the arrival of the British officer. He looked familiar, and Hassan remembered where he'd seen him. One of the men who had burst into the flat to rescue Weaver.

If both of them were involved in the hunt, how much did they know? That worried Hassan even more. Something else struck him: the way they had driven off in such a terrible hurry. Perhaps they had found the Germans? Hassan licked the hollows in his gums, remembered Tarik, and a powerful desire for revenge for what the American had done raged inside him.

"Out of the car, sir, and let's be having your papers," a sergeant ordered.

Hassan climbed out. The sergeant examined his papers carefully, as a couple of soldiers quickly checked inside the car and opened the boot.

"Your business in Alex, sir?"

"I'm visiting my father. He's very ill." If he'd been wearing a djellaba instead of a suit, and driving a donkey cart instead of the Packard, Hassan knew the sergeant wouldn't have shown him such courtesy.

"The car's clean, Sarge, but I found this."

A corporal handed over the knife. "A pretty dangerous weapon," the sergeant remarked, and raised his eyes, waiting for an explanation.

Hassan shrugged, confident he was safe. "I'm a businessman. I'm sure you know how it is, Sergeant. In Egypt, a man like myself must protect himself from hoodlums and thieves."

The sergeant didn't seem to doubt it for a minute. He handed Hassan back his knife.

"May I enquire why all this searching?"

"No, sir, you may not. Move on, please."

Hassan got back into the car and started the engine. On the long stretch of desert road up ahead, he saw the taillights of Weaver's Jeep, and the second one behind it, racing towards the city. Deacon had told him to find the policeman. But a thought suddenly sparked in Hassan's head.

He had a better idea.

FORTY-SEVEN

7:30 P.M.

Halder was woken by the sound of traffic. It was dark outside, a wash of moonlight filtering into the room through the open shutters. When he put out his hand for Rachel, she wasn't there. He reached for the revolver under the pillow, climbed out of bed, and was about to flick on the light when he saw her sitting in a cane chair near the window. "You gave me a fright—for a moment there, I thought you'd gone." He relaxed, saw the Baedeker lying open on her knees. "What are you doing?"

"Thinking."

He kissed her forehead. "I thought you wanted to sleep."

"I decided to have a look at the guidebook. There are a couple of routes we hadn't considered."

"Such as?"

"The harbour, for one. From there, we could make it to Rashid and on to Cairo." She handed him the book. "See for yourself."

Halder slipped the revolver into his trouser belt and turned on the light. He glanced at the book before putting it aside, shaking his head. "You can bet Harry and his friends will have the harbour covered. Besides, it's too slow a route, and there's nowhere to run to once you're out on the open sea."

"The book says there's an aerodrome."

"Two, actually. But how do we get past the guards?"

"You've got a military ID. You bluff your way in, and we hitch a ride."

"It's not that easy, Rachel. Even if we manage to get anywhere near an aircraft, there are all sorts of complications. They'd probably want to verify my military ID before they let us board, or they could already have been alerted in case we tried something like that."

"But we can't just sit here and wait to be caught. We have to do *something*." A note of desperation crept into her voice.

"The desert is still our best bet. Probably our only one."

"And how do we steal transport?"

"Leave that to me." He took her hand and pulled her up beside him, cupped her face in one of his palms. "Do you have any regrets about what happened between us?"

She shook her head, and then he saw tears at the edges of her eyes. "Do you want to know the truth?"

"Tell me."

"I could never make up my mind between you and Harry. You see, I loved you both."

"And now?"

She bit her lip, and seemed distracted, on the verge of tears again, and then her arms went around his neck and she pulled him close. When they had kissed, she put her head against his chest, clutching him tightly. He held her for a long time, until she said, "It's so quiet up here."

"Maybe they've forgotten about us."

"A while ago I thought I heard someone out on the landing. Maybe we should look?"

"Let's hope our friend Safa kept her end of the bargain.

I'd hate to think what might happen if she didn't."

As Halder went towards the door, they heard a screech of tyres. He flicked off the bedroom light and crossed to the window. Half a dozen army trucks had drawn up in the street below, dozens of soldiers climbing down, unslinging their rifles. He came away from the window, his face taut.

"It looks like we've got company." He took out his pistol. "Get dressed, quickly."

Suddenly they heard banging on the door, and a voice roared, "Open up! Military police."

Halder froze. A split second later there was more pounding, and another voice shouted, "Come out with your hands up—you're surrounded!"

In their panic, it took them a moment to realise that the noise hadn't come from *outside* their door, but through the open window, from one of the landings in the buildings directly opposite. Halder looked out and Rachel joined him. Soldiers and police were coming from all directions. A Jeep had pulled up and Harry Weaver was in the back. He climbed down, accompanied by the British intelligence officer, Sanson, whom Halder had shot at the station. The man's right hand was heavily bandaged. Both men raced up the steps of the building across the street.

"What's going on?" Rachel asked.

"Either they've gone to the wrong address, or it's not us they're after."

They waited anxiously, then came the crash of splintering wood from one of the landings opposite, like the sound of a door being kicked in. Five minutes later they saw Weaver and Sanson come out of the building. There was a buzz of activity as half a dozen military policemen followed them out, escorting a tall, blond young man and an Arab woman. They had their hands on their heads, and were bundled into one of the trucks and driven off.

Weaver and Sanson stayed outside on the steps, talking earnestly for several minutes, until Sanson strode over to his Jeep, climbed in, and it drove away. They saw Harry Weaver remain behind, looking totally frustrated. He glanced up and down the street, towards the busy café, studying the scene. Then his eyes moved up to the windows of the buildings around him, as if he were considering something, before he strode over to a uniformed British captain sitting in another jeep. He seemed to be arguing with the officer.

Halder stepped back into the shadows and pulled Rachel after him. "I'm afraid Harry looks like he's under stress. And I didn't like the look on his face—he's up to something."

"What was all that business about across the street?"

Halder heard an engine start up and looked out of the window again. Weaver had climbed back into the Jeep, and it moved off, its red tail-lights disappearing up the street.

"By the looks of it, they've arrested the wrong couple. Harry's gone for now, but if he decides to search the area, it won't be long before someone knocks on our door." He turned back to Rachel. "As they say in American movies—it's time to get out of Dodge City."

"Why the hell weren't all the brothels checked?" Weaver demanded angrily.

He was in Myers's Jeep, speeding towards the city centre. The captain blushed. "Well, sir, some of them are popular with our senior brass. It wouldn't do to go barging in and—"

Weaver cut him off, furious. "How many?"

"I—I couldn't rightly say, sir—probably no more than half a dozen. Besides, a bordello didn't seem a likely refuge for a couple."

Weaver gritted his teeth in frustration. Sanson had gone to oversee the checkpoints. The couple they'd arrested had turned out to be a German deserter who'd escaped from a POW camp, and a prostitute he'd befriended. Weaver had stood in the street afterwards, looking up at the shabby buildings. The red-light district was an ideal hiding place, a maze of back alleyways, seething with European refugees lodging in its run-down hotels and flophouses. Which was why, when he strode back to Myers, he'd asked if every hotel and brothel in the area had been checked, just to be certain.

"No, sir," Myers had reluctantly admitted.

Now that Weaver had heard the explanation, he exploded. "Stop the damned car," he ordered the driver. The man pulled into the kerb and Weaver rounded angrily on the captain. "Find out exactly how many were ignored, and damned fast. Get on the radio. And I don't give a fig how many generals are caught with their pants down."

"Yes—yes, sir." Myers switched on the radio, picked up the hand mike, put the receiver to his ear, and spoke for several minutes on the crackling set. "There are only five we didn't search, sir."

"Where the hell are they?" Weaver demanded.

"One's near the docks area, another's back at the Corniche. The other three are in the suburbs of San Stefano and Sidi Bishr. Most of them are high-class establishments with European girls." Myers blushed again. "I'd still suggest we don't go kicking in any doors, sir. It could upset any brass who might be visiting, and there'll be hell to pay."

"That's my worry, not yours. We'll take the docks and Corniche first, they're the nearest." Weaver tapped the driver on the shoulder. "Get moving."

7:50 P.M.

Hassan sweated as he drove the Packard through the narrow streets. He'd lost Weaver twice as the army vehicles sped towards the city, then found him again in the suburbs. Five minutes later he saw Weaver's driver enter the red-light area, and turn down a back street lined with military trucks, troops everywhere. Hassan pulled a sharp left into the kerb and hit the brakes.

It appeared that some sort of raid was in progress. Dozens of soldiers and police had cordoned off the street. Weaver and the officer with the eye patch disappeared into a building, and came out a short time later, followed by a group of MPs guarding a man and a woman with their hands on their heads. The couple were bundled into the back of a truck and driven off.

Hassan swore. They had obviously found two of the Germans.

He saw Weaver walk back towards the Jeep and argue with a captain. Hassan was trying to figure out what was going on when an Egyptian policeman came over.

"You'll have to move on, sir."

"What's happening here, Officer?"

The policeman took in Hassan's suit, the American car, and seemed to consider that he was someone of importance. He saluted. "We caught a German deserter," he said proudly.

Hassan frowned. "It seems a lot of fuss for a deserter."

The policeman simply shrugged. "I'm afraid you'll have to move on, sir."

Hassan saw Weaver climb into his Jeep again and drive off in a different direction to the truck. He couldn't understand what was going on. If they had found two of the Germans, why hadn't Weaver followed the prisoners? He started the car and tried one last time with the policeman. "Who was the woman you arrested?"

"The deserter's girlfriend. A local *sharmoota*. Move on now, sir."

A *prostitute*. Hassan grinned and understood. No wonder Weaver looked angry. The army had obviously got the wrong couple. He reversed out of the alley, shifted into forward gear, and drove after Weaver's Jeep.

7:50 P.M

Gabrielle Pirou wrung her hands in despair, feeling more perplexed by the minute.

She glanced anxiously at the telephone on her desk. The man and woman upstairs had to be the couple the army was looking for, she had convinced herself of that. She had hoped they would simply leave quietly, and save her the trouble of calling the military police, but so far that hadn't happened. When she'd crept upstairs to check, the door was locked from the inside. A raid would have been embarrassing for her clients, and disastrous for business. But the last customer had departed out of the back door more than an hour ago, and she'd given the girls the rest of the evening off.

She couldn't wait any longer for the pair to leave, and the last thing she wanted was to risk a confrontation. Trembling, she reached for the receiver and dialled the number of Military Police HQ.

A man's voice answered. "Provost's office. Sergeant-Major Squires speaking."

"I—I have some information that might interest you," Gabrielle offered.

"Who's speaking?"

Gabrielle gave her name and address, told the sergeant-major about the couple and gave their descriptions. There was a long silence, and then she heard the excitement in the man's voice. "Your address again?"

Gabrielle told him, and said anxiously, "How long before your men arrive?"

"They'll be there within ten minutes, lady. But don't do anything foolish. If it's the pair we're looking for, they're armed and highly dangerous. Just stay on the line," the sergeant-major said reassuringly. "I'll be right here until they arrive."

The poodle yapped at her feet and Gabrielle's heart skipped with fright. "Donny—please."

"Is everything all right, miss?" the voice asked.

"Yes—fine."

Ten minutes. It would be an eternity. And she certainly didn't like the armed and highly dangerous bit. The best thing she could do would be to exit quietly through the back door, and leave everything to the proper authorities. She was about to speak into the receiver, to tell the sergeant-major her plans, when she heard a soft click and looked round as the parlour door opened.

The couple stood there. The man had a gun in his hand. "You've been a naughty girl, madame. Now, please put down the telephone and do exactly as I say."

8 P.M.

As Weaver sped towards the seafront, the radio crackled on the back seat. He swung round and saw the radio operator slip on his earphones and speak into the mike. A moment later the man looked up. "Message for you, sir. There's been a phone call to the Provost's office. Some lady claims the couple we're looking for are on her premises."

Weaver's heart skipped as he told the driver to pull in. "What's the address?"

The operator told him, glanced at Myers, and tried to suppress a smile. "It's a high-class knocking shop on the Corniche, sir, popular with some of the senior brass. The

Provost's dispatched two dozen men. They should be there within minutes. But it's only a couple of streets away—we might get there sooner."

Weaver said anxiously, "Pass on the word—no one's to do anything rash until I arrive. I want the couple alive." As the radio operator spoke into the mike, Weaver shouted at the driver, "Let's move it, soldier. Put your foot down."

8:05 P.M.

The poodle yapped at Halder's feet and he said to Rachel, "Put the dog outside for now, and find a towel and some bed-sheets. Then turn off all the lights on the ground floor."

Rachel picked up the protesting animal and carried him out into the hall. Halder looked back at Madam Pirou. The woman seemed paralysed with fear, but was obviously relieved she hadn't been shot.

"What did you tell the military police?"

She told him, and Halder said, "Who else is in the building?"

"No one. Everyone's gone. I—I thought there might be trouble."

"Very thoughtful of you. Do you have a car, by any chance?"

The woman didn't answer. Halder levelled the gun and said gently, "Madame, it's really against my nature to threaten a lady, but believe me, I mean business."

"I—I have a Citroën."

"Where?"

"In the garage at the back."

"Does the garage open on to the street at the rear?"

"Y—Yes."

"Where are the keys for both?"

"In the bottom drawer of my desk."

Halder searched and found them. "I presume there's fuel in the tank?"

Gabrielle nodded, still trembling. Her military connections ensured that she always had a plentiful supply. Suddenly they both heard loud knocking. It sounded as if it was coming from the front door down the hall.

"Who's that?" barked Halder.

The Frenchwoman looked terribly frightened. "Probably a customer."

"Or your phone call got a quicker response than you expected." Halder yanked the telephone wire from the wall socket as Rachel came back with a towel and sheets. "There's someone at the front door."

"I heard." He put down his gun, twisted the bed-sheets and used them to tie the madame to one of the chairs, then secured the towel around her mouth. "Unlike some of your customers, I can't say it's been a pleasure, madame. I hope you won't be too uncomfortable for too long."

Gabrielle Pirou squealed behind the gag. The knocking down the hall became louder. Halder picked up the revolver and nodded to Rachel. "Let's go."

8:05 P.M.

Weaver pounded on the front door for the third time.

He looked up at the four-storey building. No lights were on; the place was in complete darkness. He had his pistol out and his driver, a corporal, stood beside him, a Sten gun in his hands, Myers and the radio operator waiting on the pavement, weapons at the ready. People strolling on the promenade across the Corniche looked over, and a few curious passers-by began to stop and stare. Weaver said to the corporal, "Tell them to move on."

The corporal did as he was told, and Weaver went back down the front steps and said to Myers, "You're sure this is the address?"

"Yes, sir. It's well known by reputation. Run by a Frenchwoman named Madam Pirou. You want me to try and see if there's a back way in? I think there's a side street further along that leads to the rear."

Weaver looked back at the building. If anyone was inside, they would have heard him knocking by now, but no lights had come on, and it made him deeply suspicious.

"No, I'll do it myself. You stay here and cover the front. If anyone comes out, caution them before you start any shooting. When the rest of the men arrive, tell them the same. I want the couple alive, if possible."

Weaver saw the entrance to a darkened alleyway further down the street. "Is that the way to the rear?"

"I think so, sir." Myers nodded.

Weaver cocked his pistol and raced towards the alley.

FORTY-EIGHT

Halder stepped out into the rear courtyard, Rachel behind him. He saw the outhouse he had noticed earlier from the upstairs window, and realised it was the garage. There was an entrance door off to one side, and he found it unlocked.

The place was in pitch darkness and smelled of oil. He fumbled along the walls and flicked on a light switch. A black pre-war Citroën, its chrome and bodywork brightly polished, stood gleaming under the light, and there was a pair of wooden exit doors that led outside, a small Judas-gate set in one of them.

"See if they're open." Halder yanked the driver's door of the Citroën and jumped inside.

Rachel rattled the garage doors. "They're locked."

He tossed her the keys and she found the right one and turned the lock. "Don't open them out yet—I'll do it when I'm ready," Halder told her. "Now give me back the keys."

She threw them across. He inserted one of the keys in the ignition, pressed the starter switch, and the engine spluttered and died. "Say a prayer." He tried again, twice, and it started the third time. "The gods are with us after all. Climb in."

Rachel slid into the passenger seat, then Halder went over to the Judas-gate, opened it a crack, and looked out. A cobbled back street lay outside, lit by the wash of lights from a couple of buildings and the café opposite. A few Arabs and off-duty soldiers passed by in the street. He was just about to open out the garage doors when he suddenly heard a commotion further along the alley. A man was moving at a jogging pace along the wall, coming towards the garage, carrying a pistol. Passers-by were stepping out of the man's way, and he recognised Harry Weaver at once.

Halder moved smartly back inside and shut the Judas-gate.

"It seems I spoke too soon."

"What's the matter?" Rachel asked.

"We've got company—Harry, to be precise, and he's coming this way. The madame's phone call must have brought him running."

"You . . . you're not serious?"

"Believe me, it's him. Get in the passenger seat and kill the engine. Stay in the car and don't make a sound."

Rachel did as she was told, leaning across the dashboard and turning off the ignition. The garage became deathly silent. Halder killed the light, then fumbled his way back to the Citroën. A little later they heard the creak of a gate being opened somewhere outside, then silence. After a while, Rachel seemed unable to bear the tension, and she whispered, "Where's he gone?"

"At a guess, in the back way to look for us."

"Shouldn't we get out of here before it's too late?"

Halder made to move out of the car. "There's been a slight change of plan. Stay here and don't make a sound."

"But that's crazy. Harry will—"

"Just do as I say." Halder cocked the revolver, stepped out of the seat, and disappeared into the darkness.

Weaver had counted off the rear entrances as he moved along the back wall, pistol in hand, hardly paying attention to the shocked passers-by in the street who stared at him. He came to an arched iron gate that opened into a small flagstoned courtyard, a couple of fig trees beyond. He saw a pair of double wooden doors further along the wall but he ignored them and tried the gate.

It creaked open and he stepped into the courtyard. Across the flagstones was a door into the rear of the main building. He moved towards it, tried the handle. The door opened, and he found himself in an unlit hallway. On one side was a darkened kitchen, with more rooms further along.

He was aware of an unbearable tension coiled inside him as he felt his way along the hall, pistol at the ready. He heard a noise and halted. It sounded like a dog yapping, and came from a room up the hall. He moved towards the door, halted outside.

The yapping erupted again. He readied himself, put a hand on the doorknob, turned it slowly, and burst into the room, ready to fire.

A poodle nipped at his feet. He almost shot the animal, before he saw the woman tied to a chair and gagged with a towel. He laid down his pistol, loosened the gag, and the woman sucked in air, white from trauma.

"*Merci!* Thank God you came!"

Weaver untied her and she scooped up the poodle and embraced it. "The Bosch bastards—they put *petit* Donny and me through hell!"

The woman emitted a string of French expletives before Weaver interrupted. "Madam Pirou?"

"*Oui.*"

"Where's the couple?"

Weaver stepped out into the courtyard. He saw the garage across the patio and moved towards it carefully. He hesitated before he turned the door handle. The interior was in darkness, but he could see the dim outline of a car. Halder and Rachel hadn't taken it after all. He moved inside. The garage appeared empty, and there was a strong smell of oil and must, but as he fumbled for a light switch he felt the cold tip of a gun barrel on the back of his neck.

"Not a word, Harry," a voice whispered. "Don't try to move—I'd really hate to have to kill you. Now, put the safety catch on, then drop your pistol on the ground."

Weaver did as he was told and the pistol clattered to the floor. A second later a bulb blazed on and the garage was flooded with light. Weaver stared ahead. Sitting in the Citroën's passenger seat was Rachel. She looked round and her eyes met his. Before Weaver could speak, Halder stepped out from behind, a revolver in his hand, and picked up the Colt pistol.

"We meet again, old friend, and hardly in pleasant circumstances."

"What the *hell's* going on?"

"If you don't mind, we'll save the reunion speeches for later. For now, move to the front of the car."

Weaver obeyed. Halder said, "Are any of your men outside?"

When Weaver hesitated, Halder said, "Don't lie to me, Harry, or people are liable to get killed. Us included."

"They're at the front. I came round the back way."

"Alone?"

"Yes."

"Get in the driver's seat."

"You'll never get away," Weaver told him. "The area's surrounded."

"Maybe, but I happen to have an ace up my sleeve."

"And what's that?"

Halder smiled. "I'll tell you later, Harry. Now get in the car and do exactly as you're told. Drive out on to the street, hang a left, and head east out of the city. Keep going until I tell you to stop."

"You're crazy, Jack. You won't get a hundred yards. The entire city's crawling with troops and police, looking for you."

"A fact I'm well aware of. Get in the car."

Weaver slid in beside Rachel. He looked across at her face, felt overcome with emotion. "Rachel—"

"Hello, Harry."

Before Weaver could speak further, Halder climbed into the back seat and prodded the revolver in his ribs. "See if the street's clear," he ordered Rachel. "If you spot uniforms or anything suspicious, let me know."

Rachel did as Halder instructed. She walked to the doors and peered out through the Judas-gate, then came back. "It all looks quiet, apart from a few pedestrians. I didn't see any soldiers."

"Then let's be grateful for small mercies—it sounds like maybe we're a little ahead of Harry's posse. Open out the doors, then get back in here."

She pushed out the double doors, then she came back and sat in the passenger seat. Halder said, "Start the car, Harry."

"Jack, for God's sake be sensible—we can't get far."

Halder pushed the gun harder into his ribs. "I'd appreciate it if you'd do as you're told. I don't want to do something I'll be sorry for. And don't turn on the headlights until I tell you to."

Weaver started the ignition and the engine throbbed into life first time.

"Drive on out," Halder ordered. "If anyone tries to stop us or gets in our way, put your foot down hard. And remember, don't even attempt to stop the car unless I tell you."

Weaver revved the engine. He waited until a couple of Arab pedestrians in the alley had moved out of the way, then shifted into gear and released the clutch. The Citroën jerked forward, and he swung left out of the garage.

FORTY-NINE

8:05 P.M.

Hassan pulled up on the seafront and killed the engine. He knew he couldn't keep following Weaver for much longer without being spotted. He had seen the American knock on the door of the house on the Corniche, then disappear down an alleyway while his men waited outside. He was still looking for the Germans in the red-light district, that much was obvious.

Hassan sat there in frustration. If they were inside the building, he hadn't a hope of alerting them first, not with armed troops on the street. But it looked as if Weaver was going to cover the back way, alone. He slipped the knife into his pocket and got out of the car.

He crossed the road and turned down one of the alleyways that brought him to the rear of the seafront buildings, but saw no sign of the American. As he walked along, trying to count off the houses, a pair of garage doors suddenly swung open further down the alley. A black Citroën drove out, its headlights extinguished. Weaver sat in the driver's seat, a woman in front beside him, another man wearing civilian clothes in the back. The car swung left and drove away, picking up speed. For a moment, Hassan stood there in complete bewilderment, then he raced back to the Packard.

As he came out on to the seafront again he saw an army truck screech to a halt on the promenade, followed by several Jeeps. He slowed to a walking pace, anxious not to draw attention to himself. Soldiers were appearing from everywhere now, and a section of the Corniche was being sealed off. Outside the house where Weaver had knocked, troops took up positions.

It took Hassan less than two anxious minutes to walk back to the Packard, but he knew by then he was far too late. He had lost whatever chance he had of following Weaver. He couldn't risk driving off at speed, and he hadn't a hope of finding the Citroën in the maze of back streets. He cursed as he slid into the car.

The road ahead was completely blocked with soldiers. A handful were being led towards the back streets by an officer. The fools didn't know what had happened. Two of the Germans had obviously escaped and taken Weaver with them as hostage. Hassan sat there, trying to reason things out.

The Germans might try to make for Rashid. It was probably their only hope of escape. He grinned wickedly and started the engine, an interesting thought coming to him. If he took one of the minor roads that cut on to the coast, he might even get there before them. And if he was right, and Rashid was where the Germans were headed, then he had a chance of settling his score with the American.

8:15 P.M.
Weaver drove through the twisting back streets, until Halder said, "Turn on the headlights."

They were dimmed with blue paint because of the blackout regulations, and when Weaver flicked on the beams, they hardly made a difference.

Halder leaned forward, looked left and right. "Head towards the sea. Keep your speed down, unless I tell you otherwise."

"How about telling me what's going on?"

"We'll leave the talk until later. Just concentrate on driving."

Weaver swung left and eventually came to a junction with the Corniche. Across the street, the Mediterranean shimmered in the moonlight. Suddenly an open army truck sped past along the seafront, dozens of armed troops standing in the back, followed by several Jeeps.

"Wait! Keep your foot off the pedal," Halder ordered.

The vehicles pulled up outside Madam Pirou's, men climbing down and taking up positions on the street.

"It looks like we got out just in time." Halder checked left and right. "OK, the road's clear. Pull out and turn right."

When Weaver hesitated, Halder pushed the pistol into his ribs. "You heard me, Harry. Do it."

Weaver turned right, along the Corniche. "Where am I supposed to be going?"

"Just continue east out of the city. That's all you need to know for now."

They drove on in silence along the seafront, the tension in the car unbearable. Weaver glanced across at Rachel. She looked at him.

"Keep your eyes on the road," Halder intervened.

"You'll never make it out of Alex alive. Surrender, Jack, it's your only chance."

"We have an ace, remember."

"And what's that?"

"You, Harry. You're going to get us out of this mess."

Up ahead, they all saw a barrier strung across the road, several MPs and Egyptian policemen with rifles and machineguns manning the blockade. A military truck was parked on the footpath, a radio operator sitting on the back running board.

Halder tensed. "I guess this is the acid test. When we get close, explain who you are and show your ID. Tell them you're making a checkpoint inspection. If anyone asks any questions, we're with you, and you're in a hurry. Think you can manage that?"

"And if I don't?"

"There'll be shooting, and we're all in trouble. But somehow I don't think you want that."

Weaver flicked a glance at Rachel. She looked frightened, and touched his hand. "Please, Harry. Just do as he says."

Moments later they were at the checkpoint and Weaver

eased the Citroën to a halt. A sergeant came forward and flashed a torch in their faces. Weaver rolled down the window and the sergeant saluted.

"Sorry, sir, but we'll have to check your vehicle and papers." He looked in at the passengers. "Yours too, sir, madam."

Weaver handed across his ID. "Lieutenant-Colonel Weaver, military intelligence. I'm overseeing this operation. Have you anything to report?"

The sergeant quickly examined Weaver's ID under the torch light, handed it back, and snapped to attention. "Sorry, sir. Nothing."

"Are you stopping every vehicle and pedestrian?"

"Yes, sir, civilian and military, exactly as we were ordered."

Weaver jerked a thumb at Rachel and Halder. "These people are with me, there's no need to check their documents. We're in a hurry."

The sergeant looked in at the passengers. For a second or two he hesitated, as if unsure about something, then Weaver said, "Get a move on with the barrier, Sergeant. I've got more checkpoint inspections to make and I haven't got all night."

"I'm sorry, sir, but I have orders to examine every passenger's documents—"

"Of course you have. Those were my orders. Now do as I say."

"Yes, sir. Very good, sir." The sergeant saluted and ordered his men to move the barrier. Weaver drove through. When he looked in the rear-view mirror he saw the sergeant stare after the Citroën, scratching his jaw, before he strode over to the radio sitting at the back of the truck.

Halder let out a breath. "You did well, Harry. Let's just hope our luck holds."

"What now?" Weaver asked grimly.

"Take the next turning for Rashid."

8:10 P.M.

The seafront bristled with troops, and Sanson climbed briskly out of his Jeep and went over to a corporal with a

Sten gun hanging from his shoulder. "Sanson, Intelligence. What's happening?"

"We only just got here ourselves, sir. We tried knocking on the door but got no reply."

Sanson looked up at the building. The lights were out and it appeared deserted. "You're certain this is the place?"

"Positive, sir."

"Where's Lieutenant-Colonel Weaver?"

"He went looking for a back way in."

"When?"

"About five minutes ago."

Sanson called over an officer and flashed his ID. "I'm taking charge. Get a couple of dozen men round the back—I want the alleyways sealed off."

"I believe Captain Myers and some men went round the back a few minutes ago, sir, looking for Lieutenant-Colonel Weaver."

"Have they got a radio?"

"No, sir."

"Then send some more men after them and find out what the bloody hell's going on. Make certain both ends of the street are blocked off, front and back—no one gets in or out. And find Lieutenant-Colonel Weaver."

"Yes, sir."

The officer was about to turn away when light showed through the glass above the hall door, and the corporal said to Sanson, "Something's happening, sir."

"Tell the men to take positions. No one's to shoot unless I give the order. Pass it on."

The officer barked the order and soldiers raced for cover, readied their weapons. Sanson bounded up the steps to the front entrance, drawing his pistol, a couple of men behind him. They positioned themselves on either side of the door. A moment later came the rattle of bolts.

"Is that you, Weaver?" Sanson called out. "Are you in there?"

The door began to open very slowly and an elderly woman appeared. Her face was a mask of smudged lipstick and rouge, and her mouth dropped when she saw the array of weapons pointed at her.

"Oh my God! Please don't shoot!" she screamed.

"Put your bloody hands in the air, where I can see them, and don't try anything," Sanson roared.

Behind the woman, a man's voice said, "Don't shoot, for Christ's sake!"

Myers appeared, a couple of infantrymen behind him. Sanson frowned as he lowered his gun, then he exploded. "What the *fuck* is going on? Where's Weaver?"

"We got in the back way, sir. It seems he's disappeared."

8:15 P.M.
Sanson stormed into the garage and out through the double doors. The back street was crowded with soldiers, sealing off the area. He came back into the garage. "You're absolutely certain Lieutenant-Colonel Weaver came this way?"

Gabrielle Pirou nodded. "When he heard the couple took my car keys, he went after them."

Sanson kicked one of the doors furiously, his face livid. "What's the licence number of your car?"

She told him, and a fuming Sanson said to an NCO near by, "Get on the radio and alert every patrol and checkpoint. Give them the licence number and tell them to be on the lookout for a black Citroën with three passengers. The car's got to be stopped no matter what."

Myers stumbled in through the garage doors, out of breath, and saluted. "I questioned the people in the café across the street like you said, sir."

"Well? Spit it out, man!"

"The owner claims he saw someone drive out in Madam Pirou's Citroën no more than a few minutes ago. He thinks there were three people inside, a woman and two men. A uniformed officer was behind the wheel. From the description I got, it sounds like Lieutenant-Colonel Weaver."

FIFTY

9 P.M.
The ancient fishing port of Rashid lay just over twenty miles east of Alexandria. Built on the marshlands of the Nile delta, dominated by the conquering Turks in the fif-

teenth century, and bombarded by the French during Napoleon's campaign, the port and its broad estuary had been of strategic importance ever since the time of the Pharaohs: the Nile flowed into the Mediterranean from Rashid, leaving an exposed artery running through the entire heartland of Egypt, all the way down to Cairo and Luxor.

It was pitch dark as Weaver drove through the town, a rundown shambles of Egyptian and French styles, with peeling shutters and crumbling stone buildings. "Take the next road south," Halder told him.

A smell of salt air and rotting fish wafted into the Citroën as they trundled over cobblestone past the massive granite harbour. A couple of rusting Allied frigates lay at anchor, and the whole town had a sad, neglected look.

"It's hard to believe Napoleon intended to conquer all of Egypt from here," commented Halder.

"Save me the history lesson, Jack. What do *you* intend?"

"Ask me no questions, Harry, and I'll tell you no lies."

Halder pointed towards the Nile delta, lit by the moon, the riverbank dotted with the silhouettes of tall palm trees. "You'll see a road ahead. It runs alongside some cane fields by the water. There's a track down to an old jetty. That's where you're headed."

9:05 P.M.

Hassan had taken one of the minor roads, eventually cutting on to the coast, but he hadn't seen the black Citroën on the way. He feared he might have been wrong about the Germans trying to make it to Rashid, or perhaps they had been caught *en route*. Either way, he would have to get rid of the boat. He drove to the end of a grass-strewn track lined with palms and halted. He was south of Rashid, on the delta marshlands.

A boathouse stood off to the left, a crumbling wooden affair once used by local fishermen which looked as if it hadn't been occupied in years. He saw a wooden motor vessel with a sharp prow tied up at the jetty. He got out of the Packard, took a torch from the boot, and flashed it three times. A light flashed back at him, then a small, unshaven man wearing a greasy captain's hat trotted out of the boathouse shadows, carrying a storm lamp.

He frowned, recognising Hassan. "I didn't expect to see *you* here. What's up, cousin? Have we a cargo?"

"There's been a change of plan. You must leave at once."

The man looked relieved, but at that precise moment they heard an engine noise. Hassan turned, and saw the lights of an approaching car back along the track. As it drew closer, the headlights flashed three times. Hassan's spirits rose when he saw the distinctive black Citroën. He signalled with the torch, then turned to his cousin and grinned.

"It seems your cargo's arrived after all. Get the boat ready."

"Those friends of yours had better be fast—we can't hang about all night if you want to avoid the river patrols."

The man tossed away his cigarette, scurried down to the jetty with the storm lamp and climbed into the boat. As he began to untie the ropes, Hassan saw the Citroën approach, Weaver still in the driver's seat.

He grinned to himself. "Time to settle old scores, American."

They all climbed out. Halder studied the Arab who came forward to meet them. "There are supposed to be four of you," the man said gruffly. "Where're the other two?"

"God only knows. We had some trouble—it's what delayed us." Halder jerked a thumb at Weaver. "This man's our prisoner—an American intelligence officer. We had to take him with us."

"I know all about your trouble. And I've met the American before." Hassan produced the knife, pointed the tip at Weaver's throat. "Remember me, Weaver?"

Halder saw the gleeful menace in the Arab's eyes. For a moment Weaver looked confused, until recognition sparked in his face. "I guess you can't get rid of a bad thing."

Halder frowned. "You obviously know each other. Care to explain?"

"Later," Hassan said sharply. "The boat's waiting. If you don't leave at once, you risk being spotted by the river patrols."

"You're not coming with us?"

"I return to Cairo by car."

Halder said to Rachel, "You'd better get down to the jetty."

"I—I'd like a few moments with Harry."

"You heard, there isn't time. We could have company any minute. The boatman's waiting. Go *now*."

Rachel bit her lip as she looked over at Weaver, then she moved off towards the jetty.

Halder said, "Bring the storm lamp from the boat. And find some rope to tie his hands."

"With pleasure." Hassan grinned, and moved off at a trot.

"Are you going to kill me?" Weaver asked.

"Come off it, Harry. We've been friends too long."

"You still haven't told me why you're involved in this. And why Rachel? I thought she was dead—"

"There's no time for all that, I'm afraid. With a bit of luck, someone will find you by morning. But by then, we'll be long gone."

Hassan came back with the storm lamp and a handful of rope. While he held the lamp, Halder yanked back Weaver's arms and tied them. "Now take him to the boat-house."

Hassan grinned. "And then I kill him."

"No one's going to kill anyone," Halder snapped. "Just tie him securely and gag him. Make sure he can't escape or call for help. When you're finished, ditch the Citroën in the river."

Hassan looked completely puzzled. "But he's the enemy, and he's seen our faces—"

"No buts, just do as you're told. I don't want him harmed," Halder ordered. He gave a wave, and turned towards the jetty. "So long, Harry. Be good."

Hassan shoved Weaver into the boathouse. There was a dirt floor and wooden rafters, ancient nets hanging overhead, and the place stank of rotting fish.

The Arab hung the storm lamp on one of the rafters and pushed Weaver into a corner.

"I should have killed you last time, American. It was my mistake."

Weaver heard the boat's engine start up outside, and knew what was coming. Hassan tossed the rope aside and drew his knife out again. "But don't worry, I'm going to finish it now. Slowly. Painfully." He moved closer, a blood-thirsty look on his face. "Then I'm going to cut out your heart."

Hassan slashed with the blade and Weaver stepped back. "Give in to the will of Allah, American. Death will be quicker."

Weaver lashed out helplessly with his feet and the Arab laughed. "Good. You're angry. That way, dying will be more painful."

He slashed again, and Weaver staggered back. The Arab moved in for the kill. Weaver kicked out with his foot, but Hassan caught it, twisted, and Weaver fell back into the corner. He was trapped. There was nowhere to turn.

"And now you die."

Hassan raised the knife. There was a soft click and a voice said, "Put down the toothpick, there's a good boy."

Halder stood in the doorway, the pistol in his hand, livid anger on his face. Hassan frowned. "He tried to kill me once before. Now I kill him."

He turned back smartly to finish Weaver off. The blade stabbed through the air, but before it reached its target there was a loud explosion and a bullet nicked Hassan's ear, drawing blood. The knife clattered to the floor and he yelped in pain.

"You ought to wash out your ears," Halder admonished. "And heed a warning when it's given. I told you to tie him up—not kill him. Now get outside and take care of the Citroën, before I change my mind and finish the dirty deed."

There was a curious look on the Arab's face, rage mixed with confusion, as he clutched his ear. "Fool! You don't know what you're doing—"

Halder jerked the revolver impatiently. "Outside, I said. And be quick about it. I haven't got all night."

Hassan stared over at Weaver and spat on the floor. "*Inshallah.* There'll be another time, American."

He went out, glaring at Halder, who tucked the gun into his trouser belt, took a pack of cigarettes from his pocket, selected one, and lit it. "It's so hard to find decent help these days."

Weaver struggled to move. "Stay where you are, Harry." Halder picked up the rope and tied him securely to one of the wooden posts.

"You came to kill Roosevelt and Churchill, didn't you?"

Halder raised his eyes, his shock obvious. "And what makes you think that?"

"It's true, isn't it?"

"You always were quick off the mark, Harry. But this time you really do surprise me. Maybe it's a reasonable deduction, maybe not. The question is, what makes you think so?"

"It's an insane idea, Jack—a suicide mission. It doesn't have to be this way. Give yourself up right now and—"

"And what? Face a firing squad?" Halder finished tying the knot, stepped back, and shook his head solemnly. "That's about my only option, Rachel's too, even though she's an innocent in all this. Call me an adventurous fool, but I know where our chances lie, and surrender's not one of them. Besides, I'm in far too deep to wade out again."

"Because you killed two officers?"

Halder shook his head, disgust etched on his face. "Not my doing, I promise you that."

Weaver felt a welter of confusion. "I don't understand any of this. Why you and Rachel? How is she still alive—?"

Halder put a finger to his lips. "No time for explanations, not now. Let's just hope we don't bump into each other again, at least for the duration of this war. Even the thought of us being temporary enemies is hard enough to stomach, and I'd hate to ruin whatever fellowship remains. So do me a favour and stay out of this."

"I can't do that."

Halder ground out his cigarette with his shoe, his expression grim. "Then if it comes to the worst, a flower on my grave wouldn't go amiss. One of those lilies my father was so fond of will do quite nicely. I'd do the same for you, if it came to it. But meantime let's try to look on the bright side, and pray that doesn't happen—for either of us." A tortured look crossed his face. "I beg you, stay out of it, Harry," he pleaded. "This is bigger than both of us."

"I told you—I can't."

"So be it." Halder removed his jacket, took off his shirt, and twisted it to make a gag.

"Jack, for God's sake, listen to me—"

Halder tied the gag around Weaver's mouth, then slipped his jacket back on. He retrieved the storm lamp and moved towards the door. "It's been good seeing you again, and I mean that, despite the circumstances. And I'd love to stay and finish our talk, but I've got a boat waiting and duty beckons. So long, Harry."

Weaver struggled behind the gag, the storm lamp went out, the door banged shut, and the boathouse was plunged into darkness.

PART FOUR

22–23 NOVEMBER 1943

FIFTY-ONE

The Douglas C-54 transport plane, with the Stars and
Stripes emblem on its fuselage, touched down on the heavily guarded runway at RAF Cairo West airport, exactly two
and a half hours behind schedule. After a ten-hour night
flight from Tunis over barren desert and in total radio silence, a distance of almost two thousand miles, the crew
and passengers were exhausted.

Waiting on the runway apron were dozens of troop-filled
trucks and armoured vehicles, Secret Service agents, squads
of MPs mounted on motorcycles, and a cavalcade of staff
cars. When the aircraft taxied to a halt, there was a flurry
of activity, and two of the staff cars drove up to meet the
plane.

A group of anxious-looking senior officers stepped out
of the vehicles, among them the commanding general of
US Army forces in the Middle East, Major-General Royce,
his chief of staff, and the American ambassador, Alexander
C. Kirk. They waited while the aircraft door opened, and
then the Secret Service agents on board climbed down,
tough-looking men wearing suits, felt hats, and carrying
Thompson submachine-guns, who acted like a law unto
themselves as they surrounded the plane.

The Douglas C-54, nicknamed the Sacred Cow, had
been uniquely modified by the manufacturers, for as well
as the usual exits a special hydraulic door had been installed
in the fuselage. Moments later it whirred open, and an elec-
trical elevator cage began to lower the familiar white-suited
figure of President Franklin Delano Roosevelt, seated in his
wheelchair. Once he had been surrounded and helped to
disembark by the Secret Service men, his personal entou-
rage of uniformed military and naval personnel, tired-
looking men all of them, came down the metal steps.

Ambassador Kirk was the first to step forward, offering

his hand. "Good to see you again, Mr. President. Welcome to Cairo."

Roosevelt gave a warm handshake, smiled despite his exhaustion. "Hello, Alex. I guess I kept you all waiting, but better late than never."

Kirk and his companions were visibly relieved. Because of the secrecy of the President's flight plan, his pilot had maintained total radio silence. Two different groups of fighter escorts had been appointed to rendezvous with the plane at scheduled times during the flight, but they had failed to make visual contact and returned to their bases, leaving some very anxious senior officers fearful that the aircraft had been shot down.

"You certainly caused us some concerns, Mr. President," one of them commented. "We were just about to send up search planes."

Roosevelt smiled. "You can blame Major Bryan, my pilot. He reckoned the only way to avoid any enemy fighters that might cross our path by accident or design was to fly the longest route south." He greeted each of the senior officers present by name, then turned his attention back to Kirk. "And how have you been, Alex?"

"Fine, sir. I thought I should let you know that Prime Minister Churchill sends his best wishes, and is looking forward to your preliminary private discussion at eleven a.m. at the Mena, as scheduled, after you've both had a chance to greet the chiefs of staff."

"He arrived yesterday, I believe?"

"Yes, sir." Before Ambassador Kirk could speak further, the motorised cavalcade started up and the heavily armed Secret Service detail went into action, taking up their positions, forming a solid wall of flesh as the President was wheeled towards a waiting black Packard. No one could have failed to notice the extraordinary number of troops, military vehicles, and Bofors anti-aircraft guns guarding the airfield, least of all the President. "Security seems pretty tight this morning," Roosevelt remarked lightly.

Kirk dabbed his forehead with a handkerchief, waited until the Secret Service men had quickly transferred the President to the back seat of the Packard. "Sir, there's something of importance I'd like to discuss. Would you mind if I rode with you?"

"I was kind of hoping you would. Why, is there a problem?"

"I think you could say that, Mr. President."

Four hundred yards across the airfield, a Royal Egyptian Air Force liaison officer with the RAF was on duty that morning in one of the Nissen huts. He stood at the window, watching the arrival proceedings with a pair of powerful binoculars, well out of range of the security cordon. When the cavalcade drove out through the main exit gates, he laid down the binoculars and picked up the desk telephone.

MAISON FLEUVE
8:15 A.M.

Halder came awake from a fitful doze, to the sound of lapping water and a hot sun on his face. The boatman was busy guiding the vessel through some reeds towards the private jetty of a whitewashed villa, with overgrown gardens. Rachel was asleep on Halder's shoulder and he roused her. "We're here."

Banyan trees overhung the water's edge, steps leading up to a flagstone patio at the back, a wicker table and chairs set out. The villa looked sadly neglected, the walls peeling and covered with ragged creepers. Cairo's outline rose up in the near distance, and the unmistakable Giza pyramids further west. The Arab was waiting for them on the jetty, and he didn't look happy to see them.

"Not exactly the warm welcome I'd hoped for," Halder commented.

Rachel studied the villa. "Where are we?"

"A couple of miles south of Cairo, by the looks of it. Happy to be back?"

"Under these circumstances, I'm not so sure."

"If you're still worried about Harry, don't be. He'll be perfectly safe until he's found."

"I'm more worried about what happens afterwards." Her face darkened. "He's not going to stop until he finds us, but then I presume you know that."

"I didn't think he would. But war or no war, I could

hardly kill him now, could I? Even though something tells me we might live to regret it."

The Arab helped the boatman tie the ropes, then glared at them sullenly and jerked his head towards the patio.

Halder stepped on to the jetty and held his hand out to Rachel. "Come on. There should be someone waiting to meet us."

As they stepped on to the patio, a French door opened and a rugged-looking man came out. His hands were thrust into the pockets of his linen jacket, his greying hair greased off his forehead, and he frowned worriedly as he came forward. "So, you finally made it. You must be Major Halder?" He offered his hand. "Harvey Deacon. Besheeba to my friends in Berlin. I hope your river journey wasn't too unpleasant?"

"Apart from the boatman having to hide our vessel in the reeds for two solid hours to avoid a river patrol."

"Unfortunate, but you're here now, which is what's important." Deacon turned to Rachel, the frown gone as he smiled charmingly and kissed her hand. "Berlin told me to expect a woman, but I never expected one so pretty. Delighted, I'm sure." He made a gesture towards the villa. "But perhaps for now you'd be good enough to step inside and make yourself at home? There's some private business I need to discuss with the major."

Rachel went in through the French doors, leaving Halder alone with Deacon and Hassan. When Deacon turned back, the worried look returned. "A terrible catastrophe, your aircraft crashing. It's not going to help matters."

"How did you know?"

Deacon sighed. "A long story, which I'll explain later, but among other things, I radioed Berlin last night. Your contact at the airfield sent them a signal. As of now, our friend Schellenberg isn't aware of your safe arrival in Cairo, but he'll know tonight when I send my report." He glanced at Hassan before turning back. "I believe you both had a small disagreement last night?"

"He failed to carry out my orders."

"You should have let me kill the American," Hassan said bitterly. "He'll only bring us trouble after this. You're a fool if you think otherwise."

Halder stared him down. "And you ought to remember who's in charge of this operation."

"Gentlemen," Deacon interrupted, and jerked his thumb at Hassan. "Go inside and look after the woman, then do as I told you."

When he had left, Halder lit a cigarette. "Does your friend have a name?"

Deacon plucked a cigar from his breast pocket, lit it, tossed the match into the river.

"Hassan. He tells me you already know this American intelligence officer, Weaver?"

"Since before the war." Halder explained briefly and Deacon frowned.

"I see. An unwelcome surprise. But you'll have to understand about Hassan. He's headstrong and arrogant, and never forgives a slight. But apart from that, he's worth his weight in gold. Try to humour him. He's been very useful to us."

"From now on he'll have to get used to taking my orders—so I'd suggest you make sure he follows them. We're on fragile ground as it is, and I'm not going to tolerate disobedience."

Deacon said icily, "You can talk about disobedience all you like, Major, but the fact is Hassan was right—you should have killed Weaver when you had the chance. It was *very* stupid to have let him live. He can only cause us more trouble."

Halder ignored the rebuke. "There's something much more troubling you should be aware of. He knew exactly what we're up to."

Deacon was stunned. "But—how?"

Halder shrugged. "Guesswork, or maybe there's more to it. But it's unlikely he knows of your involvement, otherwise you'd have had a visit from military intelligence long before now."

"But it doesn't bode well, does it?"

"My sentiments exactly. The fact of it is, we've been dealt a lousy hand, but we've no choice except to play the game. And it's going to be an uphill battle from now on."

"You're still committed to carrying on?"

Halder nodded. "But our misfortune rather puts you in greater danger."

Deacon had a look of steely resignation. "Risk is something I willingly accepted long ago, Major."

Halder glanced towards the jetty. "Can the boatman be trusted?"

"Absolutely."

Suddenly the strain and tiredness showed on Halder's face. "We've had a trying time of it since we crashed. We'll need to get cleaned up. And a decent meal wouldn't go astray."

"It's all been organised. I'll take you to your rooms and get you settled in. Afterwards, we'll have a talk, in private. There are some other serious difficulties you'll need to be aware of."

"You mean there's *more* bad news?"

Deacon sighed. "I'm afraid I've run into a snag with your transport." He flicked away his unfinished cigar, and it cart-wheeled into the river. "But we can discuss that later. You never told me the woman's name."

"Rachel Stern."

"Hassan informs me you've no idea what's happened to your two comrades."

"The last I knew, they tried to make their escape across the desert."

"As I said, I'll inform Berlin tonight of your arrival. But the signal I sent them last night contained some welcome news. In fact, you have a surprise in store."

Deacon looked towards the French doors as Hassan stepped out on to the patio. Behind him came Kleist and Doring, wearing fresh civilian clothes. A slow grin spread on Kleist's face. "It seems we're back in business, Herr Major."

FIFTY-TWO

MENA HOUSE
22 NOVEMBER/11:30 A.M.
The heavily guarded room on the ground floor was large and magnificent, decorated with delicate Arabic woodwork,

the walls painted a pastel blue, but the air was grey with cigarette smoke and thick with uniforms. Officially the hotel's main dining room, now it thronged with military chiefs of staff and senior Allied officers, deep in serious conversation.

Churchill was already there, wearing a white linen suit, in excellent mood as he mingled with the crowd, the usual cigar clenched between his fingers, and when they wheeled in Roosevelt there was a spontaneous round of applause from everyone present as the two great men warmly greeted each other. Finally, after they had chatted briefly with most of the senior officers, an aide in charge of the proceedings announced, "And now, gentlemen, as I'm sure you can appreciate, the Prime Minister and President need some time in private. Refreshments will be served in the room next door if you'll kindly follow me, please."

Moments later the room had been emptied, the doors had been closed, and the two men were completely alone, Roosevelt's Secret Service men and Churchill's Scotland Yard bodyguards, who accompanied him at all times, waiting politely outside.

Sitting there in his wheelchair, after the strain of so much travel, Roosevelt looked pale and sickly. There were a few moments of silence, the only sound the rattan ceiling fans whirring overhead, and then Churchill said, "So, we have a busy schedule in front of us, Franklin. I take it you're still firmly committed to Overlord going ahead?"

"As firmly as ever."

Churchill smiled. "We'll have our differences on strategy, of course, and you'll hear them in the course of the next few days."

"No doubt I will."

"But on one thing we must agree. You know how much I enjoy a good party—it's my one great weakness. Well, the day we crush Herr Hitler, I intend for us both to host the biggest bash you can bloody well imagine, and expense be damned."

"I think I could go along with that," Roosevelt answered with a slight grin. Then his face became a little more serious, and he said almost as an afterthought, "I guess you heard about this bunch of Germans on the loose?"

"The word reached me through my intelligence people. I must say, it certainly has my bodyguards on edge. They seem intent on keeping me under close watch. No doubt you're suffering the same fate." Churchill was irritated. "But if they think they're going to keep me from a private drinks party I'm scheduled to attend in Cairo tonight at the British embassy with some very dear old friends, they've got another damned think coming. I've been looking forward to it for days."

"What do you make of it all, Winston?"

There was a glint of humour in Churchill's eyes. "I think Berlin has got a bloody cheek if they really intend trying to assassinate us. It just shows how desperate Hitler must be to have agreed such a gambit, but we can both see the logic behind it. However, I have every confidence that these people who crash-landed will be quickly hunted down and dealt with—considering the odds against them, the poor fools are as good as dead. And speaking personally, I've no intention of being the first Prime Minister in British history to be assassinated."

There was a soft knock on the door, and Roosevelt said, "Enter."

One of the President's senior aides stepped into the room, a middle-aged colonel in full dress uniform, and closed the door discreetly behind him. "I know you didn't wish to be disturbed, Mr. President. But there's a General Clayton here to see both you and the Prime Minister, urgently. He's accompanied by Ambassador Kirk. I believe it has to do with these German infiltrators the ambassador informed you about, sir."

"Speak of the Devil. I guess you'd better send them in."

MAISON FLEUVE/9 A.M.

There was a meal laid out on the kitchen table, with some pitta bread and fresh lime juice. When they had eaten, Halder suggested to Rachel she go up to her room to get some rest. He went out on to the patio, where Deacon and the others sat waiting at the table.

"You mind telling me how the hell you both managed to make it across the desert without getting caught?" Halder asked as he pulled up a chair.

"It wasn't easy," Kleist answered sourly. "We'd stopped at a wadi in the late afternoon when we heard a spotter plane overhead. We had to wait until it grew dark before taking the risk of moving out again. Then our truck broke down about five miles from a village called Birqash. We tried to make it on foot to the village and were stopped by a couple of Egyptian police manning a roadblock. We cut their throats, buried the bodies, and stole their car. Once we reached the outskirts of Cairo, we ditched it, took the train, and barely made the rendezvous last night."

Halder's face sagged with distaste as he said to Deacon, "More death. My God, this war gets worse by the day."

Deacon simply shrugged. "There's no getting away from corpses in a battle, Major."

"What did Berlin say when you informed them two of your contacts had arrived safely?"

"They simply acknowledged the message. I usually don't invite too much comment on the air, and keep things to an absolute minimum. A lengthy communication time might allow the British radio detectors to pinpoint my transmitter. And I've been very careful not to let that happen. But no doubt they'll have some comment tonight. Now, we'd better get down to business. Your misfortune may well have destroyed whatever chances we had of success. It's certainly ruined the element of surprise. However, we'll return to those problems later. Facts first. Roosevelt arrives at Cairo West airfield just after nine-thirty this morning. My sources tell me he's being accommodated in the presidential suite at the Mena House. Churchill arrived yesterday, and he's also being quartered at the hotel."

"Is your source reliable?"

"He's an Egyptian Air Force officer with excellent connections, whose information is usually faultless."

"Security?"

Deacon grimly pursed his lips. "Very tight, as you'd expect. And after what's happened, you can be sure it'll be tighter still."

"Schellenberg said you'd have gathered more details by the time we arrived."

"I've done my best." Deacon reached inside his pocket and took out several folded pages. "You'll see from my report the hotel's heavily guarded. No one is allowed near the compound without the proper authorisation. Photographs were obviously out of the question, far too risky, but I got as close as I dared and made notes and drawings of everything I could see. Tanks, anti-aircraft guns on the roofs, patrols in the grounds operating at irregular intervals."

Halder studied the handwritten pages intently, then looked up. "Hardly the crock of gold I'd hoped for. We could really do with more exact information."

"Impossible, I'm afraid."

Halder gave the pages to Kleist and Doring to study. "What about this problem with the vehicles?"

Deacon sighed heavily. "You're not going to like this." He explained about Salter. "The man's a dangerous gangster with a reputation for violence. Unfortunately, I had no choice except to deal with him."

Halder said, puzzled, "What exactly does he think we're up to?"

"The fool suspects we're about to carry out a robbery, and wants a cut to ensure his silence. Otherwise, we can forget about the Jeep and trucks, and I can expect a visit from the police."

Halder stood, exasperated. "It gets even worse. When does this fellow Salter want an answer?"

"Tomorrow night. After that, there'll be trouble."

Halder sighed. "You're quite sure he knows nothing about our real intentions?"

"I doubt Salter would imagine for a moment that I'm a German agent. Apparently, valuable archaeological caches are sometimes transported to Cairo via the Shabramant airfield. Salter seems to think there might be one on its way, and has it in his stupid head we've got a plan to steal it."

"Does he know we're here at the villa?"

Deacon shook his head vigorously. "Absolutely not. I've been careful to make sure I haven't been followed since the last episode, and I've seen nobody trying to tail me. I can only assume Salter thinks we've no choice except to agree to his little proposition, and following me is a futile exercise." He gave another sigh. "Quite a mess, isn't it? Well, any suggestions? Because I certainly haven't."

Halder shook his head in despair. "Right now, not even one. But we *must* have those vehicles. Everything depends on it." He turned back to study the villa. "So, this is to be our lair?"

"I think you'll find it comfortable enough, and perfectly safe."

Halder said to Kleist and Doring, "Take a good look around. Familiarise yourselves with the surroundings and draw me a decent map. I want to plan escape routes in case we need them. And choose a couple of suitable rooms front and back that we can use as lookout points. We'll need to set up a watch roster. I don't want anyone surprising us—including this fellow Salter."

"Yes, Major."

After Kleist and Doring had left, Halder lit a cigarette. "The villa's somewhat remote. I'm not sure I'm happy about that."

"A necessary change of plan. The safe house I intended using in the city was raided by your friend Weaver, and a comrade of his, a British officer named Sanson, from GHQ."

Halder looked at him in amazement. "Why didn't you make Berlin aware of this?"

"But I did." Deacon explained what had happened. "You weren't told?"

Halder shook his head angrily. "It sounds to me like we've been walking towards trouble from the very start."

Deacon frowned. "It seems odd you weren't informed."

Halder raised an eyebrow suspiciously, still furious. "All Schellenberg is concerned with is accomplishing his plan, come hell or high water. He doesn't give a damn about people's lives. No doubt he thought I'd have no interest in his little scheme if I knew your operation had been jeopardised." He thought for a moment. "Is there any way Allied intelligence could have become aware of our plans because of the raid?"

"I seriously doubt it. What evidence could they have?"

"Maybe you're right. But it worries me how they could have known. I've already met this Sanson, by the way."

Deacon raised his eyes when Halder explained. "I'm impressed you managed to escape. I don't know about your friend Weaver, but Sanson is not someone to cross. By reputation he's a determined man, as dangerous as a cobra."

Halder stood, nodded to the villa. "Right now, I'm more worried about this place."

He strolled in through the French windows, into a large living room with cane chairs and brightly coloured Arab rugs scattered on the floor. The white-painted walls were bare except for a couple of Nubian death masks, made of polished dark wood, the primitive faces frightening, almost evil.

"The villa's called Maison Fleuve," Deacon explained. "Originally built by a French campaign general to entertain his mistresses. There's no telephone, but then most of the villas around here are used only as weekend retreats. It's also very private, so no one should bother us. The main road is a mile from here—which gives plenty of time to see anyone approaching—and leads directly into Cairo. The Mena House and Giza are only five miles away. Naturally, the motorboat will be at your disposal. You can reach the city without having to worry about being stopped and having your papers scrutinised—the river patrols don't operate this far south."

Halder examined the death masks on the wall with interest. "The wood carving's really first class. At least a couple of hundred years old, I imagine?"

Deacon nodded, took one down with a smile, brushed some dust from the wood with his sleeve. "Something the general picked up on his travels up the Nile. Along with a couple of exquisite female Nubian slaves I believe he was rather fond of."

"And what about the villa's present owner?"

"You're looking at him." Deacon replaced the mask. "Now, I believe you mentioned escape routes?"

Deacon held up the oil lamp as they went down the cellar steps. Light flickered on the arched walls, the air pleasantly cool, and Halder saw the stored racks of cobwebbed wine bottles off to one side. They moved to the end of the cellar where there was a metal door rusting on its hinges. Deacon pushed it open and brilliant sunshine flooded in. A tiny stone pier was revealed outside, well covered by tall reeds.

The Nile lay beyond, and a small rowing boat was tied up, complete with an outboard motor, an old tarpaulin thrown over it to protect the engine.

"Interesting," remarked Halder, seeing an aerial protruding outside, hidden by the reeds, the wire leading back to a wooden cabinet at the bottom of the stairs. "That's where you keep your radio?"

Deacon nodded, opened the cabinet, revealing the transmitter, his Luger pistol beside it, then closed it again. "The cellar was originally built as a *cave*. You know how fastidious the French are about storing their wine. But being a practical man, the general decided he'd be better served knocking out the end wall and using it as an escape route for his girlfriends, in case their husbands showed up, which apparently was often."

Deacon smiled, went to shut the metal door, which creaked on its hinges. "An ace in the hole, should we need it. But let's hope not. I'll leave it to you to show the others. One other precaution I should mention. There's a solid metal bar I suggest you always leave in place on the villa's main entrance door upstairs. If there's danger brewing and anyone tried to force their way in, it should give you enough time to get down here and make your escape."

"You're a cautious man, Deacon."

"It's why I've lived so long."

"Schellenberg also mentioned you'd have an overall escape route lined up, in case things went badly wrong at the airfield."

Deacon nodded. "An Egyptian friend of mine is a serving captain with the Royal Egyptian Air Force. It was he who supplied much of the information about the Shabramant airfield. If we need him, he's arranged to 'borrow' an aircraft from his unit and pick us up from a landing strip in the desert, a few miles from Sakkara. It'll be outside any air exclusion zone, and therefore less likely to get shot down."

"I know the strip you're talking about. It was used to ferry in supplies for archaeological digs."

"I believe so. My friend the captain can be in the air, on stand-by, ready to pick us up if necessary, once he sees a prearranged signal on the ground. As soon as you decide when the attack will commence and we know Skorzeny's men are on their way, I'll contact him. But then I'm assuming everything will still go ahead as planned. If not, and we have to abort, the captain will attempt to fly you out anyway, to the nearest German airbase on Crete. But we can go over everything in more detail later."

"This captain friend of yours doesn't know what we're up to, of course?"

"Naturally. But he's a fervent sympathiser, willing to help the German cause in any way he can."

They came back up the steps to the hallway and Deacon blew out the lamp.

"Two things," said Halder. "First, you don't reveal our intentions in front of the lady. She knows nothing about our plans, or our purpose here."

"I understand. Berlin explained everything."

"Second, I'll give you a list of things I'll need by this afternoon—mostly some heavy tools and digging equipment, as well as a pair of powerful binoculars, and a couple of the American uniforms you got from Salter."

Deacon saw the tension on Halder's face; the man was like a coiled spring. "You mind telling me what for?"

"My original intention was to try and bluff my way into the compound posing as an American officer, or somehow steal a pass, so I could carry out the necessary reconnaissance work. But that's just the kind of strategy the Allies would expect now that they're aware of our intentions. And one that's especially useless seeing as they know my identity. It looks to me like we now have only one option. Near Cheops pyramid, there's a tunnel, part of a natural rock cavern that runs for almost two hundred metres from a Second Dynasty burial vault. It leads from the direction of the hotel grounds."

Deacon frowned. "How do you know?"

"It was discovered some years ago by Fraulein Stern's father, a respected archaeologist. Schellenberg seems to think the passageway may lead inside the compound."

"Amazing." Deacon looked astonished, scratched his jaw. "So that's why Berlin had me confirm there was still digging going on at Giza. I wondered about that."

"What's important is that we may have a way of getting

into the compound, unseen. But the tunnel entrance will have to be reopened and the direction verified. Did you find out who's working on the site?"

"Mostly student groups from Cairo's universities."

"There's no time to waste, so we'll have to carry out the necessary exploration late this afternoon. Just you, me and Kleist. The students will have finished their work by the time it's getting dark. Is the site guarded?"

Deacon nodded. "There's usually either a few men on watch duty from one of the nearby police stations, or civilian guards from the Ministry of Antiquities."

Halder produced his wallet, and showed Deacon the documents stating that he was Paul Mallory, along with credentials from the American University. "Do you know of an expert forger? Someone trustworthy who can work fast?"

Deacon nodded. "Cairo's got no shortage of forgers who'll do anything for a price. Why?"

"Sanson checked my papers in Alex, as well as Fraulein Stern's. No doubt he'll alert the police and military to keep a lookout for our identities. But a clever forger should easily be able to alter the names without too much difficulty. Can you arrange it promptly, if I give you a couple of alternative names?"

Deacon shrugged. "It's a minor enough job, so I don't see why not. Care to tell me what you have in mind?"

"To all intents, I'll be a professor, conducting a legitimate inspection of my students' work at Giza, so it should be easy enough to bluff our way past the police, but even if it comes to the worst, and if my past experience is anything to go by, such guards are unreliable at the best of times, and totally corruptible. The poor devils are usually paid such a pittance they could probably be bribed not to bother us."

Deacon studied the documents carefully. "They certainly look impressive enough. Don't you need to bring the woman along?"

Halder shook his head. "It's pointless putting her in any further unnecessary danger. She can tell me what I need to know. But you still need to arrange to have her papers altered, just in case we have to leave the villa at any stage. I'll fetch them for you before you go."

Deacon raised his eyes. "Do I detect something between the two of you, Major?"

Halder avoided the question. "Just the three of us should be enough. Besides, a little distraction might help me mull over Salter's ultimatum. As it is, the problem has me completely stumped."

"And what if we manage to find this tunnel and it leads where you think it does?"

"Kleist and I will assess the security inside the hotel grounds, and try to find out exactly where Roosevelt and Churchill are quartered. Which is why we'll need the uniforms."

Deacon looked troubled. "But you won't have passes. And there are bound to be security checks inside the compound. Weaver and his comrades will be determined to catch you. All of which makes everything infinitely more hazardous."

"My problems to worry about. And there's really no other option besides the tunnel. Unless you can think of one."

"You've got me there, Major."

"We'll need transport. And preferably a way of getting to Giza that helps us avoid any checkpoints, if that's possible."

Deacon scratched his head. "There's a rough desert track near by that leads directly to the village of Nazlat as-Saman, near the pyramids. But the Packard's heavily built and the suspension would take a hammering, so we'd be asking for trouble." He thought for a moment. "I have a better suggestion. All of us travelling together would certainly be unwise. No doubt your friend Weaver has issued your description to every police station and military barracks from here to Luxor. Hassan has a motorcycle. Kleist and I could take the car, using the normal route, by road. You could take the motorcycle, and we can meet up on the far side of the village, near the Sphinx."

Halder crushed out his cigarette, smiled tightly. "Perfect. It's settled, then. And don't fret about Harry Weaver. He's not going to find me."

FIFTY-THREE

"What kind of an idiot are you?" Clayton banged his fist on the desk. "How the hell could you let them escape?"

Weaver sat in the general's office, his eyes raw, his body aching from exhaustion. He hadn't slept for more than a couple of minutes throughout the entire night. After eight hours of trying to free himself from the ropes, all he had managed to do was loosen the gag. A little after seven, two local fishermen heard his shouts, wandered into the boathouse, and found him. Soon after he had made the telephone call to military HQ from Rashid police station, Sanson arrived, furious that he'd allowed Halder and Rachel to escape. Two hours later, Sanson had him on a plane to Cairo, and driven straight to Clayton's office.

"I didn't have much choice, sir," Weaver answered.

Sanson sat next to him. He and the general were still seething. "It's damned ridiculous," Clayton said in astonishment. "We had half the army out, every road blocked off, and still they evaded capture. As for you, Weaver, allowing two enemy agents to dupe you into helping them escape is downright incompetence. What have you got to say for yourself?"

"I made a mistake going after them alone," Weaver said lamely.

Clayton flared. "Damned right you did. It seems to me you let personal sentiment get in the way of duty. In this instance, that's not only unforgivable, it's almost treasonable." The general rose angrily from behind his desk. "You'd better tell me everything you know about this couple."

The general stood there until Weaver had finished, then said to Sanson, "What about the boat they used?"

Sanson explained that every vessel on the waterway as far as Cairo had been stopped and boarded. "But the river patrols turned up nothing. We were obviously too late. By early morning, the boat could easily have reached any number of places along the Nile."

Clayton turned back to Weaver. "Didn't you see the registration on the Arab's car?"

He had already gone over every detail with Sanson. "I couldn't see the licence plate in the dark. The only thing I'm reasonably certain of is the car was an American model." Weaver knew the information was pretty useless without an exact model description or licence number. Cairo was full of American vehicles, military and civilian.

"That's not much help, is it?" Clayton grimaced, picked up Sanson's report from his desk, and slapped it back down again. "But there *are* a couple of things we *can* be pretty certain of. First, it's obvious we're dealing with more than just two enemy infiltrators. And second, they're most likely somewhere in the city by now."

Weaver knew from the report Sanson had delivered that two Egyptian policemen had gone missing late the previous afternoon, not far from a village called Birqash, over twenty miles north of Cairo. Their bodies had been discovered early that morning, buried in a shallow grave, their throats cut. At ten the previous evening, their car had been found abandoned near a railway station on the city outskirts. A Bedouin family living several miles from Birqash had been questioned by the police, and claimed to have seen two men driving a military truck late the previous afternoon, heading in the general direction of the village. The truck had been found a couple of miles outside—a Fiat with an Italian Army registration.

"The men were too far away for the Bedouin to provide descriptions," Sanson had told Clayton. "But we know Halder and the woman were in Alex, so it couldn't have been them. It now looks like we're dealing with at least four German agents."

The general crossed to the French windows, still enraged. "What about the Fiat? Someone must have owned the damned thing."

"So far as we can tell, it wasn't on the register of confiscated enemy vehicles," Sanson answered. "I've requested a list of all military vehicles missing in the last twenty-four hours. But the Fiat still had its original Italian Army plates on, so unless it's reported stolen, it's unlikely we'll trace the owner."

"You mind telling me why not?"

"General, there's enough surplus military hardware floating around this country to start another war. It's more than possible the truck was somebody's loot before it was stolen or borrowed by the Germans, so it's unlikely the owner would report it missing."

The general came back and slumped into his chair. "The whole thing's a goddamned mess. The President arrived this morning, Prime Minister Churchill yesterday afternoon. The fact that we've got at least four ruthless German agents at large in the same city doesn't bear thinking about."

"If I might make a suggestion," Sanson offered. "We ask the President and Prime Minister to cancel or delay their meeting until we locate these people."

The general shook his head firmly, slapped his fist on the desk. "That's not even an option. Have either of you any idea of the amount of planning that's gone into this thing? Thousands of man-hours spent at meetings, communications, organisation. VIPs and senior officers to be transported from all over the world—not an easy thing in wartime. It could take months to reorganise everything, and that's time we just don't have."

"With respect, sir, these are exceptional circumstances."

"The ambassador already put that point to the President and Prime Minister. They both refused point blank to change their schedule. You must know the kind of men they are. They're not going to be intimidated by a handful of Nazi agents. As far as the President goes, he's got a favourite saying. There's nothing to fear but fear itself. With a philosophy like that it's impossible to frighten the man. And I think I'd be right in saying Mr. Churchill is made of the same kind of iron—he doesn't scare easily. Their personal security details have been briefed about the situation, and they've assured me they'll be taking extra precautions. But it's still your job to find these people."

There was a knock on the door and the general's aide appeared. "Your car is ready to take you to the Mena House, sir."

"I'll be right there." The door closed and Clayton said sternly, "I want no more excuses—just results. What we need is a little bit of luck—and we won't have that unless we police *every* damned hotel, bar, restaurant, and bawdy-house in the city and outskirts, check *everyone's* identity papers, and haul in anyone we see who's acting suspiciously. I don't give a frig who they are or how authentic their credentials. If you suspect them, round up the sons of bitches and haul 'em in. The same applies to the home of every Nazi sympathiser on our lists. Somebody's got to be helping the Arab and Germans to hide out. And they're out there somewhere."

The general stood, picked up his cap, looked sternly at Weaver. "Muster as many men as you need, but you find every one of those fucking Krauts, damned fast. I want them dead."

As they drove back through the city, Weaver felt exhausted, oblivious to the traffic rushing past. He had tried to think everything through, but still it didn't make any sense. *Rachel was dead, and now she's alive.* And there didn't seem to be any way he could save her, or Jack Halder.

Sanson said, "I'll have a list made of all American vehicles registered in Cairo, military or civilian, including any that may have been stolen, and we'll see what it turns up. I've already put out a general alert for anyone with the identities of Mallory and Tauber to be immediately arrested, warning that they're armed and dangerous. Though my guess is they'll have the sense not to use the same identity papers again. Meanwhile, you'd better grab a few hours' sleep. If anything develops, I'll call you."

"I'll be OK."

Sanson said gruffly, "I'm not being kind to you, Weaver. We've got a busy time ahead, so take the rest while you can. Something else you ought to know. I had one of my men check back through the maritime reports at Port Said. It seems the *Izmir* went to the bottom all right, and the ship had a history of engine trouble, but there was something the newspapers neglected to mention at the time."

"What?"

"They reported that a Maltese fishing trawler rescued a

life-raft with four Turkish sailors from the *Izmir* the day after it sank. But what they didn't say was that the trawler's skipper spotted a German naval frigate in the same area."

"What are you saying?"

"The German frigate's too much of a coincidence. The Sterns were the only passengers on board the *Izmir*, according to the ship's manifest. The vessel was Turkish, and the Turks are notoriously pro-German. For all we know the frigate could have been planning a rendezvous somewhere at sea to pick them up, before things went wrong and the boat blew up."

"Pick them up for what reason?"

"The Sterns had never intended to travel on to Istanbul, but back to Germany. They were spies, one or all of them, working for the Nazis."

"Oh, come on, Sanson," Weaver said angrily. "The Germans have always used the Med. Their frigate could have been there by pure chance. Rachel or her parents were never spies. It's crazy."

They had reached Garden City, and Sanson pulled up outside GHQ. "I'll have Lieutenant Kane drop you at your villa—I've got work to do. You'd better meet me back here at six. There's someone I want you to meet who should help clear all this up."

"Who?"

"You'll find out later. But I'll tell you this much—I reckon you've got a bloody big surprise in store, Weaver. And I hope you're ready for it."

When they reached Zamalek, Helen Kane took the door key from Weaver and let them into the villa. "You look terrible. I'll run you a bath. Then I'll let you get some rest."

They went up to Weaver's room and she ran the bath and found some fresh towels. When he'd undressed, he went to lie in the steaming water. She came in with two glasses of Scotch and handed him one. "I figured you might need this. Mind if a girl keeps you company?"

He'd been away less than forty-eight hours, but it felt like as many days, and there was a tension between them he could sense. "I guess not."

She smiled uncertainly, leaned against the door frame,

and sipped her drink. "You seem distracted. Want to tell me about it?"

Weaver's mind was in turmoil. "Do I have to?"

"No, but I think from the look on your face you need to tell someone."

He lay back in the hot water, exhausted, ran a flannel over his eyes and face, and told her everything. When he had finished, she barely reacted. "You don't seem surprised."

"I have a confession to make. Sanson phoned me from Alex and had me report what happened to General Clayton."

"I see."

She put her glass down. "Except I don't understand any of it. I could accept your friend Halder being involved, but not Rachel Stern, at least not from what you told me about her. None of it makes any sense. She was dead, and now she's alive. And according to Sanson, he suspects she's a Nazi agent."

"She couldn't be, Helen. Not with her background. Even Halder made a point of telling me she was innocent in all this. Sure, the German frigate probably picked her up. After that, I would have thought prison was likely, or one of those camps we've all been hearing about."

He finished bathing, and she handed him a towel and left as he dried himself. When he had dressed and came out of the bathroom, she was sitting on the couch. She looked preoccupied, and said quietly, "Can I ask you something, Harry?"

"What?"

"Are you still in love with her?"

"Now how did I know you'd ask me that?"

"You didn't answer the question."

He hesitated. "I don't know."

She looked hurt. "That means you're still in love with her."

His heart sank as he said, "Maybe the truth is I never stopped loving her."

She bit her lip, put down her glass. "I understand." She stood, clearly upset. "I'll let you get some rest."

He put a hand to her face. "I'm sorry, Helen. But you asked for the truth."

She took his hand away, gently. "Don't feel bad. I'm just feeling sorry for myself, that's all." She gave a nervous smile, then made to go, but turned back, brushed a strand of hair from her face. "Life's never that simple, is it, Harry?" There was a hint of tears at the edges of her eyes. "I'll see you around."

Weaver heard her footsteps go down the stairs, was almost overcome by a terrible wave of guilt, but he didn't try to stop her.

FIFTY-FOUR

BERLIN
22 NOVEMBER/12:30 P.M.
The Adlon, Berlin's famous landmark hotel, was a five-minute drive from Canaris's office. It was cold and blustery when he stepped out of his staff-driven Mercedes and entered the plush foyer, leaving his coat and hat at the cloakroom desk. Looking tired and drawn, he moved past the sweeping staircase, noticed that the once splendid chandelier overhead and the ceiling plasterwork had been badly damaged by the bombing, and stepped into the dining room. Most of the lunch-time crowd hadn't yet arrived, just a few tables occupied by bleak-looking businessmen and a handful of uniformed officers.

The head waiter, hovering near the door, recognised Canaris immediately, escorted him to one of the private dining booths at the end and pulled back the red velvet curtain. Schellenberg was already there, a bottle of brandy and a full glass in front of him, a fork in his hand as he tucked into a meal of sauerkraut, potatoes and pickled beef.

"Ah, Wilhelm. You've arrived at last. I've started without you, as you can see. The beef's excellent. I'd recommend it."

"I was delayed. But no matter. I'm not hungry."

"But you'll have a brandy, of course?" Schellenberg grinned. "It's only Polish, I'm afraid, the French stocks have been depleted, so you risk losing the enamel from your teeth."

"I've risked a lot more in my time." Canaris waved the head waiter away, then took a seat opposite. "Well, what's this urgent news you spoke of?"

Schellenberg poured him a large measure of brandy. "Naturally, I couldn't tell you on the telephone."

"Then tell me now, damn you. I've heard nothing since yesterday, when you told me Halder and the others survived the crash. I've hardly slept since, so don't keep me in suspense."

Schellenberg swallowed a forkful of sauerkraut, washed it down with the remains of his brandy, and slapped the glass on the table. "It's of the good and bad news variety."

"Go on," Canaris said expectantly, ignoring his drink.

"We received a signal early this morning from Deacon. Our friends Kleist and Doring managed to arrive safely in Cairo and make contact. Which cheered me up somewhat. Not to mention Himmler and the Führer."

Canaris was on the edge of his seat. "What about Halder and the woman?"

"No news of them yet. It seems the team split up into two pairs after the crash, and tried to make it to Cairo separately. Kleist and Doring, and Halder and Rachel Stern. I've no information other than that."

"I see." Canaris sat back, and sighed inwardly with relief, not disappointment. "It still doesn't look good, then?"

Schellenberg refilled his own glass to the brim, swallowed a mouthful. "In this case, no news is hardly good news."

"But you seem rather pleased, and in good spirits. Why?"

Schellenberg smiled broadly. "Because there's a glimmer of hope, considering two of our team got through. And you should have more faith in Halder, Wilhelm. After all, he's one of your best men, and infinitely more resourceful than either Kleist or his comrade. If the pair of *them* could make it, I expect Halder can." A nervous excitement crept into Schellenberg's voice. "In fact, I *know* he'll make it, and carry on with the mission. I can feel it in my bones. Any man who can easily pass himself off as an enemy officer, British or American, as he's done in the past, must surely stand more than a chance."

"I'm well aware of Halder's abilities." Canaris glanced at the bottle on the table. "But you're sure it's not the brandy making you optimistic?"

Schellenberg's mouth tightened. "Don't be smart, Wilhelm."

"Try to see it realistically. Assuming Halder is still alive, and even *if* he manages to get to Cairo and make contact with Deacon, the Allies will be hunting him down. We have to expect that after the crash. The odds against Sphinx succeeding will be considerably diminished."

"But he's a clever man is Jack, and wily as a fox when the odds are stacked against him." Schellenberg still sounded bullish. "And I'm convinced he'll do his utmost to achieve his objectives, no matter what the obstacles. To pinpoint wherever Roosevelt and Churchill are, secure the airfield at Shabramant, transport Skorzeny and his paratroops to the required location once they land, and help them get past Allied security to carry out the necessary business. A tall enough order, I know, but unlike you, I still firmly believe Halder can accomplish what's expected of him. I wouldn't be surprised if we heard something positive from Deacon soon, in regard to Halder's safe arrival."

Canaris sighed, emptied his glass in one swallow, and tried not to show his distress at the unsettling thought of Sphinx actually succeeding. "So, what next? We wait for Deacon's next radio transmission?"

Schellenberg nodded. "Exactly. Which should be tonight, around midnight or soon after. Then we should know better where we stand. Unless Deacon is tempted to transmit earlier if he has urgent news, though long-range radio transmission and reception is always poorer during daylight hours, as you know. Something to do with the atmosphere. But Rome and Athens have firm instructions to relay any hint of a signal they receive from Cairo immediately. Naturally, the Führer wants to be informed the moment we have any information. He's anxious to know the mission status, and with every hour that goes by, he seems more convinced than ever its success is our only hope of winning this war."

"Anything else I should know about?"

Schellenberg smiled broadly again. "Just one more thing. As a sign of my good faith in Halder, I've already put Skorzeny and his men on alert. They'll be ready to fly to Cairo at a moment's notice."

CAIRO
4:30 P.M.

Halder was checking through the uniforms and the altered identity documents Deacon had delivered to his room when there was a knock on the door and Rachel came in. She had changed into a fresh blouse and khaki pants, and Halder said, "Feeling any better after your rest?"

"A little. Didn't you sleep?"

"I managed to grab a couple of hours."

The bedroom was a small affair, with a bare wooden floor. There was just an iron bed, a chair by the balcony window, and an enamel jug and washbasin on a wicker table in a corner. Dusk had begun to fall, the shutters were open, the sound of crickets and the scent of flowers carrying into the room on the warm tropical air. The view of the Nile was exquisite, the dying orange light reflected on the waters, and Rachel stepped out on to the narrow wrought-iron balcony. "Did you ever miss it here after you returned to Germany?"

Halder joined her. "The happiest time I ever had was at Sakkara. I used to think I'd like to spend my life here, excavating ruins, and retire to live in a big old villa overlooking the Nile." He smiled, took a deep breath. "God, but it's good to smell the warm air of Cairo again."

"Do you think Harry will be all right?"

"His comrades will have found him by now, I'm certain."

"You should have let me talk to him one last time before we boarded the boat."

"What good would it have done, Rachel? And there really wasn't time."

Rachel sighed, and Halder said, "What's the matter?"

"Just a feeling I have, that it could get much worse from now on. You told me when you asked Harry not to get involved he refused. It's a frightening thought, both of you being up against each other. And no doubt his superiors will want him to be resolute to catch us. I'm sure he's in a quandary, just like you."

"I'd try not to dwell on it," Halder said, dispirited. "It's hard enough as it is, just the thought of him hunting us down. I'd hate to face the prospect of either of us having to decide which came first, duty or friendship, if it ever came down to it."

As if to change the subject, Rachel pointed at an American captain's uniform laid out on the bed. "What's that for? A fancy-dress party at Shepheard's?"

"Now there's a thought." Halder went back into the room, stuffed the uniform into a kit-bag. "I've got a little work to do, along with our host and Kleist. I'll probably be gone until late, so don't wait up."

Rachel followed him inside. "What about the others?"

"Doring and our friend Hassan will be taking turns on watch."

Rachel bit her lip, a look of fear on her face. "I don't like the idea of being alone with either of them. They make me feel uneasy."

"You'll be perfectly safe. Keep your door locked, but if anyone so much as bothers you—" He slipped Falconi's automatic from his pocket, handed it to her. "Feel free to use this, and let me worry about the consequences."

She handed back the weapon and shivered. "I don't like guns. I never have."

"No matter. I'll leave it just in case." He tossed it on the bed. "There's something I need to discuss. It's about your father."

Her face darkened. "What—what do you mean?"

"Schellenberg told me about the discovery at Giza. I admit I wondered at the time what the professor was getting up to, coming back exhausted some mornings to Sakkara, looking like he'd been up half the night. I would have thought it was a risky business, not to mention highly illegal, him not informing the Egyptian authorities."

Rachel blushed, then said firmly, "There were good reasons why my father kept his work secret."

"Tell me."

"There was a war looming. The Egyptians were pro-

German. If the country had fallen, the last thing he wanted was for anything valuable he might discover to end up in Nazi hands."

"And what exactly did he find?"

"A tunnel about two hundred metres long, most of it part of a natural underground cavern in the rock, which led to an important noble's tomb from the Second Dynasty that hadn't been discovered. My father believed that the area the tunnel originated in had once been the location of living quarters for some of the craftsmen and stonemasons working on the pyramids. The passageway had obviously been extended either by them or grave-robbers who intended to reach Cheops pyramid and steal any valuables they found inside, but they obviously miscalculated and ended up in the noble's tomb instead."

Halder frowned. "The area would have been closely guarded during the Pharaoh's time. Which I presume would explain why they burrowed from such a distance away."

Rachel nodded. "We found a valuable hoard of jewellery and scarabs buried in the passageway—the treasure was probably discarded by the robbers before they were caught and executed by the royal guards. Their bodies were left in the tunnel before it was sealed up again—the normal punishment in those days—obviously as a warning to others. The skeletons were still there, or what was left of them."

"I don't understand what your father was doing at Giza in the first place. His work was at Sakkara."

"A German professor named Braun had suspected the existence of the tunnel, and secretly made some preliminary explorations a couple of months before my family were due to leave Egypt. Braun was a former colleague of my father's and confided in him, but before he could take his work further he was summoned back to Germany and conscripted. My father managed to get the necessary permission from the authorities to carry on with Braun's work, but said nothing about the passageway, for the reasons I told you."

"Schellenberg claimed it led from the direction of the Mena House. Is that where your father believed the workmen's site might originally have been?"

She nodded. "In that general area, yes. Why?"

"I can't tell you why exactly, but I'll need to have a look at the tunnel. Can you remember its exact location?"

"Yes—yes, of course."

"How difficult would it be to gain entry?"

"Not very difficult. My father sealed up the entrance again, but it's well enough hidden, so no one would suspect its existence."

"Good. We'll go over everything in detail before I leave."

"Is it dangerous what you have to do?"

"Not particularly, but you never know. Just a little reconnaissance work, and to see if we can find and enter the passageway."

"Take me with you, Jack," she said suddenly.

Halder shook his head. "For one, the army and police will be on the lookout. And I wouldn't like to take the chance of you getting caught."

"I'm well able to look after myself."

"So I've noticed."

"I'm also beginning to think I'm your good-luck charm." She half smiled and leaned over, kissed him briefly on the lips.

Something sparked in him, and he responded, drawing her close, feeling the rise of her breasts against his chest through her cotton blouse as she suddenly moved into his arms.

He smiled. "And what the devil was *that* for?"

"Does there have to be a reason?"

"No, but I think there might be."

"Take me with you. Please? I'd feel safer, rather than staying here. And I can help you find the passageway a lot quicker."

"I guess I never could say no to a beautiful woman."

ABU SAMMAR/4 P.M.

That same afternoon, Achmed Farnad was in the barn, working feverishly, sweat running down his face. He had the trapdoor open and he grabbed the Luger pistol, then hauled out the radio and battery.

Two truck-loads of British troops had swept into the village, were searching every house and hovel. There was no point tempting providence. The best thing to do was bury the radio somewhere in the desert, and get rid of the gun.

Mafouz had the donkey and cart waiting, and Achmed hefted the radio on to the cart, then the battery, and hurriedly covered them with old sackcloth and some scrap metal. "You know what to do, Mafouz. Be careful, my son. Quickly, now!"

As the boy led the donkey out, Achmed saw his wife hurrying towards them, chickens scattering in her path. "Achmed! The soldiers are coming—!"

Achmed's blood turned to ice. Pursuing her across the yard was a British officer and half a dozen of his men. Behind them was Wafa, the crabby old midwife, being helped by two more soldiers. The officer had his revolver out, and he led them into the barn. Wafa pointed an accusing finger. "That's him. He's the one!"

"Traitorous bitch!" Achmed spat. In his panic, he realised to his horror that he still had the Luger in his hand. Before he had a chance to toss it away, one of the soldiers screamed, "The sodding bastard's got a gun!"

A rifle shot cracked, a terrible pain blossomed in Achmed's side, and he clutched at his wound and keeled over. His wife and son screamed, and were held back as the troops covered him with their weapons.

"Get a medic!" the officer roared. "We want him alive."

Achmed was still conscious as the soldiers rushed forward to give him first aid. Then he saw the officer pull the sackcloth from the cart and toss aside the metal junk, revealing the radio underneath. "Achmed Farnad, I'm arresting you on suspicion of aiding and abetting enemy agents."

FIFTY-FIVE

ROME
22 NOVEMBER/4:30 P.M.

Captain Willi Neumann was unhappy.

A small man, broad and muscular, the son of a Hamburg docker, his ruddy twenty-six-year-old face looked aged before its time. Unlike his father and three generations before him who had succumbed to the lure of the sea, he'd been bitten by the flying bug and joined the Luftwaffe at seventeen. With three tours of duty in Russia flying Junkers transports behind him, in all kinds of weather imaginable and with Soviet fighter pilots and flak crews constantly doing their utmost to blast him out of the skies, Neumann had possessed the Devil's own luck, suffering nothing more than a minor shrapnel wound in his left thigh that had barely needed a half-dozen stitches.

That afternoon at Practica di Mare aerodrome, he wondered if his luck was going to change for the worse. It was bad enough having to fly over enemy territory *and* land on enemy soil, but his latest problem only added to his troubles. As the senior flying officer, he was in charge of the two crews—four Luftwaffe flight officers including himself—manning the two Dakotas detailed to fly Skorzeny and his men on their mission to Egypt. He'd worked with Skorzeny once before, dropping him and two dozen of his men on a mission behind Soviet lines in the dead of winter, and was quite certain the colonel was raving mad, even if after Mussolini's daring rescue he was considered the golden-haired boy in Berlin. Neumann didn't know exactly what the hell the colonel was getting up to in Cairo dressing his men and himself in American uniforms; his own briefings had been confined to the flying end of things and the rest wasn't his business. But the weather was—and the safety of his crews.

He held the forecast sheets in his hand as he stood outside the hangar with Skorzeny, a cool wind blowing in from the sea, less than a kilometre away, the sun still warm and bright but starting to drop, twilight beginning to creep in. Back inside the hangar, his own crews and Skorzeny's paratroops were waiting restlessly, men of action who found inactivity the worst fate of all. "It looks like we may have a problem, Colonel."

Skorzeny stood before him, his massive size dwarfing Neumann. "Explain."

"The reports indicate there's a risk of very heavy fog all along this part of the Italian coast, over the entire twenty-four hours to come, and it could be on its way very soon.

If the predictions are accurate, it may be really bad—
treacherous, in fact. Which for us means poor visibility.
And poor visibility, as you know, can hamper take-off and
landing."

"I'm not concerned with landing," Skorzeny answered
brusquely. "Only take-off, Neumann. Surely it can still be
done even if the fog's really bad?"

Neumann shrugged. "Any of my crews could take off
pretty much blind, that's not the problem. And we're all
reasonably familiar with the Dakota, having been trained
on it at the Luftwaffe special operations unit in Berlin. In
fact, two of the crew flew them while working for com-
mercial airlines before the war. But it's really a question of
safety and risk. If we have very bad fog here at the aerodrome we could find ourselves in dire trouble, on or after
take-off, if either aircraft suffered engine failure or a serious
technical problem."

"But surely control tower could help guide us down by
radio if we had to return to the airfield?"

"That's still no guarantee of a safe landing, if conditions
are bad. There's such a thing as an aircraft's operating limits, and they apply as much to weather and visibility. We
might not be able to *see* the runway lights, let alone the
runway, and that kind of thing spells nothing but danger. I
wouldn't like to take the risk of trying to land again in
dense fog with near-zero visibility, not with two aircraft
fully laden with fuel, men and munitions. It would be insane. And there's nowhere else we could try to land in these
parts. South of Rome, the Allies control the airfields—and
even there they'll have the same weather, if the forecasts
are to be believed."

Skorzeny ran a massive hand over his face and sighed,
then stared out at the coast with narrowed eyes, as if trying
to discern the weather threat for himself. "*Nothing* can be
allowed to stop us, Neumann. Not even the likelihood of
heavy fog. The signal I received from Berlin expressly says
we're on alert. Which could mean taking off at a moment's
notice if we get the word. That's unlikely until darkness
falls, I know, but that's how it stands."

"But it's the weather we're talking about, Colonel. We
can defy nature only at our peril. If anything should go

wrong, the lives of your men could be at serious risk, and those of my crews too."

"I'll defy *anything* that gets in the way of this mission, Captain, nature included. We do what we must, and we go when we have to. Fog or no fog, I want those aircraft off the ground if and when the time comes."

"But the safety of the crew and passengers—"

"You'll do as you're ordered, Neumann," Skorzeny snapped bluntly, and with that he turned smartly and strode away.

CAIRO
6 P.M.

Weaver arrived at Sanson's office to find him talking to a thin-faced Egyptian with a hook nose. His dark, hooded eyes looked faintly sinister, his skin pockmarked with old acne scars. He carried a tattered leather briefcase and wore a pale, short-sleeved tropical suit. Something about the man looked oddly familiar, but Weaver couldn't recall where he had seen him before.

Sanson made the introductions. "I'd like you to meet Captain Yosef Arkhan. Cairo Homicide."

Weaver remembered the name. The captain in charge of Mustapha Evir's murder investigation.

"A pleasure to meet you, Lieutenant-Colonel Weaver," Arkhan said in perfect English, and shook Weaver's hand.

"You mind telling me what this is about?" Weaver asked Sanson.

"Yosef and I go back a long way. Before serving with Homicide, he used to work for the secret police—the Mukhabarat."

Weaver glanced over at Arkhan. With his hooded eyes and menacing looks, the captain still had the look of a secret policeman. "I don't get it."

"You will, and very soon. Take a seat." Sanson gestured to the chairs, then nodded to Arkhan. "Tell him, Yosef—"

The Egyptian removed two worn manila files from his briefcase, and said politely to Weaver, "You were a member of an international archaeological team at Sakkara in '39."

"What of it?"

Arkhan opened one of the files, and read. "Harold Weaver. American citizen, born in New York, a graduate of engineering. Father an estate caretaker—Thomas Weaver—employed by a wealthy German-American family named Halder. Unmarried, but appears to have a platonic relationship with one Rachel Stern, German citizen, a member of same archaeological team. No known vices, apart from occasional alcohol. Mr. Weaver appears a bona fide citizen of his country, and not engaged in any espionage activity." Arkhan closed the file and looked up. "I could go on, there are lots more petty details, but I'm afraid they're really not very interesting."

Weaver stared angrily at the Egyptian. "You were watching me."

Arkhan shrugged. "My men and I watched many of the archaeological teams who came to our country. I'm sure you know the nickname by which the secret police are known—the Red Eye. The eye that never sleeps. We observed not only your team, but many other foreign visitors—anyone who interested us or we had our suspicions about. There was a long list—German and Italian oil workers and company executives, American professors at our universities. Even diplomats." He paused. "In fact, our paths crossed once, four years ago. Oddly enough, it was in the grounds of the American residency. The occasion was a farewell party."

Weaver felt stunned, remembering where he had seen Arkhan before. "I was on the veranda with Rachel Stern. You were watching us."

Arkhan gave a slight nod. "You're observant, Lieutenant-Colonel Weaver, and possessed of a good memory. Few people could recall a fleeting incident that happened so long ago."

"Why were you watching us?"

"Not only you and the young lady. We had an interest in quite a number of the party guests that night."

"You didn't answer my question."

Arkhan hesitated, and Sanson said, "Tell him, Yosef."

"Some of the people we observed during that period were entirely innocent. Others were definitely not what they pretended to be. They were spies. Italian, German, even

American. In extreme cases, we quietly expelled such people. But among the Germans at Sakkara, several especially interested us. In particular, Rachel Stern and her parents."

"Why?"

"Because we strongly suspected they were German agents. Had they not left the country when they did, they would certainly have been arrested."

Weaver looked at Sanson and said incredulously, "I can't believe this."

"Let him finish. Go on, Yosef."

"The young lady was watched discreetly for a considerable time. On different occasions, she was seen near military installations, and in the same company as a number of my countrymen suspected of working for the Nazi intelligence services. Her father was also conducting several archaeological digs in secret—an illegal act in itself. But I believe the true purpose of his work was much more dangerous."

"What do you mean?"

Arkhan glanced at Sanson before replying. "We felt certain the Germans would eventually invade North Africa, and that Egypt would be their principal target. We believed they had plans to store arms and munitions, supplies and communications equipment in secret dumps, to be used to arm an Egyptian fifth column, which would stir internal unrest once war started. After all, there was, and still is, considerable support for the Nazi cause among the officer class and the general population. We think Professor Stern's job was to locate suitable archaeological sites around Cairo, which would have been used as secret supply dumps."

"Did you find hard evidence of that?"

Arkhan hesitated. "No, but we were certain—"

"These people Rachel Stern met," Weaver interrupted. "The meetings could have been entirely innocent. She could have simply bumped into the wrong people at the wrong time—or socialised with them unknowingly. Isn't that possible?"

"Perhaps, but I don't believe so—"

"Oh, come on, Captain. I can't accept the Sterns were

spies. How many times do I have to say it? The professor hated the Nazis, and his wife was Jewish."

"His hatred of the Nazis was most certainly a cover story. And his wife's race was nothing more than a rumour we couldn't prove." Arkhan paused. "We also suspected this other German, Halder, was a spy. However, apart from his closeness to Miss Stern, we couldn't be absolutely certain. But we were positive about one thing."

"What?"

"At least four of the people in your group at Sakkara were Nazi agents. More importantly, one of them was arrested on spying charges several months after the war began. He confessed that the top Nazi agent in the Middle East was operating in Cairo at the time of your dig—under the code name Nightingale." Arkhan looked steadily at Weaver. "I believe Nightingale was none other than Rachel Stern."

Weaver almost laughed. "On what basis?"

"Instinct. Nightingale was undoubtedly the most brilliant agent the Germans had. Catching her in the act proved impossible. She was far too clever. So in the end, instincts were all we had to go by."

Sanson said, "Well, Weaver?"

"I don't buy it. You can't condemn someone on instinct alone. You need hard facts."

Arkhan offered across the second file. "Perhaps we didn't have irrefutable evidence, as you say. But instinct is often the best attribute an intelligence officer can possess. We kept a dossier that detailed the lady's meetings and the places she went. Perhaps you'd care to read it for yourself? It might help you understand our suspicions."

Weaver ignored the file. "I don't need to. You know as well as I do even the best-intentioned intelligence report can lead to false conclusions. Didn't you ever have an intuition about something that was wrong?"

"Of course, but—"

"But nothing. This time you got it wrong. You even got it wrong about me."

"Pardon?"

"I was born in Boston, not New York."

Arkhan shrugged. "A small matter." He said delicately,

"There was a certain romantic attachment between you and the young lady, was there not?"

"What's that got to do with it?"

"As we say in Egypt, a man in love can mistake a wart for a dimple. Passion can make us blind to the truth."

Weaver ignored the remark. Sanson nodded to Arkhan. "Thanks, Yosef. You can go now."

The captain replaced the files in his briefcase, tucked it under his arm, and bowed politely. "Good-day, gentlemen. It's been a pleasure meeting you, Lieutenant-Colonel Weaver."

When the Egyptian had left, Sanson looked over at Weaver. "Arkhan's a good policeman. Whenever I've had to put my faith in his judgment, I've rarely been disappointed. Like when he came to me about Evir's murder. He has a sixth sense about these things, one that's seldom been proven wrong. He knew something didn't smell right, and he was spot on. But you don't believe him, do you?"

"No, I don't."

Sanson sighed, made a steeple of his fingers. "The desert searches turned up a bit of good luck. I got a phone call from Myers just before you arrived. His men have picked up a man named Achmed Farnad, a German agent who runs a small hotel at a place called Abu Sammar, about twenty miles from Alex. He was shot and seriously wounded during the arrest, but he's still conscious, and they managed to get him to talk a little. It seems he was the link man Berlin arranged to meet their team. The plan was that they would rendezvous at a nearby deserted airfield, and Farnad would send them on their way to Cairo. They never made the rendezvous, but some hours after the crash they arrived at his hotel in the Jeep they stole from the murdered officers. Five people—the pilot, three men and a woman. The way Farnad is telling it, Halder is in charge. The pilot was badly injured in the crash, and later died. Which leaves four, as we suspected."

"When can we interrogate him?"

"It's imperative that he's thoroughly questioned, of course, but that's my business, Weaver. Though I don't know how much more he can tell us—he's probably got no idea what the Germans are really up to. But from here on, this has nothing more to do with you."

"What do you mean?"

Sanson said firmly, "It's my duty to inform you that you're no longer on the case. I can't put my trust in a man whose judgment I think is suspect."

"You can't do that, Sanson, damn you!"

"I already have, and with General Clayton's full consent. In fact, he wanted to dismiss you at our meeting this afternoon. I asked that you be given one more chance. Once you'd considered the evidence, I thought you might have changed your mind. But you've been pig-headed and ignored my professional judgment in this matter. If you'd accepted it, I might have allowed you to remain on the case. But to be truthful, I'm not sure I can rely on you to carry out your duties effectively and with proper vigour, Weaver."

"What the hell do you mean?"

"I told you when this began I needed an officer who was prepared to do his duty and follow orders—to kill the enemy if necessary. I'm not at all certain you'd be prepared to do that in this instance. You and your friends are on opposite sides of the fence, but it's obvious this friendship of yours ran very deep. And there just might be a conflict between your loyalty to your friends and your duty to your country. You might even be tempted to allow them to escape, rather than have them face military justice. And I can't have that."

Weaver fumed. "You're totally ignoring the real issue here, Sanson. There's no hard evidence Rachel Stern is a spy. Only hearsay and guesswork. You'd be killing an innocent woman."

"That's a matter of opinion. Arkhan's accusation is enough for me. Not that it really matters. These friends of yours are condemned anyway. But I wanted to give you the benefit of Arkhan's information." Sanson stood and picked up his cap, the meeting at an end. "Now, if you don't mind, I've got to attend to Farnad's interrogation. Good-day, Weaver."

Weaver pushed back his chair angrily. "You can't just dump me like that."

"The decision's made."

"Listen to me, Sanson—"

"I said good-day."

"Then just do me one favour," Weaver pleaded. "If you find Halder and Rachel Stern, at least let me attempt to talk to them before any shooting starts—let me try to convince them to surrender."

"You see? My point's proven. You still want to try and save their necks. But if you think I'm going to risk the lives of my men by pussyfooting around and asking these friends of yours to surrender, you've got another think coming. Forget it, Weaver. I won't do that."

FIFTY-SIX

6 P.M.

Halder kept his speed down as he drove the motorcycle, Rachel holding on to him in the pillion seat. The moonlit track was dark and bumpy, full of ruts and potholes, and he wore sand goggles to protect his eyes from the gritty desert air. Half an hour after leaving the villa they came to the outskirts of the busy little village of Nazlat as-Saman, at the foot of the majestic Sphinx.

"Well, we made it." Halder pulled off the goggles. "Now let's find the others."

The village was a rabbit-warren of boisterous narrow streets, carnival stalls everywhere, fire-eaters and snake-charmers giving displays, and they realised there was some kind of local festival in progress. Near the end of the main street a dirt road led up past the Sphinx, and on a rise behind it loomed the site of the Giza pyramids, a magnificent backdrop against the moonlit night sky.

As Halder inched the BSA through the noisy, good-humoured crowd, he saw two groups of American military police up ahead, stopping civilians and off-duty soldiers to check their papers.

"There's no end to it, is there?" he said over his shoulder to Rachel. "Still, there's no point in inviting trouble."

"You think it's us they're looking for?"

Halder shrugged. "It could be just routine, but somehow I doubt it. I'm sure Harry and his pals are tearing Cairo apart."

He turned down an alley, hoping to skirt around the MPs, but realised they were in a dead end. When he looked back down the alley, he saw another group of MPs stroll past on the street.

"*Damn*. We'd better keep our faces out of the way until they've gone."

"What about meeting the others?"

"They'll just have to wait." He told Rachel to dismount, then propped the motorcycle on its stand. There was an open doorway opposite, the hallway lit by an oil lamp. "Let's see if there's a way out of this dead end, just in case." He saw a beaded curtain at the end of the hallway, pushed his way through, and Rachel followed.

They were in a tiny candlelit room that smelled powerfully of incense. A young girl wearing a cotton wrap and loop earrings sat behind a rickety table, flicking through a tattered magazine, as if to pass the time. She smiled up at them. "You have come to consult with Khalil, the oracle?"

Halder realised the girl thought they had come to have their fortunes read, but he didn't miss a beat. "Indeed we have."

"This way."

The girl led them through another beaded curtain, as Rachel whispered to Halder, "What are you doing?"

"It'll keep us out of harm's way for a while. Besides, maybe we could do with a glimpse of what lies in store."

"You don't really believe in all that hocus-pocus nonsense?"

Halder laughed. "Oh, I don't know. There might be something in it. The Pharaohs put a lot of faith in their mystics, remember?"

They were in another small candlelit room. A *bassara*, an Egyptian fortune-teller, sat cross-legged on a carpet—a shabbily dressed old man with wrinkled skin the colour of walnut. One of his eyes was milky white, the blind pupil staring into nothing. In front of him was a brass tray with some tiny cups, a coffee pot heating on a tiny charcoal brazier near by.

"A couple to see you, Grandfather."

The girl left and the old man said, "So, you have come to consult with Khalil. Be seated."

They sat cross-legged on the floor. "Is it just the young lady, or you also, effendi?"

"Both of us, I think." Halder smiled as he turned to Rachel. "I'll go first, if you like. Seeing as how you're a disbeliever." He nodded to the old man. "Let's hear what the future holds, my friend."

The man poured thick Turkish coffee into one of the cups and handed it over. "Drink, effendi."

Halder swallowed the treacly black liquid and returned the cup. The fortune-teller rolled it between his palms and stared into the grounds at the bottom. "The effendi has come from a far country, but he is no stranger to this land. I see pain and trouble in his past, and more lies ahead. There is an opportunity to redeem himself, if he does not give in to evil. There is also a woman he desires very much, but he will be forced to choose between desire and duty."

Halder turned to Rachel with a smile. "What can I say to all that?"

"Something else," the old man went on solemnly. "Someone the gentleman loved has recently passed away." He hesitated, a cloud crossed his face, and he shook his head.

"That is all I see."

"Nothing more?"

"I am sorry."

Halder said to Rachel, "Now it's your turn."

"I'd rather not, Jack. It's stupid."

"Humour him."

The man said to Rachel, "Khalil doesn't lie. His gift comes from the mystic power of the pyramids. The future is there, if you wish to know it. Hold out your hand, dear lady."

Rachel held it out to the man. He filled another cup, placed it in her hand, and she drank the coffee. She returned the empty cup to Khalil, who studied the grounds, but his face clouded again, and he suddenly put it down. "I'm afraid Khalil can see nothing in the lady's future that she doesn't already know."

Rachel was silent for a moment, then she shrugged and looked at Halder. "See, I told you. It's all nonsense, anyway."

The man stared across at Halder, who placed a handful of coins on the table. "Let's get out of here."

He led Rachel out past the girl, into the hall, and lit a cigarette. "You don't seem too comfortable. Did he upset you?"

"I never believed in fortune-tellers. It's gibberish."

"You're still not impressed, are you? But one or two things he said had a ring of truth."

"You think he meant about your father's death, don't you?"

Halder's face darkened and he shivered. "Maybe, but the feeling it gave me when he mentioned a death was quite uncanny. Like someone walking over my grave. I had this vision, not of my father, but of Pauli—"

There was a morbid look on his face, a terrible unease, and Rachel quickly put a reassuring hand on his arm. "Jack, don't be silly. You're reading something into nothing."

He did his best to shrug off the feeling of dread. "Maybe you're right. You'd better wait here."

He went down the alley and peered into the street, then came back. "It looks all clear, so let's give it a try. I'm sure Deacon and Kleist are wondering what's happened to us." He retrieved the motorcycle, climbed on, helped Rachel on to the back, and started the engine.

Five minutes later he had cut around the village and was on a gravel road, halfway up to the pyramids. Deacon's car was parked off the road, Kleist in the passenger seat, and he drove up beside them. He and Rachel dismounted.

Deacon stepped out, frowning, wiping his forehead with a handkerchief. "What the devil kept you?"

Halder nodded back towards the village. "A small problem of some military police we had to avoid. Did you have any trouble getting here?"

"There were a couple of army checkpoints on the way. But fortunately your friend's papers passed the test."

Kleist said, "Are you ready, Major?"

Halder nodded. "I'll leave the motorcycle here and we'll go on together."

He wheeled the machine off the road, left it hidden behind some rocks, and climbed into the back of the car with Rachel. The massive Cheops pyramid lay ahead as they drove on up the hill, and there was a jumble of boulders on the right-hand side of the road, the tumbling ruins of several tombs. They saw a red-and-white barrier pole blocking their way, a wooden sentry box beside it, and suddenly a shabbily dressed Egyptian policeman appeared out of the shadows, wearing a red hat with a tarboosh, and a pair of scruffy sandals instead of boots. He flashed a torch for them to halt.

When Deacon pulled up, Halder said, "Leave this to me." He climbed out and showed his ID. "I'm a professor from Cairo University."

The policeman looked at the documents, a kind of awe on his face, but he said nothing, until Halder realised the poor fellow was probably barely literate. There was a noise behind him, and a stout man wearing a sergeant's uniform came out of nowhere, his thumbs stuck in his leather belt. He was obviously in charge.

"What's the trouble, Ali?" the sergeant asked.

"The effendi says he's a professor, from Cairo University."

"Some students of mine are working on the site," Halder went on quickly, and offered the sergeant his papers. "Some colleagues and I need to make an inspection of their progress. Are any of the excavating teams still here?"

"They have all gone home. The site is empty." The sergeant looked in at the passengers, then examined the documents under the torch light and scratched his head. "A thousand pardons, Professor, but is it not a little late in the evening for this sort of thing?"

Halder smiled. "Not when you're expecting an important visit from a Ministry of Antiquities delegation first thing tomorrow. We need to make absolutely certain everything's in perfect order. I'm sure you understand. Lift the barrier, there's a good fellow." Halder took out his wallet and generously slipped the sergeant a couple of banknotes. "A small token of my gratitude, for your kind help."

The money vanished instantly into the sergeant's back pocket and he bowed his thanks. "Of course, effendi. I am at your service." He clicked his fingers. "You heard the professor. Lift the barrier, Ali."

The policeman scurried away to do as he was told.

Halder climbed back into the Packard, and as they passed under the barrier, the sergeant drew himself to attention and saluted. Halder smiled at Deacon. "See. I told you. Easy."

Deacon wiped his brow with the back of his sleeve. "Let's just hope our luck holds out for the rest of it, Major."

FIFTY-SEVEN

BERLIN
22 NOVEMBER/7 P.M.
The chauffeured Mercedes glided to a halt in the enclosed courtyard at the rear of the Chancellery building and Schellenberg climbed out. An acrid smell immediately filled his nostrils, and he covered his mouth and nose with his hand. He hadn't failed to notice a couple of large, smouldering bomb craters in the Chancellery grounds, nor the dozens of thick, black oily plumes drifting up from the west of the city, and he could still hear the clanging of fire engine bells in the distance. Berlin was covered by a pall of choking smoke after another devastating air raid that late afternoon, the sky so dark it looked as if the world were going to end.

Two SS guards of the Liebstandarte Division, Hitler's private bodyguard, immaculate in their black uniforms and white gloves, snapped to attention as Schellenberg went past into the bunker lobby, where a waiting adjutant took his overcoat and led him straight down two flights of steps to the Führer's private underground office.

When Schellenberg was led into the sparse concrete room, Hitler was in an anxious mood, wringing his hands as he paced the floor. "Well?"

"I've been personally waiting in the signals room at SS headquarters since early afternoon, and will return there to be on hand, but still nothing yet, *mein Führer*. However, as I explained, we don't expect Deacon to transmit until tonight."

Hitler looked gravely disappointed. "And Skorzeny and his men?"

"On alert, and ready and waiting. The colonel informs me he can be off the ground and on his way to Cairo within five minutes of receiving our instruction."

"This afternoon Allied bombers destroyed a dozen more of our factories, not to mention direct hits to two of our railway stations."

"Yes, I heard, *mein Führer*. A terrible business."

"Terrible? It's catastrophic!" Hitler's face turned purple, the veins swelling on his neck and forehead. "Dozens of carriages destroyed, hundreds of military and civilian casualties, total disruption to our armaments shipments by rail to the Russian front, production halted in four of our tank factories and small-arms plants. It's getting worse, Walter. Every day it's getting worse. If this continues, our armies will have nothing left to fight with but sticks and stones."

"I'm certain Production Minister Speer will do his absolute utmost to rectify matters quickly."

"If he doesn't, I'll have his neck on the end of a rope." Hitler slumped into a leather armchair, his body crumpling with despair. "So, you still think Halder can get through and carry out his orders?"

"I'm convinced of it."

Hitler fixed Schellenberg with a cold stare. "As always, your optimism is enviable, Walter. But if Sphinx fails, mark my words, heads will roll. Perhaps even yours. With every day that passes, it becomes even more imperative we annihilate our two mortal enemies, Roosevelt and Churchill. Two bombs hit the Chancellery grounds this afternoon. Can you believe it? They're trying to kill me, Walter. *Me!* We must destroy them first, before they destroy us all."

"I agree totally, *mein Führer*."

"The very *second* you receive word from Deacon, you call me, personally. Dismissed."

CAIRO
8 P.M.
Weaver went up the steps past the uniformed dragomans at the entrance to Shepheard's. He found an empty seat under the palms on the front terrace. It was Friday night and the

streets were overflowing. He ordered a large Scotch and sat there, barely taking notice of the chaos of traffic that went past the hotel.

He had phoned Clayton at least half a dozen times, but the general wasn't taking his calls. He felt angry and frustrated. And there was a strange feeling he was aware of, now that he had got over the shock of seeing Rachel alive. The fact that she was with Jack Halder sent a pang of jealousy through him, so powerful it almost made him wish Halder dead. It was as if he had been wounded, a pain spreading through his entire body.

A waiter scurried past and he ordered another large Scotch. In the warm evening air, the alcohol was fast going to his head, but he didn't care.

"Hello, Harry."

He saw Helen Kane standing over him. "Mind if I join you?"

He was surprised to see her, and felt faintly embarrassed. "No, of course not. How did you know I was here?"

She pulled up a chair. "I didn't. I called at the villa but there was no one there. I was on my way back to the office and saw you on the terrace as I drove past." She looked at him sympathetically. "I heard what happened with Sanson. I thought maybe you could do with some company. And I also wanted to apologise."

"For what?"

"My behaviour this afternoon. I was being selfish, playing the spurned woman and only thinking of myself. You're a good man, Harry Weaver. And for what it's worth I believe you when you say Rachel Stern is innocent."

He put a hand on hers, and this time she didn't pull away. "I'm sorry about what happened, Helen. It's just—"

"You don't have to explain, really you don't."

Weaver felt a terrible stab of guilt, and quickly changed the subject. "You mind me asking if Sanson's made any progress?"

She blushed, took her hand away slowly. "I suppose I shouldn't be telling you this, but there was a phone call from a Sergeant Morris at the Provost's office. It had to do with the enquiry Sanson made about stolen vehicles. There were exactly four thefts in the last week—all of them in the last five days, all of them military, and from the same transport pool in Cairo."

"What kinds of vehicles?"

"A Jeep and three trucks. The sergeant seemed to think it unusual that all four should be stolen almost simultaneously. Another thing. There were three uniforms taken from a clothing store at about the same time as the Jeep, which made him faintly suspicious there might be something more to it."

"Uniforms?"

"Military police. One officer's, and two NCOs'. The sergeant suggested he might have some information about the thefts."

"What kind of information?"

"He didn't say."

Weaver perked up. "What's Sanson doing about it?"

"He's on his way back from Alex. I don't think he's had much luck interrogating the Arab agent that Myers picked up."

"How long before he gets back?"

"An hour, maybe more."

There was a spark in Weaver's face, and Helen Kane said seriously, "If you're thinking what I think you are, don't even consider it, Harry. If Sanson found out you went behind his back he'd have you court-martialled." She stood. "I'd better be going. He's got everyone working round the clock. Do you mind if I say something? I hope for your sake Rachel Stern doesn't come to a bad end in all of this, I really do." She smiled bravely, still faintly upset. "Be good, Harry."

"Helen, wait—"

But she turned, hurried down the veranda steps, and was gone.

Deacon halted the Packard near the western slope of the Cheops pyramid. Bathed in pale silver moonlight, the ancient burial site looked truly awesome, its gigantic silhouette filling the night sky. There was a scattering of ruined tombs near by, all made of massive limestone cubes, dozens of them set around the pyramids. Most of the blocks were in total disarray, as if they'd been tossed about by the force of an earthquake.

When they climbed out of the car into the shadowy darkness, Halder said to Rachel, "You'd better lead the way." He turned to Kleist and Deacon. "We'll bring the things from the car. But don't light the oil lamps just yet."

They retrieved a couple of spades, a pickaxe, several oil lamps, a large crowbar, some balls of twine and two water canteens from the boot and stumbled over the rocks, fumbling in the dark for about fifty metres, until Rachel said, "It's down there somewhere. I'm sure of it."

She pointed to the ruins of one of the tombs. It was no more than a deep gaping recess in the ground, about twelve feet square and six feet deep, surrounded by a jumble of huge limestone blocks. Some were cracked and broken and had spilled into the recess.

"My father left a marker, on a stone block above the entrance."

"What kind of marker?"

"Two parallel lines chiselled in the stone."

They climbed down into the recess, but it was impossible to see anything clearly in the moonlight. "Let's have some light on the situation," Halder said. They lit a couple of the oil lamps and searched along the walls until Kleist said suddenly, "Is this what you're looking for, Major?"

Halder and the others joined him. There was a pile of old rubble, chunks of rock and earth left stacked up near the bottom right-hand corner of the tomb. Above the pile, etched in one of the stone blocks lining the walls, was an unmistakable pair of straight lines.

"That's it," said Rachel. "The entrance should be underneath the rubble, covered by a slab of rock."

Halder grabbed the crowbar and picked away all the rubble. Below was a large round stone, about two feet in diameter, lying flat on the ground. Using the crowbar, he tried to jimmy it back, but the slab didn't budge. "It's no use— it's damned heavy and wedged hard." He stripped to the waist and tossed away his shirt, sweat pumping from him now in the clammy heat. "Give me a hand here, Kleist."

The SS man joined him and together they levered the

crowbar and applied all their strength, groaning with the effort, but still the slab didn't move.

"Bring the rest of the tools and give us some help," Halder called out to Deacon.

The three of them worked around the edge with the crowbar, shovel and pickaxe, sweating in the darkness, loosening the slab and heaving together until it began to move a little. When they finally managed to lever it back, the slab fell away with a crash, and a sudden rush of dust and foul air wafted up at them.

They covered their mouths until the air had cleared, and Halder held up the lamp. There was a small rim of rock that surrounded a round, black hole, sloping down into darkness, barely enough room for a man to crawl through. "It seems we're in the right spot."

His excitement mounting, Halder rolled off a length from one of the balls of twine, tied it to a slab. "I'll go first. Deacon, you'd better stay here and keep watch. If anyone comes by, tug hard on this a couple of times. Got that?"

"Whatever you say, Major."

Halder grabbed the oil lamp, got down on one knee, ready to crawl into the hole, and looked back up at Rachel and Kleist. "The moment of truth. If it's safe, I'll tug on the string and you follow me in."

He crawled for about five metres, the journey claustrophobic, the air stale. The ground was covered with a scattering of rough limestone chips, and when he came to the end of the passage he found himself in a narrow upright vault. It was pleasantly cool. He stood, dusted himself, and picked up the lamp.

He was in a dark and ghostly chamber, about eight feet across, the roof just touching his head. In the centre was a large stone sarcophagus, covered in a layer of thick brown dust. He ran his fingers over the grimy lid of the ancient coffin, revealing a smoothly polished surface beneath, parts of it etched with hieroglyphics. He raised the lamp and turned slowly in a circle.

The chamber walls were decorated with even more magnificent hieroglyphics, the colours still fresh and vivid de-

spite the centuries that had passed, and for several moments
he marvelled at the uncanny splendour of it all, until he
picked out with startling suddenness two skeletal remains
lying in a heap against the bottom left-hand wall, the skull
sockets staring out at him eerily. Halder shivered.

At the far end of the tomb was a gaping hole in the
ground, leading into darkness. He knelt and crawled forward on his belly. This time the passage was no more than
a couple of feet long, and it came out into a cavern. The
rock walls were about five feet wide, and the roof formed
a jagged apex a couple of feet above his head. The shaft
had obviously been formed naturally, and extended about
ten paces before it came to an archway of rock. He went
forward, ducked through the low entrance, and saw that the
passageway carried on into blackness.

He crawled back into the burial chamber, tugged hard
on the string, and called up the passage. "You can come in
now. Bring some of the tools with you, and the canteens
and kit-bag."

A few minutes later, Kleist crawled through, grunting as
he pushed the shovels and crowbar ahead of him, then came
Rachel, with the kit-bag and water canteens. "Did you find
the passageway?" she asked.

"Over there." He pointed to the entrance, then played
the lamp over the skeletons.

"The remains of the grave-robbers I told you about,"
said Rachel.

Halder shot a look at Kleist. "Not the most reassuring
of company, are they? Let's just hope they're not an omen
for us." He put down the lamp and knelt, ready to enter the
cavern again. "OK, follow me, and we'll see where the
passageway leads. And be careful how you go."

After the first ten paces, the cave floor sloped downward
for about twenty feet, then came up again. They moved
through it smoothly, the walls narrowing and widening
along the way, but it was an easy enough passage, and while
Kleist held the lamp, Halder carefully let out the string, trying to keep it from snagging on the jagged rock edges. He
counted off the number of paces. After they had gone about
two hundred, they came to the end of the tunnel.

An immense slab of stone, at least five or six tons, stretched across their path, and sloped backwards towards the high roof. Halder swung the lamp in an arc but could see no way forward. "Unless I'm very much mistaken, we're at a dead end," he told Rachel, his voice rebounding off the cavern walls.

She pointed above them, to where the slope met the roof. "You should see some rocks near the top. That's where the exit is, I think."

Halder raised the lamp. Sure enough, there was a sloping bank of rubble and stones in a recess between the top of the massive boulder and the roof. "Give me a lift up," he ordered Kleist.

The SS man cupped his hands and hefted him up. Halder balanced precariously on the sloping boulder for a couple of moments, his boots scraping on stone, then managed to get a firm grip. "Now hand me up a shovel, and try to give me some light."

Kleist did so, directing the oil lamp into the recess as Halder picked away at the rubble, his face and body streaked with sweat, the blade of the shovel flashing in the light as he worked feverishly at scouring away the rocks and clay, until a mass of debris came tumbling down, filling the passageway with choking dust. An eerie sound whispered through the cave, as a warm finger of fresh air licked their faces, causing the lamp to flicker. When the dust cleared, Halder looked up and saw an open rock shaft leading upwards, more than wide enough for him to pass through.

He wiped sweat from his face. "I'll see where it leads. Wait here."

He handed the shovel back down to Kleist and climbed up through the darkened shaft. A moment later he was securely wedged against the rock, his back against one side, his feet against the other, his hands fastening on the rock as he heaved desperately, moving his way up. After about six feet he came to the top. He saw moonlight, smelled the scent of warm perfumed air, and hauled himself out over the edge.

He was lying in a slight hollow in the ground, the area in deep shadow and partly protected by a cluttered circle of bushes. A vast manicured lawn stretched around him. At first, he saw only darkness beyond, but then he noticed a perimeter fence about eighty yards away, patrolled by dozens of armed American GIs and British squaddies, some with dogs.

Behind him was a large building, perhaps a hundred paces distant, the clipped lawns in front dotted with flowerbeds and palm trees, the windows ablaze with lights. He recognised the Mena House. Up on the roof a muzzle protruded from a sandbagged machinegun emplacement, and a short way behind it the twin fingers of an anti-aircraft gun pointed skyward. Several of the windows below the roof parapet were lit up, and he noticed a couple of Sherman tanks parked in front of the hotel.

At that precise moment, two GIs appeared from the palm trees, rifles over their shoulders, talking idly as they strolled towards him across the lawn. Halder flattened himself into the ground, waited until the men had passed a short distance away, then climbed back into the shaft, feet first. Moments later he was inching his way down the slope of the massive boulder, back into the tunnel.

"Well?" Kleist asked expectantly.

"I think we might be in business."

The SS man beamed, his excitement obvious, and Halder said to Rachel, "Take one of the lamps and make your way back to Deacon. Wait there until we return."

"Don't you need me any more?"

"No, your work's done." He smiled, touched her arm reassuringly. "I'll join you later." He saw the concern on her face.

"Whatever you're going to do, be careful, Jack."

She took one of the oil lamps and moved back into the tunnel. Halder took a swig from one of the canteens, poured some water on to his palm and cleaned his face, then said to Kleist, "Hand me the kit-bag with the uniforms, then get yourself tidied up. We're going up to have a proper look."

"You mind telling me exactly what you found up there?"

Halder explained as he struggled out of his shirt, dried his face with it, and began to change into the captain's uniform. "The shaft leads up to the hotel grounds, about a hundred paces from the main building."

The SS man beamed again. "It almost sounds too good to be true."

"Which is why we shouldn't speak too soon. There are lots of guards about, and remember, we have to confirm that the targets are inside. Even if they are, we have another concern—the entrance to the tomb, and the shaft here, will have to be widened. Dozens of paratroops in full combat gear are going to have to crawl through those holes, not to mention return the same way."

"It can be done." Kleist nodded firmly, his excitement mounting. "You can be sure of that."

"We'll see." Halder finished putting on the uniform and buttoned the tunic, while Kleist began to struggle into his. "You'd better blow out the lamp before we go up. It wouldn't do for anyone above to catch a glimpse of light down here. If anything goes wrong and I don't make it, try to get back to the others and away from here as quick as you can." A troubled look flashed in Halder's eyes. "One other thing—you don't harm the woman under any circumstances, is that understood, Kleist? If I don't return, you simply let her go—I want you to promise me that. She's more than played her part in all of this. She doesn't deserve to die."

A slight grin played across Kleist's face as he finished adjusting his uniform. "Whatever you say, Major. But I'm quite sure you'll make it back. You have something at stake, I think?"

Halder glared at him silently in reply, then tugged on his officer's cap. "Give me a lift up."

Kleist cupped his hands again. Halder scurried up on to the boulder, then helped up the SS man. A moment later he blew out the lamp, the cavern was smothered in darkness, and he climbed up through the shaft again, Kleist behind him.

FIFTY-EIGHT

Halder lay flat on his belly among the bushes in the hollow. He remained like that in the darkness for several minutes, surveying the grounds. The two sentries were nowhere to be seen, but behind him the guards were still patrolling the perimeter. When he was reasonably certain it was safe to move, he whispered down the shaft. "You can come up now, Kleist."

A minute later Kleist struggled up. "Stay flat," Halder ordered, and gave the SS man a few moments to adapt himself to his surroundings. "We'll head towards the front of the hotel. Just a nice leisurely pace like we're out for a stroll."

"What then?"

Halder dusted his clothes, ready to move. "We play the cards as they fall. So long as we keep our heads we shouldn't arouse suspicion, but you can bet the sentries have got a password system in operation, in which case we're at a disadvantage. So you'd better keep that weapon of yours handy just in case we're challenged."

They walked towards the front of the hotel. There was a flurry of activity, dispatch riders arriving and departing on the gravel driveway out front. A half-dozen white-helmeted MP sentries stood on either side of the entrance steps, and there was a desk in the open-doored foyer beyond, manned by an officer and a corporal, checking the papers of anyone who entered. On the grass lawn directly outside were the Sherman tanks, their crews sitting out around the turrets, idly talking and smoking cigarettes. Halder strolled over casually. One of the tank crew sergeants saw them and went to salute. "At ease, Sergeant. Have you got a light?"

"Sure, Captain." The man rummaged in his pocket and handed over a box of matches. Halder took his time lighting his cigarette and observed the entrance. The grounds were very heavily patrolled, sentries moving singly or in pairs out in the gardens. He could see no obvious way they could gain entrance to the hotel without being spotted or challenged.

He handed back the matches. "What's your name, Sergeant?"

"Grimes, sir."

"Where are you from, Grimes?"

"Speedwell, Tennessee, sir."

Halder smiled. "So how does it feel for a boy from the sticks to be guarding the President of the United States and the Prime Minister of England?"

The young sergeant beamed. "I guess it's quite an honour, Captain."

"You can say that again. So make sure you stay alert."

"Yes, sir." The sergeant snapped off a perfect salute, Halder returned it, and he and Kleist moved away from the tanks. The SS man let out a sigh of relief and grinned in the darkness. "I'll say this for you, Halder, you have a neck as hard as brass. And clever with it."

"If I was that, I'd never have allowed myself to get involved in this mess. And we can hardly take the sergeant's word for it that Roosevelt and Churchill are here. We'll have to make certain for ourselves."

Kleist looked aghast. "You mean you're going to try and get *inside* the hotel?"

"Let's face it, how else can we confirm their presence?"

"And what if we're caught? It would ruin everything."

"All part of the risk. And really there's no other way. Remember, a nice leisurely pace, and don't even think about reaching for that pistol unless I tell you to."

They strolled along one of the flower-bordered paths that wended around the grounds. Sandbagged machinegun nests were dotted on the front lawns, and behind the hotel hundreds of tents were visible in the pale moonlight, dozens of trucks and half-tracks parked near by. Troops were moving about them in the darkness.

"These defences are tighter than the Führer's lair," Kleist said, dispirited.

"Just keep walking. And keep your eyes open for any chink in the armour. We simply have to find a way in."

They walked on, towards the hotel grounds at the back.

It was the same everywhere they went, more sentries and gun emplacements, and on the roof they noticed another anti-aircraft position and several more machinegun nests. As they came towards the rear service entrance, Halder saw a parked army delivery truck, two soldiers in fatigues unloading crates of provisions and carrying them into the hotel kitchens, while an armed corporal with a clipboard supervised at the door. There was a busy scene inside, army cooks and soldiers in fatigues working away in clouds of steam, a wall of heat wafting out.

Halder paused, and Kleist seemed to read his thoughts. "Well, what do you think?"

"Let's give it a try."

Kleist sounded doubtful. "You're sure about this?"

"I'm sure of nothing, so be ready to cover me if anything goes wrong. Otherwise, just keep your mouth shut and do exactly as I say." Halder brazenly walked over to the corporal supervising the unloading. "What's going on here?" he demanded.

The man saluted. "Kitchen deliveries, Captain."

As one of the soldiers made to move past him carrying a crate of supplies, Halder laid a hand on the man's arm. "Did you check this man's papers, Corporal?"

"They were examined thoroughly at the gate, Captain. No one gets past without inspection—"

"I'm well aware of that, Corporal, but that wasn't the question I asked. Did *you* check them?"

The man looked flustered. "Well—no, sir, I didn't rightly see the need."

"Didn't see the need?" Halder exploded. "It's that kind of negligence that can cost us the war, Corporal. What about the supplies in the truck?"

"They were examined at the gate too, sir."

"And that's good enough for you, is it?" Halder raised an eyebrow sarcastically, and shot a look at the men. "Let me see your papers."

The men saluted and proffered them. Halder scrutinised the documents. "They look in order, right enough." He handed them back to the corporal. "But in future, you double-check every goddamned person who comes through here. And the contents of any delivery vehicle. Starting right now. Is that clear, Corporal?"

"Yes, Captain."

As he handed back the men's papers, Halder moved towards the kitchen doors and snapped back at Kleist, "Stay here, Sergeant, and make sure this vehicle is thoroughly searched and these men properly supervised. I want to make sure no one's slipped past this idiot here."

"Yes, sir."

"Captain, you can take my word—" the embarrassed corporal began, but Halder totally ignored him, stepping through the door and into the kitchen.

8:30 P.M.

The Provost's office was busy that evening. Weaver asked for Sergeant Morris at the front desk. It was ten minutes before the man appeared—a burly military policeman who looked under pressure. "Sorry for keeping you waiting, sir. How can I help?"

Weaver showed his ID. "It's about a call you made to Lieutenant-Colonel Sanson's office, concerning a number of stolen vehicles and uniforms."

The sergeant scratched his head. "You caught me at a bad time, sir. I'm up to my eyes. Is it urgent?"

"Very."

The sergeant sighed audibly. "Right. You'd better come into my office, sir."

Morris led him down the hall to a communal room with some desks and typewriters, where a couple of NCOs were busily working away. He sat down at one of the desks, searched for a file, found it, and glanced through the pages inside.

"Three Ford two and a half-ton canvas-top trucks, a Jeep, and three MPs' uniforms—all American equipment, and all stolen from Camp Huckstep stores in the last five days. You mind me asking why you're interested, sir?"

"It's a security matter," Weaver said simply. "I believe you have information about the thefts?"

"I thought if Lieutenant-Colonel Sanson had any clues about the matter, we might have been able to help each other. There's someone we think may have been responsible, but we're a bit shy on hard evidence."

"He doesn't. It was an American staff or civilian sedan we were interested in. But who's the suspect?"

"A Sergeant Wally Reed, British Army. 'Baldy' to his friends. He's a pen-pusher attached to our quartermaster's office. We believe he's been responsible for quite a bit of pilfering from army stores—everything from diesel to provisions destined for the officers' mess—except so far we can't prove a thing."

"But Reed's British Army, and the stolen vehicles and uniforms are American?"

The sergeant grinned. "Easy to explain, sir. Reed's got an arrangement with the stores master-sergeant at Camp Huckstep. If either has a shortage of vehicle parts and equipment, they help each other out. It's all perfectly above board."

"And what makes you think Reed might be responsible for the thefts?"

"I've had my eye on him for quite a while. Your MPs made enquiries and discovered he was a visitor at Camp Huckstep the day the Jeep and uniforms went missing. The same with the trucks. They questioned the stores personnel and turned up nothing—but they heard a whisper that Reed might have had a hand in it, though there isn't a shred of proof. No one saw him steal the equipment—he probably had the stores people do it for him, and paid them to keep their traps shut. You get a nose for these things after a while, and I'm pretty certain he's the culprit, but he's a slippery customer is Baldy. It'll be hard to catch him red-handed. We need to nab him in the act, or somehow link him back to the stuff he's nicked."

"What does he do with the supplies he steals?"

The sergeant shrugged. "Sells them on the black market, I should imagine. There's a lot of call for that sort of thing in Cairo. If something's not nailed down, it sprouts legs and walks. But I don't see how any of this can help you, sir. You said you were looking for a stolen sedan?"

Weaver frowned. "I am, but this sounds a lot more interesting. Any idea what anyone would want with US military vehicles?"

The sergeant scratched his head. "Now there you've got

me, which is why I phoned Lieutenant-Colonel Sanson. The Arabs wouldn't take the risk of dealing in stuff like that. An army truck isn't exactly the kind of thing you can paint over and disguise. Or a Jeep for that matter. And I reckon most of the parts wouldn't be much use to them. But it's the uniforms that really get me. Pretty odd that. Any chaps I know from here to Blighty are trying to get out of the bloody things, not into them."

"Maybe it's time you questioned this Sergeant Reed."

"Now, sir?" the sergeant protested. "But I haven't got the evidence I need. And putting the screws on Reed right now could ruin any case I try to build against him."

Weaver was already on his feet. "*Now*, Sergeant. I'll explain on the way. It could be a matter of life and death."

Halder went through the kitchen unchallenged, and halted at a pair of swing-doors at the end. There was a dining room beyond, in use as a temporary mess, dozens of officers seated at tables, being served by a battery of soldiers. The swing-doors opened and a GI came through carrying a tray of dirty dishes.

Halder moved out of the way and looked around for another exit. Off to his right was an open door, a narrow stairwell beyond, steps leading up. He went through and came up into a hallway on the first floor, doors leading off on either side. At the end of the hall he found himself in the deserted hotel lounge. Leather couches and easy chairs were scattered around the room, which was decorated in the style of an Egyptian hunting lodge, the walls lined with the trophy heads of game animals. An enormous chandelier hung from the ceiling as a striking centrepiece, and a broad staircase led down to the lobby security desk. A couple of senior officers came up the staircase.

Halder saluted as they went past, waited until they had disappeared down one of the corridors, then climbed the stairs to the next floor. At the end of a corridor, he saw two military police and a couple of burly-looking men in civilian clothes standing guard outside a room. Before he could move another step, an American two-star general came out of one of the rooms across the hall, carrying a briefcase.

Halder saluted, but the general frowned, keenly sized him up. "What's your name, Captain?"

"Kowalski, sir."

"You don't look familiar. Have I seen you before?"

"They sent me over from Camp Huckstep, sir."

"Is that a fact?" The general raised an eye. "Come down with me to the lobby, at the double."

Before Halder could reply, the general moved down the stairs, pausing to look back when Halder hesitated. "Well, what are you waiting for, Captain? Are you deaf?"

"No, sir."

Halder followed him down, not knowing what to expect, his heart pounding as he eased off his holster flap, ready to shoot the man if he had to. When they reached the lobby, the general went directly to the security desk, as the officer behind it put down a field telephone.

"Well, are we in business yet, Major?" the general asked brusquely.

"On their way, sir. They've just arrived at the gate."

The general beckoned Halder with a finger. "Follow me, Kowalski."

Halder anxiously followed the general out through the lobby and down the short flight of entrance steps. When the general appeared, the area in front of the hotel buzzed with a sudden activity, an almost palpable electricity in the air, the white-helmeted sentries bracing themselves, the tank crews jumping down from their turrets and standing to attention.

Moments later a black Packard and two Ford sedans swept up the driveway. The general checked his uniform, adjusted his cap, and said to Halder, "Captain, have a couple of the men get the ramp over here and hold it in place. And let's do it very smartly, mind."

But Halder was barely listening, a strange excitement flooding his veins. As the cavalcade came closer, he could hardly believe what he saw. In the rear of the middle car was President Franklin Delano Roosevelt, wearing a pale linen suit, a blanket draped over his legs, looking frail and exhausted.

"Captain Kowalski!" The general barked aloud as the cars moved ever closer. "Didn't you hear my order, man?

Get that damned ramp securely in place, on the double!"

For a moment, Halder was totally lost, panic almost setting in, until he suddenly noticed a sloping wooden contraption on wheels off to his left, two MPs already reacting to the general's command as they smartly wheeled it into place in front of the steps. Halder joined them in an instant, relieved that the soldiers seemed to know exactly what they were doing. "You heard the general. On the double."

"Sure, Captain," one of the men said drily, as if he were dealing with an idiot superior. "We got it under control."

The general skewered Halder with a stare. "*Christ almighty, Kowalski.* Does it always take you an age to issue a simple instruction?"

Halder didn't have a chance to reply, because the ramp was barely in place on the front steps before the vehicles halted on the gravel. Several young men in suits tumbled out of the Packard, obviously Secret Service agents, armed with Thompson submachine-guns and shotguns, as a host of senior uniformed officers carrying briefcases climbed out of the front and rear cars. With military precision, a number of the Secret Service men took up positions, and two of them began helping the President out of the car. Another agent already had the boot open, the wheelchair appeared, and Roosevelt was helped in, his thin, metal-braced legs lifted into place.

The general saluted. "Mr. President, sir."

Halder watched as the Secret Service men pushed the President's chair smartly up the ramp. When they got to the top, the wheelchair bumped as it moved on to level ground, and the blanket slipped from Roosevelt's legs. One of the Secret Service aides started to make a grab for it, but without thinking Halder reached across and beat him to it. He handed it back to the aide, who tucked the blanket around the President's legs. When it was done, Halder found himself staring directly into Roosevelt's face. "That's most kind of you, Captain," the President said charmingly.

"Not at all, sir."

"What's your name, son?"

"Kowalski, sir."

"Captain Kowalski, I thank you for your courtesy."

Halder saluted. "My pleasure, Mr. President, sir."

The President's party proceeded upstairs, four Secret Service men lifting Roosevelt's wheelchair between them, two on either side, and Halder stood watching, almost in a trance. The general came over, still riled, and whispered fiercely under his breath. "Well, Kowalski, I'm still waiting for an explanation. You took your time getting that ramp into place. What in the hell got into you?"

Halder snapped out of his reverie. "My—my apologies, sir. But to tell the truth, it's the first time I've seen the President in the flesh. I guess I was kind of awestruck."

The general appeared to soften, gave him a forgiving look, then turned to stare at his commander-in-chief being carried up the staircase. There was real emotion in his voice. "And well you should be. Goddammit, but every time I see that pitiful sight I want to weep. For a man who spends most of his life in constant agony, you'll never hear a single word of complaint. You know something, Kowalski? If half the men under my command were as courageous, we'd have won this damned war long ago."

"Yes, sir." Halder saw his chance, said to the general casually, "Will Prime Minister Churchill be returning tonight, sir?"

The general raised an eye and laughed. "Where in tarnation have you been, Captain? Don't you know the man's a night owl? He's attending a party in Cairo. At a guess, we'll be lucky to see his face before dawn."

"Of course, sir."

"That'll be all, Kowalski. Dismissed. And try to keep your wits about you in future." Halder saluted, watched as the general followed the President's party upstairs. When it reached the top, the Secret Service men put down the wheelchair, and he had a perfect view of the back of Roosevelt's head. A cold sweat broke out on Halder's face, and he was almost smothered by a powerful anger. Ten yards away was the man ultimately responsible for maiming his son and killing his father, and for a moment he stood there, teetering on the brink, one hand resting on his holster flap.

Then the party disappeared upstairs. Without regard for his own safety, Halder followed, all reason evaporated, feeling his anger swell as he bounded up the steps two at a time. When he reached the top, he was just in time to see

Roosevelt being wheeled down a corridor, towards the door with the MPs outside. As the Secret Service men began to move the President inside, a gap opened among the clutter of aides, and Halder was presented with a clear shot.

One bullet and it would be over.

He casually opened his holster flap, mesmerised by the situation, but then cold reason took hold. "Damn it, Halder," he told himself. "You must be mad."

He stood there, unable to decide if it was conscience about shooting a man in a wheelchair pricking him, or the simple fact that if he fired he'd be committing certain suicide.

Suddenly one of the Secret Service men looked back, and their eyes locked. Halder caught the cold stare, offered the man a salute, then moved off quickly, the spell broken but his anger undiminished, as he made his way back downstairs towards the kitchen.

Twenty minutes later he crawled out of the tomb, Kleist behind him. They had both changed out of uniform, and Deacon and Rachel looked relieved.

"Jack—thank God you're back." She moved into his arms, and Halder said, "You'd better get back to the car. We've overstayed our welcome here as it is. I'll be along in a moment. Kleist, take her back. We'll leave the rest of the tools and lamps here for now."

Kleist helped her climb up out of the tomb recess, and then they were gone into the darkness.

"For a while there I was worried you wouldn't make it back." Deacon dabbed his brow with a handkerchief. "What kept you? You've been gone over an hour."

Halder busied himself stashing the remaining tools and lamps in the mouth of the shaft.

"There was work to be done. We had to open up the tunnel exit."

"Well, what's the verdict?" Deacon asked expectantly.

When Halder had finished hiding the equipment, he told him everything. Deacon's amazement was obvious. "You actually *saw* the great man?"

"He was as close to me as you are. Not only that, I know exactly where he's being quartered."

"Excellent!" Deacon radiated excitement. "You've excelled yourself, Major. Well done."

"Save the congratulations. It's not over yet. We'll have our work cut out widening the tomb shafts and the exit. That's solid rock we're talking about."

"Is there a risk somebody might spot the opening you made?"

"It's somewhat protected, and in a hollow, but I took the precaution of covering it over with some bushes as best I could when I climbed back into the shaft."

"Whatever extra tools you need, I can assure you you'll have them." Deacon's face clouded. "Such a pity about that pig Churchill. You think there's a chance he might return?"

"The general didn't seem to hold out much hope. Apparently, old Winston likes his socialising and late nights."

"So I've heard, though what a triumph it would be to get both. Still, at least we definitely have the main target in our sights. And with Churchill out of the way, we'll have to intensify our efforts to get Roosevelt. But there's a more pressing problem, or have you forgotten about Salter's ultimatum? Even if Colonel Skorzeny and his men manage to land safely, without the trucks we've no way of transporting them from the airfield to here."

Halder smiled. "Ah, now there I may have an idea. A little bit of deception that just might do the trick. If Salter wants a piece of the action perhaps we shouldn't disappoint him."

"What do you mean?"

"Can you arrange for us to meet him within the next couple of hours? Somewhere safe, obviously, where there's no risk of having to go anywhere near a checkpoint."

"I think so." Deacon's eyebrows furrowed. "But what's the idea?"

Halder explained, and when he had finished, Deacon looked at him in amazement, then rubbed his hands and laughed. "You know, that's quite brilliant, Major. Simple, but brilliant. I wonder why I didn't think of it myself. You're a genius."

"Hardly. But if it works, it might just solve our problems."

"There's just one other thing that bothers me. How do

our paratroops get safely across the lawns and into the hotel building? Not the way you got in, surely? Granted, Skorzeny's men will be wearing American uniforms, but after your little foray into the hotel, they'll be checking papers at the kitchen entrance, like you told them to."

Halder nodded. "True enough, but on the way back to the tunnel I took the time to count off the rooms on the first floor—it appears the one Roosevelt's staying in has a large balcony area. It could prove a direct way of entering his quarters, if the guards in the immediate area could be silenced somehow. After that, a full-frontal assault on the room might be the best course of action, swift and brutal, the kind of thing Skorzeny excels at. But that's up to the colonel to decide, not me, and no doubt he'll have his own ideas after I fill him in on the situation once he lands. The main thing is we've discovered exactly where Roosevelt is located. Not only that, we have a secure way of entering the grounds. All in all, a good night's work."

Deacon smiled in the darkness. "You know, I'm even beginning to think we might actually have a chance of pulling this off. Assuming we can solve the tricky problem of Salter, when do we signal Berlin to send in Skorzeny's troops?"

Halder got a foothold in one of the limestone blocks, was about to climb out of the recess when he looked back solemnly. "I think we can safely assume Roosevelt has retired for the evening. We just may get lucky and Churchill will return, but as you rightly say, at least we've got our main target in our sights, so from now on Roosevelt's our priority. And all things considered, the Allies are already on our backs, which means we've got to take whatever opportunity we've got and move fast. So it's really got to be tonight, don't you agree?"

FIFTY-NINE

9:30 P.M.
Baldy Reed lay naked on the bed, watching appreciatively as the young Arab girl undressed in front of him. She was no more than eighteen, with large breasts and a full figure,

one of the best the brothel near the Rameses station could offer. He grinned in anticipation of the pleasure to come, finished smoking and stubbed his cigarette out in the beer bottle by the bed. "Get a move on, darling. I haven't got all bleeding night."

The girl finished undressing, came over to lie beside him. Reed had started to run his hands over her breasts when there was a knock on the door. "Who the fuck is that?"

The girl looked bewildered, and Reed got off the bed angrily. "A man can't even dip his wick in bloody peace." As he crossed the room to open the door, it burst in on its hinges and a couple of uniforms barged in.

"Baldy, old son, and about time. We've scoured half the city looking for you." Morris glanced over Reed's shoulder at the girl. "I see you're doing your bit to socialise with the natives?"

Reed recognised the military police sergeant instantly, but the American officer didn't look familiar. "Get your clothes on, miss," Weaver ordered the girl in Arabic, and gestured to the door. She hastily dragged her clothes on and left.

"What the bleeding hell's going on?" Reed demanded. "Since when is it against the law for a man to enjoy 'imself?"

The American jerked a thumb. "Get yours on too, Sergeant. We need to talk."

9:30 P.M.

The decaying jetty on the Nile's eastern banks looked deserted in the darkness as Halder and Deacon came alongside in the motorboat. Halder tied the ropes. As they went up the wooden steps they saw a military ambulance parked at the shore end, the telltale red cross painted on the side.

A solid-looking man stood guard, wearing a British uniform and armed with a Sten gun. Two other men waited beside him, dressed as officers, one of them swarthy and carrying a storm lamp, the other smoking a cheroot, small and vicious-looking, his uniform jacket draped casually over his shoulders, a swagger stick under his arm.

"The one smoking the cheroot is Salter," Deacon told

Halder. "The other's Costas Demiris, his partner, another deserter and all-round slimeball."

"What's the idea of the ambulance and uniforms?"

"Just one of the ways Salter moves about with impunity. He's got a barrel-load of disguises and forged papers that any intelligence service would die for."

"Let's go meet him."

They moved down the boardwalk. Salter had a grin on his face. "So you must be Harvey's mystery man. Reggie Salter's the name." He thrust out a hand. "I didn't catch yours?"

"That's entirely irrelevant," said Halder, and ignored the offered handshake.

"Have it your way." Salter shrugged. "I take it Harvey's filled you in on my little offer?"

"It seems you've left us with no option but to accept, Mr. Salter. We need those vehicles badly."

Salter's grin widened in triumph. "Supply and demand, ain't it the curse of this wicked old world? Now that the awkward bit's out of the way, you mind telling me what you have in mind?"

"A robbery, Mr. Salter. Pure and simple. There's a valuable cargo on board two Dakota aircraft due to land at Shabramant airfield."

Salter beamed. "What did I tell you, Costas?" He looked back at Halder, drew fiercely on his cheroot, the expression on his face unconcealed greed. "So what's this cargo worth?"

"It hasn't got a worth, not as such. It's priceless. Artefacts of gems and gold, mostly. But if you insist on assessing its monetary value—assuming the gold was melted down and the gems cut up—a conservative estimate would probably be two million. Pounds sterling, not dollars."

Salter whistled. "*Jesus Christ.*"

"Ten per cent makes that two hundred thousand. That's a lot of money coming your way, Mr. Salter. The question is, are you worth it?"

"Oh, I'm worth it, old son," Salter answered excitedly. "Don't fret about that. Anything you need done, or in the line of equipment and men, you've only got to ask. So how do me and Costas here get our cut?"

"We can discuss that later, when we go over details."

"You mind telling me who's involved?"

"Five of us, including Deacon here."

"Military backgrounds?"

"You might say that."

"I thought you had the look of it about you. So what's the deal?"

"Now that you're to be counted in, you'll have to earn your share. Are you prepared for that?"

"For two hundred grand? Listen, Mister Whoever-you-are, for that kind of dosh I think you can safely assume I'll give this job my undivided attention."

"Good, then let's get straight down to business. I want you and your men to secure the airfield."

Salter frowned. "What do you mean?"

"I want control of the airbase. No one goes in or out without my say-so, but at the same time, no one outside must know what's happened. It has to be done without shooting. We don't want the army or police alerted."

"I get the drift. We take over the airfield and nab the stuff when it arrives. What are the trucks and Jeep for, an escort afterwards?"

"Precisely."

Salter smiled. "I like it."

"No more than a dozen of your men ought to be enough. The tower, the barrack quarters and the entrance are our main concerns. As well as seizing and controlling all communications equipment. We estimate there shouldn't be more than half a dozen Royal Egyptian Air Force personnel on duty. I emphasise, I don't want any of them killed—just kept under lock and key, and out of harm's way until the aircraft land and our business is completed. Could you handle all that?"

"No sweat. With a dozen of my best men, I could take the Royal Palace." Salter frowned. "You mind telling me what you'll be doing while me and my lads are playing commandos?"

"Three of my men and I will accompany you to the airfield, to make sure everything goes smoothly. Assuming it does, I'll leave two of them behind, then join you later, before the aircraft land. Among other things, I have a radio link to take care of—I'll be in touch with someone at the point of departure before the aircraft take off—so that way I'll know the arrival time. Obviously, you'll need to bring the trucks to the airfield, to transport the consignment."

Salter thought for a moment, then nodded. "Sounds all right to me. When do you want to do it?"

Halder smiled. "I want the airfield secured by midnight tonight."

Salter whistled again. "Blimey! That soon? It's not giving us much time. I'd have to work like the clappers to get everything organised. Why so bloody quick?"

"We've no choice in the matter. We learned this evening the delivery has been brought forward. Which is why I'm agreeing to your demand. We'll need those trucks and the Jeep smartly. I take it you were serious about supplying anything we need?"

"Of course. Why?"

"I'll want a couple of field radios, with a minimum range of ten miles."

Salter nodded. "There's no problem there. When do you expect the aircraft to land?"

"Some time between three and four a.m. I'll go over the airfield layout and security, and tell you exactly how I want this done."

"Just one other thing." Salter looked across threateningly, pointed the swagger stick at Halder's chest. "You and your friends try to double-cross me, mister, and I'll bury the lot of you. Understand?"

Halder pushed the stick away, met Salter's stare. "I'll keep to my word. Just make sure you keep to yours." He took a map from his pocket, spread it on the ambulance bonnet, borrowed the storm lamp from Demiris. "Right, let's go over things very carefully, so nobody makes any stupid mistakes."

Twenty minutes later, Halder was back in the motorboat, headed towards the far side of the Nile.

"You think it'll work?" Deacon asked as he manoeuvred the tiller.

"There's a fair chance," Halder replied. "But Salter's going to get one hell of a shock when he sees two Dakotas landing and a hundred crack SS paratroops piling out."

Deacon smiled. "I only hope I'm there to see the bastard's face when it happens."

Salter watched from the jetty as the motorboat faded into the watery darkness. He pulled his uniform jacket around his shoulders, and lit another cheroot. "Two million quid's worth of gems and gold." He scratched his head. "Well, I'll be blowed."

Costas Demiris's face was sweaty with excitement. "It's a real treasure trove, Reggie. In the right quarters, our share could be worth an even bigger fortune. It's the kind of stuff private collectors would give their eye teeth for."

"True enough. What do you reckon about Deacon's mate?"

"A smooth customer. But he sounded on the level."

"Too bloody smooth if you ask me. And he gave in to us just like that." Salter snapped his fingers. "Which makes me suspicious. And he didn't offer to explain what Deacon was doing out at Giza. That's the little bit that baffles me."

"You think he might try and mess us about?"

"Who knows? Either way, I'm pretty sure it's something our boys can handle."

Salter's eyes narrowed and he tossed his cheroot into the water. "Deacon's mate definitely had the cut of the military, all right. I wonder who the fuck he is."

"Special forces or commandos probably, by the looks of him. And you can bet he's not going to like it when he finds out what we've got up our sleeve, Reggie. He's not going to like it one little bit."

Salter shot a sly look at Demiris and laughed. "No, he won't, will he?"

SIXTY

9:15 P.M.

"You mind telling me what this is about, sir?" The interrogation room at the Provost's office was stifling hot, and beads of perspiration were running down Baldy Reed's face.

Weaver stood over him. "I thought you were the one who could do that." He read out the list of stolen items and Reed frowned.

"I think you've got the wrong man, sir."

"We've got the right man," Sergeant Morris interrupted. "He's just singing the wrong tune. A friend of yours in the motor pool at Camp Huckstep sang the full ten verses, pointed the finger right up your nose. Claims you were behind the whole thing. So spill, Baldy."

Reed nervously licked his lips, stared back at Morris. "You're either lying, or joking."

"It ain't my style. You ought to know that."

"As God is my bleeding judge—"

"He won't be, it'll be a military court. You're already fingered. So you might as well tell us what you did with the stuff you nicked."

"I told you, there's been some kind of mistake—"

Weaver lost his patience, grabbed Reed by the lapels. "Listen to me, and listen good. Four German agents are loose in the city and playing a very dangerous game. There's a chance they might have need for the kind of military equipment that's been stolen, so I want to know what's happened to it. Now you can sing dumb all night, Reed, but so help me, if you're lying, I'll see you face a firing squad for aiding the enemy."

Reed blinked at Weaver as if he were mad. "You're— you're not serious?"

"Deadly. Get it into your thick skull."

Reed turned chalk-white, suddenly crumpled, cupping his face in his hands. "The bastards put me up to it, I swear to God they did."

"Who?"

"Reggie Salter and Costas Demiris. Said they'd have my balls for worry beads if I didn't help them."

Weaver turned to the sergeant. "Who the hell is he talking about?"

"Underworld criminals," Morris replied. "Deserters who run a stolen goods and black-market racket. Salter's the mastermind, and as nasty a gangster as they come."

Weaver addressed Reed. "Did they tell you what they wanted the stuff for?"

Reed shook his head. "Salter only mentioned he had some deal going and needed it urgently. That's the honest truth."

"What *exactly* did he want?"

"The Jeep and trucks, papers for the lot, and the three uniforms."

"Anything else?"

"Nothing, I swear it." There was an instant look of fear on Reed's face. "You've got to protect me. If Salter hears I've squealed, the bastard will skin me alive."

The sergeant couldn't help smiling. "It's nothing compared to what the army's going to do with you. I've got you at last, mate. And you've nailed yourself to the wall."

"What d'you mean?"

"No one pointed the finger, Baldy, except yourself. We bluffed about your pals squealing. And don't go thinking you can retract your admission. I've got an officer as witness."

Reed's mouth opened, his face a furious red. "You cunning bleeding bastard—"

"Shut up, Reed," Weaver interrupted, and turned to the sergeant. "Can we pull Salter in and have a word with him?"

"With respect, sir, you might as well try and catch a greased snake. We've been after his hide for over a year now, without success. Tight little number he operates. We reckon he's got about twenty men and a couple of warehouses in the city, but where they are we don't rightly know. Rumour has it he's got armed guards and lookouts posted, not to mention his hand in a few pockets hereabouts to keep him alerted to any trouble coming his way. Sad fact of life, but that's the size of it."

"We *have* to talk to him and clear this up."

The sergeant scratched his head. "You mind telling me how, sir?"

Weaver jerked a thumb at Reed. "He's dealt with Salter, he can lead us to him." He glared at the frightened prisoner. "In return, we drop all the charges. Well, have we got a deal, Reed?"

SHABRAMANT
10 P.M.

The Jeep halted a couple of hundred yards from the airfield entrance gates. Salter was in the front seat, dressed in the uniform he'd worn on the jetty, Halder in the seat behind, wearing the captain's outfit and carrying an M_3 machine-pistol, a couple of field radios beside him.

The darkened road ahead was barely lit by a quarter-moon, the perimeter wire and sentry huts just about visible. Salter tapped ash from his cheroot. "Looks quiet enough. You happy so far?"

"I'll only be that when we've taken the airfield," Halder answered.

Salter laughed. "I've broken into enough well-guarded store-houses in my day. This ought to be no different."

"Remember, no shooting if we can help it, otherwise it gives the game away. And I don't want anyone hurt unnecessarily."

"Would I let you down?" Salter clicked his fingers at the driver. "Get going, Charlie. Pull up in front of the sentry huts."

"Right, boss." The driver started up, and as they moved off Halder looked behind. The three Ford trucks were following, Kleist and Doring seated in the cab of the leading vehicle, Hassan driving. In the back were a dozen of Salter's men, all armed and wearing military uniforms. As they drove up towards the gates, Halder saw the sentries step out of their boxes, suddenly alert.

Salter idly tossed his cheroot away and said confidently, "Leave the talking to me."

The Jeep swung in towards the gates and halted. A warning sign told them to douse their lights and, as the driver did so, Halder saw the two young Egyptian sentries ready their weapons, confusion on their faces at the unexpected arrival of a military cavalcade.

Salter climbed out of the vehicle and strode up to them cockily with a swagger stick in one hand, his papers in the other. "I'm Major Cairns. Direct me to your CO, if you would. I've got some urgent business to discuss."

It happened quickly. As the bewildered sentries started to examine Salter's papers, a half-dozen men tumbled out of the back of the leading truck and rushed forward. There was a moment of uncertainty as the confused Egyptians tried to ready their weapons, but Salter's men quickly overpowered them and searched through their pockets for the keys to the gate.

"Find out exactly how many men are on the airfield and where they are," Salter ordered as he took charge of the keys. "If they don't oblige, break their frigging arms."

The two frightened sentries obviously understood, because they needed no persuasion.

"Half a dozen men," Salter remarked, when he heard the details. "Not much opposition, is it?"

"Let's not count our chickens, Salter, until the job's done," Halder told him.

"You're a cautious man, Captain." Salter grinned, and looked as if he was thoroughly enjoying himself. He unlocked the entrance gates and waved the cavalcade in. "Get a move on, sharpish. Leave the vehicles inside the gates for now; we'll go the rest of the way on foot—we don't want the bastards to hear us coming. Fan out towards the airfield buildings. And two of you get those uniforms off the guards and take their places."

He plucked a Sten gun from the Jeep as it drove in through the gates, while two of his men began to change into the guards" uniforms. "Right," he said briskly to Halder. "Let's go sort out the rest of them."

It took less than fifteen minutes to secure the airfield, and without firing a single shot. Salter's men had accounted for all the Egyptians. Halder went along the wooden veranda into the main barrack office. It was a large functional room, with a scratched desk and a couple of rusting filing cabinets. He lifted the telephone to make sure the line had been cut, then removed his cap and watched from the window as the half-dozen disarmed and bewildered Royal Egyptian Air Force men, their hands on their heads, were led past.

Salter came in with a couple of his men, looking pleased. "Don't worry about that lot. They'll be locked up in one of the huts and well guarded—we don't want anyone getting away to raise the alarm." He sat behind the desk, laid down his Sten gun, put up his feet, and looked at Halder.

"Just what the doctor ordered. Well, Captain, I think that about takes care of everything for now. Impressed?"

"You've exceeded my expectations, Mr. Salter. Before I leave I'll need to check the runway."

"What for?"

"To make certain the landing strip is operational, and the field's unobstructed."

"Fair enough."

Halder gestured to Kleist and Doring, and with Hassan they went outside to the Jeep and drove in darkness for about three hundred metres past the hangars, until they came to the nearest end of the runway. The landing strip didn't look up to much, the surface rough in places. They drove to the far end, checking for debris, and when they had doubled back, Halder raised a hand for the Jeep to stop.

"Not exactly the main runway at Tempelhof, is it? Well, what do you think, Kleist?"

"I've seen worse. I can put down some electric torches to guide the pilots in on the final leg when the time comes. There shouldn't be a problem."

"Good. So all that remains is to transmit our signal and await the arrival." Halder checked his watch and had the others synchronise theirs. "Twenty-two thirty hours exactly. If we transmit before midnight, it shouldn't take more than about three hours for Skorzeny's paratroops to get here. That gives us an ETA of oh three hundred hours, give or take. Allow another hour to get them to Giza and through the tunnel, which brings it to oh four hundred approximately."

"A perfect time to spring our surprise." Kleist grinned. "Even the sentries will be half asleep by then."

"Let's hope you're right," Halder replied doubtfully. "We'd better have a look at the hangars—we'll need to keep Skorzeny's aircraft safely out of the way until we get back here after the attack."

When they pulled up outside the first of the two hangars, the doors were open. Halder strode into the building. It reeked of grease and aviation fuel, two well-worn Gloster Gladiators parked near the front, a small two-seater training aircraft next to them. Halder shook his head. "We'll need more space than this to accommodate two Dakotas. Let's have a look at the other hangar."

The second was closer to the airfield barrack huts, and completely empty, apart from an ancient green-coloured Italian Moto Guzzi motorcycle and a couple of bicycles parked near the doors, private transport which obviously belonged to the Egyptian Air Force men.

"Excellent. This one will do perfectly well—there's more than enough space." Halder turned to Hassan and Doring. "I'm going to leave you both with Salter. He'll get a shock, of course, when our paratroops land, and he'll be fighting a losing battle if he thinks of putting up resistance. But we'll have to try and dissuade him from that idea when the moment arrives, and hope he sees the sense of giving in quietly. Kleist and I will be back at the villa, sending the signal. We'll rejoin you within a couple of hours. But if there's even a hint of any problems here, you contact us on the field radio, understood, Doring?"

"Yes, Major."

"So, it seems we're all set," Halder said grimly. "Another few hours, and one way or another it'll all be over."

When they got back to the barrack office, half a dozen of Salter's men sat about on the veranda, smoking and talking. Halder told Doring to remove one of the field radios from the Jeep and they went in with Hassan, while Kleist remained at the wheel. Salter was busy cleaning his Sten gun with an oily rag. "Well, are we in business?"

"It looks like it." Halder nodded over to Doring and Hassan. "I'm leaving two of my men. If you encounter any problems, they'll contact me by radio,. Should anyone arrive at the front gate, try to make it look like there's nothing amiss. But lock them up with the guards if you have to."

Salter nodded. "It'll be dealt with. When will you be back?"

"A couple of hours, probably less. Until then, Mr. Salter, try to keep the faith."

Halder turned to go, but Salter gripped his arm. "I meant what I said. Try and mess me about, and it'll end in tears."

"There's really no need for threats, Salter." Halder pulled away. "And I give you my personal assurance you'll be pleasantly surprised when you see the cargo."

"I'll look forward to that."

Halder moved outside and climbed in beside Kleist. They drove off, leaving Doring and Hassan behind in the office, setting up the radio. Salter strolled out on to the veranda, and watched the Jeep exit through the gates, before they were shut again by two of his men wearing the sentries' uniforms.

"What you reckon, Reggie? Are we ready?"

One of his men sidled up. Salter cradled the Sten gun in his arms, cracked his knuckles.

"Give it ten minutes for good measure, then you know what to do."

SIXTY-ONE

KHAN-EL-KHALILI BAZAAR
22 NOVEMBER / 11 P.M.

The unmarked Ford sedan pulled into the lane. Weaver sat in the passenger seat beside the military driver, Reed in the back with Sergeant Morris, all of them wearing civilian clothes.

"It's a good job you're prepared for trouble," Reed said morosely. "Because if Salter's in there, there'll be shooting and bodies, no two ways about it."

Weaver looked towards the warehouse at the end of the lane. There was a heavy metal door with a grille and shutter set in the middle, a light on above the wall on the left.

"You're sure you can't get us in peacefully?"

Reed shook his head. "Not a chance. The guards have orders to let no one past without Salter knowing about it. If anyone tries, they get blasted."

Weaver knew that if things went horribly wrong he'd be court-martialled, no question, but he'd already passed the barrier of caring about his fate. The field radio crackled on the back seat and Morris spoke into the handset, then said to Weaver, "We've got the back covered, sir. The men are ready to go as soon as they get the word."

Twenty heavily armed military police were hidden inside the delivery truck that had pulled up behind them, and combined with the two dozen ready to assault the rear,

Weaver reckoned that it ought to be enough to deal with Salter's gang. "What about the ambulances and medics?"

"Two streets away, so as not to attract attention. They'll come if we call them on the wireless."

"Let's hope they're not needed." Weaver looked at his watch anxiously. "OK, it's time. Give the word to the men."

Morris got on the radio, gave the command, then reported back to Weaver, "We're all set, sir."

"Come with me, Sergeant. Let's get it over with." Weaver picked up a heavy khaki satchel from the floor of the car, and Morris put a hand lightly on his arm, nodded at the satchel, and said, "You're sure about this, sir?"

"Can you think of any other way?"

Weaver got out of the car and went down the lane with Morris. When they reached the warehouse, he took three grenades from the satchel, placed them at the base of the metal door, then removed a Very flare pistol from the bag.

"Get back," he told Morris.

Weaver quickly pulled each of the grenade pins in turn and ran back down the lane after the sergeant. As they pressed themselves against the wall, there was a tremendous explosion, and the grenades erupted almost together. A dirty cloudburst of dust and metal splinters blew across the alleyway, echoed like a roll of thunder, and the door was blown off its hinges.

Before the dust had even settled, Weaver raised the Very gun and squeezed the trigger. A red flare exploded into the air, turning the night sky blood red, the signal to alert the men covering the rear. Already the troops were piling out of the delivery truck, weapons at the ready, as Weaver and Morris moved towards the shattered door frame.

SHABRAMANT AIRFIELD
11:30 P.M.

Doring and Hassan had finished setting up the radio on the desk when Salter strolled over. "That captain friend of yours seems an able enough sort."

Doring nodded agreeably. "Yes, he is."

"Care to tell me about his background and which unit he's from?"

Doring fell silent, and Hassan's eyes narrowed suspiciously. "Why don't you ask him yourself?"

"I wasn't talking to you." Salter glared, held the Arab's stare, then turned back to Doring. "Well, sonny? And for starters you can give me his name. And yours."

A half-dozen of Salter's men gathered ominously around them from all corners of the room. Hassan made to reach for his knife, but one of them was behind him instantly with a gun. "Try it and you'll get blasted," Salter warned. "Now put those paws in the air where I can see them."

Hassan reluctantly obeyed, and Salter came over, found the knife and took it from him, sneering. "I warned you about this before, didn't I?"

Suddenly the blade flashed in Salter's hand, and a deep gash opened on Hassan's jaw. Enraged, the Arab started to lunge at Salter, but the man behind him slammed the butt of his gun hard into his skull, and Hassan jerked and slumped to the floor.

As he lay there, unconscious, Salter put the toe of his boot to the Arab's head, tilted it over. "You ought to heed a warning when it's given." He stuck the knife into the top of the wooden desk, left it there, and walked casually over to Doring. "Well, sonny, I'm waiting."

Doring panicked, overcome by a sudden feeling of doom. In an instant he punched Salter in the face and made a desperate grab for a Sten gun behind the desk. He just managed to get his hand on the barrel when a rifle butt came crashing down on his fingers. He screamed, fists began to rain, and before he knew it he was being dragged across the room to one of the chairs.

Salter staggered over, wiping blood from his nose. He grabbed Doring savagely by the hair. "That was a fucking stupid thing to do, sonny. Very fucking stupid indeed."

Doring struggled as he was held down, features contorted in agony, his fingers a pulped mess, and Salter punched him hard in the face. There was a sickening crack, of bone splintering. Doring screamed and almost passed out as a fountain of blood spurted from his shattered nose.

"Eye for an eye, I always say. And that's just to get acquainted."

Across the room, one of Salter's men felt Hassan's neck. "He's still out of it, boss."

"Put him in one of the rooms until he comes round. We might need him later." He turned back to Doring, leaned in close, cold, evil eyes staring hard. "Now, sonny, how about you telling me who your friends are, and what exactly they've got planned after these aircraft land?"

KHAN-EL-KHALILI BAZAAR
11 P.M.

Weaver could barely contain his frustration. He was in a room on the first floor which obviously served as an office of some sort. They had stormed through the warehouse and found only three of Salter's men, who didn't have a chance of putting up much resistance. "Where are the prisoners?"

"The men are bringing them up now, sir," Sergeant Morris answered.

"Have Reed brought up from the car."

There was a clatter of feet on the stairs and three of Salter's men were led in, one of them swarthy, with a black moustache. When Reed appeared in the doorway moments later, Weaver said, "Do you recognise any of these people?"

Reed pointed to the man with the moustache. "That—that one's Costas Demiris."

The Greek clenched his teeth, livid with anger, and struggled to get free. "You fucking Judas, Reed—when Reggie gets his hands on you, you're dead!"

As Demiris was held back, Weaver said, "Bring him over here and take the others downstairs. Reed, get back down to the car."

A grateful Reed left, and Demiris was led over to a chair. Weaver said, "Where's Salter?"

"That's for me to know and you to find out," Demiris said defiantly, a slight grin playing on his face. "If you think you'll get me to squeal, you've got another think coming. Besides, Reggie's got friends in the right places. He'll soon sort this out. A case of wrongful arrest."

"You're a wanted criminal and deserter, Demiris. Unless you talk, I'll see to it personally that they toss you into a dark cell and throw away the key."

"Yeah? Want to bet?" Demiris sat there smugly, and Weaver could contain his frustration no longer. He was across the room in an instant and grasped the Greek by the hair, wrenched back his head. Demiris screamed.

"What happened to the trucks you got from Reed—?"

There was a sudden screech of tyres in the lane below, and seconds later footsteps clattered up the stairs. Weaver said, "Find out what's going on."

Before the sergeant had reached the door, Sanson burst in, crimson with rage as he stared at the scene then glared at Weaver. "What in damnation's going on here—?"

"You blatantly disobeyed orders, Weaver." Sanson stood there, his face still livid.

Weaver made to speak again, but Sanson cut him off. "We'll discuss this later. I've just spent two wasted hours of interrogation in Alex and I haven't got the patience." He shot a look at the Greek. "So, this is one of Salter's scum?"

"His name's Costas Demiris."

"Has he talked?"

"I guess he's not in a very co-operative mood right now."

"We'll soon see about that." Sanson strode over to the Greek, who had witnessed his entrance with indifference. "I'm Lieutenant-Colonel Sanson, military intelligence. Where's Salter?"

Demiris spat on the floor. "Go fuck yourself."

Sanson flushed a furious red. "Leave us, Sergeant."

"Sir?"

"You heard me! Get out! And don't come in again until I call you."

The sergeant left, closing the door after him. Sanson calmly took out his Smith and Wesson revolver, broke the barrel to make sure the chambers were loaded, then snapped the weapon shut again.

As Weaver stood watching, he calmly walked over to the Greek. "I want you to listen, and listen very carefully, Demiris. For two reasons. First, I don't have the time or the patience for wrong answers, and second, if you don't heed my advice, it's likely you'll spend the rest of your days in a wheelchair."

Demiris tensed, just slightly.

"In plain English, if you don't give me the right answers to my questions, I'm going to shoot your kneecaps off. And if you still haven't talked by then, I'm going to aim a little higher, up towards that Greek manhood of yours. Now, are you going to tell me where Salter is? And where those vehicles are?"

Demiris gave a dry, nervous laugh. "You wouldn't shoot a prisoner, Sanson. You wouldn't dare."

Sanson shot him in the left kneecap. As the weapon exploded, Demiris screamed in agony, rolling on to the floor and clutching the shattered bone. The door burst in as the sergeant came to investigate, and Sanson roared, "I said stay outside!"

The door closed abruptly. Demiris lay there, writhing, blood pumping from his wound, tears of pain streaming down his shocked face. "You mad bastard. You fucking mad bastard!"

Sanson calmly aimed the pistol at the other kneecap. "You don't know the half of it. So start talking, Demiris, and quickly."

Weaver stood aside as a white-faced Demiris was carried downstairs on a stretcher by a couple of medics, still clutching his wounded knee and moaning in agony. He turned back to Sanson. "You don't think he was lying?"

"Hardly. It all makes perfect sense." Sanson stood there, his mind ticking over furiously.

"This captain fellow sounds like Halder. As for Deacon and his Arab friend, I think we've found Halder's contacts. From the description Demiris gave us, the Arab has got to be the wily bastard we've been looking for. The rest I'm sure we can guess. A poorly guarded airfield, no more than half an hour from Giza? It sounds ideal for a covert landing, the right sort of place from which to mount an attack. As for the business of the valuable cargo, it's obviously some sort of ruse to fool Salter."

Sanson snapped his fingers at Morris. "Get on the radio and muster as many men as you can. Have them join us at the Shabramant crossroads, a mile from the airfield. And I want a raiding party sent to Deacon's nightclub. Tell them to nab him if he's there and report to me on the radio."

"Yes, sir."

"I'm coming with you," Weaver said defiantly.

Sanson glared back. "No, Weaver, you're not. And if you think you're going to worm your way out of this, think again. I'm going to finish this once and for all, and you're not in the picture. Sergeant, remove this officer's sidearm and take him into custody. He's under arrest, for disobeying orders."

SIXTY-TWO

MAISON FLEUVE
22 NOVEMBER /11:30 P.M.

When Halder pulled up outside the villa with Kleist, Deacon came out to meet them, looking anxious. "Well, what's the story?"

Halder told him the news. The excitement and relief were evident on Deacon's face.

"Excellent. If everything goes according to plan, there'll be an Iron Cross in this for all of us, presented by the Führer himself."

"Let's forget about the medals for now, Deacon. You have a signal to send."

"What about Salter?"

"He's expecting me back within a couple of hours."

"You're certain he didn't suspect anything?"

"Not so far as I could tell. Now, the radio, if you please."

He quickly followed Deacon down to the cellar, Kleist behind them. Deacon opened the cabinet and turned on the radio. While he waited for the set to warm up, he removed the Luger pistol, checked the action, and stuffed it in his pocket, before smiling up at them. "No sense in leaving a perfectly good weapon behind when it comes time to leave. I'll keep it as a memento."

Halder wrote out the message, and when the valves had warmed, Deacon slipped on the earphones and went to work on the Morse key. Ten minutes later he was jotting down the received code on a slip of paper. He took off the earphones and looked up.

"It's done."

"What's the reply?"

Deacon decoded, grinned up at Halder, and handed him the paper.

BERLIN
11:40 P.M.

The communications room in the basement of SS headquarters was a large affair, several dozen high-powered radio transmitter-receiver sets neatly arranged around the lime-coloured walls, each set manned by highly trained SD operators, day and night, who twiddled with dials and tapped on Morse keys as they dealt with the thousands of signals that flowed through the airwaves from SD Ausland agents all over the world, from such far-flung cities as Rio and Tokyo, Washington and Lisbon.

That night, a uniformed operator sat in a private communications booth, which was set apart from the main room, in a small office across the hall. His work area was illuminated by a pool of light from an electric study lamp, and he was listening intently on his earphones and jotting on a notepad with his pencil. When he had decoded, he handed the slip to Schellenberg, anxiously standing behind him and drawing fiercely on a cigarette, the duty officer by his side.

"You wish to send a specific reply, Herr General?" the operator asked.

Schellenberg read the signal almost in a trance, totally overcome with jubilation. For a moment he could hardly breathe, his pulse rapid with excitement, glittering beads of sweat rising on his temples, until he snapped out of his trance and crushed his cigarette out in a metal ashtray by the console. "Yes—yes, of course. As follows: 'Message received. Colonel departing Rome by midnight. Berlin sends best wishes for success.' "

As the operator tapped out the reply and waited for the acknowledged signal, an elated Schellenberg turned to the duty officer. "Get me a line to the Chancellery. I want to speak personally to the Führer. Then have a car ready to take me there." From his pocket he took a slip of paper he had prepared. "And this goes to Colonel Skorzeny in Rome by radio, *immediately*. The slightest delay and someone will face a firing squad."

The officer grasped the page and clicked his heels, already turning away. "*Zu Befehl*, Herr General!"

ROME
11:50 P.M.

At Practica di Mare, the aerodrome was shrouded in dense fog, great wreaths of it smothering every corner of the airfield, the hangars blanketed in a grey haze as thick and heavy as smoke. It had crept in from the sea barely an hour before, and now Skorzeny was prowling the tarmac area outside the hangar like an enraged bear, Captain Neumann by his side. They could barely see each other in the thick fog. "*Mein Gott*, it's unbelievable," muttered Skorzeny, seething with frustration.

"It's even worse than I thought," admitted Neumann. "Down to near zero. In my opinion, it would be sheer madness to take off in conditions like this."

"If I want your opinion, Neumann, I'll ask for it."

"*Colonel Skorzeny, are you there?*" Suddenly an SS major came out of the fog, waving a lighted electric torch, breathless as he almost bumped into them. "An urgent message for you, Colonel. Just received by radio from Berlin."

Skorzeny tore open the flimsy, his huge hands ripping the paper. He read the signal by the light of the torch, let out a breath with obvious relief, and said to Neumann with a broad smile, "This is it. We go immediately." He turned to the SS major. "Assuming we get airborne safely—the very moment we do—send a reply to Berlin. 'The colonel's on his way.' Simply that."

The major stared at him as if he were mad even to consider flying in such atrocious weather, but then quickly saluted. "As you wish, Colonel."

When the man had disappeared back into the fog, Skorzeny was already moving back towards the hangar. "Well, what are you waiting for, Neumann? I want your crews ready to go within five minutes."

"But we couldn't even *taxi* to the runway in these conditions without risk of getting lost. And even the runway lighting would be useless, the fog's so thick. My crews agree you're putting everyone's life in danger—"

Skorzeny stopped, turned back, put his hands on his hips. "To hell with the damned weather. You have your orders. I'll have us guided out with torches when we taxi, and give instructions for the runway lighting to be put on full power, which might help to keep us straight and narrow on take-off. Do it, Neumann, and make sure you have a quick check on the latest weather forecast for *en route*."

"With respect, what if we have to land again because of engine failure or—"

Skorzeny drew his pistol and cocked it, his expression almost savage. "Question my orders again and I'll put a bullet in you. Now, you have a simple choice—you and your flight crews. You fly or you die. So I take it you'll be a sensible man and instruct them we're taking off."

SHABRAMANT
11:45 P.M.

At the airfield, Doring had fared little better than Costas Demiris. His face was a bloodied mess and he groaned, slumped in the chair. He was barely conscious as Salter grabbed him by the roots of his hair. "Wake up, you hear me?"

Doring moaned in reply, and his head rolled to one side. Salter let go of him, gritted his teeth and crossed to the window, his mouth twisted with frustration. One of his men said, "You want me to have a go at him, boss?"

"Don't be an idiot. Another beating like the last and we'll have to bury him. We want the whole consignment, not bloody ten per cent, so I need to know *exactly* what his mates are up to before they get back."

"Not much chance of that if he won't talk."

"Douse him with a bucket of water. Then find some rope and fetch a pair of pliers from one of the toolkits in the trucks."

"What have you got in mind?"

There was a dark look in Salter's eyes. "A nail job. If it works for the Gestapo, it can work for us. I'll make the bastard talk if I have to pull them out one by one."

Behind them, Doring stirred in agony, muttered something, and his head slumped into his chest. One of the men standing over him frowned, a look of puzzlement on his face. Salter saw the reaction. "Well, what the fuck did he say?"

The confused man scratched his head. "It sounded to me like something in German, boss."

MAISON FLEUVE
11:50 P.M.

Halder went upstairs and found Rachel sitting on the bed, an oil lamp flickering on the table beside her, shadows playing around the room. She rushed over and put her arms around his neck, kissed him fiercely on the lips, and when she finally broke away, Halder smiled and put the M_3 down beside the bed. "A man could very easily get addicted to that kind of thing." He saw the concern in her eyes.

"I'm just glad you're back safely. Is everything all right?"

"It seems so, at least for now." He sighed, rubbed his eyes, then collapsed on to the bed, the strain and tiredness of the last few days suddenly showing on his face. He lay there in the dim light, his mind and body aching from exhaustion, and Rachel went to lie beside him and put her head on his chest, her fingers gently stroking his face. "Do you have to leave again?"

"In an hour, I'm afraid."

"And after that?"

"A little before dawn, and it should all be over. Then with luck, and if Schellenberg keeps to his promise, we'll be flying out of here, back to Germany and freedom." Halder tilted her face towards him, looked into her eyes, emotion in his voice. "If we make it out of this alive, and if you think you could forget about Harry and give this a chance, I want us to be together, Rachel. Start a new life. Somewhere where there's no war. I'm tired of all this killing and death, my love."

"You're sure that's what you want?"

"I've never been so sure about anything in my life."

He saw the wetness in her eyes, and she moved in close. He found her mouth, kissed her hungrily, held her until he finally felt overcome by an excruciating tiredness.

"My poor Jack, you're completely worn out. You really should try and sleep, at least for an hour. I'll wake you when it's time to go."

He was about to protest, but she blew out the lamp. He shut his eyes, and in a few moments he was resting peacefully in the darkness, her hand still gently stroking his face, until a little later he was faintly aware of her moving off the bed, the soft click of the door closing, and he gave in to his exhaustion and drifted into a deep sleep.

ROME
11:55 P.M.

Skorzeny had ordered his NCOs to assemble the men. The hangar doors had already been rolled open and the flight crews had started engines and taxied the Dakotas out on to the apron, the ground crews ready and waiting with powerful electric torches to guide them through the fog on their short journey to the runway.

As the paratroops snapped to attention, Skorzeny strode down their ranks, his baton under his arm, making a quick inspection of their American uniforms as he addressed them above the din of the Dakotas' idling engines. "Well, the moment has come. And a glorious moment it is. You've had your briefings so you all know the mission you are about to undertake *is absolutely vital* to the Reich. As you can see, the weather's not exactly to our liking for take-off, but I have every faith in our Luftwaffe crews. Remember, do your duty to your utmost. It's not only me depending on you, but the Führer himself. Good luck."

The NCOs marched the men smartly outside the hangar, and they began filing on board the two Dakotas, just as Neumann appeared, looking the worse for Skorzeny's threat, his co-pilot having taxied their aircraft out of the hangar.

"Well?" Skorzeny demanded. "What about conditions *en route*?"

"Nothing really unpleasant, so far as our Met people can tell, but they predict strong south-easterly winds from northern Sicily down to the African coast, at altitudes of up to six thousand metres. That's as far and high as the present forecasts go."

Skorzeny was pleased. "It's enough. It means the wind will be at our backs most of the way, so we could end up making excellent time, and getting to our destination quicker than we thought. That's what I like to hear, Neumann. You'd better take command of your aircraft. We're ready to go." He slapped a powerful hand on the captain's shoulder. "And cheer up, man. It could be worse."

Neumann wasn't convinced. "Not much. The fog aside, and from the little I know after our mission briefings, this whole business is going to be damned dangerous."

Skorzeny gave an almost manic grin. "You're right. In fact, I think I can promise you a very interesting night's work. Now, let's get on board."

The colonel raced up the steps to board the first Dakota, and Neumann followed, checking that the door was properly closed after the steps had been pulled away. He moved past Skorzeny and his men into the cockpit, and took his seat beside the co-pilot, noticing glinting beads of sweat on the man's forehead. Neumann tried not to show his unease. "Well, Dieter, it seems madness prevails after all. I suppose we'd better keep the colonel happy and try to get airborne."

"Ready when you are, sir. We'll be first off, I'm told."

"Why not?" replied Neumann sarcastically.

He peered out of the cockpit. Ahead of them was thick, unyielding fog, the Dakota's own take-off lights in the wings barely illuminating the solid greyness. Two ground crew were waving electric torches just a couple of metres from his nose cone, though Neumann couldn't see the men properly, just the ghostly haze from their torches. He inched the throttles forward gently and the Dakota began to move, rumbling over the tarmac.

Taxiing was painfully slow. Neumann kept to the tortuous pace the ground crews set. It took over ten minutes to reach the runway threshold and line up as best he could. To left and right of them, the runway lights were on full, but even the powerful beams they threw out were mere electric fuzz, faint yellow coronas for less than thirty metres, and then they were swallowed up by fog. Skorzeny came up to the cockpit, impatient. "Aren't we at the threshold yet?"

"We've just arrived. You'd better get back with your men, Colonel. We're about to take off."

"I'll stay here," Skorzeny answered, slipping into the vacant radio operator's seat, and strapping himself in. "Well, don't bloody hesitate, man. We haven't got all night. Go!"

Neumann didn't see the point of arguing, or even replying. He was conscious of a trickle of sweat dripping off his nose as he eased the throttles forward. The roar from the engines increased and he scanned his instruments. Suddenly the Dakota was moving. As it gained momentum, and the co-pilot called out their speed, Neumann tried his damnedest to keep the aircraft midway between the feeble strings of runway lights, using the rudder as lightly as he could. It was difficult, and with every passing second bursts of yellow from the beams shot past them to left and right, faster and faster, the dynamic rhythm almost hypnotic as they tore down the runway into a frightening wall of solid fog.

"Rotate," the co-pilot finally called out.

Neumann pulled back on the column.

The Dakota didn't budge.

For a moment, he had a sickening feeling in his stomach that something had gone terribly wrong, but then the aircraft struggled into the air with its full load. He called for the undercarriage to be retracted, and by the time the flaps had been taken in, they had burst out of the fog into clear night air.

Neumann permitted himself a quiet release of breath, wiped another drop of perspiration from his face. "So far so good. Let's check if the others made it safely."

Compared to the mess below, the visibility above the fog ceiling was excellent—a crisp night, stars sparkling in full, clear moonlight. Below them, a vast grey shroud obliterated the night-time landscape. Neumann banked left, until they were at right angles to their take-off heading, and then suddenly below them and to the left they saw the second Dakota erupt out of the fog and climb steadily after its take-off.

"Thank God for that," muttered Neumann. "No unwelcome problems." He glanced back at Skorzeny. "Except, of course, those that might lie ahead."

Skorzeny put a hand on his shoulder. "Good work, Neumann. I'll see you get a commendation for this."

"At my funeral, no doubt?"

"Don't be smart. Now, push those throttles hard forward. I want to make this crossing in record time."

SHABRAMANT
11:50 P.M.

Salter was perplexed. He wiped his brow with the back of his sleeve, the barrack office uncomfortably hot, not even an overhead fan to move the stifling air. "You're sure it was German he spoke?"

"That's what it sounded like to me, boss."

Doring stirred again, his face bathed in perspiration, twisted in agony. *"Wasser—"*

"There he goes again. I think that's what he said last time."

"Yeah, but what's he fucking saying?" Salter demanded.

"I picked up a few words when I was guarding Jerry prisoners in the Western Desert. Sounds to me like he wants water."

Salter frowned, nodded at the metal bucket. "Fetch a cup and give him some. Then ask him his name, in German this time."

Salter watched as the man ladled water from the bucket with an enamel cup, and offered it to Doring. He was still almost out of it, could barely sip. *"Was ist ihre name?"*

When Doring didn't respond, Salter grabbed a handful of hair. "Ask him again."

"Ihre name? Was ist ihre name?"

The young German groaned, eyes rolling to the ceiling. "Doring."

"What the bleeding hell's that supposed to mean?" asked Salter.

"I think he said his name's Doring. He's a Jerry, boss, no question. But what's he doing with Deacon and his mates?"

Salter's face creased in confusion. "Ask him who his friends are, and what they've got planned. Ask him—"

"Hold on a second, boss. My German ain't *that* good."

Salter exploded with exasperation, fury in his face. "Then it had better fucking improve fast. I want to know what we're fucking dealing with here!"

"But I've only got a few Jerry words—"

In a rage, Salter picked up the metal bucket and threw the contents, drenching Doring completely, then flung the bucket against the wall. It landed with a clatter, and Doring jerked and shook water from his hair, suddenly conscious.

"Well, what do you know," grinned Salter. "He's back in the land of the living. Get the ropes." As two of his men grabbed Doring's hands and secured them to the chair's armrests, Salter pulled a chair over, gripped Doring's scalp. The German's eyes snapped fully open with horror when he saw the pair of heavy pliers.

"Take a good look at these, mate. Not exactly a pleasant way to accompany a chat, but I'm afraid you've left me no option. Now, we're going to start again. Nice and easy this time. Tell me what I want to know, and you've got my word you'll walk away from here a free man. But try holding back, and I promise, it'll be blood and thorns all the way."

11:55 P.M.

Weaver felt the frustration grow inside him, and it fuelled his anger. He was in the back of the staff car as it headed towards Garden City, Sergeant Morris in the seat beside him.

There was no way he could attempt to save Rachel unless he could make it to the airfield before Sanson, and the agony was torturing him. And even if he could reach her first, what could he do?

He looked out of the window. The car was going too fast to jump, but as they came towards the Old Town, the driver slowed as they rounded a corner. Weaver saw his chance. He reached for the door, pushed it half open, but Morris grabbed him and shouted to the driver, "Stop the bloody car!"

It screeched to a halt, Weaver was flung back against the seat, and before he knew it Morris had an arm locked around his neck. "I really wouldn't try that, sir. You'll only get us both in deeper trouble."

Weaver struggled to get out of the door, but Morris produced a pair of handcuffs from his pocket, snapped them on to his wrists. "Calm down, sir, or you'll do yourself an injury."

"You don't understand—"

"You can say that again. But mine is not to reason why."

As Morris checked that the handcuffs were secure, Weaver protested. "For Christ sakes, is there really any need for these?"

"Sorry, sir, but I have my orders." Morris pulled the door shut, the car moved off again, and Weaver slumped back in even deeper frustration.

SIXTY-THREE

BERLIN
23 NOVEMBER /00:15 A.M.
When Schellenberg was led down to Hitler's private office in the Chancellery underground bunker, the Führer was already waiting. Himmler was there also, the two men in splendid mood as they relaxed in leather armchairs. They rose from their seats, and Himmler actually smiled as he raised his arm in salute. "Walter. Excellent news. Truly excellent!"

Hitler clasped a hand on Schellenberg's forearm. "This gives me hope, Walter. Lifts my spirits immeasurably. But what news of Skorzeny?"

"The word came from Rome as I left the communications room. He took off ten minutes ago, despite heavy fog. But he's well on his way by now."

Hitler was excited. "Let me see the message from Cairo."

Schellenberg handed across the decoded signal from Deacon, and said as Hitler read, "It's all happened quicker than we thought. As you can see, Halder has successfully located Roosevelt at the Mena House, breached the tunnel— which turns out to be of use to gain entry to the hotel

grounds—and has taken the airfield and successfully secured the necessary transport to ferry Skorzeny's men to
the target. He and the others are awaiting the colonel's arrival, for the final act to begin. All we can do now is bite
our nails and wait."

Hitler finished reading and looked up. "So, there's no
need for this ace you've kept up your sleeve."

Schellenberg smiled. "It seems not."

Hitler was suddenly overcome. "If Skorzeny can finish
this business, I'll make him a general. No—a field marshal!
He's an amazing man, capable of anything."

"He's certainly that, *mein Führer.*"

As Hitler handed back the signal, for a moment his expression became despondent.

"But it's hardly over yet. And I'm disappointed about
Churchill."

"But at least we have Roosevelt clearly in our sights.
And granted, it's not over. But what a promising beginning,
mein Führer."

Hitler's mood swung again, and he collapsed into his
chair, gripping the armrests, as if the excitement were too
much to bear. His joy was obvious, a radiance in his face
that neither Schellenberg nor Himmler had witnessed in a
long time. "Indeed. A very promising beginning."

SHABRAMANT
00:15 A.M.

Doring's scream rang around the room. It sounded like the
utterance of a wild animal in pain, and when it died, his
body twitched and his head fell to one side. One of Salter's
men put a hand to his neck, felt for a pulse. "He's—he's
dead, boss."

"I can bloody see that." Salter tossed the pliers on the
desk. The German hadn't told him a thing, not even after
he'd pulled out three nails. In his anger, Salter had whacked
him hard across the skull with the heavy pliers. It was a
blow too many; the German screamed, his eyes bulged
wildly, blood haemorrhaged from his nose, and then he fell
still.

Salter wiped a film of greasy sweat from his face, lit

another cheroot to steady his nerves. "You'd swear the bastard was sworn to secrecy. Anyone in his right mind would have cracked before it went this far. He was a tough nut, I'll say that much for him." He frowned suspiciously, looked at Doring's body. "I've got a funny feeling about this, a very funny feeling indeed, and I don't bloody like it. What's Deacon and that captain doing working with a German? Look at him. You ask me, he's the military type."

"Maybe he's an escaped POW?"

"Maybe." Salter looked unconvinced.

"What do we do, boss?"

Salter checked his watch. "We're in for the full shilling's worth now, ain't we? Deacon's pals get back here in less than an hour." He paced the room, mulled things over, but more frustrated than ever, the confusion eating him. He dropped the cheroot to the floor, ground it with his boot. "Get the Jerry out of the chair, and bring in the wog. I'll get to the bottom of this if it's the last bleeding thing I do."

00:20 A.M.

The staff car trundled through a rabbit-warren of side streets, five minutes away from GHQ.

Weaver's mind was working feverishly. There was no way of retrieving the handcuff key from the sergeant. The situation looked completely hopeless, but he knew he had to take his last shot, and very soon, otherwise he'd be locked up in a cell with no chance of escape. They came out of the side streets, cut right, and the car began picking up speed, heading along the darkened Nile bank. The driver, a young corporal, was concentrating on the road ahead, Morris staring idly out of the window. As the driver swung right to overtake a donkey and cart, Weaver picked his moment and lunged sideways, shoving all his weight against Morris. *"What the—"*

The sergeant gasped, exhaling, all the breath forced out of him from the impact, as Weaver reached across and slapped his palms hard against the door handle. The door opened, he grabbed at the frame, held on, and shouldered Morris. The sergeant rolled out of the moving car with a startled cry.

The corporal glanced back, horrified, slammed on the

brakes, and the car skidded to a halt thirty yards on. "Bloody hell, you could have killed—"

Weaver thrust both his fists forward, hitting the man square in the jaw. As the dazed corporal reeled back, he was already climbing out of the car.

Ten minutes later he stepped into a back-street hotel, breathless, his body drenched in sweat. An elderly Egyptian sat behind an ancient reception desk, toying with a set of worry beads. "Effendi?"

"I need to use your telephone," Weaver panted.

"Apologies, effendi. The telephone is only for hotel guests."

"Just show me the damned telephone!"

The old man noticed the handcuffs, and thought better of arguing. "Down—down the hall there is a booth."

Weaver found it at the end of the lobby, stepped in, fumbled to lift the receiver, and asked for the operator.

He heard the car pull up in the back street. His heart skipped, and he hoped it wasn't the military police. Then he saw Helen Kane come through the front door, wearing her uniform. She stared at the handcuffs. "Harry, what's going on—?"

"Did you bring the things I asked?"

"Yes, but—"

He took her arm, moved towards the door. "I'll explain on the way."

00:10 A.M.

At the Shabramant crossroads, Sanson was getting impatient. He paced up and down beside the Jeep, about to check his watch again with a torch, when one of his men called out, "I think this is them, sir."

Sanson peered along the darkened road and saw a long line of headlights coming towards him fast, from the direction of the city, clouds of dust in their wake. He counted three open-back trucks filled with British soldiers, a staff car and a Jeep, and an armoured car and a troop-carrier taking up the rear, a Bren gun mounted on top. He ran forward to meet them.

The major in the front passenger seat of the staff car had a loudhailer in his hand, and Sanson jumped on to the running board, thrust his ID through the open window, and said urgently, "Lieutenant-Colonel Sanson. How many men have you brought?"

"A hundred. You mind me asking what the reason for all this is, sir?"

Sanson ignored the question, yanked open the rear door, climbed in and said to the driver, "Move up to the head of the line and take the lead position." He turned back to address the major. "You know the airfield at Shabramant?"

"Yes, sir."

"I want you to listen to me very carefully—"

Helen Kane headed south from the city on a dark, palm-lined country road, until Weaver said, "Pull in."

She swung the staff car into the side. Weaver got out. "Bring the gun."

"You'll only get yourself in deeper trouble, Harry. Do you really think this is wise?"

"The gun, Helen."

She took a Colt automatic from under her seat. "I haven't fired a weapon since basic training."

"Now's your time to get some practice." Weaver knelt at the side of the road, placed his palm flat on the ground, stretching the handcuff chain. "Do it."

She knelt in front of him, moved the tip of the barrel close to the chain, cocked the pistol.

"Pull the trigger," Weaver urged.

She squeezed, there was an explosion, the earth kicked up a cloud of dust, and the chain shattered. Weaver stood, rubbing his wrists, the metal cuffs that remained still chafing his skin. "Did you manage to get the wire cutters?"

"No, but there's a hacksaw and some tools in a kit I put in the boot."

"They'll do. Give me the keys to the car. I'll drive back some of the way. We'll find you a taxi—"

"There isn't time. Besides, I'm going with you."

"This isn't your business, Helen, so don't be a fool. You're already risking a court-martial. I'm not going to have you risk your life as well—"

There was a sudden, steely determination in her voice.
"If you think after all this I'm going to miss the final act,
then you've got another think coming, Harry Weaver." She
found the tools in the boot, tossed them on to the back seat
and climbed back into the car. "Get in. I'm driving."

SHABRAMANT
00:25 A.M.

Sanson ordered the convoy to halt five hundred yards from
the airfield, on the dirt road that led past the entrance. Every
headlight had already been doused two miles further back
on the road, so that their approach wouldn't be seen. He
got out of the cab and studied the airfield, as much of it as
he could see in the moonlight. He could barely make out
the half-dozen or so huts and the two hangars. There was
no proper fence, just a barbed-wire run less than a couple
of metres high on the left-hand side of the road. The opposite side stretched towards desert, nothing but low-rolling
scrubland, hard-packed sand-dunes tufted with rough grass
and the odd palm tree.

He called the major over. "Pick two of your best men
and send them ahead as scouts. And bring a radio operator
up here."

"Yes, sir." The major returned minutes later with the
operator and a couple of sergeants. "These are my best men
for the job, sir."

Sanson addressed them. "I want you to recce the airfield—see if you can spot anything amiss. Keep an eye
out for any American trucks in particular. And for God's
sake make sure you're not seen. It'll ruin everything. Black
up and off you go. Try and get back here as quick as
you can."

The men blackened their faces and hands with axle
grease from one of the trucks, then moved off into the darkness, as Sanson said to the radio operator, "Get in touch
with RAF GHQ. Alert them to keep a radar watch for any
unidentified aircraft entering Cairo airspace—they may be
enemy intruders. And I want a couple of night fighters to
circle the airfield. It's absolutely imperative nothing's allowed to land there."

00:45 A.M.

"Well?" Sanson demanded, when the scouts returned.

"It looks all quiet, sir," the first man reported. "There're a couple of sentries in place at the main gate."

"Did you notice any unusual activity?"

"I can't say that we did, sir. Everything looks fairly normal. But we spotted three American trucks parked just inside the gates."

Sanson reacted, turned briskly to the major. "We're going in. Get the men ready for a quick briefing. I want to make sure they've got descriptions of who we're after, especially Salter, Halder and the woman."

1 A.M.

Hassan was doused with a bucket of water and dragged into the room, blood caked on his face from the gash Salter had inflicted. He was groggy from the blow to his skull, but when he saw Doring's body sprawled in a corner, he came suddenly awake.

"The lad should have been more co-operative," Salter remarked moodily. "Let's hope you've got more sense. Otherwise you're in for the same, or worse." He nodded at the corpse. "An interesting thing. Your pal was a Jerry, name of Doring. There's something very fucking fishy about this whole business. So how about you and me put our differences aside, and you fill me in?"

Hassan glared back at him obstinately, not a shred of fear in his face. "I tell you nothing."

Salter glanced at Doring's body. "What is it with you and your friend? You part of some kind of secret society, or what? Put him in the chair, boys. Tie down his hands."

The men held Hassan down, lashed his forearms to the armrests with the ropes, and Salter picked up the pliers. He grabbed Hassan's right hand and placed the tips of the pincers on the index fingernail. "I'll ask again, just to be polite."

Hassan spat defiantly in Salter's face.

Salter wiped away the spittle, barely able to control his rising temper, and snarled, "Tough bleeding wog, ain't you? Well, we'll see how tough you are when I've finished pulling your nails and go to work on your testicles." He grinned maliciously, tightened his grip on the pliers. "You know something, old flower? I'd be lying if I said I wasn't looking forward to this."

Salter laughed, pulled hard. The nail sheared from the finger. The Arab stiffened, beads of sweat suddenly rising on his face, its expression twisted in pain, but he didn't scream.

"Changed your mind yet?"

Hassan gritted his teeth, blood dripping from his injured finger, clenched his eyes shut against the agony.

"No? Then let's try another." As Salter moved to grip the next nail, there was a burst of machinegun fire from somewhere outside. "What the bloody hell—?" He jumped to his feet as one of his men stormed into the room.

"We got trouble on the way, boss. Lots of it."

SIXTY-FOUR

00:50 A.M.
When Weaver arrived at the Shabramant crossroads, the head-lights caught the unmistakable lattice of tyre tracks in the dust. He was filled with dread, slammed his fist into the dashboard with frustration. *"Damn!* It looks like Sanson got his reinforcements, and he's been and gone."

"What now?"

"Put your foot down, hard as you can."

SHABRAMANT
1 A.M.
Sanson and his men had crawled towards the sand-dunes opposite the gates, everything going smoothly until the last few minutes before the assault. He could make out the sentry boxes in the wash of silver moonlight, the outlines of a half-dozen barrack huts, lights on in several of the windows. But apart from the two guards, smoking and chatting as they leaned against one of the boxes, he noticed no other activity in the camp.

He gestured to the two scouts, their faces still blackened, and they slipped forward on their bellies, vanishing into the shadows like ghosts. They reappeared across the road minutes later and quickly overpowered the two guards, but one of the sentries managed to let out a muffled scream before a hand cut off his cry.

"Let's pray no one's heard the damned noise," Sanson fumed. He turned to the major.

"Get those gates open and see if you can find out from the sentries where Salter is, then bring me the loudhailer."

"Yes, sir."

Sanson led the way towards the gates, and when they were opened, he instructed the men to spread out and move forward. "Don't open fire unless I give the order."

They had hardly moved a dozen paces when the door of the nearest hut opened, fifty metres away, and a couple of men stepped out cautiously, looking as if they'd decided to investigate the disturbance.

"Get down!" Sanson ordered, and everyone threw themselves to the ground, but it was too late. The two men wore British Army uniforms and were armed with Sten guns, and when they saw the intruders they opened up, firing wildly, before vanishing back inside the hut and dousing the lights.

The major darted up beside Sanson, dropped himself flat on the ground. "Damned bad luck—we almost had them by surprise."

"Give me the loudhailer." The major handed it over, and Sanson shouted into the mouthpiece. *"This is Lieutenant-Colonel Sanson, military intelligence. We have the airfield surrounded. Put down your weapons and come out with your hands up."*

Glass shattered in one of the windows, a Sten gun was poked through, and a chatter of fire whistled above Sanson's head as he ducked for cover.

"If that's their answer, so be it. Bring up the armoured car and troop-carrier. And get some men round the back of the huts to cover the rear, just in case anyone's stupid enough to try and make a break for it."

The major spoke on the field radio, and within a minute the armoured car had roared in through the gates, followed by the troop-carrier. They drove forward and swung right, covering the troops as they crouched behind the vehicles. Sanson tapped on the car's armour plate with his revolver, a metal flap opened in the door, and the face of the machinegunner appeared.

"Rake the huts with fire, one by one," Sanson ordered. "We're going to flush them out."

Salter had doused the office lights the instant he'd heard the first rattle of gunfire. He fumbled his way to the window, where one of his men was hunched down with a Sten gun. They heard the metallic voice from the loudhailer, followed by a second burst of fire. "It's the army, boss. And it sounds like they mean business."

An armoured car and a troop-carrier with a heavy machine-gun started to hammer one of the huts with a deadly salvo of fire, and less than a hundred yards away Salter noticed shadowy figures move in the darkness. He was confused, seething with anger. "How the fucking hell did they know we were here?"

"It beats me. But we're in the shit, no two ways about it."

A stray burst of fire shattered the window, and the man went to raise the Sten gun in reply, but Salter stopped him. "Don't be bloody daft, you'll give our position away." He turned to the four of his men still in the hut. "One of you stay here, the rest try and get to the others, out the back way. Tell them we're breaking out, pronto. It's everyone for himself."

Three of the men moved towards the rear of the hut, and Salter crouched with the remaining man beside the window, saw more shadows, moving closer in the darkness. In the other buildings, the rest of his gang were putting up stiff resistance by the sound of it, answering the attack with chattering machinegun fire. "How many do you reckon there are?"

"Too many from the looks of it. And it won't be long before they have us covered, every which way."

Salter fumed in anger as one of his trucks parked outside a neighbouring hut had its tyres shredded by deliberate gunfire. "The bastards are making sure we can't escape. Well, we'll see about that. Get out to the nearest hangar at the back. See if you can find us any kind of transport. I'll be right behind you, soon as I take care of the wog."

"Right, boss." The man crawled across the floor towards the rear corridor. Salter crouched over Hassan, still tied to the chair, and pointed the tip of the Sten gun barrel in his face. "Looks like it's just you and me, sweetheart. It's time to talk or die. Where's Deacon and his friends? Tell me, and you live to fight another day. Don't, and your head's going to look like a pulped melon."

Another shower of stray fire exploded into the room, breaking glass, rounds stitching the wall and riddling the field radio's metal chassis. Salter wiped perspiration from his face, tightened his finger on the trigger, pressed the barrel into the Arab's forehead. "I don't mean to rush you, matey, but if you don't answer soon you mightn't have a bleeding choice. This is it. Last chance. Where are they?"

Sweat glistened on Hassan's face. "On the Nile bank. A villa called Maison Fleuve."

"Exactly *where* on the Nile bank?"

Hassan told him, and Salter grinned in the shadows. "You wouldn't be lying to me, would you?"

"It's the truth. Take me with you. I show you."

"Oh, don't you worry, mate, you definitely will if we get out of this alive. Your friends have a few questions to answer." Salter loosened the ropes, pointed towards the corridor with the gun, as more stray fire ripped into the hut, sending splinters of wood flying. "Outside, the back way. Fast. And keep your head down."

Hassan struggled from the chair. As he stumbled in the darkness, he knocked the table. Salter prodded him with the machinegun. "Move it! Or they'll be on top of us." Hassan noticed his knife, still planted in the desk. He stumbled again, deliberately this time, grabbed the hilt, yanked it from the wood, and slipped the blade unseen into his sleeve. "I said move it!" Salter roared.

At the back door of the hut, Salter began to panic. The gunfire was getting closer. He saw his man hurry towards them in a sweat, wheeling a battered-looking motorcycle, a green-painted Moto Guzzi, the engine already running. "What's *that*?"

"There was nothing in the hangar, boss, except a couple of push-bikes and this bloody ancient motorcycle."

"I don't give a fuck how old it is, is it working?"

"Seems to be, and there's fuel in the tank." He frowned at Hassan. "We can't take the wog. There's only room for two."

"You're right." Salter coldly brought up the Sten and squeezed the trigger, sending the stunned man reeling back, dancing in a chatter of fire.

"Get on the bike. You're driving." He pushed Hassan forward. The Arab swung round, the blade in his hand. Salter's eyes were beacons of horror as he tried desperately to raise the Sten. The knife slashed at his throat, a deep gash opened in his neck and his head went back, spouting blood. Hassan moved in for the kill, planted the blade deep in his chest.

Salter screamed, and as he staggered back Hassan snarled, "Go keep the Devil company, Englishman."

Salter collapsed, his tunic drenched in blood, and Hassan retrieved his knife, picked up the Sten, hung the weapon by its sling from his shoulder. He climbed unsteadily on to the Moto Guzzi, his jaw still on fire, just as a Jeep skidded around the corner, three soldiers on board. He raised the Sten, let go with a long chattering burst, and the vehicle reversed wildly.

Sanson led the men towards the barrack office, taking cover behind the troop-carrier. It was the last building to be stormed, the others had already been taken, Salter's gang putting up heavy resistance until they realised that the odds were overwhelming. A group of confused and shaken Egyptian Air Force men had been led out from one of the huts, their hands tied behind their backs, several injured from flying glass, but neither Halder nor Salter was among the dead or captured, and with only one building remaining, Sanson was getting anxious. "Give them a warning to surrender."

The major raised the loudhailer. *"Lay down your weapons and come out with your hands in the air. Fail to obey the order, and we open fire."*

There was no reply, and Sanson said, "Give me a couple of grenades."

The major handed over the grenades and Sanson lobbed

one through a shattered window, then another. Two flashes and two explosions followed, then he ordered the machinegunner on top of the carrier to rake the front of the building. The Bren gun stitched a hail of fire across the veranda. Wood splinters erupted, the remaining windows shattered, and the door was shot off its hinges.

When the firing died, Sanson moved forward, his pistol at the ready. "Right, let's see what we've got."

Someone switched on the lights and Sanson saw the bullet-riddled field radio, and Doring's tortured corpse sprawled in a corner. "Fetch one of the prisoners. Find out what's been happening here."

When a burly-looking prisoner with a broken nose was ushered in, his hands cuffed behind his back, Sanson went up to him. "Where's Salter?" he promptly demanded.

When the man hesitated, Sanson struck him a blow on the jaw. He reeled back, and Sanson cocked his revolver, a murderous look on his face. "If I have to ask again, you'll be minus an eye."

The man massaged his jaw. "He—he was in here last time I saw him, honest."

Sanson pointed to the body. "Who's that?"

"One—one of Deacon's mates, a Jerry name of Doring. Reggie had words with him, and the Arab—"

"You'd better tell me *everything* that went on here. *Fast*. And I want to know exactly who was present when you raided the airfield, descriptions included."

Sanson listened as Salter's man talked, then said urgently to a couple of the troops, "See if you can find the Arab and Salter, or if anyone's spotted them. They have to be still on the airfield. And be careful how you go, they're both wily bastards, and dangerous." He knelt over Doring's body. "What did he tell your boss?"

"Nothing. Kept his mouth shut to the end, the poor sod."

Sanson stood up briskly. "One of Deacon's friends you mentioned—the one dressed as an officer. I've reason to believe he's a wanted German agent named Halder. I need to find him quickly. Where is he?"

Salter's man looked totally confused. "Bloody hell!

That's news to me. You mind me asking what the *fuck's* going on?"

"Just answer the damned question."

"He was with us when we took the airfield, but left with one of his men. Only the wog and Doring stayed behind. Reggie said they'd be back before the aircraft landed."

Sanson sighed bitterly with frustration, examined the shattered radio. "Did anyone contact Doring and his friends before or after we arrived?"

"Not that I know of."

"What time are the aircraft due to land?"

"The boss wasn't sure exactly, not until Deacon's mates returned."

There was a noise behind him, as one of the men Sanson had dispatched came into the room. "The Arab's been spotted, sir. It seems our lads drove round the back a few minutes ago and saw him escape on a motorcycle. They went after him."

"What about Salter?"

"I think we found him. He's in a bad way."

They carried Salter in and laid him on the desk. His breath came in laboured gasps, his throat a crimson gash.

"We've got a medic coming. Try to hold on," Sanson told him, but knew it was useless. Salter was bleeding to death from a horrible chest wound. Lying there on the desk, he looked like a corpse already, chalk-white, his hands clutching his chest. Sanson leaned over. "Listen to me, Salter. Deacon's friends, they're German infiltrators. I've got to find them. Do you understand me?"

Salter coughed up blood, stared up at the ceiling, eyes wide. For a few moments it seemed as if he had regained his senses. He managed to claw Sanson's tunic, raw anger in his eyes, his voice a hoarse rattle. "The—sodding bastard Arab—he did for me—"

Sanson could barely control his impatience. "If you know where they are, tell me, man!"

Salter gurgled, relaxed his grip, his breath coming in tortured gasps.

"Hang in there. The medic's on his way," Sanson urged.

"No—no good. Won't help me—"

"Where are they, Salter? If you know, for Christ's sake tell me!"

Weaver saw the flashes of light two hundred yards from the airfield. Gunfire crackle and grenade explosions filled the night air, and his heart sank. He told Helen Kane to pull up and he climbed out of the car. "We're too late. It's already started."

She got out of the driver's seat and came up beside him. Weaver looked towards the airfield, his face grim, watching the flashes of light from the welter of small-arms fire. She put a hand on his arm. "There's nothing you could have done, Harry. I hate to say it, but it's over for your friends. Now let's get out of here, before we both get shot."

He took the pistol from the car, made to move off into the darkness. "If I'm not back in fifteen minutes, get out of here and back to Cairo."

"Harry, please—by now it's pointless."

"I need to know what's happened."

SIXTY-FIVE

Hassan revved the Moto Guzzi as he sped along the edge of the runway.

A burst of machinegun fire ripped into the ground to his right, and he glanced over his shoulder. A Jeep raced after him in the darkness, three soldiers on board, clouds of dust pluming in its wake. Hassan revved the throttle harder, tried to widen the gap, but he was barely able to control the motorcycle, his hand ablaze with pain as he gripped the handlebars.

Suddenly, the runway came to an abrupt end and he veered left on to open ground. He was on hard-packed sand that rolled beneath the wheels in rough waves, bouncing the front absorber struts madly, sending agonising shock waves through his body. He peered ahead into the moonlit darkness but saw only more rolling scrubland all the way to the barbed-wire perimeter. He was trapped. Gunfire raked the soil ahead of him and he glanced back again. The

Jeep bounced over the rough ground, gaining on him fast.

He drove on, zigzagging, frantically searching for a sharp rise somewhere near the perimeter, until he saw a long, rising mound no more than fifty yards to his left, near the edge of the wire. Another burst of fire riddled the ground dangerously close on his left, and he swung right, then veered left again in a narrow arc, straightened the front wheel, and headed directly towards the mound, revving hard.

The Moto Guzzi accelerated sharply, eating up the final twenty yards at full power, until it looked certain he was about to crash into the mound. At the last moment, he jerked up the handlebars and opened the throttle full. The engine screamed, the back wheels hit the rise at ferocious speed, and he sailed through the air. The motorcycle rose for a few terrifying seconds, he felt something claw savagely at his leg as he cleared the wire, and then he started to sink fast. The front wheel hit the ground forcefully, the Moto Guzzi bucked, and he came off and landed hard, grunting, the breath knocked out of him.

Dazed, he looked back to see the driver slam on his brakes to avoid hitting the mound. Too late, he skidded, and the Jeep kicked up a cloud of dust and rolled over on its side. One of the soldiers was thrown free, his body hurtling through the air, the Jeep rolled again, landed on top of the wire, and Hassan heard the muffled screams of the other two men as they were crushed beneath the vehicle.

He staggered painfully to his feet and checked the Moto Guzzi. The engine was still running, and he climbed back on and pushed the machine forward to assess the damage. The front wheel had been slightly warped. It still spun, but grated against the forks and would slow him down. The Sten gun had bruised his side when he'd fallen, the barbed wire had cut a jagged gash down his right calf, and his jaw had started to bleed again.

Suddenly he heard the roar of an aircraft as a Spitfire came in low, its engines snarling, then another on its tail, the landing lights of both ablaze as they flew over the airfield, before they screamed up into the night. As he revved the motorcycle, he saw the soldier who had been thrown clear stagger to his feet, clutching his shoulder. He brought up the Sten, squeezed off a burst and, as the dazed man dropped for cover, sped away.

Weaver was halfway along the airfield perimeter road, moving fast, when he heard a motorcycle engine somewhere behind him and looked back.

A hundred yards beyond the wire he saw a rider being pursued by a Jeep, one of the passengers firing wildly at the motorcycle as it twisted across the rough scrubland. To Weaver's amazement, the rider started to drive at high speed towards the barbed-wire run. A split second before the bike hit the wire, the front wheel lifted, and the machine roared over the fence, its engine whining. The pursuing Jeep skidded wildly, rolled twice, and crashed, belly up.

Weaver had started to run back when he saw the rider get to his feet and check his machine, as a Spitfire howled low over-head, then another, before the motorcyclist let off a volley of machinegun fire and roared off in the opposite direction.

When Weaver reached the wire he saw a sergeant sway to his feet on the other side, clutching his shoulder. He climbed over the wrecked Jeep towards him. "Lieutenant-Colonel Weaver, military intelligence. What's happened here?"

The sergeant fell to his knees. Weaver reached him just as he was about to keel over. The man's face was creased in agony, his arm limp, and it looked as if his shoulder was broken. He stared over at the tangled bodies under the wreckage. "The poor bastards."

"What happened? Where's Lieutenant-Colonel Sanson?"

"Back at the airfield, mopping up, sir."

Weaver removed the sergeant's belt and buckled it. He made a crude sling, placed the arm inside, and the sergeant groaned. "Who was on the motorcycle?"

"An Arab escaped from one of the huts. We went after him."

Weaver said urgently, "Two Germans. A man and a woman. Were they caught?"

"I didn't hear about no woman being caught, sir. Or Germans either."

Weaver heard the sound of engines. A string of blue-painted headlights raced towards him across the scrubland. Frantically, he looked back along the road where the motorcycle had disappeared. It had left a distinct wheel track in the sandy dirt. Weaver made the decision instantly. "Help's on its way, sergeant. They'll get you to a medic." He clambered over the wreckage and raced back towards Helen Kane's car.

"We lost the Arab, sir."

Sanson fumed when he heard what had happened. "Send out a couple of men to try and pick up his trail. And have them take a radio operator with them to keep in touch."

"We'll do our best, sir, though we're probably a bit late. But it seems an American officer arrived on the scene and might have gone after him. Name of Weaver, sir."

"*What?*"

"Lieutenant-Colonel Weaver—at least I'm told that's how he identified himself, sir. He gave first aid to the injured sergeant then left in a hurry, hared off in the same direction as the Arab."

Sanson flared. "Detail some men to get after him. Have them search along the road. Weaver's to be arrested on sight."

"*Sir?*"

"You heard me," Sanson was enraged. "He's an escaped prisoner. Now get me a map of Cairo, *fast.*"

The confused major relayed the orders to one of his officers, and came back promptly with a map. He looked at Salter, lying unconscious on a stretcher in a corner as a medic attended him. "Do you think he'll make it, sir?"

"I don't give a damn if he does or not," Sanson snapped back, then rolled out the map, slammed a fist on the table to hold it down. "This villa he mentioned on the western bank, Maison Fleuve, have you ever heard of it?"

"I'm afraid not."

"On second thoughts, have the radio operator remain here, just in case the Germans attempt to try and land, and reinforcements are needed. But first, have him get in touch with the American embassy and pass on the message to General Clayton, urgently. Let him know exactly what's happened here."

"What about the airfield, sir?"

"Put a couple of trucks on the field and make absolutely *certain* nothing can land. I want twenty of your men to come with me, the rest to stay here and guard the prisoners. Seeing as the field radio's out, the villa could be where the Arab's headed. And if Salter's right, that's where Deacon and the Germans are holed up."

MAISON FLEUVE
1:30 A.M.

Halder jerked awake with a cry, his body drenched in sweat. Rachel sat curled up in a chair by the window, and she came over and put a hand on his brow. "It's all right, Jack. I'm here."

"What—what happened?"

"I think you had a bad dream, that's all. You tossed and turned in your sleep."

He sat up in the bed, covered in perspiration. Rachel found a towel, dabbed his body.

"What were you dreaming about?"

His face darkened as he remembered. "That fortune-teller must have set my mind on edge. I had a terrible nightmare, about Pauli. There were bombs—he was dying. I couldn't save him—"

"Jack, that's nonsense."

He got off the bed with sudden unease, went over to the enamel basin, splashed water on his face. "The ancients called dreams the prophecies of the soul, a kind of warning from the gods. Sometimes I think they knew more than we do."

"That's superstitious drivel."

As he went to dry himself, there was an unsettling disquiet in his eyes, his features drawn. She came up behind him, put her arms around his waist reassuringly, her head against his back. "With all that's happening, your mind's working overtime. That's why you had such a terrible nightmare. You know, for a grown man, sometimes you can be so irrational. Please, try and forget about it, Jack."

He turned round, took her in his arms, looked into her face. "You know something? You're far too good for me, Rachel Stern. Practical, your feet on the ground."

She put a finger to his lips, smiled, but the tension showed in her eyes. "You'd better go downstairs. The sooner you return, the better." She touched his cheek, brushed it with a kiss, looked into his face. "Promise me you'll come back safely? For both our sakes."

He went down to the patio, and found Deacon and Kleist waiting restlessly at the table, the field radio in front of them. The Nile was dotted in the distance with the lanterns of small fishing boats, the vast, dark river incredibly placid, and on the far banks the silhouettes of palm trees were motionless in the heavy night air. "It's like the calm before the storm," Halder commented.

"It's the waiting that kills you." Deacon was on edge as he wiped his neck with a handkerchief. "You rested well?"

"Not half well enough." There was a pot of Turkish coffee and some cups on the table and Halder helped himself. "Did anything come through on the field radio?"

"It's been as dead as the morgue."

Halder nodded to Kleist. "We'd better give them a call before we head back, just to make certain."

Kleist went to the radio, flicked a switch, and put on the headphones. *"Raider One to Raider Two, are you receiving me? Over."* He repeated the message half a dozen times, then frowned. "There's no reply. It's dead the other end."

"You're sure the radio's working properly and you've got the right frequency?"

Kleist checked, to be certain, and nodded. "Try it yourself, if you wish."

Halder did, but heard just endless crackle in reply. As he put down the headphones Deacon stood, worriedly. "Do you think something's wrong?"

"We checked both the field radios before we took the airfield, and they worked perfectly. There might just be a technical problem, but you never know. Get out to the vehicle, Kleist. We're heading back."

When Kleist had left, Halder said uneasily, "Do you think there's a chance Salter has overplayed his hand?"

Deacon's expression darkened. "I wouldn't have thought so, not when he thinks he's got a fortune coming. But with a thoroughgoing snake like him, I suppose there's no telling what he might get up to. You think you can handle it, if that's the case?"

"Let's hope so. The main thing is to stall him. Salter's going to have to hang around until the aircraft land, that's for sure. After that, we won't have to worry about him either way." Halder tapped his fingers on the radio. "But the fact there's no reply worries me."

"You and me both."

Halder tugged on his cap. "If we can sort out the problem with the radio, I'll call you and let you know when Skorzeny's men have landed. Otherwise, one of us will have to drive back to keep you informed. God willing, it'll all be over one way or another before dawn, and we'll meet for the final rendezvous. Look after the lady while I'm gone."

Deacon offered a firm handshake. "Good luck, Major."

Halder turned to go, realised he'd left the M_3 upstairs in the bedroom. He moved towards the hall, heard the distinct sound of an engine roaring into the front courtyard. He removed his pistol, said to Deacon, "Who the devil's that?"

As they both went towards the front door, Kleist came rushing in, his face taut. "You'd better come outside."

SIXTY-SIX

Weaver kept the headlights off for the entire journey, following the track the Arab had left on the desert road, until eventually they spotted the motorcycle's dust cloud. The only light came from the quarter-moon, and every now and then the motorcycle wove drunkenly, as if the driver were having difficulty steering.

Weaver tried to watch the road, to make sure they kept well enough behind, hoping they wouldn't be spotted, and when they'd gone a couple of miles, he said to Helen Kane, "I might be wrong, but from the way he's driving he could be injured. Don't take your eyes off him for a second. I don't want to lose him."

At that hour of the morning there was barely any traffic, and they crossed the English Bridge ten minutes later and came to the city outskirts along the sparsely populated western bank. They passed several big old Nile villas set in their own grounds, and saw the Arab turn down a narrow private track alongside the river. A mile further on the motorcycle disappeared in through the open gates of a white-walled villa.

Weaver immediately pulled the car in off the road, killed the engine, and for a few seconds heard the throb of the motorcycle engine before it died abruptly. He stepped out of the car and peered into the darkness.

Helen Kane frowned. "What do you think he's up to?"

Weaver checked the Colt pistol, tucked it into his waistband. "Stay here. I'm going ahead to have a look. If I'm not back in twenty minutes, get to the nearest telephone and contact Sanson."

She saw a kind of possession in his expression. "Harry, you're being reckless. What can it achieve? Why don't we simply contact Sanson now?"

"I've come this far, I might as well follow it through. Remember—stay here."

They moved Hassan into a chair, and Deacon went to get a towel and a bowl of water. When he came back, he dabbed the badly gashed cheek.

"What happened?" Halder said anxiously.

The Arab gritted his teeth in agony, held the towel to his jaw, his speech broken. When he had managed to tell them, Deacon exploded with rage. "The conniving bastard—Salter's double-crossed us and ruined everything."

"Anger won't get us anywhere," Halder admonished. "What concerns me is how the army knew about the airfield. Not Salter's fault, surely?"

Hassan shook his head, words an effort. "All I know is the aircraft can't land. Not with the army and British Spitfires waiting to shoot them down."

Halder sighed, resignation on his face. "Are you sure you weren't followed?"

The Arab struggled from the chair, still holding the towel to his face. "I'm sure of nothing, except I've killed that pig Salter."

"Kleist, get outside and have a good look around."

Halder made the decision instantly. "Then we're getting out of here."

The SS man left hurriedly, and Deacon said, "You mind telling me where?"

"Anywhere will do for now, until we figure out what to do next. If the army knew about the airfield, there's no telling what else they know. To remain here would be madness. You'd better get a signal off to Berlin, fast as you can, while there's still enough time for Skorzeny to abort. Make absolutely certain they acknowledge the message. Then get out to the boat. We'll stick to the river—it might be safer than the roads."

As he went to fetch Rachel, Deacon grabbed his arm. "Listen to me, Halder. We can still finish this. If one of us could make it through the tunnel—"

Halder pulled his arm away. "See sense, Deacon. Without our paratroops, it's hopeless. If you want to volunteer for a suicide mission, be my guest. But for me, it's over. You have my orders—send the signal, and let's get out of here."

There was a footstep behind them. "It's over for all of you."

They looked round. Weaver stood on the patio. "No one's going anywhere."

He moved into the room, brandishing the Colt. "All of you put your hands up where I can see them. Very slowly."

Halder obeyed, Deacon and Hassan followed. "Now take the gun out of your holster, Jack, nice and easy, then place it on the floor and kick it over here."

Halder did so, tipped the weapon with his foot and slid it across. The shock hadn't left his face. "It seems the fateful day has come. I wasn't relishing this, Harry. You and me face to face, up against each other, like in some cheap western. It seems to tarnish whatever good there was between us. You mind telling me how you found me?"

Weaver flicked the pistol towards Hassan. "I followed your friend. The other one's Deacon, I presume? The second half of the double act."

"I'm impressed, Harry. Obviously you've been hotter on our trail than I thought."

Hassan said sourly, "You should have let me kill him when I had the chance."

"Regrets, I'm afraid, will get us nowhere," said Halder, and he looked over at Weaver. "Simply to satisfy my curiosity, how did the army know about the airfield?"

"Those stolen trucks of yours led to Salter. The rest I'm sure you can guess."

"I see." Halder looked totally resigned. "Then I suppose the only question is what happens next?"

"I think you already know the answer, Jack. Sanson and his men are on their way. After that, it's either a rope or a firing squad. That uniform you're wearing is in itself enough to warrant a bullet, for impersonating a US Army officer."

"You wouldn't be lying about Sanson, would you?"

"Not a chance."

Halder said, hopelessly, "Then try not to forget the lily on my grave, will you, old friend? I never was one for roses, I'm afraid."

Weaver knelt, picked up Halder's gun. "Where's Rachel?"

"She's not a part of this, Harry." There was a pleading look on Halder's face. "The rest of us are as guilty as sin, but she's been used from the very start. You have to let her go."

"I asked where she is."

"I'm here."

There was a noise behind him, and Weaver turned.

Rachel moved into the doorway, Halder's M_3 machine-pistol cradled in her hands.

"Now, please, put down the gun, Harry."

Kleist appeared behind her, holding Helen Kane roughly by the arm, his pistol aimed at her head. "Let go of me—"

She struggled to get free, but Kleist manhandled her into the room. "I found her outside, a friend of the American's. Waiting alone in a staff car back along the track."

The SS man glared over. "You heard the order. Put down the gun."

Weaver made to raise the Colt in anger, but Kleist said

viciously, "Another move like that, and the bitch won't have a brain."

"Harry, I think you'd better do as he says," Halder said quietly. "It seems the tables have turned. So perhaps you should drop the weapon and introduce the lady."

Weaver stared back at Rachel, said hoarsely, "You don't know what you're doing—"

"Shut up," Kleist interrupted. "Drop the gun, and be quick about it."

Weaver dropped the Colt, it clattered to the floor, and Deacon picked it up, while Halder crossed the room, his hand held out to Rachel for the machine-pistol. "For a woman who hates firearms, you did remarkably well. Now, you'd better give me that, before someone gets hurt."

She made no move to hand over the weapon. "Move away, Jack."

Halder frowned, totally confused. A shadow crossed his face. He was about to speak, but Rachel gestured with the machine-pistol. "Over there, by the wall. You too, Harry." She nodded to Kleist. "Take the woman down to the cellar. Tie her securely. Make sure she can't go anywhere."

Kleist roughly bundled Helen Kane out of the room, and Rachel said to Hassan, "Go outside and keep watch. If you see or hear anything, get back here, quickly."

The Arab looked totally bemused, his pain forgotten, and Deacon snapped, "You heard the order. Obey it. I'll explain later."

When Hassan had left, Rachel looked at Deacon. "Send Berlin the signal. You know what to tell them."

Deacon left the room hurriedly, his footsteps fading into the cellar, and then the three of them were alone.

The blood had drained completely from Weaver's face, a terrible truth dawning, and Halder was as white as death. "You know, suddenly I've got this horrible feeling Harry and I have lived with a delusion for years."

"I think it's time you both knew the truth."

SIXTY-SEVEN

Schellenberg had just finished a late supper in his private rooms at SS headquarters when the signal was delivered to him personally in a wax-sealed envelope. The bombing had stopped and he had returned to his office on the second floor, heavy rain streaking the taped windows, a blanket of dismal clouds hanging over night-time Berlin. He broke the red wax seal and read the decoded contents quickly. His face tightened, then he picked up the internal telephone and summoned his adjutant. "Call Admiral Canaris at once. Inform him I wish to see him urgently."

"Herr General, it's after midnight—"

"I'm well aware of the damned time! Just do it."

Half an hour after Schellenberg had made the necessary phone calls, a rain-soaked Canaris finally arrived, looking tired and bothered as he was led in by the adjutant, who then withdrew. "What is it you want?"

Schellenberg handed him the signal flimsy. "Some urgent news just in from Cairo. I thought you'd want to see."

When Canaris had finished reading, he grimly shook his head, tossed the flimsy on the desk with a damning flourish. "It's just as I thought. The whole thing has come to nothing in the end. Lives wasted for nothing. No doubt they'll all be apprehended and shot."

Schellenberg picked up his cigarette case from the desk, selected a cigarette, lit it and inhaled slowly, as if savouring what was about to come. "It's a calamity, no question. And so close to the end. Skorzeny's aircraft had already taken off, and were *en route*. I've had to give the order that they return to Rome—the Allies would certainly have shot them out of the skies before they landed. But there's an unfortunate communications problem with Rome—the signal keeps breaking up and we can't get in touch. We'll keep trying, of course, but as a precaution I've urgently instructed that our Luftwaffe night fighters operating out of

Crete try and intercept Skorzeny's Dakotas before it's too late. Let's just pray we can get to the colonel in time. The Führer is bitterly disappointed, of course. I spoke to him by telephone before you arrived, and his mood really wasn't the best after I'd told him. But he's not completely without hope."

Canaris stared at Schellenberg as if he were insane. "Not without hope? But it's over, for God's sake."

"Not yet. In fact, the interesting part just begins."

Canaris scowled. "I don't follow."

Schellenberg stood up from his desk. "I didn't think you would. But now, my dear Wilhelm, it's time you knew the truth. No doubt you recall the first rule of good intelligence work—one must always try to be one step ahead of the game. You see, I've kept my best card until last. And I think you're going to be surprised."

Schellenberg crossed to the window, looked out at the teeming rain, one hand behind his back, a cigarette poised in the other. "I recall you admitted having heard rumours about my agent, Nightingale?"

"I've certainly heard whispers. Why?"

"And what exactly did the gossip-mongers say?"

Canaris shrugged. "That no one but the Führer and a handful of trusted, high-ranking SD know his real identity. That he's the best agent your organisation ever trained. Ruthless. Clever. Totally dedicated."

Schellenberg gave an approving nod. "An accurate appraisal. Nightingale was certainly one of the most professional agents we ever recruited. Highly intelligent and extremely resourceful. Calm under pressure, totally lacking in fear, and absolutely committed to the task in hand. I think you'd agree those same attributes would probably describe a very capable assassin?"

Canaris's mouth went suddenly dry. "What are you trying to say?"

"Nightingale is among the team we sent to Cairo, and will attempt to succeed where Halder and Skorzeny have failed."

Canaris stared at him blankly as Schellenberg went on. "I told you, Wilhelm, above all Roosevelt is our prime tar-

get. As of now, he's our *only* target. And Nightingale is
our last card—the only remaining hope we have for the
success of the mission. Our ace in the hole."

Canaris was astounded. "But—who is he?"

Schellenberg shook his head. "Not he. She. To be precise, Rachel Stern."

The shock on Canaris's face was total. Schellenberg let the
impact sink in. "Not her real name, of course, but it'll do
perfectly well for now."

"This is some kind of joke, surely."

Schellenberg looked affronted as he came back from the
window and sat. "This is not a matter I'd jest about."

"But—but it's quite unbelievable."

"There are some facts you should be aware of. Before
the war, she was our top agent in Egypt, and provided us
with much invaluable information. About military installations, about the nationalist groups which were a thorn in
the British side, and much else besides." Schellenberg
raised an eyebrow, smugly. "Believe me, you've really no
idea how good she was back then. Better than all of our
people put together. She'd have made even the best of them
look like complete amateurs."

"But—Rachel Stern is half Jewish?"

Schellenberg smiled broadly. "Ah, now that's where it
becomes a little devious. When we first decided to send her
to Egypt, she needed a plausible background. Professor
Stern and his wife were, in fact, SD agents all along. His
wife's Jewish background and the professor's anti-Nazi
sentiment were a fabrication, all part of their cover story,
of course, and an excellent ready-made one at that. So,
someone in the SD office simply invented a daughter for
the Sterns—I think you can imagine the rest."

Canaris's mind was ticking over furiously. "And their
arrest by the Gestapo when they were returned to Germany?"

"More trickery, I'm afraid. A Kriegsmarine vessel was
scheduled to pick them up *en route* to Istanbul, when the
Izmir sank. Fortunately for us, the professor and Nightingale were rescued. But their apparent arrest was simply to

protect their cover. They were, in fact, taken away for debriefing."

"But—why was she imprisoned at Ravensbruck?"

Schellenberg smiled. "I'm surprised you can't see the reasoning behind it, Wilhelm. But then I can see you're still in shock. It was another trick, pure and simple."

"I don't follow."

"Halder hadn't seen Rachel Stern since they parted company in Cairo. The professor's anti-Nazi remarks and his wife's supposed Jewish blood would have suggested an unpleasant fate for the family had they returned to Germany. Which is exactly what Halder would have expected—anything less would have made him suspicious. As for the camp, it was an easy enough matter to arrange—a ragged camp uniform, a doctor to administer small amounts of cordite to give her a washed-out appearance. And to top it all, a fictitious camp officer who had been a pupil of her father's, to explain why she was still in reasonably good health, and hadn't been all that badly treated."

Canaris said palely, "It seems you thought of everything."

Schellenberg grinned wickedly. "I always try to. Details are so important. It was never a case of Halder making certain the woman did what was expected of her, but the other way round. He might have been the ideal man for the job, but Himmler had some doubts from the very start about Halder's true allegiance, considering he's part American—and whether he'd really do his best to carry the whole thing through. The woman was there to make sure he did. And with the future of the entire Reich at stake, we had to have a back-up plan if we couldn't get Skorzeny's paratroops into Cairo or if Halder failed."

"Why didn't you simply tell him the truth from the start?"

"It was perfectly obvious Halder still had feelings for Rachel Stern. And he'd do his utmost to make sure they made it to Cairo, whatever the obstacles. If we had told him the truth it would have completely shattered his illusions. Then there was the risk he might not even have agreed to go along with us in the first place.

"We also wanted Nightingale's cover story to be believable and beyond suspicion. If she was caught, she would simply be a victim, used by us, and not one of Germany's most brilliant agents, to be tried and sent to the gallows by the Allies. That would have given them something to boast about, and wouldn't have done our esteem any good at all."

There was a long pause, and Canaris suddenly looked angry. "Why did you keep all this from me?"

"Not my doing, Wilhelm. The Führer decided that keeping it secret was the best course—the less who knew the better."

"And no doubt he's enjoying a laugh at my expense. I've always known he doesn't trust me," Canaris said without bitterness. "This only confirms it."

Schellenberg shrugged. "That's a matter for you to pursue."

The curiosity was palpable in Canaris's voice, hoarse and very quiet now. "Who is she, Walter? What's her background?"

Schellenberg lit another cigarette. "Does it really matter at this late stage?"

"For someone to risk laying down their life on a last-ditch mission like this, she must either be a fanatic or a fool. Why would she agree to it?"

Schellenberg smiled thinly. "Because these are desperate times we find ourselves in. And she's a patriot."

Canaris looked sceptical. "That sly look on your face says there's more to it. I have a feeling there's another reason."

"You always look for an ulterior motive, don't you, Wilhelm? And rightly so." Schellenberg blew out smoke, sighed grimly. "Very well, I shall give you one. General Pieter Ulrich. You've heard of him?"

Canaris nodded. "By reputation, he's an upstanding and highly respected Wehrmacht officer. A brave and honourable man, much decorated."

"He's also the woman's father. And no longer a respected officer, but one of these insane, traitorous plotters against the Führer. In fact, the last time I paid him a visit in the Gestapo cells, he really had gone quite mad. Solitary confinement appears to have sent him over the edge."

"The—the general has been imprisoned?" Canaris stammered. "The last I heard, Ulrich had been posted to the Russian front."

"I'm afraid it's much worse than that. He and his entire family were arrested secretly some months ago on a charge of treason. All, that is, except his daughter. She wasn't considered party to his crime. Nevertheless, we decided to offer her a proposition."

Canaris's face darkened knowingly. "You played the same dirty game with her that you played with Halder?"

Schellenberg gave a shrug. "It's an old routine in our business, as you well know, but always effective. In her case, all charges dropped against her family—if she agreed to go along with this, and if necessary, to give up her life for the Fatherland. A small price, I think you'll agree, for the survival of the Reich and the release of her entire family. Both her parents, and her two younger brothers, who are also presently being held in the cellars."

"But General Ulrich's sons—I think I met them once. They must be only in their teens. Boys, both of them. How could they be guilty of such treason?"

Schellenberg gave a shrug. "You'd have to ask Himmler that—their arrest had nothing to do with me. But I've been keeping a close personal watch on all of them, you'll be glad to know, and they're being reasonably well treated— no more beatings or interrogation. At least until this is over and their fate decided."

Canaris's mouth tightened with disgust. "And what if the general's daughter fails?"

"Let's try not to contemplate failure," Schellenberg answered moodily. "I've had quite enough for one night. And the truth of it is, you must believe me when I tell you that the woman probably stands as good a chance as Skorzeny's paratroops. Halder will probably be devastated if he's learned the truth."

Canaris sat back, dazed, his brain racing, trying to fit the rest of the pieces into place. "What will happen to him now?"

"Assuming, of course, there *are* survivors, the same plan we arranged with Deacon still applies—to fly them out when it's over, Halder included. Not that I honestly expect such an outcome. But certainly if Nightingale manages to carry this off, she'll be the toast of the Reich. Dead or alive, her name will have established its place in history."

Canaris sat there for a time, mulling it all over. "No doubt she never cared a whit for Halder. It was all a charade."

"She's a splendid actress, of course, when the occasion demands," Schellenberg admitted. "But as for not caring about Halder, I'm really not so sure."

"Explain."

"I read her reports when she returned from Egypt. It seems that apart from Halder, she maintained a friendship with another young man, an American. She intended the relationships purely as a convenience, of course, all part of her cover. But as you well know, when you're an experienced intelligence officer, you train yourself to try to read minds, and the true meanings behind words."

"What are you saying?"

"I got the distinct feeling that had she not left Egypt when she did, she might have been torn between her personal feelings and her duty. When I debriefed her, I asked her out of curiosity how she felt about both men. She admitted that she had strong feelings for each."

"You're saying she loved them?"

"I'm saying that whatever she felt was perfectly understandable. She was a young woman in an exotic setting, the romantic attention flattered her, and she found herself responding, despite her best efforts not to. You know as well as I do that the finest agents are never the unfeeling brutes—they're the ones with hearts and minds." Schellenberg shrugged. "She's also a woman. And we both know how unfathomable a species *they* are. Anything is possible. But she was certainly caught up in a conflict of emotions."

"What do you mean?"

"She changed after she returned to Germany. Lost her appetite for her work. She was distracted, lacked focus, until eventually, after a couple of disastrous missions in Istanbul, she was relegated to agent training here in Berlin. And that's where she's been ever since. If you must have an honest appraisal, I'd say she fell in love with both men and couldn't get over them, but didn't want to admit it to herself. However, this time she's perfectly focused, and in no doubt about the importance of what must be done."

Canaris sat there, feeling oddly unmoved by the revelation. "You still haven't told me what happens now."

"She and Deacon will do whatever is necessary to carry this through. We now know the passageway is usable, and Roosevelt is inside the compound. The rest is up to them."

"Deacon knows about her?"

"He's been aware of our plans from the start. Kleist too. I insisted on it. With that temper of his, he was likely to have tried to kill the woman once she had outlived her apparent usefulness." Schellenberg smiled. "Not that he would have succeeded for a moment. She's more than capable of looking after herself, and a truly excellent shot."

Canaris still hadn't got over the shock. He shivered, looked out at the rain, the grim black clouds hanging over night-time Berlin. His anger was gone. It seemed pointless; everything was beyond his control. After a time, he turned back. "But do you honestly believe she can kill Roosevelt?"

"Believe me, if there's even a slim hope that anyone can finish this, Nightingale can."

SIXTY-EIGHT

MAISON FLEUVE
23 NOVEMBER /1:30 A.M.
Weaver sat there, his face as if carved in stone, every muscle taut. It was very still in the room, the silence overpowering. Halder didn't utter a word, thunderstruck, until Rachel Stern had finished talking.

"I have to admit, you fooled me completely," he said very quietly, still in shock, his voice almost a whisper. "The business of the camp, the reasons why Schellenberg wanted you as part of this, the hostility towards me at first. They all rang true. But I can see now I was gravely mistaken. It was all a sham."

A look like remorse crossed her face. "None of it my fault, Jack. Like you, I was caught between the Devil and the deep blue sea, obliged to do Schellenberg's bidding." She came back slowly from the window. "You look stricken, Harry. Have I disappointed you that much?"

Weaver felt at a total loss for words. He flinched, as if he'd received a physical blow, managed to whisper hoarsely, "More than you'll ever know."

"I'm sorry it had to be this way."

Halder said bitterly, "Very touching, but you can keep the phoney anguish, it doesn't mean a thing. You never had an ounce of feeling for either Harry or me, ever. Did you? It was all a game."

She looked at them both steadily, a kind of grief in her eyes. "Is that what you really believe, Jack?"

"I believe I've been an utter fool—the rest of it is really immaterial. Except what happens next."

"You're coming with Deacon and me. You got close to Roosevelt once already. You can do it again. But this time you'll have me as company. And if by any chance there's an afterwards, we're flying out of here."

"You mind telling me how?"

"The way Deacon arranged in case of emergency. His Egyptian officer friend will make the pick-up from a desert strip near Sakkara, and fly us to a German airbase on Crete."

"Take it from me, even if anyone makes it on board they'll be blasted out of the skies."

"Deacon doesn't seem to think so. The route's been worked out. Once the aircraft is north of Port Said, German night fighters will be waiting to guide it to safety."

"And who's going to do the dirty deed at the hotel?"

"Me. That was the intention—if you failed, or Skorzeny's men didn't arrive."

"How?" Halder shook his head. "You won't stand a chance in hell of getting near Roosevelt, never mind killing him and getting away with it."

"I'm afraid I'm going to have to play that particular hand as it falls. But as for the how—" Rachel produced Deacon's Luger, put down the machine-pistol and took something from her pocket. Halder instantly recognised the oblong metal shape. She fitted it on the end of the Luger. "A new silencer the SD has developed. The best they've ever produced. If I fired behind your back you wouldn't even know about it."

She quickly pointed the gun at Halder, squeezed the trigger. There was a barely audible sound, like a tiny cough, and a slug whispered past Halder's ear, embedded itself in the plasterwork behind. She fired again, deliberately to the right this time, hitting one of the Nubian death masks on the wall, a clean shot between the eyes.

"I'm impressed," Halder said, glancing at the result. "So, I lead you in through the passageway and you take your chances?"

"Is there any other option?"

"You could always forget about the whole damned thing."

She looked at him solemnly, shook her head. "I can't do that, Jack. And now you know the reasons why."

"You can't really believe in all that Nazi nonsense? The thousand-year Reich, one people, one Führer?"

She hesitated, and a shadow crossed her face, emotion welling in the corners of her eyes.

"What I believe in is really of no consequence. Except I have a family rotting in the Gestapo's cellars, and I really don't want them to die there. And a country that's being bombed to ruins night and day. If it doesn't stop soon, there'll be nothing left for anyone, nothing fit for decent people."

"You poor, stupid fool. Don't you see? It may be a deadly game we're playing here, but it's still only a game. Nothing you do will make the slightest bit of difference. The Allies will still win the war."

Rachel didn't reply, and as Weaver sat there, ashen-faced, listening to it all, totally puzzled, he looked at Halder. "You mentioned a passageway," he said hoarsely. "What did you mean?"

"I'm afraid you're way behind in the game, Harry. There's a fatal weakness in your President's defences."

Halder explained about the tunnel, and Weaver couldn't control his anger as he stared at Rachel, his voice full of emotion, almost savage. "Killing Roosevelt isn't going to end this war, it's only going to make it worse. There's not an American soldier alive who wouldn't feel outraged and want revenge. They'd want to see Germany on its knees. And they'd keep on fighting for as long as it took, and they'd never give up. Not till hell freezes over."

"All of which changes nothing, Harry, I'm afraid," Rachel said to him. "I still have a mission to complete. As for you and your friend, you won't be harmed, not so long as you do as you're told. You'll be tied up and left somewhere where you'll be in no danger of being discovered, until long after this is over. And now, Jack, I really think it's time we left. Harry may be bluffing, but if he's not, we might have company soon."

"There's one slight problem."

"What?"

"I'm not going with you."

Rachel levelled the gun. Halder said with resignation, his face very calm, "Shoot me if you have to, but the answer's still no. It stops here. I've had my bellyful of death and destruction. I've played my part and come to the end of the tracks."

"What about your son?"

Halder struggled to contain his emotions. "I think I accepted I'd never see Pauli again the moment I agreed to go along with this insanity. And the answer's still the same."

There was a frightening look of pain on his face as he stared levelly at Rachel Stern. Finally, she said in defeat, "Very well, Jack. Have it your way."

The door opened and Deacon came back, Kleist behind him. "The signal's been acknowledged."

"And the woman?"

"In the cellar, tied securely," Kleist answered. He carried Helen Kane's uniform on his arm. "I thought this might come in useful."

To Weaver's horror, he held up her ID, grinning broadly. "And you'll never believe what I found in her pocket. A special pass for the compound."

As Rachel studied the pass, Deacon eagerly crossed the room, tugged at Weaver's tunic pocket, and removed his ID wallet. "They're both carrying special passes. It seems Lady Luck might be on our side after all."

Weaver was totally dismayed. Halder said to Deacon, "So, you knew the truth of it all along."

"Kleist too, obviously. A sad state of affairs when one

German can't completely trust another, but there you have it, Major."

"Don't you think there's been enough killing, Deacon? The war's over for Germany, even the dogs in the bazaar know that. You'll be wasting your lives continuing with this."

Deacon ignored him, turned to Rachel. "Are we ready?"

"I'm afraid the major's not coming. It's just you and me."

Deacon scowled, nodded at the gun in her hand. "Can't you change his mind?"

"It's pointless. We'll have to take our chances alone."

Deacon regarded Halder with contempt. "Such a pity you chose to be a traitor. You've probably missed your chance to be part of history." He looked back at Rachel. "What do you want me to do with him?"

"He still gets on the plane. Even if we don't."

Deacon didn't argue. "Very well. And the other one?"

She gave Weaver a lingering look. "You'll have to keep him and the woman safely out of the way until long after we've gone."

Kleist had a bloodthirsty glint in his eyes. "Better to kill them all, here and now."

She turned on him, fiercely. "None of them are to be harmed, that's an order. You'll do as I say." She handed him the M_3 machine-pistol. "Take this. Use it—but only if you have to. And I mean that, Kleist."

Kleist tucked his pistol into his waistband and took the machine-pistol sullenly, as Rachel shot Weaver and Halder a meaningful look. "I just hope you'll both take the chance I've offered you. Play it correctly, and you'll live."

Deacon said, "Seeing as the major's deserted us, I suggest we take the motorcycle—it'll be faster. A straight run across the desert to the village of Nazlat as-Saman, like you did earlier."

Weaver looked at Rachel with sudden vehemence. "You'll never get near Roosevelt. You'll be dead before you get ten paces across the lawns."

There was a strange look on her face, unfathomable pain or remorse, and for a moment her eyes softened. "I'm afraid I've crossed the river on this one, Harry, and it's far too late to turn back. So if you don't see me again, think of me sometimes." She looked at Halder. "You too, Jack. Or is that too much to ask?"

There was a long silence. Neither of them replied, and she turned briskly to Deacon, as if she couldn't bear to see their accusing stares a second longer. "Let's go."

She left the room, and as Deacon made to follow her out, he said to Kleist, "Take the boat south as far as Memphis with Hassan, and go by foot to the landing area." He checked his watch. "Give us until oh three thirty hours at the latest, the time Captain Rahman's aircraft is scheduled to land."

"And if you don't show by then?"

"You leave without us," Deacon answered grimly. "You heard what to do about Weaver and his lady friend. The same with Halder."

"Don't worry, they're in safe hands."

Deacon shot a pointed glance at Kleist, and lowered his voice. "I hope not. Personally, I think the woman's making a grave mistake letting them live. A bad case of sentiment, I'm sure."

Kleist grinned at him, cradled the machine-pistol in his arms. "You'd have given different orders?"

"Wouldn't you?"

SIXTY-NINE

1:40 A.M.

In the Presidential Suite of the Mena House, Agent Jim Griffith heard the telephone jangle like an alarm bell.

He jolted, came wide awake. He'd been resting on one of the couches in the suite's reception room, and when he reached for the phone he saw his shift leader, Howie Anderson, stretch his arms as he lounged in the chair opposite. "*Jeez*, ain't there no rest for the wicked?"

"Not if they happen to work for the Secret Service." Griffith smiled, and spoke into the receiver. "Watch number one. Griffith."

He listened, then said, "Yes, sir, got it," and replaced

the receiver, as Anderson yawned and looked at his wrist-watch. "What's up?"

"Two visitors on their way from the lobby. Ambassador Kirk and General George Clayton. They want to see the Chief."

"At this hour?" Anderson rubbed his eyes, already knew that both men's names were on the special visitor list, and that they would have been cleared by the outer perimeter, but he checked the clipboard just the same. "Must be darned important. You want to wake him?"

"Sure." Griffith was about to move towards the short corridor that led to the President's bedroom when the knock came from the guard outside.

"Seems like the Chief's guests are in one hell of a hurry," remarked Anderson, and he picked up the Thompson submachine-gun lying propped beside the door, readying the drum magazine in the crook of his arm. "They must have taken the stairs five at a time."

Griffith kept his hand on the butt of his holstered Smith and Wesson .38, crossed the room, knocked back, and asked the guard outside for the password. When he received it, he opened the door, Anderson already a couple of steps behind, covering him with the Thompson.

Ambassador Alex Kirk and General George Clayton stood impatiently in the corridor. Griffith scrutinised their security passes. "The President," said Kirk bluntly.

"He's still asleep, sir."

"Then wake him. Quickly."

MAISON FLEUVE
1:40 A.M.

Hassan came back, and they heard the motorcycle start up outside. Kleist still had the M_3 in his hands, a gloating look on his face. "So, you finally got to know the truth, Halder? Though I'm hardly surprised you turned out to be a cowardly traitor. Well, what have you got to say for yourself?"

"Whatever it is, you'd never listen, so go to hell."

Kleist quickly crossed the room, hatred burning like coal in his eyes, and grabbed Halder tightly by the hair. "You and your Prussian kind make me sick. Arrogant, the lot of you. I asked you a question."

Halder ignored him, said to Weaver, "You're looking at the animal responsible for murdering those two officers in cold blood at the crash site. As well as butchering a couple of Egyptian policemen."

The SS man grinned, stared into his face. "You haven't got the stomach for war, Halder. How they ever put a coward like you in uniform is beyond me."

"You always were a thoroughgoing bastard, Kleist. I should have shot you when I had the chance."

Kleist struck him savagely across the face with the butt of the machine-pistol, and Halder reeled back, blood on his lips.

"A little foretaste of what's to come, the down payment on an old score." Kleist's face split into a tight grin. "And I must say, I'm going to enjoy settling the rest of it."

Outside, they heard the motorcycle rev up and drive away. Kleist looked at Halder maliciously. "If you think I'm taking you back on the plane, you've got another think coming. Even if those two manage to finish the business, something tells me they'll never get out alive. Which means you're dead."

His boot came up, lashed into Halder's groin, and he crumpled to the floor. Weaver moved to help him up, but Kleist shoved the machine-pistol in his face. "Don't tempt me, American. Besides, I believe someone else has a bone to pick."

Hassan stepped forward. The curved knife appeared in his hand, and there was a look of intense pleasure in his eyes. "The evil day has finally arrived. Get ready to say your prayers."

Kleist put a hand on his arm. "Not here. I've something much more interesting in mind. Fetch the woman and get her on to the boat, quickly." He touched the barrel of the M_3 to Halder's forehead, smirked. "We'll give the Nile crocodiles something to chew over, and get rid of the major and his friends on the river."

1:45 A.M.

Neumann had made excellent time, much better than he had anticipated, the strong south-easterly winds at their backs all the way. They were at five thousand metres, and there was very little cloud. The second Dakota had moved slightly ahead of them, taking the lead, and they could make out its faint outline no more than a mile away. In the darkened cockpit, lit only by the dim glow of the instrument panel and the pale moonlight, Skorzeny was getting impatient.

"How much longer?"

"If the winds stay in our favour, no more than fifteen minutes to the Egyptian coast. Less than an hour to our target airfield—assuming, that is, we don't come across any enemy aircraft that may have other ideas." Neumann glanced round. "This business of keeping our altitude extremely low approaching Cairo, it's going to be damned tricky, you know?"

Skorzeny put a hand on his shoulder, grinned. "Neumann, I have every faith in you."

At that precise moment, they were startled by a sudden blaze of tracer fire arcing through the night sky, its target the Dakota ahead of them. From nowhere, two Tomahawk fighters with RAF markings rocketed out of the darkness from the east, cannons blazing.

"Christ!" muttered Neumann. "We've got company."

Instinctively, he pulled up sharply, and the Dakota in front tried to do the same, as one of the Tomahawks attacked its port side with withering cannon fire. The Dakota took a hit, the port wing almost disintegrating in the hail of lead, and the aircraft exploded like a massive firework, its flaming debris plunging towards the sea.

"*Oh my God*. The poor bastards!"

"For Christ's sake, Neumann, get us out of here," Skorzeny roared above the engine noise.

"It's pointless," Neumann answered frantically. "The Tomahawks have us for speed."

"Do something, man!" Skorzeny screamed.

Neumann pushed the column hard forward, and the Dakota nosed down sharply, speeding towards the sea below at a frightening rate of knots. Sweat on his face, Neumann said, "Better hold tight, Colonel. We're in for a rough ride."

MENA HOUSE
1:45 A.M.

The suite had a small lounge area for guests, complete with a couple of leather couches and a coffee table, the white-painted walls adorned with Arab prints and wood carvings. As the ambassador and the general waited anxiously, Griffith wheeled in Roosevelt. He wore a dressing gown, his silver hair was tousled, and he looked the worse for having been woken. But there was no sign of bad temper, just a wry smile. "I'm hoping you gentlemen have a good reason for this. You know how an old man like me needs his sleep."

"We have, sir," Kirk answered, and told him the news.

"So," Roosevelt said flatly, no triumph in his voice. "It's over. Berlin tried and failed."

"I'm afraid it's not completely over yet, Mr. President," Clayton explained. "Three of the Germans escaped and they're on the run. But they haven't a chance in hell of getting anywhere near the hotel. Not that it's likely they'll try and continue with their mission with a posse after them, every barracks alerted, and a ring of steel around the compound, but we're doubling the patrols to make absolutely certain."

"That's reassuring to hear, General. I guess if over a thousand troops can't protect me, no one can."

"There's really no threat, sir. We've put every available fighter aircraft we've got in North Africa on alert, and air patrols are scouring the skies as we speak. The extra measures are purely a precaution. I'm pretty confident we'll have those Krauts rounded up pretty soon."

"But no doubt there were casualties?"

"Half a dozen troops wounded, and six dead, so far as we know. Two of our own men, and four others. It could have been a lot worse."

Roosevelt sighed heavily. "The sooner this damned war is over, the better." He glanced at his watch. "I guess there's nothing more to be said. Except I owe you and your men a debt of gratitude, General."

Clayton saluted. "I can assure you you're in safe hands, Mr. President."

"Of that, I've no doubt. And now, I'd better let you both get back to whatever it is you have to do. Gentlemen, I'll bid you good morning."

1:49 A.M.

In the Dakota, the tension was frightening. Neumann kept the column pushed hard forward as they continued their rapid descent. He hadn't the faintest belief that he could shake off the high-speed Tomahawks, and knew with certainty that it was all over, nothing but primitive animal instinct keeping him in there, fighting against the odds.

Although he couldn't see the Tomahawks behind him, their tracer fire streaked past on the left and right as the attacking aircraft followed him down all the way, the Dakota jolting fiercely with the mounting speed, the vibrations unbearable, the engines screaming in protest.

Neumann shot a glance at his altimeter; the hands were spinning down fast, the Dakota plunging headlong towards the sea, and he could barely read the instrument with the vibration.

A thousand metres.

"We'd better pull up soon, sir!" the co-pilot shouted anxiously. "We won't be able to break out of our dive!"

"Wait!" screamed Neumann.

Eight hundred.

Five hundred.

"Sir! We'll never make it!"

The Tomahawks were still on his tail, tracers hurtling past, raking into the sea directly ahead of him. Neumann chose his moment and pulled back hard on the column and the Dakota lifted, sluggishly at first, then swooping up, just barely clearing the water. He was hoping that one or both Tomahawks, faster machines, wouldn't be able to pull up in time and would crash into the sea, but he was out of luck, because within seconds of levelling out the tracers started hammering at him again. "I'm afraid that's it," he said to Skorzeny in defeat. "We're finished."

"More enemy aircraft, sir! Dead ahead!" the co-pilot interrupted.

Neumann felt his stomach sink. Sure enough, the dark figures of three aircraft were hurtling towards them, coming in low over the sea. Their cannons erupted, spewing flame, and Neumann instinctively moved to shield his face.

"They're ours!" the co-pilot screamed with joy. "109s!"

Neumann looked again. They were Messerschmitt 109s

all right, and they weren't firing at him, but at the Tomahawks. The 109s shot past, one above him, and one each to port and starboard. They'd make short work of the Tomahawks, of that Neumann was certain. "Thank Christ for that," he breathed. "It was a close thing—I'm still bloody shaking."

Before he could even bank to glimpse the dogfight, another two 109s appeared either side of him. He glimpsed the pilot on his port side giving him a series of hand signals.

"What does he want?" Skorzeny asked.

"To talk on the radio." Neumann tuned in, found the frequency, listened, then said to Skorzeny, "The mission's aborted. We're to follow him back to Crete."

"What?"

"Orders from Berlin. And I have no objection to that."

"Let me talk to him."

Neumann handed Skorzeny the headphones and neck microphone. The colonel slipped them on, made contact with the 109 pilot, and barked, "Repeat your orders."

He listened, his face twisting with disgust, then tore off the headset and mike and tossed them back at Neumann. "Damn it. Damn it to hell!"

Neumann glanced back. "You don't look too happy to be alive, Colonel."

"You don't understand. It's a catastrophe."

"True. Our men in the other aircraft—"

"I didn't mean that." Skorzeny was utterly depressed. "I meant the damned mission. Aborting could lose us the war."

"It's that bad?"

"You've absolutely no idea, Neumann."

GIZA
2:15 A.M.

Ali liked being a policeman. The pay was miserly but the work had advantages. Not least of all a good dinner at the station house each day, a free uniform, and the envious respect of his friends. Best of all was the opportunity to make a little baksheesh.

He had a fifty-piastre note tucked into his pocket, not as much as the sergeant, because the greedy son of a flea-ridden whore had pocketed most of the money the American professor had given him, but at least Ali had got a share. The sergeant was gone now, slipped off home to lie with his grumbling wife, leaving Ali alone to guard the barrier.

Half asleep, looking up at the stars as he lay on a rush mat he'd placed on one of the boulders near the sentry box, his rifle propped at his elbow, he heard the sound of an engine approaching. He yawned, scratched himself as he rose lazily, then picked up his rifle and dusted his uniform. He wondered who it could be at such an hour.

Some nights, Allied soldiers brought women out from the city in taxis or horse-drawn gharries, begged Ali to let them visit the tombs and pyramids by moonlight, and for a little baksheesh he would always oblige. He licked his lips in anticipation as the vehicle approached up the incline. With luck, he might be able to add to his fifty piastres. In the moonlit darkness, he could make out a motorcycle, two people on board. As it came closer he flicked on his torch, frowned as he recognised the faces of the man and woman from the professor's car earlier in the evening.

Ali relaxed his grip on the rifle as the motorcycle halted and the couple climbed off. It was well after midnight. What did they want this time? He bowed his head politely. "Effendi, madam."

"You remember us?" Deacon said in perfect Arabic.

"Of course."

"There's a problem," Deacon went on. "We left something at the excavation site and have to return. I need to speak to your sergeant."

"The sergeant is not here, effendi."

"Then where is he?"

Ali hesitated. The sergeant was asleep in his bed when he should have been on duty, but to tell the truth would have been unthinkable, so he simply said, "He's away on important police business, and will return by sunrise."

Deacon nodded, understanding. "So, you're alone here?"

"Alas, effendi, I am the only person on duty." Ali grinned, the grin he always used when the smell of baksheesh was in the air. He rubbed his forefinger and thumb together in the universal gesture, so the man would notice.

"Perhaps it might be possible for you to return to the site."

Deacon smiled back, made to reach inside his jacket for his wallet. "Of course."

Ali hadn't been watching the woman, which was his mistake. For some reason, she had gone over to search among the boulders off to one side of the barrier, and when she came back she nodded to her companion. "He's telling the truth. The sergeant's not here."

Ali frowned in puzzlement, knowing something wasn't right, and as he turned back the man brought out his hand, not with a wallet, but with a pistol. The metal smashed hard against the side of Ali's skull, there was a ringing pain that made him want to vomit, and a blanket of darkness smothered him.

SEVENTY

MAISON FLEUVE
23 NOVEMBER /1:35 A.M.
Sanson squinted through the binoculars. With only one good eye, he could barely see the villa in the silvery darkness.

"No wonder we couldn't find Halder and the woman after they fled Rashid—this is probably where they've been hiding out. And I'll make a bet it's where Deacon's been making his radio transmissions from too."

"Sir?"

Sanson put down the binoculars, looked back at the major. "Another part of the story. Remind me to tell you some time."

They had halted on the private road leading up to the villa, left the Jeep and truck-load of troops behind them, and walked ahead in the darkness—Sanson, the major, and one of the men—until they came to a small rise, within a hundred and fifty yards of the property. Without the binoculars this time, Sanson peered towards the whitewashed villa, the walled gardens dotted with palm trees. He saw no lights on and the windows were shuttered, but he thought he'd noticed what looked like the end of a private pier, jutting into the Nile from the back of the property.

"You'd better send half a dozen men down to the water to try and secure the rear. It's likely Deacon and his friends have a boat. I don't want anyone getting away. These people *have* to be caught, dead or alive."

The major didn't reply, but squinted ahead into the darkness, and Sanson said, "What's the matter?"

"There's a vehicle parked just forward, to the right of the track. If I'm not mistaken, it looks like a staff car."

The major pointed. Sanson saw the shadowy outline of a staff Humber, drew his pistol. "Let's have a look."

When they approached the Humber it was empty, the front doors ajar, the keys still in the ignition. The major shone a torch as Sanson looked inside. He caught sight of the hacksawed remains of a pair of handcuffs discarded on the passenger floor, and his mouth tightened in fury. "*Weaver.* I might have bloody known."

Suddenly, from the direction of the villa, they heard the rasp of an engine starting up, and Sanson cocked an ear. "What was that?"

"It sounded like a motorcycle, sir."

Sanson heard the engine rev and fade. "The bastards may be on the move. Signal the men at once. We're going in."

1:40 A.M.

In the cellar, Helen Kane struggled with the ropes. Perspiration ran down her slip. Her wrists were tied painfully tight, and it was impossible to free herself. A crack of moonlight seeped through a metal door at the far end of the cellar, barely enough to see by. She heard something move in the semi-darkness, and recoiled in horror as a rat scurried past her legs.

She tried to move the chair, with great effort managed to shift it round, almost toppling over in the process. She looked over at the racks of wine bottles. If she could only manage to break one of the bottles, she might be able to use the glass to cut the ropes. She inched forward, grating her heels against the stone floor, every tiny movement an effort. She reached the nearest rack, tilted her head forward, and tried to nudge out a cob-webbed bottle with her mouth.

It moved an inch, but no more. She tried again. This time the bottle moved out a little further.

She brushed it with her cheek, teased it out. The bottle crashed to the stone floor, splashing liquid, glass shards splintering everywhere. She inched back, tilted the chair, and crashed to the floor, landing painfully on some glass chips, grazing her arm and shoulder in the process.

She muffled her cry, but at that precise moment the cellar door opened and Hassan stood in the doorway with the lamp. He scowled dangerously and was down the steps in an instant. "Bitch!" he roared, and slapped her hard across the face, grabbed her by the hair and dragged her upstairs.

1:42 A.M.

As Kleist ushered Weaver and Halder towards the French windows at gunpoint, they all heard the roar of engines outside, followed by the screech of tyres.

Hassan pushed Helen Kane roughly into the room and moved quickly to the window, peered through a crack in the shutters. "We've got company—soldiers, many of them."

"Scheisse!" Kleist pushed Helen Kane over to join Halder and Weaver. "Cover them," he told Hassan, and crossed to the nearest window, the M_3 at the ready. He peered through the shutter, and in the darkness outside saw a uniformed officer, a patch over one eye, his pistol drawn as he rushed through the open gate. Before Kleist had a chance to open the shutters and fire the machine-pistol, the man darted into the blackness of the garden and vanished, soldiers jumping down from a truck as it drew up outside the villa's walls.

Orders were being screamed in the darkness, and suddenly there was the sound of wood splintering out in the hallway, someone trying to force the front door. Kleist turned frantically to Hassan. "Get down to the cellar. Quickly!"

Hassan glared at Weaver and the others. "What about them?"

"Leave it to me." As Hassan moved off towards the door, Kleist swung the M_3 round. "This is where it ends for you and your friends, Halder. No time for prayers, I'm afraid." He laughed like a madman and brought up the machine-pistol, his finger tightening on the trigger.

There was a click, and nothing happened. The laughter died in Kleist's throat and his face sagged, but in one fluid movement he recocked the weapon, ejected an unspent cartridge on to the floor, and squeezed the trigger again.

Click.

"You're right," Halder said. "This is where it ends." He lunged forward, his fist smashing hard into Kleist's jaw, sending the SS man reeling back. At the door, Hassan was already reacting, turning as he moved to bring up his pistol, but Halder was quicker. He yanked the pistol from Kleist's trouser belt, firing as he rolled on to the floor, hitting the Arab in the chest, sending him flying backwards, another shot catching him in the throat, the pistol flying from his grasp, his body reeling in an obscene dance of death.

As a dazed Kleist made to scramble to his feet and reach for Hassan's weapon, Weaver got to it first, shot him twice in the chest, punching the SS man back, then fired again, hitting him in the head.

"You did better than I expected, old friend." Halder bent to pick up the M₃. "Either the gods are smiling on us, or Kleist was one unlucky bastard—two dud cartridges one after another almost beggars belief." He drew back the bolt of the machine-pistol, examined it, raised an eye. "Looks like I'm wrong on both counts. The firing pin's been tampered with. Very thoughtful of someone."

Weaver turned white. "Rachel?"

"It's a distinct possibility, considering she deliberately gave Kleist the weapon." A look like remorse crossed his face. "So, she's redeemed herself, at least on our account. And maybe that says something. But I'm quite sure your President's another matter."

From the hallway came further sounds of splintering wood, and they could hear the clatter of boots out beyond the French windows, troops moving round the back. A heavy burst of fire splintered one of the wooden shutters, and lead ripped in through the windows, shattering glass.

"Down!" roared Weaver. He grabbed Helen Kane and the three of them dropped to the floor.

As Halder lay there, he looked at Weaver. "Your friends

will be on top of us any second. The bar on the front door isn't going to hold out for ever. Well, what's it to be, Harry? Surrender? Or do we try to put the brakes on this before it's too late?"

"What do you mean?"

"Me, I'm a dead man walking. But Rachel might be a different matter. I'd hate to stake my life on it, but when you consider why she's doing this, I'd like to think a military court might at least spare her the noose. That's assuming we can stop her in time. If we can somehow make it out to Giza, we just might stand a chance. It's your decision."

"You mind telling me how we're supposed to get out of here?"

"If we reach the hall, there's a way out through the cellar, and a boat waiting for us on the river."

"And after that?"

"For now, let's just worry about getting out alive. Well?"

Another burst of fire stitched across the shutters, chunks of wall masonry exploding, splinters of wood flying into the room. Weaver nodded. "Let's go."

1:43 A.M.
Sanson was enraged. He kicked savagely at the front door again, and in frustration fired another two rounds into the lock, then heaved against it with his shoulder, but it still wouldn't budge.

"Give me a grenade," he said to the private nearest him. The man handed him a grenade from his pouch.

"Stand back." Sanson placed it against the bottom of the door, ordered the men to move for cover, pulled the pin, and flattened himself against the side wall. The explosion came seconds later, a tremendous crump that blew the door off its hinges.

1:45 A.M.
Sanson stood in the middle of the room, surveying the carnage. The Arab's body lay on the floor, and another corpse sprawled in a corner, blood still pumping from two bullet wounds to his chest and another through the head.

The major rushed into the room. "There's no sign of anyone alive. Upstairs or down."

"You're *sure* the men didn't see anyone escape on the river?" Sanson asked, livid.

"No, sir. We didn't hear an engine, and there's a motorboat still out there. I don't see how anyone could have got away. Unless they left on the motorcycle we heard earlier?"

"Have the men *thoroughly* search outside."

"They're already doing that, sir." The major nodded towards Kleist's body. "One of the Germans?"

"If it is, it's not Halder. Check every room again. Go through them with a fine-tooth comb—every closet and nook and cranny, upstairs and down. And see if there's a cellar."

1:45 A.M.

They had heard the grenade explosion as they hurried down the darkened cellar steps. Halder pulled open the metal door at the end of the room and a draught of fresh warm air greeted them, moonlight washing in. The boat was still there, nestled among the reeds, and he pulled off the tarpaulin. "We'll use the oars. The engine noise will only give us away. And we'd better try to stay among the reeds—we might be spotted if we move out on to open water." He looked back grimly at Weaver. "It might be wiser if the lady remained and tried to surrender. No sense in risking her life if we're fired on out on the river." Before Helen Kane could say a word, Halder took her hand, brushed it with a kiss. "You've been a very brave woman, Helen. Another time, and different circumstances, and I'm sure it could have been a pleasure to get to know you. But forgive me. Harry and I have serious work to do. I'm sure he'll explain."

Weaver quickly told her, explaining what had to be done. "Try and stall Sanson until we get away, then tell him to get in touch with the Mena as fast as he can, and let them know what's been happening. And make sure he knows about Deacon's aircraft pick-up near Sakkara. Think you can manage that?"

"If you say so."

"Give us a couple of minutes, then scream your head off. Let them know whose side you're on, in case anyone comes down the cellar stairs shooting first before they ask questions."

Halder was already in the boat, and as Weaver moved to join him, she touched his arm. "The car—it might still be where we parked, if you can get to it. And for God's sake, watch yourself, Harry."

Weaver saw the genuine concern on her face, kissed her on the cheek. "You're a wonderful woman, you know that?"

"Or just a damned silly fool."

"Let's move," Halder said urgently.

Weaver climbed into the boat, and Halder sank the oar into the water and pushed them out through the reeds.

1:48 A.M.

Sanson was still fuming as he paced one of the bedrooms upstairs, supervising the search, when he heard a scream from somewhere downstairs, then a sudden commotion. He raced down the stairs just as two soldiers came up out of the cellar, Helen Kane between them. Her uniform was gone, and she stood there in her slip, hugging herself.

Sanson looked astounded. "Helen—!"

"We found the lady in the cellar, sir," one of the soldiers said.

Sanson was red-faced, tried to compose himself as he stared at her. "What the devil are you doing here? Where's Weaver? Where's Halder and the woman?"

"You've got to listen to me. There's no time to lose."

1:51 A.M.

Less than a hundred metres along the river, Halder eased the boat through the reeds and pushed it into the bank. They stepped out into the darkness, climbed up through the reeds, and Weaver led the way towards the private track. They saw the staff Humber still parked there, scurried towards it and climbed in. "You really think this thing can make it across rough desert?" Halder asked doubtfully.

"We'll have to try."

"With the head start that Deacon's got, let's hope it's not a wasted trip."

Weaver hit the ignition, and it started first time. "You still haven't told me how you got yourself into this mess."

"Unless you want a dead President, just drive like hell, Harry. Time enough to explain on the way."

Suddenly, up ahead, they saw troops pile out of the villa and climb back into the Jeep and truck, engines roaring to life. "It looks like Sanson got the message. Let's see if we can beat him to it." Weaver yanked the steering wheel round, hit the accelerator, the wheels kicked up dust, and they sped towards the desert track that led to Nazlat as-Saman.

GIZA
2:30 A.M.

Deacon led the way through the passageway, holding up one of the storm lamps they had left in the tomb recess. When they came to the end and saw the boulder, he put down the lamp, looked back at Rachel Stern. "You'd better change into that uniform. Meanwhile, I'll see how the land lies."

He climbed up on to the rock, struggled up through the shaft, and five minutes later came back down again and slid from the boulder. "There're a couple of sentries about a hundred metres away, but they're on the move, so they'll pass soon enough and then it should be safe for you to go up." There was a fanatical glint in his eyes, his voice almost hoarse with excitement. "Well, the moment of truth's arrived. Are you ready to do your duty, Fraulein Stern?"

She had already changed into Helen Kane's uniform, and looked back at him grimly, her face strained, marble-white. "Is that what you call it?"

"What else?" Deacon clapped a hand firmly on her shoulder, his expression uncompromising. "From this moment on, the future of the Reich depends on your success. Don't let the Führer down. And if you make it back, I can promise you a night to remember in Berlin—champagne and roses all the way. Good luck."

Deacon looked as if he were about to stretch out his arm and give her the Nazi salute, but she pushed his hand from her shoulder, before tucking the silenced Luger inside her tunic. "Forget the Nazi sentiment, Deacon. It's not why I'm doing this."

Deacon raised an eyebrow, grinned. "Motives don't interest me, *liebchen*, so long as you do what needs to be done. And let's just hope that traitor Halder told me the truth about the location of Roosevelt's room. Now, you'd better move."

He gave her a hand on to the boulder, and she climbed up, before disappearing through the shaft.

Moments later, Deacon stepped well back into the passageway, dimmed the lamp to a faint glow, and the light in the tunnel faded to a ghostly semi-darkness. He lit a cigar from the tiny flame to steady his nerves, blew out a puff of smoke. "You poor bitch," he whispered softly to himself. "Whatever your chances of pulling this off, I'll bet you haven't a hope of making it back alive."

SEVENTY-ONE

MENA HOUSE
23 NOVEMBER /1:55 A.M.
"Move me over to the window, son. I'd like to see them again."

"Yes, sir."

Griffith wheeled Roosevelt to the bedroom's French windows and pulled back the hinged mosquito screen. A large covered patio with terra-cotta tiles lay outside, scattered with earthenware flowerpots, some cane tables and chairs. In the gardens one floor below, armed sentries paced the darkened lawns. Several hundred yards away the massive shapes of the pyramids loomed, almost obliterating the night sky. It was a truly awesome scene, and Roosevelt marvelled at the view from his private room.

"Quite a sight, isn't it, Jim?"

The President nearly always called his personal bodyguards by their first names, a familiarity that charmed them. Duty aside, Griffith knew with certainty there wasn't a guy on the roster who wouldn't lay down his life for the man, including himself and Howie Anderson, whom he'd left back in the lounge, flicking through some magazines to pass the time, now that the ambassador and general had gone. "Yes, sir. It sure is."

"You know, all this excitement isn't good for an old man. One of the Seven Wonders of the World right on my doorstep, *and* a team of German commandos hell-bent on trying to kill me. I guess you might say it's been an interesting trip."

Griffith smiled. "I guess you're right, sir. But let's be grateful the general's pretty much wrapped up those Germans. Are you ready to go back to bed, Mr. President?"

Roosevelt had looked restless since he'd been woken, the heat in the room unbearable. There was a ceiling fan overhead, but it made little difference. "While I'm up, I've a mind to have a look at some paperwork. Bring me my briefcase, will you, Jim?"

"Whatever you say, Mr. President."

Griffith pulled the wheelchair back from the window, put the mosquito screen back in place, then fetched the briefcase. He knew from experience that whenever Roosevelt woke in the middle of the night, it could be hours before the man went back to sleep. "Will there be anything else, sir?"

"I guess that'll be all."

"Yes, sir." Griffith moved towards the bedroom door to let himself out, out of habit made one final check, glanced back. "You're sure you'll be OK, Mr. President?"

"Just fine." Roosevelt nodded at the metal bell he always kept by his bedside. "But if I need anything I'll ring." Suddenly a thoughtful look appeared on his face as he made to open the briefcase. He sighed, adjusted the glasses on his nose, and his expression sagged, hinting at some private torment. "You know, it all seems such a waste. A terrible, futile waste."

"Sir?"

"Those casualties—Germans included. It pains me deeply, the loss of more fine young lives, and all in vain."

"I guess that's the price of war, Mr. President."

"And what a high price it is, son."

2:15 A.M.

Weaver kept his foot hard on the accelerator, the Humber's engine straining, kicking up a formidable plume of dust as they sped along the desert track, the suspension taking an almighty hammering. "Another five minutes and we should make Nazlat as-Saman."

"You mean assuming this crate doesn't blow a track or a gasket."

Weaver tried to concentrate on the track ahead, the blue-painted headlights barely illuminating the way. "From what you told me, your friend Schellenberg sounds like a conniving bastard."

"It's just a game to him, Harry. People's lives don't figure at all."

"What happened to your father and son—I'm really sorry, Jack."

Halder barely nodded in reply, his face grim with remorse, before he peered back through the rear window. It was impossible to see through the dust cloud behind them, as the Humber bumped and skidded along at over fifty miles an hour. He opened the passenger door, made to step out. "Try not to hit any bumps. I don't want you to lose me."

"What?"

"I need to see if we've got company." He kept a foot on the running board, held on to the open door and leaned out as far as he could. Back through the dust haze, he could make out a pair of blue headlights in the near distance. He pulled himself back into the cab, shut the door.

"We've got company. Your friend Sanson, no doubt, and he's hot on our heels, about a mile back, I'd say."

"You'd better hold on. This is where it starts to get interesting." Weaver pushed his foot hard to the floor, giving it everything. The wheels skidded, gripped, and the Humber's engine snarled like an enraged animal.

2:16 A.M.

"I think I see them."

Sanson had on a pair of sand goggles as he stood upright in the passenger seat, gripping the Jeep's dust shield as they bumped over the rock-strewn ground. The desert was a ghostly silver-grey under the quarter-moon, but about a mile ahead he could distinguish a ferocious plume of dust.

"I'd say it's definitely a vehicle, sir," the major said from the back, squinting through his sand goggles.

"Too bloody right it is," Sanson answered. "And you can bet it's Weaver and Halder."

"I just hope Lieutenant Kane gets the message through to the hotel in time."

Sanson sat down in the Jeep, his face covered in sweat. He'd sent Helen Kane and the rest of the men back towards Cairo in the truck to search for a telephone. "If she doesn't, I've got a feeling we can whistle goodbye to a victory parade through the streets of Berlin." He slapped the driver on the shoulder. "Get that foot down hard, man!"

2:17 A.M.

She lay in the hollow in the ground, aware of the intense pounding in her chest, her palms wet with perspiration. She saw the two sentries pass fifty metres away, and when they had gone, she dusted her uniform and stood, moved out from the bushes, and started to walk towards the hotel building.

She had barely gone twenty paces when she saw another two GI sentries on patrol, their MI carbines slung over their shoulders. She started to reach for the Luger, but the men snapped off salutes as they went past. For a second she almost forgot she was wearing the lieutenant's uniform, and there was a moment of blind panic before she returned the salute.

One of the sentries noticed the reaction, stopped and came back. "Is everything all right, Lieutenant?"

"I—I just needed some air, Corporal. It's pretty hot inside the hotel. But thank you."

The corporal studied her suspiciously. When she looked down she saw a heavy patch of dust on her uniform. She brushed it away. The corporal frowned, as if seeking an explanation.

"I was feeling a little faint and had to sit down, I'm afraid. But I'm fine now."

The corporal noticed the green Intelligence Corps flash on her uniform sleeve, the moment of suspicion seemed to pass, and he saluted again. "You need any help, Lieutenant, or you want us to find you a doc, you let us know."

"That's very kind of you, Corporal. But I'll be OK."

The truck rattled along the narrow road, slowed as it came towards a private villa with high walls, and Helen Kane shouted, "Stop!"

The driver kept the engine running. She clambered out of the cab, and a sergeant armed with a Sten gun joined her. They approached a padlocked wrought-iron gate, a stone lily pond and some jacaranda and palm trees visible beyond in the gardens. The villa's shutters were closed, the place in darkness, looking totally deserted, but there was a bell-pull by the gate, and she tugged at it frantically, heard a hollow ring somewhere inside.

"It looks like there's no one at home, Lieutenant."

"There's *got* to be," Helen Kane answered. It was the second property they had tried in the last ten minutes, but she knew most of the big villas on the Giza side of the Nile were secluded weekend retreats for Cairo's wealthy, vacant during the week except for servants. At the first one they had tried, they had managed to rouse the elderly caretaker from his bed, but the confused man told them the villa hadn't got a telephone.

She tugged desperately at the bell again, and rattled the locked gates. The sergeant was busy scanning the garden, then peered away, down the road. "There isn't a telephone pole in sight, Lieutenant. I reckon they haven't got a line."

"But we simply *have* to find one." Helen looked frantically along the darkened road, made a decision instantly and moved back towards the truck. "There's a police station a couple of miles further on, towards the English Bridge. We'll have to try there."

Weaver drove into Nazlat as-Saman like a thunderbolt, the Humber bumping like mad through the rutted streets, the darkened village deserted, except for a couple of mangy dogs who darted for cover when they heard the roar of the engine. He sped up past the Sphinx towards the pyramids, and a hundred yards up the hill saw the red-and-white police barrier strung across the road.

He slammed on the brakes and Halder jumped out. "I'll move it."

As he raised the pole, he saw the policeman tied up in the sentry hut, unconscious, a gag around his mouth. He felt the man's pulse, then ran back to the car and climbed in as Weaver accelerated away. "Well?"

"They've been. The guard's out cold." Halder pointed up the hill towards the tomb ruins, sweat on his face. "Keep going, straight on up until I tell you to stop."

Sanson roared in through the village two minutes behind them. It was deathly quiet, no sign of Weaver's car. "Carry on up the hill," he ordered the driver frantically, and pointed up towards the road leading past the Sphinx.

When they reached the sentry box and the raised barrier, he told the driver to slow as they drove past. He saw the policeman, gagged and tied, then scanned among the shadows of the crumbling ruins and pyramids, looming at them out of the darkness, his frustration boiling. "Where the hell are they?"

"Shouldn't we be looking for this tunnel, sir?" the major asked.

"There isn't time, not now—the woman's got too much of a head start. And if our message hasn't got through we're already in trouble." Sanson drew his revolver, his eyes wild as he slapped the driver on the shoulder. "Drive straight to the hotel—as fast as you can bloody can. I want Rachel Stern dead as soon as she's spotted."

SEVENTY-TWO

GIZA
23 NOVEMBER / 2:18 A.M.

Weaver climbed out of the car, saw the motorcycle propped against one of the rocks near the tomb recess. Halder ignored it, led the way down towards the shaft opening. The tools he'd left earlier had been removed, lay scattered about. He lit one of the lamps, and when they had crawled down through the opening and entered the tomb area, for a split second Weaver marvelled at the splendid hieroglyphics, the undisturbed ancient stone coffin, but Halder was already kneeling in front of the rock shaft that led to the passageway. He wiped sweat from his face, ready to push himself through. "Be careful how you go. Deacon might be about."

2:20 A.M.

She waited until the sentries had moved away, then strolled towards the hotel. As she came on to the lawns at the side of the building, she noticed the anti-aircraft and machine-gun emplacements on the roof. Her eyes were instinctively drawn to a light in one of the rooms, one floor below the roof parapet.

A square terraced balcony with French windows jutted out from the room, protected by a safety railing. On the right-hand wall, a heavy wooden trellis clad with flowered creepers led up to the balcony, the entire area below it in shadow. The French windows appeared closed, but there was a light on beyond a gauze mosquito screen. She stood there for several moments, taking deep breaths, nausea in the pit of her stomach, then she moved towards the shadowed trellis, put a hand on the wood and tugged. It felt secure. She started to climb towards the balcony.

2:21 A.M.

Deacon was getting restless. He checked his watch again. Fifteen minutes had passed. He heard a noise behind him in the passageway, froze, then stepped back into a corner of the cave and quickly extinguished the lamp, his chest pounding.

To his horror, he saw a wash of light, shadows flickering on the walls. His fear and confusion mounted, and then Halder stepped through, followed by Weaver. He waited until Halder had climbed up on to the boulder, then stepped out, his pistol raised.

"I really don't think that would be wise, Major, unless you've changed your mind about being a traitor. Get down off the rock, very slowly. Both of you remove your firearms and toss them on the ground."

Weaver didn't move, but Halder slid off the boulder,

stood there fearlessly. "Shoot me, Deacon, and you'll give the game away to the guards above. But then I'm sure you thought of that. So on second thoughts, why don't you go ahead and pull the trigger?"

Deacon's brow glistened, and he nervously licked his lips. "Don't tempt me, Halder, or you'll be on your way to the undertakers."

"Then let's see if you've got the guts to do it." Halder stepped closer, and for just a brief second there was blind panic on Deacon's face, but it was long enough. Halder made a grab for the pistol and it exploded with an almighty bang, the shot ricocheting off the walls. Deacon struggled fiercely, but Halder punched him in the face, and Weaver stepped in, slammed the butt of the pistol into the back of Deacon's skull. He gave a muffled cry and slumped to the ground.

"Get his belt, Harry. Tie his wrists."

The gunshot seemed to go on for ever, before fading to a ghostly echo. Deacon was unconscious as Weaver quickly removed his belt and secured his hands behind his back.

"You took a risk—he could have killed you, Jack."

"It seems it's my day for playing hero—easy enough when you've nothing to lose. And I could have been wrong about the guards—the walls probably muffled the shot." Halder wiped away a gloss of sweat with his sleeve, nodded up towards the roof shaft.

"Ready?"

"As I'll ever be. I just hope Rachel hasn't already gone too far with this."

"We'll soon find out." Halder climbed up on to the boulder, offered Weaver his hand, and pulled him up.

2:24 A.M.

In the signals room of the Mena House, a telephone jangled. Private Sparky Johnson blinked, came awake with a yawn. He had his feet up, enjoying a short nap during his shift.

At that hour of the morning, the communications traffic was pretty thin. In front of him, the two radio transmitter-receivers and the array of six telephones on the table had been relatively quiet for the last hour. The duty captain was across the room, making the most of the lull, fast asleep and snoring, his head cradled in his arms on the desk.

A second telephone jangled.

Johnson picked up the first.

Out of the corner of his eye he saw the captain wake with a yawn. "Signals room, Mena compound," Johnson said into the mouthpiece.

The second phone kept ringing.

Johnson ignored it, listening to the first caller. He frowned deeply, swivelled round, beckoned the captain, saw him stand and hitch up his pants.

"Got it, sir!" Johnson replied smartly into the receiver, and without a moment's pause picked up the second phone and barked, "Signals room, Mena."

He listened again, and this time it seemed as if someone had slit his veins.

The captain came over, yawned. "A problem, Sparky?"

Johnson had a finger in the air, asking for silence as he listened to the caller, cold beads of sweat rising on his brow. "Yes, Lieutenant, I *sure* hear what you're saying—I sure do—but one moment, please." He covered the mouthpiece and looked up, frantic. "First call's from the front gate, sir. An intelligence officer named Sanson from GHQ just passed through, on his way to the President's suite. He's issued a security warning, wants the Secret Service detail alerted immediately."

The captain frowned. "What the hell for?"

Johnson thrust the receiver into the captain's face, desperately snatched up another phone and began to dial. "There's a frantic woman on the other line. Claims she's Lieutenant Kane, British Intelligence Corps. And *Jeez*, I think you'd better listen to what she's saying."

2:25 A.M.

She climbed to the top of the trellis, staying in the shadows, then slipped over the railing on to the tiled balcony. The light was still on beyond the mosquito screen, and when she peered into the room she saw the familiar figure of Roosevelt, alone, seated in a wheelchair, a pair of spectacles on as he read through some papers.

Her heart raced. She removed the silenced Luger from

her tunic and cocked it. Using her identity card, slipping it carefully into the crack between the French windows, she silently lifted the safety latch, and in an instant she had moved into the bedroom.

Roosevelt looked up, startled, the glasses almost falling from his face. He saw the young woman standing there threateningly, the silenced Luger in her hand. "Don't you think it's a little late for callers, Lieutenant?" he said casually.

He saw something in her face then, not fear, but a kind of self-loathing that was almost pitiful, just as she aimed the pistol at his head. "Sir, I truly regret having to do this."

Roosevelt looked into her eyes, held her stare, then his gaze shifted to the metal bell by the bedside. Too far to reach. There was just a frightening second of hesitation, then he looked back at the woman and said very calmly, "Madam, if you're going to shoot, I suggest you do it now."

2:25 A.M.

Griffith was napping in the suite's lounge when the telephone rang. He picked it up, and at the same moment there was a loud, urgent knocking on the door, Anderson on his feet in an instant, moving towards it, the Thompson machinegun at the ready. "I've got it."

But Griffith was barely listening, concentrating on the frantic voice from the signals room at the other end of the line. His face draining, he jumped to his feet, tugging the Smith & Wesson from his shoulder holster, shouting at Anderson, already opening the door to the password.

"Leave it, Howie! Battle stations! We've got an assassin in the grounds—!"

But everything seemed to be happening at once, loud voices in the hallway now, a kind of desperate bedlam as a flurry of anxious Secret Service men burst in, their weapons drawn, taking positions by instinct, covering the doorway, hall and lounge window. A breathless Sanson pushed in behind them, screamed, "For God's sake get to the President!"

But Sanson's words were redundant, drowned by a clatter of frantic activity, barked orders, and Griffith already lunging recklessly down the short hall that led to Roosevelt's bedroom, Anderson behind him.

2:25 A.M.

They lay in the hollow until it was safe to move, then Weaver led the way smartly across the lawns towards the front of the hotel, Halder beside him. They saw a sudden eruption of chaotic activity, dozens of sentries and military police appearing from nowhere. There was an abandoned Jeep parked out front on the gravel, the two Sherman tanks were starting up, their engines roaring to life, the anti-aircraft batteries on the roof coming alert, swivelling their guns skyward.

A flustered MP lieutenant went past. Weaver grabbed his arm. "What's going on?"

"There's a security alert in operation, sir. We've reason to believe there's a—"

At that precise moment gunfire erupted from somewhere, two quick shots, and then a siren went off, filling the air with a pitiful wail. The lieutenant darted into the hotel, screaming at a group of military police to follow, dozens of them piling into the lobby after him.

Halder's face tightened, said it all. "We're too late."

Weaver's heart pounded. His expression was drawn but he was still in command of himself. He nodded towards the side of the building. "The gunfire came from round there." He started to move away. More troops were already racing into the hotel from the compound, orders being shouted by confused-looking officers.

"Don't run, Jack. It'll only attract attention. And whatever you do, stay close to me."

When Griffith burst into the bedroom, Anderson was right behind him, the Thompson cocked and ready, Sanson charging in after them, his revolver drawn, more Secret Service men barrelling in behind.

One of the French windows was open wide. The woman dressed as a lieutenant was standing a couple of feet from Roosevelt, the silenced pistol raised in her hand. She started, panicked, jerked the gun and fired, hitting Anderson in the hand. He dropped the Thompson, but Griffith brought up his .38, got off a shot that hit the woman in the shoulder, then another, the force sending her flying back through the open French window, as a wounded Anderson threw himself bodily across Roosevelt as a human shield.

There was brief but utter bedlam in the room, Griffith giving cover while Anderson yanked the wheelchair round, aided by two more Secret Service men, and they pushed Roosevelt from the room and out into the corridor with frightening speed, chaos reigning outside in the hall and lounge as more Secret Service men swiftly helped move the President away from danger and out of the suite.

Back in the bedroom, Sanson grabbed the Thompson and darted through the open French window on to the balcony, just as the sirens went off. He scoured the shadows but saw nothing moving, the silenced Luger lying discarded on the tiles, then he raced to the end of the balcony and looked down, just as a uniformed figure moved away from the trellis below the balcony and ran across the lawn.

"Halt or I fire!"

The woman kept moving, clutching her shoulder. He brought up the Thompson, fired from the hip, a ragged burst that tore up the lawns, but the woman was still moving, fleeing towards the darkness of the gardens. He fired again, a long sustained burst this time, and finally the woman spun, as if hit, stumbled and fell forward. This time Sanson raised the machine-gun fully, got her in his sights and squeezed the trigger again.

Click.

The magazine had emptied. Out in the garden the woman got up, clutching her side, dragging herself away. He yanked out his pistol, aimed, managed to fire off two quick rounds before she disappeared into shadows.

Down on the lawns, dozens of confused troops piled into the gardens. "Stop that woman!" Sanson roared from the balcony, pointing. "Get after her!"

When they reached the side of the hotel, they saw Sanson on the balcony, a Thompson in his hands, the machinegun spouting flame as he directed his fire out towards the darkened lawns in a sustained and savage burst.

Halder pointed to a moving figure out in the gardens. "She's over there. *Rachel!*"

Weaver saw her hit by the tail-end of Sanson's burst of fire. She spun, stumbled and fell, clutching her side, before Sanson's firing ended abruptly and she staggered to her feet.

Up on the balcony, Sanson was yanking out his pistol, firing wildly, the siren still sounding as Rachel vanished into the shadows. Troops appeared from everywhere, and Sanson roared orders at them, then quickly moved back inside the French windows. With barely a second's pause, Halder touched Weaver's arm, and they ran across the lawns towards where Rachel had disappeared.

2:36 A.M.

The heavily guarded room at the far end of the hotel was bustling with Secret Service men, and dozens of anxious military police standing guard in the corridors outside. The bedlam had subsided, controlled now, and in the middle of the room Roosevelt looked at Griffith, who was shaking a little, his face bleached. "Are you OK, son?"

"I—I think so, Mr. President. That sure was close."

"Let's pray it never gets any closer. Where's Howie, son? Is he badly wounded?" Roosevelt asked, deeply concerned.

"The doc's attending to him right now—it's nothing serious. He'll be fine, sir."

"Thank God for that. Where's the lieutenant-colonel? I believe I owe him my thanks."

"They're bringing him now, sir."

A passageway was cleared in the throng, and when Sanson pushed through, Roosevelt thrust out his hand. "Lieutenant-Colonel Sanson, I presume? They tell me you're the man who helped save my life. And in the nick of time."

"I think your own men deserve credit for that, sir," Sanson replied honestly.

"From what I hear, you more than played your part, and I'm deeply indebted to you." Roosevelt's face darkened, and he said quietly, "What about the young woman?"

Sanson flushed with embarrassment. "I'm afraid we're

still trying to apprehend her, sir. It's just taking a little longer than we thought."

"That uniform she wore sure looked pretty convincing. But how in the hell did she get past our security?"

Sanson explained and Roosevelt's eyebrows rose. "Well, I'll be darned—so that's how she did it."

"We think she made it back to the tunnel. But we've got over five hundred troops scouring the compound, as well as a couple of truck-loads of GIs on their way to search the area around the pyramids. And one of my majors and his men are trying to find the tunnel entrance. One way or another, she won't get away, you can be certain of that."

"I'm sure she won't," Roosevelt said flatly, with no hint of pleasure. He looked puzzled. "But you know, it's the strangest thing."

"Sir?"

"She had her chance, but didn't take it. She heard the commotion in the hallway before you burst into the room, and yet she still didn't fire. Just stood there, looking at me, like her heart wasn't in it—almost as if she wanted to fail." The President removed his glasses, looked up. "It seems to me she was either a very brave woman with a conscience, or a very foolish one with a death wish."

There was a commotion at the door, and Sanson saw the major trying to make his way into the room, his uniform scuffed with dirt, the Secret Service men blocking his way. He said to Roosevelt, "Would you excuse me, sir? There's something I need to attend to urgently."

"Of course, work away. And again, you have my deepest gratitude, Lieutenant-Colonel Sanson. You've done a remarkable job."

Sanson snapped off a salute, turned smartly and made his way to the door. "He's with me," he vouched to the guards, as the major saluted. "Well?" Sanson demanded. "Did you find her?"

"We found the tunnel shaft, sir. Only it seems Weaver might have gone down after her, along with Halder."

"What?"

The major swallowed. "From what I can gather, somehow they managed to reach the shaft just before my men got to it. I sent a search party down after them with torches."

"And?"

"We think we've found Deacon, tied up and unconscious. And there're signs of blood in the passageway. You definitely must have wounded the woman, sir. But she's gone."

"What do you mean, *gone?*"

"Disappeared."

"Where, for God's sake?"

"One of my men crawled through into the tomb. He says he's pretty certain he heard an engine roar away."

Sanson's jaw tightened, as if he were grinding his teeth to dust. "She's probably trying to make it to the landing strip. You'd better make certain Lieutenant Kane's information about the desert rendezvous near Sakkara was passed on to GHQ."

The major nodded. "I already did. They've got a convoy on its way to the location right now. And I've got our Jeep waiting outside to join them, whenever you're ready, sir."

"I'm ready now." Sanson moved briskly down the hall and pushed through the military guards, taking two steps at a time towards the foyer. "The woman will be lucky to make the landing strip if she's been wounded. But even if she does, she'll have a bloody big surprise in store." Almost as an afterthought, he asked, "What about Weaver and Halder?"

"They've disappeared too, sir."

SEVENTY-THREE

3:25 A.M.

Captain Omar Rahman had taken off from the Royal Egyptian Air Force field at Almaza, north-east of Heliopolis. Twenty minutes later he banked the Bristol sharply, the aircraft jolting a little as he came in at three thousand feet over the cane fields above Memphis, where the rich Nile delta ended and the desert began. He was looking for marker lights in the silvery blackness of the sands below, telling him where to land.

He saw none.

It was odd, his passengers should have been down there by now, and he checked his watch. He was right on time. He nudged the control stick forward and the Bristol dropped lower. The terrain was endlessly flat, apart from the Sakkara pyramids, and he could easily make out their giant silhouettes, five or six miles away.

As Rahman scanned the ground again, ahead of him in the dark of the desert a light sprang on. Then another, and finally one more, the three lights marking out the shape of an "L." He smiled to himself. "Excellent! You made it, my friends." He nudged the stick and the Bristol descended.

SAKKARA

They had tried to follow Rachel's motorcycle across the desert from Giza, chasing the single tyre track in the sand, until they saw the trail weave up towards the Sakkara pyramids. Weaver came to the end of the gravel road that led up to the site and they saw the Moto Guzzi lying discarded on the ground. He grabbed the torch from the car, removed his pistol, and when they had climbed out, Halder went over and knelt as he examined the machine. "A bullet ruptured the tank. She must have run out of fuel."

Weaver looked at the damage in the torchlight, noticed dark stains on the machine, more of them on the ground near by. He knelt, touched wet blood, his face darkening. "She's badly wounded by the looks of it. She could have tried to make it on foot to the landing zone."

Beyond the pyramids, they saw nothing move in the endless moonlit desert. Halder gestured towards the entrance to the ruins. "We'd better have a look inside, just to be certain."

A stone archway led into the pyramids site, crumbling sandstone walls falling away on either side. As Weaver played the torch, they went through and along a short, darkened passageway.

It came out into an open courtyard, bathed in shadowy moonlight, ghostly quiet. The towering pyramid of Pharaoh Zoser rose up off to the right, and straight ahead were the ancient remains of a scattering of nobles' burial chambers, steps of solid rock leading down to the tomb entrances. They moved towards the nearest, and as soon as the torchlight hit the chamber's pitch-dark entrance mouth, a flock of bats suddenly erupted from the blackness. The flurry of wings died away, and it was still again.

"Give me the torch," Halder said suddenly.

"What's wrong?"

"I think I see something."

Weaver handed it over and Halder shone the cone of light on to the ground ahead.

"She's been here." He pointed to several more dark patches of blood in the sand, a couple of metres away, between two of the other tombs.

Weaver nodded towards the steps leading down to the first. "Let's try this one."

They heard the distant rasp of an aircraft engine overhead, and they both searched the night sky, but saw nothing. The sound of the engine grew closer. "I'll bet it's Deacon's pick-up," said Halder. "Maybe she's already made it to the landing area."

"We'd still better make sure." Shining the torch, Weaver quickly scrambled down the steps towards the mouth of the tomb, and Halder moved after him.

Rahman came in low, his flaps already deployed, lining up the nose of the plane with the lights, trickles of sweat running down his face. Landing on a coarse desert strip was tricky enough at the best of times. In almost complete darkness, it was positively deadly. If he hit too much unseen debris he might damage the undercarriage, or slew into soft sand, and it might be impossible to take off again.

"Nice and easy does it." He gently eased the stick forward a little, keeping his eyes on the L-shaped lights dead ahead. He was almost two hundred feet from the ground, getting ready to touch down, when he flicked on his landing lights.

The desert strip was sharply illuminated, and he quickly scanned for any debris or obstacles. His blood turned to ice. Dozens of army trucks loomed to his left and right.

It was a trap.

"Bastards," he screamed, and pushed the throttles hard forward, at the same time taking in the flaps, pulling back on the stick, and the Bristol began to climb steeply, the engine snarling. Headlights sprang on below, and suddenly an almighty hail of machinegun bullets and tracer fire erupted from the vehicles, ripping into the air around him.

The cockpit window shattered and a burst of lead hit him in the shoulder, spun him around, another burst ripping into his back. He shrieked, his body jerking forward on to the control stick.

He was already dead when the nose dipped violently, the black earth rushed up, and the Bristol screamed into the ground and exploded in a ball of orange flame.

They found her lying against one of the tomb walls, her tunic tied around her waist to cover a serious wound in her side. The material was drenched with crimson, and she looked like a little girl, lost and helpless. Her breathing was shallow, sweat ran down her face, and she was choking on her own blood. When she saw them her eyelids fluttered in recognition.

Weaver knelt beside her, his eyes welling with emotion. "Don't try to move. Take it easy."

She seemed to drift in and out of consciousness, her voice hoarse. She whispered, "I—I really think it might be better if you left me be, Harry."

"You'll bleed to death, for God's sake."

Halder moved beside her, gently loosened her tunic, examined the gaping wound the machinegun had inflicted in her side. Then he looked into her eyes, touched her cheek, his voice anguished. "The firing pin on Kleist's weapon—why did you do it?"

Pain contorted her face, and she coughed up blood. "You—you both know why. And now it's time one of you returned the favour. Finish it here and now."

A trickle of crimson spilled down her chin. "Let it end where it began."

Weaver stood, desperation in his reply. "I'll get help—"

Halder gripped his arm, said hopelessly, "I'm afraid it's gone far beyond that."

Rachel cried out, a terrible sound like that of an animal

in torment, her eyes wet. "For God's sake, have you no mercy? Will one of you *please* shoot me."

She moaned again, looked delirious with pain, and her eyes closed tightly. Weaver couldn't bear it any longer, tugged out his pistol, stood over her. His hand shook as he aimed at her head, beads of perspiration running down his face, and for a long time he just stood there, his finger on the trigger, looking down at her, unable to act, and for the first time since childhood he felt like crying.

"Please . . ."

He heard a click, looked over at Halder, whose eyes were wet as he raised his gun.

The explosion rang around the stone walls.

They carried her body from the tomb, laid it on the sand, and then Weaver removed his tunic and covered her face. For a long time there was nothing but a harrowing silence between them, until Halder said in a trembling voice, "It was the only way, my friend. An act of mercy."

Weaver's face was ashen. "I could have got help—"

"It still wouldn't have saved her. You know that, Harry."

Weaver felt desolate, looked out towards the desert, saw a peppering of small bright fires, the burning wreckage of the aircraft. "It looks like Sanson got his reception committee to the landing strip."

Halder's face was grim, and he took out his pistol, swallowed hard. "I guess we all go to hell in our own way. And now it's time you left me alone, and let me do the honourable thing."

"Another death isn't going to make any difference. It's over, Jack. Put the gun away."

"There's really no other way, I'm afraid. If you arrest me, then it's either a bullet or a noose. And I'd really rather not have to dangle from a rope." Halder cocked the gun. "So if you don't mind, do me a favour and step away."

Very deliberately, Weaver put out a hand, gripped the barrel. "I said put it away, Jack."

"You're not making this any easier."

"Take the car. Drive south, as far as you can. With luck, you can reach Luxor by morning. After that, God only knows."

Halder was stunned into silence, and Weaver said, "Just leave, while you still have the chance, before Sanson's men get here."

"They'll want to know what's happened to me."

"Let me worry about the afterwards. Go. Before it's too late."

Halder was almost overcome, and knelt beside Rachel's body, pulled back the tunic and touched her face. It was almost too much to bear. "Promise me you'll make sure she's given a proper burial." He looked out towards the desert, his voice thick with emotion. "Somewhere out there. Where we were all happy together, before this madness started."

Weaver nodded. "And now, you really had better go."

There was a sudden rage in Halder's voice, and he looked on the verge of a breakdown. "What a terrible thing this lousy war has been. It's destroyed us all in the end."

Weaver didn't reply, for there was really no answer, and Halder touched his arm in a final gesture. "Take care of yourself, Harry. I'm not sure we'll ever meet again, but even so, try to get through the rest of this in one piece."

He climbed into the staff car, started up, gave a final wave, and then the olive-green Humber moved off into the darkness, faded like a departing spirit.

Weaver slumped on his knees in the sand. He cradled Rachel's head in his arms, buried his face in her hair, faintly aware of the noise of the car dying away. And then there was nothing but the sound of his own sobbing, and the vast and empty silence of the desert.

THE
PRESENT

SEVENTY-FOUR

CAIRO

It was almost three in the morning when Weaver finished talking. The hotel lobby was empty and the bar staff had gone home. The *khamsin* had stopped blowing hours ago, a heavy mist had crept in, covering the city in a ghostly veil, and somewhere out on the Nile a foghorn sounded. It faded, and he put down his glass. "Well, Carney, there you have your tale."

I looked at him with amazement. "It's almost unbelievable."

"Almost, certainly, but it's the God's honest truth of what happened. I take it you'll keep to your promise not to publish anything until after I die? If you still want to write about it, that is."

"Of course, you have my word. It's just that I wonder if anyone would believe such a story." I hesitated. "May I ask you something?"

"Ask away."

"How did you know about the body at the morgue? And what made you suspect that Halder might still be alive after all these years?"

"I have a lawyer friend in Cairo, an old man now, someone whom I hired many years ago to try to help me find Jack. Like you, he read the piece in the newspaper, and immediately contacted me. The name and the age of the dead man, along with his German nationality, seemed too much of a coincidence not to investigate. So I got on the first flight I could, arriving yesterday afternoon. Damned lucky to make it, too. Those winds shut the airport down less than ten minutes after we landed."

"And you had no stronger evidence than that?"

"Some, but it went back a long time."

"How long?"

"I discovered some years after the war that the Halders' family estate in New York had been sold through a Swiss bank attorney, in Zurich. Jack's parents were both dead so naturally I wondered who had authorised the sale. I contacted the bank but they refused to give me any information. You know the Swiss, they're absolutely paranoid about secrecy and protecting their clients' interests, so my enquiries led absolutely nowhere, despite help from old intelligence contacts. Then out of the blue, some months later, I received a single postcard from Casablanca. It said simply, *'All is well, Jack.'*"

"So he did escape and survive."

Weaver nodded. "I tried to find him over the years, but it proved impossible. Franz Halder had been a much-liked and respected man, with lots of important contacts in the Middle East, people who would have been glad to help his son. Jack could have moved anywhere in the region. Besides, his father had been a wealthy man. I'm sure there was a little something salted away in a bank account somewhere, and with the proceeds from the estate, it would have helped him remain anonymous for the rest of his life."

"Do you think Jack Halder learned the truth of what happened to his own son?"

"I've no doubt he did. I visited Pauli's grave in Berlin many years ago. The boy is buried with his mother." Weaver paused. "You know what was odd? There were two fresh lilies on the gravestone, one for each of them. Apparently, the flowers were delivered from a Berlin florist's once a month. White lilies, exactly the kind my father grew for Halder's mother. I eventually discovered that the instructions came from the same bank in Zurich, which led me absolutely nowhere. The last time I visited the graves was five years ago. The fresh flowers were there, as before. Another fact that made me suspect that Jack might still be alive."

I went to refill my glass; the bottle in front of us was empty. I put it down again. "And the others. What happened to them?"

"Canaris I'm sure you know about. Soon after Sphinx failed, the Abwehr was dissolved and its functions taken over by the SD. He was arrested as part of the group that plotted against Hitler, and later hanged. It eventually came out that he'd been supplying important information to the Allies for years, through contacts in British Intelligence.

Schellenberg, true to form, carried on thinking up more insane plots. A week after Sphinx, he tried much the same trick, in Teheran this time, where Roosevelt, Churchill and Stalin were meeting. Again, he came close to succeeding, but ultimately failed once more. He was captured by the Allies and sentenced at Nuremberg in 1949. He escaped the gallows but was sent to prison as a war criminal, then released two years later because of ill-health, and died shortly after from lung cancer. Himmler was caught too, trying to escape disguised as a private, but committed suicide before he could be brought to trial, by taking a vial of cyanide concealed in his mouth. As for the rest of them, Reggie Salter survived his wounds, believe it or not, but six months later he was found guilty of desertion and murder by a military court, and executed by firing squad. Harvey Deacon met the same fate, on charges of spying."

"And what about Sanson, and Helen Kane?"

"Sanson had been right all along, of course. And I'd have to admit, a good soldier, despite our differences. The kind of Englishman you'd want on your side in a difficult battle—driven, relentless, determined not to give the enemy any quarter. He served out the rest of the war in Cairo, then returned to Britain. Surprisingly, he ran a successful public relations business for many years, until he eventually retired. He passed away ten years ago in London." Weaver hesitated, and his eyes misted. "As for Helen Kane, she learned that her boyfriend was a prisoner in a German camp in Greece. They were reunited after Athens was liberated, married, and eventually settled in England. God knows if she's still alive. But I often think of her. She was a remarkable woman."

"You know what amazes me? How such a story could have been kept hushed up for all this time. It seems incredible."

"There's been a veiled hint or two in certain history books over the years, but I agree nothing substantial has ever come out, and certainly not the full truth. That it was kept secret shouldn't really surprise you, not when you think about it. At such a critical stage in the war, the American and British public would have been totally demoralised to learn that the Nazis had come dangerously close to killing their leaders, not to mention the effect it would have had on the troops. Washington and London put a security clamp on the whole thing, as tight as anything I've ever seen.

"Berlin wasn't too keen to admit failure, either. In late 1943, the Nazis were beginning to find their backs to the wall, and needed victories, not defeats. The humiliation wouldn't exactly have been a morale-booster for their armed forces, so Hitler gave instructions that all the papers on Sphinx be destroyed, and any personnel who knew about it sworn to secrecy. Besides, there were so many stories flying around in those days—some true, others incredible. The Allies were planning to assassinate Hitler, or kidnap Rommel, and Hitler was going to get Roosevelt and Churchill, or some top Allied commander or other. It was hard to distinguish fact from fiction. After the war ended, I guess Sphinx got lost among the bunch of them."

"What happened to you?"

A tiny, wry smile played across Weaver's lips. "I was never court-martialled, if that's what you'd like to know. And that was the odd thing. For some reason best known to himself, Sanson never brought charges against me. The question of Halder's disappearance came up, of course, but it wasn't pursued, or the matter discussed further. Maybe behind it all, Sanson really knew what I was going through—a conflict between duty and love and friendship. After that, I became an unwitting expert in presidential security. What could I say? That Roosevelt's life had been saved in part by a German agent, sent to help kill him, and I'd aided his escape? It would have caused unwelcome questions about what had really happened to Jack. So I guess I let sleeping dogs lie."

"How did you learn all the facts about Rachel Stern's true identity?"

"Some of the SD's personnel files fell into Allied hands in '45. Hers was among them, and I managed to get a copy. I was also lucky enough to wangle an interview with Schellenberg while he was in prison. It was he who filled me in on the rest of the story."

I looked at Weaver's face. "Do you reckon she really loved both of you?"

For a moment he said nothing, a wistful look in his eyes, a hint of infinite sadness. "You know, I guess I'll never truly know the answer to that question. I'll take it with me to my grave. And perhaps that's the way it should be. Some questions are best left unanswered. But if you want the *honest* truth, I always liked to think she really did."

"What happened to her body?"

"She was buried in an unmarked grave, in the desert near Sakkara. No proper religious ceremony, just a military burial detail, and a sergeant read a brief passage from Revelations, which seemed oddly appropriate under the circumstances." Weaver shook his head. "I didn't attend, I'm afraid. I guess I really didn't feel up to it. But afterwards I drove out to the spot and said a prayer, for whatever good it did."

"And her family?"

"Himmler, of course, was never one to keep his promises. Despite Schellenberg's pleas for clemency, her father was executed with the other conspirators against Hitler, along with her two beloved younger brothers, innocents who had absolutely nothing to do with the plot. Only her mother was spared, but she passed away soon after, poor woman."

I looked at Weaver steadily. "Why do you think Halder never tried to see you again? And why would he stay in hiding all these years? You said the United States could have hanged him as a traitor. But that was an outside chance, surely? He was a soldier, not a war criminal. And why the secrecy?"

He took a deep breath, sighed. "You're probably right. God knows I've thought about it often enough, but there are only a couple of reasons I can think of as to why he hid himself away and never got in touch with me again, both of them connected. One, he was quite a proud man. I think in some way he felt he had let his mother's country down by going along with the Nazis in the first place. But he had no choice, really. Like so many good Germans, he'd been swept along by the current. And he only agreed to play his part in Schellenberg's plan because of his son. But you also have to remember he came from a strong Prussian background. Honour matters. The German word—*pflicht*—

that Jack was driven by. It translates as 'duty,' but I've learned it means much, much more than that. It means you don't dishonour those closest to you. I think he felt he had somehow dishonoured our friendship, and believed he could never face me again. But who knows?

"As far as the second reason, it seems the most plausible. After all the pain Jack had been through—the loss of his wife and child, and his father's death, not to mention what happened in Egypt on the mission—perhaps he simply wanted to put everything behind him, to start a new life and try to erase the torment of the past. I believe it happens, you know. It's not been unknown for people who have been through unbearable trauma to cut themselves off totally from their old lives and try to start afresh. Give themselves a clean break—new identities, new families, new careers—and obliterate anything associated with their past. A kind of cleansing of the soul, I suppose. I'm sure the psychologists could explain it in better detail, but it seems to me to make some kind of sense. And I have a feeling it might be what Jack tried to do. You might say he never forgot his wife and son, and didn't cut himself off completely by having flowers regularly delivered to their graves, but then I guess if you'd lost a family you'd dearly loved, you wouldn't forget their memory entirely."

There was a sound behind us. A couple of hotel cleaning staff on the night shift came in. They looked surprised to see anyone still in the bar, but they promptly ignored us and got down to work, clearing away tables and chairs. Weaver glanced at his watch.

"It looks like we're overstaying our welcome. Well, I must get some sleep, Carney." He stood. "I've got a flight to arrange tomorrow, back to the States."

He offered a firm handshake and I walked with him to the elevator. "I've one more question."

"Oh? And what's that?"

"You're certain the body in the morgue wasn't Halder's?"

"Jack had a noticeable scar on his left leg, an old injury from childhood when we used to play together in the grounds of his mother's estate. The poor soul in the morgue had none. As to who he really was, we'll probably never know."

"But it seems an odd coincidence. He was about the same age and had the same name as Halder."

"He also had papers in the name of Hans Meyer, I believe."

I nodded. "A contact I know in the Cairo police told me they found old identity documents in that name hidden at the flat."

"I suppose you heard that many Germans came to Egypt after the war? Some were wanted Nazis, others were young scientists, hired to work on Nasser's secret rocket programme at Helwan, out in the desert. There are still a few of them alive, I believe. They're old men now, too old to return home, living out their last days anonymously, in squalid flats in places like Imbaba. In many cases, when they first arrived in Egypt, they gave themselves new identities or aliases, to try and cover their tracks. I think when the facts are finally known you'll find the old man at the morgue was one of them, and that the name Johann Halder was an alias. There's nothing remarkable about the name—it's common enough in Germany. So is Hans Meyer. I'd place a bet that both identities were probably covers the dead man had used over the years." Weaver paused.

"You still look doubtful, Carney."

I shrugged. "I guess it's because I'm a journalist, but I don't like unfinished stories. I would have liked to have known once and for all if Halder was still alive."

"You mean you'd like to find out what happened to his father's collection?"

"Oddly enough, if I'm to be honest, I think it's Jack Halder himself who intrigues me more."

Weaver shook his head. "For all I know he could be long dead. There aren't too many of us old survivors still around these days. The flowers on the graves of his wife and son once a month could easily have been arranged to continue after his death. It's just the kind of touch I would have expected of Jack. A pity if he's dead, though. I would have liked to have seen him again, at least one more time." There was genuine regret in Weaver's voice, an almost tangible sadness. "But everything that happened was all such a long time ago. What was it some writer once said? 'The older I get, the more it seems that little by little I drift away from the shores of my past, until they become just a far-off, distant memory.' It certainly seems that way."

"But you recall it very well."

Weaver hesitated, then slowly reached into his pocket, took out his wallet, and handed something to me. "That's because I have this to remind me."

It was a very old, faded black-and-white photograph, kept preciously in a protective plastic cover, the paper wrinkled and cracked. Three young people stood among the tombs near the Step pyramid, their faces healthy and tanned, their arms around one another's waists as they smiled out at the camera. I recognised Harry Weaver at once, as a young man. Beside him stood a striking woman. She was very beautiful, her features finely chiselled, her blond hair bleached from the sun. Next to her was a handsome man, a smile etched on his face. Jack Halder and Rachel Stern.

I stared down at the photograph for a long time, the images suddenly real, faces to go with the story, then silently handed it back, stuck for something to say. There was really nothing I could think of.

Weaver returned the photograph to his wallet. "I'm glad we talked, Carney. If ever you're back Stateside, I'm always happy to see visitors, so do look me up some time. There are so few old friends still around these days—they seem to pass away with monotonous regularity."

"I'll do that."

"Well, goodnight, or should I say good morning."

"Good morning, sir."

He entered the elevator, the doors closed, and he was gone.

I walked back to my apartment but couldn't sleep. For some reason, I kept going over Weaver's story in my mind. I sat there restlessly, drinking coffee, watching the sun come up, thinking about everything Weaver had told me, until a little later I got dressed and went down to the street and walked towards the deserted Kasr-el-Nil Bridge. When a solitary taxi drove past, I hailed it. The driver looked surprised to see a customer at such an early hour.

"Where to, sir?"

"Sakkara."

He didn't register astonishment that someone would want to visit the famous site at dawn, but simply shrugged as I climbed in. We drove out along the Pyramids Road before turning south, out into the green Nile countryside and along the canal, the shabby villages along the way deserted, hardly a sinner in sight, and then we came to the ruins of the fabled city of Memphis, and at last Sakkara, that awesome monument to a long-dead king, loomed ahead.

It looked a very beautiful place just after dawn, truly glorious, sky and earth the colour of fiery sandstone, a tangerine sunrise washing over the oldest pyramid in Egypt, where the most fertile land on earth, the lush Nile delta, ended abruptly with a thick forest of palms and the barren desert began. There was a hut where the tourist police checked the incoming traffic, but there was no one about so early in the morning, and I told the driver to carry on, up the steep winding road to the site. When we reached the gravel carpark below the entrance, I got out.

"Wait here, please."

I walked up the hill. It was still cool in the desert after the freezing cold of night, and the place was desolate—no hordes of tourists, or annoying camel drivers and guides offering their services. I walked among the ruins and stood in the pale shadows of the splendour of Zoser's pyramid. There was a sign near by, saying that an international archaeological team was at work, another dig in progress, but I saw no one, so I went to sit on one of the stone blocks at the base.

There were faded initials carved into the stepped layers of ancient brown rock, hundreds and hundreds of them, scratched and chiselled by visitors and victors over countless centuries. Primitive marks left by Roman legionnaires, ciphers scraped into the weathered stone by Napoleon's conquering armies, and endless forgotten memorials to lovers, long dead. I searched for a long time, brushing away sand, moving from stone to stone, the rock so badly eroded in places that it was impossible to read some of the inscriptions, until finally a chill went through me as I found what I was looking for, the letters so badly worn I had to trace their faded outline with the tip of my finger.

But there they were. *RS, HW, JH. 1939.*

I thought of that summer when Harry Weaver had first come to Sakkara. I thought of Jack Halder and Rachel Stern, and all the dead names from the past, their bodies long gone to dust, with their passions and pain, hates and intrigues, and I thought how none of it mattered any more. Above all, I wondered if Jack Halder was still alive. He'd be a very old man now, but really it was no use wondering.

Like Weaver had said, little by little we drift from the shores of the past, until they become just a distant memory. All that remained of the truth was a worn old photograph, and these neglected initials chiselled in stone. But for me, they were truth enough.

I stood, dusted my hands, and walked back down the hill.

I never discovered what happened to Franz Halder's collection, and I never saw Harry Weaver again. He passed away almost four months later in a New York hospital, a few days after suffering a stroke. The prominent newspapers all had obituaries. He was to be buried in a local church cemetery in his home town, where he and Jack Halder had spent their childhood together.

I was back in New York on leave at the time and I decided to hire a car and make the long drive upstate to pay my final respects. There was a bad storm, I was delayed, and by the time I arrived the funeral had ended. There were dozens of mourners, and more than a few familiar White House faces. Rain drifted in across the cemetery in sheets, and it didn't take long for the crowd to disperse back to their cars as the sound of thunder rolled above us, and then I was alone.

Beyond the white-painted wooden church, on a distant rise, I could see what had once been the site of the residence belonging to Jack Halder's family. It was long gone now, a shopping mall and a parking lot in its place. For some reason I thought about two small boys who had once played there and become friends, until passion and circumstance had made them enemies, and their love for a woman had almost destroyed them both.

As I stood there, drenched by the rain, I let my eyes wander over the grave. It was covered with wreaths and bouquets of every description. More than a few were from the Pentagon and the veteran associations, and there were even two from former American Presidents.

But among the wreaths and flowers I noticed a solitary snow-white lily, lying at the base of the black marble slab. A cold shiver ran through me. I picked up the envelope, read the plain white card inside, the handwriting frail and scratched, but the words unmistakable.

They said: "*A promise kept. Jack.*"

AUTHOR'S NOTE

As ever, no book is written without help, and of the many people who assisted my research I would especially like to mention James H. Griffith, former Secret Service agent to President Roosevelt, who experienced the Cairo conference in 1943 at first hand; Secret Service archivist Mike Sampson, and H. Terrence Samway, Assistant Director, Office of Government Liaison and Public Affairs, Washington, for their kind help in providing archival material; Ted Allbeury, author, and Stephen Franke (Lieutenant-Colonel, US Army, Retired) of the Middle-East Services Group, for their much-valued advice on intelligence matters; John Hackett, a true English gentleman, with more stories to tell than any writer could hope to hear in a lifetime; and Samir Raafat, author and historian, for his expert knowledge of wartime Cairo, and for the courtesy and kindness he extended to me during my research in Egypt.

The Sands of Sakkara is a work of fiction tempered with a measure of truth, and any errors—historical, intended, or otherwise—are solely mine. That the Nazis intended to assassinate President Roosevelt and Prime Minister Churchill during the series of important Allied conferences that took place in the Middle East in late 1943 is historical fact.

The Sphinx mission is loosely based in part on Operation Long Jump, a daring top-secret plan conceived by Heinrich Himmler and Walter Schellenberg, after the infamous Nazi spy in Turkey, Cicero, provided the information—stolen from the safe of the British ambassador—that the American President and British Prime Minister were to visit Cairo, and then Teheran, for secret talks.

An initial plan was devised jointly by the SD and the Abwehr, using a special team of agents to pinpoint the exact whereabouts of the Allied leaders. When the final stage of the operation was imminent, Berlin dispatched two plane-loads of crack SS paratroops, the intention being to storm the conference location and kill Roosevelt and Churchill—the principal target being the American President. Though it came perilously close to succeeding, the objective failed virtually at the last minute, when a captured German agent revealed the conspiracy. The vital radio set that was to have guided down the aircraft, and which had been hidden in an ancient tomb, was destroyed, resulting in one of the Luftwaffe transports of SS troops being shot down, and the second forced to turn back. Until the remaining infiltrators had been killed or captured, President Roosevelt was hastily moved to a secret location by his Secret Service team.

So much of what happened during those dark, intriguing and exciting days of the Second World War is veiled by the clouds of time and distance. Old intelligence hands fade away, and take untold secrets with them to the grave. Whether Sphinx ever really came close to changing the course of world history will forever remain a mystery.